HERBS AND SPICES

Herbs are the leaves of annual or perennial shrubs. Spices are derived from the bark, roots, fruits or berries of perennial plants.

GINGER	MACE	MARJORAM	NUTMEG	OREGANO	SAGE	THYME
Beef Roasts Beef Steaks Macaroni and Cheese Baked Beans Rice Dishes	Meat Loaf Meatballs Veal Quiche Lorraine Welsh Rabbit	Beef Hamburgers Pork Lamb Veal	Pot Roasts Meat Loaf Meatballs	Swiss Steak Hamburgers Veal Liver Pizza Spaghetti	Cold Roast Beef Pork Lamb Veal Cheese Fondue	Roasts Variety Meats
Seafood Roast Chicken Roast Cornish Hens Roast Duckling	Baked Fish Fillets Shrimp Creole Chicken Fricassee	Salmon Loaf Shellfish Chicken, Turkey Venison Scrambled Eggs Omelets Soufflés	Seafood Fried Chicken	Broiled Seafood Shellfish Chicken Pheasant Boiled Eggs Egg Sandwiches	Fish Fillets Chicken Turkey Duckling Poultry Stuffing Omelets	Tuna Fried Chicken Roast Duckling Poultry Stuffing Scrambled Eggs Omelets Soufflés
Bean Soup Onion Soup Potato Soup Cocktail Sauce	Vegetable Soup Veal Stew Oyster Stew	Chicken Soup Onion Soup Potato Soup Gravy	Oyster Stew Mushroom Sauce	Beef Soup Bouillon Stews Butter Sauces Mushroom Sauce	Consommé Chicken Soup Tomato Soup Stews Cheese Sauces	Clam Chowder Borsch Stews
French Dressing Fruit Salad Dressings	Fruit	Seafood Chicken Egg Greens French Dressing	Sweet Salad Dressings	Seafood Egg Vegetable Guacamole Dip	Chicken French Dressing	Chicken Cottage Cheese Greens Tomato Tomato Aspic
Beets Carrots Squash Sweet Potatoes	Broccoli Brussels Sprouts Cabbage Succotash	Celery Eggplant Greens Potatoes Zucchini	Beans Carrots Cauliflower Corn Onions	Broccoli Cabbage Mushrooms Onions Tomatoes	Brussels Sprouts Eggplant Lima Beans Squash Tomatoes	Artichokes Carrots Green Beans Mushrooms Peas Potatoes
Nut Bread	Banana Bread Doughnuts	Fruit Juice	Nut Bread Coffee Cakes Sweet Rolls		Biscuits Corn Bread Hot Milk Tea	Biscuits Corn Bread
Steamed Pudding Cookies Broiled Grapefruit Pears Stewed Dried Fruit	Chocolate Desserts Custards Citrus Desserts	Fruit Cup Cooked Fruits	Custards Apple Pie Pumpkin Pie Vanilla Ice Cream Hard Sauce			Custards

Betty Crocker's COOKBOOK

NEW AND REVISED EDITION

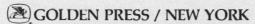

GOLDEN PRESS / NEW YORK
Western Publishing Company, Inc.
Racine, Wisconsin

Seventh Printing, 1982
Copyright © 1978, 1969 by General Mills, Inc., Minneapolis, Minnesota.
All rights reserved. Produced in the U.S.A.
Library of Congress Catalog Card Number: 78-52003
Golden® and Golden Press® are trademarks of Western Publishing Company, Inc.
ISBN 0-307-09800-1 (ringbound); ISBN 0-307-09823-0 (wirebound); ISBN 0-307-09822-2 (casebound)

CONFIDENCE – FROM BETTY CROCKER'S COOKBOOK

Confidence is what you find in *Betty Crocker's Cookbook*—the certainty that every recipe will work for you. That confidence has always been there and still is. With so many changes taking place around us, it's good to know that some things don't change. You know that you can still count on a Betty Crocker recipe. Here's why.

Months of dedicated work went into developing and testing every recipe in this book. First, we studied family lifestyles so we could design the book and select the recipes that interest you most.

Then work began in the Betty Crocker Kitchens. Skilled home economists developed needed new recipes with careful kitchen testing; they retested the tried-and-true ones, too. Next, each recipe was prepared by another home economist or kitchen technician who had never seen it before. Experienced staff members "taste tested" the results, asking questions, suggesting changes, recommending variations.

To make certain that each recipe would work in your kitchen, it was submitted to rigorous testing to take into account individual differences in equipment, ingredients and methods. It was tested with higher and lower temperatures, then shorter and longer baking times. Tests were run with larger and smaller eggs, less and more liquid. Shorter and longer mixing times were tested, too. All these changes were thoroughly checked to assure success despite such variations.

Finally, the recipe went into kitchens like yours in all parts of the country. There, home testers who are not trained home economists shopped for ingredients, followed directions and served the results to their families. And they answered a two-page questionnaire with queries like these:

"Were the ingredients easy to find where you live?" "Was the recipe too expensive?" "Were the directions clear and easy to follow?" "Did your family like it?" "Would you serve it again? How often?" We studied their reports, making any needed adjustments, until the results were as nearly perfect as time, effort and skill could make them. Then, and only then, was each recipe ready to go into our cookbook—and into your kitchen.

This careful planning and testing are the heart of *Betty Crocker's Cookbook*. They make the difference that you can rely on. And they provide the confidence that you'll have successful results with every recipe, every time.

CONTENTS

FOREWORD

Especially for the new you—this new and revised edition of *Betty Crocker's Cookbook* is the result of two years of intensive research and planning at the Betty Crocker Food and Nutrition Center. All 1,500 recipes, 299 beautiful color photographs and hundreds of tips and special helps were designed to meet your new needs—to complement the way you live today and want to live tomorrow.

We know your days are fuller. You're more time-conscious, energy-conscious, dollar-conscious. In every area you demand quality and reliability. And more than ever you're concerned about nutrition.

Today you like to cook from scratch with fresh ingredients, so the only mixes you'll find in this book are those you make yourself. You've asked for—so we've given you—recipes both nostalgic and new; imaginative money-saving uses for leftovers; bread-baking help; and techniques for preserving food at home. Included, too, are microwave directions—but only where they can help you the most. You'll also find the tried-and-true charts, guidelines and pictures that help you carve meats, select cheeses, flute pastry shells, and much more. And we've put this all together in six big, streamlined chapters, organized just the way you plan a meal.

You'll find the keystone of your menus, meats and main dishes, where you'd naturally look first—right in the beginning of the book. Along with meats, seafood and poultry are egg and cheese dishes, dried beans, and make-a-meal soups, sandwiches and salads—because today's main course doesn't have to be traditional hearty fare. Then turn to Salads and Vegetables; Breads, Pasta and Rice; Desserts; and a versatile chapter of Appetizers, Snacks and Beverages. Finally, look to Special Helps when you need any kind of kitchen know-how: It's a treasury of advice, tips and pointers on everything from the foods you need daily to care of your freezer.

Enjoy this new book. And remember—our standard of excellence has not changed. Every recipe has been developed and tested in the Betty Crocker Kitchens, then tested again in homes just like yours.

The Betty Crocker Editors

Pictured opposite: Chicken-Sesame Salad (page 90), Budget Bouillabaisse (page 74) and Pork Roast with Onions (page 45)

MEATS
AND MAIN DISHES

ABOUT MEATS

MEAT IN YOUR MENUS

Traditionally, meat is the mainstay of American menus, the food around which the rest of the meal is planned. While it is true that meat contains protein (so important for body building and repair), most Americans now eat much more meat than they need for protein requirements. As a result, they may be skimping on other foods—vegetables, fruits, breads, cereals and dairy products—that are *all* necessary for a balanced diet.

For this reason, we have based serving amounts for meats and main dishes in this chapter on at least one-fourth of the day's protein requirement for an adult. The breads, cereals, milk and other foods usually eaten at mealtime and for snacks also provide some protein (see page 354). Servings in this chapter may seem small, but each is nutritionally adequate for protein. For heartier appetites, count on fewer servings per recipe, or serve a greater variety of other foods to go with the meat.

HOW MUCH MEAT SHOULD YOU BUY?
This list will help you when you shop:
Boneless meat: about ¼ pound per serving (ground meat, tenderloin slices)

Boneless roasts: about ¼ pound per serving (beef, veal, pork, lamb)

Small bone-in: about ½ pound per serving (pork loin, rib roasts, ham)

Medium bone-in: about ½ pound per serving (pot roasts, country-style ribs)

Large bone-in: about ¾ pound per serving (shanks, spareribs, back ribs, short ribs)

Check the storage space in your refrigerator and freezer before you buy. Plan on leftovers from big cuts requiring long cooking. Plan on more than one serving for hearty appetites but remember—an average adult serving is 2 to 3 ounces of cooked lean meat, not counting bone or fat.

WHAT THE MEAT LABEL TELLS YOU
Brand name and/or *government grade* is a guide to quality; *name of the cut,* an indication of how to cook the meat. *Weight* gives a clue to cooking time of steaks, oven roasts and pot roasts, as well as to number of servings. The *price* is on the label two ways, per pound and per package: a guide to help you stay within your budget.

GRADES OF MEAT AND WHAT THEY MEAN
The round stamp bearing the abbreviations for "U.S. Inspected and Passed" is your guarantee that the meat on which the stamp appears is wholesome and that the plant in which the meat was processed has met federal standards of cleanliness. The stamp need not be trimmed from the meat; the marking fluid used is a harmless vegetable coloring.

The U.S. Department of Agriculture's grades of meat quality are found in a shield-shaped stamp. In descending order, these grades are USDA Prime, Choice, Good, Standard, Commercial and Utility. Many meat packers use special brand names to denote quality.

Most meats sold in retail stores are Choice. Prime is usually available only in special restaurants. Grades below Good are ordinarily used by the packers in combination meats and are not sold in retail stores.

As you shop for meat, look for flecks of fat within the lean; this is "marbling." It increases juiciness, flavor and tenderness.

Ribs and loins of high-quality beef, lamb and mutton are usually aged. Aging develops additional tenderness and characteristic flavor. You can ask your retailer to give you aged meat.

HOW TO STORE MEATS
Meats will begin to lose flavor and spoil if you don't store them quickly and properly right after you buy them. Fresh meats, to be at their best, should be used within 2 to 3 days; ground meat and variety meats, within 24 hours. Store them in the coldest part of the refrigerator. The temperature should be as low as possible but not freezing.

If it is to be used within 1 or 2 days, fresh prepackaged meat can be refrigerated in its original wrapper; if the meat is to be kept for a longer period, loosen the ends of the wrapper or store as described below.

Fresh meat that is not prepackaged should be stored unwrapped or wrapped loosely in waxed paper, plastic wrap or aluminum foil. This allows the air to partially dry the surface of the meat and thus retard the growth of bacteria.

Meat should never be washed. Cured and smoked meats, sausages and ready-to-serve meats may be stored in their original wrappings.

Cooked meats and the liquid in which meats have been cooked should be cooled quickly, then covered and refrigerated. Cooling can be hastened by placing the pan in cold water.

HOW TO FREEZE AND DEFROST MEAT

Just about all meats freeze well and maintain their quality if wrapped properly, frozen quickly and kept at a temperature of 0° or below. (Don't use the ice cube compartment of your refrigerator as a substitute for a freezer for more than a week.) And keep in mind that the condition of the meat at defrosting will be the same as it was at freezing. Therefore, if you do plan to freeze meat, do so as soon as possible after marketing.

Before wrapping, prepare the meat for final use by trimming off excess fat and, to conserve freezer space, by removing bones where possible. Do not salt. Choose moistureproof, vaporproof wrap and follow directions for its use. Wrap the meat tightly, then label and date before placing in freezer.

For top quality, most frozen meats should be used within 3 months; corned beef briskets, whole smoked hams and pork sausage should be used within 2 weeks. Do not freeze smoked arm picnics, canned hams or other canned meats; flavor will deteriorate.

Frozen roasts require more cooking time than usual—small roasts, about one-third longer; large roasts, closer to one-half.

To defrost meat, allow enough time for it to thaw in the refrigerator. This is an energy saver—as the cold meat thaws, it helps keep the refrigerator cold.

This timetable will help you when defrosting frozen meats in the refrigerator:

Large roast	4 to 7 hours per pound
Small roast	3 to 5 hours per pound
1-inch steak	12 to 14 hours

For last-minute thawing, use your microwave.

Refreezing defrosted meat is not recommended except in emergencies. Meat may deteriorate between defrosting and refreezing.

HOW TO COOK MEAT

Cooked by the wrong method, the most tender cut of meat can become leathery; cooked by the right method, a tough cut can become tender. Know the method recommended for the cut you plan to use.

There are six basic methods for cooking meat (at right) and two types of heat—dry (without liquid), used for roasting, broiling, panbroiling and panfrying, and moist (with steam or liquid), used for braising and water cooking. If you refer to the recommendation on the Meat Charts and to the general cooking methods on this page, you should be able to cook any cut of meat.

GENERAL COOKING METHODS

ROASTING
Cuts: Large, tender cuts of meat.

Method: Place meat fat side up on rack in shallow pan. Do not cover. Do not add water. See Timetables for specific meats. The old method of searing (browning the surface of the meat by a short application of intense heat) is rarely used.

BROILING
Cuts: Tender steaks, chops, sliced ham or bacon or ground meat. (Steaks and chops should be at least ¾ inch thick; ham slices, ½ inch.)

Method: Place meat on rack 2 to 5 inches from heat. Broil until brown; turn and broil other side until desired degree of doneness. (Cut small slit in meat and note color.)

PANBROILING
Cuts: Thin cuts (no more than 1 inch thick) of same type recommended for broiling.

Method: Use a heavy pan or griddle; do not preheat. For very lean cuts, brush pan with small amount of shortening if desired; otherwise, do not add fat or water. Cook meat slowly, turning occasionally and pouring off fat as it accumulates, until desired degree of doneness. Do not cover.

PANFRYING
Cuts: Thin, tender pieces of meat that have been made more tender by scoring, cubing or grinding.

Method: Add small amount of fat to pan or allow fat to accumulate as meat cooks. Cook meat on both sides over medium heat, turning occasionally, until desired degree of doneness. Do not cover.

BRAISING
Cuts: Less tender cuts of meat and certain tender cuts from meats such as pork.

Method: Brown meat slowly in heavy pan. Pour off drippings, season and, if necessary, add small amount of liquid to tougher cuts. Cover; simmer on top of range or in 300 to 325° oven until tender.

COOKING IN LIQUID
Cuts: Large, less tender cuts and stew meat.

Method: Brown meat on all sides if desired. Cover meat with liquid as directed and season. Cover and simmer until tender; do not boil.

We are indebted to Reba Staggs of the National Live Stock and Meat Board for broiling and roasting charts and other materials.

BEEF

HOW TO ROAST BEEF

Select beef roast from those listed in chart below. Allow about ½ pound per person (less for boneless roasts). If desired, sprinkle with salt and pepper before, during or after roasting (salt permeates meat only ¼ to ½ inch).

Place beef fat side up on rack in shallow roasting pan. The rack keeps the meat out of the drippings. (With a rib roast, the ribs form a natural rack.) It is not necessary to baste.

Insert meat thermometer so tip is in center of thickest part of beef and does not touch bone or rest in fat. Do not add water. Do not cover.

Roast in 325° oven. (It is not necessary to preheat oven.) Roast to desired degree of doneness (see Timetable), using the thermometer reading as a final guide.

Roasts are easier to carve if allowed to set 15 to 20 minutes after removing from oven. Meat continues to cook after removal from oven; if roast is to set, it should be removed from oven when thermometer registers 5 to 10° lower than desired doneness. To serve au jus, spoon beef juices over carved beef. Or serve beef with Oven-browned Potatoes (below), Pan Gravy (page 10) or Yorkshire Pudding (page 10).

NOTE: For help in carving a rib roast, see page 9.

OVEN-BROWNED POTATOES

About 1½ hours before beef roast is done, prepare and boil 6 medium potatoes as directed on page 185 except—decrease the cooking time to 10 minutes. (Make thin crosswise cuts almost through potatoes, before cooking, if desired.) Place potatoes in beef drippings in pan, turning each potato to coat completely. Or brush potatoes with margarine or butter, melted, and place on rack with beef. Continue cooking, turning potatoes once, until tender and golden brown, about 1¼ hours. Sprinkle with salt and pepper.   6 SERVINGS.

TIMETABLE FOR ROASTING BEEF
(Oven Temperature 325°F)

Cut	Approximate Weight (Pounds)	Meat Thermometer Reading (°F)		Approximate Cooking Time (Minutes per Pound)
Rib	6 to 8	140° (rare)		23 to 25
		160° (medium)		27 to 30
		170° (well)		32 to 35
Boneless Rib	4 to 6	140° (rare)		26 to 32
		160° (medium)		34 to 38
		170° (well)		40 to 42
Rib Eye (Delmonico)*	5 to 7	140° (rare)		32
		160° (medium)		38
		170° (well)		48
	4 to 6	140° (rare)		18 to 20
		160° (medium)		20 to 22
		170° (well)		22 to 24
Rolled Rump (high quality)	4 to 6	150 to 170°		25 to 30
Tip (high quality)	3½ to 4	140 to 170°		35 to 40
Tenderloin (whole)**	4 to 6	140° (rare)	Total Time	45 to 60 minutes
Tenderloin (half)**	2 to 3	140° (rare)		45 to 50 minutes

*Roast at 350° **Roast at 425°

HOW TO CARVE BEEF

STANDING RIB ROAST

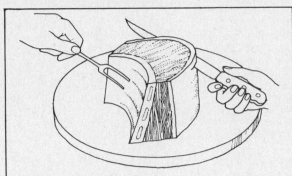

1. Place roast with large side down on a platter. If necessary, remove wedge-shaped slice from large end so roast will stand firmly. To carve, insert fork below first rib. Slice from outside of roast toward rib side.

2. After making several slices, cut along inner side of rib bone with knife. As each slice is released, slide knife under it and lift to plate.

BLADE POT ROAST

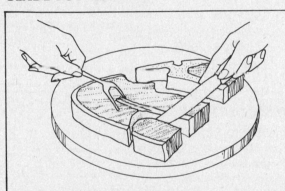

1. With fork in meat, cut between the muscles and around the bones (bones are easily removed). Remove one solid section of pot roast at a time.

2. Turn section so that meat grain runs parallel to platter. Carve across the grain of meat; slices should be about ¼ inch thick.

PORTERHOUSE STEAK

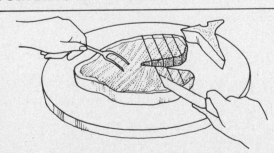

Place steak on a platter with bone to carver's right as shown. Insert fork in steak; cut around bone as closely as possible. Set bone aside. Holding meat with fork, carve 1-inch-wide slices across the full width of steak. For thick steaks, slice on the diagonal instead. (See Corned Beef Brisket instructions at right.)

CORNED BEEF BRISKET

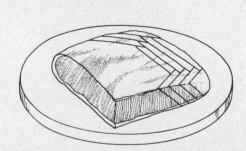

Place beef brisket on platter as shown. Carve across the 2 or 3 "faces" of brisket as shown. Make slices in rotation so that the "faces" will remain equal to each other in size. Cut *thin* slices at a slight angle, always across the grain.

PAN GRAVY FOR ROAST BEEF

For each cup gravy:

2 tablespoons drippings (fat and juices)
2 tablespoons flour
1 cup liquid* (meat juices, broth, water)
  Salt and pepper

Place meat on warm platter; keep warm while preparing gravy. Pour drippings from pan into bowl, leaving brown particles in pan. Return 2 tablespoons drippings to pan. (Measure accurately because too little fat makes gravy lumpy.)

Stir in flour. (Measure accurately so gravy is not greasy.) Cook over low heat, stirring constantly, until mixture is smooth and bubbly; remove from heat. Stir in liquid. Heat to boiling, stirring constantly. Boil and stir 1 minute. Stir in few drops bottled brown bouquet sauce if desired. Sprinkle with salt and pepper.

*Vegetable cooking water, consommé or tomato or vegetable juice can be substituted for part of the liquid.

Creamy Gravy (for turkey, chicken, chops and veal): Substitute milk for half of the liquid.

Mushroom Gravy (for beef, veal and chicken): Before blending flour, cook and stir 8 ounces mushrooms, sliced, in drippings until light brown. Stir ½ teaspoon Worcestershire sauce into gravy.

Thin Gravy: Decrease drippings to 1 tablespoon and flour to 1 tablespoon.

YORKSHIRE PUDDING WITH BEEF

1 cup all-purpose flour*
1 cup milk
2 eggs
½ teaspoon salt

Thirty minutes before beef rib roast or boneless rib roast is done, mix all ingredients with hand beater just until smooth. Heat square pan, 9x9x2 inches, in oven. Remove beef from oven; spoon off drippings and add enough melted shortening, if necessary, to measure ½ cup.

Increase oven temperature to 425°. Return beef to oven. Place hot drippings in heated square pan; pour in pudding batter. Bake 10 minutes. Remove beef; continue baking pudding until deep golden brown, 25 to 30 minutes longer. Cut pudding into squares; serve with beef.   6 TO 9 SERVINGS.

*Do not use self-rising flour in this recipe.

BEEF TENDERLOIN BEARNAISE

Brush 4-pound beef tenderloin with margarine, melted. Place on rack in shallow roasting pan; insert thermometer. Roast uncovered in 425° oven until thermometer registers 140°, 45 to 60 minutes. Serve with Béarnaise Sauce (below).   12 SERVINGS.

BEARNAISE SAUCE
2 egg yolks
3 tablespoons lemon juice
½ cup firm margarine or butter
2 tablespoons white wine or 1 tablespoon
    white wine vinegar
1 tablespoon finely chopped onion
1 teaspoon dried tarragon leaves
½ teaspoon dried chervil leaves

Stir egg yolks and lemon juice vigorously in 1-quart saucepan with wooden spoon. Add half of the margarine. Heat over very low heat, stirring constantly, until margarine is melted. Add remaining margarine. Cook, stirring vigorously, until margarine is melted and sauce thickens. (Be sure margarine melts slowly because this gives eggs time to cook and thicken sauce without curdling.) Stir in remaining ingredients.

MARINATED ROAST BEEF

4-pound beef tip, heel of round or
    rolled rump roast
1½ cups beer or apple cider
⅓ cup vegetable oil
1 teaspoon salt
¼ teaspoon garlic powder
¼ teaspoon pepper
¼ cup cold water
2 tablespoons flour
2 teaspoons instant beef bouillon

Prick beef roast thoroughly with fork. Place beef in deep glass bowl. Mix beer, oil, salt, garlic powder and pepper; pour on beef. Cover and refrigerate, turning occasionally, at least 12 hours.

Place beef fat side up on rack in shallow pan. Reserve 1 cup of the marinade. Insert thermometer so tip is in center of thickest part of beef and does not rest in fat. Roast uncovered in 325° oven until thermometer registers 160°, about 3 hours.

Remove beef to warm platter. Heat reserved marinade over medium heat until hot. Shake water, flour and instant bouillon in covered container; stir gradually into marinade. Heat to boiling, stirring constantly. Boil and stir 1 minute. Serve gravy with beef.   ABOUT 14 SERVINGS.

BEEF CUTS

From the Chuck: Boneless chuck eye roast,* chuck short ribs, blade pot roast or steak, arm pot roast or steak, boneless shoulder pot roast or steak, cross rib pot roast (braise, cook in liquid).

From the Rib: Rib roast, rib steak, boneless rib steak, rib eye or Delmonico roast or steak (roast, broil, panfry).

From the Short Loin: T-bone steak, porterhouse steak, top loin steak, boneless top loin steak, tenderloin or filet mignon steak or roast (roast, broil, panfry).

From the Sirloin: Pin bone sirloin steak, flat bone sirloin steak, wedge bone sirloin steak, boneless sirloin steak (broil, panfry).

From the Round: Rolled rump roast,* round steak, top round steak,* bottom round steak or roast,* eye of round, heel of round, cubed steak* (braise, cook in liquid).

From the Tip: Tip roast or steak,* tip kabobs* (braise).

From the Flank: Flank steak,* flank steak roll* (braise, cook in liquid).

From the Short Plate: Short ribs, skirt steak roll (braise, cook in liquid).

From the Brisket: Fresh brisket, corned brisket (braise, cook in liquid).

From the Shank: Foreshank cross cuts (braise, cook in liquid).

Hamburger and beef for stew come from the flank, short plate, foreshank, chuck or round.

Some cuts from very high quality beef may be roasted, broiled or panfried instead of braised.

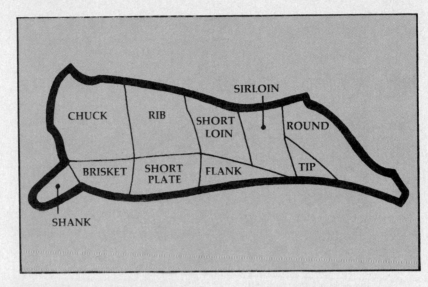

BEEF CUTS YOU SHOULD KNOW

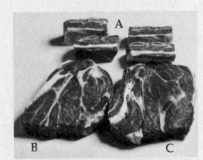

A. Chuck short ribs   B. Blade steak
C. Cross rib pot roast

D. Rib eye (Delmonico) roast
E. Rib steaks

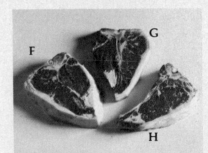

F. Porterhouse steak
G. T-bone steak   H. Top loin steak

I. Tip roast
J. Wedge bone sirloin steak

K. Rolled rump roast
L. Top round steak   M. Eye of round
N. Bottom round steak

O. Short ribs (short plate)
P. Beef for stew   Q. Cubed steak

NEW ENGLAND POT ROAST

4-pound beef arm, blade or cross rib pot roast*
1 tablespoon salt
1 teaspoon pepper
1 jar (5 ounces) prepared horseradish
1 cup water
8 small potatoes, cut into halves
8 medium carrots, each cut into fourths
8 small onions
Kettle Gravy (below)

Cook beef in Dutch oven over medium heat until brown; reduce heat. Sprinkle with salt and pepper. Spread horseradish over both sides of beef. Add water. Heat to boiling; reduce heat. Cover; simmer on top of range or cook in 325° oven 2½ hours. Add vegetables. Cover; cook until tender, about 1 hour. Remove to warm platter. Prepare gravy; serve with beef.   8 SERVINGS.

*3-pound beef bottom round, rolled rump, tip or chuck eye roast can be substituted. Use 2 teaspoons salt.

KETTLE GRAVY

Skim excess fat from broth. Add enough water to broth to measure 2 cups. Shake ½ cup cold water and ¼ cup all-purpose flour in tightly covered container; stir gradually into broth. Heat to boiling, stirring constantly. Boil and stir 1 minute.

Barbecue Pot Roast: Decrease salt to 1½ teaspoons. Omit horseradish and water. Mix 1 can (8 ounces) tomato sauce, ¼ cup water, 1 tablespoon packed brown sugar, 1 tablespoon prepared horseradish and 1 teaspoon prepared mustard; pour on beef.

Herbed Pot Roast: Omit horseradish. Sprinkle beef with 1 teaspoon dried marjoram leaves and 2 cloves garlic, crushed. Substitute 1 cup apple cider for the water and 4 medium white turnips, each cut into fourths, for the potatoes. Add 2 medium stalks celery, cut into 1-inch pieces, and 1 medium green pepper, cut into 1-inch pieces.

Savory Pot Roast: Omit horseradish. Sprinkle beef with 1 teaspoon dried dill weed. Prepare gravy as directed except—add water to measure 1½ cups. After boiling, reduce heat. Stir in ½ cup dairy sour cream and 1 teaspoon dried dill weed; heat.

Spicy Pot Roast: Omit horseradish. Stir ¼ cup catsup, 2 tablespoons vinegar, 2 cloves garlic, crushed, and ¼ teaspoon ground ginger into the gravy. Heat to boiling; reduce heat. Simmer uncovered, stirring occasionally, 10 minutes.

Wine Pot Roast: Omit horseradish and water. Mix ¾ cup dry red wine, ¾ cup dairy sour cream, 2 cloves garlic, crushed, and ½ teaspoon dried thyme leaves; pour on beef. Stir 2 tablespoons lemon juice into the gravy.

POT ROAST IN FOIL

4-pound beef arm, blade or cross rib
    pot roast*
1 can (10¾ ounces) cream of mushroom soup
    Bouillon-Onion Mix (below)
8 small potatoes
8 medium carrots, cut crosswise into halves
2 tablespoons water

Place piece of foil, 30x18 inches, in ungreased pan, 13x9x2 inches. Place beef in pan. Mix soup and Bouillon-Onion Mix; spread over beef. Add vegetables; sprinkle with water. Fold foil over and seal. Cook in 300° oven 4 hours. Skim fat from gravy; serve gravy with beef.   8 SERVINGS.

*3-pound beef bottom round, rolled rump, tip or chuck eye roast can be substituted for the bone-in beef.

BOUILLON-ONION MIX

Mix ¼ cup instant minced onion, 2 tablespoons instant beef bouillon and ½ teaspoon onion powder. (To make soup, stir mix into 4 cups boiling water; reduce heat. Cover; simmer 5 minutes.)

NOTE: 1 package (1⅜ ounces) onion soup mix can be substituted for the Bouillon-Onion Mix.

BRAISED BEEF ROAST

4-pound beef tip, heel of round or rolled
    rump roast
1 tablespoon vegetable oil
1 tablespoon cracked pepper
3¼ cups water
2 tablespoons instant beef bouillon or
    6 beef bouillon cubes
¾ cup cold water
⅓ cup all-purpose flour

Cook beef roast in oil in Dutch oven over medium to low heat until brown; sprinkle with pepper. Add 3¼ cups water and the instant bouillon. Heat to boiling; reduce heat. Cover; simmer on top of range or cook in 325° oven until tender, about 3 hours.

Remove beef to warm platter. Reserve 3 cups drippings in Dutch oven; skim excess fat. Shake ¾ cup cold water and the flour in tightly covered container; stir gradually into broth. Heat to boiling, stirring constantly. Boil and stir 1 minute. Serve gravy with beef.   ABOUT 14 SERVINGS.

NOTE: To serve au jus, do not thicken beef broth.

Cranberry Beef Roast: Substitute cranberry juice cocktail for the 3¼ cups water and the ¾ cup cold water. Decrease instant bouillon to 1 tablespoon.

BEEF BRISKET BARBECUE

Serve this picnic style—thin-sliced on buns—with corn on the cob, Coleslaw (page 138) and Brownies (page 271).

2½-pound well-trimmed fresh beef boneless
    brisket
1½ teaspoons salt
1 medium onion, finely chopped (about
    ½ cup)
½ cup catsup
¼ cup vinegar
1 tablespoon Worcestershire sauce
1½ teaspoons liquid smoke
¼ teaspoon pepper
1 bay leaf, crumbled

Sprinkle beef with salt. Place in ungreased oblong baking dish, 13½x9x2 inches. Mix remaining ingredients; pour on beef. Cover and cook in 325° oven until beef is tender, about 2 hours.
10 SERVINGS.

NOTE: For assistance in carving a beef brisket, see page 9.

CORNED BEEF AND CABBAGE

2-pound well-trimmed corned beef
    boneless brisket or round
1 small onion, cut into fourths
1 clove garlic, crushed
1 small head green cabbage, cut into
    6 wedges

Pour enough cold water on corned beef in 5-quart Dutch oven just to cover. Add onion and garlic. Heat to boiling; reduce heat. Cover and simmer until beef is tender, about 2 hours.

Remove beef to warm platter; keep warm. Skim fat from broth. Add cabbage. Heat to boiling; reduce heat. Simmer uncovered 15 minutes.   6 to 8 SERVINGS.

NOTE: For assistance in carving a beef brisket, see page 9.

New England Boiled Dinner: Decrease simmering time of beef to 1 hour 40 minutes. Skim fat from broth. Add 6 small onions, 6 medium carrots, 3 potatoes, cut into halves, and, if desired, 3 turnips, cut into cubes. Cover and simmer 20 minutes. Remove beef to warm platter; keep warm. Add cabbage. Heat to boiling; reduce heat. Simmer uncovered until vegetables are tender, about 15 minutes.

WISE BEEF BUYS

Less tender beef cuts such as pot roasts, round steak and beef for stew are as nutritious as the more expensive tender cuts. Braise or cook in liquid slowly over low to moderate heat until tender and well done to develop full flavor. But don't overcook—you will have more beef to serve. A pressure cooker does the trick, too, and speeds up the process. Or marinate the meat in a commercial or homemade marinade several hours. Leftover roasts and cooked beef in sauce freeze well, too; store no longer than 6 months.

SAVORY BEEF PIE

    1 small onion, chopped (about ¼ cup)
    2 tablespoons chopped green pepper
    2 tablespoons shortening
    2 cups bite-size pieces cooked beef
    1 package (10 ounces) frozen mixed
        vegetables, broken apart
    1 cup beef gravy
    ¼ cup water
      Sesame Drop Biscuits (below)

Cook and stir onion and green pepper in shortening in 10-inch skillet until tender. Stir in beef, frozen vegetables, gravy and water; heat until hot, about 5 minutes. Pour into ungreased oblong baking dish, 12x7½x2 inches, or square baking dish, 8x8x2 inches. Prepare Sesame Drop Biscuits; drop onto hot beef mixture. Cook uncovered in 450° oven until biscuits are light brown, 15 to 20 minutes. 6 SERVINGS.

SESAME DROP BISCUITS
    ⅓ cup shortening
    1¾ cups all-purpose flour*
    2½ teaspoons baking powder
    ¾ teaspoon salt
    1 cup milk
    ¼ cup sesame seed

Cut shortening into flour, baking powder and salt with pastry blender until mixture resembles fine crumbs. Stir in milk just until soft dough forms (dough will be sticky). Drop dough by 12 spoonfuls into sesame seed, coating all sides.

*If using self-rising flour, omit baking powder and salt.

SKILLET HASH

For crisp hash, use baking potatoes (good with skins on, too). Chop finely so flavors will permeate.

    2 cups chopped cooked beef or corned beef
        (lean only)
    4 small potatoes, cooked and chopped
        (about 2 cups)
    1 medium onion, chopped (about ½ cup)
    1 tablespoon snipped parsley
    ½ teaspoon salt
    ⅛ teaspoon pepper
    ¼ cup shortening

Mix beef, potatoes, onion, parsley, salt and pepper. Heat shortening in 10-inch skillet over medium heat until melted. Spread beef mixture evenly in skillet. Fry, turning frequently, until browned, 10 to 15 minutes. 4 SERVINGS.

Oven Hash: Omit shortening. Spread beef mixture evenly in greased square baking dish, 8x8x2 inches. Cook uncovered in 350° oven 20 minutes.

Red Flannel Skillet Hash: Use 1½ cups chopped corned beef and 3 small potatoes (about 1½ cups). Mix in 1 can (16 ounces) diced or shoestring beets, drained.

CALIFORNIA STIR-FRY

    10 Taco Shells (page 32)
     1 tablespoon margarine or butter
     1 teaspoon cornstarch
     2 medium tomatoes, chopped (about
         1 cup)
     1 small green pepper, chopped (about
         ½ cup)
     1 small onion, chopped (about ¼ cup)
     1 clove garlic, crushed
     2 cups bite-size pieces cooked beef
     3 tablespoons raisins
     ½ teaspoon salt

Prepare Taco Shells. Heat margarine in 10-inch skillet until melted; stir in cornstarch. Add tomatoes, green pepper, onion and garlic. Cook and stir over low heat until hot, about 5 minutes. Stir in beef, raisins and salt. Cook and stir until beef and raisins are hot, about 5 minutes. Spoon about ⅓ cup beef mixture into each taco shell. 5 SERVINGS.

CHEF'S SALAD

½ cup ¼-inch strips cooked meat (beef, smoked ham or tongue)
½ cup ¼-inch strips cooked chicken
½ cup ¼-inch strips Swiss cheese
1 medium head lettuce, torn into bite-size pieces
1 small bunch romaine, torn into bite-size pieces
½ cup chopped green onions
1 medium stalk celery, sliced (about ½ cup)
½ cup mayonnaise or salad dressing
¼ cup French Dressing or Garlic French Dressing (right)
2 hard-cooked eggs, sliced
2 tomatoes, cut into wedges
Ripe olives

Reserve a few strips of meat, chicken and cheese. Toss remaining meat, chicken and cheese, the lettuce, romaine, onions and celery.

Mix mayonnaise and French Dressing; pour on lettuce mixture and toss. Top with reserved meat, chicken and cheese strips, the eggs, tomatoes and olives.   5 SERVINGS.

FRENCH DRESSING

¼ cup olive or vegetable oil or combination
1 tablespoon vinegar
1 tablespoon lemon juice
¼ teaspoon salt
⅛ teaspoon dry mustard
⅛ teaspoon paprika

Shake all ingredients in tightly covered jar; refrigerate. Shake before serving.

Garlic French Dressing: Stir 1 small clove garlic, crushed, and dash of freshly ground pepper into French Dressing.

BEEF-BULGUR SALAD

½ cup uncooked bulgur wheat
  Tomato-Cucumber Dressing (below)
½ cup alfalfa sprouts
2 cups bite-size pieces cooked beef
6 medium tomatoes

Pour enough water on bulgur just to cover. Let stand 15 minutes; drain. Prepare Tomato-Cucumber Dressing; stir in bulgur, alfalfa sprouts and beef.

Place tomatoes stem sides down; cut each almost through to bottom into sixths. Spoon about ½ cup beef mixture into each tomato. Garnish with onion slices, ripe olives or alfalfa sprouts if desired. 6 SERVINGS.

TOMATO-CUCUMBER DRESSING

½ cup mayonnaise or salad dressing
1 medium tomato, chopped and drained
    (about ¾ cup)
½ medium cucumber, chopped (about ½ cup)
½ teaspoon salt
¼ teaspoon dried sage leaves

Mix all ingredients.

BEEF SANDWICH FILLING

1 cup cut-up cooked beef
1 medium stalk celery, finely chopped
    (about ½ cup)
2 tablespoons finely chopped onion
2 tablespoons sweet pickle relish, drained
1 tablespoon lemon juice
½ teaspoon salt
⅛ teaspoon pepper
⅓ cup mayonnaise or salad dressing

Mix all ingredients.   1½ CUPS FILLING (ENOUGH FOR 4 SANDWICHES).

FREEZING HERBS AND ONIONS

Freezer-stored fresh herbs (basil, dill, marjoram, oregano, sage, thyme) or chopped onion add zip to beef sandwiches. To preserve herbs, wash and drain; wrap in foil or plastic bag. Put in carton or glass jar and store in freezer. Peel, wash and quarter onions; chop, then scald for 1½ minutes. Chill in iced water. Drain, package and freeze immediately. When ready to use, remove from freezer and let come to room temperature.

CORNED BEEF SANDWICH FILLING

1 cup cut-up cooked corned beef
½ cup mayonnaise or salad dressing
⅓ cup finely chopped celery
1 tablespoon finely chopped onion
2 teaspoons prepared mustard

Mix all ingredients.   1½ CUPS FILLING (ENOUGH FOR 4 SANDWICHES).

REUBEN SANDWICHES

⅓ cup mayonnaise or salad dressing
1 tablespoon chili sauce
12 slices rye bread
6 slices Swiss cheese
6 slices cooked corned beef
1 can (16 ounces) sauerkraut, drained

Mix mayonnaise and chili sauce; spread over 6 slices bread. Arrange cheese, corned beef and sauerkraut on mayonnaise mixture; top with remaining bread slices. (If desired, spread margarine over both sides of each sandwich. Cook over low heat until bottom is golden and cheese begins to melt, about 10 minutes. Turn and cook other side.)   6 SANDWICHES.

Rachel Sandwiches: Substitute 1½ cups coleslaw for the sauerkraut.

ZESTY BARBECUE SANDWICHES

Prepare Zesty Barbecue Sauce (below). Stir 3 cups 1-inch strips thinly sliced cooked beef into sauce. Cover and simmer until beef is hot, about 5 minutes. Fill 6 hamburger buns with beef mixture. 6 SANDWICHES.

ZESTY BARBECUE SAUCE

½ cup catsup
¼ cup vinegar
2 tablespoons chopped onion
1 tablespoon Worcestershire sauce
2 teaspoons packed brown sugar
¼ teaspoon dry mustard
1 clove garlic, crushed

Heat all ingredients to boiling over medium heat, stirring constantly; reduce heat. Simmer uncovered, stirring occasionally, 15 minutes.

Quick Zesty Barbecue Sandwiches: Substitute 3 packages (3 ounces each) sliced smoked beef, chicken, ham, turkey or pastrami, cut into 1-inch strips, for the beef.

HOW TO BROIL BEEF STEAKS

For each serving, allow about ½ pound of any steak with a bone; allow about ¼ pound for boneless cuts.

Slash diagonally outer edge of fat on beef steaks at 1-inch intervals to prevent curling (do not cut into lean). Set oven control to broil and/or 550°. Place steaks on rack in broiler pan; place broiler pan so tops of ¾- to 1-inch steaks are 2 to 3 inches from heat, 1- to 2-inch steaks are 3 to 5 inches from heat. Broil until brown. The steaks should be about half done (see Timetable).

Sprinkle brown side with salt and pepper if desired. (Always season after browning because salt tends to draw moisture to the surface, delaying browning.) Turn steaks; broil until brown. Serve with your choice of toppings (right).

TIMETABLE FOR BROILING BEEF STEAKS

Cut	Approximate Total Cooking Time (Minutes)	
	Rare (140°F)	Medium (160°F)
Tenderloin (filet mignon, 4 to 8 ounces)	10 to 15	15 to 20
T-bone Steak		
1 inch	20	25
1½ inches	30	35
Porterhouse Steak		
1 inch	20	25
1½ inches	30	35
Sirloin Steak		
1 inch	20	25
1½ inches	30	35
Top Loin Steak		
1 inch	15	20
1½ inches	25	30
2 inches	35	45
Rib or Rib Eye Steak		
1 inch	15	20
1½ inches	25	30
2 inches	35	45
Chuck Eye Steak (high quality)		
1 inch	24	30
1½ inches	40	45

TOPPINGS FOR STEAKS

Spread a zesty topping on steaks just as soon as they're removed from the broiler or grill. Each of the following recipes serves four.

Blue Cheese Topping: Mix 2 ounces crumbled blue cheese and ½ teaspoon Worcestershire sauce.

Mushroom-Onion Topping: Cook and stir 1 medium onion, sliced, ½ cup sliced mushrooms, ½ teaspoon salt and 2 cloves garlic, crushed, in 2 tablespoons margarine or butter until onion is tender.

Mustard Butter: Mix ¼ cup margarine or butter, softened, 1 tablespoon snipped parsley, 2 tablespoons prepared mustard and ¼ teaspoon onion salt.

Sesame Butter: Beat ¼ cup margarine or butter, softened, 1 teaspoon Worcestershire sauce and ½ teaspoon garlic salt. Stir in 1 tablespoon toasted sesame seed.

BEEF-SAUSAGE ROLLS

1 cup soft bread crumbs (about 2 slices bread)
1 small stalk celery, chopped (about ¼ cup)
2 tablespoons finely chopped onion
⅛ teaspoon ground sage
⅛ teaspoon dried thyme leaves
½ pound bulk pork sausage
4 beef cubed steaks (about 3 ounces each)
1 can (10¾ ounces) condensed cream of mushroom soup
¼ cup water
1 can (16 ounces) French-style green beans, drained

Mix bread crumbs, celery, onion, sage and thyme. Cook and stir pork sausage in 10-inch skillet over medium heat until brown; drain. Stir sausage into bread crumb mixture. Press about ¼ cup sausage mixture evenly onto each beef cubed steak. Roll up, beginning at short side; secure with wooden picks.

Cook meat rolls in same skillet over medium heat until brown; reduce heat. Mix soup and water; pour into skillet around rolls. Cover and simmer until tender, about 45 minutes.

Stir in beans. Cover and simmer until beans are hot, about 10 minutes. Serve gravy over meat rolls.
4 SERVINGS.

MINUTE STEAKS

½ cup all-purpose flour
½ teaspoon salt
¼ teaspoon pepper
4 beef cubed steaks (about 3 ounces
   each)
¼ cup shortening
2 tablespoons margarine or butter
   (optional)

Mix flour, salt and pepper. Coat beef steaks with flour mixture. Cook beef in shortening over medium-high heat until brown and crispy, about 4 minutes on each side. Top each with 1½ teaspoons margarine.   4 SERVINGS.

Steaks Stroganoff: Cook and stir 1 medium onion, thinly sliced, in 1 tablespoon margarine or butter in 10-inch skillet until tender. Remove onion; reserve.

Cook beef in same skillet as directed except—omit salt and pepper. Remove beef to warm platter; keep warm. Pour fat from skillet. Mix onion, ½ cup dairy sour cream and ½ teaspoon salt in skillet; heat through. Serve over beef.

FLANK STEAK ROLLS

1-pound beef flank steak
1 clove garlic, cut into halves
1 teaspoon salt
¼ teaspoon pepper
4 slices bacon
1 can (8 ounces) tomato sauce
1 medium onion, finely chopped
   (about ½ cup)
¼ cup water
1 tablespoon snipped parsley
½ teaspoon salt
⅛ teaspoon dried marjoram leaves

Cut both sides of beef steak into diamond pattern ⅛ inch deep. Rub beef with garlic; sprinkle with 1 teaspoon salt and the pepper. Cut beef lengthwise into halves. Cut each half crosswise into halves.

Fry bacon until limp. Drain bacon, reserving fat. Place 1 slice bacon on each part beef. Roll up, beginning at long side; secure with wooden picks. Fry beef in bacon fat over medium heat until brown; drain.

Mix remaining ingredients; pour over beef. Cover and simmer until beef is tender, 45 to 60 minutes. Remove beef to warm platter; remove wooden picks. Pour sauce over beef.   4 SERVINGS.

LONDON BROIL

Not-so-tender flank steak is not usually broiled, but if done very rare and cut across the grain, it's delicious. Add sophisticated Caesar Salad (page 131) and a crusty loaf of Sourdough Bread (page 211); for dessert, offer fresh fruit, cheese and crackers.

1-pound high-quality beef flank steak
2 medium onions, thinly sliced
¼ teaspoon salt
1 tablespoon margarine or butter
2 tablespoons vegetable oil
1 teaspoon lemon juice
2 cloves garlic, crushed
½ teaspoon salt
¼ teaspoon pepper

Cut both sides of beef steak into diamond pattern ⅛ inch deep. Cook and stir onions and ¼ teaspoon salt in margarine until onions are tender; keep warm. Mix remaining ingredients; brush half of the mixture on beef.

Set oven control to broil and/or 550°. Broil beef with top 2 to 3 inches from heat until brown, about 5 minutes. Turn beef; brush with remaining oil mixture and broil 5 minutes longer.

Cut beef across grain at slanted angle into thin slices; serve with onions.   4 SERVINGS.

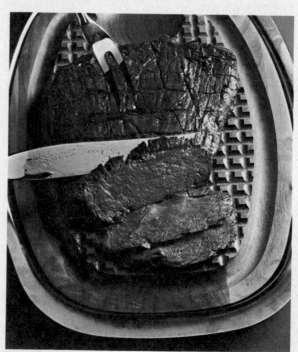

London Broil

BRAISED STEAK BARBECUE

2 tablespoons flour
¼ teaspoon salt
⅛ teaspoon pepper
1-pound beef boneless bottom or top round,
  tip or shoulder steak, ½ inch thick*
1 tablespoon shortening
  Barbecue Sauce (below)
¼ cup cold water
1 tablespoon cornstarch

Mix flour, salt and pepper. Sprinkle one side of beef steak with half of the flour mixture; pound in. Turn beef and pound in remaining flour mixture. Cut beef into 5 serving pieces.

Heat shortening in 10-inch skillet until melted. Cook beef over medium heat until brown, about 15 minutes. Prepare Barbecue Sauce; pour on beef. Heat to boiling; reduce heat. Cover and simmer until beef is tender, about 45 minutes. Add small amount of water if necessary.

Remove beef to warm platter. Shake cold water and cornstarch in tightly covered container; stir gradually into sauce. Heat to boiling. Boil and stir 1 minute. Pour sauce on beef.   5 SERVINGS.

*1½-pound beef bone-in round or chuck steak, ½ inch thick, can be substituted for the boneless beef.

BARBECUE SAUCE

½ cup catsup
¼ cup vinegar
¼ cup water
1 small onion, chopped (about ¼ cup)
1½ teaspoons packed brown sugar
1½ teaspoons prepared mustard
1½ teaspoons Worcestershire sauce
¼ teaspoon salt
⅛ teaspoon pepper

Mix all ingredients.

Braised Steak Skillet: Add ½ teaspoon dried oregano leaves to the flour mixture. Substitute Garlic Tomato Sauce (page 24) for the Barbecue Sauce; pour on beef. Heat to boiling; reduce heat. Cover and simmer 15 minutes. Add 1 package (9 ounces) frozen Italian green beans and 1 can (16 ounces) whole onions, drained. Heat to boiling; reduce heat. Cover and simmer about 30 minutes. Continue as directed.

SWISS STEAK

2 tablespoons flour
¼ teaspoon salt
⅛ teaspoon pepper
1-pound beef boneless bottom or top round,
  tip or chuck steak, ½ inch thick*
1 tablespoon shortening
1 can (8 ounces) whole tomatoes
1 medium onion, chopped (about ½ cup)
½ small green pepper, finely chopped
  (about ¼ cup)
½ teaspoon salt
⅛ teaspoon pepper

Mix flour, ¼ teaspoon salt and ⅛ teaspoon pepper. Sprinkle 1 side of beef steak with half of the flour mixture; pound in. Turn beef and pound in remaining flour mixture. Cut beef into 4 or 5 serving pieces.

Heat shortening in 10-inch skillet until melted. Cook beef over medium heat until brown, about 15 minutes. Mix tomatoes (with liquid) and remaining ingredients; pour on beef. Heat to boiling; reduce heat. Cover and simmer until beef is tender, about 45 minutes.   4 OR 5 SERVINGS.

*1½ pounds beef bone-in round or chuck steak, ½ inch thick, can be substituted for the boneless beef.

Onion Swiss Steak: Omit salt in flour mixture. Mix 1 can (10¾ ounces) condensed cream of mushroom soup, 1 can (4 ounces) sliced mushrooms, drained (optional), ½ cup water and the Bouillon-Onion Mix (page 13); substitute for the tomato mixture.

MUSTARD SHORT RIBS

4 pounds beef short ribs, cut into pieces
⅓ cup prepared mustard
1 tablespoon sugar
2 tablespoons lemon juice
1 teaspoon salt
½ teaspoon pepper
2 cloves garlic, crushed
4 medium onions, sliced

Place beef ribs in shallow glass dish. Mix mustard, sugar, lemon juice, salt, pepper and garlic; spread over beef. Top with onions. Cover and refrigerate, turning beef occasionally, 24 hours.

Cook beef in 4-quart Dutch oven over medium heat until brown; drain. Add onions and pour marinade on beef. Cover and cook in 350° oven until tender, about 2 hours.   4 SERVINGS.

BEEF TERIYAKI

1½ pounds beef boneless top loin
    or sirloin steak*
¼ cup soy sauce
¼ cup vegetable oil
2 tablespoons dry white wine
1 teaspoon sugar
½ teaspoon ground ginger
1 clove garlic, crushed
1 tablespoon cornstarch
    Rice (below)

Trim fat and bone from beef steak; cut beef across grain into ⅛-inch slices. Mix soy sauce, oil, wine, sugar, ginger and garlic. Stir in beef, coating each slice thoroughly. Cover and refrigerate 1 hour.

Drain beef, reserving marinade. Cook and stir beef in 10-inch skillet over medium heat, stirring frequently, just until beef is light brown, about 5 minutes.

Add enough cold water to reserved marinade to measure ½ cup. Shake marinade-water mixture and cornstarch in tightly covered container; stir gradually into beef. Heat to boiling, stirring constantly; reduce heat. Simmer uncovered 5 minutes. For each serving, spoon about ½ cup beef mixture onto about ½ cup hot Rice.   6 SERVINGS.

*2¼ pounds beef bone-in short loin or sirloin steaks can be substituted for the boneless beef.

NOTE: Beef is easier to slice if partially frozen.

RICE
Heat 1 cup uncooked regular rice, 2 cups water and 1 teaspoon salt to boiling, stirring once or twice; reduce heat. Cover and simmer 14 minutes. (Do not lift cover or stir.) Remove from heat. Fluff rice lightly with fork; cover and let steam 5 to 10 minutes.

ABOUT GREEN PEPPERS
Tender young green peppers, available year round, turn red as they mature. Only 15 calories each, peppers are high in vitamin C (for healthy gums and skin). One raw pepper furnishes more than the daily adult requirement of vitamin C; a cooked pepper provides almost enough for a day. Look for medium to dark green color, a glossy sheen and firm sides. Slice peppers into salads, cut them into pieces and use for dippers, or stuff and bake or microwave them (page 38).

BEEF AND MUSHROOM SALADS

1½ pounds beef sirloin steak, 1½ inches thick
1 jar (4½ ounces) sliced mushrooms, drained
1 medium green pepper, thinly sliced
    into rings
⅓ cup red wine vinegar
¼ cup vegetable oil
1 teaspoon salt
½ teaspoon onion salt
½ teaspoon Worcestershire sauce
¼ teaspoon pepper
¼ teaspoon dried tarragon leaves
2 cloves garlic, crushed
    Lettuce cups

Set oven control to broil and/or 550°. Broil beef steak with top about 2 inches from heat until medium, about 13 minutes on each side. Cool; cut into ⅜-inch strips. Arrange in ungreased oblong baking dish, 13½x9x2 inches. Arrange mushrooms on beef; top with green pepper rings.

Mix vinegar, oil, salt, onion salt, Worcestershire sauce, pepper, tarragon and garlic; pour on beef and vegetables. Cover and refrigerate, spooning dressing over vegetables occasionally, at least 3 hours. Remove vegetables to lettuce cups with slotted spoon. Arrange beef beside vegetables.
4 TO 6 SERVINGS.

BEEF KABOBS

2 pounds high-quality beef tip or round, cut
    into 1¼-inch cubes
1 can (10½ ounces) condensed beef consommé
⅓ cup dry white wine or apple juice
2 tablespoons soy sauce
2 cloves garlic, crushed
¼ teaspoon onion powder
1 tablespoon plus 1 teaspoon cornstarch

Place beef in oblong baking dish, 13½x9x2 inches. Heat consommé, wine, soy sauce, garlic and onion powder to boiling; reduce heat. Simmer uncovered 5 minutes; cool. Pour mixture on beef. Cover and refrigerate, spooning mixture over beef occasionally, at least 3 hours.

Thread 4 or 5 beef cubes on each of 6 to 8 skewers. Stir marinade gradually into cornstarch in saucepan. Cook, stirring constantly, until mixture thickens. Boil and stir 1 minute. Brush over kabobs. Set oven control to broil and/or 550°. Broil kabobs with tops about 4 inches from heat 7 minutes; turn. Brush with sauce and broil 7 minutes. Place on hot platter; spoon on remaining sauce.   8 SERVINGS.

BEEF FONDUE

Several hours before serving, trim fat from 1 to 2 pounds beef tenderloin or boneless top loin steak, 1 inch thick. Cut beef into 1-inch cubes. Cover and refrigerate. Prepare choice of sauces (below and right).

About 15 minutes before serving, mound beef cubes on bed of salad greens. Pour peanut or vegetable oil into metal fondue pot to depth of 1 to 1½ inches. Margarine or butter can be substituted for ¼ of the oil if desired. Heat until a bread cube browns in 1 minute. Carefully place pot on stand and ignite denatured alcohol burner or canned cooking fuel.

Guests use long-handled forks to spear beef cubes, dip into hot oil and cook until crusty on the outside, juicy and rare inside. Since the long fork will be very hot by this time, beef should be dipped in sauce and eaten with a second fork. 4 TO 6 SERVINGS.

ANCHOVY BUTTER SAUCE

Drain 1 can (2 ounces) anchovy fillets. Mix ½ cup margarine or butter, softened, the anchovy fillets and ⅛ teaspoon pepper. Cover and refrigerate. Bring to room temperature before serving.

BLUE CHEESE SAUCE

½ cup dairy sour cream
¼ cup crumbled blue cheese
1 teaspoon Worcestershire sauce
¼ teaspoon salt

Mix all ingredients. Cover and refrigerate until serving time.

GARLIC BUTTER SAUCE

Beat ½ cup margarine or butter, softened, until fluffy. Stir in 1 tablespoon snipped parsley and 1 clove garlic, crushed. Cover and refrigerate. Bring to room temperature before serving.

HORSERADISH SAUCE

Mix 1 cup dairy sour cream, 2 tablespoons prepared horseradish, ½ teaspoon lemon juice, ¼ teaspoon Worcestershire sauce, ⅛ teaspoon salt and ⅛ teaspoon pepper. Cover and refrigerate until serving time.

ABOUT FONDUES

Plan everything ahead, then relax. It's simple to entertain in this leisurely style where guests can do it themselves. You'll need:

☐ A metal pot with a broad base, secure handle, sloping sides or partial cover to prevent spattering, and a well-balanced stand. (An electric pot is the best all-purpose pot for cooking and heating.)

☐ A sturdy, level table that provides easy reach for those sharing the fondue pot. (Four is an ideal number for fondue.)

☐ A heatproof tray for the pot to rest on.

☐ Fondue forks (10 to 12 inches long, with insulated handles color coded for convenience).

☐ Dinner forks. Hot food is transferred to these from fondue forks.

☐ Service plates with indentations for sauces.

☐ Vinyl cloth or wipe-clean fabric to protect your table from spills.

Fuels for Fondues: An *alcohol burner* contains a wick or fiber pad. Fill only half full; wipe dry with cloth before lighting. Regulate heat by raising or lowering wick or closing or opening damper. Never refuel while alcohol is burning or while container is hot. Empty and dry alcohol burner before using. *Canned heat* is solidified alcohol. Regulate heat with movable cover or use lid. Keep both fondue fuels out of the reach of children.

Sliced Beef with Mushrooms

SLICED BEEF WITH MUSHROOMS

½ cup thinly sliced mushrooms
2 tablespoons finely chopped onion
1 teaspoon lemon juice
1 teaspoon Worcestershire sauce
⅛ teaspoon salt
1 clove garlic, crushed
¼ cup margarine or butter
2 tablespoons snipped parsley
1-pound beef tenderloin or rib eye
　　(Delmonico), cut into 8 slices
2 tablespoons margarine or butter

Cook and stir mushrooms, onion, lemon juice, Worcestershire sauce, salt and garlic in ¼ cup margarine until mushrooms are tender. Stir in parsley; keep warm.

Cook beef in 2 tablespoons margarine over medium-high heat, turning once, until desired doneness, 3 to 4 minutes on each side. Serve with mushroom sauce.　4 SERVINGS.

VEGETABLE GO-WITHS FOR BEEF

In addition to the usual potatoes, carrots and onions, try one of the following to complement the robust flavor of beef: broccoli, cabbage, cauliflower, celery, green beans, tomatoes, beets and beet greens, mushrooms, eggplant, white turnips, parsnips or kohlrabi. You'll be adding vitamins A and C and some minerals at the same time.

ECONOMY BEEF WITH PEA PODS

1 pound beef round steak, ½ inch thick
1 tablespoon soy sauce
1 thin slice gingerroot, crushed*
1 clove garlic, crushed*
2 tablespoons vegetable oil
1 can (13¾ ounces) chicken broth (about
　　1⅔ cups)
1 package (6 ounces) frozen Chinese pea pods
4 ounces mushrooms, sliced
3 stalks Chinese cabbage, cut diagonally
　　into ¼-inch slices (about 2 cups)
1 medium onion, sliced
1 can (8½ ounces) water chestnuts, drained
　　and thinly sliced
1 can (8½ ounces) bamboo shoots, drained
2 tablespoons vegetable oil
3 tablespoons cornstarch
2 tablespoons soy sauce
½ teaspoon salt
¼ teaspoon sugar
1⅓ cups chow mein noodles or 3½ cups hot
　　cooked rice (page 225)

Cut beef across grain into ⅛-inch slices. Mix 1 tablespoon soy sauce, the gingerroot and garlic; toss with beef. Cover and refrigerate at least 1 hour.

Cook and stir beef in 2 tablespoons oil in 10-inch skillet over medium-high heat until brown. Stir in 1 cup of the broth. Heat to boiling; reduce heat. Cover and simmer until beef is tender, about 20 minutes. Remove beef and broth from skillet.

Rinse pea pods under cold water to separate; drain. Cook and stir mushrooms, cabbage, onion, water chestnuts and bamboo shoots in 2 tablespoons oil over high heat 2 minutes. Stir in beef, broth and pea pods. Cover; cook over medium heat 2 minutes.

Shake remaining broth, the cornstarch, 2 tablespoons soy sauce, the salt and sugar in tightly covered container; stir gradually into skillet. Heat to boiling, stirring constantly. Boil and stir 1 minute. Serve over noodles.　5 SERVINGS.

*Pound gingerroot and garlic between waxed paper.

NOTE: Beef is easier to slice if partially frozen.

Classic Beef with Pea Pods: Substitute ¾ pound beef tenderloin or boneless top loin steak for the round steak. Marinate 30 minutes. Cook and stir beef in oil until brown; remove from skillet (do not simmer). Stir the 1 cup broth into vegetable mixture with the pea pods. Continue as directed except—stir in beef after boiling and stirring vegetable mixture 1 minute. Heat until beef is hot.

ABOUT MUSHROOMS

Fresh mushrooms are available year-round but peak in November and December. Look for clean, firm, fresh-looking mushrooms that are white, creamy or tan. Avoid withered (old) mushrooms. Caps should be closed around the stem or slightly open. Fresh mushrooms can be refrigerated for 4 or 5 days in their carton; cover loosely. Eventually they will oxidize and turn dark. Do not peel mushrooms; much of the flavor is in the skin. If the bottom of the stem looks dry and brown, trim away a thin slice and discard. Never soak them; just whisk under cool water and pat dry. Unless you want the mushroom flavor to mingle with others, do not overcook—4 or 5 minutes is plenty. Overcooking dries them out and makes them tough.

ECONOMY SUKIYAKI

1 pound beef boneless round steak
⅓ cup soy sauce
2 tablespoons sugar
2 tablespoons vegetable oil
1 beef bouillon cube
½ cup boiling water
8 ounces mushrooms, thinly sliced
1 bunch green onions (about 8 medium), cut into 1½-inch pieces
2 large onions, thinly sliced
3 medium stalks celery, cut into diagonal slices (about 1½ cups)
1 can (8½ ounces) bamboo shoots, drained
3 ounces spinach, torn into bite-size pieces (about 3 cups)
3 cups hot cooked rice (page 225)

Cut beef steak across grain into strips, each about 2x¼-inch. Mix soy sauce and sugar; toss with beef. Cover and refrigerate 2 hours.

Drain beef, reserving marinade. Cook and stir beef in oil in 12-inch skillet or Dutch oven over medium-high heat until brown. Push beef to side of skillet. Dissolve bouillon cube in water; stir in reserved marinade. Pour into skillet. Arrange mushrooms, onions, celery and bamboo shoots in separate sections of skillet. Cover; simmer until beef is tender, about 10 minutes. Add spinach. Cover; simmer 5 minutes longer. Serve with rice.   4 SERVINGS.

Classic Sukiyaki: Substitute beef boneless top loin steak or tenderloin for the round steak. Do not marinate. Stir in soy sauce and sugar with the bouillon.

BEEF STEW

1 pound beef boneless chuck, tip or round, cut into 1-inch cubes
1 tablespoon shortening
3 cups hot water
½ teaspoon salt
⅛ teaspoon pepper
1 large potato, cut into 1½-inch pieces (about 1¼ cups)
1 medium turnip, cut into 1-inch pieces (about 1 cup)
2 medium carrots, cut into 1-inch pieces (about 1 cup)
1 medium green pepper, cut into 1-inch pieces (about 1 cup)
1 medium stalk celery, cut into 1-inch pieces (about ½ cup)
1 small onion, chopped
½ teaspoon bottled brown bouquet sauce
1½ teaspoons salt
1 beef bouillon cube
1 bay leaf
Parsley Dumplings (page 195)
½ cup cold water
2 tablespoons flour

Cook and stir beef in shortening in 12-inch skillet or Dutch oven until beef is brown, about 15 minutes. Add 3 cups hot water, ½ teaspoon salt and the pepper. Heat to boiling; reduce heat. Cover and simmer until beef is almost tender, 2 to 2½ hours.

Stir in potato, turnip, carrots, green pepper, celery, onion, bouquet sauce, 1½ teaspoons salt, the bouillon cube and bay leaf. Cover and simmer until vegetables are tender, about 30 minutes.

Prepare Parsley Dumplings. Shake ½ cup cold water and the flour in tightly covered container; stir gradually into stew. Heat to boiling, stirring constantly. Boil and stir 1 minute; reduce heat.

Drop dumpling dough by 10 to 12 spoonfuls onto hot stew (do not drop directly into liquid). Cook uncovered 10 minutes. Cover and cook 10 minutes longer.   5 OR 6 SERVINGS.

Do-ahead Tip: After boiling and stirring 1 minute, stew can be covered and refrigerated no longer than 48 hours. To serve, heat to boiling over medium-high heat. Continue as directed.

Chicken Stew: Substitute 1½- to 2-pound stewing chicken, cut up, for the beef and chicken bouillon cube for the beef bouillon cube.

Oxtail Stew: Substitute 2 pounds oxtails for the beef. Increase first simmering time to 3½ hours.

COOKING WITH WINE

Wine brings out the finest taste and aroma of many foods. When wine is heated, the alcoholic content disappears, leaving only its essence to impart a subtle flavor.

Recipes in this book were tested with drinking wines—not those labeled "Cooking Wine," which have salt added. When a recipe calls for dry, medium or sweet wines, follow this guide:

Dry Red Wines: Barbera, Baco Noir, Bordeaux, Burgundy, Cabernet Sauvignon, Chianti, claret, Côtes du Rhône, Gamay, Gamay Beaujolais, Grignolino, Grignolino rosé, Pinot Noir, Pinot St. George, Rioja reds, Zinfandel, Zinfandel rosé

Medium Red Wines: Anjou rosé, Catawba red, Concord, Grenach rosé, Lake Country red, Lambrusco, medium-dry sherry, vino rosso

Sweet Red Wines: Aleatico, kosher Concord, Malaga, port (ruby, tawny, tinta), red Malvasia, sweet (red) vermouth

Dry White Wines: white Burgundy, Chablis, Chenin Blanc, white Chianti, green Hungarian, grey Riesling, Johannisberg Riesling, Muscadet, Pinot Blanc, Pinot Chardonnay, dry Rhine, dry sauterne, dry Semillon, dry sherry, Soave, Sylvaner Riesling, dry (white) vermouth

Medium White Wines: white Anjou, Gewürztraminer, Lake Country white, Liebfraumilch, Orvieto, Rhine, Riesling, Vouvray

Sweet White Wines: Angelica, Barsac, cream sherry, Haut-Sauternes, white kosher wines, Malvasia, Marsala, Muscat-deré-de-Frontignan, Muscatel, sauternes, sweet Semillon, Tokay

BEEF WITH SPAGHETTI

    Garlic Tomato Sauce (right)
1½ pounds beef boneless chuck, tip or
      round, cut into 1-inch pieces
¼ cup instant minced onion
2 tablespoons instant beef bouillon
½ teaspoon onion powder
½ cup dry red wine
7 or 8 ounces uncooked spaghetti

Prepare Garlic Tomato Sauce. Mix beef, onion, bouillon, onion powder, wine and sauce in Dutch oven. Cover and cook in 350° oven, stirring occasionally, until beef is tender, 2½ to 3 hours. (Add water or wine during cooking if necessary).

Cook spaghetti as directed on page 221. Serve beef mixture over spaghetti.   6 SERVINGS.

GARLIC TOMATO SAUCE
1 clove garlic, cut into halves
1 tablespoon olive oil
1 can (16 ounces) whole tomatoes
1 small onion, chopped (about
    ¼ cup)
1 tablespoon margarine or butter
½ teaspoon salt
¼ teaspoon sugar
¼ teaspoon dried basil leaves
¼ teaspoon dried rosemary leaves (optional)
    Dash of pepper

Cook and stir garlic in oil in 1½-quart saucepan over low heat until garlic is brown; discard garlic. Stir in tomatoes (with liquid) and remaining ingredients; break up tomatoes with fork. Heat to boiling; reduce heat. Simmer uncovered, stirring frequently, until sauce thickens, 40 to 50 minutes.

BEEF-VEGETABLE SOUP

1 pound beef boneless chuck, tip or round,
    cut into ½-inch cubes
1 tablespoon vegetable oil
1 cup water
2 teaspoons instant beef bouillon
1½ teaspoons salt
¼ teaspoon dried marjoram leaves
¼ teaspoon dried thyme leaves
¼ teaspoon monosodium glutamate
⅛ teaspoon pepper
1 bay leaf
4 cups water
3 medium carrots, sliced (about 1 cup)
1 large stalk celery, sliced
1 medium onion, chopped (about ½ cup)
1 can (16 ounces) whole tomatoes

Cook and stir beef in oil in 4-quart Dutch oven over medium heat until brown. Stir in 1 cup water, the instant bouillon, salt, marjoram, thyme, monosodium glutamate, pepper and bay leaf. Cover and simmer until beef is tender, 1 to 1½ hours.

Stir in 4 cups water, the carrots, celery, onion and tomatoes (with liquid). Heat to boiling; reduce heat. Cover and simmer until carrots are tender, about 35 minutes.   5 SERVINGS.

Beef-Barley Vegetable Soup: Add ½ cup uncooked barley or bulgur wheat with the tomatoes.

Beef-Pasta Vegetable Soup: Cover and simmer until carrots are crisp-tender, about 30 minutes. Stir in ½ cup uncooked macaroni rings. Cover; simmer until macaroni is tender, 7 to 10 minutes.

ECONOMY BEEF STROGANOFF

1½ pounds beef for stew, cut into ⅛-inch
    slices
2 tablespoons margarine or butter
1½ cups beef bouillon
2 tablespoons catsup
1 small clove garlic, finely chopped, or
    ⅛ teaspoon instant minced garlic
1 teaspoon salt
8 ounces mushrooms, sliced
1 medium onion, chopped (about
    ½ cup)
3 tablespoons flour
1 cup dairy sour cream
3 or 4 cups hot cooked noodles
    (page 221)
1 tablespoon margarine or butter
1 teaspoon poppy seed

Cook and stir beef in 2 tablespoons margarine in 10-inch skillet over low heat until brown. Reserve ⅓ cup of the bouillon. Stir remaining bouillon, the catsup, garlic and salt into skillet. Heat to boiling; reduce heat. Cover and simmer until beef is tender, 1 to 1½ hours.

Stir in mushrooms and onion. Cover and simmer until onion is tender, about 5 minutes. Shake reserved bouillon and the flour in tightly covered container; stir gradually into beef mixture. Heat to boiling, stirring constantly. Boil and stir 1 minute; reduce heat. Stir in sour cream; heat through.

Toss noodles with 1 tablespoon margarine and the poppy seed. Serve beef mixture over hot noodles. 6 SERVINGS.

NOTE: Beef is easier to slice if partially frozen.

Classic Beef Stroganoff: Substitute 1½ pounds beef tenderloin or boneless top loin, about ½ inch thick, for the beef for stew. Cut beef across grain into strips, each 1½x½ inch. Decrease first simmering time to 10 minutes.

ABOUT DAIRY SOUR CREAM

Store dairy sour cream in the original container in the coldest part of the refrigerator. Do not freeze sour cream, even though some foods prepared with it do freeze well. When you cook with sour cream, protect its smooth texture by heating gently; do not boil. Add to other ingredients just before serving. If the mixture does curdle, only the appearance will be affected, not the taste.

HUNGARIAN GOULASH

2 pounds beef for stew, cut into 1-inch
    cubes
1 medium onion, sliced
1 small clove garlic, finely chopped, or
    ⅛ teaspoon instant minced garlic
¼ cup shortening
1½ cups water
¾ cup catsup
2 tablespoons Worcestershire sauce
1 tablespoon packed brown sugar
2 teaspoons salt
2 teaspoons paprika
½ teaspoon dry mustard
    Dash of cayenne red pepper
¼ cup cold water
2 tablespoons flour
    Noodles (below)

Cook and stir beef, onion and garlic in shortening until beef is brown; drain. Stir in 1½ cups water, the catsup, Worcestershire sauce, brown sugar, salt, paprika, mustard and red pepper. Heat to boiling; reduce heat. Cover and simmer until beef is tender, 2 to 2½ hours.

Shake ¼ cup cold water and the flour in tightly covered container; stir gradually into beef mixture. Heat to boiling, stirring constantly. Boil and stir 1 minute. Serve over hot Noodles. 6 TO 8 SERVINGS.

NOODLES

Drop 8 ounces uncooked noodles into 6 cups rapidly boiling salted water (4 teaspoons salt). Heat to rapid boiling. Cook, stirring constantly, 3 minutes. Cover tightly. Remove from heat and let stand 10 minutes; drain.

Do-ahead Tip: Hungarian Goulash can be covered and frozen no longer than 4 months. Cover and heat frozen goulash and ½ cup water over medium-low heat, turning occasionally, until hot and bubbly, about 30 minutes.

MEAT LOAF

1½ pounds hamburger
 1 cup dry or soft bread crumbs, cracker
    crumbs or dry bread cubes and
    1¼ cups milk; or 3 slices bread, torn
    into pieces, and 1 cup milk; or ¾ cup
    oatmeal and 1 cup milk
 1 egg
 1 small onion, chopped (about ¼ cup)
 1 tablespoon Worcestershire sauce
1½ teaspoons salt
 ½ teaspoon dry mustard
 ¼ teaspoon pepper
 ¼ teaspoon ground sage
 1 clove garlic, crushed (optional)
    Mushroom Gravy (below)

Mix all ingredients except Mushroom Gravy.
Spread in ungreased loaf pan, 9x5x3 inches. Cook
uncovered in 350° oven until done, about 1½
hours. Serve with Mushroom Gravy.   6 SERVINGS.

MUSHROOM GRAVY

 1 can (4 ounces) mushroom stems and pieces,
    drained (reserve liquid)
 2 tablespoons flour
 2 tablespoons vegetable oil
 1 beef bouillon cube
 4 drops bottled brown bouquet sauce

Cook mushrooms and flour in oil over low heat,
stirring constantly, until mixture is bubbly; remove
from heat. Add enough water to reserved mushroom liquid to measure 1 cup; stir into mushroom
mixture. Add bouillon cube. Heat to boiling, stirring constantly. Boil and stir 1 minute. Stir in
bouquet sauce.

■ **To Microwave:** Spread meat loaf mixture in
ungreased 2-quart round glass casserole. Cover and
microwave 7 minutes; turn casserole one quarter
turn. Microwave until done, 8 to 10 minutes longer.
Let stand 5 minutes. Cut into wedges and serve
immediately.

Applesauce Meat Loaf: Substitute 1 cup applesauce for the milk. Spread mixture of 1 cup applesauce and ¼ teaspoon ground ginger over meat loaf
mixture in pan. Sprinkle with ground cinnamon if
desired. Omit gravy.

Barbecue Meat Loaf: Spread ½ cup barbecue sauce,
catsup or chili sauce over meat loaf mixture in pan.
Omit gravy.

Blue Cheese Meat Loaf: Mix in 2 ounces crumbled
blue cheese. Omit gravy.

Individual Meat Loaves: Shape meat loaf mixture
into 6 small loaves; place in ungreased oblong pan,
13x9x2 inches. Cook uncovered 45 minutes.

Mushroom Meat Loaf: Mix in 8 ounces mushrooms, finely chopped.

Spanish Meat Loaf: Substitute ⅓ cup tomato sauce
and ⅔ cup milk for the milk. Mix in 8 large pimiento-stuffed olives, sliced. Spread ⅔ cup tomato sauce over meat loaf mixture in pan. Omit gravy.

Wine Meat Loaf: Substitute ½ cup sweet red wine
for ½ cup of the milk. Mix in 2 small carrots, finely
chopped, and 1 medium stalk celery, finely
chopped. Increase salt to 2½ teaspoons.

HAMBURGER KNOW-HOW

Hamburger is another word for ground beef; however, federal laws specify the amount of fat permitted in the various types of ground beef, so it is
actually the amount of fat that determines the
classification. Any ground beef bearing the label
hamburger can contain up to 30% fat. *Ground beef* can
also contain 30% fat, but only the fat attached to the
particular cut of beef being ground; no other beef
fat can be added.

Lean ground beef (*ground chuck*) has 20% or less fat;
extra lean ground beef (*ground round*), 15% or less.
Recipes in this book were tested with hamburger.

Since hamburger is far more perishable than other
beef cuts, use within 24 hours of purchase. Store in
the meat keeper or coldest part of the refrigerator.
If prepackaged, leave in the package; if ground to
order, rewrap loosely in waxed paper or aluminum
foil and refrigerate. If you plan to store hamburger
longer than 24 hours, freeze it.

Freezer storage time for beef at 0° F:

Hamburger or other ground beef	3 to 4 months
Most cuts of beef	9 months
Beef for stew	4 months
Liver, heart, tongue	3 to 4 months
Cooked beef	2 months

To prepare for freezing: Do not season. For easy
separation, place double layer of freezer wrap
between hamburger patties, steaks or chops. Use
moistureproof, vaporproof wrap; wrap closely to
eliminate air. Prepackaged meat can be frozen in its
wrapper up to 2 weeks. Cook meat thawed or frozen.

To cook: Thaw wrapped meat in refrigerator or
broil frozen patties and steaks farther than normal
distance from heat.

Spread broccoli on rectangle.

Roll up, using foil to lift.

Meat Loaf Roll

MEAT LOAF ROLL

 1 package (10 ounces) frozen chopped
     broccoli or leaf spinach
 2 pounds hamburger
 2 eggs
 ¾ cup soft bread crumbs (about 1 slice bread)
 ¼ cup catsup
 ¼ cup milk
 ½ teaspoon salt
 ¼ teaspoon pepper
 ¼ teaspoon dried oregano leaves
 1 teaspoon salt
 1 package (3 ounces) smoked sliced ham
 3 slices mozzarella cheese, each 3x3 inches,
     cut diagonally into halves (optional)

Rinse frozen broccoli under running cold water to
separate; drain. Mix hamburger, eggs, bread
crumbs, catsup, milk, ½ teaspoon salt, the pepper
and oregano. Pat hamburger mixture into rectangle, 12x10 inches, on piece of aluminum foil, 18x15
inches.

Arrange broccoli on hamburger mixture to within
½ inch of edges; sprinkle with 1 teaspoon salt.
Arrange ham on broccoli. Roll up rectangle carefully, beginning at 10-inch side and using foil to lift.
Press edges and ends of roll to seal.

Place on rack in shallow roasting pan. Cook uncovered in 350° oven 1¼ hours. Overlap cheese on
top; cook just until cheese begins to melt, about 1
minute longer. (Center of meat loaf roll may be
slightly pink due to ham.) Garnish with celery
leaves if desired.   8 SERVINGS.

Do-ahead Tip: After rolling, cover and refrigerate meat loaf no longer than 24 hours. Cook as
directed except—increase first cooking time to
1½ hours.

Sweet-and-Sour Meatballs (page 29) and Economy Beef with Pea Pods (page 22)

MEATBALLS

1 pound hamburger
½ cup dry bread crumbs
¼ cup milk
2 tablespoons finely chopped onion
1 teaspoon salt
½ teaspoon Worcestershire sauce
1 egg

Mix ingredients; shape into twenty 1½-inch balls. Cook over medium heat, turning occasionally, until brown, about 20 minutes. Or cook in ungreased oblong pan, 13x9x2 inches, in 400° oven until light brown, 20 to 25 minutes.   4 SERVINGS.

Swedish Meatballs: Substitute ½ pound ground pork for ½ pound of the hamburger and half-and-half for the milk. Mix in ½ teaspoon ground allspice. Cook in skillet.

SWEET-AND-SOUR MEATBALLS

Meatballs (above)
½ cup packed brown sugar
1 tablespoon cornstarch
1 can (13¼ ounces) pineapple chunks
⅓ cup vinegar
1 tablespoon soy sauce
1 small green pepper, coarsely chopped

Cook Meatballs in skillet; remove. Drain fat from skillet. Mix brown sugar and cornstarch in skillet. Stir in pineapple (with syrup), vinegar and soy sauce. Heat to boiling, stirring constantly; reduce heat. Add meatballs. Cover; simmer, stirring occasionally, 10 minutes. Stir in green pepper. Cover; simmer until crisp-tender, 5 minutes.   4 SERVINGS.

SAUCY MEATBALLS

Meatballs (above)
1 can (10¾ ounces) condensed cream of
    chicken soup
⅓ cup milk
⅛ teaspoon ground nutmeg
½ cup dairy sour cream

Cook Meatballs in skillet; drain. Stir in soup, milk and nutmeg. Heat to boiling, stirring occasionally; reduce heat. Cover and simmer 15 minutes. Stir in sour cream; heat through.   4 SERVINGS.

■ **To Microwave:** Cover and microwave Meatballs in ungreased baking dish, 8x8x2 inches, until almost done, about 6 minutes; drain. Mix soup, milk, nutmeg and sour cream; stir into meatballs. Cover; microwave until bubbly, about 5 minutes.

PORCUPINES

1 pound hamburger
½ cup uncooked regular rice
½ cup water
⅓ cup chopped onion
1 teaspoon salt
½ teaspoon celery salt
⅛ teaspoon garlic powder
⅛ teaspoon pepper
1 can (15 ounces) tomato sauce
1 cup water
2 teaspoons Worcestershire sauce

Mix hamburger, rice, ½ cup water, the onion, salt, celery salt, garlic powder and pepper. Shape mixture by rounded tablespoonfuls into 12 balls. Cook meatballs in 10-inch skillet until brown on all sides; drain.

Mix remaining ingredients; pour over meatballs. Heat to boiling; reduce heat. Cover and simmer 45 minutes. (Add water during cooking if necessary.)   4 OR 5 SERVINGS.

Oven Porcupines: Place meatballs in square baking dish, 8x8x2 inches. Mix remaining ingredients; pour over meatballs. Cover and cook in 350° oven 45 minutes. Uncover and cook 15 minutes longer.

WINE-MARINATED KABOBS

1 pound hamburger
8 ounces large mushrooms
½ cup dry red wine
¼ cup vegetable oil
1 teaspoon dried marjoram leaves
½ teaspoon salt
⅛ teaspoon instant minced garlic
1 teaspoon Worcestershire sauce
2 tablespoons catsup

Shape hamburger by tablespoonfuls into 24 balls. Place meatballs and mushrooms in glass bowl or plastic bag. Mix remaining ingredients; pour on meatballs and mushrooms. Cover and refrigerate, turning meatballs and mushrooms occasionally, at least 8 hours.

Remove meatballs and mushrooms, reserving marinade. Alternate 6 meatballs with mushrooms on each of four 12-inch metal skewers, leaving space between foods.

Set oven control to broil and/or 550°. Broil kabobs with tops about 4 inches from heat, turning and brushing occasionally with marinade, until done, 15 to 20 minutes.   4 SERVINGS.

HAMBURGERS

1 pound hamburger
3 tablespoons finely chopped onion
3 tablespoons water
1 teaspoon salt
¼ to ½ teaspoon pepper

Mix all ingredients. Shape mixture into 4 patties, each about 1 inch thick.   4 SERVINGS.

To Broil: Set oven control to broil and/or 550°. Broil with tops about 3 inches from heat until desired doneness (5 to 7 minutes on each side for medium).

To Oven-bake: Place patties on rack in broiler pan. Cook in 350° oven until desired doneness (about 30 minutes for medium).

To Panfry: Cook in 10-inch skillet over medium heat, turning frequently, until desired doneness (about 10 minutes for medium).

Horseradish Burgers: Mix in 1½ teaspoons prepared horseradish.

Mustard-Pickle Burgers: Mix in 1 tablespoon dry mustard and 2 tablespoons drained pickle relish.

ZESTY HAMBURGERS

2 tablespoons margarine or butter
1 small onion, sliced
3 ounces mushrooms, sliced
1 teaspoon Worcestershire sauce
¼ teaspoon lemon juice
1 clove garlic, finely chopped
  Hamburgers (above)

Heat margarine in 10-inch skillet until melted. Add onion, mushrooms, Worcestershire sauce, lemon juice and garlic. Cook and stir over medium heat 2 minutes; remove from heat.

Prepare Hamburgers. Push mushroom mixture to side of skillet. Cook patties in same skillet as directed. Serve mushroom mixture over patties. 4 SERVINGS.

■ **To Microwave:** Microwave margarine uncovered in 1-quart glass measuring cup until melted, about 30 seconds. Stir in onion, mushrooms, Worcestershire sauce, lemon juice and garlic. Cover and microwave until onion is crisp-tender, about 2 minutes; reserve. Cover and microwave hamburger patties in ungreased square glass baking dish, 8x8x2 inches, until almost done, 6 to 7 minutes; drain. Spoon mushroom mixture onto hamburgers. Cover and microwave until hot, about 1 minute.

DOUBLE-DECKER HAMBURGERS

Prepare Hamburgers as directed at left except—mix in ¼ cup dry bread crumbs and 1 egg. Shape mixture into 6 patties, each about ½ inch thick. Top 3 of the patties with dill pickle slices, prepared mustard, catsup, onion slices, tomato slices and/or process American or Cheddar cheese slices to within ½ inch of edges. Top each patty with a remaining patty and seal edge firmly.   3 SERVINGS.

AVOCADO CHEESEBURGERS

  Hamburgers (left)
½ cup cold water
1 tablespoon chili powder
1 teaspoon cornstarch
¼ teaspoon ground cumin
¼ teaspoon salt
1 clove garlic, crushed
1 avocado or 1 medium tomato
1 cup shredded Cheddar cheese

Prepare Hamburgers. Cook patties in 10-inch skillet over medium-high heat, turning once, until brown. Remove patties; drain fat from skillet.

Mix water, chili powder, cornstarch, cumin, salt and garlic in same skillet. Heat to boiling, stirring constantly; reduce heat. Return patties to skillet and turn to coat with sauce.

Cut avocado into 4 rings. Top each patty with avocado ring. Cover and simmer 10 minutes; sprinkle with cheese. Cover and simmer until cheese is melted, about 2 minutes longer. Spoon sauce onto patties.   4 SERVINGS.

BACON-WRAPPED HAMBURGERS

1½ pounds hamburger
1 egg
½ cup water
¼ cup dry bread crumbs
1 small onion, chopped
½ small green pepper, chopped
¼ cup lemon juice
1 teaspoon salt
½ teaspoon instant beef bouillon
6 or 7 thin slices bacon, cut into halves

Mix all ingredients except bacon. Shape mixture into 6 or 7 patties, each about ¾ inch thick. Crisscross 2 half-slices bacon on each patty, tucking ends under. Place patties on rack in shallow roasting pan. Cook uncovered in 350° oven 50 minutes.   6 OR 7 SERVINGS.

SLOPPY JOES

 1 pound hamburger
 1 medium onion, chopped (about ½ cup)
⅓ cup chopped celery
⅓ cup chopped green pepper
⅓ cup catsup
¼ cup water
 1 tablespoon Worcestershire sauce
⅛ teaspoon red pepper sauce
 1 teaspoon salt
 5 hamburger buns, split and toasted

Cook and stir hamburger and onion in 10-inch skillet until hamburger is light brown; drain. Stir in remaining ingredients except buns. Cover and cook over low heat just until vegetables are tender, 10 to 15 minutes. Fill buns with beef mixture.
5 SANDWICHES.

NOTE: For saucier Sloppy Joes, use ½ cup catsup.

CHILI

 1 pound hamburger
 1 large onion, chopped (about 1 cup)
 2 cloves garlic, crushed
 1 can (16 ounces) whole tomatoes
 2 medium stalks celery, sliced (about 1 cup)
 2 to 3 tablespoons chili powder
 2 teaspoons salt
 1 teaspoon sugar
 1 teaspoon Worcestershire sauce
½ teaspoon red pepper sauce (optional)
 1 can (15 ounces) kidney beans, drained

Cook and stir hamburger, onion and garlic in 3-quart saucepan until hamburger is light brown; drain. Stir in tomatoes (with liquid), celery, chili powder, salt, sugar, Worcestershire sauce and pepper sauce. Heat to boiling; reduce heat. Cover and simmer 1 hour.

Stir in beans. Heat to boiling; reduce heat. Simmer uncovered until hot, about 15 minutes. (For thicker chili, continue simmering, stirring occasionally, until desired consistency.)   5 SERVINGS (ABOUT 1 CUP EACH).

Do-ahead Tip: After simmering 1 hour, hamburger mixture can be covered and frozen no longer than 4 months. To serve, drain beans, reserving liquid. Place reserved bean liquid and frozen hamburger mixture in saucepan. Cover and cook over medium-high heat, turning occasionally, 25 minutes. Uncover and cook 15 minutes. Stir in beans; cook uncovered 5 minutes longer. Stir in additional chili powder if desired.

Chili with Pinto Beans: Omit kidney beans. Heat 3 cups water and 8 ounces dried pinto beans (about 1¼ cups) to boiling in 3-quart saucepan; remove from heat. Cover and let stand 1 hour. Heat beans to boiling; reduce heat. Cover and simmer until beans are tender, 1 to 1½ hours. Stir hamburger mixture, tomatoes (with liquid) and remaining ingredients into beans. Continue as directed.

ENCHILADAS

 8 Tortillas (page 206)
 1 pound hamburger
 1 medium onion, chopped (2)
½ cup dairy sour cream
 1 cup shredded Cheddar cheese
 2 tablespoons snipped parsley
 1 teaspoon salt
¼ teaspoon pepper
 1 can (15 ounces) tomato sauce 8 oz.
⅔ cup water
⅓ cup chopped green pepper
 1 tablespoon chili powder
½ teaspoon dried oregano leaves
¼ teaspoon ground cumin
 2 whole green chilies, chopped (optional)
 1 clove garlic, finely chopped
   Tomato-Chili Sauce (page 33)

Prepare Tortillas. Cook and stir hamburger in 10-inch skillet over medium heat until light brown. Remove from heat; drain. Stir in onion, sour cream, cheese, parsley, salt and pepper. Cover and reserve.

Heat remaining ingredients except Tomato-Chili Sauce to boiling, stirring occasionally; reduce heat. Simmer uncovered 5 minutes. Pour sauce into ungreased 8- or 9-inch pie plate.

Dip each tortilla into sauce to coat both sides. Spoon about ¼ cup hamburger mixture onto each tortilla; roll tortilla around filling. Arrange in ungreased oblong baking dish, 12x7½x2 inches. Pour remaining sauce over enchiladas. Cook uncovered in 350° oven until bubbly, about 20 minutes. Garnish with shredded cheese, dairy sour cream and chopped onions or lime wedges if desired. Serve with Tomato-Chili Sauce.   4 SERVINGS.

Cheese Enchiladas: Substitute 2 cups shredded Monterey Jack cheese (about 8 ounces) for the hamburger; mix with onion, sour cream, Cheddar cheese, parsley, salt and pepper. Sprinkle ¼ cup shredded Cheddar cheese (about 1 ounce) on enchiladas before cooking. Garnish with sour cream and chopped onions or lime wedges if desired.

TACOS

8 Taco Shells (right)
1 pound hamburger
¾ cup water
1 medium onion, chopped (about ½ cup)
2 tablespoons chili powder
1 teaspoon salt
½ teaspoon ground cumin
1 clove garlic, crushed
1 cup shredded lettuce
1 medium onion, chopped (about ½ cup)
1 cup shredded Cheddar cheese (about 4 ounces)
1 large tomato, chopped (about 1 cup)
½ cup dairy sour cream

Prepare Taco Shells. Cook and stir hamburger in 10-inch skillet until light brown; drain. Stir in water, ½ cup onion, the chili powder, salt, cumin and garlic. Heat to boiling; reduce heat. Simmer uncovered, stirring occasionally, until thickened, about 10 minutes.

Spoon about ¼ cup hamburger mixture into each shell. Top with shredded lettuce, chopped onion, shredded cheese, chopped tomato and sour cream. 8 TACOS.

TACO SHELLS

1½ cups cold water
1 cup all-purpose flour*
½ cup cornmeal
¼ teaspoon salt
1 egg
Vegetable oil

Heat 8-inch skillet over medium-low heat just until hot. Grease skillet if necessary. (To test skillet, sprinkle with few drops water. If bubbles skitter around, heat is just right.)

Beat water, flour, cornmeal, salt and egg with hand beater until smooth. Pour scant ¼ cup of the batter into skillet; immediately rotate skillet until batter forms very thin tortilla about 6 inches in diameter. Cook tortilla until dry around edge, about 2 minutes. Turn and cook other side until golden, about 2 minutes longer.

Heat oil (1 inch) in 3-quart saucepan to 375°. Slide tortilla into oil. Fold in half with tongs or two forks and hold so 1-inch space remains between halves of tortilla. Fry, turning occasionally, until crisp and golden brown; drain on paper towel. ABOUT 1 DOZEN SHELLS.

*Do not use self-rising flour in this recipe.

Rotate skillet to form the tortilla.

Fold over tortilla to make taco shell.

Tacos

KEEPING HAMBURGER SAFE

Cook hamburger thoroughly—it's handled often in preparation and bacteria can get mixed in. Don't eat raw or rare ground meat—it's not safe. Raw hamburger is more perishable than other beef cuts and should be refrigerated as soon as possible after you buy it; use within 24 hours or freeze.

MEATY BEAN BURRITOS

    Refried Beans (below)
8 Tortillas (page 206)
1 pound hamburger
¾ cup water
1 medium onion, chopped (about ½ cup)
2 tablespoons chili powder
1 teaspoon salt
½ teaspoon ground cumin
1 clove garlic, crushed
    Tomato-Chili Sauce (right)

Prepare Refried Beans and Tortillas. Cook and stir hamburger in 10-inch skillet until light brown; drain. Stir in water, onion, chili powder, salt, cumin and garlic. Heat to boiling; reduce heat. Simmer uncovered, stirring occasionally, until thickened, about 10 minutes.

Spread about ⅓ cup refried beans over each tortilla. Spoon about ¼ cup hamburger mixture onto center of each tortilla; roll tortilla around filling. Arrange burritos in ungreased oblong baking dish, 12x7½x2 inches, or square baking dish, 8x8x2 inches. Cook uncovered in 350° oven until hot, about 20 minutes. Garnish with Guacamole (page 322), shredded Cheddar or Monterey Jack cheese, dairy sour cream and chopped onions or lime wedges if desired. Serve with Tomato-Chili Sauce.　4 SERVINGS.

REFRIED BEANS

2 cups water
8 ounces dried pinto beans (about 1¼ cups)
1 medium onion, chopped (about ½ cup)
¼ cup margarine or butter
¾ teaspoon salt
½ cup shredded Cheddar cheese

Mix water, beans and onion in 2-quart saucepan. Cover and heat to boiling; boil 2 minutes. Remove from heat; let stand 1 hour.

Add just enough water to beans to cover. Heat to boiling; reduce heat. Cover and boil gently, stirring occasionally, until beans are very tender, about 1½ hours. (Add water during cooking if necessary.)

Mash beans. Stir in margarine and salt until margarine is completely absorbed. Stir in cheese.

TOMATO-CHILI SAUCE

2 medium tomatoes, finely chopped
    (about 1½ cups)
1 to 3 jalapeño peppers, finely chopped
1 medium onion, chopped (about ½ cup)
1 teaspoon salt
¼ teaspoon ground cumin
⅛ clove garlic, crushed

Mix all ingredients. Cover and refrigerate no longer than 1 week. Serve with enchiladas, tacos, tostadas, burritos or refried beans.

Chili Sauce: Substitute 1 can (8 ounces) tomato sauce for the tomatoes. Mix all ingredients in saucepan. Heat to boiling, stirring constantly; reduce heat. Simmer uncovered, stirring occasionally, 10 minutes. Serve with meat loaf, hamburger or fish.

HAMBURGER-BEAN BAKE

4 slices bacon
1½ pounds hamburger
3 medium onions, finely chopped (about
    1½ cups)
1 medium stalk celery, chopped (about
    ½ cup)
1 beef bouillon cube
⅓ cup boiling water
½ to 1 clove garlic, crushed
¾ cup catsup
2 tablespoons prepared mustard
¾ teaspoon salt
¼ teaspoon pepper
1 can (17 ounces) lima beans, drained
1 can (15½ ounces) kidney beans, drained

Fry bacon in 10-inch skillet until crisp; drain on paper towels. Drain fat from skillet. Cook and stir hamburger, onions and celery in same skillet until hamburger is light brown; drain.

Dissolve bouillon cube in boiling water. Stir bouillon, garlic, catsup, mustard, salt, pepper and beans into hamburger mixture. Pour into ungreased 2-quart casserole. Cover and cook in 375° oven until hot and bubbly, about 30 minutes. Arrange bacon on or crumble over beans.
8 SERVINGS.

Deep-Dish Pizza (page 40) and Hamburger-Corn Pie (page 35)

HAMBURGER STROGANOFF

1 pound hamburger
1 medium onion, chopped (about ½ cup)
¼ cup margarine or butter
2 tablespoons flour
1 teaspoon salt
1 clove garlic, finely chopped, or 1 teaspoon
    garlic salt
¼ teaspoon pepper
1 can (4 ounces) mushroom stems and
    pieces, drained
1 can (10¾ ounces) condensed cream of
    chicken soup
1 cup dairy sour cream or unflavored yogurt
2 or 3 cups hot cooked noodles (page 221) or
    rice (page 225)

Cook and stir hamburger and onion in margarine in 10-inch skillet until hamburger is light brown. Stir in flour, salt, garlic, pepper and mushrooms. Cook, stirring constantly, 5 minutes. Stir in soup. Heat to boiling, stirring constantly; reduce heat. Simmer uncovered 10 minutes. Stir in sour cream; heat through. Serve over hot noodles and, if desired, sprinkle with snipped parsley.   4 SERVINGS.

HAMBURGER-CORN PIE

1 pound hamburger
¼ pound bulk pork sausage
1 small onion, chopped (about ¼ cup)
1 clove garlic, finely chopped
1 can (16 ounces) whole tomatoes
1 can (16 ounces) whole kernel corn,
    drained
20 to 24 pitted ripe olives
1½ to 3 teaspoons chili powder
1½ teaspoons salt
1 cup cornmeal
1 cup milk
2 eggs, well beaten
1 cup shredded Cheddar cheese (about
    4 ounces)

Cook and stir hamburger, pork sausage, onion and garlic until meat is brown; drain. Stir in tomatoes (with liquid), corn, olives, chili powder and salt. Heat to boiling. Pour into ungreased baking dish, 9x9x2 or 12x7½x2 inches, or 2-quart casserole.

Mix cornmeal, milk and eggs; pour over meat mixture. Sprinkle with cheese. Cook in 350° oven until golden brown, 40 to 50 minutes. Garnish with parsley sprigs and black olives if desired.
8 SERVINGS.

BEEF-BEAN COMBO

1 pound hamburger
1 medium onion, chopped
1 can (16 ounces) cut green beans
1 can (10¾ ounces) condensed cream of
    mushroom soup
1 can (4 ounces) mushroom stems and
    pieces, drained
1 small green pepper, chopped (about
    ½ cup)
1 medium stalk celery, chopped
1 cup milk
1 tablespoon Worcestershire sauce
1 teaspoon salt
4 ounces uncooked noodles

Cook and stir hamburger and onion in 12-inch skillet or Dutch oven until hamburger is light brown; drain. Stir in green beans (with liquid) and remaining ingredients. Heat to boiling; reduce heat. Cover and simmer, stirring occasionally, until noodles are tender, 25 to 30 minutes. Or cover and cook in 350° oven 35 minutes.   6 SERVINGS.

Beef-Tomato Combo: Omit mushrooms and milk. Stir in 1 can (28 ounces) whole tomatoes (with liquid) and ½ cup catsup with the remaining ingredients.

CHOW MEIN CASSEROLE

1 pound hamburger
1 large stalk celery, chopped (about
    ¾ cup)
¾ cup chopped onion
1¼ cups boiling water
½ cup uncooked parboiled (converted) rice
½ teaspoon salt
1 can (10½ ounces) condensed chicken
    with rice soup
1 can (4 ounces) mushroom stems and
    pieces, drained
1 tablespoon packed brown sugar
2 tablespoons soy sauce
1 teaspoon margarine or butter
1½ cups chow mein noodles

Cook and stir hamburger, celery and onion in 10-inch skillet until hamburger is light brown; drain.

Pour boiling water on rice and salt in greased 2-quart casserole. Stir in hamburger mixture, soup, mushrooms, brown sugar, soy sauce and margarine. Cover and cook in 350° oven 30 minutes; stir. Cook uncovered 30 minutes longer. Stir in noodles; serve immediately.   5 OR 6 SERVINGS.

HAMBURGER-NOODLE BAKE

½ pound hamburger
1 medium onion, chopped (about ½ cup)
1 can (15 ounces) tomato sauce
¼ teaspoon salt
⅛ teaspoon garlic powder
5 uncooked lasagne noodles
1 carton (12 ounces) creamed cottage cheese
    (1½ cups)
¼ cup grated Parmesan cheese
2 teaspoons dried parsley flakes
1 cup shredded mozzarella cheese (about
    4 ounces)

Cook and stir hamburger and onion in 2-quart saucepan until hamburger is light brown; drain. Stir in tomato sauce, salt and garlic powder. Heat to boiling; reduce heat. Simmer uncovered, stirring occasionally, 30 minutes.

Cook noodles as directed on page 221. Mix cottage cheese, Parmesan cheese and parsley. Layer half each of the noodles, sauce, mozzarella cheese and cottage cheese mixture in ungreased oblong baking dish, 12x7½x2 inches, or square baking dish, 8x8x2 inches; repeat. Cover and cook in 350° oven 40 minutes. Let stand 10 minutes before cutting.
6 SERVINGS.

ONE-SKILLET SPAGHETTI

1 pound hamburger
2 medium onions, chopped (about 1 cup)
1 can (28 ounces) whole tomatoes
¾ cup chopped green pepper
½ cup water
1 can (4 ounces) mushroom stems and
    pieces, drained
2 teaspoons salt
1 teaspoon sugar
1 teaspoon chili powder
7 ounces uncooked thin spaghetti, broken
    into pieces
1 cup shredded Cheddar cheese (about
    4 ounces)

Cook and stir hamburger and onions in 10-inch skillet or Dutch oven until hamburger is light brown; drain. Stir in tomatoes (with liquid), green pepper, water, mushrooms, salt, sugar, chili powder and spaghetti; break up tomatoes with fork. Heat to boiling; reduce heat. Cover and simmer, stirring occasionally, until spaghetti is tender, about 30 minutes. (Add water during cooking if necessary.) Sprinkle with cheese. Cover and heat until cheese is melted.　7 SERVINGS.

Oven Spaghetti: After breaking up tomatoes, pour mixture into ungreased 2- or 2½-quart casserole. Cover and cook in 375° oven, stirring occasionally, until spaghetti is tender, about 45 minutes. Sprinkle with cheese; cook uncovered 5 minutes longer.

ITALIAN SPAGHETTI

1 pound hamburger
1 large onion, chopped (about 1 cup)
1 clove garlic, crushed
1 cup water
1 teaspoon salt
1 teaspoon sugar
1 teaspoon dried oregano leaves
¾ teaspoon dried basil leaves
½ teaspoon dried marjoram leaves
¼ teaspoon dried rosemary leaves (optional)
1 bay leaf
1 can (8 ounces) tomato sauce
1 can (6 ounces) tomato paste
4 cups hot cooked spaghetti (page 221)

Cook and stir hamburger, onion and garlic in 10-inch skillet until hamburger is light brown; drain. Stir in remaining ingredients except spaghetti. Heat to boiling; reduce heat. Cover and simmer, stirring occasionally, 1 hour.

Serve sauce over hot spaghetti. Sprinkle with grated Parmesan cheese if desired.　6 SERVINGS.

Do-ahead Tip: After simmering, sauce can be covered and refrigerated no longer than 2 days or frozen no longer than 4 months. To serve, cover and heat frozen sauce over medium heat, turning occasionally, until thawed, 20 to 30 minutes. Reduce heat; cook uncovered 10 minutes.

Chicken Spaghetti: Omit hamburger. Cover and simmer sauce, stirring occasionally, 30 minutes. Stir in 1½ cups 1-inch pieces cooked chicken. Cover and simmer, stirring occasionally, 30 minutes longer.

STUFFED CABBAGE ROLLS

12 cabbage leaves*
 1 pound hamburger
½ cup uncooked instant rice
 1 medium onion, chopped (about
      ½ cup)
 1 can (4 ounces) mushroom stems
      and pieces
 1 teaspoon salt
⅛ teaspoon pepper
⅛ teaspoon garlic salt
 1 can (15 ounces) tomato sauce
 1 teaspoon sugar
½ teaspoon lemon juice
 1 tablespoon cornstarch
 1 tablespoon water

Cover cabbage leaves with boiling water. Cover and let stand until leaves are limp, about 10 minutes. Remove leaves; drain.

Mix hamburger, rice, onion, mushrooms (with liquid), salt, pepper, garlic salt and ½ cup of the tomato sauce. Place about ⅓ cup hamburger mixture at stem end of each leaf. Roll leaf around hamburger mixture, tucking in sides.

Place cabbage rolls seam sides down in ungreased square baking dish, 8x8x2 inches. Mix remaining tomato sauce, the sugar and lemon juice; pour over cabbage rolls. Cover and cook in 350° oven until hamburger is done, about 45 minutes.

Mix cornstarch and 1 tablespoon water in saucepan. Stir in liquid from cabbage rolls. Heat to boiling, stirring constantly. Boil and stir 1 minute. Serve sauce with cabbage rolls. Garnish with parsley if desired.   4 OR 5 SERVINGS.

*To separate leaves from cabbage head, remove core and cover cabbage with cold water. Let stand about 10 minutes; remove leaves.

■ **To Microwave:** Cover and microwave cabbage leaves and ¼ cup cold water in 3-quart round glass casserole until limp, 4 to 5 minutes. Continue as directed except—mix remaining tomato sauce, the sugar, lemon juice, cornstarch and 1 tablespoon water; pour over cabbage rolls. Cover with plastic wrap and microwave 7 minutes; turn dish one quarter turn. Microwave until hamburger is done, 8 to 9 minutes longer. Let stand 1 minute. Remove cabbage rolls to platter. Stir sauce in dish with fork; pour over cabbage rolls.

Cover and microwave prepared green peppers until hot.

Stuff peppers with hamburger mixture; add sauce.

Microwave 30 seconds to melt cheese topping if desired.

STUFFED GREEN PEPPERS

6 large green peppers
1 pound hamburger
2 tablespoons chopped onion
1 teaspoon salt
⅛ teaspoon garlic salt
1 cup cooked rice (page 225)
1 can (15 ounces) tomato sauce
¾ cup shredded mozzarella cheese

Cut thin slice from stem end of each pepper. Remove seeds and membranes; rinse. Cook peppers in enough boiling water to cover 5 minutes; drain.

Cook and stir hamburger and onion in 10-inch skillet until hamburger is light brown; drain. Stir in salt, garlic salt, rice and 1 cup of the tomato sauce; heat through.

Stuff each pepper with hamburger mixture; stand upright in ungreased baking dish, 8x8x2 inches. Pour remaining sauce over peppers. Cover; cook in 350° oven 45 minutes. Uncover; cook 15 minutes longer. Sprinkle with cheese.   6 SERVINGS.

Do-ahead Tip: Reserve ⅓ cup of the tomato sauce; pour remaining sauce over stuffed green peppers. Cover and cook 30 minutes. Refrigerate green peppers and reserved tomato sauce no longer than 24 hours. Pour reserved sauce over green peppers. Cook uncovered in 350° oven 35 minutes.

■ **To Microwave:** Prepare green peppers as directed (do not cook). Place peppers cut sides up in ungreased 9- or 10-inch glass pie plate. Cover with plastic wrap; microwave until hot, 3 to 3½ minutes. Mix cooked rice, uncooked hamburger, onion, salt, garlic salt and 1 cup of the tomato sauce. Stuff each pepper with about ½ cup hamburger mixture. Pour remaining sauce over peppers. Cover with plastic wrap; microwave 6 minutes. Turn plate one-quarter turn; microwave until mixture is done, 6 to 7 minutes longer. Sprinkle with cheese.

MICROWAVING BEEF

Hamburger is a natural for microwaving. If you have a varied-temperature microwave, you can cook even the less tender cuts of beef. You won't notice the lack of browning if you add sauces or toppings, or you can brown hamburgers or steaks on the grill, then freeze them. Thawing and heating in the microwave can be done as needed, and meats won't have any "leftover" flavor.

BEEF-LENTIL SOUP

1 pound hamburger
1 medium onion, chopped (about ½ cup)
1 clove garlic, finely chopped
1 can (4 ounces) mushroom stems and
    pieces
1 can (16 ounces) stewed tomatoes
1 medium stalk celery, sliced (about ½ cup)
1 large carrot, sliced (about ¾ cup)
6 ounces dried lentils (about 1 cup)
3 cups water
¼ cup red wine (optional)
1 bay leaf
2 tablespoons snipped parsley
2 teaspoons salt
1 teaspoon instant beef bouillon
¼ teaspoon pepper

Cook and stir hamburger, onion and garlic in Dutch oven until hamburger is light brown; drain. Stir in mushrooms (with liquid) and remaining ingredients. Heat to boiling; reduce heat. Cover and simmer, stirring occasionally, until lentils are tender, about 40 minutes.   6 SERVINGS (ABOUT 1⅓ CUPS EACH).

HAMBURGER-VEGETABLE SOUP

An easy supper treat—serve in mugs, with toast triangles, a fresh fruit salad and warm Gingerbread (page 257).

1½ pounds hamburger
3 cups water
3 medium carrots, chopped (about 1 cup)
2 medium stalks celery, chopped (about
    1 cup)
1 large potato, cut into ½-inch pieces
    (about 1 cup)
2 medium onions, chopped (about 1 cup)
2 teaspoons salt
1 teaspoon bottled brown bouquet sauce
¼ to ½ teaspoon pepper
1 bay leaf
⅛ teaspoon dried basil leaves
1 can (28 ounces) whole tomatoes

Cook and stir hamburger in Dutch oven until light brown; drain. Stir in remaining ingredients; break up tomatoes with fork. Heat to boiling; reduce heat. Cover and simmer just until vegetables are tender, about 20 minutes.   6 SERVINGS (ABOUT 1½ CUPS EACH).

MEATBALL STEW

4½ cups water
8 ounces dried large lima beans (about 1 cup)
½ cup cold water
2 to 3 tablespoons flour
1 can (16 ounces) whole tomatoes
2 medium stalks celery, sliced (about 1 cup)
3 medium carrots, cut into 2-inch pieces
1 medium onion, chopped (about ½ cup)
1 tablespoon salt
¼ teaspoon pepper
1 bay leaf
½ recipe Meatballs (page 29)

Heat 4½ cups water and the beans to boiling in Dutch oven. Boil 2 minutes; remove from heat. Cover and let stand 1 hour.

Shake cold water and flour in covered container; stir gradually into beans. Heat to boiling, stirring occasionally. Stir in tomatoes (with liquid), celery, carrots, onion, salt, pepper and bay leaf. Heat to boiling. Cover and cook in 375° oven 1 hour.

Prepare ½ recipe Meatballs as directed except— shape into 1-inch balls and decrease cooking time to 10 minutes. Add meatballs to bean mixture. Cover and cook until meatballs are hot, about 30 minutes.   5 SERVINGS (1¼ CUPS EACH).

EMERGENCY SEASONINGS

If the recipe calls for:	You can substitute:
1 clove garlic	¼ teaspoon instant minced garlic or ⅛ teaspoon garlic powder
1 tablespoon snipped fresh chives	1 teaspoon freeze-dried chives
1 tablespoon snipped fresh herbs	1 teaspoon dried herbs or ¼ teaspoon ground herbs
1 pound fresh mushrooms, cooked	6-ounce can mushrooms, drained, or 3 ounces dried mushrooms
½ cup chopped onion	2 tablespoons instant minced onion or onion flakes or 1 teaspoon onion powder or 2 teaspoons onion salt (decrease regular salt by 1 teaspoon)
1 teaspoon dry mustard	2 to 3 teaspoons prepared mustard

PIZZA

- ½ pound hamburger
  Pizza Dough (below)
- 1 can (8 ounces) tomato sauce
- 2 teaspoons dried oregano leaves
- 1¼ teaspoons salt
- ⅛ teaspoon instant minced garlic
- ⅛ teaspoon pepper
- ¼ cup grated Parmesan cheese
- 1 medium onion, chopped (about ½ cup)
- ½ small green pepper, chopped
- 2 cups shredded mozzarella cheese (about
      8 ounces)

Cook and stir hamburger until light brown; drain. Prepare Pizza Dough. Mix tomato sauce, oregano, salt, garlic and pepper.

Divide dough into halves. Pat each half into 11-inch circle on lightly greased cookie sheet with floured fingers. Spread sauce over circles. Sprinkle with Parmesan cheese, hamburger, onion, green pepper and mozzarella cheese. Cook in 425° oven until cheese is light brown, 20 to 25 minutes.   2 PIZZAS.

PIZZA DOUGH

- 1 package active dry yeast
- 1 cup warm water (105 to 115°)
- 1 teaspoon sugar
- 1 teaspoon salt
- 2 tablespoons vegetable oil
- 2½ cups all-purpose* or whole wheat flour

Dissolve yeast in warm water. Stir in remaining ingredients; beat vigorously 20 strokes. Let rest about 5 minutes.

*If using self-rising flour, omit salt.

Combination Pizza: Sprinkle with ½ cup sliced mushrooms and ½ cup sliced pitted ripe olives before adding mozzarella cheese.

Frankfurter Pizza: Substitute 3 frankfurters, sliced, for the hamburger and 1 cup shredded Cheddar cheese (about 4 ounces) for 1 cup of the mozzarella cheese. Decrease salt in sauce to ¼ teaspoon.

Italian Sausage Pizza: Substitute ½ pound bulk Italian sausage for the hamburger. Decrease salt in sauce to ¼ teaspoon.

Miniature Pizzas: Divide dough into 6 equal parts. Pat each part into 6-inch circle on lightly greased cookie sheet. Layer sauce and toppings on each. Cook 15 to 20 minutes.

Pepperoni Pizza: Substitute 1 cup sliced pepperoni (about 4 ounces) for the hamburger. Decrease salt in sauce to ¼ teaspoon.

Shrimp Pizza: Substitute 1 can (4½ ounces) broken shrimp, rinsed and drained, for the hamburger. Decrease salt in sauce to ¼ teaspoon.

Tuna Pizza: Substitute 1 can (6½ ounces) tuna, drained, for the hamburger. Decrease salt in sauce to ¼ teaspoon.

DEEP-DISH PIZZA

- 1 pound hamburger
  Pizza Dough (left)
- 1 can (16 ounces) whole tomatoes, drained
- 1 tablespoon instant minced onion
- 1 teaspoon dried oregano leaves
- ¼ teaspoon salt
- ¼ teaspoon pepper
- ⅛ teaspoon garlic powder
- 1 teaspoon salt
- 1 small green pepper, cut into thin strips
- 1 can (4 ounces) mushroom stems and
      pieces, drained
- 1 cup shredded mozzarella cheese (about
      4 ounces)

Cook and stir hamburger until light brown; drain. Prepare Pizza Dough. Mix tomatoes, onion, oregano, ¼ teaspoon salt, the pepper and garlic powder; break up tomatoes with fork.

Press dough evenly on bottom and halfway up sides of greased oblong baking dish, 13x9x2 inches. Sprinkle hamburger over dough; sprinkle with 1 teaspoon salt. Spoon sauce onto hamburger; top with green pepper, mushrooms and cheese. Cook in 425° oven until cheese is light brown, 20 to 25 minutes.   8 SERVINGS.

MENU-MAKING SECRETS

Contrast is the secret of appetizing meals:

Flavor contrast: Balance a spicy pizza with a mild, cool salad or a delicately flavored dessert.

Color contrast: Imagine how the food will look on the plate, then choose a bright garnish or vegetable if needed.

Texture contrast: Serve something soft with something crisp; combine chewy with smooth, dry with moist.

Shape contrast: Cut vegetables diagonally or into sticks or rounds. Or leave them whole.

Temperature contrast: Serve a hot soup with a chilled salad, an icy sherbet with chow mein.

PORK

HOW TO ROAST PORK

Select fresh or smoked pork roast from those listed in chart (page 43). Allow about ⅓ pound per person —less for boneless roasts, more for roasts with a bone. Sprinkle fresh pork roasts with salt and pepper, if desired, before, during or after roasting (salt permeates the meat only ¼ to ½ inch).

Place pork fat side up on rack in shallow roasting pan. The rack keeps the meat out of the drippings. (With a rib roast, the ribs form a natural rack.) It is not necessary to baste.

Insert meat thermometer so tip is in center of thickest part of pork and does not touch bone or rest in fat. Do not add water. Do not cover.

Roast in 325° oven. (It is not necessary to preheat oven.) Roast to desired degree of doneness (see Timetable, page 43), using thermometer reading as final guide.

Roasts are easier to carve if allowed to set 15 to 20 minutes after removing from oven. Since meat continues to cook after removal from oven, if roast is to set, it should be removed from oven when thermometer registers 5° lower than desired doneness.

NOTE: For assistance in carving a whole smoked ham, smoked picnic shoulder or fresh loin roast, see page 42.

GLAZES FOR FRESH PORK ROAST

Instead of using any other seasoning, during the last hour of roasting, brush pork every 15 minutes with one of the following glazes (enough for a 4-pound roast). Serve any remaining glaze as a sauce.

Currant Glaze: Heat 1 jar (10 ounces) currant jelly, ¼ cup prepared mustard and ½ teaspoon onion salt over low heat, stirring constantly, until jelly is melted. Heat to boiling. Boil and stir 3 minutes.

Orange Glaze: Heat 1 can (6 ounces) frozen orange juice concentrate, ½ cup honey and ½ teaspoon ground ginger to boiling, stirring constantly. Boil and stir 3 minutes.

HERBS FOR FRESH PORK ROAST

Before roasting, sprinkle pork with one of the following seasonings (enough for 4-pound roast).

Caraway Salt: Mix 2 tablespoons caraway seed, crushed, 1 teaspoon salt, ½ teaspoon garlic powder and ¼ teaspoon pepper.

Herb Salt: Cut 1 clove garlic into halves; rub pork with garlic. Mix 1 teaspoon dried sage leaves, 1 teaspoon marjoram leaves and 1 teaspoon salt.

GLAZES FOR SMOKED PORK ROAST

Remove pork roast from oven 30 minutes before it is done. Pour drippings from pan. Remove any skin from pork. Cut fat surface of pork in diamond pattern ¼ inch deep. Insert whole cloves in each diamond if desired. Spread with one of the following glazes (enough for 5-pound roast); continue roasting 30 minutes. Or omit glaze and serve with Gingered Cranberry Sauce (below).

Honey Glaze: Mix ¼ cup honey, ½ teaspoon dry mustard and ¼ teaspoon ground cloves.

Horseradish Glaze: Mix ½ cup packed brown sugar, 2 tablespoons prepared horseradish and 2 tablespoons lemon juice.

Marmalade Glaze: Mix ½ cup orange marmalade, ⅓ cup sweet white wine, 1 tablespoon prepared mustard and ⅛ teaspoon ground cloves.

Gingered Cranberry Sauce: Heat 1 can (16 ounces) whole cranberry sauce, 1 teaspoon grated orange peel, ½ teaspoon ground ginger and ¼ teaspoon ground allspice, stirring occasionally, until hot.

ENERGY SAVERS—OVEN AND RANGE

Oven: Preheat oven only when specified in the recipe (all roasts and most casseroles can start in a cold oven). Plan complete oven meals. When using two racks, stagger pans so one is not directly over another or touching a pan or oven wall.

Range Top: Use flat-bottomed pans of medium weight for even, quick conduction of heat. With a gas range, adjust flame to pan size; with electric range, adjust pan to size of unit. Use lowest flame or temperature possible for different cooking methods. When long cooking is required, consider a pressure cooker.

HOW TO CARVE PORK

WHOLE HAM

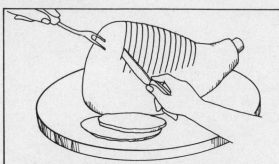

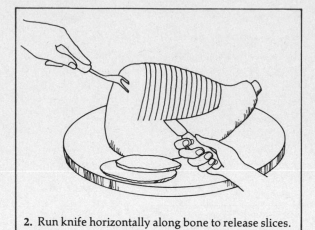

1. Place ham on platter with fat side up and shank facing right. Cut a few slices from the thin side (thin side will face toward carver if ham is a left leg and away from carver if ham is a right leg). Turn ham so it rests on cut side. Make slices down to bone.

2. Run knife horizontally along bone to release slices.

ARM PICNIC

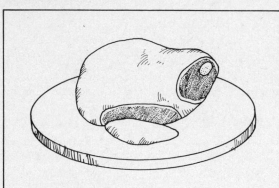

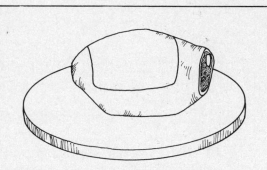

1. Cut off a lengthwise slice from picnic. Turn meat so that it rests on this cut surface.

2. Make vertical cuts as shown; turn knife and cut horizontally along bone to remove boneless piece for carving. For additional servings, remove remaining meat from arm bone and carve.

LOIN ROAST

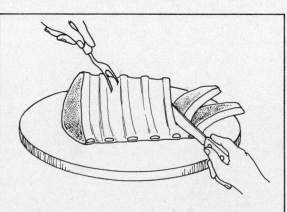

1. After cooking loin roast, remove backbone from ribs to facilitate carving. Place roast with the rib side toward carver.

2. With fork inserted in roast, cut slices on each side of rib bones. (Every other slice will contain a bone.)

TIMETABLE FOR ROASTING FRESH AND SMOKED PORK
(Oven Temperature 325°F)

Cut	Approximate Weight (Pounds)	Meat Thermometer Reading (°F)	Approximate Cooking Time (Minutes per Pound)
Fresh Loin			
Center	3 to 5	170°	30 to 35
Half	5 to 7	170°	35 to 40
Blade or			
Sirloin	3 to 4	170°	40 to 45
Boneless Top			
(double)	3 to 5	170°	35 to 45
Boneless Top	2 to 4	170°	30 to 35
Smoked Loin	3 to 5	160°	25 to 30
Fresh Arm Picnic	5 to 8	170°	30 to 35
Smoked Arm Picnic			
(cook before eating)	5 to 8	170°	30 to 35
(fully cooked)	5 to 8	140°	25 to 30
Fresh Boston			
Shoulder			
Boneless Blade			
Boston	3 to 5	170°	35 to 40
Blade Boston	4 to 6	170°	40 to 45
Smoked Shoulder			
Roll (butt)	2 to 3	170°	35 to 40
Fresh Leg (ham)			
Whole (bone-in)	12 to 14	170°	22 to 26
Boneless	10 to 14	170°	24 to 28
Half (bone in)	5 to 8	170°	35 to 40
Smoked Ham			
(cook before eating)			
Whole	10 to 14	160°	18 to 20
Half	5 to 7	160°	22 to 25
Shank Portion	3 to 4	160°	35 to 40
Rump (butt)			
Portion	3 to 4	160°	35 to 40
Smoked Ham			
(fully cooked)			
Whole	10 to 15	140°	15 to 18
Half	5 to 7	140°	18 to 24
Canadian-style			
Bacon	2 to 4	160°	35 to 40
Fresh Tenderloin	½ to 1	Total Time	¾ to 1 hour
Fresh Spareribs, Back Ribs and Country-style Ribs*			1½ to 2½ hours

*All three are always cooked until well done.

PORK CUTS

From the Boston Shoulder: Blade Boston roast, boneless blade Boston roast (braise, roast); smoked shoulder roll (roast, cook in liquid); blade steak (braise, panfry).

From the Loin: Boneless top loin roast, blade loin roast, center loin roast, sirloin roast (roast); tenderloin (roast, braise, panfry); back ribs, country-style ribs (roast, braise, cook in liquid); Canadian-style bacon (roast, broil, panfry); rib chop, loin chop, sirloin chop, top loin chop, blade chop, butterfly chop, sirloin cutlet (braise, broil, panfry); smoked loin chop (broil, panfry).

From the Leg (Ham): Smoked ham—shank or rump (butt) portion (roast, cook in liquid); boneless leg or fresh ham, boneless smoked ham, canned ham (roast); center smoked ham slice (broil, panfry).

From the Spareribs—Bacon (Side Pork): Salt pork (broil, panfry, cook in liquid, bake); spareribs (roast, braise, cook in liquid); sliced bacon, slab bacon (broil, panfry, bake).

From the Picnic Shoulder: Fresh hock, smoked hock (braise, cook in liquid); neckbones (cook in liquid); fresh arm picnic (roast); smoked arm picnic (roast, cook in liquid);

arm roast (roast); arm steak (braise, panfry).

From the Jowl: Smoked jowl (cook in liquid, broil, panfry).

From the Forefoot and Hindfoot: Pig's feet (cook in liquid, braise).

Pork cubes, cubed steak, ground pork and sausage may come from several sections.

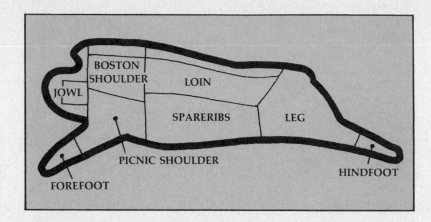

PORK CUTS YOU SHOULD KNOW

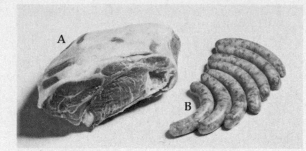

A. Blade Boston roast   **B.** Link sausage

C. Sirloin chop   **D.** Canadian-style bacon
E. Loin chop   **F.** Back ribs

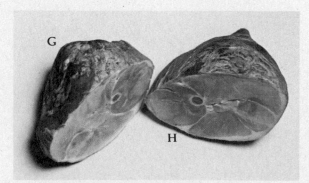

G. Smoked ham, rump (butt) portion
H. Smoked ham, shank portion

I. Sliced bacon   **J.** Smoked arm picnic   **K.** Spareribs
L. Fresh hocks

PORK ROAST WITH ONIONS

4-pound pork boneless top loin roast
Salt and pepper
2 pounds medium onions
1¼ teaspoons ground sage
1 teaspoon salt
¼ teaspoon pepper
Pork Pan Gravy (below)

Place pork roast fat side up on rack in shallow roasting pan; sprinkle with salt and pepper. Insert meat thermometer so tip is in center of thickest part of pork and does not rest in fat. Roast uncovered in 325° oven 1½ hours.

Heat 2 inches water to boiling. Add onions. Cover and heat to boiling. Cook until tender, 15 to 20 minutes; drain. Chop onions coarsely; stir in sage, 1 teaspoon salt and ¼ teaspoon pepper. Remove pork and rack from pan; drain drippings from pan, reserving ¼ cup. Mound onion mixture in center of pan; place pork on top. Roast uncovered until thermometer registers 170°, about 1 hour. Prepare Pork Pan Gravy; serve with pork.   10 TO 14 SERVINGS.

PORK PAN GRAVY

Pour reserved pork drippings into saucepan. Stir in ¼ cup all-purpose flour. Cook over low heat, stirring constantly, until mixture is smooth and bubbly; remove from heat. Stir in 2 cups water. Heat to boiling, stirring constantly. Boil and stir 1 minute. Sprinkle with salt and pepper.

Pork Roast with Sauerkraut: Omit onions, sage, 1 teaspoon salt, ¼ teaspoon pepper and the Pork Pan Gravy. Mix 1 can (27 ounces) sauerkraut, drained, 1 medium onion, chopped (about ½ cup), ¼ cup water, 2 teaspoons sugar and 1 teaspoon instant beef bouillon. Mound in center of pan; place pork on top. Roast as directed. Garnish sauerkraut with chopped pimiento if desired.

GO-WITHS FOR PORK

Tangy dill pickles, sauerkraut, tart cranberry relish or preserved kumquats add zest to the rich pork flavor. Or try cauliflower, celery, green beans, raw spinach, greens (collards, kale, mustard, turnip, beet), tomatoes or summer squash. This vegetable group provides vitamins A and C, potassium (spinach) and iron (mustard greens). Pork, one of the best sources of thiamine, is a good source of other B vitamins and minerals, especially iron.

LUAU ROAST

3-pound fresh pork boneless blade Boston
  or arm picnic roast
¼ cup pineapple juice
¼ cup vegetable oil
¼ cup dark corn syrup
2 tablespoons lime juice
1 small clove garlic, crushed
1½ teaspoons packed brown sugar
1½ teaspoons prepared mustard
1½ teaspoons soy sauce
1 teaspoon salt
½ teaspoon ground coriander
¼ teaspoon ground ginger

Place pork roast in plastic bag or shallow baking dish. Mix remaining ingredients; pour on pork. Fasten bag securely or cover dish with plastic wrap. Refrigerate, turning occasionally, at least 8 hours but no longer than 24 hours.

Place pork fat side up on rack in shallow roasting pan or baking dish; reserve marinade. Insert meat thermometer so tip is in center of thickest part of pork and does not rest in fat. Roast uncovered in 325° oven, brushing occasionally with reserved marinade, until thermometer registers 170°, about 2½ hours.   10 SERVINGS.

HAM WITH SPICED FRUITS

2 bananas, each cut into fourths
1 can (8 ounces) sliced peaches
1 can (8 ounces) sliced pears
12 maraschino cherries, cut into halves
¼ teaspoon pumpkin pie spice
1½-pound fully cooked boneless smoked ham
1 can (23 ounces) sweet potatoes, drained
  and cut into halves
1 cup packed brown sugar
1 teaspoon dry mustard

Mix bananas, peaches (with syrup), pears (with syrup), cherries and pumpkin pie spice. Remove ½ cup syrup from fruit mixture; reserve. Refrigerate fruit mixture.

Place ham in ungreased oblong baking dish, 12x7½x2 inches, or square baking dish, 8x8x2 inches. Arrange sweet potatoes around ham. Mix brown sugar, reserved fruit syrup and the mustard; pour over ham and potatoes. Cook uncovered in 350° oven, spooning sauce onto ham and potatoes occasionally, 30 minutes.

Drain fruit mixture; arrange on top of and around ham. Cook uncovered 15 minutes.   6 SERVINGS.

PORK WITH BROWNED RICE

Serve with a salad of tossed greens sparked with chopped watermelon pickles.

2 medium stalks celery, cut diagonally
    into slices (about 1 cup)
⅔ cup uncooked regular rice
1 medium onion, chopped (about ½ cup)
2 tablespoons vegetable oil
1½ cups boiling water
1 teaspoon instant chicken or beef bouillon
2 tablespoons soy sauce
2 cups 1-inch pieces cooked smoked pork
1 medium green pepper, chopped
    (about 1 cup)

Cook and stir celery, rice and onion in oil in 10-inch skillet over medium heat until rice is golden brown and onion is tender. Stir in water, instant bouillon, soy sauce and pork. Heat to boiling; reduce heat. Cover and simmer until rice is tender and liquid is absorbed, 18 to 20 minutes. Stir in green pepper. Cover and simmer 10 minutes longer.
4 SERVINGS.

Beef with Browned Rice: Substitute 1½ cups 1-inch pieces cooked beef for the pork and decrease soy sauce to 2 teaspoons.

SUBGUM

Serve with cantaloupe wedges drizzled with lime juice.

1 can (4 ounces) sliced mushrooms
1½ cups ¾-inch pieces cooked pork
4 medium stalks celery, sliced (about
    2 cups)
1 tablespoon margarine or butter
1½ cups pork or beef gravy
1 can (16 ounces) bean sprouts, drained
2 to 3 cups chow mein noodles or hot
    cooked rice (page 225)

Cook and stir mushrooms (with liquid), pork and celery in margarine until celery is tender, about 10 minutes. Stir in gravy. Heat to boiling; reduce heat. Cover and simmer 15 minutes. Stir in bean sprouts; heat through. Serve over noodles.   4 SERVINGS.

HAM AND SCALLOPED POTATOES

Prepare Creamy Scalloped Potatoes (page 185) as directed except—arrange 1½ cups cubed or ½ pound sliced fully cooked smoked ham between layers of potatoes.   4 TO 6 SERVINGS.

HAM AND RYE PINWHEELS

  Rye Dough (below)
6 to 8 thin slices fully cooked smoked ham or
    1 package (3 ounces) smoked sliced ham
1 cup shredded process cheese spread loaf
1 can (4 ounces) mushroom stems and pieces,
    drained
⅓ cup chopped onion
2 tablespoons margarine or butter, melted

Prepare Rye Dough; roll into rectangle, 12x8 inches. Arrange ham on rectangle; sprinkle with cheese, mushrooms and onion. Roll up, beginning at 8-inch side; cut into 1-inch slices.

Place slices in greased square pan, 8x8x2 inches; brush with margarine. Cook uncovered in 400° oven 30 minutes.   4 SERVINGS.

RYE DOUGH

⅓ cup shortening
1 cup all-purpose flour*
¾ cup rye or all-purpose* flour
2½ teaspoons baking powder
¾ teaspoon salt
¼ teaspoon dry mustard
  About ¾ cup milk

Cut shortening into flours, baking powder, salt and mustard with pastry blender until mixture resembles fine crumbs. Stir in just enough milk until dough leaves side of bowl and rounds up into a ball. (Too much milk makes dough sticky, not enough makes dough dry.)

*If using self-rising flour, omit baking powder and salt.

FREEZER STORAGE TIME FOR PORK AT 0°F

Most cuts	4 to 5 months
Ground pork	2 months
Sausage	2 months
Cooked pork	2 months
Ham (unsliced)	2 months

Ham slices, bacon and frankfurters lose quality when frozen. See packaging tips and general freezing tips, pages 380–81.

HAM-MUSHROOM SANDWICHES

8 ounces mushrooms, sliced (reserve 4 caps)
1 small onion, sliced
2 cloves garlic, crushed
2 tablespoons margarine or butter
2 hard rolls or kaiser rolls, cut into halves
4 thin slices fully cooked smoked ham
4 slices Swiss cheese

Cook and stir mushrooms, mushroom caps, onion, garlic and margarine in 10-inch skillet until mushrooms are tender, about 3 minutes. Cover and remove from heat.

Set oven control to broil and/or 550°. Place rolls cut sides up on ungreased cookie sheet. Broil with tops about 3 inches from heat until toasted. Place 1 ham slice on each half. Spoon about ¼ of the mushroom mixture, reserving caps, onto each half. Top with cheese slices; broil just until cheese is melted. Garnish with mushroom caps and, if desired, parsley sprigs.   4 OPEN-FACE SANDWICHES.

HAM AND ORANGE SALAD

1 clove garlic, cut into halves
2 cups diced fully cooked smoked ham
2 medium stalks celery, thinly sliced
    (about 1 cup)
½ cup chopped walnuts
⅓ cup chopped green onions
1 can (11 ounces) mandarin orange
    segments, drained
⅓ cup mayonnaise or salad dressing
2 tablespoons half-and-half
1 tablespoon vinegar
¼ teaspoon pepper

Rub salad bowl with garlic. Mix ham, celery, walnuts, onions and orange segments. Cover and refrigerate.

Just before serving, mix remaining ingredients; pour on ham mixture and toss. Garnish with watercress or snipped mint leaves if desired.
5 SERVINGS.

Submarine Sandwich (page 57) and Ham-Mushroom Sandwiches (above)

HOW TO COOK
SMOKED HAM SLICES

Slash diagonally outer edge of fat of fully cooked smoked ham slice at 1-inch intervals to prevent curling.

To Bake: Place ham slice (about 1 inch thick) in ungreased baking dish. Cook uncovered in 325° oven 30 minutes.

To Broil: Set oven control to broil and/or 550°. Broil ham slice (about 1 inch thick) with top about 3 inches from heat until light brown, about 10 minutes. Turn; broil until light brown, about 6 minutes longer. Brush ham with 3 tablespoons jelly, slightly beaten, during last 2 minutes of broiling if desired.

To Panfry: Rub skillet with small piece of fat cut from ham slice (ham slice should be about ½ inch thick). Cook over medium heat until light brown, about 3 minutes. Turn; cook until light brown, about 3 minutes longer.

HAM SLICES WITH SPINACH

  1 package (10 ounces) frozen chopped
     spinach
  1 small stalk celery, finely chopped
  1 can (4 ounces) mushroom stems and
     pieces, drained
  2 tablespoons chopped onion
  2 tablespoons vegetable oil
  ¼ teaspoon salt
  ⅛ teaspoon pepper
  2 fully cooked smoked ham slices, ½ inch
     thick (about 1½ pounds)
  1 tablespoon margarine or butter, melted
    Horseradish Sauce (below)

Cook spinach as directed on package; drain. Cook and stir celery, mushrooms and onion in oil until celery is tender. Stir in spinach, salt and pepper.

Place 1 ham slice in ungreased shallow baking dish; spread with spinach mixture. Top with second ham slice; brush with margarine. Cover and cook in 325° oven 15 minutes. Uncover and cook 15 minutes longer. Serve with Horseradish Sauce.
6 SERVINGS.

HORSERADISH SAUCE
Beat ½ cup chilled whipping cream in chilled bowl until stiff. Fold in 3 tablespoons well-drained prepared horseradish and ½ teaspoon salt.

Do-ahead Tip: After brushing with margarine, cover and refrigerate stuffed ham no longer than 24 hours. Increase both cooking times to 30 minutes.

HAM SLICE WITH MARMALADE

Place 1 fully cooked smoked ham slice, 1 inch thick, in ungreased oblong pan, 13x9x2 inches; brush with ¼ cup marmalade. Sprinkle with ground ginger. Cook in 350° oven, brushing once with marmalade, until hot, about 30 minutes.
4 SERVINGS.

Curried Ham Slice: Substitute mixture of 3 tablespoons margarine, melted, 2 tablespoons wine vinegar, 2 teaspoons curry powder and ½ teaspoon dry mustard for the marmalade and ginger.

PORK MORNAY

  6 pork cubed steaks
  2 eggs, beaten
  ⅔ cup dry bread crumbs
  3 tablespoons vegetable oil
  2 tablespoons water
  6 tablespoons tomato sauce or catsup
    Mornay Sauce (below)
    Paprika

Dip pork steaks into egg; coat with bread crumbs. Heat oil in 10-inch skillet. Fry pork over medium heat until brown. Add water. Spoon 1 tablespoon tomato sauce onto each pork steak; reduce heat. Cover and cook until done, about 30 minutes.

Remove pork steaks to platter; top with Mornay Sauce. Sprinkle with paprika.   6 SERVINGS.

MORNAY SAUCE
  2 teaspoons margarine or butter
  2 teaspoons flour
    Dash of salt
    Dash of ground nutmeg
    Dash of cayenne red pepper
  ¼ cup chicken bouillon
  ¼ cup half-and-half
  ¼ cup shredded Cheddar cheese (about
     1 ounce)

Heat margarine in saucepan until melted. Blend in flour, salt, nutmeg and red pepper. Cook over low heat, stirring constantly, until mixture is smooth and bubbly. Immediately stir in bouillon and half-and-half. Heat to boiling, stirring constantly. Boil and stir 1 minute. Stir in cheese until melted.

HOW TO BROIL FRESH PORK

Slash diagonally outer edge of fat on pork chops or steaks at 1-inch intervals to prevent curling (do not cut into lean). Set oven control to broil and/or 550°. Place pork on rack in broiler pan; place broiler pan so top of pork is 3 to 5 inches from heat. Broil until light brown. The pork should be about half done (see Timetable).

Sprinkle brown side with salt and pepper. (Always season after browning because salt tends to draw moisture to surface, delaying browning.) Turn pork; broil until brown. Serve with Mushroom Topping (right) if desired.

TIMETABLE FOR BROILING FRESH PORK

Cut	Approximate Total Cooking Time
Chops	
¾ to 1 inch	20 to 25 minutes
Blade Steaks	
½ to ¾ inch	20 to 22 minutes
Kabobs	
1½x1½x¾ inch	22 to 25 minutes
Patties	
1 inch	20 to 25 minutes

CRANBERRY PORK CHOP BROIL

6 pork loin or rib chops, about ¾ inch thick
  Salt
1 can (8 ounces) jellied cranberry sauce
1 teaspoon lemon juice
½ teaspoon almond extract
¼ teaspoon ground nutmeg
1 can (29 ounces) peach halves, drained

Set oven control to broil and/or 550°. Broil pork chops with tops 3 to 5 inches from heat 5 minutes. Sprinkle with salt. Turn; broil 5 minutes longer. Sprinkle with salt.

Heat cranberry sauce, lemon juice, almond extract and nutmeg over low heat. Brush pork with sauce. Continue broiling, turning and brushing with sauce, until done, 10 to 15 minutes longer. Remove pork chops to platter; brush with sauce. Fill each peach half with about 1 teaspoon sauce; serve with pork. 6 SERVINGS.

MUSHROOM TOPPING FOR PORK

Cook and stir 8 ounces mushrooms, sliced, 1 teaspoon water, 1 teaspoon instant beef bouillon and ¼ teaspoon dried thyme leaves over medium heat until mushrooms are hot. 4 SERVINGS.

BREADED PORK CHOPS

Prepare Pork Coating Mix (below). Dip 4 pork rib or loin chops, ½ to ¾ inch thick, into ¼ cup milk. Shake each in Pork Coating Mix, coating both sides. Cook on rack in shallow roasting pan in 425° oven until done and brown, 30 to 35 minutes. 4 SERVINGS.

PORK COATING MIX

2 tablespoons yellow cornmeal
2 tablespoons whole wheat flour
1 teaspoon salt
1 teaspoon ground sage
½ teaspoon onion powder
½ teaspoon sugar
½ teaspoon paprika
½ teaspoon monosodium glutamate

Shake ingredients in medium plastic or paper bag.

BRAISED PORK CHOPS

4 pork loin or rib chops, about ½ inch thick
1 teaspoon salt
¼ teaspoon pepper
¼ cup pineapple juice, apple juice or water
  Pan Gravy (below)

Cook pork chops over medium heat until brown; drain. Sprinkle with salt and pepper. Reduce heat; pour pineapple juice on pork. Cover and simmer until done, 20 to 25 minutes.

Remove pork chops to warm platter; keep warm. Prepare Pan Gravy; serve with pork chops. 4 SERVINGS.

PAN GRAVY

Pour pork drippings into bowl, leaving brown particles in pan. Let fat rise to top of drippings; skim off fat, reserving ¼ cup. Return reserved fat to pan. Stir in ¼ cup all-purpose flour. Cook over low heat, stirring constantly, until mixture is smooth and bubbly; remove from heat. Stir in 2 cups water. Heat to boiling, stirring constantly. Boil and stir 1 minute. Sprinkle with salt and pepper.

Pockets cut into bone side hold stuffing securely.

Corn-stuffed Pork Chops

CORN-STUFFED PORK CHOPS

1 can (7 ounces) vacuum-pack whole kernel
  corn with peppers
1 cup soft bread cubes
1 small onion, finely chopped (about ¼ cup)
1 teaspoon salt
½ teaspoon ground sage
6 pork rib chops, about 1 inch thick (with
  pockets cut into chops on bone side)
2 tablespoons shortening

Mix corn (with liquid), bread cubes, onion, salt and
sage. Stuff pork chop pockets with corn mixture.

Fry pork chops in shortening until brown, about 15
minutes; reduce heat. Cover and simmer until pork
chops are done, about 1 hour.   6 SERVINGS.

PORK CHOPS SUPREME

4 pork loin or rib chops, about ¾ inch thick
  Salt
4 thin onion slices
4 thin lemon slices
¼ cup packed brown sugar
¼ cup catsup

Sprinkle both sides of pork chops with salt. Place
pork chops in ungreased shallow baking pan or
dish. Top each pork chop with onion slice, lemon
slice, 1 tablespoon brown sugar and 1 tablespoon
catsup. Cover and cook in 350° oven 30 minutes.
Uncover and cook, spooning sauce onto pork chops
occasionally, until done, about 30 minutes
longer.   4 SERVINGS.

PORK CHOP-EGGPLANT MEDLEY

4 pork rib chops, about ½ inch thick
1 tablespoon vegetable oil
1 teaspoon salt
⅛ teaspoon pepper
1 can (16 ounces) stewed tomatoes
1 small eggplant (about 1 pound), cut into
  ½-inch pieces (about 5 cups)
2 small zucchini, cut into ½-inch slices
  (about 2 cups)
1 teaspoon garlic salt
½ teaspoon dried oregano leaves
¼ cup cold water
1 tablespoon cornstarch

Cook pork chops in oil in 10-inch skillet over
medium heat until brown; sprinkle with salt and
pepper. Pour tomatoes over pork. Heat to boiling;
reduce heat. Cover and simmer until pork is almost
tender, 25 to 30 minutes.

Add eggplant and zucchini; sprinkle with garlic salt
and oregano. Heat to boiling; reduce heat. Cover
and simmer until pork is done and vegetables are
crisp-tender, about 10 minutes.

Remove pork to warm platter; keep warm. Shake
cold water and cornstarch in tightly covered container; stir gradually into vegetables. Heat to
boiling, stirring constantly. Boil and stir 1 minute.
Serve vegetable mixture with pork.   4 SERVINGS.

Pork Chops and Rice: Omit eggplant, zucchini,
garlic salt and oregano. After browning, top each
pork chop with green pepper ring; fill each ring
with 1 tablespoon uncooked regular rice. Pour ¼
cup stewed tomatoes carefully on rice in each ring.
Pour remaining tomatoes into skillet. Cover and
simmer until rice is tender, about 35 minutes.

PORK AND SQUASH IN FOIL

4 pork loin or rib chops, about ½ inch thick
½ teaspoon salt
¼ teaspoon pepper
2 acorn squash, cut into halves
¼ cup packed brown sugar
¼ cup honey
¼ cup margarine or butter
   Paprika

Trim excess fat from pork chops. Place each pork chop on piece of heavy-duty aluminum foil, 18x12 inches; sprinkle with salt and pepper.

Fill hollow of each squash half with 1 tablespoon brown sugar, 1 tablespoon honey and 1 tablespoon margarine; sprinkle with paprika. Place 1 squash half on each pork chop; wrap securely in foil. Cook on ungreased cookie sheet in 400° oven until squash is tender and pork is done, about 55 minutes. 4 SERVINGS.

PINEAPPLE-STUFFED SPARERIBS

3-pound rack fresh pork spareribs
   Stuffing (below)
1 can (13¼ ounces) pineapple chunks,
   drained (reserve syrup)
¼ teaspoon ground cloves

Tie pork spareribs in circle; place spareribs bone tips up on rack in shallow roasting pan. Roast uncovered in 325° oven 2 hours.

Prepare Stuffing; stir in pineapple, cloves and, if necessary, enough reserved pineapple syrup to moisten. Spoon stuffing into circle of spareribs. Roast uncovered until spareribs are done, about 30 minutes. 6 SERVINGS.

STUFFING

1 medium stalk celery, chopped
1 small onion, chopped (about ¼ cup)
⅓ cup margarine or butter
5 cups soft bread cubes (about 10 slices
   bread)
1 teaspoon salt
½ teaspoon rubbed sage
¼ teaspoon dried thyme leaves
   Dash of pepper

Cook and stir celery and onion in margarine in 3-quart saucepan until tender. Add remaining ingredients; toss.

OVEN-BARBECUED SPARERIBS

Place 4½ pounds fresh pork spareribs, cut into serving pieces, meaty sides up on rack in shallow roasting pan. Roast uncovered in 325° oven 1 hour.

Brush pork with Mustard Barbecue Sauce (below). Roast, turning and brushing frequently with sauce, until spareribs are done, about 45 minutes.
6 OR 7 SERVINGS.

MUSTARD BARBECUE SAUCE

Mix ⅓ cup prepared Dijon-style mustard and ⅓ cup molasses; stir in ⅓ cup cider vinegar.

PLUM-BARBECUED SPARERIBS

For this succulent finger food, you'll want to have plenty of napkins—or even a moist fingertip towel—for each person.

4 pounds fresh pork spareribs, cut into
   serving pieces
1 tablespoon salt
1 can (16 ounces) whole purple plums,
   drained (reserve syrup)
1 tablespoon packed brown sugar
3 tablespoons chopped onion
2 teaspoons soy sauce
¼ teaspoon grated lemon peel
¼ teaspoon ground cinnamon
   Dash of ground cloves
   Dash of ground nutmeg
3 drops red food color

Place pork spareribs in Dutch oven. Add enough water to cover spareribs (about 3 quarts) and the salt. Heat to boiling; reduce heat. Cover and simmer 40 minutes; drain.

Remove pits from plums. Sieve plums into 2-quart saucepan. Stir reserved plum syrup and the remaining ingredients into plum pulp. Heat to boiling, stirring constantly. Cook, stirring constantly, 3 minutes. Arrange spareribs meaty sides up on rack in shallow roasting pan. Spread with ⅔ cup of the plum sauce. Roast uncovered in 375° oven, basting with remaining plum sauce 3 times during roasting period, until done and glazed, about 45 minutes. 6 SERVINGS.

SMOKED PORK HOCKS

4 smoked pork hocks (about 4 pounds)
4 cups water
1 onion, sliced
½ teaspoon dried marjoram leaves
2 cans (16 ounces each) sauerkraut, drained
½ teaspoon celery seed
1 apple, cut into eighths

Heat pork hocks, water, onion and marjoram to boiling in Dutch oven; reduce heat. Cover and simmer 1½ hours. Drain liquid from Dutch oven, reserving 1 cup. Stir reserved liquid, the sauerkraut and celery seed into pork hocks. Cover and simmer 15 minutes. Add apple; cover and simmer 15 minutes longer.   4 SERVINGS.

BEER STEW

1 pound pork shoulder roll or smoked
    hocks, cut into 1-inch pieces
1 pound beef boneless chuck, tip or round,
    cut into 1-inch pieces
3 tablespoons vegetable oil
1 can or bottle (12 ounces) beer
1 tablespoon instant beef bouillon
1½ teaspoons salt
½ teaspoon garlic salt
⅛ teaspoon ground marjoram
⅛ teaspoon ground thyme
⅛ teaspoon dried basil leaves
6 carrots, cut into 1-inch pieces
3 potatoes, cut into 1-inch pieces
1 medium onion, thinly sliced
½ cup cold water
¼ cup all-purpose flour
¾ cup walnut halves (optional)
1 tablespoon margarine or butter, melted
    (optional)

Cook pork and beef in oil over medium heat, stirring frequently, until beef is brown, about 8 minutes; drain. Add enough water to beer to measure 2 cups; pour on pork and beef. Add bouillon, salt, garlic salt, marjoram, thyme and basil. Heat to boiling. Add carrots, potatoes and onion.

Cover and cook in 325° oven until beef is tender and pork is done, about 1½ hours.

Shake cold water and flour in tightly covered container; stir gradually into stew. Cover and cook 10 minutes. Stir walnut halves in margarine; sprinkle stew with walnuts.   8 SERVINGS.

NOTE: The beef in this recipe will assume a pink color because of the smoked pork.

SWEET-AND-SOUR PORK

¼ cup all-purpose flour
2 teaspoons ground ginger
1 pound pork boneless shoulder, cut into
    ½-inch cubes
¼ cup vegetable oil
1 can (13¼ ounces) pineapple chunks,
    drained (reserve syrup)
¼ cup vinegar
¼ cup soy sauce
1½ teaspoons Worcestershire sauce
⅓ cup sugar
1½ teaspoons salt
¼ teaspoon pepper
1 small green pepper, cut into ¼-inch strips
1 can (16 ounces) bean sprouts, drained
1 can (8 ounces) water chestnuts, drained
    and thinly sliced
1 tablespoon chili sauce
2½ to 3½ cups hot cooked rice (page 225)

Mix 2 tablespoons of the flour and the ginger. Coat pork with flour mixture. Heat oil in 10-inch skillet. Fry pork until brown; remove from skillet.

Add enough water to reserved pineapple syrup to measure 1 cup. Shake remaining flour and the syrup-water mixture in tightly covered container. Stir flour mixture, vinegar, soy sauce and Worcestershire sauce into fat in skillet. Heat to boiling, stirring constantly. Boil and stir 1 minute; reduce heat. Stir in sugar, salt, pepper and pork. Cover and simmer, stirring occasionally, until pork is tender, about 45 minutes.

Add pineapple and green pepper; cook uncovered 10 minutes. Stir in bean sprouts, water chestnuts and chili sauce; cook uncovered 5 minutes longer. Serve over hot rice.   5 SERVINGS.

QUICK PORK TRICKS

Kabob Combos: Alternate fully cooked smoked ham cubes and pieces of fruit on skewers; broil with tops about 4 inches from heat until hot.

Links in Blankets: Wrap hot oval-shaped pancakes around hot cooked fresh or smoked sausage links. Serve with syrup.

Sausage Fondue: Dip pieces of hot cooked fresh or smoked sausage links into cheese fondue.

Scrambled Eggs in Bologna Cups: Panfry slices of bologna or salami to form cups (they will curl as they cook). Fill with scrambled eggs.

Braised Pork and Vegetables

BRAISED PORK AND VEGETABLES

1 pound pork boneless shoulder, cut into
     ¾-inch pieces
2 tablespoons vegetable oil
1 medium onion, chopped (about ½ cup)
1 clove garlic, finely chopped
3 carrots, cut into 2x½-inch strips
1 cup water
1 teaspoon instant chicken bouillon
1 teaspoon salt
½ teaspoon dried basil leaves
¼ teaspoon dried thyme leaves
¼ teaspoon pepper
½ cup water
1 package (10 ounces) frozen Brussels sprouts
8 ounces thin spaghetti
2 tablespoons margarine or butter
¼ cup grated Parmesan cheese

Cook and stir pork in oil in 10-inch skillet over medium heat until brown; drain on paper towels. Cook and stir onion and garlic in same skillet until onion is tender. Stir in pork, carrots, 1 cup water, the bouillon, salt, basil, thyme and pepper. Heat to boiling; reduce heat. Cover and simmer 45 minutes.

Add ½ cup water and the Brussels sprouts. Heat to boiling; reduce heat. Cover and simmer until Brussels sprouts are tender, 10 to 15 minutes.

Cook spaghetti as directed on page 221. Stir in margarine and cheese. Serve pork and vegetables over spaghetti.   6 SERVINGS.

PORK CHOW MEIN

For dessert—scoops of fruit sherbet and crisp ginger cookies.

1-pound pork blade or arm steak
2 cups beef bouillon
2 medium stalks celery, sliced (about 1 cup)
1 medium onion, chopped (about ½ cup)
3 tablespoons soy sauce
1 teaspoon monosodium glutamate
1 can (4 ounces) mushroom stems and pieces,
     drained (reserve ¼ cup liquid)
3 tablespoons cornstarch
1 can (16 ounces) Chinese vegetables, drained
2 tablespoons brown gravy sauce (molasses type)
3 to 4 cups chow mein noodles

Trim excess fat from pork steak. Cut pork diagonally into very thin strips. Grease lightly 10-inch skillet with fat cut from pork. Fry pork until brown. Stir in bouillon, celery, onion, soy sauce and monosodium glutamate. Heat to boiling; reduce heat. Cover and simmer 30 minutes.

Shake reserved mushroom liquid and the cornstarch in tightly covered container; stir gradually into pork. Add mushrooms, Chinese vegetables and gravy sauce. Heat to boiling, stirring constantly. Boil and stir 1 minute. Serve over noodles.
4 OR 5 SERVINGS.

Wine Chow Mein: Substitute 1 cup dry red wine, 1 cup boiling water and 2 teaspoons instant beef bouillon for the bouillon.

HAM LOAF

    1 pound ground ham
    ½ pound ground lean pork
    2 eggs
 1¼ cups soft bread crumbs
    ¾ cup milk
    ½ cup packed brown sugar
    4 teaspoons prepared mustard
    ¼ teaspoon pepper

Mix ham, pork, eggs, bread crumbs, milk, ¼ cup of the brown sugar, 2 teaspoons of the mustard and the pepper. Spread ham mixture in ungreased loaf pan, 9x5x3 or 8½x4½x2½ inches. Mix remaining brown sugar and mustard; spread over ham mixture. Cook uncovered in 350° oven until done, about 1½ hours.   8 SERVINGS.

HOW TO COOK SAUSAGE (UNCOOKED SMOKED OR FRESH)

To Bake: Arrange sausages in single layer in shallow baking pan. Cook uncovered in 400° oven, turning sausages to brown evenly, until well done, 20 to 30 minutes. Spoon off drippings as they accumulate.

To Panfry: Place pork sausage links or patties in cold skillet. Add 2 to 4 tablespoons water. Cover and cook slowly until done, 5 to 8 minutes (depending on size or thickness). Uncover and cook, turning sausages to brown evenly, until well done.

SAUSAGE-BROWN RICE CASSEROLE

    1 pound bulk pork sausage
    2 cups cooked brown rice (page 225)
    ¾ cup milk
    1 large stalk celery, chopped (about
          ¾ cup)
    ⅓ cup chopped green pepper
    1 small onion, chopped (about ¼ cup)
    1 can (10¾ ounces) condensed cream of
          mushroom soup
    1 can (4 ounces) sliced mushrooms,
          drained
    ½ cup shredded process American cheese
          (about 2 ounces)

Cook and stir pork sausage in Dutch oven until brown; drain. Stir in rice, milk, celery, green pepper, onion, soup and mushrooms. Pour into ungreased 2-quart casserole; sprinkle with cheese. Cook uncovered in 350° oven until center is bubbly, about 45 minutes.   4 SERVINGS.

LASAGNE

At its best served with breadsticks and a tossed salad of greens with black olives and zucchini slices; follow with spumoni ice cream.

    1 pound bulk Italian sausage or hamburger
    1 medium onion, chopped (about ½ cup)
    1 clove garlic, pressed
    1 can (16 ounces) whole tomatoes
    1 can (15 ounces) tomato sauce
    2 tablespoons dried parsley flakes
    1 teaspoon sugar
    1 teaspoon dried basil leaves
    ½ teaspoon salt
    9 uncooked lasagne noodles (about
          8 ounces)
    1 carton (16 ounces) ricotta or creamed
          cottage cheese (about 2 cups)
    ¼ cup grated Parmesan cheese
    1 tablespoon dried parsley flakes
 1½ teaspoons salt
 1½ teaspoons dried oregano leaves
    2 cups shredded mozzarella cheese (about
          8 ounces)
    ¼ cup grated Parmesan cheese

Cook and stir Italian sausage, onion and garlic in 10-inch skillet until sausage is light brown; drain. Add tomatoes (with liquid), tomato sauce, 2 tablespoons parsley, the sugar, basil and ½ teaspoon salt. Heat to boiling, stirring occasionally; reduce heat. Simmer uncovered until mixture is consistency of thick spaghetti sauce, about 1 hour.

Cook noodles as directed on page 221. Reserve ½ cup of the sauce mixture. Mix ricotta cheese, ¼ cup Parmesan cheese, 1 tablespoon parsley, 1½ teaspoons salt and the oregano. Layer ⅓ each of the noodles, remaining sauce mixture, mozzarella cheese and ricotta cheese mixture in ungreased oblong pan, 13x9x2 inches. Repeat 2 times. Spoon reserved sauce mixture onto top; sprinkle with ¼ cup Parmesan cheese. Cook uncovered in 350° oven 45 minutes. Let stand 15 minutes before cutting.   8 TO 10 SERVINGS.

Do-ahead Tip: After cooking, lasagne can be covered and frozen no longer than 3 weeks. To serve, cook uncovered in 375° oven until bubbly, about 1 hour.

HOW TO COOK FRANKFURTERS AND SMOKED SAUSAGES

Frankfurters or other cooked smoked sausage links do not require cooking; they need only be heated. Do not pierce with fork.

To Broil: Brush frankfurters with margarine, butter or shortening. Set oven control to broil and/or 550°. Broil with tops about 3 inches from heat, turning with tongs, until evenly brown.

To Panbroil: Cook frankfurters in 1 to 2 tablespoons shortening, turning with tongs, until brown.

To Simmer: Drop frankfurters into boiling water; reduce heat. Cover and simmer until hot, 5 to 10 minutes (depending on size of sausages).

CORN DOGS

  1 pound frankfurters
    Vegetable oil
  1 cup all-purpose flour*
  2 tablespoons cornmeal
1½ teaspoons baking powder
 ½ teaspoon salt
  3 tablespoons shortening
 ¾ cup milk
  1 egg, beaten
  1 medium onion, grated (optional)

Pat frankfurters dry with paper towels. Heat oil (2 to 3 inches) to 365°. Mix flour, cornmeal, baking powder and salt. Cut in shortening. Stir in remaining ingredients. Dip frankfurters into batter, allowing excess batter to drip into bowl. Fry, turning once, until brown, about 6 minutes; drain on paper towels. Insert wooden skewer in end of each frankfurter if desired.   4 SERVINGS.

*If using self-rising flour, omit baking powder and salt.

Mini Corn Dogs: Cut frankfurters into 1-inch slices before dipping into batter. Fry 4 to 5 minutes.

CHEESE BOATS

Cut 1 pound frankfurters lengthwise almost through to bottoms. Place 1 strip sharp process cheese, 2½x½x¼ inch, in cut of each frankfurter. Wrap each with slice of bacon; secure with wooden picks. Place cut sides down on rack in broiler pan.

Set oven control to broil and/or 550°. Broil with tops about 5 inches from heat, turning when bacon is crisp, until done, about 15 minutes.   5 SERVINGS.

HOT DOG KABOBS

    Soy Glaze (below)
10 frankfurters (1 pound), each cut into fifths
  2 dill pickle spears, each cut into fifths
  1 medium green pepper, cut into 1-inch pieces
  1 can (8¼ ounces) pineapple chunks, drained
  1 can (8½ ounces) whole small onions, drained

Prepare Soy Glaze. Alternate 5 frankfurter pieces, 1 dill pickle piece, 2 or 3 green pepper pieces, 2 or 3 pineapple chunks and 1 onion on each of ten 8-inch wooden skewers. Brush kabobs with glaze.

Set oven control to broil and/or 550°. Broil kabobs with tops about 3 inches from heat 3 minutes. Turn kabobs; brush with glaze. Broil 3 minutes longer. 3 SERVINGS.

SOY GLAZE

Mix ¼ cup soy sauce, 2 tablespoons packed brown sugar and 1 clove garlic, crushed, in saucepan. Heat to boiling, stirring constantly; reduce heat. Simmer uncovered, stirring occasionally, 5 minutes.

CREOLE WIENERS

  8 slices bacon, finely chopped
  3 large onions, finely chopped (about 3 cups)
  1 can (16 ounces) whole tomatoes
 ¾ teaspoon salt
 ⅛ teaspoon pepper
  1 pound frankfurters

Fry bacon and onions in 10-inch skillet until bacon is crisp and onions are tender; drain, reserving 2 tablespoons bacon fat in skillet. Stir in tomatoes (with liquid), salt and pepper. Heat to boiling; reduce heat. Simmer uncovered, stirring occasionally, 15 minutes. Add frankfurters; cover and simmer 15 minutes longer.   4 SERVINGS.

POLISH SAUSAGE-BEER BOIL

Cover and heat ½ to ¾ cup beer or water and 1 pound precooked Polish sausage to boiling; reduce heat. Cover and simmer 10 minutes. (If using uncooked Polish sausage, increase cooking time to 20 minutes.)   4 SERVINGS.

Bratwurst-Beer Boil: Substitute 1 pound fully cooked bratwurst for the Polish sausage; cook bratwurst in 2 teaspoons margarine or butter until brown before cooking in beer.

CURRIED BRATWURST

Hearty and homestyle with chilled Potato Salad (page 141) or hot fried hominy.

- ¾ cup catsup
- 1 tablespoon Worcestershire sauce
- 1¼ teaspoons curry powder
- ¾ teaspoon paprika
- 6 precooked bratwurst sausage links, each about 5½ inches long (about 1 pound)
- 6 slices pumpernickel bread

Mix catsup, Worcestershire sauce, curry powder and paprika. Cut each bratwurst lengthwise almost through to bottom; spread open. Fry over medium heat, turning occasionally, until brown, about 15 minutes.

Place each bratwurst on 1 slice bread. Spoon about 2 tablespoons sauce onto each bratwurst.
6 SERVINGS.

HOW TO COOK BACON

To Bake: Place separated slices of bacon on rack in broiler pan. Cook in 400° oven without turning until brown, about 10 minutes.

To Broil: Set oven control to broil and/or 550°. Broil separated slices of bacon about 3 inches from heat until brown, about 2 minutes. Turn; broil 1 minute.

To Panfry: Place slices of bacon in cold skillet. Cook over low heat, turning bacon to brown evenly on both sides, 8 to 10 minutes.

Bacon Curls: Cut bacon slices into halves. Roll up; secure with wooden picks. Set oven control to broil and/or 550°. Broil with tops 4 to 5 inches from heat 2 minutes. Turn; broil until crisp, about 2 minutes.

HOW TO COOK CANADIAN-STYLE BACON

To Bake: Place 2-pound piece Canadian-style bacon fat side up on rack in shallow pan. Insert meat thermometer so tip is in center of bacon. Cook uncovered in 325° oven until thermometer registers 160°, 1 to 1¼ hours.

To Broil: Set oven control to broil and/or 550°. Broil ¼-inch slices Canadian-style bacon with tops 2 to 3 inches from heat until brown, about 3 minutes. Turn; broil 3 minutes longer.

To Panfry: Place ⅛-inch slices Canadian-style bacon in cold skillet. Cook over low heat, turning bacon to brown evenly on both sides, 8 to 10 minutes.

SPANISH RICE

- ½ pound bacon (about 10 slices), cut into ¾-inch pieces
- ½ pound hamburger
- 1 medium onion, chopped (about ½ cup)
- 2 cups water
- 1 cup uncooked regular rice
- ⅔ cup chopped green pepper
- 1 can (16 ounces) stewed tomatoes
- 1 teaspoon chili powder
- ½ teaspoon dried oregano leaves
- 1¼ teaspoons salt
- ⅛ teaspoon pepper

Fry bacon until crisp; drain on paper towels. Cook and stir hamburger and onion in 10-inch skillet until hamburger is light brown; drain. Stir in bacon and remaining ingredients. Heat to boiling; reduce heat. Cover and simmer, stirring occasionally, until rice is tender, about 30 minutes. (Add small amount water during cooking if necessary.)
6 SERVINGS.

Oven Spanish Rice: Stir hamburger mixture into bacon and remaining ingredients in ungreased 2-quart casserole. Cover and cook in 375° oven, stirring occasionally, about 45 minutes.

BACON-TURKEY CLUB SALAD

- 5 slices bacon
- 1 small head iceberg lettuce, torn into bite-size pieces (about 6 cups)
- 1 large tomato, cut into eighths
- 1½ cups cut-up cooked turkey
- 1 hard-cooked egg, sliced
  Barbecue Dressing (below)

Fry bacon until crisp; drain and crumble. Toss lettuce, bacon, tomato and turkey. Garnish with egg slices; serve with Barbecue Dressing. 4 SERVINGS.

BARBECUE DRESSING

- ¼ cup mayonnaise or salad dressing
- 2 tablespoons barbecue sauce
- 2 teaspoons instant minced onion
- 2 teaspoons lemon juice
- ¼ teaspoon salt
- ⅛ teaspoon pepper

Mix all ingredients.

SERVE-YOURSELF SALAD

    Buttermilk Dressing (page 159)
1 medium head lettuce, torn into bite-size
    pieces (about 8 cups)
12 ounces assorted sliced luncheon meat
    (about 16 slices)
8 ounces cheese (Cheddar, Swiss, American
    or Monterey Jack), sliced (about
    8 slices)
2 medium carrots, cut diagonally into
    ¼-inch slices (about 1 cup)
1 cup shredded red cabbage
1 cup broccoli flowerets
1 cup sliced cauliflowerets or 2 small
    turnips, thinly sliced
½ cup sliced radishes or 1 cup cherry
    tomatoes, cut into halves
1 small cucumber, cut into ½-inch cubes

Prepare Buttermilk Dressing. Place lettuce in salad bowl. Arrange luncheon meat and cheese on large platter (roll, fold or cut into attractive shapes). Arrange carrots, cabbage, broccoli, cauliflower, radishes and cucumber on platter. Garnish with ripe olives, if desired, and serve with Buttermilk Dressing.   8 SERVINGS.

SUBMARINE SANDWICH

1 loaf (1 pound) French bread
    Margarine or butter, softened
4 or 5 lettuce leaves
½ pound salami, sliced
2 tomatoes, sliced
    Salt and pepper
4 ounces Swiss cheese, sliced
½ pound boiled ham (luncheon meat),
    sliced
½ cucumber, thinly sliced
1 medium onion, sliced
3 tablespoons prepared mustard

Cut bread horizontally into halves. Spread bottom half of bread with margarine. Layer lettuce, salami and tomatoes on buttered half; sprinkle with salt and pepper. Layer cheese, ham, cucumber and onion on tomatoes.

Spread top half of bread with mustard; place on bottom half of bread. Secure with wooden skewers.   8 SERVINGS.

Spicy Submarine Sandwich: Omit mustard. Before layering, dip lettuce leaves into mixture of 1 tablespoon wine vinegar, 1 tablespoon olive oil and ¼ teaspoon garlic salt.

HEARTY SANDWICH LOAF

1 loaf (1 pound) unsliced white bread (about
    8 inches long)
½ cup margarine or butter, softened
3 tablespoons instant minced onion
1 tablespoon poppy seed
3 tablespoons prepared mustard
1 tablespoon lemon juice
    Dash of cayenne red pepper
6 slices Swiss cheese (about 8 ounces)
6 thin slices luncheon meat or fully cooked
    ham (about 6 ounces)

Slice crust from top of bread. Make 5 diagonal cuts in bread at equal intervals almost through to bottom. Place on lightly greased cookie sheet. Mix margarine, onion, poppy seed, mustard, lemon juice and red pepper; reserve about 3 tablespoons. Spread remaining margarine mixture between cuts. Place 1 slice cheese and 1 slice meat in each of 4 cuts; alternate 2 slices cheese and 2 slices meat in last cut.

Spread reserved margarine mixture over top and sides of bread. Cook in 350° oven 25 minutes; cover with aluminum foil during last 10 minutes of cooking.   6 SERVINGS.

Do-ahead Tip: Before cooking, wrap assembled bread in heavy-duty aluminum foil. Refrigerate no longer than 24 hours. Place wrapped loaf on ungreased cookie sheet; open foil. Cook in 350° oven 30 minutes. Close foil and cook until hot, about 20 minutes longer.

PORK-PINEAPPLE BAKE

1 can (12 ounces) pork luncheon meat
2 teaspoons prepared mustard
4 slices pineapple, cut into halves
2 tablespoons packed brown sugar

Cut pork luncheon meat slightly more than halfway through loaf into 8 sections. Place pork in ungreased baking dish. Spoon ½ teaspoon mustard between every other cut. Insert half-slice pineapple in each cut; top with remaining half-slice pineapple. Insert whole cloves in pineapple if desired. Sprinkle brown sugar over pork. Cook in 375° oven 20 minutes.   3 SERVINGS.

LAMB

HOW TO ROAST LAMB

Select lamb roast from those listed in chart (page 59). Do not remove fell (the paperlike covering). A lamb roast keeps its shape better, cooks in less time and is juicier when the fell is left on.

If desired, sprinkle with salt and pepper before, during or after roasting (salt permeates meat only ¼ to ½ inch). For a quick seasoning, 4 or 5 small slits can be cut in lamb with tip of sharp knife and slivers of garlic inserted; be sure to remove garlic before serving.

Place lamb fat side up on rack in shallow roasting pan. The rack keeps the meat out of the drippings. (With a rib roast, the ribs form a natural rack.) It is not necessary to baste.

Insert meat thermometer so tip is in center of thickest part of lamb and does not touch bone or rest in fat. Do not add water. Do not cover.

Roast in 325° oven. (It is not necessary to preheat oven.) Roast to desired degree of doneness (see Timetable, page 59), using thermometer reading as final guide. The times and temperatures are for well done. Lamb can also be roasted to 140° (rare) or 160° (medium).

Roasts are easier to carve if allowed to set 15 to 20 minutes after removing from oven. Since meat continues to cook after removal from oven, if roast is to set, it should be removed from oven when thermometer registers 5 to 10° lower than desired doneness.

SEASONINGS FOR LAMB ROAST

Before roasting, sprinkle lamb with one of the following seasonings (enough for 4-pound roast).

Curried Onion Salt: Mix 2 teaspoons curry powder, 1½ teaspoons instant minced onion, ½ teaspoon salt and ¼ teaspoon pepper.

Dill-Rosemary Salt: Mix 2 teaspoons dried dill weed, 1 teaspoon salt, ½ teaspoon dried rosemary leaves and ¼ teaspoon pepper.

Herbed Salt: Mix 2 teaspoons ground cumin, ½ teaspoon dried basil leaves, ¼ teaspoon salt and ¼ teaspoon chili powder.

GLAZES FOR LAMB ROAST

Instead of using any other seasoning or inserting garlic in lamb during the last hour of roasting, brush lamb every 15 minutes with one of the following glazes (enough for 4-pound roast). Serve any remaining glaze as a sauce.

Apricot Glaze: Heat ¼ cup mint-flavored apple jelly until melted. Stir in 2 jars (4¾ ounces each) strained apricots (baby food).

Minted Glaze: Heat 1 jar (10 ounces) mint-flavored apple jelly, 2 cloves garlic, crushed, and 1 tablespoon water, stirring constantly, until jelly melts.

Wine Glaze: Mix 2 tablespoons packed brown sugar, 2 teaspoons cornstarch and ½ teaspoon dried basil leaves in saucepan. Stir in ¼ cup soy sauce and ¼ cup dry white wine or apple juice. Cook, stirring constantly, until mixture thickens and boils. Boil and stir 1 minute.

STUFFED CROWN ROAST

For very special occasions, you may want to serve a lamb crown roast centered with a bread stuffing.

Sprinkle lamb with salt and pepper. Place lamb bone ends up in shallow roasting pan; wrap bone ends with aluminum foil to prevent excessive browning. To hold shape, place a small ovenproof cup or bowl in crown.

Insert meat thermometer so tip is in center of thickest part of lamb and does not touch bone or rest in fat. Do not add water. Do not cover.

Roast in 325° oven until desired degree of doneness (see Timetable, page 59).

One hour before lamb is done, remove cup or bowl from crown; fill crown with Bread Stuffing (page 85). (Use about 2 cups stuffing for 4-pound lamb crown.) Cover just the stuffing with aluminum foil during first 30 minutes of roasting. When lamb is done, remove foil from bone ends and, if desired, replace with paper frills. To carve, cut between ribs.

CARVING A LEG OF LAMB

Place the roast with the shank bone to your right (or to left if left-handed). Cut a few lengthwise slices from the thin side. Turn the leg over so that it rests on the cut side. Make vertical slices to the leg bone, then cut horizontally along bone to release slices.

Roast Leg of Lamb

TIMETABLE FOR ROASTING LAMB
(Oven Temperature 325°F)

Cut	Approximate Weight (Pounds)	Meat Thermometer Reading (°F)	Approximate Cooking Time (Minutes per Pound)
Crown Roast	2½ to 4	170 to 180°	40 to 45
Rib (roast at 375°)	1½ to 3	170 to 180°	35 to 45
Leg	5 to 9	170 to 180°	30 to 35
Rolled Leg	4 to 7	170 to 180°	35 to 40
Shoulder			
Square	4 to 6	170 to 180°	30 to 35
Boneless	3½ to 5	170 to 180°	40 to 45
Cushion	3½ to 5	170 to 180°	30 to 35

LAMB CUTS

From the Neck: Neck slices (braise).

From the Shoulder: Cushion shoulder roast, boneless shoulder roast, square shoulder roast (roast); arm chop, blade chop, boneless blade or Saratoga chop (broil, panfry).

From the Rib: Rib roast, crown roast (roast); rib chop, Frenched rib chop (broil, panfry).

From the Loin: Loin roast, boneless double loin roast (roast); boneless double loin chop, loin chop (broil, panfry).

From the Sirloin—Leg: Sirloin roast, sirloin half of leg, shank half of leg, American leg, French-style leg, center leg, rolled leg, combination leg (roast); leg chop (steak), sirloin chop (broil, panfry).

From the Breast: Breast, rolled breast, stuffed breast (roast, braise); riblets (braise); spareribs (braise, roast); stuffed chop (broil, panfry).

From the Shank: Foreshank, hindshank (braise, cook in liquid).

Lamb cubes, cubed steak and ground lamb may come from any section.

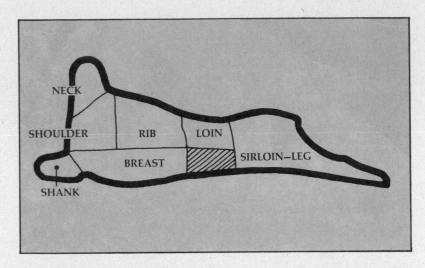

LAMB CUTS YOU SHOULD KNOW

A. Square shoulder roast

B. Neck slice
C. Boneless blade or Saratoga chop

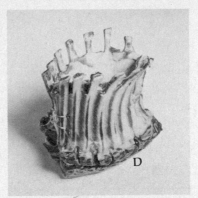

D. Crown roast

E. Loin chops

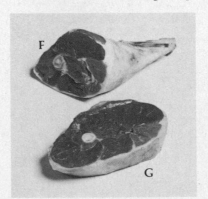

F. Hindshank   **G.** Leg chop (steak)

H. Foreshank   **I.** Boneless riblets
J. Riblets

HOW TO BROIL LAMB CHOPS

Choose loin, rib or shoulder lamb chops, allowing 1 or 2 chops for each person. Remove fell (the paperlike covering) if it is on chops. Slash diagonally outer edge of fat on lamb chops at 1-inch intervals to prevent curling (do not cut into lean).

Set oven control to broil and/or 550°. Place chops on rack in broiler pan; place broiler pan so tops of ¾- to 1-inch chops are 2 to 3 inches from heat, 1- to 2-inch chops are 3 to 5 inches from heat. Broil until brown. The chops should be about half done (see Timetable).

Sprinkle brown side with salt and pepper if desired. (Always season after browning because salt tends to draw moisture to surface, delaying browning.) Turn chops; broil until brown.

TIMETABLE FOR BROILING LAMB CHOPS AND PATTIES

Thickness	Approximate Total Cooking Time*
¾ to 1 inch	12 minutes
1½ inches	18 minutes
2 inches	22 minutes

*Time given is for medium doneness; lamb chops are not usually served rare.

CHEESY LAMB CHOPS

　4　lamb loin or sirloin chops or
　　　8 rib chops, about ¾ inch thick
　4　or 8 slices process Swiss cheese
　4　or 8 thin onion slices

Set oven control to broil and/or 550°. Broil lamb chops with tops about 3 inches from heat until brown, about 7 minutes. Cut cheese to fit chops.

Turn lamb chops; broil until done, 5 to 7 minutes longer. Place onion and cheese slice on each lamb chop; broil until cheese begins to melt, about 30 seconds.　4 SERVINGS.

Glazed Lamb Chops: Omit cheese and onion slices. Heat ¼ cup prepared mustard, ¼ cup honey, ⅛ teaspoon onion salt and ⅛ teaspoon pepper over low heat, stirring occasionally; keep warm. Brush lamb chops with mustard mixture before and after turning. Pour remaining mustard mixture over lamb chops.

LAMB CHOPS WITH PINEAPPLE

　1　can (13¼ ounces) pineapple chunks,
　　　drained (reserve syrup)
　¼　cup soy sauce
　¼　cup vinegar
　½　teaspoon dry mustard
　4　lamb shoulder chops, about ½ inch thick
　¼　cup packed brown sugar
　1　teaspoon cornstarch

Mix reserved pineapple syrup, the soy sauce, vinegar and mustard; pour on lamb chops in shallow glass dish. Cover and refrigerate, turning occasionally, at least 4 hours.

Drain lamb, reserving marinade. Cook lamb over medium-low heat until brown. Add ¼ cup reserved marinade. Cover and cook over low heat until lamb is tender, 30 to 45 minutes.

Mix brown sugar and cornstarch in saucepan; stir in remaining reserved marinade. Heat to boiling; reduce heat. Simmer uncovered 5 minutes. Add pineapple; heat through. Top lamb with pineapple glaze.　4 SERVINGS.

LAMB-NOODLE SKILLET

　2　pounds lamb shoulder chops, about
　　　½ inch thick
　2　tablespoons water
　3　cups water
　1　can (6 ounces) tomato paste
　1½　teaspoons salt
　⅛　teaspoon pepper
　　　Dash of cayenne red pepper
　1　bay leaf, crumbled
　1　large clove garlic, finely chopped
　4　ounces uncooked wide egg noodles
　½　cup shredded Cheddar cheese

Cook lamb slowly in 10-inch skillet until brown; drain. Add 2 tablespoons water. Cover and simmer until lamb is done, about 1 hour. Cool; remove lamb from bones.

Return lamb to skillet. Stir in 3 cups water, the tomato paste, salt, pepper, red pepper, bay leaf and garlic. Heat to boiling; reduce heat. Cover and simmer 30 minutes. Stir in noodles. Cover and cook until noodles are tender, about 12 minutes. Sprinkle with cheese.　5 SERVINGS.

ITALIAN LAMB SHANKS

1 cup Italian Dressing (page 157)
4 lamb shanks (each about 12 ounces)
½ cup grated Parmesan cheese
¼ cup all-purpose flour
1 tablespoon dried parsley flakes
½ teaspoon salt
¼ teaspoon onion salt
⅓ cup shortening
   Grated Parmesan cheese

Pour dressing on lamb shanks in shallow glass dish. Cover and refrigerate, turning lamb occasionally, at least 5 hours.

Remove lamb, reserving marinade. Mix ½ cup cheese, the flour, parsley, salt and onion salt. Coat lamb with cheese mixture, reserving remaining cheese mixture.

Heat shortening in 12-inch skillet or Dutch oven until melted. Cook lamb in hot shortening, turning occasionally, until brown; reduce heat. Sprinkle remaining cheese mixture over lamb. Add reserved marinade. Cover and simmer, turning occasionally, until tender, about 2½ hours. Serve with cheese. 4 SERVINGS.

Italian Chicken: Substitute 2½-pound broiler-fryer chicken, cut up, for the lamb and decrease simmering time to 1 hour. 6 SERVINGS.

MARINATED LAMB KABOBS

   French Dressing (page 157)
1 pound lamb boneless shoulder, cut into
   ¾-inch cubes
1 green pepper, cut into 1-inch pieces
1 medium onion, cut into eighths
1 pint cherry tomatoes

Pour dressing on lamb. Cover and refrigerate, stirring occasionally, at least 4 hours.

Remove lamb, reserving marinade. Thread lamb on four 11-inch metal skewers, leaving space between each. Set oven control to broil and/or 550°. Broil lamb with tops about 3 inches from heat 5 minutes. Turn; brush with reserved marinade. Broil 5 minutes longer.

Alternate green pepper, onion and tomatoes on four 11-inch metal skewers, leaving space between foods. Place vegetables on rack in broiler pan with lamb. Turn lamb; brush lamb and vegetables with reserved marinade. Broil kabobs, turning and brushing with reserved marinade every 2 minutes, until evenly brown, 3 to 4 minutes. 4 SERVINGS.

LAMB CURRY

1 medium onion, chopped (about ½ cup)
½ small green pepper, chopped (about
   ¼ cup)
1 small stalk celery, chopped (about ¼ cup)
1 apple, thinly sliced
¼ cup margarine or butter
¼ cup all-purpose flour
1 to 2 teaspoons curry powder
¼ to ½ teaspoon salt
2 cups chicken broth
2 cups cubed cooked lamb
3 cups hot cooked rice (page 225)
¼ to ½ cup chopped peanuts or chutney

Cook and stir onion, green pepper, celery and apple in margarine until onion is tender. Blend in flour, curry powder and salt. Cook over low heat, stirring constantly, until mixture is hot and bubbly; remove from heat. Stir in broth gradually. Heat to boiling, stirring constantly. Boil and stir 1 minute. Stir in lamb. Heat, stirring occasionally, until hot, about 10 minutes. Spoon onto hot rice. Serve with peanuts to sprinkle over top. 4 SERVINGS.

Do-ahead Tip: After cooking, Lamb Curry can be covered and frozen no longer than 4 months. To serve, cover and heat frozen lamb mixture and ½ cup water over medium heat, turning occasionally, until hot and bubbly, about 30 minutes.

BROILED LAMB PATTIES

1 pound ground lamb
2 tablespoons dry bread crumbs
1 tablespoon snipped parsley
½ teaspoon salt
¼ teaspoon dried dill weed
1 egg
1 clove garlic, crushed
4 slices bacon

Mix lamb, bread crumbs, parsley, salt, dill weed, egg and garlic. Shape mixture into 4 patties, each about 1 inch thick. Wrap bacon slice around edge of each patty and secure with wooden picks.

Set oven control to broil and/or 550°. Broil patties with tops about 3 inches from heat, turning once, until done, about 15 minutes. 4 SERVINGS.

VEAL

HOW TO ROAST VEAL

Select roast from those in chart below. Allow about ⅓ pound per person—less for boneless roasts, more for roasts with a bone. If desired, sprinkle with salt and pepper.

Place veal fat side up on rack in shallow pan. (With a rib roast, the ribs form a natural rack.) It is not necessary to baste. If roast has little or no fat, place 2 or 3 slices bacon or salt pork on top.

Insert meat thermometer so tip is in center of thickest part of veal and does not touch bone or rest in fat. Do not add water. Do not cover.

Roast in 325° oven to desired doneness (see Timetable), using thermometer as final guide. Roasts are easier to carve if allowed to set 15 to 20 minutes after removing from oven. Meat continues to cook out of the oven; it should be removed when thermometer registers 5 to 10° lower than desired doneness.

TIMETABLE FOR ROASTING VEAL
(Oven Temperature 325°F)

Cut	Approximate Weight (Pounds)	Cooking Time* (Minutes per Pound)
Round or Sirloin	5 to 8	25 to 35
Loin	4 to 6	30 to 35
Rib	3 to 5	35 to 40
Boneless Rump	3 to 5	40 to 45
Boneless Shoulder	4 to 6	40 to 45

*Meat thermometer reading 170°F.

LIME GLAZE FOR ROAST VEAL

½ cup margarine or butter, melted
1 tablespoon grated lime peel
¼ cup lime juice
1 teaspoon dried marjoram leaves
½ teaspoon dried thyme leaves

Mix all ingredients; brush over veal occasionally during roasting.

VEAL MUSTARD

4 veal rib or loin chops, ½ inch thick (about 1 pound)
1 tablespoon prepared mustard
1 teaspoon salt
½ teaspoon pepper
½ cup finely chopped bacon
¾ cup half-and-half
2 tablespoons capers

Brush both sides of each veal chop lightly with mustard; sprinkle tops with salt and pepper. Place veal in ungreased square pan, 9x9x2 inches. Sprinkle bacon over and around veal. Cook uncovered in 350° oven until veal is tender, 45 to 60 minutes.

Remove veal to warm platter. Pour all but 1 tablespoon drippings from pan, leaving bacon and mustard in pan. Stir in half-and-half and capers. Heat to boiling, stirring constantly; reduce heat. Simmer uncovered, stirring frequently, until thickened, about 8 minutes. Pour sauce over veal.   4 SERVINGS.

VEAL WITH SOUR CREAM

1 medium onion, finely chopped
2 tablespoons margarine or butter
1 pound veal shoulder steak, about ½ inch thick
1 can (4 ounces) mushroom stems and pieces, drained
1 chicken bouillon cube
⅓ cup boiling water
½ teaspoon paprika
¼ teaspoon salt
¼ teaspoon dried dill weed
⅛ teaspoon pepper
2 one-inch strips lemon peel
½ cup dairy sour cream
¼ cup cold water
1½ teaspoons cornstarch

Cook and stir onion in margarine in 10-inch skillet until tender. Remove onion from skillet. Cook veal in same skillet over medium heat, turning once, until golden; sprinkle with mushrooms and onion.

Dissolve bouillon in boiling water; stir in paprika, salt, dill weed, pepper and peel. Add to veal. Cover; simmer until veal is tender, 30 to 40 minutes.

Remove veal to warm platter. Stir in sour cream gradually. Cook and stir over medium heat until hot. Shake water and cornstarch in tightly covered container; stir gradually into sour cream sauce. Heat to boiling, stirring constantly. Boil and stir 1 minute. Pour on veal.   4 SERVINGS.

VEAL CUTS

From the Shoulder: Arm roast, blade roast, boneless shoulder roast (roast, braise); arm steak, blade steak (braise, panfry); veal for stew (braise, cook in liquid).

From the Rib: Rib roast, crown roast (roast); rib chop, boneless rib chop (braise, panfry).

From the Loin: Loin roast (roast, braise); loin chop, kidney chop, top loin chop (braise, panfry).

From the Sirloin—Round (Leg): Sirloin roast, boneless sirloin roast (roast); rump roast, boneless rump roast, round roast (roast, braise); sirloin chop, round steak, cutlet (braise, panfry).

From the Breast: Breast, stuffed breast (roast, braise); riblets, boneless riblets (braise, cook in liquid); stuffed chop (braise, panfry).

From the Shank: Shank, shank cross cut (braise, cook in liquid).

Ground veal, mock chicken legs and city chicken come from any section.

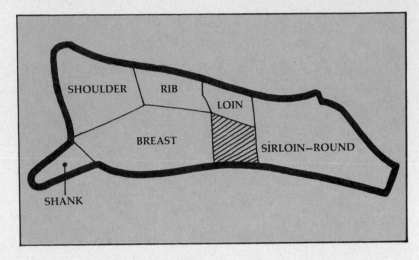

VEAL CUTS YOU SHOULD KNOW

A. Boneless shoulder roast
B. Arm steak   **C.** Blade steak

D. Loin chop   **E.** Kidney chop
F. Rib chop

G. Rump roast

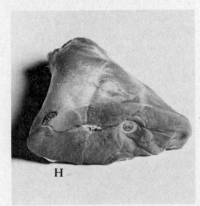

H. Round roast

I. Cutlets

J. Riblets   **K.** City chicken
L. Mock chicken legs

SPANISH VEAL

    1 package (10 ounces) frozen cut green
        beans
  1½ pounds veal boneless shoulder, cut into
        ¾-inch cubes
    3 tablespoons vegetable oil
    1 can (16 ounces) whole tomatoes
    1 tablespoon chopped onion
    1 teaspoon salt
    ¼ teaspoon pepper
    1 bay leaf
    1 clove garlic, cut into halves
    ½ cup cold water
    2 tablespoons flour

Cook beans as directed on package; drain. Cook veal in oil in 10-inch skillet until brown. Stir in tomatoes (with liquid), onion, salt, pepper, bay leaf and garlic. Heat to boiling; reduce heat. Cover and simmer until veal is tender, about 1½ hours.

Remove garlic from veal mixture. Shake cold water and flour in tightly covered container; stir gradually into veal mixture. Stir in beans; heat through. Serve over hot cooked rice (page 225) if desired.
6 SERVINGS.

SPICY STUFFED VEAL

    4 pork link sausages
    4 veal cutlets (each about 3 ounces) or
        ¾-pound veal round steak, about
        ½ inch thick
    2 tablespoons flour
    1 teaspoon salt
    1 medium onion, sliced
    ½ cup uncooked regular rice
    1 can (16 ounces) stewed tomatoes
    2 teaspoons sugar
    1 teaspoon salt

Cook and stir sausages in skillet until brown. If using veal round steak, cut into 4 serving pieces. Pound veal to ¼-inch thickness. Wrap each piece veal around 1 sausage; secure with wooden picks. Mix flour and salt; coat veal rolls with flour mixture. Cook veal rolls on all sides in sausage fat in skillet until brown; drain on paper towels.

Drain fat from skillet; add veal rolls, onion, rice, tomatoes, sugar and salt. Heat to boiling; reduce heat. Cover and simmer, stirring occasionally, until veal and rice are tender and liquid has been absorbed, about 40 minutes. Garnish with parsley sprigs if desired.   4 SERVINGS.

Veal Cordon Bleu

VEAL CORDON BLEU

    4 veal cutlets (each about 3 ounces) or
        ¾-pound veal round steak, about
        ½ inch thick
    4 thin slices smoked sliced ham
    4 thin slices Swiss cheese
    2 tablespoons flour
    ½ teaspoon salt
    ¼ teaspoon pepper
    ¼ teaspoon ground allspice
    1 egg, slightly beaten
    ½ cup dry bread crumbs
    3 tablespoons shortening
    2 tablespoons water

If using veal round steak, cut into 4 serving pieces. Pound veal to ¼-inch thickness. Place 1 slice each ham and cheese on each piece veal. Roll up carefully, beginning at narrow end; secure with wooden picks.

Mix flour, salt, pepper and allspice; coat rolls with flour mixture. Dip rolls into egg, then roll in bread crumbs.

Heat shortening in 10-inch skillet until melted. Cook rolls in shortening until brown, about 5 minutes. Add water. Heat to boiling; reduce heat. Cover and simmer until veal is tender, about 45 minutes. Remove cover during last 2 to 3 minutes to crisp veal slightly.   4 SERVINGS.

VARIETY MEATS

VARIETY MEATS FOR HEALTH

Variety meats—liver, brains, kidneys, tripe, sweetbreads, heart and tongue—are excellent sources of many essential nutrients, including protein, B vitamins, iron and phosphorus. In fact, liver is so rich in iron and vitamin A that if your family won't eat it plain, offer it with barbecue sauce, catsup or onions. Liver and other variety meats are more perishable than other meats; cook and serve them as soon as possible after you buy them.

LIVER

Beef and pork livers are frequently braised, panfried or deep-fat fried and are sometimes ground for loaves and patties. (If liver is to be ground, cook slowly in 2 to 3 tablespoons vegetable oil about 5 minutes. This makes grinding much easier.) Baby beef, veal (calf) and lamb livers are usually panfried or broiled. Peel or trim any membrane from liver before cooking.

To Braise (whole): Coat beef or pork liver with flour. Heat shortening until melted. Fry liver until brown; sprinkle with salt. Add ⅓ to ½ cup liquid. Heat to boiling; reduce heat. Cover and simmer on top of range or cook in 350° oven until done, about 30 minutes per pound. Sliced or cubed vegetables can be simmered with the liver if desired.

To Braise (sliced): Prepare as directed for whole liver except—have beef or pork liver sliced ½ to ¾ inch thick and decrease liquid to ¼ cup. Cover and simmer 20 to 30 minutes.

To Broil: Have veal or lamb liver sliced ½ to ¾ inch thick. Dip into melted bacon fat, margarine or butter. Set oven control to broil and/or 550°. Broil with tops 3 to 5 inches from heat just long enough to change color and become brown, about 3 minutes on each side.

To Deep-fat Fry: Have beef or pork liver cut into long, thin strips. Coat with flour. Or dip into egg, then coat with crumbs. Heat vegetable oil to 350° Fry liver until brown.

To Panfry: Have liver sliced ½ to ¾ inch thick. Coat with flour. Heat 2 tablespoons shortening until melted. Fry liver over medium-high heat until brown, 2 to 3 minutes on each side.

LIVER AND ONIONS

Have 1 pound liver sliced ½ to ¾ inch thick. Cook and stir 2 medium onions, thinly sliced, and 3 tablespoons margarine or butter in 10-inch skillet until tender. Remove from skillet; keep warm.

Heat ¼ cup shortening in same skillet until melted. Coat liver slices with flour. Fry liver in shortening over medium heat until brown, 2 to 3 minutes on each side. Sprinkle with salt and pepper. Add the onions during last minute of cooking to heat through.   5 SERVINGS.

BRAINS AND SWEETBREADS

Brains and sweetbreads, soft in consistency and very tender, have a delicate flavor. If not cooked immediately after purchase, they should be precooked. Precooking makes them firm; then they can be broiled, fried or braised.

To Precook: Heat 1 quart water, 1 teaspoon salt and 1 tablespoon lemon juice to boiling. Add 1 pound brains or sweetbreads. Heat to boiling; reduce heat. Cover and simmer 20 minutes. Drain; plunge into cold water. Remove membrane with sharp knife.

Precooked brains or sweetbreads can be broken into small pieces and scrambled with eggs: reheated in a rich cream sauce, well-seasoned tomato sauce (see Garlic Tomato Sauce, page 24) or Cheese Sauce (page 173); dipped into slightly beaten egg, then into crumbs and fried until delicate golden brown; made into croquettes; served in salads.

To Broil (after precooking): Mix ¼ cup margarine or butter, melted, and 1 clove garlic, crushed. Brush half of the margarine mixture over 1 pound brains or sweetbreads. Set oven control to broil and/or 550°. Broil with tops about 3 inches from heat 5 minutes. Turn; brush with remaining margarine. Broil 5 minutes longer.

To Braise (without precooking): Remove membrane with sharp knife. Coat brains or sweetbreads with flour. Heat shortening until melted. Fry brains until brown. Cover and cook until done, about 20 minutes.

To Panfry (without precooking): Prepare as directed for braised except—do not cover. Fry, turning occasionally, until done, about 20 minutes.

KIDNEYS

Kidneys are considered a great delicacy and are served in a variety of gourmet dishes. Beef kidney is less tender than other kidneys and should be cooked in liquid or braised. Lamb, pork and veal kidneys can be cooked in liquid, braised or broiled. Remove membrane and hard parts from kidney before cooking.

To Cook in Liquid: Cover with liquid (usually water). Heat to boiling; reduce heat. Cover and simmer until tender, 1 to 1½ hours for beef kidney, ¾ to 1 hour for lamb, pork or veal kidney.

To Braise: Roll halves or pieces of kidney in flour or crumbs seasoned with salt and pepper. Heat vegetable oil in skillet. Cook kidney until brown. Add small amount liquid. Cover and cook until tender, 1½ to 2 hours for beef kidney, ¾ to 1 hour for lamb kidney, 1 to 1½ hours for pork or veal kidney.

To Broil: Cut lamb kidney lengthwise into halves or leave whole. Cut veal kidney into slices. Brush kidney with margarine or butter, melted, or marinate in French Dressing (page 157). Set oven control to broil and/or 550°. Broil until done, about 5 minutes on each side. Kidney can also be wrapped in slices of bacon and broiled, or broiled on a skewer.

TRIPE

Tripe can be purchased fresh, pickled or canned. It has a very delicate flavor and is one of the less tender variety meats, requiring long, slow cooking in liquid. Tripe is already partially cooked when purchased; however, precooking in water is essential to all ways of serving. Tripe can also be purchased fully cooked, then broiled.

To Precook: Cover tripe with salted water; add 1 teaspoon salt for each quart water. Heat to boiling; reduce heat. Cover and simmer until tender, 1 to 1½ hours.

To Broil (after precooking): Brush tripe with margarine or butter, melted. Set oven control to broil and/or 550°. Broil until light brown on both sides, 10 to 15 minutes.

Cooked tripe can also be served topped with a well-seasoned tomato sauce (see Garlic Tomato Sauce, page 24); creamed; spread with dressing and baked; dipped into fritter batter and fried.

HEART

Heart is flavorful but one of the less tender variety meats. Braising and cooking in liquid are the preferred methods of cooking.

To Braise (whole): Cook heart on all sides in small amount vegetable oil until brown. Add small amount liquid (about ½ cup). Sprinkle with salt and pepper. Heat to boiling; reduce heat. Cover and simmer on top of range or in 300 to 325° oven until tender, 3 to 4 hours for beef heart, 2½ to 3 hours for lamb, pork or veal heart.

To Braise (sliced): Prepare as directed for whole heart except—cook 1½ to 2 hours for beef heart, 2½ to 3 hours for lamb, pork or veal heart.

To Cook in Liquid: Cover heart with water; add 1 teaspoon salt for each quart water. Heat to boiling; reduce heat. Cover and simmer until tender, 3 to 4 hours for beef heart, 2½ to 3 hours for lamb, pork or veal heart.

TONGUE

Tongue can be purchased fresh, pickled, corned, smoked or canned. Tongue is one of the less tender variety meats, requiring long, slow cooking in liquid. Smoked, corned or pickled tongue may require soaking before cooking. Lamb and pork tongues are usually sold ready-to-serve.

To Cook in Liquid: Cover tongue with water. If cooking fresh tongue, add 1 teaspoon salt for each quart water. Heat to boiling; reduce heat. Cover and simmer until tender, 3 to 4 hours for beef tongue, 2 to 3 hours for veal tongue. Drain; plunge into cold water. Peel skin from tongue; cut away roots, bones and cartilage.

After cooking, tongue can be served hot or cold (whole or sliced) in a spicy sauce. Hot tongue is delicious served with buttered chopped spinach or Harvard Beets (page 168). If tongue is served cold, reserve cooking liquid. After removing skin, roots, bones and cartilage, allow tongue to cool in reserved liquid. Serve sliced cold tongue with Horseradish Sauce (page 48).

GLAZED BEEF TONGUE

Cook 3- to 3½-pound beef tongue as directed above. Place in ungreased oblong pan, 13x9x2 inches. Mix 1 can (8¼ ounces) crushed pineapple, drained, ¼ cup packed brown sugar and 1 teaspoon grated orange peel; spread over tongue. Cover and cook in 350° oven 30 minutes.   6 TO 8 SERVINGS.

SEAFOOD

SEAFOOD IN YOUR MENUS

Fish is a high-protein food. It takes only 2 to 3 ounces of fish or shellfish (not counting bones or shells) to provide the protein needed for one meal—about one-fourth of the day's protein requirement. If the servings in our recipes (based on protein needs per meal) seem small for hearty appetites, count on fewer servings per recipe or increase the variety or amount of foods you serve with the fish.

HOW MUCH SHOULD YOU BUY?
How much fish you buy will depend on what form and kind you select. Use these guidelines the first time you shop if you are uncertain about amounts.

Whole fish (just as it comes from the water): about 1 pound per serving

Drawn fish (whole but eviscerated): about ¾ pound per serving

Dressed or pan-dressed (less than 1 pound): about ½ pound per serving

Steaks (cross-section slices, about ¾ inch thick, from large dressed fish): about ⅓ pound per serving

Fillets (sides of fish cut lengthwise away from backbone—almost boneless): ¼ pound or less per serving

Butterfly fillets (double fillets held together by skin): about ¼ pound per serving

Sticks (cuts from frozen blocks of fish fillets—breaded, partly cooked and frozen): about 4 sticks per serving

HOW TO BUY SEAFOOD
Whole fresh fish: Look for bright, clear bulging eyes; firm flesh that springs back when pressed; reddish pink gills; shiny, bright-colored scales, close to the skin; fresh smell, not too strong.

Frozen fish: Be sure it is frozen solid, no discoloration with little or no odor, little or no airspace between fish and wrapping.

Shellfish: Available canned, frozen, smoked, breaded and, in some areas, live; consult recipe or dealer for amount to buy.

STORING AND FREEZING SEAFOOD
Refrigerate fresh fish in the coldest section. If you don't plan to use it within a day or two, freeze it. If you buy frozen fish, keep it solidly frozen.

To freeze fresh fish (cleaned and scaled), wash under running cold water, drain, gently pat dry and wrap tightly in moistureproof, vaporproof wrap, or place in freezer container and cover with water. Separate steaks and fillets with a double thickness of aluminum foil or waxed paper, then tightly wrap, label, date and freeze.

To thaw frozen fish, leave in the refrigerator only long enough for ease of handling (about 24 hours for a 1-pound package). Do not thaw fish at room temperature.

If thawing process must be speeded up, immerse fish (wrapped in waterproof package) in cold water or under running cold water. Use immediately after thawing; dry thawed fish before cooking. Fillets or steaks can be broiled, poached or fried (if they are not breaded) without being completely thawed. Allow additional cooking time.

Frozen breaded fish fillets, portions or sticks should go directly from freezer to pan without thawing. If they thaw, use immediately; don't refreeze.

After cooking, fish can be refrigerated in covered container no longer than 3 days or frozen no longer than 3 months.

LEAN AND FAT SEAFOOD
Low Fat-High Protein Seafood (less than 5% fat, more than 15% protein): Tuna and halibut (may contain up to 25% protein); cod, flounder, haddock, pollack, mullet, ocean perch and other rockfish, carp, whiting, crabs, scallops, shrimp, lobster

Medium Fat-High Protein Seafood (5 to 15% fat, more than 15% protein): Anchovies, herring, mackerel, salmon, sardines

High Fat-Low Protein Seafood (more than 15% fat, less than 15% protein): Certain species of lake trout and, during some seasons, herring, mackerel and sardines

Low Fat-Low Protein Seafood: Oysters and clams (80% water)

METHODS OF COOKING SEAFOOD
The most important rule is: Don't overcook. Fish can be steamed, poached, fried, boiled, broiled, baked or planked (literally, cooked on a wooden plank). Broiling, baking or planking usually are best for fat fish, while lean fish remain firm and moist when steamed or poached. Exceptions can be made if lean fish are basted. Both fat and lean fish are suitable for frying. Shellfish are usually steamed, boiled, fried, broiled or baked.

BAKED FISH

1 pound fish fillets
½ teaspoon salt
 Dash of pepper
2 tablespoons margarine or butter, melted
1 tablespoon lemon juice
1 teaspoon grated onion

If fish fillets are large, cut into 5 or 6 serving pieces. Sprinkle both sides of fish with salt and pepper. Mix margarine, lemon juice and onion. Dip fish into margarine mixture; arrange in ungreased square pan, 9x9x2 inches. Pour remaining margarine mixture over fish.

Cook uncovered in 350° oven until fish flakes easily with fork, 25 to 30 minutes. Sprinkle with paprika if desired.   5 OR 6 SERVINGS.

■ **To Microwave:** Microwave margarine, lemon juice and onion uncovered in 1-cup glass measuring cup until melted; stir. Arrange fish in ungreased 1½-quart round glass casserole; sprinkle with salt and pepper. Pour margarine mixture over fish. Cover and microwave until fish flakes easily with fork, 4 to 4½ minutes.

TOMATOED FISH BAKE

1 package (16 ounces) frozen fish fillets
½ teaspoon salt
1 can (10¾ ounces) condensed tomato soup
1 small stalk celery, finely chopped (about
    ¼ cup)
¼ teaspoon dried oregano leaves
 Small onion slices, cut into halves
 Small lemon slices, cut into halves

Cut frozen fish crosswise into 5 or 6 serving pieces (let fish stand at room temperature 10 minutes before cutting). Arrange fish in ungreased square baking dish, 8x8x2 inches, or oblong baking dish, 12x7½x2 inches; sprinkle with salt.

Mix soup, celery and oregano; pour over fish. Top each part fish with 1 half-slice onion and 1 half-slice lemon. Cook uncovered in 450° oven until fish flakes easily with fork, 20 to 25 minutes. Garnish with snipped parsley if desired.   5 or 6 SERVINGS.

■ **To Microwave:** Cover and microwave frozen fish in ungreased square glass baking dish, 8x8x2 inches, 45 seconds; cut crosswise into 5 or 6 serving pieces. Continue as directed except—cover and microwave until fish flakes easily with fork, 14 to 15 minutes.

CREOLE FLOUNDER

1 pound flounder or pollack fillets
1 medium tomato, chopped (about ¾ cup)
½ small green pepper, chopped (about
    ¼ cup)
3 tablespoons lemon juice
1½ teaspoons vegetable oil
1 teaspoon salt
1 teaspoon finely chopped onion
½ teaspoon dried basil leaves
⅛ teaspoon coarsely ground pepper
2 drops red pepper sauce

If fish fillets are large, cut into 5 or 6 serving pieces. Place fish in greased oblong baking dish, 13½x9x2 inches. Mix remaining ingredients; spoon onto fish. Cook uncovered in 400° oven until fish flakes easily with fork, about 10 minutes. Garnish with green pepper rings and tomato wedges if desired.   5 OR 6 SERVINGS.

FISH FIESTA

1 pound fish fillets
1 teaspoon salt
¼ teaspoon pepper
1 small onion, thinly sliced
1 tomato, cut into ½-inch slices
1 tablespoon lime juice
1 tablespoon vegetable oil
1 tablespoon snipped parsley

If fish fillets are large, cut into 5 or 6 serving pieces. Arrange fish in ungreased square baking dish, 8x8x2 inches; sprinkle with salt and pepper. Top with onion and tomato slices; sprinkle with lime juice, oil and parsley. Cover and cook in 375° oven 15 minutes. Uncover and cook until fish flakes easily with fork, about 15 minutes longer. Garnish with lime wedges if desired.   5 OR 6 SERVINGS.

Do-ahead Tip: Before cooking, cover and refrigerate fish mixture no longer than 24 hours. Increase first cooking time to 30 minutes.

■ **To Microwave:** Place fish in ungreased square glass baking dish, 8x8x2 inches; sprinkle with salt and pepper. Cover and microwave until fish is almost done, 3½ to 4 minutes. Continue as directed except—cover and microwave until vegetables are crisp-tender and fish flakes easily with fork, 2 to 3 minutes.

Fish and Spinach Salad (page 73), Fish-Vegetable Medley (page 71) and Jellied Salmon Mold (page 76)

FISH-VEGETABLE MEDLEY

1 pound fish fillets
1 teaspoon salt
¼ teaspoon pepper
1 package (10 ounces) frozen green peas
1 medium cucumber, cut lengthwise into
    fourths, then crosswise into 1-inch pieces
1 medium stalk celery, cut diagonally into
    ¼-inch slices (about ½ cup)
1 small onion, cut into ¼-inch slices
½ teaspoon salt
1 tablespoon lemon juice
¼ cup margarine or butter

If fish fillets are large, cut into 5 or 6 serving pieces. Arrange fish in ungreased oblong baking dish, 12x7½x2 inches, or 2-quart casserole. Sprinkle with 1 teaspoon salt and the pepper.

Rinse frozen peas under running cold water to separate; drain. Spoon peas, cucumber, celery and onion onto fish; sprinkle with ½ teaspoon salt and the lemon juice. Dot with margarine.

Cover and cook in 350° oven until fish flakes easily with fork, 20 to 30 minutes. Sprinkle with paprika and garnish with lemon wedges if desired.
5 OR 6 SERVINGS.

■ **To Microwave:** Place fish in ungreased 2-quart round glass casserole; sprinkle with 1 teaspoon salt and the pepper. Cover and microwave until fish is almost done, 3½ to 4 minutes. Continue as directed except—cover and microwave until vegetables are crisp-tender and fish flakes easily with fork, about 6 minutes.

BAKED PARMESAN FISH

6 to 8 small fish fillets (about 1 pound)
½ teaspoon salt
⅛ teaspoon pepper
½ cup dairy sour cream
2 tablespoons grated Parmesan cheese
¼ teaspoon paprika
⅛ teaspoon dried tarragon leaves
3 green onions (with tops), sliced
    (about 3 tablespoons)

Roll up fish fillets; place seam sides down in ungreased square baking dish, 8x8x2 inches. Sprinkle with salt and pepper. Mix sour cream, cheese, paprika and tarragon; spread over fish. Cook uncovered in 350° oven until fish flakes easily with fork, 20 to 30 minutes. Sprinkle with onions. Garnish with cherry tomato halves if desired.
6 TO 8 SERVINGS.

FISH WITH LEMON SPINACH

2 small onions, cut into ¼-inch slices
2 tablespoons margarine or butter
2 tablespoons flour
1 cup milk
1 teaspoon instant chicken bouillon
1 package (16 ounces) frozen fish fillets,
    partially thawed and separated
½ teaspoon salt
2 packages (10 ounces each) frozen chopped
    spinach, thawed and drained
3 tablespoons lemon juice
2 tablespoons grated Parmesan cheese
  Paprika

Cook and stir onions in margarine until tender. Stir in flour. Cook over low heat, stirring constantly, until mixture is smooth and bubbly; remove from heat. Stir in milk and instant bouillon. Heat to boiling, stirring constantly. Boil and stir 1 minute.

If fish fillets are large, cut into 8 serving pieces. Arrange in ungreased oblong baking dish, 12x7½x2 inches, or square baking dish, 8x8x2 inches; sprinkle with salt. Spoon spinach around fish; drizzle lemon juice over spinach. Spoon sauce evenly onto fish and spinach.

Cook uncovered in 350° oven until fish flakes easily with fork, 20 to 25 minutes. Sprinkle with cheese and paprika.   8 SERVINGS.

■ **To Microwave:** Microwave margarine uncovered in 1-quart glass measuring cup until melted, 30 to 45 seconds. Stir in onions. Cover and microwave until onions are tender, about 1 minute. Stir in flour. Cover and microwave until bubbly, about 45 seconds. Stir in milk and instant bouillon gradually; cover and microwave until thickened, about 4 minutes. Arrange fish in ungreased square glass baking dish, 8x8x2 inches; sprinkle with salt. Cover and microwave until almost done, about 4 minutes. Continue as directed except—cover and microwave until fish flakes easily with fork, 3 to 4 minutes.

FREEZER STORAGE TIME FOR FISH

At 0°F, cod, yellow perch, bluefish, haddock and pollock can be frozen 9 months; lake bass, flounder, bluegill, sunfish and sole, 7 to 8 months; whitefish, lake trout, catfish, northern pike and shrimp, 4 to 5 months. Fish frozen in ice, glazed or kept in a freezer at -10°F can be stored an additional 1 or 2 months.

FISH WITH CRUNCHY VEGETABLES

1 pound fish fillets
½ teaspoon salt
⅛ teaspoon pepper
⅛ teaspoon paprika
1 medium carrot, shredded (about ½ cup)
1 large stalk celery, finely chopped (about
    ¾ cup)
3 green onions, finely chopped (about
    ⅓ cup)
½ teaspoon salt
1 tablespoon lemon juice
2 tablespoons margarine or butter

If fish fillets are large, cut into 5 or 6 serving pieces. Arrange fish in ungreased oblong baking dish, 12x7½x2 inches, or square baking dish, 8x8x2 inches. Sprinkle with ½ teaspoon salt, the pepper and paprika.

Spoon carrot, celery and onions onto fish; sprinkle with ½ teaspoon salt and the lemon juice. Dot with margarine. Cover and cook in 350° oven until fish flakes easily with fork, about 30 minutes.
5 OR 6 SERVINGS.

Do-ahead Tip: Before cooking, cover and refrigerate fish and vegetables no longer than 24 hours. Increase cooking time to about 45 minutes.

■ **To Microwave:** Place fish in ungreased square glass baking dish, 8x8x2 inches. Sprinkle with ½ teaspoon salt, the pepper and paprika. Cover and microwave until fish is almost done, 3½ to 4 minutes. Continue as directed except—cover and microwave until vegetables are crisp-tender and fish flakes easily with fork, 2 to 3 minutes.

OVEN-FRIED FISH

1 pound fish fillets or steaks
1½ teaspoons salt
¼ cup milk
½ cup dry bread crumbs
2 tablespoons margarine or butter, melted

If fish fillets are large, cut into 5 serving pieces. Stir salt into milk. Dip fish into milk, then coat with bread crumbs. Place in well-greased oblong pan, 13x9x2 inches.

Pour melted margarine over fish. Place pan on rack that is slightly above middle of oven. Cook uncovered in 500° oven until fish flakes easily with fork, 10 to 12 minutes.   5 SERVINGS.

BAKED STUFFED FISH

8-to 10-pound fish (salmon, cod, snapper
    or lake trout), cleaned
Salt and pepper
Garden Vegetable Stuffing (below)
Vegetable oil
½ cup margarine or butter, melted
¼ cup lemon juice

Rub cavity of fish with salt and pepper; stuff with Garden Vegetable Stuffing. Close opening with skewers and lace with string. Spoon any extra stuffing into baking dish; cover and refrigerate. Heat in oven 20 minutes before serving.

Brush fish with oil; place in shallow roasting pan. Mix margarine and lemon juice. Cook fish uncovered in 350° oven, brushing occasionally with margarine mixture, until fish flakes easily with fork, about 1½ hours.   10 TO 12 SERVINGS.

GARDEN VEGETABLE STUFFING

2 medium onions, chopped (about 1 cup)
¼ cup margarine or butter
2 cups dry bread cubes
1 cup coarsely shredded carrot
3 ounces mushrooms, chopped
½ cup snipped parsley
1 tablespoon plus 1½ teaspoons lemon juice
1 egg
1 clove garlic, finely chopped
2 teaspoons salt
¼ teaspoon dried marjoram leaves
¼ teaspoon pepper

Cook and stir onions in margarine until tender. Stir in remaining ingredients gently.

POACHED FISH

1 medium onion, sliced
3 slices lemon
3 sprigs parsley
1 bay leaf
1 teaspoon salt
2 peppercorns
1 pound fish fillets

Heat 1½ inches water, the onion, lemon, parsley, bay leaf, salt and peppercorns to boiling in 10-inch skillet; reduce heat.

Arrange fish in single layer in skillet. Simmer uncovered until fish flakes easily with fork, 4 to 6 minutes.   5 or 6 SERVINGS.

FISH AND SPINACH SALAD

    Ginger Dressing (below)
1 pound fish fillets*
6 ounces spinach, torn into bite-size pieces
    (about 7 cups)
1 can (16 ounces) bean sprouts, chilled and
    drained
1 medium stalk celery, cut diagonally into
    ¼-inch slices (about ½ cup)
4 large green onions, sliced (about ⅔ cup)
12 cherry tomatoes, each cut into halves

Prepare Ginger Dressing. Poach fish as directed for Poached Fish (page 72). Break fish into bite-size pieces. Pour dressing on fish. Cover and refrigerate at least 1 hour.

Toss spinach, bean sprouts, celery, onions and tomatoes. Add fish and dressing; toss.   5 or 6 SERVINGS.

*2 cups bite-size pieces cooked fish can be substituted for the fish fillets; do not poach.

GINGER DRESSING
¼ cup vegetable oil
3 tablespoons white vinegar
2 teaspoons sugar
1½ teaspoons salt
1 teaspoon soy sauce
½ teaspoon ground ginger
⅛ teaspoon pepper

Shake all ingredients in tightly covered container.

PARSLEY-BUTTERED TORSK

⅓ cup sugar
1 teaspoon salt
1 pound torsk or cod fillets
    Parsley Butter (below)

Heat 1½ inches water, the sugar and salt to boiling in 10-inch skillet; reduce heat. Arrange fish in single layer in skillet. Simmer uncovered until fish flakes easily with fork, 4 to 6 minutes. Serve with Parsley Butter.   5 or 6 SERVINGS.

PARSLEY BUTTER
¼ cup margarine or butter
1 tablespoon lemon juice
1 tablespoon snipped parsley
¼ teaspoon salt
⅛ teaspoon red pepper sauce

Heat all ingredients over low heat, stirring occasionally, until margarine is melted.

DEEP-FRIED FISH

    Vegetable oil or shortening
2 pounds fish fillets, steaks or pan-dressed
    fish
1 cup all-purpose flour*
1 teaspoon salt
⅛ teaspoon pepper
2 eggs, slightly beaten
1 cup dry bread crumbs

Heat oil (2 to 3 inches) in deep-fat fryer or kettle to 375° or heat oil (1½ to 2 inches) in skillet until hot. If fish fillets are large, cut into 10 to 12 serving pieces. Mix flour, salt and pepper. Coat fish with flour mixture; dip into eggs, then coat with bread crumbs. Fry in deep-fat fryer or skillet until golden brown, about 4 minutes.   10 to 12 SERVINGS.

*If using self-rising flour, omit salt.

Batter-fried Fish: Prepare Thin Fritter Batter (page 206). Coat fish with flour, then dip into batter. Fry in deep-fat fryer until golden brown, about 3 minutes, or fry in skillet until golden brown, about 4 minutes.

FISH AND CHIPS

    Vegetable oil
    French-fried Potatoes (page 187)
1 pound fish fillets, cut into halves
¾ cup all-purpose flour*
2 teaspoons dried dill weed
½ teaspoon salt
½ teaspoon baking soda
1 tablespoon vinegar
¾ cup water
    Vinegar
    Salt

Heat oil (2 to 3 inches) in deep-fat fryer or kettle to 375°. Prepare French-fried Potatoes, allowing 1 potato for each person; keep warm. Dry fish fillets thoroughly. Mix flour, dill weed and ½ teaspoon salt. Mix baking soda and 1 tablespoon vinegar; stir into flour mixture. Stir in water; beat until smooth.

Dip fish into batter, allowing excess batter to drip into bowl. Fry, turning once, until brown, about 5 minutes. Sprinkle fish and potatoes with vinegar and salt.   5 OR 6 SERVINGS.

*If using self-rising flour, omit salt.

PANFRIED FISH

2 pounds fish fillets, steaks or pan-dressed
    fish
1 teaspoon salt
⅛ teaspoon pepper
1 egg
1 tablespoon water
1 cup all-purpose flour,* cornmeal or
    grated Parmesan cheese
    Shortening (part margarine or butter)

If fish fillets are large, cut into 10 to 12 serving
pieces. Sprinkle both sides of fish with salt and
pepper. Beat egg and water until blended. Dip fish
into egg, then coat with flour.

Heat shortening (⅛ inch) in skillet until hot. Fry fish
in hot shortening over medium heat, turning fish
carefully, until brown on both sides, about 10
minutes.   10 to 12 SERVINGS.

*If using self-rising flour, omit salt.

BROILED FISH

1 pound fish fillets or steaks, about 1 inch
    thick
½ teaspoon salt
    Dash of pepper
2 tablespoons margarine or butter, melted

If fish fillets are large, cut into 5 or 6 serving pieces.
Sprinkle both sides of fish with salt and pepper. If
fish has not been skinned, place skin sides up on
rack in broiler pan; brush with half the margarine.

Set oven control to broil and/or 550°. Broil with
tops 2 to 3 inches from heat until light brown, about
5 minutes. Brush fish with margarine; turn carefully
and brush other sides. Broil until fish flakes easily
with fork, 5 to 8 minutes longer.   5 or 6 SERVINGS.

Broiled Fish Italiano: Omit salt and pepper. Substitute 2 tablespoons Italian Dressing (page 157) for
the margarine.

Herb Broiled Fish: Mix 2 tablespoons margarine or
butter, softened, ⅛ teaspoon dried dill weed, dash
of dried thyme leaves and dash of onion powder;
substitute for the margarine.

Lemon Broiled Fish: Omit salt and pepper. Mix 1
tablespoon grated onion, 1 tablespoon margarine
or butter, softened, ½ teaspoon salt, 1 teaspoon
lemon juice, ⅛ teaspoon pepper and ⅛ teaspoon
dried marjoram leaves; substitute for margarine.

BUDGET BOUILLABAISSE

1 medium onion, chopped
1 small stalk celery, chopped
1 tablespoon vegetable oil
1 can (28 ounces) whole tomatoes
1 tablespoon snipped parsley
½ teaspoon lemon juice
¼ teaspoon salt
¼ teaspoon dried thyme leaves
⅛ teaspoon dried oregano leaves
⅛ teaspoon fennel seed
1 clove garlic, finely chopped
1 small bay leaf
    Dash of cayenne red pepper
2 cans (10¾ ounces each) condensed
    chicken broth
½ cup water
2 tablespoons cornstarch
1 pound frozen cod, partially thawed and
    cut into 1-inch pieces

Cook and stir onion and celery in oil in 3-quart
saucepan over medium heat until onion is tender
and celery is crisp-tender, about 4 minutes. Stir in
tomatoes (with liquid), parsley, lemon juice, salt,
thyme, oregano, fennel seed, garlic, bay leaf and
red pepper. Heat to boiling; reduce heat. Simmer
uncovered 15 minutes. Stir in broth. Mix water and
cornstarch; stir into broth mixture. Cook, stirring
constantly, until mixture thickens and boils. Stir in
cod. Simmer uncovered until cod flakes easily with
fork, about 10 minutes. Sprinkle with salt and
pepper if desired.   7 SERVINGS.

FRUIT-GLAZED FISH STICKS

Cook 1 package (8 ounces) frozen fish sticks as
directed on package for oven method except—
blend ¼ cup orange marmalade, melted, and 2
tablespoons lemon juice; spoon onto fish sticks
during last 5 minutes of cooking.   2 SERVINGS.

FISH STICKS WITH MUSHROOMS

1 package (8 ounces) frozen fish sticks
1 can (4 ounces) mushroom stems and
    pieces, drained
1 small onion, chopped
¼ cup margarine or butter, melted
¼ cup chopped pecans

Arrange frozen fish sticks in ungreased jelly roll
pan, 15½x10½x1 inch. Mix remaining ingredients;
spoon onto fish sticks. Cook as directed on package
for oven method.   2 SERVINGS.

GARNISHES FOR FISH

Spiral Mushrooms

Lemon Rose

Citrus Blossom

Vegetable Daisies

Cherry Tomato Blossoms

Carrot and Celery Curls

SPIRAL MUSHROOMS

Remove stems and skin from large mushrooms. Cut 5 curved slits from center to outer edge on the rounded side of each cap. Make a second set of cuts parallel to previous cuts; lift out small wedge of mushroom between each cut.

LEMON OR LIME ROSE

Cut thin slice from stem end of lemon or lime. Starting just above cut end, cut around lemon in a continuous motion to form a spiral of peel. Carefully curl peel spiral to resemble a rose.

CITRUS BLOSSOM

Cut thin slice from stem end of large lemon or lime. Holding cut end down, make slanted gashes in staggered fashion around side of fruit. Cut one short gash across top. Cut a smaller lemon or lime crosswise into thin slices; cut slices into halves. Insert slices peel sides out in gashes as pictured.

VEGETABLE DAISIES

Cut pared small turnip or rutabaga into thin slices; cut out circles with scalloped or round cutter. Make V-shaped notches around plain circles to form petals. Attach thin carrot shapes to center of each circle with dab of cream cheese.

CHERRY TOMATO BLOSSOMS

Hollow out stem end of each cherry tomato slightly. Pipe about ½ teaspoon softened cream cheese into center. Or make 5 cuts almost to bottom of tomato and insert five ⅛-inch slices water chestnut in cuts. Garnish with parsley.

CARROT AND CELERY CURLS

Cut carrots lengthwise into paper-thin slices with parer. Roll up; secure with picks. Chill in iced water. Place ripe olive in center. Cut celery into pieces. Slit ends almost to center. Chill in iced water.

SALMON PUFF

2 tablespoons margarine or butter, melted
½ cup milk
4 slices bread, torn into pieces
1 can (15½ ounces) salmon, drained and
   flaked
2 eggs, separated
3 tablespoons lemon juice
2 teaspoons finely chopped onion
1 teaspoon salt
½ teaspoon pepper
   Paprika

Mix margarine, milk and bread; stir in salmon, egg yolks, lemon juice, onion, salt and pepper. Beat egg whites until stiff; fold into salmon mixture. Pour into greased 1½-quart casserole; sprinkle with paprika. Cook uncovered in 350° oven 1 hour. 6 SERVINGS.

■ **To Microwave:** Use round glass casserole; do not grease. Microwave uncovered until top is dry and set, 5 to 7 minutes.

SALMON-MACARONI SLAW

3 ounces uncooked elbow macaroni
   (about ¾ cup)
1 can (15½ ounces) salmon, drained and
   flaked
3 cups finely shredded cabbage
1 medium stalk celery, chopped (about
   ½ cup)
1 medium green pepper, chopped (about
   1 cup)
2 tablespoons finely chopped onion
1½ teaspoons salt
1½ teaspoons pepper
¼ cup vegetable oil
2 tablespoons vinegar

Cook macaroni as directed on page 221. Mix macaroni, salmon, cabbage, celery, green pepper and onion. Mix salt, pepper, oil and vinegar; pour over macaroni mixture and toss. Cover and refrigerate 30 minutes. (If a moister salad is desired, stir in ⅔ cup mayonnaise or salad dressing.) 6 SERVINGS.

Shrimp-Macaroni Slaw: Substitute 3 cans (4½ ounces each) tiny shrimp, rinsed and drained, for the salmon.

Tuna-Macaroni Slaw: Substitute 1 can (9¼ ounces) tuna, drained, for the salmon. Stir in ½ cup shredded Cheddar cheese (about 2 ounces).

JELLIED SALMON MOLD

1 envelope unflavored gelatin
¼ cup cold water
¾ cup boiling water
2 tablespoons lemon juice
1½ teaspoons vinegar
1 teaspoon salt
1 medium stalk celery, chopped
⅓ cup chopped cucumber
   About 10 thin slices cucumber
1 can (15½ ounces) red salmon, drained
   and flaked
   Salad Greens
   Sour Cream Sauce (below)

Sprinkle gelatin on cold water to soften; stir in boiling water gradually. Stir until gelatin is dissolved. Stir in lemon juice, vinegar and salt; cool.

Mix celery and chopped cucumber. Arrange the cucumber slices in bottom of 4-cup mold. Layer half of the salmon, the celery-cucumber mixture and the remaining salmon on cucumber. Pour gelatin on salmon. Refrigerate until set, about 3 hours.

Unmold jellied salmon on salad greens. Serve with Sour Cream Sauce.   6 SERVINGS.

SOUR CREAM SAUCE

¼ cup plus 2 tablespoons dairy sour cream
½ small green pepper, finely chopped
1 teaspoon snipped parsley
1 teaspoon snipped chives
¼ teaspoon salt
   Dash of pepper

Mix all ingredients; refrigerate until serving time.

TUNA AND CHIPS

1 can (10¾ ounces) condensed cream of
   mushroom soup
½ cup milk
1 can (6½ ounces) tuna, drained
1¼ cups crushed potato chips
1 cup cooked green peas

Mix soup and milk in ungreased 1-quart casserole. Stir in tuna, 1 cup chips and the peas. Sprinkle with remaining chips. Cook uncovered in 350° oven until hot, about 25 minutes.   4 SERVINGS.

■ **To Microwave:** Use round glass casserole. Do not sprinkle remaining potato chips over casserole. Microwave uncovered 5 minutes; sprinkle remaining potato chips over casserole. Microwave uncovered until hot and bubbly, about 4 minutes.

TOASTY TUNA CASSEROLE

12 slices sandwich bread (crusts
    removed), toasted
1 can (6½ ounces) tuna, drained
1 small onion, chopped (about
    ¼ cup)
¼ cup mayonnaise or salad dressing
6 slices process American cheese
1 package (10 ounces) frozen mixed
    vegetables or 1 package (10 ounces)
    frozen chopped broccoli, thawed
1 can (10¾ ounces) condensed cream
    of celery soup
¼ cup milk
¼ teaspoon salt

Arrange 6 slices toast in ungreased oblong baking dish, 12x7½x2 inches, or oblong pan, 13x9x2 inches. Mix tuna, onion and mayonnaise; spread over toast in dish. Top each slice toast with 1 slice cheese; place remaining slices toast on cheese.

Mix remaining ingredients; pour on center of toast, spreading to within 2 inches of edges. Cook uncovered in 350° oven until hot and bubbly, 25 to 30 minutes.　6 SERVINGS.

TUNA MANICOTTI CREPES

  Manicotti Crepes (right)
1 can (6½ ounces) tuna, drained
1 can (15 ounces) tomato sauce
1 medium stalk celery, chopped (about
    ½ cup)
1 egg
1 cup creamed cottage cheese
½ teaspoon garlic salt
⅛ teaspoon pepper
1 cup shredded mozzarella or Cheddar
    cheese (about 4 ounces)

Prepare Manicotti Crepes. Heat tuna, tomato sauce and celery until hot, 3 to 5 minutes. Pour ⅓ of the sauce into ungreased oblong baking dish, 12x7½x2 inches, or oblong pan, 13x9x2 inches.

Mix egg, cottage cheese, garlic salt and pepper. Spread about 1 tablespoon cheese mixture down center of each crepe. Reserve ½ cup mozzarella cheese. Sprinkle about 1 teaspoon remaining mozzarella cheese on each crepe; roll up. Place seam sides down in baking dish; pour remaining sauce over crepes. Sprinkle reserved mozzarella cheese down center of crepes. Cook uncovered in 350° oven until hot and bubbly, about 30 minutes.
6 SERVINGS.

MANICOTTI CREPES

½ cup all-purpose flour
½ teaspoon salt
2 eggs
½ cup water
2 teaspoons vegetable oil

Mix all ingredients; beat with hand beater until smooth, about 1 minute.

Lightly butter 7-inch skillet; heat over medium heat until bubbly. For each crepe, pour about 2 tablespoons batter into skillet; *immediately* rotate skillet until thin film of batter covers bottom. Cook until top looks dull and dry and bottom is light brown, about 30 seconds.

TUNA LOAF SANDWICHES

1 can (9¼ ounces) tuna, drained
½ cup cracker crumbs
2 eggs, slightly beaten
1 tablespoon finely chopped green onion
1 teaspoon lemon juice
½ teaspoon salt
¼ teaspoon lemon pepper
¼ teaspoon chili powder
  Dash of red pepper sauce
  Lettuce leaves
4 hamburger buns, split and toasted
  Tartar Sauce (below)
2 tomatoes, sliced

Mix tuna, cracker crumbs, eggs, onion, lemon juice, salt, lemon pepper, chili powder and pepper sauce. Press in greased loaf pan, 8½x4½x2½ inches. Cook uncovered in 350° oven until firm and juicy, about 25 minutes. Cool in pan about 2 minutes; remove from pan.

Cut loaf into fourths; split each fourth horizontally into halves. Place lettuce and 1 tuna slice on each bun half; spread with about 1 tablespoon Tartar Sauce and top with tomato slice.　4 SERVINGS
(2 OPEN-FACE SANDWICHES PER SERVING).

TARTAR SAUCE

½ cup mayonnaise or salad dressing
1 tablespoon finely chopped dill pickle
1½ teaspoons snipped parsley
1 teaspoon chopped pimiento
½ teaspoon grated onion

Mix all ingredients; refrigerate until serving.

TUNA CAKES

2 slices white bread (crusts removed),
    torn into small pieces
1 can (6½ ounces) tuna, drained
1 egg
1 teaspoon Worcestershire sauce
½ teaspoon dry mustard
¼ teaspoon salt
1 tablespoon vegetable oil
    Dill Sauce (below)

Mix bread, tuna, egg, Worcestershire sauce, mustard and salt. Shape mixture into 3 firm patties, each about ½ inch thick.

Fry patties in oil over medium heat until golden brown on both sides, 4 to 5 minutes. Top with Dill Sauce.   3 SERVINGS.

DILL SAUCE
Mix ¼ cup mayonnaise or salad dressing, 1 tablespoon chopped pimiento-stuffed olives and ⅛ teaspoon dried dill weed.

■ **To Microwave:** Cover and microwave patties in ungreased 9-inch glass pie plate 2 minutes. Turn patties over; cover and microwave until set, 2 to 3 minutes longer.

Fish Cakes: Substitute 1 cup flaked cooked fish for the tuna.

Salmon Cakes: Substitute 1 can (7¾ ounces) salmon, drained, for the tuna.

Shrimp Cakes: Substitute 1 can (4½ ounces) tiny shrimp, drained and chopped, for the tuna.

TUNA CHEESIES

1 can (6½ ounces) tuna, drained
2 medium stalks celery, chopped (about
    1 cup)
½ cup diced process American cheese
    loaf
1 tablespoon instant minced onion
¼ teaspoon salt
⅛ teaspoon pepper
¼ cup mayonnaise or salad dressing
6 hamburger buns, split
    Margarine or butter, softened

Mix tuna, celery, cheese, onion, salt, pepper and mayonnaise. Spread buns with margarine. Fill buns with tuna mixture. Place each sandwich on piece of aluminum foil and fold edges securely; place on ungreased cookie sheet. Cook in 350° oven until hot, about 20 minutes.   6 SANDWICHES.

TUNA SALAD SANDWICH FILLING

1 can (6½ ounces) tuna, drained
¼ cup finely chopped sweet pickle
½ cup mayonnaise or salad dressing
¼ teaspoon salt

Mix all ingredients; refrigerate until serving time. 1¼ CUPS FILLING (ENOUGH FOR 3 OR 4 SANDWICHES).

Tuna-Olive Sandwich Filling: Substitute ¼ cup sliced pimiento-stuffed olives for the sweet pickle.

Tuna-Ripe Olive Sandwich Filling: Substitute ¼ cup sliced pitted ripe olives for the sweet pickle.

TUNA SALAD IN PUFF BOWL

½ cup water
¼ cup margarine or butter
½ cup all-purpose flour*
⅛ teaspoon salt
½ to 1 teaspoon caraway seed
2 eggs
    Tuna Salad (below)

Heat water and margarine to rolling boil. Quickly stir in flour, salt and caraway seed. Stir vigorously over low heat until mixture forms a ball, about 1 minute; remove from heat. Beat in eggs, both at once; continue beating until smooth. Spread batter evenly in greased 9-inch pie plate (do not spread up side). Cook uncovered in 400° oven until golden brown, 45 to 50 minutes; cool.

Just before serving, mound Tuna Salad in puff bowl. Garnish with parsley, sliced tomatoes or hard-cooked eggs if desired.   8 SERVINGS.

*Self-rising flour can be used in this recipe.

TUNA SALAD

2 cans (6½ ounces each) tuna, drained
2 medium stalks celery, chopped (about
    1 cup)
½ cup cubed avocado or ½ cup chopped
    green or pitted ripe olives
1 small onion, chopped (about ¼ cup)
1 tablespoon lemon juice
3 hard-cooked eggs, cut up
½ teaspoon curry powder (optional)
¾ to 1 cup mayonnaise or salad dressing

Mix all ingredients except mayonnaise. Cover and refrigerate. Just before serving, fold mayonnaise into tuna mixture.

Chicken Salad in Puff Bowl: Substitute 2 cups cut-up cooked chicken for the tuna.

BOILED DUNGENESS CRABS

Have your fish retailer dress 3 live Dungeness crabs for eating. Wash body cavity of each. Heat 8 quarts water and ½ cup salt to boiling in large kettle. Drop crabs into kettle. Cover and heat to boiling; reduce heat. Simmer 15 minutes; drain.

Crack claws and legs. Serve hot with margarine or butter, melted, or chill crabs and serve with mayonnaise or salad dressing.   6 SERVINGS.

FRIED SOFT-SHELL CRABS

12 soft-shell blue crabs
 2 eggs
¼ cup milk
 2 teaspoons salt
¾ cup all-purpose flour*
¾ cup dry bread crumbs
   Shortening

Have your fish retailer dress the crabs for eating. Rinse in cold water; drain.

Beat eggs, milk and salt until blended. Mix flour and bread crumbs. Dip crabs into egg mixture, then coat with flour mixture.

Heat shortening (⅛ inch) in 10-inch skillet. Fry crabs in shortening over medium heat, turning carefully, until brown, 8 to 10 minutes. Serve with lemon wedges if desired.   6 SERVINGS.

*If using self-rising flour, decrease salt to 1¼ teaspoons.

Deep-fried Soft-shell Crabs: Heat oil (2 to 3 inches) in deep-fat fryer or large kettle to 375°. Fry until brown, 3 to 4 minutes.

BOILED HARD-SHELL CRABS

 6 quarts water
⅓ cup salt
24 live hard-shell blue crabs
   Cocktail Sauce (page 132)

Heat water and salt to boiling in large kettle. Drop crabs into kettle. Cover and heat to boiling; reduce heat. Simmer 15 minutes; drain. Serve crabs hot or cold with Cocktail Sauce.   6 SERVINGS.

NOTE: To remove meat, grasp body of crab. Break off large claws. Pull off top shell. Cut or break off legs. Scrape off the gills; carefully remove digestive and other organs located in center part of body.

Crab Louis—an individual serving

CRAB LOUIS

 2 cans (7½ ounces each) crabmeat or
    2 packages (6 ounces each) frozen
    cooked crabmeat, thawed
   Louis Dressing (below)
 4 or 5 medium tomatoes, each cut into
    fourths
 4 or 5 hard-cooked eggs, each cut into
    fourths
18 pitted ripe or green olives
 4 cups bite-size pieces salad greens

Drain crabmeat and remove cartilage; cover and refrigerate until chilled. Prepare Louis Dressing. Arrange crabmeat, tomatoes, eggs and olives on salad greens; pour dressing over salad.
6 SERVINGS.

LOUIS DRESSING

¾ cup chili sauce
½ cup mayonnaise or salad dressing
 1 teaspoon instant minced onion
½ teaspoon sugar
¼ teaspoon Worcestershire sauce

Mix all ingredients. Cover and refrigerate at least 30 minutes.

CRAB-AVOCADO SALADS

2 cans (7½ ounces each) crabmeat, drained
    and cartilage removed
2 hard-cooked eggs, chopped
¼ cup finely chopped sweet pickle or pickle
    relish
⅓ cup mayonnaise, salad dressing or dairy
    sour cream
¼ teaspoon salt
⅛ teaspoon red pepper sauce
3 avocados
½ cup shredded Swiss cheese (about
    2 ounces)

Mix crabmeat, eggs, pickle, mayonnaise, salt and pepper sauce. Cut avocados lengthwise into halves; remove pits. Place avocados cut sides up in ungreased square pan, 9x9x2 inches. Fill each half with about ½ cup crabmeat mixture; sprinkle with cheese. Cook uncovered in 400° oven until hot and bubbly, about 20 minutes.   6 SERVINGS.

Do-ahead Tip: After sprinkling with cheese, salads can be covered and refrigerated no longer than 24 hours.

CRAB-CHEESE BUNS

Served with pickles, Carrot and Celery Curls (page 75) and strawberry sundaes, these make a meal to remember.

2 cups shredded process American cheese
    (about 8 ounces)
⅓ cup margarine or butter
1 can (7½ ounces) crabmeat, drained and
    cartilage removed
6 hamburger buns, split

Heat cheese and margarine in saucepan over low heat until melted; remove from heat. Stir in crabmeat. Place buns cut sides up on rack in broiler pan. Spread with crabmeat mixture.

Set oven control to broil and/or 550°. Broil with tops 4 to 5 inches from heat until slightly brown and bubbly, about 2 minutes.   6 SERVINGS
(2 OPEN-FACE SANDWICHES PER SERVING).

ABOUT CRABMEAT

Elegant crabmeat provides a good supply of protein, calcium and minerals. Combine crabmeat with less expensive fish in sauces, salads, chowders and dips. Crabs are available live (near place of capture), frozen (cooked in the shell) and canned.

DEEP-FRIED SHELLFISH

  Vegetable oil
½ cup all-purpose flour*
1 teaspoon salt
¼ teaspoon pepper
  Shellfish (below)
2 eggs, slightly beaten
1 cup dry bread crumbs

Heat oil (2 to 3 inches) in deep-fat fryer or large kettle to 375°. Mix flour, salt and pepper. Coat shellfish with flour mixture; dip into beaten eggs, then coat with bread crumbs. Fry until golden brown (see Timetable).

*If using self-rising flour, decrease salt to ½ teaspoon.

Batter-fried Shellfish: Prepare Thin Batter (page 206). Coat shellfish with flour; dip into batter. Fry in deep-fat fryer, turning once, until golden brown (see Timetable).

Panfried Oysters or Clams: Fry oysters or clams in ⅛ inch melted margarine or butter over medium heat about 2 minutes on each side.

TIMETABLE FOR DEEP-FRYING SHELLFISH

Shellfish	Cooking Time
Deep-fried	
1 pound shrimp	2 to 3 minutes
12 ounces scallops	3 to 4 minutes
1 pint oysters	2 to 3 minutes
1 pint clams	2 to 3 minutes
Batter-fried	
1 pound shrimp	4 to 5 minutes
12 ounces scallops	3 to 4 minutes

BOILED LOBSTER

Heat 3 quarts water and 3 tablespoons salt to boiling in large kettle. Plunge 2 live lobsters (about 1 pound each) headfirst into water. Cover and heat to boiling; reduce heat. Simmer 10 minutes; drain. Place each lobster on its back. Cut lengthwise into halves with sharp knife.

Remove the stomach, which is just behind the head, and the intestinal vein, which runs from the stomach to the tip of the tail. Do not discard green liver and coral roe. Crack claws.   2 SERVINGS.

Clockwise: Broiled Lobster Tails (below), Deep-fried Fish (page 73) and a double recipe of Creole Flounder (page 69)

BROILED LOBSTER TAILS

2 quarts water
2 tablespoons salt
1 package (24 ounces) frozen South
   African rock lobster tails
⅓ cup margarine or butter,
   melted
   Lemon Butter Sauce (right)

Heat water and salt to boiling in saucepan. Add lobster tails. Cover and heat to boiling; reduce heat. Simmer 15 minutes; drain.

Cut away thin undershell (covering meat of lobster tails) with kitchen scissors. To prevent tail from curling, insert long metal skewer from meat side through tail to shell side, then back through shell and meat at opposite end. Place tails meat sides up on broiler rack. Brush with margarine.

Set oven control to broil and/or 550°. Broil about 3 inches from heat until hot, 2 to 3 minutes. Remove skewers and serve with Lemon Butter Sauce in lemon cups.   3 OR 4 SERVINGS.

LEMON BUTTER SAUCE

½ cup margarine or butter
1 tablespoon lemon juice
1 tablespoon snipped parsley
¼ teaspoon red pepper sauce

Heat all ingredients over low heat, stirring constantly, until margarine is melted; keep warm.

COOKED SHRIMP

1½ pounds fresh or frozen raw shrimp
   (in shells)
 4 cups water
 2 tablespoons salt

Peel shrimp. (If shrimp is frozen, do not thaw; peel under running cold water.) Make a shallow cut lengthwise down back of each shrimp; wash out sand vein.

Heat water to boiling. Add salt and shrimp. Cover and heat to boiling; reduce heat. Simmer 5 minutes; drain. Remove any remaining particles of sand vein.   2 CUPS CLEANED COOKED SHRIMP (¾ POUND).

NOTE: To cook shrimp before peeling, increase salt to ¼ cup. After cooking shrimp, drain and peel. Remove sand vein.

SHRIMP-ARTICHOKE SALADS

   Russian Dressing (page 158)
½ medium head lettuce, shredded (about
   4½ cups)
 1 large tomato, cut into 3 slices
 3 large canned artichoke hearts
 1 can (4½ ounces) tiny shrimp, drained
 3 hard-cooked eggs, finely chopped

Prepare Russian Dressing. Divide lettuce among 3 salad plates. Place 1 tomato slice on each salad. Place 1 artichoke heart on each tomato slice. Sprinkle about ⅓ cup shrimp over each salad. Sprinkle chopped eggs around edge of lettuce on each plate. Serve with dressing.   3 SERVINGS.

Chicken-Artichoke Salads: Substitute 1 cup bite-size pieces cooked chicken for the shrimp.

Crabmeat-Artichoke Salads: Substitute 1 can (7½ ounces) crabmeat, drained and cartilage removed, for the shrimp.

TYPES OF SHRIMP

Raw shrimp (heads removed) are greenish or pink and are sold frozen or refrigerated by the pound. One and a half pounds raw shrimp will yield ¾ pound cooked (about 2 cups). Cooked shrimp (shells removed) are pink and are sold by the pound. Canned shrimp can be used interchangeably with cooked shrimp.

Shrimp are low in calories—there are only 100 calories in a 3-ounce serving.

QUICK SHRIMP AND RICE

¼ cup dry bread crumbs
 1 tablespoon margarine or butter, softened
 3 cups cooked shrimp or other seafood
¼ cup margarine or butter
 1 can (10¾ ounces) condensed cream of
   shrimp soup
 1 cup milk
 2 tablespoons lemon juice
 3 cups hot cooked rice (page 225)

Toss bread crumbs with 1 tablespoon margarine. Cook and stir shrimp in ¼ cup margarine until hot. Stir in soup, milk and lemon juice. Heat, stirring frequently, until hot. Serve over hot rice; sprinkle with bread crumbs.   4 OR 5 SERVINGS.

SHRIMP CREOLE

 1 medium onion, finely chopped
 2 tablespoons margarine or butter
 1 small green pepper, chopped
 1 small stalk celery, chopped (about ¼ cup)
 1 bay leaf, crushed
 1 teaspoon snipped parsley
 1 teaspoon salt
⅛ teaspoon cayenne red pepper
 1 can (6 ounces) tomato paste
 2 cups water
 2 cups cleaned cooked shrimp (left)
 3 cups hot cooked rice (page 225)

Cook and stir onion in margarine in 2-quart saucepan until onion is tender. Stir in remaining ingredients except shrimp and rice. Cook over low heat, stirring occasionally, 30 minutes. Stir in shrimp; heat through. Serve over rice.   6 SERVINGS.

SCALLOPED OYSTERS

 1 pint shucked select or large oysters
½ to ¾ cup half-and-half
 3 cups soft bread crumbs
½ cup margarine or butter, melted
 1 teaspoon salt
 2 teaspoons celery seed
¼ teaspoon pepper

Arrange oysters (with liquid) in greased baking dish, 12x7½x2 inches. Pour about half of the half-and-half over oysters.

Mix remaining ingredients; sprinkle over oysters. Top with remaining half-and-half (liquid should come about ¾ of the way up on oysters). Sprinkle with paprika if desired. Cook uncovered in 375° oven until hot, 30 to 40 minutes.   4 SERVINGS.

STEAMED CLAMS

Wash 6 pounds shell clams ("steamers") thoroughly, discarding any broken-shell or open (dead) clams. Place in a steamer* with ½ cup boiling water. Steam until clams open, 5 to 10 minutes. Serve hot in shells with melted margarine or butter and cups of broth.   6 TO 8 SERVINGS.

*If a steamer is not available, add 1 inch water to kettle with clams. Cover tightly.

MANHATTAN CLAM CHOWDER

¼ cup finely cut-up lean salt pork or
      bacon, or margarine or butter
1 small onion, finely chopped (about
      ¼ cup)
2 cans (8 ounces each) minced or whole
      clams*
2 cups finely chopped potatoes
1 cup water
⅓ cup chopped celery
1 can (16 ounces) whole tomatoes
2 teaspoons snipped parsley
1 teaspoon salt
¼ teaspoon dried thyme leaves
⅛ teaspoon pepper

Cook and stir salt pork and onion in large kettle until pork is crisp and onion is tender. Drain clams, reserving liquid. Add clam liquid, potatoes, water and celery to onion and pork. Cook until potatoes are tender, about 10 minutes.

Add clams, tomatoes (with liquid) and the remaining ingredients. Heat to boiling, stirring occasionally. Serve with assorted crackers if desired.
4 TO 6 SERVINGS.

*1 pint shucked fresh clams with liquid can be substituted for the canned clams. Chop clams and add with the potatoes.

Corn Chowder: Decrease onion to 2 tablespoons. Substitute 1 can (16 ounces) cream-style corn for the clams. Use 1 cup boiling water and increase celery to 1 cup. Add 2 medium carrots, chopped (about 1 cup), with the celery.

Vegetable-Clam Chowder: Add 2 tablespoons finely chopped green pepper with the onion. Add 1 small carrot, finely chopped (about ¼ cup), 1 small stalk celery, finely chopped (about ¼ cup), and ½ cup green peas with the potatoes; increase water to 1 cup. Add broken soda crackers and 1 tablespoon margarine or butter just before serving.

NEW ENGLAND CLAM CHOWDER

1 medium onion, chopped (about
      ½ cup)
¼ cup cut-up bacon or lean salt pork
2 cans (8 ounces each) minced clams,
      drained (reserve liquid)
1 cup finely chopped potato
½ teaspoon salt
    Dash of pepper
2 cups milk

Cook and stir onion and bacon in 2-quart saucepan until onion is tender and bacon is crisp. Add enough water, if necessary, to reserved clam liquid to measure 1 cup. Stir clams, liquid, potato, salt and pepper into onion mixture. Heat to boiling; reduce heat. Cover and simmer until potato is tender, about 15 minutes. Stir in milk; heat through, stirring occasionally.   6 SERVINGS.

SCALLOP CASSEROLE

1 package (12 ounces) frozen scallops,
      thawed, or 12 ounces fresh scallops
¾ cup half-and-half
1 cup dry bread crumbs
½ cup margarine or butter, melted
2 teaspoons celery seed
1 teaspoon salt
¼ teaspoon pepper
    Paprika

If scallops are large, cut into 1½-inch pieces. Remove any shell particles and wash scallops. Arrange in greased oblong baking dish, 12x7½x2 inches, or square pan, 9x9x2 inches.

Pour about half of the half-and-half on scallops. Mix bread crumbs, margarine, celery seed, salt and pepper; sprinkle over scallops. Top with remaining half-and-half (liquid should come about ¾ of the way up on scallops). Sprinkle with paprika. Cook uncovered in 375° oven until hot and bubbly, 25 to 30 minutes.   5 SERVINGS.

POULTRY

POULTRY IN YOUR MENUS

Poultry ranks with meats and fish as a good protein source. For an adequate protein serving for one meal, you need only 1 small chicken leg or thigh, ½ small chicken breast or 2 slices (4x2x¼ inch) of chicken, turkey, duck or game hen. In our recipes, servings (based on protein needs) may seem small, but they are nutritionally adequate. For heartier appetites, allow fewer servings or add a variety of breads, vegetables and fruits to go with the poultry.

WISE CHICKEN BUYS

The best bargain of the popular broiler-fryers is the whole bird (the bigger the bird, the more meat in proportion to the bone). Cut-up chicken is a convenience and some extra cost per pound should be expected for this service. Some chicken parts sold separately will contain more meat per pound than a whole broiler-fryer; some will contain less, depending on the parts:

Chicken Parts Packaged Separately	Proportion of Meat per Pound Compared to Whole Bird
Wings	About 19% less
Drumsticks	About 3% more
Drumstick-thigh cuts	About 6% more
Thighs	About 10% more
Breasts with ribs	About 32% more
Breasts without ribs	About 36% more

Drumsticks, at a few pennies more per pound than whole broiler-fryers, are still a good bargain because they contain a little more meat per pound.

As the amount of meat per pound of the chicken parts increases—from the wings to the meatiest breasts—the price will go up accordingly, and the chicken parts may still be a wise buy.

WHICH CHICKEN TO BUY?

Consider how you want to prepare it and how many you are planning to serve. A good rule of thumb is to allow about ½ pound chicken per serving.

Rock Cornish hens (game hens) weigh 1½ pounds or less. Allow one-half to one small hen per person. Best stuffed and roasted or split and broiled.

Broiler-fryers weigh 1½ to 3 pounds. Best broiled or fried, they can also be roasted or stewed.

Roasters weigh 2½ to 5 pounds. Best roasted.

Capons, with a lot of white meat, weigh 4½ to 7 pounds. Best roasted.

Stewing chickens (hens) weigh 2½ to 5 pounds. They provide a generous amount of meat. Best used in fricassees, stews and soups.

STORING POULTRY

To store fresh poultry: Wrap loosely and refrigerate immediately after buying; store in coldest part of refrigerator 1 to 2 days.

To store leftover poultry: Refrigerate meat, giblets, dressing and gravy separately 1 to 2 days. Meal-size portions can be frozen up to 1 month.

FREEZING POULTRY

To freeze fresh poultry: Wash, pat dry and wrap tightly in freezer wrap (giblets separately). At 0°F, chicken and turkey can be frozen 9 months; ducks and geese 6 months; giblets 3 months.

To freeze cooked poultry: Meal-size portions of cooked poultry can be frozen in broth or gravy no longer than 3 weeks.

To thaw frozen chicken: Thaw, wrapped, in refrigerator about 12 hours. (As it thaws, the frozen chicken keeps the refrigerator cold and saves energy.)

CARVING CHICKEN OR TURKEY

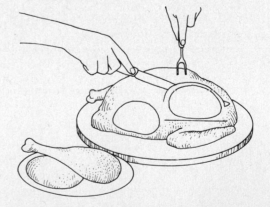

Gently pulling leg away from body, cut through joint between leg and body. Remove leg. Cut between drumstick and thigh; slice off meat. Next, make a deep horizontal cut into breast just above wing. Insert fork in top of breast and, starting halfway up breast, carve thin slices down to the cut, working upward. (To carve duckling, cut into quarters or halves with shears.)

ROAST CHICKEN

Rub cavity of chicken lightly with salt if desired. Do not salt cavity if chicken is to be stuffed. Stuff chicken just before roasting—not ahead of time. (See Bread Stuffing, right.) Fill wishbone area with stuffing first. Fasten neck skin to back with skewer. Fold wings across back with tips touching. Fill body cavity lightly. (Do not pack—stuffing will expand while cooking.) Tie or skewer drumsticks to tail. Place chicken breast side up on rack in shallow roasting pan. Brush with melted margarine or butter. Do not add water. Do not cover.

Follow Timetable (below). Chicken is done when thickest parts are done and drumstick meat feels very soft when pressed between fingers.

TIMETABLE FOR ROASTING CHICKEN

Ready-to-Cook Weight	Oven Temperature (°F)	Approximate Total Cooking Time
Broiler-Fryer		
1½ to 2 pounds	400°	¾ to 1 hour
2 to 2½ pounds	400°	1 to 1¼ hours
2½ to 3 pounds	375°	1¼ to 1¾ hours
3 to 4 pounds	375°	1¾ to 2¼ hours
Capon (stuffed)		
5 to 8 pounds	325°	2½ to 3½ hours

Times given are for unstuffed chickens; stuffed chickens require about 15 minutes longer.

NOTE: To roast an unstuffed goose, follow directions for Roast Chicken (above) except—allow 2½ to 3 hours in 350° oven for 7- to 9-pound goose, 3 to 3½ hours for 9- to 11-pound goose, 3½ to 4 hours for 11- to 13-pound goose. For a stuffed goose, add ½ to ¾ hour. For an unstuffed duckling, allow 2 hours in 325° oven for 3½-pound duckling, 3 hours for 5½-pound duckling.

GIBLETS

Cover gizzard, heart and neck with water; sprinkle with ½ teaspoon salt, 2 peppercorns, 2 cloves, a small bay leaf and a little onion. Heat to boiling; reduce heat. Simmer uncovered until gizzard is fork-tender. Liver is very tender and can be fried, broiled or simmered in water 5 to 10 minutes.

Giblet broth can be used in stuffing, gravy (page 10) and recipes where broth is specified. Cooked giblets can be cut up and added to gravy or stuffing.

BREAD STUFFING

Allow ¾ cup stuffing for each pound of ready-to-cook chicken or turkey. A 1- to 1¼-pound Rock Cornish hen requires about 1 cup stuffing. Allow ¼ to ⅓ cup stuffing for each rib pork chop and about ½ cup per pound of dressed fish. This recipe makes enough for a 12-pound turkey.

  ¾ cup finely chopped onion
1½ cups chopped celery (with leaves)
  1 cup margarine or butter
  9 cups soft bread cubes
  2 teaspoons salt
1½ teaspoons dried sage leaves
  1 teaspoon dried thyme leaves
  ½ teaspoon pepper

Cook and stir onion and celery in margarine in 10-inch skillet until onion is tender. Stir in about ⅓ of the bread cubes. Turn into deep bowl. Add remaining ingredients; toss. Stuff turkey just before roasting. 9 CUPS STUFFING.

Apple-Raisin Stuffing. Decrease bread cubes to 7 cups and increase salt to 1 tablespoon. Add 3 cups finely chopped apples and ¾ cup raisins with the remaining ingredients.

Corn Bread Stuffing: Substitute corn bread cubes for the soft bread cubes.

Corn Stuffing: Decrease bread cubes to 8 cups and add 1 can (12 ounces) whole kernel corn, drained, and 1 small green pepper, chopped (about ½ cup), with the remaining ingredients.

Giblet Stuffing: Simmer heart, gizzard and neck from chicken or turkey in seasoned water until tender, 1 to 2 hours. Add the liver during the last 5 to 15 minutes of cooking. Drain giblets; chop and add with the remaining ingredients.

Oyster Stuffing: Decrease bread cubes to 8 cups and add 2 cans (8 ounces each) oysters, drained and chopped, with the remaining ingredients.

Sausage Stuffing: Decrease bread cubes to 8 cups and omit salt. Add 1 pound bulk pork sausage, crumbled and browned, with the remaining ingredients. Substitute sausage drippings for part of the margarine.

Stuffing Balls: Shape stuffing by ½ cupfuls into balls; place in greased baking dish. Cover and cook in 325° oven 30 minutes. Uncover and cook 15 minutes longer. 10 STUFFING BALLS.

Chicken-Noodle Soup with Vegetables

STEWED CHICKEN

4- to 5-pound stewing chicken, cut up
1 sprig parsley
½ cup chopped celery (with leaves)
1 medium carrot, sliced (about ½ cup)
1 small onion, sliced
2 teaspoons salt
½ teaspoon pepper

Remove any excess pieces of fat from chicken. Place chicken, giblets and neck in kettle. Add just enough water to cover. Add remaining ingredients. Heat to boiling; reduce heat. Cover and simmer until thickest pieces are tender, 2½ to 3½ hours. If not serving immediately, refrigerate chicken in broth until cool.

When cool, remove chicken from bones and skin in pieces as large as possible. Skim fat from broth. Cover and refrigerate chicken pieces and broth separately; use within 24 hours. For longer storage, freeze chicken and broth together.   ABOUT 5 CUPS CUT-UP COOKED CHICKEN AND 5 TO 6 CUPS BROTH.

NOTE: To stew a 3- to 4-pound broiler-fryer chicken, decrease simmering time to about 45 minutes. 3 TO 4 CUPS CUT-UP COOKED CHICKEN AND 2 TO 3½ CUPS BROTH.

CHICKEN-NOODLE SOUP WITH VEGETABLES

2½-pound broiler-fryer chicken, cut up
1 quart water
4 medium carrots, cut into ½-inch slices (about 2 cups)
4 medium stalks celery, cut into ½-inch slices (about 2 cups)
1 tablespoon salt
1 tablespoon monosodium glutamate (optional)
1 teaspoon sugar
¼ teaspoon pepper
3 chicken bouillon cubes
2 cups uncooked thin egg noodles

Heat all ingredients except noodles to boiling in 4-quart Dutch oven; reduce heat. Cover and simmer until chicken is done, about 45 minutes. Skim fat if necessary.

Cook noodles as directed on page 221. Remove chicken from broth; cool slightly. Remove chicken from bones and skin. Cut chicken into 1-inch pieces. Add chicken and noodles to broth; heat until hot, about 5 minutes.   8 SERVINGS (ABOUT 1 CUP EACH).

CHICKEN POT PIE

⅓ cup margarine, butter or chicken fat
⅓ cup all-purpose flour*
⅓ cup chopped onion
½ teaspoon salt
¼ teaspoon pepper
1¾ cups chicken or turkey broth
⅔ cup milk
2 cups cut-up cooked chicken or turkey
1 package (10 ounces) frozen peas and carrots
Celery Seed Pastry (below)

Heat margarine over low heat until melted. Blend in flour, onion, salt and pepper. Cook over low heat, stirring constantly, until mixture is smooth and bubbly; remove from heat. Stir in broth and milk. Heat to boiling, stirring constantly. Boil and stir 1 minute. Stir in chicken and frozen vegetables; reserve.

Prepare Celery Seed Pastry. Roll ⅔ of pastry into 13-inch square on lightly floured cloth-covered board. Ease pastry into square pan, 9x9x2 inches; pour chicken filling into pastry-lined pan. Roll remaining dough into 11-inch square; place over filling. Roll edges under, flute. Cut slits in center to allow steam to escape. Cook uncovered in 425° oven until crust is brown, 30 to 35 minutes. 6 SERVINGS.

CELERY SEED PASTRY

⅔ cup plus 2 tablespoons shortening or ⅔ cup lard
2 cups all-purpose flour*
2 teaspoons celery seed
1 teaspoon salt
4 to 5 tablespoons water

Cut shortening into flour, celery seed and salt until particles are size of small peas. Sprinkle in water, 1 tablespoon at a time, tossing with fork until all flour is moistened and pastry almost cleans side of bowl (1 to 2 teaspoons water can be added if necessary). Gather pastry into ball.

*If using self-rising flour, omit salt.

VEGETABLE GO-WITHS FOR POULTRY

Try any of these vegetables to enhance the flavor of poultry: asparagus, broccoli, corn, lima beans, mushrooms, green peas, sweet potatoes, tomatoes. You'll be getting vitamins A and C plus some iron (asparagus and lima beans) and other minerals.

ABOUT WHITE SAUCES

Mushroom Sauce (right) is a variation of Medium White Sauce, which is incorporated into many recipes throughout this book. Thin White Sauce (page 162) and Cheese Sauce (page 173) are often used for vegetables. For Medium White Sauce, increase flour and margarine in Thin White Sauce to 2 tablespoons each; for Thick White Sauce, to ¼ cup each.

EASY CHICKEN GUMBO

    3 tablespoons margarine or butter
    1 can (16 ounces) cut okra, drained
    1 small onion, chopped (about ¼ cup)
    ½ small green pepper, chopped
    4 cups chicken or turkey broth
    1 can (16 ounces) whole tomatoes
    1 small bay leaf
    1 teaspoon salt
      Dash of pepper
    2 cups cut-up cooked chicken or turkey
    1 tablespoon snipped parsley
    3 cups hot cooked rice (page 225)

Heat margarine in 3-quart saucepan until melted. Add okra, onion and green pepper; cook and stir until onion is tender. Stir in broth, tomatoes (with liquid), bay leaf, salt and pepper. Heat to boiling; reduce heat. Simmer uncovered 15 minutes. Stir in chicken and parsley; heat through. Serve chicken mixture over hot rice.   6 SERVINGS.

CHICKEN-MUSHROOM CASSEROLE

    1 can (4 ounces) mushroom stems and
      pieces, drained
    1½ cups soft bread crumbs
    1½ cups cut-up cooked chicken or turkey
    ½ cup chicken or turkey broth
    ½ cup milk
    1 egg, beaten
    1 tablespoon chopped onion
    ¾ teaspoon salt
      Dash of pepper
      Mushroom Sauce (right)

Reserve 2 tablespoons mushrooms for sauce. Mix remaining mushrooms, the bread crumbs, chicken, broth, milk, egg, onion, salt and pepper. Pour into ungreased 1-quart casserole.

Cook uncovered in 350° oven until knife inserted 1 inch from edge comes out clean, about 1 hour. Serve with Mushroom Sauce.   4 SERVINGS.

MUSHROOM SAUCE

    2 tablespoons reserved mushrooms
    2 tablespoons chopped onion
    2 tablespoons margarine or butter
    2 tablespoons flour
    1 cup chicken or turkey broth
    ¼ teaspoon salt
    ⅛ teaspoon pepper
    ⅛ teaspoon Worcestershire sauce

Cook and stir mushrooms and onion in margarine over low heat until golden brown. Stir in flour. Cook over low heat, stirring constantly, until flour is deep brown; remove from heat. Stir in broth. Heat to boiling, stirring constantly. Boil and stir 1 minute. Stir in remaining ingredients.

CHICKEN-RICE CASSEROLE

    ¼ cup margarine or butter
    ⅓ cup all-purpose flour*
    1½ teaspoons salt
    ⅛ teaspoon pepper
    1 cup chicken broth
    1½ cups milk
    1½ cups cooked white rice or wild rice
      (page 225)
    2 cups cut-up cooked chicken or turkey
    1 can (4 ounces) mushroom stems and
      pieces, drained
    ⅓ cup chopped green pepper
    2 tablespoons chopped pimiento
    ¼ cup slivered almonds

Heat margarine in 2-quart saucepan until melted. Blend in flour, salt and pepper. Cook over low heat, stirring constantly, until bubbly; remove from heat. Stir in broth and milk. Heat to boiling, stirring constantly. Boil and stir 1 minute. Stir in remaining ingredients. Pour into ungreased 2-quart casserole or oblong baking dish, 10x6x1½ inches. Cook uncovered in 350° oven until bubbly, 40 to 45 minutes. Garnish with parsley if desired.   6 SERVINGS.

*Self-rising flour can be used in this recipe.

■ **To Microwave:** Microwave margarine uncovered in 1-pint glass measuring cup until melted, about 45 seconds. Blend in flour, salt and pepper. Cover and microwave until hot and bubbly, 45 to 60 seconds. Decrease milk to ½ cup. Stir broth and milk into margarine mixture. Cover and microwave 4 minutes; stir. Cover and microwave 2 minutes longer. Pour into ungreased 2-quart round glass casserole. Stir in remaining ingredients. Continue as directed except—cover and microwave until hot and bubbly, about 5 minutes.

CHICKEN A LA KING

- 1 can (4 ounces) mushroom stems and pieces, drained (reserve liquid)
- 1 small green pepper, chopped (about ½ cup)
- ½ cup margarine or butter
- ½ cup all-purpose flour
- 1 teaspoon salt
- ¼ teaspoon pepper
- 1½ teaspoons instant chicken bouillon
- 1½ cups milk
- 1¼ cups hot water
- 2 cups cut-up cooked chicken or turkey
- 1 jar (4 ounces) whole pimiento, chopped

  Toast, hot mashed potatoes, waffles, cooked rice or noodles

Cook and stir mushrooms and green pepper in margarine over medium heat 5 minutes; remove from heat. Blend in flour, salt and pepper. Cook over low heat, stirring constantly, until mixture is bubbly; remove from heat. Stir in instant bouillon, milk, water and reserved mushroom liquid. Heat to boiling, stirring constantly. Boil and stir 1 minute. Stir in chicken and pimiento; heat through. Serve over toast. 6 SERVINGS.

YIELDS FOR COOKED POULTRY

Cook more chicken or turkey than you need and have a base for recipes using leftovers of each. Here are the amounts you can expect:

Kind and Size	Approximate Cooked Yield
3- to 4-pound broiler-fryer chicken	3 to 4 cups
5- to 6-pound turkey roast	10 to 12 cups
12-pound turkey	14 cups

To cook chicken for leftovers, see Stewed Chicken (page 87). An easy way to cook turkey for leftovers is poaching. Cut turkey into quarters; place in large kettle with enough water to cover bottom of kettle. Sprinkle with 2 tablespoons salt and 2 teaspoons white pepper. Heat to boiling; reduce heat. Cover and simmer until turkey is done, 2 to 2½ hours. Remove turkey from broth; refrigerate at least 1 hour but no longer than 2 days. Remove meat from bones and cut up.

CHICKEN CREPES

- Crepes (below)
- 3 tablespoons margarine or butter
- 3 tablespoons flour
- ½ teaspoon salt
- 2 cups chicken or turkey broth
- 1½ cups finely cut-up cooked chicken or turkey
- ⅔ cup chopped apple
- 1 medium stalk celery, chopped (about ½ cup)
- 2 tablespoons chopped onion

Prepare Crepes; keep covered to prevent them from drying out. Heat margarine over low heat until melted. Blend in flour and salt. Cook over low heat, stirring constantly, until mixture is smooth and bubbly; remove from heat. Stir in broth. Heat to boiling, stirring constantly. Boil and stir 1 minute.

Mix chicken, apple, celery, onion and ¾ cup of the thickened broth. Place scant ¼ cup chicken mixture on center of each crepe; roll up. Place crepes seam sides down in ungreased oblong baking dish, 13½x9x2 inches. Pour remaining broth over crepes. Cook uncovered in 350° oven until crepes are hot, about 20 minutes. 6 SERVINGS.

CREPES

- 1 cup all-purpose flour*
- ¼ teaspoon baking powder
- ¼ teaspoon salt
- 1¼ cups milk
- 1 egg
- 1 tablespoon margarine or butter, melted

Mix flour, baking powder and salt. Stir in remaining ingredients. Beat with hand beater until smooth.

Lightly butter 7- or 8-inch skillet; heat over medium heat until bubbly. For each crepe, pour scant ¼ cup of the batter into skillet; *immediately* rotate skillet until thin film of batter covers bottom. Cook until light brown. Run wide spatula around edge to loosen; turn and cook other side until light brown. Stack crepes, placing waxed paper or paper towel between each. (To freeze crepes, see page 307.)

*If using self-rising flour, omit baking powder and salt.

CHICKEN-SESAME SALAD

A perfect salad for leftover chicken or turkey, too. Sprinkle it with a dash of ground ginger.

    3 chicken breast halves (about 1½ pounds)
    ¼ teaspoon ground ginger
    ½ teaspoon salt
    1 medium head lettuce, torn into pieces
    3 green onions, cut into 1½-inch strips
    2 medium tomatoes, cut into thin wedges
    2 tablespoons toasted sesame seed
      Oil and Vinegar Dressing (below)

Place chicken in 2-quart saucepan; add just enough water to cover. Add ginger and salt. Heat to boiling; reduce heat. Cover and simmer until chicken is tender, 30 to 40 minutes.

Remove chicken from bones and skin; cut into 1-inch pieces (2½ cups). Refrigerate until chilled. Toss with remaining ingredients.   6 TO 8 SERVINGS.

OIL AND VINEGAR DRESSING

    1 tablespoon sugar
    2 tablespoons vinegar
    1 tablespoon vegetable oil
    1½ teaspoons salt
    1 teaspoon monosodium glutamate
    ½ teaspoon pepper

Shake all ingredients in tightly covered container.

Do-ahead Tip: After simmering, chicken can be refrigerated in broth. When cool, remove chicken from bones and skin; skim fat from broth. Cover and refrigerate separately no longer than 24 hours.

FRUITED CHICKEN SALAD

    1½ cups cut-up cooked chicken or turkey
    1 can (8¼ ounces) green grapes, drained,
      or 1 cup fresh seedless green grapes
    1 can (8 ounces) water chestnuts,
      drained and chopped
    1 can (11 ounces) mandarin orange
      segments, drained
    ½ cup mayonnaise or salad dressing
    ½ teaspoon salt or 1 teaspoon soy sauce
    ¼ teaspoon curry powder

Mix chicken, grapes, water chestnuts and orange segments. Mix remaining ingredients; toss with chicken mixture.   4 SERVINGS.

Fruited Chicken-Macaroni Salad: Cook 1½ cups elbow macaroni (6 ounces) as directed on page 221. Mix with remaining ingredients.

PRESSED CHICKEN

    3- to 4-pound stewing chicken, cut up
    ½ cup chopped celery (with leaves)
    1 medium carrot, sliced (about ½ cup)
    1 bay leaf, crumbled
    2 teaspoons salt
    ½ teaspoon pepper
    4 cups water
      Salad greens

Place chicken in kettle with giblets and neck. Add celery, carrot, bay leaf, salt, pepper and water. Heat to boiling; reduce heat. Cover and simmer until chicken is tender, 2½ to 3½ hours. Refrigerate chicken in broth until cool.

When cool, remove chicken from bones and skin. Cut chicken into pieces and arrange in ungreased loaf pan, 9x5x3 or 8½x4½x2½ inches, or 1½-quart mold. Skim fat from broth; strain broth. Heat broth to boiling; boil until reduced to 2 cups. Pour over chicken. Refrigerate until firm, at least 12 hours. Unmold on salad greens. Serve with mayonnaise or salad dressing if desired.   8 TO 10 SERVINGS.

CHILI CHICKEN SALAD

    1½ cups cut-up cooked chicken or turkey
    1 can (15½ ounces) kidney beans, drained
    2 green onions, sliced
    1 small head iceberg lettuce or 10 ounces
      spinach, torn into bite-size pieces
      Mexicali Dressing (below)
    1 medium avocado
    1 cup broken tortilla chips
    1 medium tomato, cut into wedges
      Ripe olives

Place chicken, beans, onions and lettuce in large bowl. Cover and refrigerate at least 3 hours. Prepare Mexicali Dressing.

Just before serving, cut avocado into bite-size pieces. Add avocado and dressing to chicken mixture; toss. Sprinkle with tortilla chips; garnish with tomato wedges and olives.   6 SERVINGS.

MEXICALI DRESSING

    ½ cup mayonnaise or salad dressing
    ¼ cup catsup
    1 teaspoon chili powder
    ½ teaspoon garlic salt

Mix all ingredients; refrigerate.

Cheesy Chicken Salad: Substitute ¾ cup shredded Cheddar or jalapeño pepper cheese (about 3 ounces) for ½ cup of the chicken.

CLUB SANDWICHES

Mayonnaise or salad dressing
18 slices white bread, toasted
12 lettuce leaves
6 slices cooked chicken or turkey
18 slices tomato (about 3 medium)
12 slices bacon, crisply fried
Salt and pepper

Spread mayonnaise over 1 side of each slice toast. Place 1 lettuce leaf and 1 slice chicken on each of 6 toast slices. Cover with second slice toast. Top with lettuce leaf, 3 slices tomato and 2 slices bacon. Sprinkle with salt and pepper. Cover with third slice toast; secure with wooden picks. To serve, cut diagonally into triangles. 6 SERVINGS.

NOTE: Cheddar or Swiss cheese, salami, fully cooked ham, hard-cooked eggs or green pepper rings can be added to sandwiches if desired.

CURRIED CHICKEN SANDWICHES

Margarine or butter, softened
8 slices bread, toasted
1 cup cut-up cooked chicken or 1 can (5½ ounces) boned chicken, chopped
1 medium onion, chopped (about ½ cup)
½ small green pepper, chopped (about ¼ cup)
½ cup chopped salted peanuts
½ cup mayonnaise or salad dressing
1 tablespoon lemon juice
¾ teaspoon curry powder

Spread margarine over 1 side of each slice toast. Mix remaining ingredients. Spread to edges of toast. Set oven control to broil and/or 550°. Broil with tops about 3 inches from heat until hot and bubbly, about 3 minutes. 4 SERVINGS (8 OPEN-FACE SANDWICHES).

Club Sandwich

FRIED CHICKEN

Here's a quick and easy trick for coating chicken. Place flour mixture in paper or plastic bag. Add a few pieces of chicken to bag and shake until well coated; repeat.

2½-pound broiler-fryer chicken
  ½ cup all-purpose flour*
  1 teaspoon salt
  1 teaspoon paprika
  ¼ teaspoon pepper
  Vegetable oil

Cut chicken into pieces; cut each breast half into halves. Mix flour, salt, paprika and pepper. Coat chicken with flour mixture.

Heat oil (¼ inch) in 12-inch skillet. Cook chicken in oil over medium heat until light brown, 15 to 20 minutes; reduce heat. Cover tightly and simmer, turning once or twice, until thickest pieces are done, 30 to 40 minutes. If skillet cannot be covered tightly, add 1 to 2 tablespoons water. Remove cover during last 5 minutes of cooking to crisp chicken. 8 SERVINGS.

*If using self-rising flour, decrease salt to ½ teaspoon.

Maryland Fried Chicken: Blend 2 eggs and 2 tablespoons water; after coating chicken with flour, dip pieces into egg mixture, then into 2 cups cracker crumbs or dry bread crumbs.

Oven-fried Chicken: Omit vegetable oil. Heat ¼ cup margarine or butter and ¼ cup shortening in oblong pan, 13x9x2 inches, in 425° oven until melted. Place coated chicken skin sides down in pan. Cook uncovered 30 minutes. Turn chicken; cook uncovered about 30 minutes longer.

Sherried Chicken: Substitute ¼ teaspoon ground ginger for the paprika. After browning chicken, place skin sides up in ungreased oblong pan, 13x9x2 inches. Mix ½ cup chicken broth, ¼ cup sherry or apple juice and 1 clove garlic, crushed. Pour ¼ of the broth mixture over chicken. Cover and cook in 325° oven, brushing occasionally with remaining broth mixture, until done, 45 to 50 minutes. Remove cover during last 5 minutes of cooking to crisp chicken.

BROILED CHICKEN

Young chickens weighing 2½ pounds or less can be broiled. They should be cut into halves, quarters or pieces.

For halves or quarters, turn wing tips onto back side. Set oven control to broil and/or 550°. Brush chicken with margarine or butter, melted. Place chicken skin side down on rack in broiler pan; place broiler pan so top of chicken is 7 to 9 inches from heat. (If not possible to place broiler pan this far from heat, reduce oven temperature to 450°.)

Broil chicken 30 minutes. Sprinkle brown side with salt and pepper. Turn chicken; brush with margarine or butter, melted. Broil until chicken is brown and crisp and thickest pieces are done, 20 to 30 minutes longer.

CHICKEN-BROCCOLI BAKE

 2 tablespoons margarine or butter
 2 tablespoons vegetable oil
 6 small chicken breasts (about 2 pounds)
 ½ teaspoon garlic salt
 1 can (10¾ ounces) condensed cream of chicken soup
 1 can (4 ounces) mushroom stems and pieces
 ¼ cup water
 1 teaspoon Worcestershire sauce
 ½ teaspoon dried thyme leaves
 2 packages (10 ounces each) frozen broccoli spears
 ½ teaspoon salt

Heat margarine and oil in oblong baking dish, 13½x9x2 inches, in 400° oven until margarine is melted. Place chicken in dish, turning to coat with margarine mixture. Arrange chicken skin sides up; sprinkle with garlic salt. Cook uncovered 30 minutes.

Mix soup, mushrooms (with liquid), water, Worcestershire sauce and thyme. Rinse broccoli under running cold water to separate; drain. Remove chicken from oven; drain fat from dish. Arrange broccoli along sides of chicken; sprinkle with salt. Spoon soup mixture over broccoli.

Cook uncovered until chicken is done and broccoli is tender, about 30 minutes. Garnish with paprika and ripe olives if desired.   6 SERVINGS.

CHICKEN-CAULIFLOWER SKILLET

 2½-pound broiler-fryer chicken
 ⅓ cup all-purpose flour*
 1 teaspoon salt
 ½ teaspoon paprika
 ⅛ teaspoon pepper
 3 tablespoons vegetable oil
 ¼ cup water
 ½ teaspoon dried thyme leaves
 1 package (10 ounces) frozen cauliflower
 1 package (10 ounces) frozen green peas
 1 medium stalk celery, cut diagonally into ¼-inch slices (about ½ cup)
 1 small onion, cut into ¼-inch slices
 ¼ cup water
 1 medium tomato, cut into sixths**
 1 teaspoon salt

Cut chicken into pieces; cut each breast half into halves. Mix flour, 1 teaspoon salt, the paprika and pepper. Coat chicken with flour mixture.

Heat oil in 12-inch skillet or Dutch oven. Fry chicken over medium heat until light brown, 10 to 15 minutes. Add ¼ cup water and the thyme. Heat to boiling; reduce heat. Cover and simmer 20 minutes.

Add frozen cauliflower, frozen peas, celery, onion and ¼ cup water. Heat to boiling; reduce heat. Cover and simmer until chicken is done and vegetables are crisp-tender, 15 to 20 minutes. Add tomato and sprinkle with 1 teaspoon salt. Cover and simmer until tomato is hot, 2 to 3 minutes longer. Garnish with snipped parsley if desired.
8 SERVINGS.

*If using self-rising flour, decrease salt in flour mixture to ½ teaspoon.

**1 medium red pepper, sliced, can be substituted for the tomato; add with the cauliflower.

Chicken-Artichoke Skillet: Substitute 1 package (10 ounces) frozen artichoke hearts for the cauliflower.

Chicken-Green Bean Skillet: Substitute 1 package (10 ounces) frozen green beans and 2 medium carrots, cut diagonally into ¼-inch slices, for the cauliflower and peas.

Chicken-Squash Skillet: Substitute 1 crookneck squash, cut lengthwise into halves, and 1 package (10 ounces) frozen French-style green beans for the cauliflower and peas. Heat to boiling; reduce heat. Cover and simmer until vegetables are tender, 20 to 25 minutes. Continue as directed.

ABOUT BACON

Bacon enhances poultry as well as eggs with its smoky-sweet flavor. It comes mild or heavily smoked, lean or fat, sliced thick or thin. Look for uniform slices with fine ribbons of lean throughout. The best bacon is about ⅓ lean. It should cook to a crisp, golden brown and crumble easily. Use bacon within a week after package is opened; wrap tightly after each use to protect from the air. Refrigerate but do not freeze.

CHICKEN IN WINE

2½-pound broiler-fryer chicken
 ½ cup all-purpose flour*
 1 teaspoon salt
 ¼ teaspoon pepper
 8 slices bacon
 8 small onions
 8 ounces mushrooms, sliced
 4 carrots, cut into halves
 1 cup chicken broth
 1 cup dry red wine
 1 clove garlic, crushed
 ½ teaspoon salt
    Bouquet Garni (below)

Cut chicken into pieces; cut each breast half into halves. Mix flour, 1 teaspoon salt and the pepper. Coat chicken with flour mixture. Fry bacon in 12-inch skillet until crisp; drain on paper towels. Cook chicken in hot bacon fat until brown.

Push chicken to side; add onions and mushrooms. Cook and stir until mushrooms are tender. Drain fat from skillet. Crumble bacon and stir into vegetables with the remaining ingredients. Cover and simmer until thickest pieces of chicken are done, about 35 minutes. Remove Bouquet Garni; skim off excess fat. Sprinkle chicken with snipped parsley if desired.   8 SERVINGS.

*If using self-rising flour, decrease salt to ½ teaspoon.

BOUQUET GARNI
Tie ½ teaspoon dried thyme leaves, 1 bay leaf and 2 large sprigs parsley in cheesecloth bag.

TOMATO-PEPPER CHICKEN

2½-pound broiler-fryer chicken
 ¼ cup shortening
 ½ cup all-purpose flour
 2 cups thinly sliced onion rings
 1 small green pepper, chopped (about
    ½ cup)
 2 cloves garlic, crushed
 1 can (16 ounces) whole tomatoes, drained
 1 can (8 ounces) tomato sauce
 1 can (4 ounces) mushroom stems and
    pieces, drained
 1 teaspoon salt
 ¼ teaspoon dried oregano leaves

Cut chicken into pieces; cut each breast half into halves. Heat shortening in 12-inch skillet. Coat chicken with flour. Cook chicken in shortening over medium heat until light brown, 15 to 20 minutes. Remove chicken from skillet.

Add onion rings, green pepper and garlic to skillet; cook and stir over medium heat until onion and green pepper are tender. Stir in remaining ingredients. Add chicken. Cover tightly and simmer until thickest pieces are done, 30 to 40 minutes. 8 SERVINGS.

BEER-BATTER CHICKEN

¾ cup beer
2½-pound broiler-fryer chicken
    Vegetable oil
 2 eggs, separated
 ¾ cup all-purpose flour
 ¾ teaspoon salt
1½ teaspoons vegetable oil
 ¼ teaspoon garlic powder

Let beer stand at room temperature until flat, about 45 minutes. Cut chicken into pieces; cut each breast half into halves. Pour enough water on chicken in Dutch oven just to cover. Heat to boiling; reduce heat. Cover and simmer 25 minutes. Remove chicken from broth; drain and pat dry.

Heat oil (2 to 3 inches) in deep-fat fryer or kettle to 375°. Beat egg whites until stiff. Beat beer, flour, salt, 1½ teaspoons oil, the garlic powder and egg yolks until smooth. Fold egg whites into beer mixture.

Dip chicken pieces one at a time into batter. Fry 3 or 4 at a time until golden brown, 5 to 7 minutes. 8 SERVINGS.

CHICKEN FRICASSEE

1 cup all-purpose flour
2 teaspoons salt
¼ teaspoon pepper
2 teaspoons paprika (optional)
4-pound stewing chicken, cut up
  Shortening or vegetable oil
1 cup water
3 tablespoons flour
  Milk
  Chive Dumplings (see Parsley
    Dumplings, page 195)

Mix 1 cup flour, the salt, pepper and paprika. Coat chicken with flour mixture. Heat thin layer of shortening in 12-inch skillet. Cook chicken until brown on all sides. Drain fat from skillet; reserve. Add water and, if desired, chopped onion, lemon juice or herbs, such as dried rosemary or thyme leaves, to chicken. Cover and cook over low heat, adding water if necessary, until chicken is done, 2½ to 3½ hours. Remove chicken to warm platter; keep warm. Drain liquid from skillet; reserve.

Heat 3 tablespoons reserved fat in skillet. Blend in 3 tablespoons flour. Cook over low heat, stirring constantly, until mixture is smooth and bubbly; remove from heat. Add enough milk to reserved liquid to measure 3 cups; pour into skillet. Heat to boiling, stirring constantly. Boil and stir 1 minute. Return chicken to gravy.

Prepare Chive Dumplings; drop by spoonfuls onto hot chicken. Cook uncovered 10 minutes; cover and cook 20 minutes longer.   8 SERVINGS.

NOTE: To fricassee a 3-pound broiler-fryer chicken, cook over low heat about 45 minutes.

CHICKEN ALMOND

  2 **tablespoons vegetable oil**
  ½ **teaspoon salt**
  1 **pound chicken breasts (about 2 large),
      boned, skinned and cut into ⅛-inch
      strips (about 1 cup)**
  1 **can (8½ ounces) bamboo shoots, drained**
  1 **large stalk celery, cut diagonally into
      ¼-inch slices (about ¾ cup)**
  8 **ounces mushrooms, cut into ¼-inch slices**
  ½ **teaspoon monosodium glutamate**
  ¼ **teaspoon ground ginger**
  ¾ **cup chicken broth**
  2 **teaspoons soy sauce**
  3 **tablespoons cold water**
  2 **tablespoons cornstarch**
  ½ **cup toasted whole blanched almonds**
  2 to 3 **cups hot cooked rice (page 225)**

Heat oil and salt in 10-inch skillet until few drops water sprinkled in skillet skitter around. Add chicken. Cook and stir over medium-high heat until almost done, about 6 minutes.

Add bamboo shoots, celery, mushrooms, monosodium glutamate and ginger. Cook and stir 1 minute. Stir in broth and soy sauce; reduce heat. Cover and simmer until vegetables are crisp-tender and chicken is done, 3 to 5 minutes.

Shake cold water and cornstarch in tightly covered container; stir gradually into chicken mixture. Heat to boiling, stirring constantly. Boil and stir 1 minute. Top with almonds and serve with hot rice.
4 SERVINGS.

Chicken Almond with Pea Pods: Substitute 1 medium onion, cut into ¼-inch slices, for the bamboo shoots. Rinse 1 package (6 ounces) frozen Chinese pea pods under running cold water to separate; drain. Add pea pods to chicken with the celery.

BONING A CHICKEN BREAST

Turn chicken breast bone side up. To remove breast bone, cut through only the white gristle at neck end. Bend breast halves back to pop out keel bone (the wide center bone between the rib cages). Loosen keel bone and pull back and away from chicken breast. Cut rib cages away from breast, cutting through shoulder joint. Turn chicken breast over and cut away wishbone. If desired, split breast after pulling and cutting the tendons.

CHICKEN-VEGETABLE FONDUE

  2 **pounds chicken breasts (about 4 large), boned,
      skinned and cut into bite-size pieces**
  1 **pound broccoli, separated into flowerets**
  8 **ounces mushrooms, sliced**
  1 **bunch green onions, cut into ½-inch pieces**
  4 or 5 **cups hot cooked rice (page 225)**
  8 **cups chicken broth
      Lemon-Soy Sauce (below)**

Arrange chicken, broccoli, mushrooms and onions on serving tray. Divide rice among 8 small bowls.

Heat broth in electric skillet to 225°. Guests spear foods with chopsticks or fondue forks and cook in hot broth until done, 2 to 4 minutes, then dip in Lemon-Soy Sauce. At end of main course, guests ladle broth over remaining rice in bowls and eat as soup.   8 SERVINGS.

LEMON-SOY SAUCE
Mix ½ cup soy sauce, ½ cup lemon juice and ¼ cup dry white wine.

CHICKEN-ASPARAGUS BAKE

  1 **package (10 ounces) frozen cut asparagus**
  1 **package (3 ounces) smoked sliced chicken
      or turkey, cut up**
  ½ **teaspoon dried marjoram leaves**
  ¼ to ½ **teaspoon ground sage**
  1 **cup shredded process American cheese**
  ½ **cup milk**
  2 **eggs, beaten**
  1 **cup all-purpose flour***
  2 **teaspoons baking powder**
  1 **teaspoon salt
      Quick Cheese Sauce (below)**

Cook asparagus as directed on package; drain. Arrange asparagus in ungreased square baking dish, 8x8x2 inches. Arrange chicken on asparagus; sprinkle with marjoram and sage. Mix cheese, milk and eggs. Stir in flour, baking powder and salt; spread over chicken. Cook uncovered in 350° oven until golden brown, 25 to 30 minutes. Serve with Quick Cheese Sauce.   6 SERVINGS.

*If using self-rising flour, omit baking powder and salt.

QUICK CHEESE SAUCE
  1 **can (11 ounces) condensed Cheddar
      cheese soup**
  ⅓ **cup milk**
  ¼ **teaspoon dry mustard**
  ¼ **teaspoon Worcestershire sauce**

Heat ingredients just to boiling, stirring frequently.

ROCK CORNISH HENS

10 slices dried beef
½ cup margarine or butter
1 medium onion, chopped (about ½ cup)
¾ cup chopped celery (with leaves)
¼ teaspoon finely chopped garlic
2 tablespoons snipped parsley
½ teaspoon poultry seasoning
¼ teaspoon pepper
1¾ cups soft bread cubes
3 Rock Cornish hens (about 1¼ pounds each), thawed
    Margarine or butter, melted
    Cranberry Sauce or Cranberry-Ginger Relish (below)

Snip dried beef into small pieces. Heat ½ cup margarine in 12-inch skillet until melted. Add dried beef, onion, celery and garlic. Cook and stir until onion and celery are tender, about 6 minutes; remove from heat. Stir in parsley, poultry seasoning, pepper and bread cubes; toss.

Stuff each hen with about 6 tablespoons stuffing. Secure opening with skewers. Fasten neck skin to back. Place hens breast sides up on rack in shallow roasting pan. Brush with margarine. Roast hens uncovered in 350° oven, brushing with margarine 5 or 6 times, until golden brown and done, about 1 hour. To serve, cut hens with kitchen scissors, cutting along backbone from tail to neck. Serve with Cranberry Sauce.   6 SERVINGS.

CRANBERRY SAUCE

Mix 2 cups water and 2 cups sugar in Dutch oven. Heat to boiling; boil 5 minutes. Stir in 4 cups cranberries. Heat to boiling; boil rapidly 5 minutes longer. Cool; cover and refrigerate at least 8 hours.

CRANBERRY-GINGER RELISH

1 can (16 ounces) whole cranberry sauce
1 orange (pulp and peel), finely chopped
½ cup golden raisins
2 tablespoons finely chopped crystallized ginger

Mix all ingredients. Cover and refrigerate at least 3 hours.

Duckling with Orange Sauce

DUCKLING WITH ORANGE SAUCE

1 ready-to-cook duckling (4 to 5 pounds)
2 tablespoons finely chopped onion
¼ teaspoon dried tarragon leaves
2 tablespoons margarine or butter
2 tablespoons shredded orange peel
½ cup orange juice
⅛ teaspoon salt
⅛ teaspoon dry mustard
¼ cup currant jelly
2 tablespoons sweet red wine or cranberry juice cocktail
1 orange, pared and sectioned
1½ teaspoons cornstarch

Fasten neck skin of duckling to back with skewers. Lift wing tips up and over back for natural brace. Place duckling breast side up on rack in shallow roasting pan.

Cook and stir onion and tarragon in margarine until onion is tender. Add orange peel, orange juice, salt, mustard and jelly. Heat over medium heat, stirring constantly, until jelly is melted. Reduce heat; stir in wine and orange sections.

Measure sauce; reserve half for glaze. Brush duckling with part of remaining orange sauce. Roast uncovered in 325° oven, pricking skin with fork and brushing occasionally with remaining orange sauce, until done, about 2½ hours. If duckling becomes too brown, place piece of aluminum foil lightly over breast. Duckling is done when drumstick meat feels very soft.

Stir reserved orange sauce slowly into cornstarch in saucepan. Cook over medium heat, stirring constantly, until mixture thickens and boils. Boil and stir 1 minute. Pour sauce over duckling just before serving.   6 TO 8 SERVINGS.

ROAST TURKEY

When buying turkeys under 12 pounds, allow about ¾ pound per serving. For heavier turkeys (12 pounds and over) allow about ½ pound per serving.

Rub cavity of turkey lightly with salt if desired. Do not salt cavity if turkey is to be stuffed.

Stuff turkey just before roasting—not ahead of time. (See Bread Stuffing, page 85.) Fill wishbone area with stuffing first. Fasten neck skin to back with skewer. Fold wings across back with tips touching. Fill body cavity lightly. (Do not pack—stuffing will expand while cooking.) Tuck drumsticks under band of skin at tail or tie together with heavy string, then tie to tail.

Place turkey breast side up on rack in shallow roasting pan. Brush with shortening, oil, margarine or butter. Insert meat thermometer so tip is in thickest part of inside thigh muscle or thickest part of breast meat and does not touch bone. Do not add water. Do not cover.

Roast in 325° oven. Follow Timetable (below) for approximate total cooking time. Place a tent of aluminum foil loosely over turkey when it begins to turn golden. When ⅔ done, cut band of skin or string holding legs.

TIMETABLE FOR ROASTING TURKEY

Ready-to-Cook Weight	Approximate Total Cooking Time	Internal Temperature (°F)
6 to 8 pounds	3 to 3½ hours	185°
8 to 12 pounds	3½ to 4½ hours	185°
12 to 16 pounds	4½ to 5½ hours	185°
16 to 20 pounds	5½ to 6½ hours	185°
20 to 24 pounds	6½ to 7 hours	185°

This timetable is based on chilled or completely thawed stuffed turkeys at a temperature of about 40°. Time will be slightly less for unstuffed turkeys. Differences in the shape and tenderness of individual turkeys can also necessitate increasing or decreasing the cooking time slightly. For best results, use a meat thermometer. For prestuffed turkeys, follow package directions very carefully; do not use Timetable.

There is no substitute for a meat thermometer for determining the doneness of a turkey. Placed in the thigh muscle, it should register 185° when turkey is done. If turkey is stuffed, the thermometer point can be inserted in the center of stuffing and will

register 165° when done. If a thermometer is not used, test for doneness about 30 minutes before Timetable so indicates. Move drumstick up and down—if done, the joint should give readily or break. Or press drumstick meat between fingers; meat should be very soft.

When turkey is done, remove from oven and allow to stand about 20 minutes for easiest carving. As soon as possible after serving, remove every bit of stuffing from turkey. Cool stuffing, turkey meat and gravy (page 10) promptly; refrigerate separately. Use gravy or stuffing within 1 or 2 days; heat them thoroughly before serving. Serve cooked turkey meat within 2 or 3 days after roasting. If frozen, it can be kept up to 3 weeks.

BONELESS ROASTS OR ROLLS

Follow package directions; if not available, follow directions for Roast Turkey except—if roast is not preseasoned, sprinkle with salt and pepper. Brush turkey with margarine, butter or pan drippings during roasting. Continue roasting until meat thermometer inserted in center registers 170°.

TIMETABLE FOR BONELESS ROASTS/ROLLS

Ready-to-Cook Weight	Approximate Total Cooking Time*	Internal Temperature (°F)
3 to 5 pounds	2½ to 3 hours	170°
5 to 7 pounds	3 to 3½ hours	170°
7 to 9 pounds	3½ to 4 hours	170°

*Allow 30 minutes additional time if frozen.

HALVES AND QUARTERS

Prepare half and quarter turkey according to basic instructions for whole turkey except—skewer skin to meat along cut edges to prevent shrinking from meat during roasting. Place skin side up on rack in shallow roasting pan. Place meat thermometer in thickest part of inside thigh muscle or thickest part of breast. Be sure it does not touch bone.

TIMETABLE FOR ROAST HALVES AND QUARTERS

Ready-to-Cook Weight	Approximate Total Cooking Time	Internal Temperature (°F)
5 to 8 pounds	2½ to 3 hours	185°
8 to 10 pounds	3 to 3½ hours	185°
10 to 12 pounds	3½ to 4 hours	185°

HOW TO COOK TURKEY IN FOIL

Prepare turkey as directed for Roast Turkey (page 98). To wrap, place turkey breast side up in middle of large sheet of heavy-duty aluminum foil. (For larger turkeys, join 2 widths of foil.)

Brush with shortening, oil, margarine or butter. Place small pieces of aluminum foil over ends of legs, tail and wing tips to prevent puncturing. Bring long ends of aluminum foil up over the breast of turkey and overlap 3 inches. Close open ends by folding foil up so drippings will not run into pan. Wrap loosely; do not seal airtight. Place wrapped turkey breast side up in shallow roasting pan.

Cook in 450° oven. Follow Timetable. Open foil once or twice during cooking to judge doneness. When thigh joint and breast meat begin to soften, fold back foil completely to brown turkey and crisp skin. Insert thermometer at this time.

TIMETABLE FOR TURKEY IN FOIL

Ready-to-Cook Weight	Approximate Total Cooking Time	Internal Temperature (°F)
7 to 9 pounds	2¼ to 2½ hours	185°
10 to 13 pounds	2¾ to 3 hours	185°
14 to 17 pounds	3½ to 4 hours	185°
18 to 21 pounds	4½ to 5 hours	185°
22 to 24 pounds	5½ to 6 hours	185°

TURKEY THAWING DIRECTIONS

To Cook Immediately: Remove wrap. Place frozen turkey on rack in shallow pan. Cook uncovered in 325° oven 1 hour. Remove neck and giblets. Immediately return to oven.

To Cook Later the Same Day: Leave in wrap. Thaw in frequently changed cold water (about 30 minutes per pound). Cook or refrigerate immediately.

To Cook the Following Day: Leave in wrap. Wrap frozen turkey in 2 or 3 layers of newspaper. Place on tray. Thaw at room temperature (about 1 hour per pound). Cook or refrigerate immediately.

To Cook Two Days Later: Thaw wrapped turkey in refrigerator. (A large turkey may take up to 3 days.)

Important: Don't allow thawed turkey to stand at room temperature. Don't thaw commercially stuffed turkeys. Don't prepare stuffing and stuff turkey until ready to cook.

TURKEY WITH CORNMEAL BISCUITS

     Cornmeal Biscuits (below)
 1 package (10 ounces) frozen chopped
     broccoli
 ¼ cup margarine or butter
 ¼ cup all-purpose flour
 ¼ teaspoon pepper
 ¼ teaspoon ground sage
 ¾ cup half-and-half
 1 can (13¾ ounces) chicken broth (about
     1¾ cups)
 2 packages (3 ounces each) sliced smoked
     turkey or chicken, cut up
 ¼ cup shredded Cheddar cheese (about
     1 ounce)

Prepare Cornmeal Biscuits. Cook broccoli as directed on package; drain.

Heat margarine in 10-inch skillet over low heat until melted. Blend in flour, pepper and sage. Cook, stirring constantly, until mixture is smooth and bubbly; remove from heat. Stir in half-and-half and broth. Heat to boiling, stirring constantly. Boil and stir 1 minute. Stir in broccoli and turkey; heat through. Sprinkle with cheese; cover until cheese is melted. Serve over hot biscuits.   6 SERVINGS.

CORNMEAL BISCUITS
 ⅓ cup shortening
 1¼ cups all-purpose flour*
 ½ cup cornmeal
 2½ teaspoons baking powder
 ¾ teaspoon salt
 ¾ cup milk
     Cornmeal

Heat oven to 450°. Cut shortening into flour, ½ cup cornmeal, the baking powder and salt with pastry blender until mixture resembles fine crumbs. Stir in just enough milk so dough leaves side of bowl and rounds up into a ball. (Too much milk makes dough sticky, not enough makes biscuits dry.)

Turn dough onto lightly floured surface. Knead lightly 10 times. Roll ½ inch thick. Cut with floured 2-inch biscuit cutter. Sprinkle ungreased cookie sheet with cornmeal. Place rounds on cookie sheet about 1 inch apart for crusty sides, touching for soft sides. Sprinkle with cornmeal. Bake until golden brown, 10 to 12 minutes. Immediately remove from cookie sheet.

*If using self-rising flour, omit baking powder and salt.

NOTE: For recipes using leftover turkey, see pages 87–91.

PHEASANT WITH BROWN GRAVY

1 pheasant or 2-pound broiler-fryer
   chicken, cut into fourths
1 can (10¾ ounces) condensed cream of
   chicken soup
½ cup apple cider
1 tablespoon plus 1 teaspoon Worcestershire
   sauce
¾ teaspoon salt
⅓ cup chopped onion
1 clove garlic, finely chopped
1 can (4 ounces) mushroom stems
   and pieces, drained
   Paprika

Place pheasant in ungreased square baking dish, 9x9x2 inches. Mix soup, cider, Worcestershire sauce, salt, onion, garlic and mushrooms; pour over pheasant. Sprinkle generously with paprika.

Cook uncovered in 350° oven, spooning sauce onto pheasant occasionally, until done, 1½ to 2 hours. After cooking pheasant 1 hour, sprinkle generously again with paprika.　2 OR 3 SERVINGS.

BRAISED RABBIT

2 domestic rabbits (2 to 2½ pounds each) or
   4 wild rabbits, cut up
1½ cups cider vinegar
1 medium onion, chopped (about ½ cup)
2 tablespoons packed light brown sugar
1 tablespoon dry mustard
2 teaspoons salt
1 cup all-purpose flour
1 tablespoon granulated sugar
½ teaspoon pepper
¼ teaspoon grated nutmeg
   Vegetable oil, lard, shortening or bacon fat
½ cup all-purpose flour
3 cups water

Place rabbit in shallow glass dish. Mix vinegar, onion, brown sugar, mustard and salt; pour over rabbit. Cover and refrigerate, turning occasionally, at least 12 hours but no longer than 24 hours.

Drain rabbit and pat dry. Mix 1 cup flour, the granulated sugar, pepper and nutmeg. Coat rabbit with flour mixture. Heat oil (¼ inch) in 12-inch skillet. Cook rabbit until brown; remove from skillet. Drain oil, reserving ½ cup. Stir in ½ cup flour; stir in water slowly. Heat to boiling, stirring constantly. Boil and stir 1 minute. Place rabbit in gravy; reduce heat. Cover and simmer until tender, 1 to 1½ hours. Stir in additional water if necessary.　4 TO 6 SERVINGS.

VENISON SAUERBRATEN

3- to 3½-pound venison chuck roast
2 onions, sliced
2 bay leaves
12 peppercorns
12 juniper berries (optional)
6 whole cloves
2 teaspoons salt
1½ cups red wine vinegar
1 cup boiling water
2 tablespoons shortening
12 gingersnaps, crushed (about ¾ cup)
2 teaspoons sugar

Place venison roast in glass bowl or baking dish with onions, bay leaves, peppercorns, berries, cloves, salt, vinegar and boiling water. Cover tightly and refrigerate, turning venison twice a day, at least 3 days. Never pierce when turning.

Drain venison, reserving marinade. Cook venison in shortening in heavy skillet until brown on all sides. Add marinade mixture. Heat to boiling; reduce heat. Cover and simmer until venison is tender, 3 to 3½ hours. Remove venison and onions from skillet; keep warm.

Strain and measure liquid in skillet. Add enough water, if necessary, to measure 2½ cups. Pour liquid into skillet. Cover and simmer 10 minutes. Stir gingersnaps and sugar into liquid. Cover and simmer 3 minutes. Serve venison and onions with gravy.　10 TO 12 SERVINGS.

FRUIT GARNISHES FOR MEATS

For each garnish, cut 1 peach, nectarine or apricot into halves and remove pit; or core 1 pear and cut into halves. Make a few partial cuts through fruit. Brush each half with ¼ to ½ teaspoon margarine, softened; top with one of the following:

☐ Brush with soy sauce; sprinkle with ground ginger.

☐ Spread with mixture of 2 tablespoons orange marmalade and ¼ teaspoon dry mustard.

☐ Drizzle with dry white wine or brandy; sprinkle with grated orange peel.

☐ Drizzle with honey or maple-flavored syrup; sprinkle with ground cinnamon.

☐ Drizzle with lemon or lime juice; sprinkle with ½ teaspoon brown sugar and dash of ground nutmeg.

Set oven control to broil and/or 550°. Broil fruit halves with tops about 5 inches from heat until bubbly, 4 to 6 minutes.

EGGS AND CHEESE

EGGS AND CHEESE IN YOUR MENUS

Eggs and cheese are good partners—in so many ways that we have put them together in this chapter. Both eggs and cheese are sources of complete animal protein and the best kind of meat stretchers and meat substitutes. Servings in these recipes are nutritionally adequate for protein. Since eggs and cheese are often combined with such bulky foods as pasta, rice and bread, you will find the servings larger than some of the nutritionally adequate servings of meats, poultry and fish.

BUYING EGGS

Size: Eggs are most often available as extra large, large and medium. Our recipes were tested with large eggs. When it is essential to the recipe's success, amounts are also given in liquid measure.

Grade: Federal standards classify eggs as AA, A, B and C. AA and A are best for poaching, frying and eating in the shell. The yolks are firm, round and high. The thick white stands high around the yolk; there is less of the thin white. Grade B eggs are more economical and have the same nutritive value as AA and A; they are good for uses other than poaching, frying or eating in the shell.

Color: Brown eggs or white, deep yellow yolks or pale yellow ones—the flavor, nutritive value and cooking performance are the same. The shell color is the result of pigment; the yolk color, of feed.

STORING EGGS

Refrigerate eggs right after you buy them (with the large ends up to hold the yolks in the centers) and use them within a week. Leftover egg whites will keep in the refrigerator in a covered jar 7 to 10 days. Cover leftover yolks with water and store in a covered jar 2 to 3 days. Use the leftover yolks for Classic Hollandaise Sauce (page 164) or Cooked Salad Dressing (page 158). Use the whites for Meringue Shell (page 311) or Angel Food Cake Deluxe (page 243).

EGG EQUIVALENTS

To measure 1 cup, you need 4 to 6 whole eggs or 8 to 10 whites or 12 to 14 yolks.

KINDS OF CHEESE

Natural cheese: Made from cow, sheep or goat milk, or cream; usually cured or aged to develop flavor. (See Cheese Charts, pages 112–13.)

Pasteurized process cheese: A blend of one or more lots of cheese, processed using heat, water and emulsifier.

Cheese food: A mixture of one or more cheeses, processed using milk solids, salt, emulsifier.

Cheese spread: Higher in moisture and lower in milk fats than cheese food. Sometimes flavored with pimiento, olives or other ingredients.

Coldpack (club) cheese: One or more kinds of natural cheese, mixed without heat or emulsifier.

BUYING CHEESE

☐ Domestic cheese often costs less than imported cheese of the same kind and quality.

☐ Pasteurized process cheese usually costs less than mild natural cheese.

☐ Mild natural cheese often costs less than sharp, aged cheese.

☐ Process cheese loaves cost less than the spreads.

☐ Blocks of cheese usually cost less than sliced or shredded cheese.

STORING CHEESE

☐ All cheese needs refrigeration. For freezing tips, see page 104.

☐ Store soft cheese (Camembert, cream cheese, cottage cheese) tightly covered.

☐ Cottage cheese keeps for 3 to 5 days; other soft cheese keeps for 2 weeks.

☐ Hard cheese (Swiss, Cheddar, Parmesan) keeps for several months. Store unopened in original wrappers. After opening, wrap tightly with aluminum foil or plastic wrap.

☐ If you find mold on natural cheese, cut it off.

☐ If mold has penetrated the cheese, discard cheese.

☐ In mold-ripened cheese (blue, Gorgonzola) the mold contributes distinctive flavor and color.

COOKING CHEESE

Keep cooking temperatures low and avoid overcooking to prevent stringiness and toughness in cheese. Add the cheese to other ingredients in small pieces—it spreads evenly and cooks in a shorter time. For even shorter cooking time, use your microwave.

POACHED EGGS

1. Hold cup close to water's surface; slip egg into water.

2. Lift eggs carefully from skillet with slotted spatula.

FRIED EGGS

1. Spoon margarine onto eggs, forming film over yolks.

2. Or, when edges turn white, spoon water into skillet.

BAKED (SHIRRED) EGGS

Cook until whites are set; yolks should be soft.

SCRAMBLED EGGS

Lift set portions; uncooked portion will flow to bottom.

POACHED EGGS

Heat water (1½ to 2 inches) to boiling; reduce to simmer. Break each egg into measuring cup or saucer; holding cup or saucer close to water's surface, slip 1 egg at a time into water.

Cook until desired doneness, 3 to 5 minutes. Remove eggs from water with slotted spatula.

Eggs Poached in Bouillon: Add 2 chicken or beef bouillon cubes to the water before boiling.

Eggs Poached in Egg Poacher: Pour water into poacher to just below bottom of egg cups; heat to boiling. Break eggs into buttered metal egg cups. Set egg cups in frame over boiling water. Cover and steam until desired doneness, 3 to 5 minutes.

Eggs Poached in Milk: Substitute milk for the water. To serve, pour hot milk over eggs on hot toast.

EGGS BENEDICT

Prepare Classic Hollandaise Sauce (page 164); keep warm. Split 3 English muffins; toast. Spread margarine or butter over each half. Fry 6 thin slices fully cooked smoked ham in margarine or butter until light brown. Prepare Poached Eggs (above). Place 1 ham slice on split side of each muffin; top with poached egg. Spoon warm sauce onto eggs. 6 SERVINGS.

FRIED EGGS

Heat margarine, butter or bacon drippings in heavy skillet to ⅛-inch depth just until hot enough to sizzle a drop of water. Break each egg into measuring cup or saucer; carefully slip 1 egg at a time into skillet. Immediately reduce heat.

Cook slowly, spooning margarine onto eggs until whites are set and a film forms over yolks (sunnyside up). Or turn eggs over gently when whites are set and cook until desired doneness.

Poached-Fried Eggs: Heat just enough margarine or bacon drippings to grease skillet. Cook eggs over low heat until edges turn white. Add ½ teaspoon water for 1 egg, decreasing proportion slightly for each additional egg. Cover and cook until desired doneness.

BAKED (SHIRRED) EGGS

For each serving, break 1 egg carefully into buttered 6-ounce custard cup. Sprinkle with salt and pepper. If desired, top each with 1 tablespoon milk or half-and-half, dot with margarine or butter, softened, or sprinkle with 1 tablespoon shredded Cheddar cheese. Cook eggs uncovered in 325° oven until desired doneness, 15 to 18 minutes. (Whites should be set but yolks soft.)

SOFT-COOKED EGGS

Cold Water Method: Place eggs in saucepan; add enough cold water to come at least 1 inch above eggs. Heat rapidly to boiling; remove from heat. Cover and let stand until desired doneness, 1 to 3 minutes. Immediately cool eggs in cold water several seconds to prevent further cooking. Cut eggs into halves; scoop eggs from shells.

Boiling Water Method: Place eggs in bowl of warm water to prevent shells from cracking. Fill saucepan with enough water to come at least 1 inch above eggs; heat to boiling. Transfer eggs from warm water to boiling water with spoon; remove from heat. Cover and let stand until desired doneness, 6 to 8 minutes. Immediately cool eggs in cold water several seconds to prevent further cooking. Cut eggs into halves; scoop eggs from shells.

HARD-COOKED EGGS

Cold Water Method: Place eggs in saucepan; add enough cold water to come at least 1 inch above eggs. Heat rapidly to boiling; remove from heat. Cover and let stand 22 to 24 minutes. Immediately cool eggs in cold water to prevent further cooking. Tap egg to crackle shell. Roll egg between hands to loosen shell, then peel. Hold egg under running cold water to help ease off shell.

Boiling Water Method: Place eggs in bowl of warm water to prevent shells from cracking. Fill saucepan with enough water to come at least 1 inch above eggs; heat to boiling. Transfer eggs from warm water to boiling water with spoon; reduce heat to below simmering. Cook uncovered 20 minutes. Immediately cool eggs in cold water to prevent further cooking. Tap egg to crackle shell. Roll egg between hands to loosen shell, then peel. Hold egg under running cold water to help ease off shell.

SCRAMBLED EGGS

For each serving, break 2 eggs into bowl with 2 tablespoons milk or cream, ¼ teaspoon salt and dash of pepper. Mix with fork, stirring thoroughly for a uniform yellow, or mixing just slightly if streaks of white and yellow are preferred.

Heat 1½ teaspoons margarine or butter in skillet over medium heat just until hot enough to sizzle a drop of water. Pour egg mixture into skillet.

As mixture begins to set at bottom and side, gently lift cooked portions with spatula so that thin, uncooked portion can flow to bottom. Avoid constant stirring. Cook until eggs are thickened throughout but still moist, 3 to 5 minutes. Sprinkle with a little Fines Herbes (below) if desired.

FINES HERBES
1 tablespoon dried basil leaves
1 tablespoon dried marjoram leaves
1 tablespoon dried oregano leaves
1 tablespoon dried tarragon leaves
1 tablespoon dried thyme leaves
2 teaspoons dried rosemary leaves
2 teaspoons dried sage leaves

Place all ingredients in blender container. Cover and blend on high speed 10 seconds. Store in tightly covered container.

Scrambled Eggs in Double Boiler: Cook egg mixture in top of double boiler over simmering (not boiling) water, stirring occasionally, until thick and creamy.

Party Scrambled Eggs: For each serving, mix in 2 tablespoons of one of the following: shredded Cheddar, Monterey Jack or Swiss cheese, chopped mushrooms, snipped chives, snipped parsley, crisply fried and crumbled bacon,* finely shredded dried beef,* chopped fully cooked smoked ham.*

*Omit salt.

FREEZING CHEESE

Freeze cheese (preferably in 8-ounce piece or less) in unopened wrapping, overwrapped with freezer wrap. Slices and loaves of natural cheese (such as Cheddar and Swiss) and pasteurized process cheese products can be frozen up to three months. Before using, thaw frozen cheese in its wrapping in the refrigerator.

EGG FOO YONG
2 tablespoons vegetable oil
3 eggs
1 cup bean sprouts, drained
½ cup chopped cooked pork
2 tablespoons chopped onion
¾ teaspoon salt
   Sauce (below)

Heat oil in 10-inch skillet. Beat eggs until thick and lemon colored, about 5 minutes. Stir in bean sprouts, pork, onion and salt.

Pour ¼ cup egg mixture at a time into skillet. Push cooked egg up over pork with broad spatula to form a patty. Cook until patty is set; turn. Cook over medium heat until other side is brown. Serve with Sauce.   2 SERVINGS.

SAUCE
½ cup water
1 teaspoon cornstarch
1 teaspoon sugar
1 teaspoon vinegar
2 tablespoons plus 1½ teaspoons soy sauce

Cook all ingredients, stirring constantly, until mixture thickens and boils. Boil and stir 1 minute.

Do-ahead Tip: Cover and freeze cooked patties no longer than 1 month. Heat frozen patties uncovered in 375° oven until hot, about 15 minutes.

EASY DENVER SANDWICHES
   Margarine or butter, softened
8 slices bread or toast
1 small onion, finely chopped (about ¼ cup)
½ small green pepper, finely chopped
1 tablespoon margarine or butter
1 tablespoon shortening
4 eggs
½ cup chopped fully cooked smoked ham
¼ teaspoon salt
⅛ teaspoon pepper

Spread margarine over 4 slices bread. Cook and stir onion and green pepper in 1 tablespoon margarine and the shortening in 10-inch skillet until onion is tender. Beat eggs slightly; stir in remaining ingredients. Pour egg mixture into skillet. Cook over low heat just until set. Cut into four wedges; turn. Cook until light brown. Serve between bread slices.   4 SANDWICHES.

Deviled Denver Sandwiches: Substitute 1 can (2¼ ounces) deviled ham and ¼ teaspoon Worcestershire sauce for the ham.

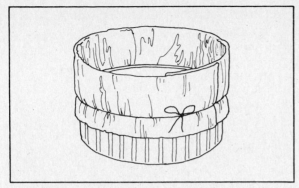

Add height to a soufflé dish by tying a buttered 4-inch band of aluminum foil around the rim.

CHEESE SOUFFLE

¼ cup margarine or butter
¼ cup all-purpose flour
½ teaspoon salt
¼ teaspoon dry mustard
  Dash of cayenne red pepper
1 cup milk
1 cup shredded Cheddar cheese
3 eggs, separated
¼ teaspoon cream of tartar

Heat oven to 350°. Butter 4-cup soufflé dish or 1-quart casserole. Make a 4-inch band of triple-thickness aluminum foil 2 inches longer than circumference of dish; butter 1 side. Secure foil band, buttered side in, around dish as pictured above.

Heat margarine in saucepan over low heat until melted. Blend in flour, salt, mustard and red pepper. Cook over low heat, stirring constantly, until mixture is smooth and bubbly; remove from heat. Stir in milk. Heat to boiling, stirring constantly. Boil and stir 1 minute. Stir in cheese until melted; remove from heat.

Beat egg whites and cream of tartar until stiff but not dry. Beat egg yolks until very thick and lemon colored, about 5 minutes; stir into cheese mixture. Stir about ¼ of the egg whites into cheese mixture. Fold cheese mixture into remaining egg whites.

Carefully pour into soufflé dish. Cook uncovered until knife inserted halfway between center and edge comes out clean, 50 to 60 minutes. Serve immediately. Carefully remove foil band and divide soufflé into sections with 2 forks.   3 SERVINGS.

Shrimp Soufflé: Omit mustard, red pepper and cheese. Add 1 can (4½ ounces) tiny shrimp, rinsed and drained, and 1 teaspoon dried tarragon leaves to sauce mixture before adding the beaten yolks.

SPINACH PUFF

1 pound fresh spinach or Swiss chard
¼ cup margarine or butter
¼ cup all-purpose flour
¼ teaspoon salt
⅛ teaspoon pepper
1 cup milk
1 tablespoon finely chopped onion
1 teaspoon salt
⅛ teaspoon ground nutmeg
3 eggs, separated
¼ teaspoon cream of tartar

Prepare and cook spinach or Swiss chard as directed on page 179; chop and drain completely.

Heat oven to 350°. Butter 4-cup soufflé dish or 1-quart casserole. Heat margarine in saucepan over low heat until melted. Blend in flour, ¼ teaspoon salt and the pepper. Cook over low heat, stirring constantly, until mixture is smooth and bubbly; remove from heat. Stir in milk. Heat to boiling, stirring constantly. Boil and stir 1 minute; remove from heat. Stir in onion, 1 teaspoon salt and the nutmeg.

Beat egg whites and cream of tartar in large mixer bowl until stiff. Beat egg yolks in small mixer bowl until very thick and lemon colored; stir into white sauce mixture. Stir in spinach.

Stir about ¼ of the egg whites into sauce mixture; fold into remaining egg whites.

Carefully pour into soufflé dish. Set soufflé dish in pan of water (1 inch deep). Bake until puffed and golden and until knife inserted halfway between center and edge comes out clean, 50 to 60 minutes. Serve immediately.   4 TO 6 SERVINGS.

Broccoli Puff: Substitute 1 pound broccoli, prepared and cooked as directed on page 169, or 1 package (10 ounces) frozen chopped broccoli, cooked and drained, for the spinach.

BEATING EGG WHITES

Be sure that both bowl and beaters are spotlessly clean and dry—and that there is no yolk in the white. Egg whites will not beat properly if bowl or beater is even slightly moist or greasy or if there is the tiniest speck of yolk in the white. Properly beaten whites should more than triple their volume. Eggs separate more easily when cold but beat to higher volume faster at room temperature.

PUFFY OMELET

4 eggs, separated
¼ cup water
¼ teaspoon salt
⅛ teaspoon pepper
1 tablespoon margarine or butter

Beat egg whites, water and salt in small mixer bowl until stiff but not dry. Beat egg yolks and pepper in another mixer bowl until very thick and lemon colored, about 5 minutes. Fold into egg whites.

Heat margarine in 10-inch ovenproof skillet just until hot enough to sizzle drop of water. Pour omelet mixture into skillet; level surface gently. Reduce heat. Cook slowly until puffy and light brown on bottom, about 5 minutes. (Lift omelet at edge to judge color.) Cook uncovered in 325° oven until knife inserted in center comes out clean, 12 to 15 minutes.

Tilt skillet; slip pancake turner or spatula under omelet to loosen. Fold omelet in half, being careful not to break it. Slip onto warm plate. Serve with Avocado Sauce or Shrimp-Mushroom Sauce (below) if desired.   2 SERVINGS.

AVOCADO SAUCE

¾ cup dairy sour cream
½ teaspoon salt
⅛ teaspoon dried dill weed
1 large tomato, diced and drained
1 small avocado, diced

Heat sour cream, salt and dill weed. Stir in tomato gently; heat 1 minute. Stir in avocado carefully.

SHRIMP-MUSHROOM SAUCE

½ cup milk
1 can (10¾ ounces) condensed cream of
    mushroom soup
1 small stalk celery, finely chopped (about
    ¼ cup)
1 teaspoon finely chopped onion
1 tablespoon lemon juice
3 drops red pepper sauce
1 can (4½ ounces) tiny shrimp, rinsed and
    drained

Stir milk gradually into soup in saucepan. Heat over medium heat, stirring constantly, until sauce is bubbly. Stir in celery, onion, lemon juice and pepper sauce. Fold in shrimp; heat through.

CHEESE-CHILI OVEN OMELET

2 cups shredded Cheddar cheese
1 can (4 ounces) chopped green chilies,
    drained
2 cups shredded Monterey Jack cheese
1¼ cups milk
3 tablespoons flour
½ teaspoon salt
3 eggs
1 can (8 ounces) tomato sauce

Layer Cheddar cheese, chilies and Monterey Jack cheese in greased square baking dish, 8x8x2 inches. Beat milk, flour, salt and eggs; pour over cheese mixture. Cook uncovered in 350° oven until set in center and top is golden brown, about 40 minutes. Let stand 10 minutes before cutting. Heat tomato sauce; serve with omelet.   8 SERVINGS.

HAM-CHEESE OVEN OMELET

8 eggs
1 cup milk
½ teaspoon Seasoned Salt (below)
1 package (3 ounces) smoked sliced ham, beef
    or corned beef, torn into small pieces
1 cup shredded Cheddar, Swiss or
    mozzarella cheese (about 4 ounces)
3 tablespoons finely chopped onion

Beat eggs, milk and Seasoned Salt. Stir in remaining ingredients. Pour into greased oblong baking dish, 12x7½x2 inches, or square baking dish, 8x8x2 inches. Cook uncovered in 325° oven until omelet is set and top is golden brown, 40 to 45 minutes. 6 SERVINGS.

SEASONED SALT

½ cup salt
1 tablespoon celery salt
1 tablespoon garlic salt
1 tablespoon paprika
1 teaspoon dry mustard
1 teaspoon onion powder
1 teaspoon pepper

Place all ingredients in blender container. Cover and blend on high speed 20 seconds. Store in tightly covered container.

Do-ahead Tip: After pouring into baking dish, cover and refrigerate omelet no longer than 24 hours.

NOTE: Recipe can be doubled. Double all ingredients and cook in greased oblong baking dish, 13½x9x2 inches, 45 to 50 minutes.

FRENCH OMELET

Mix 3 eggs with fork just until whites and yolks are blended. Heat about 1 tablespoon margarine or butter in 8-inch skillet or omelet pan over medium-high heat. As margarine melts, tilt skillet in all directions to coat side thoroughly. When margarine just begins to brown, skillet is hot enough to use.

Quickly pour eggs all at once into skillet. Start sliding skillet back and forth rapidly over heat. At the same time, stir quickly with fork to spread eggs continuously over bottom of skillet as they thicken. Let stand over heat a few seconds to lightly brown bottom of omelet. (Do not overcook—omelet will continue to cook after folding.)

Tilt skillet; run fork under edge of omelet, then jerk skillet sharply to loosen eggs from bottom of skillet. Fold portion of omelet nearest you just to center. (Allow for portion of omelet to slide up side of skillet.)

Grasp skillet handle; turn omelet onto warm plate, flipping folded portion of omelet over so far side is on bottom. Tuck sides of omelet under if necessary. Brush omelet with margarine or butter to make it shine if desired.   1 SERVING.

Bacon Omelet: Just before folding omelet, sprinkle with 3 slices bacon, crisply fried and crumbled.

Cheese Omelet: Just before folding omelet, sprinkle with ¼ cup shredded Cheddar cheese.

Chive Omelet: Just before folding omelet, sprinkle with 1 tablespoon snipped chives.

Herbed Omelet: Just before folding omelet, sprinkle with dried basil, chervil, thyme or marjoram leaves, 1 tablespoon snipped chives and 1 tablespoon snipped parsley.

Jelly Omelet: Just before folding omelet, drizzle with 2 tablespoons jelly or preserves.

Western Omelet: Mix in ¼ cup finely chopped fully cooked smoked ham, 2 tablespoons chopped onion and 2 tablespoons chopped green pepper.

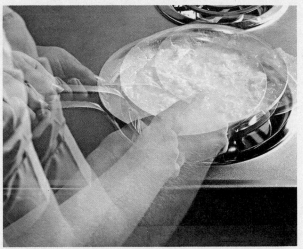

Stir quickly, sliding skillet back and forth over heat.

Tilt skillet; fold nearest omelet edge just to center.

Turn onto plate; far side flips over onto unfolded portion.

EGGS AU GRATIN

¼ cup margarine or butter
⅓ cup all-purpose flour
¾ teaspoon salt
¼ teaspoon pepper
2 cups water
1 cup milk
2 chicken bouillon cubes
½ teaspoon Worcestershire sauce
1 cup shredded Cheddar cheese (about
    4 ounces)
12 hard-cooked eggs
⅓ cup dry bread crumbs
2 tablespoons margarine or butter, melted
⅓ to ½ cup grated Parmesan cheese

Heat ¼ cup margarine in saucepan until melted. Blend in flour, salt and pepper. Cook over low heat, stirring constantly, until mixture is smooth and bubbly; remove from heat. Stir in water, milk and bouillon cubes. Heat to boiling, stirring constantly. Boil and stir 1 minute; remove from heat. Stir in Worcestershire sauce and Cheddar cheese until cheese is melted.

Cut peeled eggs lengthwise into halves. Arrange eggs in ungreased oblong baking dish, 13½x9x2 inches. Pour cheese sauce over eggs. Toss bread crumbs with 2 tablespoons margarine and the Parmesan cheese; sprinkle over top.

Cook uncovered in 350° oven until mixture bubbles and crumbs are brown, 20 to 25 minutes. Garnish with parsley if desired.   8 SERVINGS.

EGG-BACON BAKE

¼ cup dry bread crumbs
1 tablespoon margarine or butter, melted
5 hard-cooked eggs, peeled and sliced
3 slices bacon, chopped
1 cup dairy sour cream
3 tablespoons finely chopped onion
1 tablespoon milk
½ teaspoon salt
¼ teaspoon paprika
⅛ teaspoon pepper
½ cup shredded Cheddar cheese

Toss bread crumbs and margarine; divide among 4 buttered 10-ounce custard cups. Layer egg slices over bread crumbs.

Fry bacon until crisp; drain. Mix bacon, sour cream, onion, milk, salt, paprika and pepper; spoon onto eggs. Top with cheese. Cook uncovered in 350° oven until cheese is melted, 10 to 15 minutes.
4 SERVINGS.

CREAMED EGGS WITH HAM

3 tablespoons margarine or butter
3 tablespoons flour
½ teaspoon dry mustard
¼ teaspoon salt
⅛ teaspoon pepper
2¼ cups milk
1 cup diced fully cooked smoked ham
4 hard-cooked eggs, each peeled and cut
    into fourths

Heat margarine in saucepan over low heat until melted. Blend in flour, mustard, salt and pepper. Cook over low heat, stirring constantly, until mixture is smooth and bubbly; remove from heat. Stir in milk. Heat to boiling, stirring constantly. Boil and stir 1 minute. Stir in ham and eggs gently; heat through.   5 SERVINGS.

Creamed Eggs: Omit mustard and ham and increase eggs to 6.

Creamed Eggs with Seafood: Omit mustard and ham; stir 1 can (7¾ ounces) salmon, drained and flaked, or 1 can (6½ ounces) tuna, drained, into white sauce with the eggs.

EGGS WITH CHEESE AND SHRIMP

9 hard-cooked eggs
3 tablespoons mayonnaise or salad dressing
1 tablespoon chopped sweet pickle
2 teaspoons vinegar
½ teaspoon dry mustard
    Dash of Worcestershire sauce
    Dash of pepper
1 can (4 ounces) mushroom stems and
    pieces, drained
1 can (4½ ounces) tiny shrimp, rinsed and
    drained
¾ cup milk
1 can (11 ounces) condensed Cheddar
    cheese soup
4 cups cooked rice (page 225)

Cut peeled eggs lengthwise into halves. Slip out yolks; mash with fork. Mix yolks, mayonnaise, pickle, vinegar, mustard, Worcestershire sauce and pepper. Fill egg whites with egg yolk mixture, heaping it lightly.

Heat mushrooms, shrimp, milk and soup just to boiling, stirring occasionally. Spread rice in ungreased oblong baking dish, 12x7½x2 inches, or square pan, 9x9x2 inches. Arrange eggs in 3 rows on top; pour soup mixture over eggs and rice. Cook uncovered in 350° oven 15 minutes. 8 SERVINGS.

EGG-CHEESE BAKE

Margarine or butter, softened
6 slices caraway rye bread
1 medium onion, sliced
1 tablespoon margarine or butter
8 hard-cooked eggs, peeled and sliced
2 cups shredded process Swiss cheese
   (about 8 ounces)
1 can (10¾ ounces) condensed cream of
   mushroom soup
¾ cup milk
1 teaspoon prepared mustard
½ teaspoon seasoned salt
¼ teaspoon dried dill weed
¼ teaspoon pepper

Spread margarine over 1 side of each slice bread. Cut each slice diagonally into 4 triangles. Cook and stir onion in 1 tablespoon margarine until onion is tender. Spread mixture in oblong baking dish, 12x7½x2 inches, or square baking dish, 9x9x2 inches. Top with egg slices; sprinkle with cheese. Beat remaining ingredients with hand beater; pour over cheese. Overlap bread slices on casserole.

Cook uncovered in 350° oven until hot, 30 to 35 minutes. Set oven control to broil and/or 550°. Broil about 5 inches from heat until bread is toasted, about 1 minute.   6 SERVINGS.

PUFFY CHEESE BAKE

Margarine or butter, softened
4 slices bread
2 eggs
1 cup half-and-half
2 tablespoons margarine or butter, melted
½ teaspoon salt
½ teaspoon dry mustard
¼ teaspoon paprika
Dash of cayenne red pepper
1½ cups shredded process American cheese
   (about 6 ounces)

Spread margarine over 1 side of each slice bread. Cut each slice diagonally into 4 triangles. Line bottom and sides of ungreased square baking dish, 8x8x2 inches, with bread triangles, buttered sides down. (For crown effect, place 8 triangles upright against sides of dish. Arrange remaining triangles in bottom of dish.)

Beat eggs slightly; mix in remaining ingredients. Pour into baking dish. Cook uncovered in 350° oven 40 minutes. Let stand 10 minutes before cutting.   4 SERVINGS.

CHEESE STRATA

⅓ cup margarine or butter, softened
1 clove garlic, crushed
½ teaspoon dry mustard
10 slices white bread (crusts removed)
2 cups shredded sharp Cheddar cheese
   (about 8 ounces)
2 tablespoons snipped parsley
2 tablespoons chopped onion
1 teaspoon salt
½ teaspoon Worcestershire sauce
⅛ teaspoon pepper
Dash of cayenne red pepper
4 eggs
2⅓ cups milk
⅔ cup dry white wine (optional)*

Mix margarine, garlic and mustard. Spread over 1 side of each slice bread. Cut each slice into thirds. Line bottom and sides of ungreased square baking dish, 8x8x2 inches, with some of the bread slices, buttered sides down.

Mix cheese, parsley, onion, salt, Worcestershire sauce, pepper and red pepper; spread evenly in dish. Top with remaining bread slices, buttered sides up. Beat eggs; blend in milk and wine. Pour over bread. Cover and refrigerate at least 2 hours.

Cook uncovered in 325° oven until knife inserted in center comes out clean, about 1¼ hours. Let stand 10 minutes before cutting.   6 SERVINGS.

*Wine can be omitted; increase milk to 2½ cups.

RICE AND CORN BAKE

3 eggs, separated
1 can (8¾ ounces) whole kernel corn,
   drained
1½ cups cooked rice (page 225)
1 cup shredded Cheddar cheese (about
   4 ounces)
½ cup milk
1 teaspoon salt
¾ teaspoon dry mustard
⅛ teaspoon pepper

Heat oven to 350°. Mix egg yolks and remaining ingredients. Beat egg whites until stiff peaks form; fold into rice mixture. Pour into greased 1-quart casserole or 5-cup soufflé dish. Cook uncovered until knife inserted in center comes out clean, 40 to 45 minutes.   4 SERVINGS.

READ THE LABEL

Many food labels now include clear, readable information to help you determine food value and calories per serving. All fortified foods (such as macaroni) and those for which a nutrition claim has been made must carry this information: serving size; servings per container; calories per serving; grams of protein, carbohydrates and fat per serving; percent of U.S. RDA of protein, major vitamins, calcium and iron per serving.

CHEESE AND MACARONI SALAD

- 1½ cups uncooked elbow macaroni (about 6 ounces)
- 1 package (10 ounces) frozen green peas
- 2 cups shredded Cheddar cheese (about 8 ounces)
- 4 green onions, sliced (about ½ cup)
- 1 medium stalk celery, sliced (about ½ cup)
- ¾ cup mayonnaise or salad dressing
- ⅓ cup sweet pickle relish
- ½ teaspoon salt
- ½ head iceberg lettuce, torn into bite-size pieces (about 3 cups)
- ⅓ cup imitation bacon

Cook macaroni as directed on page 221. Rinse frozen peas under running cold water to separate. Mix macaroni, peas, cheese, onions, celery, mayonnaise, relish and salt. Cover and refrigerate. Just before serving, toss with lettuce and imitation bacon.   6 SERVINGS.

Cheese and Bologna Salad: Substitute 1 cup cut-up bologna (about 4 ounces) for the imitation bacon.

Cheese and Chicken Salad: Substitute ½ cup cut-up cooked chicken or turkey for 1 cup of the cheese.

Cheese and Frank Salad: Substitute 3 frankfurters, sliced, for the imitation bacon.

Cheese and Shrimp Salad: Substitute 1 can (4½ ounces) tiny shrimp, rinsed and drained, for 1 cup of the cheese.

MACARONI SHELL SALAD

- Herbed Dressing (below)
- 7 ounces uncooked macaroni shells (about 2 cups)
- 1 cup shredded pizza cheese
- ½ cup sliced pimiento-stuffed olives
- 3 medium zucchini, chopped
- Salad greens
- ¼ cup grated Parmesan cheese

Prepare Herbed Dressing. Cook macaroni as directed on page 221. Toss macaroni, pizza cheese, olives and zucchini with dressing. Cover and refrigerate at least 3 hours. Serve on greens and sprinkle with Parmesan cheese. Garnish with parsley if desired.   6 SERVINGS.

HERBED DRESSING

- 1 can (8 ounces) tomato sauce
- ½ cup mayonnaise or salad dressing
- 1 teaspoon salt
- ½ teaspoon garlic salt
- ½ teaspoon dried oregano leaves

Place ingredients in blender container. Cover; blend on medium speed until smooth, about 10 seconds.

COTTAGE CHEESE-EGG SALAD

- 1 cup boiling water
- 1 package (3 ounces) lemon-flavored gelatin
- 1½ teaspoons salt
- ¾ cup cold water
- ¼ cup vinegar
- 9 hard-cooked eggs
- 1 medium cucumber, shredded and well drained
- 1 tablespoon grated onion
- 1½ cups creamed cottage cheese
- ½ teaspoon dried tarragon leaves
- 5 drops red pepper sauce

Pour boiling water on gelatin and salt in large bowl; stir until gelatin is dissolved. Stir in cold water and vinegar. Refrigerate until mixture is slightly thickened but not set.

Cut peeled eggs crosswise into halves. Spread 1 cup of the gelatin in oblong baking dish, 12x7½x2 inches, or square pan, 9x9x2 inches. Press eggs cut sides down gently into gelatin.

Beat remaining gelatin until light and fluffy; stir in remaining ingredients. Pour gelatin mixture over eggs. Cover and refrigerate until firm, at least 8 hours.   6 SERVINGS.

CHEESE-PINEAPPLE BOATS

1 pineapple
1 cup strawberries, cut into halves (reserve
     4 whole berries)
2 cups cantaloupe or honeydew melon balls
¼ teaspoon ground ginger
2 tablespoons lime juice
8 ounces Cheddar, Muenster or Monterey
     Jack cheese, cut into ½-inch cubes
2 tablespoons coarsely chopped dry roasted
     almonds
     Ground ginger
     Pineapple yogurt

Select a pineapple with fresh green leaves. Cut
pineapple lengthwise into quarters through green
top. Cut along curved edges of quarters with
grapefruit knife to remove fruit. Cut off pineapple
core; cut fruit into chunks. Drain fruit and invert
shells to drain.

Place pineapple chunks, halved strawberries and
melon balls in large bowl. Sprinkle with ¼ teaspoon ginger and the lime juice; toss. Cover and refrigerate 1 hour.

Stir in cheese; spoon mixture into shells. Sprinkle
with almonds and ginger. Spoon yogurt onto each
serving and garnish with whole strawberries.
4 SERVINGS.

SOFT CHEESES

Brie (bree): French origin. Edible crust. Mild to pungent. Appetizer, dessert.

Camembert (kam'-embear): French origin. Pungent. Appetizer, dessert.

Club: Canadian origin. Often flavored. Appetizer, sandwich, dessert.

Cottage: Large or small curds, dry or creamed. Salad, snack, cooking.

Cream: U.S. origin. Very mild. Chill slightly. Salad, snack, dessert.

Gourmandise: French origin. Cherry brandy flavor. Appetizer, dessert.

Liederkranz: U.S. origin. Edible crust. Pungent. As an appetizer, for dessert.

Ricotta (rih-kah'-tuh): Italian origin. Mild. Curd or dry. Cooking, dessert.

SEMISOFT CHEESES

Bel Paese (bel-pah-ay'-ze): Italian origin. Mild. As an appetizer, for dessert.

Brick: U.S. origin. Mild to sharp flavor. Firm to soft. As a snack, in sandwiches.

Monterey Jack: California origin. Mild. Appetizer, cooking, sandwich.

Mozzarella, Scamorze: Italian origin. Mild. For cooking, as a snack.

Muenster (mun'-ster): German origin. Mild to sharp. Appetizer, sandwich.

Port du Salut (por-du-salu): French origin. Mild to robust. Appetizer, dessert.

Roquefort (roke-for): Of French origin. Sharp, salty. Appetizer, salad, dessert.

Samsoe: Danish origin. Mild. Softer than Swiss. "Eyes." Sandwich, snack.

FIRM-TO-HARD CHEESES

Blue: Probable French origin. Tangy, sharp. Appetizer, salad, dessert.

Cheddar: English origin. Mild to very sharp. Snack, cooking, dessert.

Cheshire: English origin. Crumbly texture. Snack, cooking (Welsh rarebit).

Edam, Gouda: Dutch origin. Inedible casing. Mild. Appetizer, dessert.

Fontina (fahn-tee'-nah): Italian origin. Mellow. Appetizer, dessert.

Gjetost (yate'-ohst): Norwegian origin. Caramel flavor. Sandwich, snack.

Gorgonzola: Italian origin. Piquant flavor; crumbly. In salads, for dessert.

Gruyère (gree-air'): Swiss origin. Nutty, sharper than Swiss. Cooking, dessert.

VERY HARD CHEESES

Kashkaval (kotch-kah-vaih'): Yugoslavian. Salty. Appetizer, snack, dessert.

Noekkelost(nee-ke-lohst): Norwegian origin. Mild. Seeded. Sandwich, snack.

Provolone (pro-vo-lo'-nee): Italian. Smoked. Mild to sharp. Cooking, snack.

Swiss: Mild, nutty, sweet flavor. Appetizer, sandwich, cooking, dessert.

Parmesan: Italian origin. Inedible casing. Sharp. Usually grated for cooking.

Romano: Italian origin. Piquant. Granular. Usually grated, also as a snack.

Sapsago (sap-say'-go): Swiss origin. Clover flavor. Usually grated.

Sbrinz: Of Swiss origin. Medium to sharp. Often grated, also as a snack.

Clockwise from top: Cheese Soufflé (page 105), Puffy Omelet (page 106) and Quiche Lorraine (page 115)

QUICHE LORRAINE

Pastry for 9-inch One-Crust Pie
(page 289)
12 slices bacon, crisply fried and crumbled
1 cup shredded natural Swiss cheese (about
4 ounces)
⅓ cup finely chopped onion
4 eggs
2 cups half-and-half
¾ teaspoon salt
¼ teaspoon pepper
⅛ teaspoon cayenne red pepper

Prepare pastry. Sprinkle bacon, cheese and onion
in pastry-lined pie plate. Beat eggs slightly; beat in
remaining ingredients. Pour egg mixture into pie
plate. Cook uncovered in 425° oven 15 minutes.

Reduce oven temperature to 300°. Cook uncovered
until knife inserted halfway between center and
edge comes out clean, about 30 minutes longer. Let
stand 10 minutes before cutting.   6 SERVINGS.

Do-ahead Tip: After sprinkling pastry with bacon,
cheese and onion, cover and refrigerate. Beat
remaining ingredients; cover and refrigerate. Store
no longer than 24 hours. Stir egg mixture before
pouring into pie plate. Continue as directed
except—increase second cooking time to about 45
minutes.

Chicken Quiche: Substitute 1 cup cut-up cooked
chicken for the bacon and ½ teaspoon dried thyme
leaves for the red pepper. Increase salt to 1
teaspoon.

Crab Quiche: Substitute 1 can (7½ ounces) crabmeat, drained and cartilage removed, for the bacon.
Pat crabmeat dry with paper towels. Increase salt to
1 teaspoon.

Deviled Ham Quiche: Substitute 2 cans (4½
ounces each) deviled ham for the bacon. Mix ham
with ¼ cup dry bread crumbs. Decrease half-and-
half to 1½ cups.

ENERGY SAVERS

Save energy by preheating your oven only when it
is specified in the recipe. Preheating is needed for
cakes, pastries, breads, quick breads and soufflés.
Roasts, casseroles and some egg dishes can be
started in a cold oven. Another energy saver: When
baking more than one item at a time, stagger pans
on racks and allow airspace all around them.

CHEDDAR CHEESE PIE

9-inch Baked Pie Shell (page 289)
3 cups shredded sharp natural Cheddar
cheese (about 12 ounces)
1 tablespoon finely chopped onion
½ teaspoon salt
½ teaspoon dry mustard
½ teaspoon Worcestershire sauce
3 eggs
6 medium tomatoes
Salt and pepper
Grated Parmesan cheese (optional)

Bake pie shell. Heat Cheddar cheese, onion, salt,
mustard and Worcestershire sauce over low heat,
stirring constantly, until cheese is melted; remove
from heat. Beat eggs in large bowl until foamy; beat
in cheese mixture gradually. Pour into pie shell.
Cook uncovered in 325° oven just until set, about
25 minutes.

Cut tomatoes into thin slices. Overlap slices around
edge of pie to form a wreath; sprinkle with salt,
pepper and Parmesan cheese. Cook uncovered 15
minutes longer.   6 SERVINGS.

CHEESE-RICE PIE

1½ cups hot cooked regular rice (page 225)
1 tablespoon snipped chives
1 egg white
1 package (3 ounces) smoked sliced beef,
torn into small pieces
3 eggs plus 1 egg yolk
1 can (13 ounces) evaporated milk
¼ teaspoon salt
½ cup shredded mozzarella or Monterey
Jack cheese (about 2 ounces)
⅓ cup finely chopped onion
¼ teaspoon dried sage leaves
6 tomato slices
Grated Parmesan cheese (optional)

Beat rice, chives and egg white with fork. Turn
mixture into greased 9- or 10-inch pie plate. Spread
evenly with rubber scraper over bottom and halfway up side of pie plate (do not leave any holes).
Cook uncovered in 350° oven 5 minutes.

Sprinkle beef over rice crust. Beat eggs, egg yolk,
milk and salt; stir in mozzarella cheese, sage and
onion. Pour carefully into crust. Cook uncovered in
350° oven until knife inserted in center comes out
clean, about 45 minutes. Immediately run knife
around edge to loosen crust. Let stand 10 minutes
before cutting. Top each serving with tomato slice;
sprinkle with Parmesan cheese.   6 SERVINGS.

COTTAGE CHEESE

Try cottage cheese as an inexpensive meat substitute or meat stretcher. One-half cup of creamed cottage cheese (120 calories) has about the same amount of protein as a 2-ounce serving of cooked meat, poultry or fish, or 2 slices Cheddar cheese, or 2 eggs. Store cottage cheese as you would fresh milk and use within a few days. Creamed cottage cheese should not be frozen; when it thaws it separates. Uncreamed cottage cheese can be frozen in its container no longer than 1 month.

CHEESE-TUNA SPAGHETTI

7 ounces uncooked thin spaghetti
¼ cup margarine or butter
¼ cup all-purpose flour
½ teaspoon salt
¼ teaspoon pepper
1 cup milk
¾ cup water
¼ cup dry red wine
1 teaspoon instant chicken bouillon
1 can (6½ ounces) tuna, drained
1½ cups shredded sharp Cheddar cheese (about 6 ounces)
1 jar (2½ ounces) sliced mushrooms, drained
1 jar (2 ounces) pimiento, drained and chopped
½ cup grated Parmesan cheese

Cook spaghetti as directed on page 221. Heat margarine in 10-inch skillet over low heat until melted. Stir in flour, salt and pepper. Cook over low heat, stirring constantly, until mixture is smooth and bubbly; remove from heat.

Stir in milk, water, wine and instant bouillon. Heat to boiling, stirring constantly. Boil and stir 1 minute. Stir in tuna, Cheddar cheese, spaghetti, mushrooms and pimiento. Pour into ungreased 2-quart casserole; sprinkle with Parmesan cheese.

Cook uncovered in 350° oven until bubbly, about 30 minutes. Set oven control to broil and/or 550°. Broil just until brown. 7 OR 8 SERVINGS.

Tuna Spaghetti: Increase tuna to 2 cans and omit Cheddar cheese.

CHEESY SPAGHETTI AND SPROUTS

1 package (10 ounces) frozen Brussels sprouts
1 can (11 ounces) condensed Cheddar cheese soup
⅓ cup milk
3 teaspoons salt
3½ ounces uncooked thin spaghetti
½ cup shredded Swiss cheese (about 2 ounces)

Cook Brussels sprouts as directed on package except—decrease cooking time by 5 minutes; drain. Mix soup and milk in same saucepan. Stir in Brussels sprouts. Cook over medium heat, stirring occasionally, until hot, about 5 minutes.

Cook spaghetti as directed on page 221. Serve sauce over hot spaghetti; sprinkle with cheese.
4 SERVINGS.

SPAGHETTI-CHEESE PIE

7 ounces uncooked spaghetti
1 cup creamed cottage cheese
2 eggs, slightly beaten
1½ teaspoons salt
⅛ teaspoon pepper
¾ cup shredded sharp Cheddar cheese (about 3 ounces)
1 egg, beaten
2 tablespoons grated Parmesan cheese

Cook spaghetti as directed on page 221. Mix cottage cheese, 2 eggs, the salt, pepper, Cheddar cheese and spaghetti. Turn into buttered 9-inch pie plate. Mix 1 egg and the Parmesan cheese; spread over spaghetti mixture.

Cook uncovered in 350° oven until knife inserted in center comes out clean, 45 to 50 minutes. Serve with Quick Mushroom Sauce or Tomato Sauce (below) if desired. 5 SERVINGS.

QUICK MUSHROOM SAUCE
Heat 1 can (10¾ ounces) condensed cream of mushroom soup and ½ cup milk just to boiling, stirring frequently.

TOMATO SAUCE
1 tablespoon margarine or butter, melted
2 tablespoons chopped onion
2 tablespoons chopped green pepper
1 can (8 ounces) tomato sauce
Salt and pepper

Heat margarine in saucepan until melted. Add onion and green pepper; cook and stir until tender. Stir in tomato sauce, salt and pepper; heat through over low heat.

PARMESAN-EGGPLANT SPAGHETTI

½ cup vegetable oil
1 eggplant (about 1 pound), cut into
   ½-inch cubes
1 medium onion, finely chopped
   (about ½ cup)
1 clove garlic, crushed
2 teaspoons dried parsley flakes
1 can (28 ounces) whole tomatoes
1 can (12 ounces) tomato paste
½ cup dry red wine
1 can (4 ounces) mushroom stems and
   pieces, drained
2 teaspoons dried oregano leaves
1 teaspoon salt
1 teaspoon sugar
16 ounces uncooked spaghetti
1 cup grated Parmesan cheese

Heat oil in Dutch oven over medium-high heat. Cook and stir eggplant, onion, garlic and parsley in oil until onion is tender, about 8 minutes. Stir in tomatoes (with liquid), tomato paste, wine, mushrooms, oregano, salt and sugar; break up tomatoes with fork. Heat to boiling; reduce heat. Cover and simmer, stirring occasionally, 15 minutes.

Cook spaghetti as directed on page 221. Serve eggplant sauce over hot spaghetti; sprinkle with cheese.   6 SERVINGS.

STUFFED MANICOTTI SHELLS

1 package (8 ounces) manicotti shells
1 small onion, chopped (about ¼ cup)
1 package (10 ounces) frozen chopped
   spinach, thawed and drained
1 tablespoon instant chicken bouillon
½ teaspoon garlic powder
⅛ teaspoon dried thyme leaves
1½ cups creamed cottage cheese
2 eggs
¼ cup grated Parmesan cheese
1 can (8 ounces) tomato sauce
1 cup shredded mozzarella cheese (about
   4 ounces)

Cook manicotti shells as directed on package; drain. Mix onion, spinach, instant bouillon, garlic powder, thyme, cottage cheese, eggs and Parmesan cheese. Fill manicotti shells with spinach mixture; arrange in greased oblong pan, 13x9x2 inches. Pour tomato sauce over manicotti; sprinkle with mozzarella cheese. Cover and cook in 350° oven until hot and bubbly, about 25 minutes.   5 SERVINGS.

MACARONI AND CHEESE

1 to 1½ cups uncooked elbow macaroni,
   rigatoni or spinach egg noodles (about
   6 ounces)
¼ cup margarine or butter
1 small onion, chopped (about ¼ cup)
½ teaspoon salt
¼ teaspoon pepper
¼ cup all-purpose flour
1¾ cups milk
8 ounces process sharp American or Swiss
   cheese, process American cheese loaf
   or process cheese spread loaf, cut into
   ½-inch cubes

Cook macaroni as directed on page 221. Cook and stir margarine, onion, salt and pepper over medium heat until onion is slightly tender. Blend in flour. Cook over low heat, stirring constantly, until mixture is smooth and bubbly; remove from heat. Stir in milk. Heat to boiling, stirring constantly. Boil and stir 1 minute; remove from heat. Stir in cheese until melted.

Place macaroni in ungreased 1½-quart casserole. Stir cheese sauce into macaroni. Cook uncovered in 375° oven 30 minutes.   5 SERVINGS.

Garden Macaroni and Cheese: Stir 1 package (10 ounces) frozen green peas or green beans into cheese sauce.

Ham Macaroni and Cheese: Stir 1 cup cut-up fully cooked smoked ham into cheese sauce.
7 SERVINGS.

Hot Dog Macaroni and Cheese: Stir 1 cup sliced frankfurters (about 3) or cut-up luncheon meat into cheese sauce.   6 SERVINGS.

Olive Macaroni and Cheese: Stir ¼ cup chopped pimiento-stuffed olives into cheese sauce.

Pepper Macaroni and Cheese: Stir ⅓ cup chopped green and/or red peppers or 1 can (4 ounces) green chilies, drained and chopped, into cheese sauce.

Tomato Macaroni and Cheese: Stir ¼ cup sliced ripe olives into macaroni in casserole. Arrange 1 large tomato, cut into 5 slices, around edge of casserole before cooking.

Tuna Macaroni and Cheese: Stir 1 can (6½ ounces) tuna, drained, into cheese sauce.   7 SERVINGS.

NOURISHING SANDWICHES

Swiss cheese, baked ham, sliced cucumber—on raisin rye

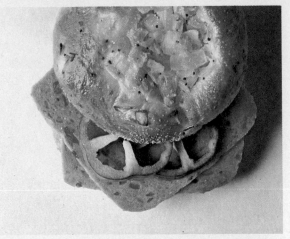

Luncheon meat, green pepper rings—on an onion roll

Roast beef, radish slices—on an English muffin

Tuna salad, spinach leaves, tomato—on pumpernickel

SANDWICH CHART

Sandwich Breads and Rolls		Fillings	Filling Companions
French	Biscuits	Cheese	Sliced cucumber
Italian	Corn muffins	Sliced cooked beef, ham, lamb,	Sliced green pepper
Onion	English muffins	pork, turkey or chicken	Lettuce leaves
Potato	Frankfurter buns	Tongue	Sliced olives
Pumpernickel	Hamburger buns	Assorted cold cuts	Sliced onion
Raisin	Hard rolls	Bacon	Sliced radishes
Rye		Canned luncheon meats	Sliced tomato
Vienna		Sliced hard-cooked eggs	Spinach leaves
White		Jelly	
Whole wheat		Peanut butter	
		Softened cream cheese	

EGG SALAD SANDWICH FILLING

    6 hard-cooked eggs, chopped
    1 medium stalk celery, chopped (about
         ½ cup)
    1 tablespoon finely chopped onion
    ⅓ cup mayonnaise or salad dressing
    ¼ teaspoon salt
       Dash of pepper

Mix all ingredients.   2 CUPS FILLING (ENOUGH FOR
6 SANDWICHES).

CRUNCHY COTTAGE CHEESE SANDWICHES

       Margarine or butter, softened
    6 slices rye bread
    1½ cups creamed cottage cheese
    1 small green pepper or 1 medium stalk
         celery, finely chopped (about ½ cup)
    1 dill pickle, finely chopped
    1 tablespoon snipped chives
    ⅛ teaspoon salt
    ¼ cup grated Parmesan cheese

Spread margarine over 1 side of each slice bread.
Mix cottage cheese, green pepper, pickle, chives
and salt. Spread over buttered sides of bread;
sprinkle with Parmesan cheese.   6 OPEN-FACE
SANDWICHES.

PUFFY CHEESE SLICES

    5 slices bread
    2 cups shredded Cheddar or mozzarella
         cheese (about 8 ounces)
    1 egg, slightly beaten
    ½ teaspoon dry mustard
    ½ teaspoon salt

Set oven control to broil and/or 550°. Broil bread 5
inches from heat until golden brown on 1 side;
turn. Blend cheese, egg, mustard and salt; spread
over untoasted sides of bread. Broil until cheese
bubbles. Serve with Pickle Fans or Radish Roses
(below) if desired.   5 OPEN-FACE SANDWICHES.

PICKLE FANS

Cut 4 lengthwise slits from one end of sweet or dill
pickle almost to the other end. Spread gently to
form an open fan.

RADISH ROSES

Remove stems and root ends from large radishes.
Cut thin petals around radishes. Chill in bowl of ice
and water until crisp and petals open.

CHILI-CHEESE SANDWICHES

    8 ounces Monterey Jack cheese, cut into
         16 slices
    8 slices rye bread
    4 tablespoons chili sauce
    1 can (4 ounces) green chilies, drained
    ¼ cup milk
    1 egg
    ¼ teaspoon ground cumin
    ¼ teaspoon salt
    1 tablespoon margarine or butter

Place 4 slices cheese on each of 4 slices bread;
spread each with 1 tablespoon chili sauce. Divide
chilies equally among sandwiches. Top with
remaining slices bread.

Beat milk, egg, cumin and salt with fork in 9-inch
pie plate until smooth. Dip both sides of sandwiches into egg mixture.

Heat margarine in 12-inch skillet until hot and
bubbly; reduce heat. Cover and cook sandwiches
over low heat 5 minutes; turn. Cover and cook until
cheese is melted and bread is light brown, about 5
minutes longer.   4 SANDWICHES.

CHEESE CLUB SANDWICH

Set oven control to broil and/or 550°. For each
sandwich, broil bread slice 5 inches from heat until
golden brown on 1 side; turn. Broil until golden
brown on second side. Spread second side with
margarine or butter. Top with tomato slice. Place 2
or 3 slices crisply fried bacon on tomato and top
with cheese slice. Broil until cheese is melted.

CHEESE-ZUCCHINI SANDWICH

    1 slice Italian bread, toasted
    1 slice provolone cheese, cut to fit bread
    ½ small zucchini, sliced
    1 thin slice Bermuda onion
       Dash of dried oregano leaves
    2 tablespoons shredded provolone cheese
    1 slice bacon, crisply fried and crumbled,
         or 1½ teaspoons imitation bacon
         (optional)

For each serving, top toast with cheese slice, zucchini and onion; sprinkle with oregano, shredded
cheese and bacon. Cook uncovered on ungreased
cookie sheet in 350° oven until cheese is melted,
about 5 minutes.

WELSH RABBIT

¼ cup margarine or butter
¼ cup all-purpose flour
½ teaspoon salt
¼ teaspoon pepper
¼ teaspoon dry mustard
¼ teaspoon Worcestershire sauce
1 cup milk
½ cup beer or medium white wine*
2 cups shredded Cheddar cheese (about
    8 ounces)
4 to 6 slices toast

Heat margarine in saucepan over low heat until melted. Blend in flour, salt, pepper, mustard and Worcestershire sauce. Cook over low heat, stirring constantly, until mixture is smooth and bubbly; remove from heat. Stir in milk. Heat to boiling, stirring constantly. Boil and stir 1 minute. Add beer gradually. Stir in cheese. Heat over low heat, stirring constantly, until cheese is melted. Serve over toast. Sprinkle with paprika if desired.
4 TO 6 SERVINGS.

*Beer or wine can be omitted; increase milk to 1½ cups.

CHEESE FONDUE

1 clove garlic, cut into halves
2 cups dry white wine
1 tablespoon lemon juice
2 tablespoons flour
4 cups shredded Swiss cheese* (about
    16 ounces)
3 tablespoons kirsch
    Salt and pepper
    French bread, cut into 1-inch cubes

Rub cut clove of garlic on bottom and side of earthenware fondue dish or heavy skillet. Add wine; heat over low heat until bubbles rise to surface (wine must not boil). Stir in lemon juice.

Sprinkle flour over cheese; toss until cheese is coated. Keeping fondue dish over low heat, add cheese, about ½ cup at a time, stirring constantly with wooden spoon, until cheese is melted.

Stir in kirsch, salt and pepper. Stir in nutmeg to taste if desired. Keep warm over low heat.

Use long-handled forks to spear bread cubes, then dip and swirl in fondue with stirring motion to keep fondue from sticking. If fondue becomes too thick, add a little heated wine.   4 TO 6 SERVINGS.

*The Swiss cheese should be natural (not process) and aged at least 6 months.

CHEESE-POTATO SOUP

3 medium potatoes, chopped (about 2 cups)
1 large onion, chopped (about 1 cup)
1½ cups water
2 teaspoons instant chicken bouillon
8 ounces process cheese spread loaf, cut up
¼ cup imitation bacon

Heat potatotes, onion, water and instant bouillon to boiling in 2-quart saucepan. Cover and cook until potatoes are tender, about 10 minutes. Place in blender container; add cheese. Cover and blend on high speed until uniform consistency. Sprinkle each serving with 1 tablespoon imitation bacon.
4 SERVINGS (ABOUT 1 CUP EACH).

CREAM OF CHEESE SOUP

3 green onions (with tops), thinly sliced
    (about 3 tablespoons)
1 medium stalk celery, thinly sliced (about
    ½ cup)
2 tablespoon margarine or butter
1¼ cups water
½ cup half-and-half
⅔ cup pasteurized process cheese spread
1 teaspoon instant chicken bouillon
⅛ teaspoon ground nutmeg
⅓ cup dry white wine
    Paprika

Cook and stir onions and celery in margarine in 3-quart saucepan over medium heat until onions are tender, about 8 minutes. Stir in water, half-and-half, cheese spread, instant bouillon and nutmeg. Heat to boiling over medium heat, stirring constantly; stir in wine. Heat to boiling. Boil and stir 1 minute. Sprinkle each serving with paprika and, if desired, garnish with croutons.   3 SERVINGS (ABOUT 1 CUP EACH).

CHEDDAR CHEESE CHOWDER

1 package (10 ounces) frozen mixed
    vegetables
1 can (10¾ ounces) condensed cream of
    chicken soup
1 soup can milk
1 cup shredded Cheddar cheese (about
    4 ounces)

Cook vegetables as directed on package; drain. Stir soup and milk into vegetables in saucepan. Heat, stirring occasionally, until hot. Sprinkle ⅓ cup cheese on each serving.   3 SERVINGS (ABOUT 1⅓ CUPS EACH).

DRIED BEANS

DRIED BEAN DISHES IN YOUR MENUS

Dried beans (and dried peas and lentils) are excellent sources of vegetable protein. Combine them with meats or dairy foods—the proteins fortify each other. Beans also supply iron, thiamin, riboflavin and niacin.

COOKING DRIED BEANS

Don't be afraid to substitute a similar bean if you can't find the kind indicated in the recipe. To prevent foaming during the first cooking, add a tablespoon of oil or shortening; for very hard water, add ⅛ to ¼ teaspoon baking soda for each cup of beans. Later, cook slowly over low heat; test for doneness by piercing a bean with a knife.

STORING DRIED BEANS

Dried beans can be stored in your kitchen in a tightly covered container 6 to 8 months; cooked dried beans can be refrigerated as long as 4 days or frozen as long as 3 months.

SPLIT PEAS

Split peas, like dried beans, are high in vegetable protein and their nutritional value is enhanced when they are combined with meats (most commonly in hearty soups). Soak them before cooking. They can be stored as you would dried beans.

LENTILS

Lentils are round like peas but disk shaped. While they also are high in vegetable protein, they don't need to be presoaked and cook faster than dried beans. Often cooked in soups, they are flavorful in casseroles and salads too. Available year-round. Store in the same manner as dried beans.

SOY BEANS

Dried soy beans contain 1½ as much protein as other beans. It is such high-quality protein that soy beans are often used for meat extenders. (See page 126 for information about textured protein derived from soy beans.) These beans, even after cooking, will be firmer than other dried beans. They can be stored in the same way as other beans.

BAKED BEANS

    4 cups water
    1 pound dried navy or pea beans (about 2 cups)
    1 medium onion, sliced
    ¼ pound salt pork (with rind), thinly sliced
    ¼ cup packed brown sugar
    3 tablespoons molasses
    1 teaspoon salt
    ¼ teaspoon dry mustard
    ⅛ teaspoon pepper

Heat water and beans to boiling in Dutch oven; boil 2 minutes. Remove from heat; cover and let stand 1 hour.

Add enough water to beans to cover if necessary. Heat to boiling; reduce heat. Cover and simmer until tender, 1 to 1½ hours (do not boil or beans will burst). Drain beans, reserving liquid.

Layer beans, onion and salt pork in ungreased 3- or 4-quart bean pot, casserole or Dutch oven. Mix brown sugar, molasses, salt, mustard, pepper and reserved bean liquid; pour over beans. Add enough water to almost cover beans. Cover and cook in 350° oven, stirring occasionally, 3 hours. Uncover and cook until beans are desired consistency, about 30 minutes.   6 SERVINGS.

Do-ahead Tip: Soak beans in 4 cups water overnight. Heat beans to boiling in same water; cover and simmer until tender, 1 to 2 hours. Drain beans, reserving liquid. Continue as directed.

Baked Soybeans: Substitute dried soybeans for the navy beans. After boiling 2 minutes, skim off loose bean skins. Cover and let stand 1 hour.

Boston Baked Beans: Decrease brown sugar to 2 tablespoons. Increase molasses to ½ cup and mustard to ¾ teaspoon.

QUICK CHEESY BEANS

Mix 1 can (20¾ ounces) pork and beans in tomato sauce, 1 cup shredded process sharp American cheese (about 4 ounces) and 1 small green pepper, chopped (about ½ cup), in ungreased 1-quart casserole. Cover and cook in 350° oven 30 minutes. Uncover and cook 15 minutes longer.   4 SERVINGS.

SKILLET BEANS

3 slices bacon, cut into 1-inch pieces
1 medium onion, chopped (about ½ cup)
2 cans (16 ounces each) pork and beans
¼ cup chili sauce
1 teaspoon prepared mustard

Cook and stir bacon and onion in 10-inch skillet until bacon is crisp. Stir in remaining ingredients. Heat to boiling; reduce heat. Simmer uncovered, stirring occasionally, until liquid is absorbed, 15 to 20 minutes.   4 SERVINGS.

TOMATOED BEANS

4 cups water
1 pound dried lima or Great Northern
      beans (about 2 cups)
2 teaspoons salt
2 tablespoons margarine or butter
¾ cup chopped onion
¾ cup chopped green pepper
1 clove garlic, finely chopped
1 can (6 ounces) tomato paste
½ cup chopped pitted ripe olives
¼ cup grated Parmesan cheese
2 to 3 teaspoons chili powder
1 teaspoon salt

Heat water and beans to boiling; boil 2 minutes. Remove from heat; cover and let stand 1 hour.

Add enough water to beans to cover if necessary. Add 2 teaspoons salt. Heat to boiling; reduce heat. Cover and simmer until tender, 45 to 60 minutes (do not boil or beans will burst). Drain beans, reserving liquid. Add enough water to bean liquid, if necessary, to measure 1 cup.

Heat margarine in 10-inch skillet until melted. Add onion, green pepper and garlic; cook and stir until onion is tender. Mix in beans, reserved bean liquid and the remaining ingredients. Pour into ungreased 2-quart casserole. Cook uncovered in 375° oven 30 minutes.   6 SERVINGS.

COUNTRY LIMAS

8 ounces dried lima or Great Northern
      beans (about 1 cup)
1 small onion, cut into ¼-inch slices
½ cup tomato juice
2 tablespoons light molasses
1 tablespoon packed brown sugar
1 tablespoon chili sauce
1 teaspoon salt
½ teaspoon dry mustard
2 tablespoons imitation bacon

Heat beans and enough water to cover to boiling; boil 2 minutes. Remove from heat; cover and let stand 1 hour.

Add enough water to beans to cover if necessary. Heat to boiling; reduce heat. Simmer uncovered until tender, about 30 minutes (do not boil or beans will burst). Drain beans, reserving liquid.

Layer beans and onion in ungreased 1½-quart casserole. Mix tomato juice, molasses, brown sugar, chili sauce, salt and mustard; pour over beans. Add enough reserved bean liquid to cover. Cover and cook in 300° oven 1 hour. Stir in imitation bacon.   7 SERVINGS.

TEXAS PINTO BEANS

4 cups water
1 pound dried pinto beans (about
      1¼ cups)
¼-pound salt pork (with rind)
2 teaspoons chili powder
¼ teaspoon red pepper sauce

Heat water and beans to boiling in 3-quart saucepan; boil 2 minutes. Remove from heat; cover and let stand 1 hour.

Stir in remaining ingredients. Heat to boiling; reduce heat. Cover and simmer until beans are tender, about 1½ hours (do not boil or beans will burst). Remove salt pork; slice and stir into beans.   6 SERVINGS.

Soybean Salad (page 126). Left to right in background: blackeye beans or peas; pinto beans (top), kidney beans (bottom); lentils; split peas (top), kidney beans (bottom); navy beans; garbanzo beans or chick peas; lima beans.

Clockwise from upper left: Northern Bean Soup, Split Pea Soup, Biscuit Sticks (page 194) and Lentil Soup

NORTHERN BEAN SOUP

    8 cups water
    1 pound dried Great Northern or lima
        beans (about 2 cups)
    1 can (8 ounces) tomato sauce
 2¼ pounds smoked pork hocks
    1 large onion, chopped (about 1 cup)
    1 tablespoon instant beef bouillon
    1 teaspoon salt
  ½ teaspoon pepper
    1 clove garlic, crushed
    2 cups Mashed Potatoes (page 185)
    2 medium carrots, cut into ½-inch pieces
    2 medium stalks celery, cut into ½-inch
        pieces (about 1 cup)

Heat water and beans to boiling in Dutch oven; boil 2 minutes. Remove from heat; cover and let stand 1 hour.

Add tomato sauce, pork hocks, onion, instant bouillon, salt, pepper and garlic to beans. Heat to boiling; reduce heat. Cover and simmer until beans are tender, about 2 hours (do not boil or beans will burst). Skim fat if necessary.

Remove pork hocks; trim fat and bone from pork. Cut pork into ½-inch pieces. Stir pork, potatoes, carrots and celery into soup. Heat to boiling; reduce heat. Cover and simmer until vegetables are tender, about 45 minutes. Stir in 1 to 2 cups milk or water for thinner consistency.   8 SERVINGS (ABOUT 1½ CUPS EACH).

NAVY BEAN SOUP

    7 cups water
    1 pound dried navy or pea beans (about
        2 cups)
    2 cups cubed cooked smoked ham
    1 ham bone
    1 small onion, finely chopped (about ¼ cup)
  ½ teaspoon salt
    1 bay leaf
      Dash of pepper

Heat water and beans to boiling in Dutch oven; boil 2 minutes. Remove from heat; cover and let stand 1 hour.

Stir in remaining ingredients. Heat to boiling; reduce heat. Cover and simmer, skimming off foam occasionally, until beans are tender, about 1¼ hours (do not boil or beans will burst). Add water during cooking if necessary.

Remove ham bone; trim ham from bone and stir into soup.   7 SERVINGS (ABOUT 1 CUP EACH).

SPLIT PEA SOUP

    8 cups water
    1 pound dried split peas (about 2¼ cups)
    2-pound smoked ham
    1 medium onion, chopped (about ½ cup)
    1 teaspoon salt
  ¼ teaspoon pepper
    2 medium carrots, cut into ½-inch pieces
        (about 1 cup)
    2 medium stalks celery, cut into ½-inch
        pieces (about 1 cup)

Heat water and peas to boiling in Dutch oven; boil 2 minutes. Remove from heat; cover and let stand 1 hour.

Stir ham, onion, salt and pepper into peas. Heat to boiling; reduce heat. Cover and simmer until peas are tender, about 1 hour. Skim fat if necessary.

Remove ham; trim fat and bone from ham. Cut ham into ½-inch pieces (about 4 cups). Stir ham, carrots and celery into soup. Heat to boiling; reduce heat. Cover and simmer until vegetables are tender, about 45 minutes.   8 SERVINGS (ABOUT 1½ CUPS EACH).

LENTIL SOUP

    3 slices bacon, cut into 2-inch pieces
    1 medium onion, sliced
    1 large carrot, sliced (about ¾ cup)
    1 large stalk celery, sliced (about ¾ cup)
    1 clove garlic, finely chopped
    4 cups water
  12 ounces dried lentils (about 2 cups)
    1 chicken bouillon cube
    2 tablespoons snipped parsley
    1 tablespoon salt
  ½ teaspoon pepper
  ¼ to ½ teaspoon dried thyme leaves
    1 bay leaf
    1 can (28 ounces) whole tomatoes
    1 cup water

Fry bacon in 3-quart saucepan or Dutch oven until limp; drain on paper towels. Add onion, carrot, celery and garlic to bacon fat; cook and stir over medium heat until celery is tender, about 10 minutes. Stir in bacon, 4 cups water, the lentils, bouillon cube, parsley, salt, pepper, thyme and bay leaf. Heat to boiling; reduce heat. Cover and simmer until soup thickens, about 1 hour.

Stir in tomatoes (with liquid) and 1 cup water. Simmer uncovered 15 minutes.   6 SERVINGS (ABOUT 1½ CUPS EACH).

BLACK BEAN SOUP

3 cups water
4 ounces dried black beans (about ½ cup)
1 ham bone or 1 pound ham shank or
    smoked pork hocks
1 medium carrot, sliced (about ½ cup)
1 medium stalk celery, chopped (about
    ½ cup)
1 medium onion, chopped (about ½ cup)
1 clove garlic, finely chopped
½ small dried hot pepper, crumbled
1 small bay leaf
½ teaspoon salt
3 lemon slices
3 hard-cooked eggs, shredded
2 tablespoons chopped red onion
    Dry white wine (optional)

Heat water and beans to boiling in 2-quart saucepan; boil 2 minutes. Remove from heat; cover and let stand 1 hour.

Add ham bone. Heat to boiling; reduce heat. Cover and simmer until beans are tender, about 2 hours (do not boil or beans will burst).

Stir in carrot, celery, ½ cup onion, the garlic, hot pepper, bay leaf and salt. Cover and simmer 1 hour.

Remove ham bone and bay leaf. (Soup can be pressed through food mill. Or place in blender container; cover and blend until uniform consistency.) Trim ham from bone and stir into soup. Serve with lemon slices, shredded eggs and chopped red onion. (The wine can be stirred into soup if desired.)   6 SERVINGS (ABOUT 1 CUP EACH).

ABOUT TEXTURED SOY PROTEIN

From the soy bean comes the highest quality vegetable protein (comparable to animal protein in helping with body growth and energy.) *Soy flour or grits* and *soy protein concentrate* (textured or powdered) are used commercially in baked goods, baby foods, candy, cereals and some sausages. *Isolated soy protein* (extracted) is used in sausages and cold cuts, whipped toppings, frozen desserts, dips, sauces, gravies and snacks. *Textured soy protein* (from the three products above) is used for meat extenders or substitutes, including imitation bacon. While soy foods will not replace meats, they provide protein in a variety of low-cost ways.

SOYBEAN SALAD

3 cups water
8 ounces dried soybeans (about 1¼ cups)
1 teaspoon salt
1 cup French Dressing (page 157)
2 tablespoons sugar
1 can (16 ounces) lima beans, drained, or
    1 package (10 ounces) frozen lima beans,
    cooked and drained
1 medium stalk celery, cut diagonally into slices
3 green onions, sliced (about ⅓ cup)
12 cherry tomatoes, each cut into fourths
¼ cup sliced pitted ripe olives (about 6)
    Lettuce leaves
1 tablespoon imitation bacon

Heat water and soybeans to boiling; boil 2 minutes. Remove from heat; cover and let stand 1 hour.

Stir salt into soybeans. Heat to boiling; reduce heat. Cover and simmer until tender, 2 to 3 hours. (Add water during cooking if necessary.)

Drain beans; cool. Prepare French Dressing; stir in sugar. Mix soybeans, lima beans, celery, onions, tomatoes and olives; stir in dressing. Cover and refrigerate at least 2 hours.

Remove bean mixture to lettuce-lined salad bowl with slotted spoon. Sprinkle with imitation bacon.
6 SERVINGS.

BEAN AND EGG SALAD

½ cup mayonnaise or salad dressing
3 tablespoons shredded Cheddar cheese
1 tablespoon prepared mustard
    Few drops Worcestershire sauce
1 can (15 ounces) kidney beans or 1 can
    (16 ounces) garbanzo beans, drained
1 small stalk celery, chopped (about ¼ cup)
2 hard-cooked eggs, sliced
3 dill or sweet pickles, chopped
1 small onion, finely chopped (about ¼ cup)
½ teaspoon salt
⅛ teaspoon pepper
2 hard-cooked eggs, each cut into fourths
½ cup shredded Cheddar cheese
    Salad greens

Mix mayonnaise, 3 tablespoons cheese, the mustard and Worcestershire sauce. Cover and refrigerate until chilled.

Mix beans, celery, sliced eggs, pickles, onion, salt and pepper; stir in mayonnaise mixture. Garnish with quartered eggs and ½ cup cheese. Serve on salad greens.   4 SERVINGS.

FREEZER DINNERS

A piping hot dinner from freezer to oven to table in 25 to 35 minutes! Use leftover cooked meats and gravy and frozen, canned or left-over vegetables —include a surprise to make your dinner special.

PREPARING, STORING AND HEATING

Save foil trays from commercially frozen dinners. Or use foil broiler pans, cake or pie pans; shape divider compartments of foil to place in these pans. Fill trays, cover tightly with foil, label and freeze no longer than 3 weeks.

When ready to serve, heat oven to 450°. Heat frozen dinners in foil-covered commercial foil pans 25 minutes, in foil-covered homemade foil pans 35 minutes. (When heating two or more dinners in same oven, allow 5 minutes longer.) When the dinner includes French-fried or mashed potatoes, fold back foil to expose potatoes. Just before serving, stir gravy; spoon gravy onto meat and sprinkle with salt. (Meats lose some flavor after freezing.)

INDIVIDUAL PORTIONS

Meat: 2 or 3 ounces with ⅓ to ½ cup gravy (below) or ½ cup meat juices. (Meat frozen without a gravy or sauce is dry and tastes reheated.)

Potatoes or Rice: ½ cup Mashed Potatoes (page 128) with 1 teaspoon margarine or butter; ½ cup frozen French-fried potatoes or instant mashed potatoes; Instant Rice (page 128).

Vegetables: ½ cup uncooked frozen vegetables (mixed vegetables, corn, peas or green beans) with ½ teaspoon margarine or butter; ½ cup frozen carrots with 2 tablespoons water; ⅓ to ½ cup canned or leftover vegetables with 2 tablespoons liquid and ½ teaspoon margarine or butter.

Gravies: Add ½ cup water to 1 cup Pan Gravy (page 10) or Kettle Gravy (page 12); add ¾ cup water to 1 can (10¾ ounces) gravy; add 1½ cups water to 1 packet (1¼ ounces) gravy mix. (Gravies for frozen dinners must be thinner than other gravies.)

Accompaniments: 2 to 3 tablespoons cranberry sauce, mint jelly, chutney, fruit pie filling with a dash of ground cinnamon (place in separate compartment); Cherry Sauce or Mustard Sauce (page 128).

Shape foil dividers for trays.

Expose fried potatoes to brown.

Freezer Dinners

FREEZER DINNER MENUS

Roast Beef with Gravy
Sliced Peaches or Peach Pie
  Filling with Cinnamon
Twice-baked Potatoes
Buttered Peas

Baked Ham with Cherry
  Sauce
Shredded Potato Rounds
Buttered Asparagus
Buttered Carrots
French Puff

Meat Loaf Slices with Gravy
Buttered Mashed Potatoes
Buttered Carrots
Orange Muffin

Roast Lamb with Gravy
Chutney or Mint Jelly
Curried Instant Rice
Buttered Mixed Vegetables

Roast Veal with Gravy
Buttered Green Beans
Mustard Sauce
French-fried Potatoes

Roast Pork with Gravy
Spiced Crab Apple
Buttered Corn
Buttered Broccoli Spears
Chocolate Pudding

Roast Turkey with Gravy
Cranberry Sauce
Buttered Sweet Potatoes
Buttered Green Beans
Blueberry Muffin

FREEZER DINNER RECIPES

MASHED POTATOES

Prepare Mashed Potatoes as directed on page 185; cool. Or prepare instant mashed potatoes as directed on package for desired number of servings except—increase milk by 1 tablespoon for each serving; cool.

INSTANT RICE

 3 tablespoons uncooked instant rice
¼ cup water
½ teaspoon margarine or butter
⅛ teaspoon salt
  Dash of curry powder (optional)

Place all ingredients in foil pan; freeze. When cooking frozen dinner, cover rice with foil. 1 SERVING.

CHERRY SAUCE

Mix ½ cup cherry pie filling, ¼ cup water and 1 teaspoon lemon juice; pour on ham.   ENOUGH SAUCE FOR 2 FREEZER DINNERS.

MUSTARD SAUCE

 1 tablespoon margarine or butter
 1 tablespoon flour
½ teaspoon salt
¼ teaspoon pepper
 1 cup milk
 3 tablespoons prepared mustard
 1 tablespoon prepared horseradish

Heat margarine over low heat until melted. Blend in flour, salt and pepper. Cook over low heat, stirring constantly, until smooth and bubbly; remove from heat. Stir in milk. Heat to boiling, stirring constantly. Boil and stir 1 minute. Stir in mustard and horseradish. Heat until hot; cool. Pour on beef, veal or ham.   ENOUGH SAUCE FOR 6 FREEZER DINNERS.

SUBSTITUTIONS

If you are using large trays, you may have space to add some special treats or you may want to substitute them for meat accompaniments or potatoes. For a change of pace, try baked muffins or ⅓ to ½ cup chocolate or vanilla pudding.

Pictured opposite: Chive-buttered Carrots (page 172), Caesar Salad (page 131), Broccoli-Tomato Salad (page 142) and Italian Cabbage Wedges (page 170)

SALADS
AND VEGETABLES

SALADS

Tossed Salads

Salads add color and texture to meals and, more importantly, are an easy, natural way to include the four servings of fruits and vegetables (rich in vitamins A and C) that are needed for a day's good nutrition (see page 353.) Greens have some vitamin A—the darker the green, the higher the content.

ABOUT SALAD GREENS

Four main groups of the many varieties of lettuce are commonly available. *Crisphead* (notably *iceberg*) is so popular that other varieties are sometimes overlooked: *butterhead*, including *Boston* and *Bibb*, with its tender leaves; *romaine* (also called *cos*), with crisp, elongated dark leaves; and *leaf lettuce*, red or green, with tender "leafy" leaves that don't form heads. The *endive* family includes *curly endive* (sometimes miscalled chicory), a frilly, narrow-leaved, bushy plant; *escarole*, a less frilly, broader-leaved variety; and *Belgian* or *French endive*, with narrow, blanched leaves in tight upright clusters.

Of the hundreds of green cousins, look for watercress, parsley, fresh beet and mustard tops, Chinese cabbage, even dandelion and nasturtium leaves! Always choose crisp, tender greens.

STORING SALAD GREENS

Greens belong in the refrigerator as fast as you can get them there, usually in a covered container, a plastic bag or the crisper section. However, watercress, parsley and fresh herbs should be refrigerated in large screwtop jars. These, as well as romaine and iceberg lettuce, will keep up to a week. Most other greens will droop within a few days.

Wash greens several hours before using—they need time to crisp. Wash thoroughly under running cold water, then shake off the excess moisture. Toss in a cloth towel or blot dry with paper towels to remove the remaining moisture; refrigerate.

If you're going to use iceberg lettuce within a day or so, remove the core before washing. Strike the core end against a flat surface, then twist and lift out core. Hold the head, cored end up, under running cold water to separate and clean leaves. Turn right side up and drain thoroughly. Refrigerate in a plastic bag or bowl with an airtight lid.

SERVING SALAD GREENS

Mix dark greens with light, crisp with tender and straight with curly. Team pale iceberg lettuce with dark green spinach, romaine and/or curly endive. Bronze lettuce provides color and delicate flavor. Beet greens and red cabbage add color accents too. Fresh herbs and other salad "sparkers" perk up the simplest combinations.

Tear—do not cut—salad greens into bite-size pieces. (Exceptions are shredded lettuce, cut wedges of iceberg lettuce and lengthwise quarters or pulled-off leaves of Belgian endive.) With the easily bruised butterheads, use the small inner whole leaves for the salad; save the outer ones for lettuce "beds."

Dry any leftover moisture you find in the crevices; the drier the greens the better. Pour on the dressing just before serving. Use only enough to coat the ingredients lightly, then toss.

Romaine

Boston lettuce

Curly endive

Belgian endive

Escarole

Red leaf (bronze) lettuce

TOSSED SALAD CHART
(for 6 to 8 servings)

Basic Greens	Add Salad Sparkers		Toss with	Garnish with
Choose one or more to total 12 cups	*Choose one or more to total 1½ cups*		*Shake to mix*	*Choose one or two to total ⅓ to ½ cup*
Iceberg lettuce	Fresh vegetables:	Cooked vegetables:	¼ cup vegetable	French-fried onions
Boston lettuce	Alfalfa sprouts	Artichoke bottoms	or olive oil or	Croutons
Bibb lettuce	Asparagus,	or hearts, plain	combination	Bacon, crisply fried,
Bronze lettuce	diagonally	or marinated	2 tablespoons	crumbled
Leaf lettuce	sliced	Dill green beans	cider, wine or	Hard-cooked eggs,
Romaine	Carrots, thinly	Green peas, beans	tarragon vinegar	sliced
Escarole	sliced	or sliced carrots,	¾ teaspoon salt	Salted nuts
Spinach	Cauliflowerets	marinated	⅛ to ¼ teaspoon	Blue cheese,
Watercress	Cucumbers, sliced		pepper	crumbled
Endive (French	Green peppers,	Meat and fish:	1 small clove	Toasted wheat
or Belgian)	diced or sliced	Turkey or chicken,	garlic, crushed	germ
Curly endive	Mushrooms, sliced	ham, tongue,		Sunflower nuts
	Onions, sliced or	cold cuts, cut into		Olives, sliced
	diced	¼-inch strips or		
	Radishes, sliced	cubes		
	Tomatoes, cut into	Shrimp, crabmeat		
	wedges	or lobster, cut up		
	Zucchini, sliced			
		Cheese:		
	Fruit:	Swiss or Cheddar,		
	Apple wedges	cut into ¼-inch		
	Avocados, sliced	strips or cubes		
	Orange sections			

CAESAR SALAD

Baked Croutons (right)
Coddled Egg (right)
1 clove garlic, cut into halves
8 anchovy fillets, cut up
⅓ cup olive oil
1 teaspoon Worcestershire sauce
½ teaspoon salt
¼ teaspoon dry mustard
Freshly ground pepper
1 large or 2 small bunches romaine, torn into bite-size pieces
1 lemon, cut into halves
⅓ cup grated Parmesan cheese

Prepare Baked Croutons and Coddled Egg. Rub large wooden salad bowl with cut clove of garlic. Allow a few small pieces of garlic to remain in bowl if desired. Mix anchovies, oil, Worcestershire sauce, salt, mustard and pepper in bowl; toss with romaine until leaves glisten. Break egg onto salad. Squeeze lemon over salad; toss. Sprinkle croutons and cheese over salad; toss. 6 SERVINGS.

BAKED CROUTONS
Trim crusts from 4 slices white bread. Butter both sides of bread slices generously; sprinkle with ¼ teaspoon garlic powder. Cut into ½-inch cubes. Bake in 400° oven on ungreased cookie sheet, stirring occasionally, until golden brown and crisp, 10 to 15 minutes.

CODDLED EGG
Place cold egg in warm water. Heat enough water to boiling to cover egg completely. Immerse egg in boiling water with spoon; remove from heat. Cover and let stand 30 seconds. Immediately cool egg in cold water to prevent further cooking; refrigerate.

OLYMPIAN SALAD

- ½ medium head lettuce, torn into bite-size pieces
- 1 small bunch romaine, torn into bite-size pieces
- 8 radishes, sliced
- 1 medium cucumber, sliced
- 4 scallions, cut into short pieces
    Oregano Dressing (below)
- 18 pitted ripe olives
- ¼ cup crumbled blue or feta cheese
- 1 can (2 ounces) rolled anchovies with capers, drained

Place lettuce, romaine, radishes, cucumber and scallions in large plastic bag; close bag and refrigerate. Prepare Oregano Dressing.

Just before serving, shake dressing. Add olives and dressing to vegetables in bag. Close bag tightly and shake until ingredients are well coated. Pour salad into large bowl; top with cheese and anchovies.
6 SERVINGS.

OREGANO DRESSING

- ½ cup vegetable oil
- ⅓ cup wine vinegar
- 1½ teaspoons salt
- 1½ teaspoons dried oregano leaves

Shake all ingredients in tightly covered jar; refrigerate.

SPINACH-BEAN SPROUT SALAD

- 8 ounces spinach or curly endive, torn into bite-size pieces
- 1 can (16 ounces) bean sprouts, drained
- 1 can (8 ounces) water chestnuts, drained and sliced
    Sesame Dressing (below)
- 1 cup croutons (optional)

Toss spinach, bean sprouts, water chestnuts and Sesame Dressing. Sprinkle with croutons.
6 SERVINGS.

SESAME DRESSING

- ¼ cup soy sauce
- 2 tablespoons toasted sesame seed
- 2 tablespoons lemon juice
- 1 tablespoon finely chopped onion
- ½ teaspoon sugar
- ¼ teaspoon pepper

Mix all ingredients.

TANGY MUSHROOM SALAD

For each serving, tear Bibb or Boston lettuce into bite-size pieces (¾ cup). Add ¼ cup sliced fresh mushrooms and 1 to 2 tablespoons Cocktail Sauce (below); toss.

COCKTAIL SAUCE

- 1 bottle (12 ounces) chili sauce
- 1 tablespoon prepared horseradish
- 1 tablespoon lemon juice
- ½ teaspoon Worcestershire sauce
- ¼ teaspoon salt
    Dash of pepper

Mix all ingredients. Cover and refrigerate any leftover sauce.

Tangy Shrimp Appetizer Salad: Add ¼ cup cleaned cooked shrimp with the mushrooms.

FLORENTINE SALAD

- 1 clove garlic, slivered
- ⅓ cup vegetable oil
- ¼ cup wine vinegar
- ¼ teaspoon salt
    Dash of pepper
- 12 ounces spinach, torn into bite-size pieces
- 1 hard-cooked egg, chopped
- 2 slices bacon, crisply fried and crumbled

Let garlic stand in oil 1 hour; discard garlic. Mix oil, vinegar, salt and pepper in salad bowl. Add spinach; toss until leaves are well coated. Sprinkle with egg and bacon; toss.   3 SERVINGS.

Hot Florentine Salad: Prepare as directed except —heat oil, vinegar, salt and pepper in chafing dish or saucepan over low heat, stirring constantly, until hot.

MUSHROOM-SPINACH TOSS

- 2 tablespoons tarragon or wine vinegar
- ¾ teaspoon salt
- 1 small clove garlic, crushed
    Generous dash of freshly ground pepper
- 8 ounces mushrooms, sliced (about 3 cups)
- 16 ounces spinach, torn into bite-size pieces
- ¼ cup vegetable oil

Mix vinegar, salt, garlic and pepper; toss with mushrooms and let stand 15 minutes. Toss spinach and oil until leaves glisten. Toss mushroom mixture with spinach.   4 TO 6 SERVINGS.

Zucchini Toss

ZUCCHINI TOSS

1 small bunch romaine, torn into pieces
2 tablespoons olive or vegetable oil
1 medium zucchini, thinly sliced
½ cup sliced radishes
3 green onions, sliced (about 3 tablespoons)
2 tablespoons crumbled blue cheese
1 tablespoon tarragon or wine vinegar
½ teaspoon salt
1 small clove garlic, crushed
¼ teaspoon monosodium glutamate
   Dash of freshly ground pepper

Toss romaine and oil until leaves glisten. Add remaining ingredients; toss.   8 SERVINGS.

SPINACH-APPLE-BACON TOSS

8 ounces spinach, torn into bite-size pieces
4 slices bacon, crisply fried and crumbled
1 red apple, sliced
⅓ cup mayonnaise or salad dressing
3 tablespoons frozen orange juice
   concentrate, thawed

Toss spinach, bacon and apple. Mix mayonnaise and orange juice concentrate; serve with salad.
6 SERVINGS.

MEDITERRANEAN SALAD BOWL

1 small eggplant (about 1 pound), cut into
   cubes
   Sour Cream-Lemon Dressing (below)
1 cup croutons
2 tablespoons margarine or butter, melted
4 cups bite-size pieces salad greens

Heat 1 inch salted water (½ teaspoon salt to 1 cup water) to boiling. Add eggplant. Heat to boiling; reduce heat. Cover and cook just until tender, about 5 minutes; drain completely. Refrigerate until chilled. Prepare Sour Cream-Lemon Dressing. Toss croutons with margarine.

Just before serving, toss eggplant with salad greens, dressing and croutons. Garnish with pitted ripe olives if desired.   5 OR 6 SERVINGS.

SOUR CREAM-LEMON DRESSING

½ cup dairy sour cream
1 tablespoon lemon juice
1 tablespoon snipped parsley
½ teaspoon salt
½ teaspoon dried dill weed
¼ teaspoon coarsely ground pepper
1 small clove garlic, crushed

Mix all ingredients; cover and refrigerate until chilled.

Stir cooled almonds to separate.

Add almonds to salad in bag.   Mandarin Salad

MANDARIN SALAD

¼ cup sliced almonds
1 tablespoon plus 1 teaspoon sugar
¼ head lettuce, torn into bite-size pieces
¼ bunch romaine, torn into bite-size pieces
2 medium stalks celery, chopped (about
    1 cup)
2 green onions (with tops), thinly sliced
    (about 2 tablespoons)
    Sweet-Sour Dressing (right)
1 can (11 ounces) mandarin orange
    segments, drained

Cook almonds and sugar over low heat, stirring constantly, until sugar is melted and almonds are coated. Cool and break apart. Store at room temperature.

Place lettuce and romaine in plastic bag; add celery and onions. Pour Sweet-Sour Dressing into bag; add orange segments. Close bag tightly and shake until salad greens and orange segments are well coated. Add almonds and shake.   4 TO 6 SERVINGS.

SWEET-SOUR DRESSING
¼ cup vegetable oil
2 tablespoons sugar
2 tablespoons vinegar
1 tablespoon snipped parsley
½ teaspoon salt
    Dash of pepper
    Dash of red pepper sauce

Shake all ingredients in tightly covered jar; refrigerate.

Do-ahead Tip: Before dressing is added, bag of salad greens can be closed tightly and refrigerated no longer than 24 hours.

Pineapple Salad: Substitute 1 can (13¼ ounces) pineapple chunks, drained, for the mandarin orange segments and snipped mint leaves for the parsley.

TOSSED AVOCADO SALAD

Tear 1 small head lettuce into bite-size pieces. Cut 1 small avocado lengthwise into halves; cut halves crosswise into slices. Toss lettuce and avocado with ½ cup Lorenzo Dressing (page 157).   5 SERVINGS.

Tossed Avocado-Apple Salad: Add 1 red apple, sliced.

Tossed Avocado-Grapefruit Salad: Add 1 can (8½ ounces) grapefruit sections, drained, or 1 medium grapefruit, pared and sectioned.

Tossed Avocado-Radish Salad: Add ½ cup sliced radishes.

Tossed Cauliflower Salad: Substitute ¼ small cauliflower, separated into flowerets (about 1 cup), for the avocado.

Tossed Cucumber Salad: Substitute 1 small cucumber, diced (about 1 cup), for the avocado.

Tossed Vegetable Salad: Substitute 1 cup cooked vegetables (green beans, lima beans, peas or mixed vegetables) for the avocado.

Tossed Zucchini Salad: Substitute 1 small zucchini, sliced, for the avocado.

EASY-DO SALAD

    1 large head lettuce, torn into bite-size pieces
    4 ounces spinach, torn into bite-size pieces
    ½ cup pitted ripe olives
    1 jar (about 7 ounces) marinated artichoke
        hearts
    ½ cup Herb Dressing or Tomato Dressing
        (page 157)

Place lettuce and spinach in large plastic bag; refrigerate. Just before serving, add artichoke hearts (with liquid) and Herb Dressing to bag. Close bag tightly and shake vigorously. Serve in large bowl. 6 SERVINGS.

SWEET-SOUR LETTUCE

    ½ cup half-and-half
    3 to 4 tablespoons vinegar
      About 1 tablespoon sugar
    ¼ teaspoon salt
    2 bunches leaf lettuce, torn into bite-size
        pieces

Mix half-and-half, vinegar, sugar and salt in salad bowl. Add lettuce; toss.   5 OR 6 SERVINGS.

WILTED LETTUCE SALAD

    4 slices bacon, diced
    ¼ cup vinegar
    2 bunches leaf lettuce, shredded
    5 green onions (with tops), chopped
        (about ⅓ cup)
    2 teaspoons sugar
    ¼ teaspoon salt
    ⅛ teaspoon pepper

Fry bacon in 12-inch skillet until crisp. Add vinegar; heat through. Remove from heat; add lettuce and onions. Sprinkle with sugar, salt and pepper; toss until lettuce is wilted, 1 to 2 minutes. 4 SERVINGS.

Dill Wilted Lettuce Salad: Stir ½ teaspoon dried dill weed and ½ teaspoon dry mustard into vinegar.

BACON-CAULIFLOWER TOSS

    ½ medium bunch romaine, torn into
        bite-size pieces
    8 slices bacon, crisply fried and crumbled
    ½ small head cauliflower, broken into tiny
        flowerets (about 2 cups)
    ¼ cup sliced radishes
    ¼ cup mayonnaise or salad dressing
    ¼ cup dairy sour cream
    2 green onions, sliced (about 2 tablespoons)
    ¼ teaspoon dried dill weed
      Freshly ground pepper

Layer half each of the romaine, bacon and cauliflower in glass salad bowl. Top with radishes and the remaining romaine, bacon and cauliflower.

Mix mayonnaise, sour cream and onions; drop by spoonfuls onto cauliflower. Sprinkle with dill weed and pepper. Cover and refrigerate at least 2 hours. Just before serving, toss.   4 SERVINGS.

CAULIFLOWER-ORANGE SALADS

    2 cans (11 ounces each) mandarin orange
        segments, drained
    ½ small cauliflower, separated into flowerets
        (about 2 cups)
    ½ small green pepper, chopped (about ¼ cup)
    2 ounces spinach, torn into bite-size pieces
    ¼ cup Sweet French Dressing (page 157)
      Lettuce cups

Toss orange segments, cauliflowerets, green pepper, spinach and Sweet French Dressing. Serve in lettuce cups.   5 OR 6 SERVINGS.

GOURMET TOSSED GREEN SALAD

½ small head lettuce, torn into bite-size pieces
3 ounces mushrooms, sliced (about 1 cup)
½ small cauliflower, separated into tiny
    flowerets (about 2 cups)
½ small Bermuda onion, thinly sliced and
    separated into rings
½ medium green pepper, diced (about ⅓ cup)
¼ cup sliced pimiento-stuffed olives
¼ cup crumbled blue cheese
    Gourmet French Dressing (below)

Toss all ingredients except Gourmet French
Dressing. Cover and refrigerate until chilled, at
least 1 hour. Just before serving, toss with dressing
as directed below.   6 SERVINGS.

GOURMET FRENCH DRESSING

2 tablespoons olive or vegetable oil or
    combination
1 tablespoon tarragon or wine vinegar
1 small clove garlic, crushed
½ teaspoon salt
    Dash of monosodium glutamate
    Generous dash of freshly ground pepper

Toss salad with oil until leaves glisten. Mix remaining ingredients; pour over salad and toss.

CRUNCHY NOODLE SALAD

    Oil and Vinegar Dressing (below)
2 tablespoons margarine or butter
½ teaspoon garlic powder
2 cups chow mein noodles
2 tablespoons grated Romano cheese
1 small bunch romaine, torn into pieces
2 green onions, sliced (about 2 tablespoons)

Prepare Oil and Vinegar Dressing. Heat margarine
in square pan, 9x9x2 inches, in 200° oven until
melted; sprinkle with garlic powder. Stir in noodles
gently until coated with margarine mixture; sprinkle with cheese. Bake uncovered 20 minutes.

Toss hot noodles, romaine and onions with
dressing.   4 SERVINGS.

OIL AND VINEGAR DRESSING

2 tablespoons vegetable oil
1 tablespoon tarragon or wine vinegar
¼ teaspoon salt
⅛ teaspoon monosodium glutamate
    Dash of freshly ground pepper

Shake all ingredients in tightly covered jar; refrigerate. Shake before serving.

SWISS SALAD

2 cups bite-size pieces salad greens
½ cup shredded Swiss cheese (about
    2 ounces)
2 tablespoons sliced pimiento-stuffed olives
1 hard-cooked egg, chopped
    Creamy Mustard Dressing (below)

Mix salad greens, cheese, olives and egg; toss with
Creamy Mustard Dressing. Garnish with tomato
wedges if desired.   3 OR 4 SERVINGS.

CREAMY MUSTARD DRESSING

¼ cup mayonnaise or salad dressing
1 tablespoon half-and-half
½ teaspoon dry mustard
¼ teaspoon salt
⅛ teaspoon pepper

Mix all ingredients.

TOSSED SALAD COMBOS

*Crisp, refreshing combos. Toss with your favorite dressing,
Creamy Onion Dressing (page 158) or Italian Dressing
(page 157).*

□ Romaine, iceberg lettuce, tomato wedges, ripe
olives, anchovies, crumbled blue or feta cheese

□ Leaf lettuce, escarole, avocado wedges, mushrooms, chopped salted peanuts, a sprinkle of curry
powder

□ Iceberg lettuce, curly endive, tomato wedges,
marinated artichoke hearts, zucchini, a sprinkle of
grated Parmesan cheese

□ Leaf lettuce, radishes, cucumber, carrots (cut into
diagonal slices), cauliflowerets, green onions

□ Iceberg lettuce chunks (line bowl with bright
outer leaves), onion rings, ripe olives, corn chips,
pickled red chili peppers

□ Spinach leaves, sliced hard-cooked egg, ¼-inch
strips of Swiss cheese, onion rings, imitation bacon

□ Romaine, beets (or any cooked vegetable), red
onion rings, sour cream, black or red caviar

□ Boston or Bibb lettuce, drained canned mandarin
orange segments, sliced water chestnuts

□ Spinach leaves, iceberg lettuce, cauliflowerets,
pimiento-stuffed olives, cherry tomatoes, green
pepper rings

Vegetable Salads

Versatile, health-packed vegetables: How could anyone ever find them dull when they're seasoned, dressed and served up as a zestful salad?

BACON-AND-EGG BEAN SALADS

2 cans (16 ounces each) whole green beans, drained
1 medium onion, chopped (about ½ cup)
⅓ cup vegetable oil
¼ cup vinegar
½ teaspoon salt
¼ teaspoon pepper
4 hard-cooked eggs, chopped
¼ cup mayonnaise or salad dressing
2 teaspoons vinegar
1 teaspoon prepared mustard
¼ teaspoon salt
4 slices bacon, crisply fried and crumbled
   Lettuce leaves
   Paprika

Toss beans, onion, oil, ¼ cup vinegar, ½ teaspoon salt and the pepper. Cover and refrigerate. Mix eggs, mayonnaise, 2 teaspoons vinegar, the mustard and ¼ teaspoon salt. Cover and refrigerate.

Just before serving, drain bean mixture. Add bacon; toss. Arrange lettuce on salad plates. Top each serving with spoonful of beans and scoop of egg mixture; sprinkle with paprika.   6 SERVINGS.

GARBANZO-KIDNEY BEAN SALAD

1 can (20 ounces) white kidney beans, drained
1 can (15 ounces) red kidney beans, drained
1 can (15 ounces) garbanzo beans, drained
3 medium tomatoes, diced (about 1½ cups)
1 hot pepper, seeded and finely chopped
1 medium red or sweet white onion, chopped (about ¾ cup)
½ large green or red pepper, chopped
5 green onions, sliced (about ⅓ cup)
1 cup Garlic French Dressing (page 157)
½ teaspoon salt
2 or 3 drops red pepper sauce
   Lettuce leaves

Mix all ingredients except lettuce. Cover and refrigerate, stirring occasionally, at least 3 hours.

Just before serving, remove salad to lettuce-lined salad bowl with slotted spoon.   10 TO 12 SERVINGS.

BEAN BONANZA

½ cup vinegar
½ cup vegetable oil
⅓ cup sugar
1 teaspoon salt
¼ teaspoon pepper
1 can (16 ounces) cut green beans, drained
1 can (15 ounces) kidney beans or garbanzo beans, drained
1 small green pepper, finely chopped
1 small onion, finely chopped (about ¼ cup)

Mix vinegar, oil, sugar, salt and pepper; mix in beans, green pepper and onion. Cover and refrigerate at least 8 hours. Just before serving, remove to salad bowl with slotted spoon.   4 TO 6 SERVINGS.

THREE-BEAN SALAD

1 can (16 ounces) green beans, drained
1 can (16 ounces) wax beans, drained
1 can (15 ounces) kidney beans, drained
4 green onions, chopped (about ¼ cup)
¼ cup snipped parsley
1 cup Italian Dressing (page 157)
1 tablespoon sugar
2 cloves garlic, crushed
   Lettuce leaves

Mix beans, onions and parsley in large bowl. Mix Italian Dressing, sugar and garlic; pour over salad and toss. Cover and refrigerate, stirring occasionally, at least 3 hours.

Just before serving, remove to lettuce-lined salad bowl with slotted spoon.   5 OR 6 SERVINGS.

Cauliflower-Bean Salad: Omit wax beans. Mix in ½ small head cauliflower, coarsely chopped (about 2 cups), with the kidney beans and ½ teaspoon dry mustard with the dressing.

Crunchy Three-Bean Salad: Just before serving, stir in ¼ cup imitation bacon.

BRIGHT BEAN SALAD

1 medium carrot, finely chopped
1 can (16 ounces) French-style green beans, drained, or 1 package (9 ounces) frozen green beans, cooked and drained
2 tablespoons chopped onion
⅛ teaspoon salt
3 tablespoons Herb Dressing (page 157)

Mix all ingredients. Cover and refrigerate at least 4 hours.   4 SERVINGS.

COLESLAW

¼ cup dairy sour cream
2 tablespoons mayonnaise or salad dressing
¼ teaspoon seasoned salt
¼ teaspoon dry mustard
  Dash of pepper
¼ medium head green cabbage, finely
    chopped or shredded (about 2 cups)
½ small onion, chopped (about 2 tablespoons)
  Paprika or dried dill weed

Mix sour cream, mayonnaise, seasoned salt, mustard and pepper; toss with cabbage and onion. Sprinkle with paprika.   ABOUT 4 SERVINGS.

NOTE: To chop cabbage and onion in blender, cut cabbage into 2-inch pieces and onion into halves. Place cabbage and onion in blender container; add enough water to cover. Cover and blend on high speed until desired size; drain completely.

Apple-Cheese Coleslaw: Omit mustard, pepper and onion. Toss 1 tart apple, chopped, and ¼ cup crumbled blue cheese with the cabbage.

Green Pea Coleslaw: Rinse 1 package (10 ounces) frozen green peas under running cold water to separate; drain. Sprinkle peas with ¼ teaspoon salt; toss with the cabbage.

Herbed Coleslaw: Omit mustard and pepper; mix in ½ teaspoon celery seed and ¼ teaspoon dried chervil leaves.

Pineapple-Marshmallow Coleslaw: Omit onion; toss 1 can (8¼ ounces) pineapple chunks, drained, ½ cup miniature marshmallows and 1½ teaspoons lemon juice with the cabbage.

Red Cabbage Coleslaw: Substitute 1 cup red cabbage for 1 cup of the green cabbage.

OLD-FASHIONED CABBAGE SALAD

½ medium head green cabbage, finely
    shredded or chopped (about 4 cups)
⅓ cup white vinegar
½ small green pepper, chopped (about ¼ cup)
3 tablespoons vegetable oil
2 tablespoons sugar
1 tablespoon chopped pimiento
1 teaspoon instant minced onion
1 teaspoon salt
½ teaspoon celery seed
½ teaspoon dry mustard
¼ teaspoon pepper

Mix all ingredients. Cover and refrigerate 3 hours. Just before serving, drain salad.   6 SERVINGS.

SAUERKRAUT SLAW

1 can (16 ounces) sauerkraut, drained
2 medium stalks celery, cut diagonally into
    slices (about 1 cup)
1 small green pepper, cut into strips
1 medium onion, chopped (about ½ cup)
¼ cup sugar
⅓ cup dairy sour cream or ¼ cup
    half-and-half
½ teaspoon celery seed

Chop sauerkraut into short pieces. Mix in remaining ingredients. Cover and refrigerate, stirring occasionally, at least 24 hours.   8 SERVINGS.

CARROT-RAISIN SALADS

3 to 4 medium carrots, finely shredded
    (about 2 cups)
⅓ cup raisins
1 tablespoon snipped chives
¼ teaspoon salt
  Cooked Salad Dressing (page 158)
  Lettuce cups

Mix carrots, raisins, chives and salt. Add just enough Cooked Salad Dressing to moisten; toss. Spoon into lettuce cups.   4 OR 5 SERVINGS.

NOTE: To chop carrots in blender, cut into ½-inch slices. Place half of the carrot slices in blender container; add just enough water to cover. Cover and blend on high speed just until carrots are finely chopped, 3 to 5 seconds; drain completely. Repeat.

RED AND GREEN SALAD

2 packages (10 ounces each) frozen
    Brussels sprouts
¼ cup vinegar
¼ cup vegetable oil
1½ teaspoons dried chervil leaves
1 teaspoon salt
¼ teaspoon pepper
1 tomato
  Spinach leaves
  Snipped parsley

Cook Brussels sprouts as directed on package; drain. Shake vinegar, oil, chervil, salt and pepper in tightly covered jar; pour over hot Brussels sprouts, turning each until well coated. Cover and refrigerate at least 3 hours.

Just before serving, cut tomato into wedges; toss with Brussels sprouts. Serve on spinach; sprinkle with parsley.   6 SERVINGS.

Cauliflower-Bean Salad (page 137), Mushroom-Spinach Toss (page 132), and Green Pea Coleslaw (page 138)

CARROT-SPROUT SALAD

Heat ½ cup Classic French Dressing (page 157) and 1 package (10 ounces) frozen Brussels sprouts to boiling; reduce heat. Cover and simmer 8 minutes. Add 1 can (16 ounces) sliced carrots, drained; cook until Brussels sprouts are tender. Cover and refrigerate, stirring occasionally, at least 6 hours but no longer than 48 hours. Serve on salad greens. 6 TO 8 SERVINGS.

CUCUMBER SALAD

    2 to 3 medium cucumbers
    1 tablespoon salt
    ¾ cup white vinegar
    2 tablespoons sugar
    ¼ teaspoon pepper

Score cucumbers lengthwise with tines of fork. Cut into paper-thin slices to measure 4 cups.

Layer cucumber slices in deep bowl, sprinkling every few layers with salt. Cover cucumbers with a plate and weight them down with a heavy object (a can of fruit or coffee). Let stand at room temperature 2 hours.

Drain cucumbers completely, pressing out remaining liquid. Mix remaining ingredients; pour over slices. Cover and refrigerate at least 4 hours. Drain salad before serving.   4 TO 6 SERVINGS.

CUCUMBER-STUFFED TOMATOES

    6 medium tomatoes
    1 small cucumber, cut into ½-inch pieces
       (about 1 cup)
    ⅓ cup mayonnaise or salad dressing
    1 clove garlic, crushed
    1 tablespoon snipped parsley
       Dash of salt
       Lettuce cups

Remove stem ends from tomatoes; cut thin slice from bottom of each tomato to prevent tipping. Remove pulp from each tomato; drain and reserve pulp. Invert tomato shells on paper towels; refrigerate at least 2 hours.

Finely chop reserved tomato pulp; drain. Stir in cucumber, mayonnaise, garlic, parsley and salt. Cover and refrigerate at least 2 hours.

Just before serving, arrange each tomato shell in lettuce cup. Fill tomatoes with cucumber mixture. Garnish each with small parsley sprig and small cooked shrimp if desired.   6 SERVINGS.

DILLY CUCUMBER SALAD

    ¾ cup dairy sour cream
    1 small clove garlic, crushed
    1 teaspoon sugar
    ½ teaspoon salt
    ¼ teaspoon dried dill weed
    2 medium cucumbers or zucchini,
       thinly sliced

Mix sour cream, garlic, sugar, salt and dill weed; stir in cucumbers. Sprinkle with snipped parsley if desired. Serve immediately.   6 SERVINGS.

HOT GERMAN POTATO SALAD

    1½ pounds potatoes (about 4 medium), cut
       into halves
    3 slices bacon
    1 medium onion, chopped (about ½ cup)
    1 tablespoon flour
    1 tablespoon sugar
    1 teaspoon salt
    ¼ teaspoon celery seed
       Dash of pepper
    ½ cup water
    ¼ cup vinegar

Heat 1 inch salted water (½ teaspoon salt to 1 cup water) to boiling. Add potatoes. Heat to boiling; reduce heat. Cover and cook until tender, 20 to 25 minutes. Drain and cool.

Fry bacon in 8-inch skillet until crisp; drain bacon on paper towels. Cook and stir onion in bacon fat until tender. Stir in flour, sugar, salt, celery seed and pepper. Cook over low heat, stirring constantly, until mixture is bubbly; remove from heat. Stir in water and vinegar. Heat to boiling, stirring constantly. Boil and stir 1 minute; remove from heat.

Crumble bacon into hot mixture, then slice in warm potatoes. Cook, stirring gently to coat potato slices, until hot and bubbly.   5 OR 6 SERVINGS.

■ **To Microwave:** Microwave potatoes as directed on page 185. Microwave bacon uncovered in square glass baking dish, 8x8x2 inches, until crisp, 4¼ to 4½ minutes; drain bacon on paper towels.

Stir onion into bacon fat. Microwave uncovered until onion is tender, about 2 minutes. Stir in flour, sugar, salt, celery seed, pepper, water and vinegar. Microwave uncovered, stirring every 2 minutes, until mixture is thick and bubbly, about 5 minutes.

Slice potatoes into hot mixture; stir gently. Microwave uncovered until potatoes are hot, about 1 minute. Crumble bacon into potato mixture; stir.

POTATO SALAD

2 pounds potatoes (about 6 medium)
1 small onion, finely chopped (about ¼ cup)
¼ cup Italian Dressing (page 157)
1 teaspoon salt
⅛ teaspoon pepper
½ cup mayonnaise or salad dressing
1 medium stalk celery, chopped (about ½ cup)
2 hard-cooked eggs, coarsely chopped

Heat 1 inch salted water (½ teaspoon salt to 1 cup water) to boiling. Add potatoes. Heat to boiling; reduce heat. Cover and cook until tender, 30 to 35 minutes. Drain and cool.

Cut potatoes into cubes; stir in onion, Italian Dressing, salt and pepper. Cover and refrigerate at least 2 hours.

Just before serving, toss with mayonnaise until potatoes are well coated. Stir in celery and eggs.
4 TO 6 SERVINGS.

Garden Potato Salad: Stir in ½ cup thinly sliced radishes, 1 small cucumber, cut into cubes (about ½ cup), 1 small green pepper, chopped (about ½ cup), and ½ teaspoon celery salt.

Golden Potato Salad: Increase eggs to 6 and stir in 3 tablespoons prepared mustard.

Herring Potato Salad: Stir in 1 jar (8 ounces) pickled herring, drained and chopped, and 1 teaspoon dried dill weed.

Italian Potato Salad: Increase mayonnaise to ¾ cup. Stir in ½ cup sliced pimiento-stuffed olives or pitted ripe olives, ⅓ cup grated Parmesan cheese and 1 tablespoon dried oregano leaves.

GREEN AND GOLD SALAD

1 package (10 ounces) frozen green peas or 1 can (8 ounces) green peas, drained
½ cup shredded natural Cheddar cheese (about 2 ounces)
2 tablespoons chopped onion
2 tablespoons mayonnaise or salad dressing
1½ teaspoons prepared mustard
¼ teaspoon salt
Salad greens

Rinse frozen peas under running cold water to separate; drain. Mix peas, cheese, onion, mayonnaise, mustard and salt. Serve on salad greens.
4 OR 5 SERVINGS.

For Tomato Flowers, cut crosswise, then diagonally.

TOMATO FLOWERS

Cut stem ends from 4 chilled medium tomatoes. Place tomatoes cut sides down; cut each into sixths to within 1 inch of bottom. Carefully spread out sections, forming a "flower." Sprinkle insides of tomatoes with salt. Fill with your favorite potato or tuna salad or cottage cheese.   4 TOMATO FLOWERS.

PICNIC SALADS

1 medium cucumber
6 radishes
4 green onions
2 cups creamed cottage cheese
⅓ cup dairy sour cream
1 teaspoon salt
¼ teaspoon pepper
Dash of cayenne red pepper
Lettuce cups

Cut cucumber lengthwise into fourths, then into 1½-inch pieces. Cut radishes into halves and onions into 1½-inch pieces. Place vegetables in blender container; add enough water to cover. Cover and blend on high speed until finely chopped; drain completely. (Or vegetables can be finely chopped by hand.)

Mix cottage cheese, sour cream, salt, pepper and red pepper; stir in vegetables. Spoon into lettuce cups and, if desired, garnish with sliced ripe olives.   6 TO 8 SERVINGS.

BROCCOLI-TOMATO SALAD

2 medium tomatoes, cut into wedges
8 ounces broccoli, cut into bite-size pieces
    (about 2 cups)
½ small head iceberg lettuce, torn into
    bite-size pieces
    Green Goddess Dressing (page 157) or
    Parsley Cheese Dressing (page 158)

Arrange tomato wedges and broccoli on lettuce; serve with Green Goddess Dressing.   4 SERVINGS.

VEGETABLE SALAD COMBOS

Vitamin-packed combos. Serve on salad greens with your favorite tangy dressing, Buttermilk Dressing (page 159), Blue Cheese Dressing (page 158), Curried French Dressing (page 157) or Russian Dressing (page 158).

□ Cooked green peas, cooked French-style green beans, chopped green pepper, onion and celery; marinate in oil and vinegar dressing overnight and garnish with pimiento

□ Shredded carrots and drained crushed pineapple or finely chopped celery; mix with raisins

□ Sliced zucchini and cauliflowerets or thinly sliced radishes; toss with greens

□ Tomato wedges, cucumber slices and cauliflowerets; marinate in French salad dressing and serve on lettuce leaves

□ Cooked baby lima beans, sliced mushrooms and sliced green onions; season with oregano

□ Overlapping slices of tomato, unpared cucumber slices and onion rings or slices

□ Shredded parsnips, chopped sweet onion, chopped celery and tiny pimiento-stuffed olives; toss with greens

□ Tomato stuffed with cottage cheese or cabbage salad; sprinkle with snipped chives, parsley or toasted almonds

□ Mound of cottage cheese with diced green and/or red pepper, cucumber and onions

□ Asparagus tips on thick tomato slices; sprinkle with shredded cheese

□ Shredded carrots and diced celery; mix with raisins or nuts

□ Chilled tomato halves; sprinkle with snipped parsley, chives or green onions

□ Shredded carrots, chopped sweet onion, chopped celery, grated orange peel and orange sections

VINAIGRETTE VEGETABLE PLATE

1 pound whole green beans or 2 bunches
    asparagus
1 cauliflower, separated into flowerets
1 jar (about 7 ounces) artichoke hearts,
    drained
    Classic French Dressing or Curried
    French Dressing (page 157)

Cook beans and cauliflower in 1 inch boiling salted water (½ teaspoon salt to 1 cup water) in separate saucepans just until tender; drain. Arrange cooked vegetables and artichoke hearts in separate sections in shallow glass dish.

Pour Classic French Dressing over vegetables. Cover and refrigerate, spooning dressing over vegetables occasionally, at least 2 hours. To serve, remove vegetables with slotted spoon. Garnish with cherry tomatoes and parsley sprigs if desired.
4 SERVINGS.

Shrimp Vegetable Plate: Add 1 can (4½ ounces) tiny shrimp, rinsed and drained, or 1 cup cleaned cooked shrimp.

VEGETABLE ANTIPASTO PLATTER

Serve this help-yourself salad tray as a snack, appetizer or accompaniment to an Italian-style main dish.

1 can (15 ounces) garbanzo beans, drained
1 cup Italian Dressing (page 157)
4 Deviled Eggs (page 327)
1 can (16 ounces) tiny whole beets, chilled
1 can (11 ounces) hot green cherry peppers,
    chilled
1 can (6 ounces) pitted ripe olives, chilled
2 jars (about 7 ounces each) marinated
    artichoke hearts, chilled
    Celery sticks
1 can (2 ounces) anchovy fillets

Place beans in glass or plastic jar. Pour Italian Dressing on beans. Cover and refrigerate, stirring occasionally, at least 8 hours. Prepare Deviled Eggs; refrigerate.

Just before serving, drain beans, beets, peppers, olives and artichoke hearts. Cut beets into halves. Arrange vegetables and eggs in separate sections on platter. Place anchovy fillets on eggs.   8 SERVINGS.

Vegetable Salad Combos (page 142)

Macaroni Toss surrounded by Tomatoes Vinaigrette

TOMATOES VINAIGRETTE

- 2 medium tomatoes, sliced
- ½ cup olive or vegetable oil
- 3 tablespoons wine vinegar
- 1 teaspoon dried oregano leaves
- ½ teaspoon salt
- ¼ teaspoon pepper
- ¼ teaspoon dry mustard
- 1 clove garlic, crushed
  Lettuce leaves
- 4 green onions, finely chopped
- 1 tablespoon snipped parsley

Arrange tomatoes in glass baking dish, 8x8x2 inches. Shake oil, vinegar, oregano, salt, pepper, mustard and garlic in tightly covered jar; pour over tomatoes. Cover and refrigerate, spooning dressing over tomatoes occasionally, at least 2 hours.

Arrange tomatoes on lettuce; sprinkle with onions and parsley. Drizzle with dressing.   4 SERVINGS.

PREPARING AVOCADOS

To cut up an avocado, cut it lengthwise around the pit and twist to separate the halves. To remove the pit, strike it with a sharp knife, then twist gently with knife and lift out. Pare skin, place avocado cut side down; cut lengthwise and/or crosswise. For avocado balls, scoop from unpared halves.

MACARONI TOSS

- 7 ounces uncooked elbow, shell or ring macaroni
- 1 package (10 ounces) frozen green peas
- 1 cup cubed Cheddar cheese (about 4 ounces)
- 1 cup sliced gherkins
- ¾ cup mayonnaise or salad dressing
- 1 medium onion, chopped (about ½ cup)
  Salt and pepper

Cook macaroni as directed on page 221. Cook peas as directed on package; drain. Mix macaroni, peas, cheese, gherkins, mayonnaise and onion; sprinkle with salt and pepper. Cover and refrigerate at least 2 hours.   6 TO 8 SERVINGS.

MEXICAN SALAD

- 2 avocados, cut up
- 3 tablespoons grated onion
- 1 tablespoon lemon or lime juice
- 1 teaspoon salt
- 1 canned green hot pepper, finely chopped
- 1 medium tomato, chopped
  Shredded lettuce

Mash avocados with fork. Add onion, lemon juice, salt and hot pepper; beat until creamy. Fold in tomato. Cover and refrigerate no longer than 3 hours. Serve on lettuce.   5 OR 6 SERVINGS.

Molded Salads

These jewellike beauties show off your talents and make a big splash of delicious color. Busy? Make a molded salad early in the morning or even the day before, then refrigerate. Unmold at serving time.

MAKING MOLDED SALADS

Salad molds: The molds can be plain or fancy, large or small; you can even use a substitute—an ice cube tray, a stainless steel bowl, custard cups. Gelatin will thicken more quickly and unmold more easily in thin metal containers.

Capacity of molds: Find the size of an unmarked mold by filling it with water, then measure the water. Don't try to adjust ingredient amounts to fit odd-size molds. Just pour the extra into smaller containers for snacks or other meals.

Flavored and unflavored gelatins: Follow directions carefully for these; they are dissolved by different methods.

Adding solids: Before you add fruits or vegetables, allow the gelatin mixture to thicken to the consistency of unbeaten egg white. Vegetables and fruits should be thoroughly drained.

Arranging fruits and vegetables: Make a kaleidoscope of a salad by arranging the fruits or other solids in bottom of the mold, then carefully add the thickened gelatin. Or pour a layer of gelatin into the mold and arrange solids in desired pattern. Allow each layer to set before going on to the next one. Make a rainbow effect by layering different colors of gelatin.

To speed up thickening: Place the gelatin mixture in the freezer or in a bowl of ice and water. Remove it when it starts to thicken. If it has set too solidly, soften over hot water.

Unmolding salads: To unmold a salad, quickly dip into hot water to top of mold. Loosen the edge of salad with tip of paring knife. Place a plate on top of the mold and, holding tightly, invert plate and mold. Shake mold gently and remove carefully. It may be necessary to repeat the process. Or place a plate on top of the mold first, then, holding firmly, invert both. Soak a cloth towel in hot water, wring it out and press it around the mold and into any crevices. Shake mold gently and remove carefully. If the salad does not slide out easily, reapply the hot damp towel until it does.

TANGY TOMATO ASPIC

    Parsley Cheese Dressing (below)
1¼ cups boiling water
 1 package (3 ounces) lemon-flavored
      gelatin
 1 can (8 ounces) tomato sauce
 1 tablespoon plus 1½ teaspoons
      vinegar
 ½ teaspoon salt
 ½ teaspoon onion juice
 ⅛ teaspoon red pepper sauce
    Dash of ground cloves
 2 cups chopped celery

Prepare Parsley Cheese Dressing. Pour boiling water on gelatin in bowl; stir until gelatin is dissolved. Stir in tomato sauce, vinegar, salt, onion juice, pepper sauce and cloves. Refrigerate until slightly thickened but not set.

Stir in celery. Pour into 4-cup mold or 6 individual molds. Refrigerate until firm. Unmold on serving plate and, if desired, garnish with ripe olives and parsley. Serve with dressing.   6 SERVINGS.

PARSLEY CHEESE DRESSING

Mix 1 cup mayonnaise or salad dressing, ¼ cup pasteurized process sharp American cheese spread and 1 tablespoon snipped parsley. Cover and refrigerate at least 4 hours.

CONFETTI CABBAGE MOLD

 1 cup boiling water
 1 package (3 ounces) lemon-flavored
      gelatin
 ½ cup mayonnaise or salad dressing
 ½ cup cold water
 2 tablespoons vinegar
 ¼ teaspoon salt
1½ cups finely shredded cabbage
 ½ cup sliced radishes
 ½ cup diced celery
 2 to 4 tablespoons chopped green pepper
 1 tablespoon chopped onion
    Salad greens

Pour boiling water on gelatin in bowl; stir until gelatin is dissolved. Mix in mayonnaise, cold water, vinegar and salt. Refrigerate until mixture mounds slightly when dropped from a spoon.

Beat until fluffy. Add remaining ingredients. Pour into 4-cup mold or 6 to 8 individual molds. Refrigerate until firm. Unmold on salad greens and, if desired, garnish with radish slices.   6 TO 8 SERVINGS.

To unmold salad, press hot damp towel into crevices.

Or quickly dip mold into hot water to top of salad.

CELERY-CABBAGE MOLDS

1 cup boiling water
1 package (3 ounces) lemon-flavored gelatin
2 tablespoons lemon juice or vinegar
1 teaspoon salt
1 cup cold water
1 cup finely chopped celery
1 cup finely shredded cabbage
2 tablespoons finely chopped pimiento
⅓ cup chopped sweet pickles
  Salad greens

Pour boiling water on gelatin in bowl; stir until gelatin is dissolved. Stir in lemon juice, salt and cold water. Refrigerate until slightly thickened but not set.

Stir in celery, cabbage, pimiento and sweet pickles. Pour into 6 to 8 individual molds. Refrigerate until firm. Unmold on salad greens.   6 TO 8 SERVINGS.

BEET AND HORSERADISH MOLD

1 cup boiling water
1 package (3 ounces) lemon-flavored gelatin
1 can (16 ounces) diced beets, drained
    (reserve 1 cup liquid)
¾ cup chopped celery
2 tablespoons chopped green onion
2 tablespoons prepared horseradish
  Buttermilk Dressing (page 159)

Pour boiling water on gelatin in large bowl; stir until gelatin is dissolved. Stir in reserved beet liquid, the beets, celery, onion and horseradish. Refrigerate until slightly thickened but not set.

Pour into 4-cup mold or 6 to 8 individual molds. Refrigerate until firm. Unmold and serve with Buttermilk Dressing.   6 TO 8 SERVINGS.

CUCUMBER-RELISH MOLD

1½ cups boiling water
1 package (3 ounces) lime-flavored gelatin
1 cup drained shredded cucumber
1 cup thinly sliced celery
3 tablespoons thinly sliced green onions
½ teaspoon salt

Pour boiling water on gelatin in bowl; stir until gelatin is dissolved. Refrigerate until slightly thickened but not set.

Stir in cucumber, celery, onions and salt. Pour into 4-cup mold or 4 to 6 individual molds. Refrigerate until firm; unmold.   4 TO 6 SERVINGS.

PARTY CHEESE-LIME SALAD

3 cups boiling water
2 packages (3 ounces each) lime-flavored
    gelatin
1 cup pineapple juice
1 teaspoon vinegar
½ teaspoon salt
2 cups creamed cottage cheese
1 teaspoon finely chopped onion
1 teaspoon finely chopped green pepper
½ cup coarsely chopped cucumber
½ cup coarsely chopped celery

Pour boiling water on gelatin in bowl; stir until gelatin is dissolved. Stir in pineapple juice, vinegar and salt. Pour 1 cup of the gelatin mixture into 8-cup ring mold. Refrigerate until firm.

Refrigerate remaining mixture until slightly thickened but not set; beat with hand beater until light and fluffy. Mix in remaining ingredients; pour on gelatin layer in mold. Refrigerate until firm. Unmold on serving plate.   10 SERVINGS.

MELON MOLD

1 cup boiling water
1 package (3 ounces) orange-flavored gelatin
¾ cup orange juice
¼ teaspoon ground ginger
2 cups small melon balls (cantaloupe and/or honeydew)
  Salad greens
  Fruited Cream Dressing (page 158)

Pour boiling water on gelatin in bowl; stir until gelatin is dissolved. Stir in orange juice and ginger. Refrigerate until slightly thickened but not set.

Stir in melon balls. Pour into 4-cup mold or 6 individual molds. Refrigerate until firm, at least 4 hours. Unmold on salad greens and serve with Fruited Cream Dressing.   6 SERVINGS.

CHERRY-ALMOND MOLD

1 cup boiling liquid (water or fruit syrup)
1 package (3 ounces) cherry-flavored gelatin
1 cup dairy sour cream
1 cup pitted dark sweet cherries
⅓ cup slivered blanched almonds
  Salad greens

Pour boiling liquid on gelatin in small mixer bowl; stir until gelatin is dissolved. Cool; add sour cream. Beat until smooth. Refrigerate until slightly thickened but not set.

Stir in cherries and almonds. Pour into 4-cup ring mold or 5 individual molds. Refrigerate until firm. Unmold on salad greens.   5 SERVINGS.

APRICOT-CINNAMON MOLD

1 can (30 ounces) apricot halves, drained (reserve syrup)
¼ cup vinegar
1 teaspoon whole cloves
1 four-inch stick cinnamon
1 package (3 ounces) orange-flavored gelatin
  Salad greens

Cut apricot halves into fourths; place in 4-cup mold or 8 individual molds. Heat reserved syrup, vinegar, cloves and cinnamon to boiling. Reduce heat; simmer uncovered 10 minutes. Remove cloves and cinnamon. Add enough hot water to hot syrup mixture to measure 2 cups. Pour on gelatin in bowl; stir until gelatin is dissolved. Pour gelatin mixture on apricots. Refrigerate until firm. Unmold on salad greens.   8 SERVINGS.

PINEAPPLE-CARROT SALAD

1 cup boiling water
1 package (3 ounces) lemon-flavored gelatin
½ cup cold water
1 can (8¼ ounces) crushed pineapple
⅛ teaspoon salt
½ cup shredded carrots
  Salad greens

Pour boiling water on gelatin in bowl; stir until gelatin is dissolved. Stir in cold water, pineapple (with syrup) and salt. Refrigerate until slightly thickened but not set. Stir in carrots. Pour into 4-cup ring mold or 6 individual molds. Refrigerate until firm. Unmold on salad greens.   6 SERVINGS.

PINEAPPLE-CHEESE MOLD

1 cup boiling water
1 package (3 ounces) lemon-flavored gelatin
2 tablespoons lemon juice or vinegar
1 can (8¼ ounces) crushed pineapple, drained (reserve syrup)
1 cup shredded Cheddar cheese (about 4 ounces)
1 cup chilled whipping cream
  Salad greens

Pour boiling water on gelatin in bowl; stir until gelatin is dissolved. Add lemon juice and enough water to reserved pineapple syrup to measure 1 cup; stir into gelatin. Refrigerate until slightly thickened but not set.

Stir in pineapple and cheese. Beat whipping cream in chilled bowl until stiff; fold into gelatin mixture. Pour into 4-cup mold or 8 individual molds. Refrigerate until firm. Unmold on salad greens.
8 SERVINGS.

MOLDED WALDORF SALAD

1 cup boiling water
1 package (3 ounces) lemon-flavored gelatin
1 can (11 ounces) mandarin orange segments
1 can (8¼ ounces) pineapple chunks
1 medium apple, diced
1 medium banana, sliced
¼ cup coarsely chopped nuts
  Salad greens

Pour boiling water on gelatin in bowl; stir until gelatin is dissolved. Stir in orange segments (with syrup), pineapple (with syrup), apple, banana and nuts. Pour into 5-cup mold. Refrigerate until firm. Unmold on salad greens.   6 TO 8 SERVINGS.

STRAWBERRY SNOWBALL SALAD

1 cup boiling water
1 package (3 ounces) strawberry-flavored
    gelatin
½ cup sweet red wine or cranberry juice
    cocktail
¼ cup cold water
1 package (3 ounces) cream cheese, softened
⅓ cup finely chopped nuts
2 cups strawberries
1 tablespoon sugar

Pour boiling water on gelatin in bowl; stir until gelatin is dissolved. Stir in wine and cold water. Refrigerate until slightly thickened.

Shape cream cheese into 18 balls; roll in nuts. Mix strawberries and sugar. Pour ⅓ cup thickened gelatin into 6-cup ring mold. Arrange cheese balls evenly in gelatin. Spoon strawberries over cheese balls. Carefully pour remaining gelatin over strawberries. Refrigerate until firm. Unmold.   6 TO 8 SERVINGS.

Strawberry Salad Glacé: Omit cold water. Substitute 1 package (16 ounces) frozen strawberry halves for the fresh strawberries. Add frozen strawberries and wine to dissolved gelatin. Stir until gelatin begins to thicken. Continue as directed.

LIME-SOUR CREAM SALAD

1 can (8¼ ounces) crushed pineapple
1 package (3 ounces) lime-flavored gelatin
1 cup dairy sour cream
½ cup seedless green grapes
    Salad greens
    Banana-Cream Dressing (below)

Drain pineapple, reserving syrup. Add enough water to reserved pineapple syrup to measure 1 cup; heat until hot. Stir gelatin into hot syrup until dissolved. Refrigerate until slightly thickened. Fold in pineapple, sour cream and grapes. Pour into 4-cup mold or 6 to 8 individual molds. Refrigerate until firm. Unmold on salad greens. Serve with Banana-Cream Dressing. If desired, garnish with grape clusters.   6 TO 8 SERVINGS.

BANANA-CREAM DRESSING

1 banana, sliced
½ cup dairy sour cream
2 tablespoons packed brown sugar
1½ teaspoons lemon juice

Place ingredients in blender container. Cover; blend until smooth, 12 to 15 seconds. Refrigerate.

TRIPLE ORANGE SALAD

2 cups boiling liquid (water or fruit syrup)
1 package (6 ounces) orange-flavored gelatin
1 pint orange sherbet
2 cans (11 ounces each) mandarin orange
    segments, drained
1 can (13¼ ounces) pineapple chunks,
    drained
1 cup flaked coconut
1 cup miniature marshmallows
1 cup dairy sour cream or ½ cup chilled
    whipping cream, whipped

Pour boiling liquid on gelatin in bowl; stir until gelatin is dissolved. Add orange sherbet; stir until melted. Stir in 1 can orange segments. Pour into 6-cup ring mold; refrigerate until firm.

Mix remaining orange segments, the pineapple, coconut and marshmallows. Fold in sour cream. Refrigerate at least 3 hours. Unmold and fill center with fruit mixture.   10 TO 12 SERVINGS.

CRANBERRY-RASPBERRY MOLD

2 cups boiling water
1 package (6 ounces) raspberry-flavored
    gelatin
1⅓ cups dairy sour cream
⅔ cup whole cranberry sauce

Pour boiling water on gelatin in bowl; stir until gelatin is dissolved. Refrigerate until very thick but not set. Beat in sour cream and cranberry sauce with hand beater. Pour into 5-cup mold. Refrigerate until firm; unmold.   8 TO 10 SERVINGS.

CRANBERRY-RELISH MOLD

1 cup boiling water
1 package (3 ounces) lemon-flavored
    gelatin
1 package (10 ounces) frozen
    cranberry-orange relish
1 can (8¼ ounces) crushed pineapple
1 tart apple, chopped
½ cup chopped celery
⅓ cup chopped nuts (optional)

Pour boiling water on gelatin in bowl; stir until gelatin is dissolved. Add relish, pineapple (with syrup), apple, celery and nuts; stir until relish is thawed. Pour into 4-cup mold or 6 to 8 individual molds. Refrigerate until firm. Unmold on serving plate.   6 TO 8 SERVINGS.

Cauliflower-Orange Salad (page 135), Lime-Sour Cream Salad (page 148), Melon-Cucumber Salad (page 154)

WHITE WINE MOLD

¾ cup sugar
2 envelopes unflavored gelatin
1 cup dry white wine
1 can (6 ounces) frozen orange juice
    concentrate, thawed
2 cups water
2 tablespoons lemon juice
    Grated peel of 1 lemon
2 cups chilled whipping cream
    Salad greens

Mix sugar and gelatin in 3-quart saucepan; stir in wine, orange juice concentrate, water and lemon juice. Heat to boiling, stirring constantly. Boil and stir 1 minute. Remove from heat; stir in lemon peel. Refrigerate until mixture mounds slightly when dropped from a spoon, about 2½ hours.

Beat whipping cream in chilled small mixer bowl until stiff. Fold chilled gelatin mixture into whipped cream. Pour into 7-cup mold. Refrigerate until firm, about 12 hours. Unmold on salad greens and, if desired, garnish with orange slices.   10 TO 12 SERVINGS.

RHUBARBERRY MOLD

1 package (20 ounces) frozen unsweetened
    rhubarb
1 package (3 ounces) strawberry-flavored
    gelatin
1 or 2 drops red food color (optional)
1 can (8 ounces) crushed pineapple in
    juice
¼ cup chopped nuts
    Salad greens
    Crushed Pineapple Dressing (below)

Prepare Rhubarb Sauce as directed on package of frozen rhubarb; remove from heat. Stir in gelatin and food color. Refrigerate until very thick, about 1½ hours.

Reserve 2 tablespoons pineapple for Crushed Pineapple Dressing. Stir remaining pineapple (with juice) and nuts into gelatin mixture; pour into 4-cup mold. Refrigerate until firm, at least 4 hours. Unmold on salad greens. Serve with Crushed Pineapple Dressing.   6 SERVINGS.

CRUSHED PINEAPPLE DRESSING

Mix ½ cup frozen whipped topping (thawed), ¼ cup mayonnaise or salad dressing and 2 tablespoons reserved crushed pineapple.

FROZEN FRUIT SALAD

2 cups dairy sour cream
¾ cup sugar
1 tablespoon plus 1 teaspoon lemon juice
1 can (30 ounces) fruit cocktail, drained
2 medium bananas, cut into ¼-inch slices
½ cup coarsely chopped walnuts
1 jar (10 ounces) maraschino cherries,
    cut into halves
    Salad greens

Mix sour cream, sugar and lemon juice. Stir in remaining ingredients. Pour into 2 ice cube trays. Cover and freeze at least 24 hours but no longer than 1 month.

Remove trays from freezer and refrigerate 15 minutes. Cut into serving pieces. Serve on salad greens.   16 SERVINGS.

CREAMY FROZEN SALAD

1 package (8 ounces) Neufchâtel cheese,
    softened
1 cup dairy sour cream
¼ cup sugar
¼ teaspoon salt
1 can (17 ounces) apricot halves, drained
1 can (16 ounces) pitted dark sweet cherries,
    drained
1 can (8¼ ounces) crushed pineapple,
    drained
1 cup miniature marshmallows
    Salad greens

Beat cheese in large mixer bowl until smooth. Beat in sour cream, sugar and salt on low speed.

Cut apricots into halves. Reserve a few cherries for garnish. Stir apricots, remaining cherries, the pineapple and marshmallows into cheese mixture. Pour into 4½-cup mold or 6 to 8 individual molds. Freeze at least 8 hours.

Remove mold(s) from freezer and let stand at room temperature 10 to 15 minutes. Unmold on salad greens. Garnish with reserved cherries.   6 TO 8 SERVINGS.

FROZEN CRAN-APPLE SALAD

1 can (20 ounces) crushed pineapple, well
    drained
1 can (16 ounces) whole cranberry sauce
1 cup dairy sour cream
¼ cup coarsely chopped pecans
    Salad greens

Mix pineapple, cranberry sauce, sour cream and
pecans; pour into ice cube tray. Freeze until firm, at
least 3 hours.

Remove tray from freezer and refrigerate 30 minutes. Cut into serving pieces and serve on salad
greens.   6 TO 8 SERVINGS.

FROZEN RASPBERRY SALAD

½ cup boiling water
1 package (3 ounces) raspberry-flavored
    gelatin
1 package (10 ounces) frozen raspberries,
    thawed
2 packages (3 ounces each) cream cheese,
    softened
1 cup dairy sour cream
1 can (16 ounces) whole cranberry sauce
⅛ teaspoon salt
    Salad greens
    Lime-flavored or raspberry-flavored
    yogurt or Fluffy Yogurt Dressing
    (page 159)

Pour boiling water on gelatin in bowl; stir until
gelatin is dissolved. Stir in raspberries (with syrup).
Mix cream cheese, sour cream, cranberry sauce and
salt; stir into gelatin mixture. (Salad will be slightly
lumpy.) Pour into square pan, 8x8x2 or 9x9x2
inches. Cover and freeze at least 24 hours but no
longer than 2 months.

Remove pan from freezer and let stand at room
temperature 10 minutes. Cut into serving pieces.
Arrange on salad greens; serve with yogurt.
9 TO 12 SERVINGS.

24-HOUR SALAD

1 can (17 ounces) pitted light or dark sweet
    cherries, drained
2 cans (13¼ ounces each) pineapple chunks,
    drained (reserve 2 tablespoons syrup)
3 oranges, pared, sectioned and cut up, or
    2 cans (11 ounces each) mandarin
    orange segments, drained
1 cup miniature marshmallows
    Old-fashioned Pineapple Dressing (below)
    Lettuce leaves

Mix cherries, pineapple, oranges and marshmallows; toss with Old-fashioned Pineapple Dressing.
Cover and refrigerate at least 12 hours but no
longer than 24 hours. Spoon into lettuce-lined
salad bowl or lettuce cups and, if desired, garnish
with orange sections.   8 TO 10 SERVINGS.

OLD-FASHIONED PINEAPPLE DRESSING

2 eggs, beaten
2 tablespoons sugar
2 tablespoons vinegar or lemon juice
2 tablespoons reserved pineapple syrup
1 tablespoon margarine or butter
    Dash of salt
¾ cup chilled whipping cream

Mix all ingredients except whipping cream in
saucepan. Heat just to boiling, stirring constantly;
cool. Beat whipping cream in chilled small mixer
bowl until stiff; fold in egg mixture.

MACARONI FRUIT SALAD

1½ cups uncooked macaroni rings
1 tablespoon cornstarch
1 tablespoon sugar
1 can (30 ounces) fruit cocktail
2 tablespoons lemon juice
½ cup chilled whipping cream
1 tablespoon sugar
¼ cup maraschino cherries, cut into halves

Cook macaroni as directed on page 221. Blend
cornstarch and 1 tablespoon sugar in saucepan.
Drain fruit cocktail, reserving ½ cup syrup. Stir
reserved syrup and the lemon juice gradually into
cornstarch mixture. Cook over medium heat, stirring constantly, until mixture thickens and boils.
Boil and stir 1 minute. Stir into hot macaroni rings.
Cover and refrigerate at least 4 hours.

Just before serving, beat whipping cream and 1
tablespoon sugar in chilled small mixer bowl until
stiff. Fold whipped cream, fruit cocktail and cherries into macaroni mixture.   4 TO 6 SERVINGS.

Fruit Salads

Sparkling fruit salads, so refreshing and juicy. You'll find first course fruit salads on pages 316–17 and a make-a-meal salad on page 111.

WALDORF SALADS

2 medium apples, diced (about 2 cups)
2 medium stalks celery, chopped
    (about 1 cup)
⅓ cup coarsely chopped nuts
½ cup mayonnaise or salad dressing
    Lettuce cups

Toss apples, celery and nuts with mayonnaise. Spoon into lettuce cups and, if desired, garnish with maraschino cherries.   4 TO 6 SERVINGS.

Waldorf Salads Supreme: Decrease celery to 1 medium stalk and nuts to ¼ cup. Stir in 1 can (8¼ ounces) pineapple chunks, drained, ½ cup miniature marshmallows and ⅓ cup cut-up dates.

APPLE-ORANGE-GRAPE SALAD

1 small apple, thinly sliced
1 can (8¼ ounces) seedless green grapes,
    drained, or 1 cup fresh seedless green
    grapes
1 can (11 ounces) mandarin orange segments,
    drained
    Honey-Spice Dressing (below)
    Salad greens

Mix apple, grapes and orange segments. Pour Honey-Spice Dressing over fruit. Cover and refrigerate. Just before serving, toss fruit until coated with dressing; serve on greens.   4 OR 5 SERVINGS.

HONEY-SPICE DRESSING
Mix 2 tablespoons lemon juice, 2 tablespoons honey and ¼ teaspoon ground cinnamon.

Banana-Pineapple Salad: Substitute banana pieces (dipped in pineapple syrup and rolled in chopped peanuts) and pineapple chunks for the apple, grapes and orange segments.

California Salad: Substitute orange and grapefruit sections and avocado slices for the apple, grapes and orange segments.

Melon Salad: Substitute honeydew melon slices and cantaloupe and watermelon balls for the apple, grapes and orange segments.

DOUBLE APPLE SALAD

1 jar (14 ounces) spiced apple rings, chilled
3 medium apples, sliced
    Salad greens
1 medium stalk celery, finely chopped
    (about ½ cup)
    Mayonnaise or salad dressing

Cut apple rings into halves; arrange with fresh apple slices on salad greens. Sprinkle with celery. Serve with mayonnaise.   6 SERVINGS.

AMBROSIA SALADS

1 can (11 ounces) mandarin orange segments,
    drained
1 medium apple, chopped
2 medium bananas, sliced
¼ cup cut-up sugar-rolled dates
2 tablespoons Piquant Dressing (page 157)
    Lettuce cups
    Plain or toasted coconut

Toss orange segments, apple, bananas, dates and Piquant Dressing. Spoon into lettuce cups; sprinkle with coconut.   4 OR 5 SERVINGS.

CITRUS SALAD

Arrange 1 orange and 1 grapefruit, each pared and sectioned, in pinwheel design on salad greens. Garnish with maraschino cherries if desired. Serve with Ruby-Red Dressing (below).   2 SERVINGS.

RUBY-RED DRESSING
Beat ¼ cup currant or cranberry jelly and 2 tablespoons Oil and Vinegar Dressing (page 136) until smooth.

AVOCADO-CITRUS SALAD

1 avocado
    Lemon juice
    Salt
1 orange or grapefruit, pared and sectioned
    Lettuce
    Sweet French Dressing (page 157)

Cut avocado crosswise into halves; cut halves into ¼-inch slices. Sprinkle with lemon juice and salt.

Arrange avocado slices and fruit sections on lettuce. Garnish with watercress or parsley sprigs if desired. Serve with Sweet French Dressing.
4 SERVINGS.

ORANGE TOSS

    Blue Cheese-Lemon Dressing (below)
1 clove garlic, cut into halves
1 small head iceberg lettuce or 2 small heads
    Boston lettuce
2 medium oranges
¼ teaspoon salt
    Freshly ground pepper

Prepare Blue Cheese-Lemon Dressing. Just before serving, rub salad bowl with garlic. Tear lettuce into bite-size pieces. Pare and section oranges; add to greens. Sprinkle with salt and pepper; toss with dressing.   6 SERVINGS.

BLUE CHEESE-LEMON DRESSING

2 tablespoons crumbled blue cheese
2 tablespoons vegetable oil
¼ cup dairy sour cream
2 teaspoons lemon juice
¼ teaspoon grated lemon peel
    Dash of salt
    Dash of garlic salt

Mash cheese with fork; beat in oil until mixture is smooth. Mix in remaining ingredients. Cover and refrigerate at least 2 hours. Bring dressing to room temperature before serving; stir.

SPICY PEACH SALAD

1 can (16 ounces) peach halves, drained
    (reserve ¼ cup syrup)
½ cup water
1 tablespoon lemon juice
1 stick cinnamon, broken into 1-inch pieces
4 whole cloves
⅛ teaspoon ground ginger
1 can (14¼ ounces) sliced pineapple, drained
    Salad greens
    Strawberry or raspberry preserves or jam

Heat peaches, reserved peach syrup, the water, lemon juice, cinnamon, cloves and ginger in saucepan to boiling, stirring gently. Reduce heat; simmer uncovered 10 minutes. Spoon peaches and spices into pint jar. Pour hot syrup over peaches. Cover and refrigerate at least 4 hours but no longer than 4 days.

Arrange pineapple slices on salad greens. Place 1 peach half cut side up on each pineapple slice and spoon about ½ teaspoon preserves into center. 4 SERVINGS.

ORANGE-ONION SALADS

Toss 2 cans (11 ounces each) mandarin orange segments, drained, and 3 tablespoons finely chopped mild onion. Spoon into lettuce cups. Top each with 1 to 2 tablespoons Buttermilk Dressing (page 159) or Blue Cheese Dressing (page 158). 4 SERVINGS.

GRAPE-CHERRY-NUT SALADS

2 cups fresh seedless green grapes or 2 cans
    (8¼ ounces each) seedless green grapes,
    drained
4 medium stalks celery, chopped (about
    2 cups)
1 cup pitted dark sweet cherries or
    maraschino cherries, cut into halves
½ cup coarsely chopped nuts
¼ cup Limeade Dressing (page 159)
    Lettuce cups

Toss grapes, celery, cherries, nuts and Limeade Dressing. Serve in lettuce cups.   4 TO 6 SERVINGS.

STUFFED PEAR SALAD

Arrange 1 can (16 ounces) pear halves, drained, on salad greens. Fill centers of pear halves with cranberry relish or sauce, raspberry or strawberry jelly, fruit-flavored gelatin cubes, crunchy peanut butter or shredded Cheddar cheese.   4 SERVINGS.

CHERRY-PINEAPPLE SALAD

1 medium pineapple
⅓ cup sugar
½ pound dark sweet cherries, pitted
    Salad greens
    Poppy Seed Dressing (page 157)
    Crumbled blue cheese

Cut pineapple into chunks as directed on page 156. Place pineapple in shallow dish; sprinkle with sugar. Cover and refrigerate.

Just before serving, drain pineapple. Arrange pineapple and cherries on salad greens. Drizzle Poppy Seed Dressing over fruit and sprinkle with blue cheese.   6 SERVINGS.

Winter Cherry-Pineapple Salad: Substitute 1 can (20 ounces) pineapple chunks, drained, and 1 can (16 ounces) pitted dark sweet cherries, drained, for the fresh pineapple and cherries.

FIVE-FRUIT SALADS

Honey-Lime Dressing (below)
1 can (8¼ ounces) sliced pineapple, drained
  Lettuce cups
1 banana
  Lemon juice
1 orange, pared and sectioned
1 cup seedless green grapes
1 cup melon pieces

Prepare Honey-Lime Dressing. Place pineapple in lettuce cups. Slice banana; dip slices into lemon juice to prevent darkening. Mix banana, orange, grapes and melon; arrange on pineapple. Drizzle dressing over salads.   4 TO 6 SERVINGS.

HONEY-LIME DRESSING

¼ cup vegetable oil
¼ teaspoon grated lime peel
3 tablespoons lime juice
3 tablespoons honey
½ teaspoon dry mustard
¼ teaspoon seasoned salt
¼ teaspoon paprika
  Dash of white pepper

Shake all ingredients in tightly covered jar; refrigerate. Bring dressing to room temperature before serving; shake.

WATERMELON STAR SALAD

½ slice medium watermelon (1 inch thick)
  Salad greens
½ cup creamed cottage cheese
1 tablespoon blueberries
  1-2-3 Fruit Dressing (page 159)

Cut watermelon slice into 5 wedges. Cut rind from wedges. Arrange wedges on salad greens in circle with points outward to resemble star. Spoon cottage cheese into center of watermelon star; sprinkle with blueberries. Serve with 1-2-3 Fruit Dressing.   1 SERVING.

FRUIT FOR VITAMINS

Vitamins C and A (for healthy gums and skin and normal night vision) can be found in many fresh fruits. Good sources of vitamin C are grapefruit, lemons, oranges, papayas and strawberries. Cantaloupes are a good source of both vitamins, while apricots, persimmons and watermelons are the best fruit sources of vitamin A.

MELON-CUCUMBER SALAD

¼ cup vegetable oil
2 tablespoons lemon juice
1 teaspoon sugar
½ teaspoon salt
  Dash of freshly ground pepper
1 medium cucumber, thinly sliced
2 cups ¾-inch pieces melon (honeydew,
    cantaloupe and/or watermelon)
  Salad greens

Mix oil, lemon juice, sugar, salt and pepper. Toss with cucumber and melon. Cover and refrigerate. To serve, remove to salad greens with slotted spoon.   4 SERVINGS.

Pear-Cucumber Salad: Substitute cut-up pears for the melon.

FRUIT SALAD COMBOS

Color-packed combos. Serve on salad greens with your favorite sweet fruit dressing, Cranberry Dressing (page 158) or Honey-Peanut Dressing (page 159).

□ Orange or mandarin orange segments and diced apple or banana slices; garnish with coconut

□ Pineapple spears and banana slices; roll in chopped peanuts

□ Long slices of banana and cubes of jellied cranberry sauce

□ Fresh or canned pineapple spears, strawberries and halves of blue plums

□ Cantaloupe balls, dark sweet cherries and green grapes

□ Pineapple chunks, dark sweet cherries and pecans

□ Orange and grapefruit sections and avocado slices or slices of unpared red apples; garnish with pomegranate seeds or sliced strawberries

□ Apricot, peach or pear half or pineapple slice; top with tiny cream cheese balls rolled in chopped nuts (pistachios are especially attractive)

□ Sliced fresh pears and halved Tokay grapes

□ Halved green grapes or cherries in hollows of pear or peach halves

□ Peach slices or peach halves; top with mayonnaise and shredded Cheddar cheese

□ Fresh peach slices, green grapes and peanuts

□ Slices of pineapple topped with round slices of jellied cranberry sauce

SUMMER FRUIT SALADS

½ cup strawberries, cut into halves, or
   1 cup whole raspberries
½ cup seedless green grapes, cut into
   halves
2 medium peaches or nectarines
2 small bananas
   Lettuce cups
   Mint Cloud Dressing or Honey-Sour Cream
   Dressing (below)

Mix strawberries and grapes. Slice peaches and
bananas into fruit; toss. Spoon salad into lettuce
cups and, if desired, garnish with mint leaves. Serve
with Mint Cloud Dressing.   4 OR 5 SERVINGS.

MINT CLOUD DRESSING

Beat 1 cup dairy sour cream, 3 tablespoons mint
jelly and 1 or 2 drops green food color until smooth,
about 30 seconds. Cover and refrigerate 1 hour.

HONEY-SOUR CREAM DRESSING

Mix 1 cup dairy sour cream, 2 tablespoons honey
and 2 tablespoons orange or grapefruit juice. Cover
and refrigerate 1 hour.

WINTER FRUIT BOWL

1 can (8¼ ounces) pineapple chunks,
   chilled
1 can (11 ounces) mandarin orange
   segments, chilled and drained
1 can (8¾ ounces) seedless green grapes,
   chilled and drained
1 red apple, sliced
   Salad greens
   Pineapple Creme Dressing (below)

Drain pineapple, reserving 1 tablespoon syrup for
dressing. Mix pineapple, orange segments, grapes
and apple. Serve on salad greens. Sprinkle with
pomegranate seeds if desired. Serve with Pineapple
Creme Dressing.   4 SERVINGS.

PINEAPPLE CREME DRESSING

1¼ cups marshmallow creme
 1 tablespoon reserved pineapple syrup
 3 tablespoons mayonnaise or salad
   dressing
 ¼ teaspoon vanilla

Blend marshmallow creme and pineapple syrup.
Stir in mayonnaise and vanilla.

FRUITS FOR SALADS

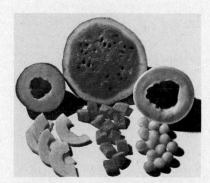
Cantaloupe, watermelon, honeydew

Pomegranate, guava, kiwi

Grapefruit, orange

Mango, papaya, persimmon

Fruit salad platter—improvise your own combination!

HOW TO CUT A PINEAPPLE

1. Twist out top; cut pineapple in half, then quarters.

2. Hold pineapple quarter securely; slice fruit from rind.

3. Cut off the pineapple core and remove any "eyes."

4. For chunks, slice quarter lengthwise, then crosswise.

SUNBURST FRUIT PLATE

Each of these party salad dress-ups—sherbet, cottage cheese, tangy dressing—is also refreshing enough to be served alone with your choice of fruits.

Curried Cottage Cheese (right)
Three-Fruit Dressing (right) or
  Limeade Dressing (page 159)
Pineapple chunks or slices
Orange slices or sections
Grape clusters
Melon balls or slices
Strawberries
Banana
Orange and lime sherbets
Salad greens

Prepare Curried Cottage Cheese and one of the dressings. Refrigerate all fruit except banana.

Just before serving, slice banana; dip slices into lemon juice to prevent darkening. Arrange fruit, Curried Cottage Cheese and scoops of sherbet on salad greens. Serve with dressing.   4 SERVINGS.

CURRIED COTTAGE CHEESE

1½ cups creamed cottage cheese
 ¼ cup toasted slivered almonds
  1 tablespoon mayonnaise or salad
       dressing
 ½ teaspoon curry powder

Mix all ingredients. Cover and refrigerate at least 1 hour.

THREE-FRUIT DRESSING

 ½ cup sugar
  1 tablespoon plus 1½ teaspoons
       cornstarch
 ½ cup unsweetened pineapple juice
       Grated peels of 1 small lemon and
       1 small orange
  2 tablespoons lemon juice
  2 tablespoons orange juice

Mix sugar and cornstarch in saucepan. Stir in pineapple juice. Cook, stirring constantly, until mixture thickens and boils. Boil and stir 1 minute; remove from heat. Stir in remaining ingredients; cool.

Salad Dressings

Salad dressings should accent but not overpower the other flavors of the salad. Dressings also act as flavor counterpoints for the other dishes you're serving. Try a robust salad dressing, for instance, with a hearty steak. Salad greens welcome a clear or creamy dressing, sharply or delicately seasoned; tart fruits, a sweet or creamy dressing. Add dressing with discretion—too much will make even the crispest greens limp.

FRENCH DRESSING

 1 cup olive or vegetable oil or
    combination
¼ cup vinegar
¼ cup lemon juice
 1 teaspoon salt
½ teaspoon dry mustard
½ teaspoon paprika

Shake all ingredients in tightly covered jar; refrigerate. Shake before serving.   1½ CUPS DRESSING.

Curried French Dressing: Mix ½ cup French Dressing and ⅛ teaspoon curry powder.   ABOUT ½ CUP DRESSING.

Garlic French Dressing: Mix ½ cup French Dressing, 1 clove garlic, crushed, and generous dash of freshly ground pepper.   ABOUT ½ CUP DRESSING.

Herb Dressing: Mix ½ cup French Dressing, 2 teaspoons snipped parsley, ½ teaspoon dried oregano leaves and ⅛ teaspoon dried thyme leaves.   ABOUT ½ CUP DRESSING.

Lorenzo Dressing: Mix ½ cup French Dressing and 1 tablespoon chili sauce.   ABOUT ½ CUP DRESSING.

Piquant Dressing: Mix ½ cup French Dressing, 2 tablespoons sugar, ½ teaspoon celery seed and ½ teaspoon grated onion. Cut 1 clove garlic crosswise into halves; let stand in dressing 1 hour.   ABOUT ½ CUP DRESSING.

Poppy Seed Dressing: Mix ½ cup French Dressing and ½ teaspoon poppy seed.   ABOUT ½ CUP DRESSING.

Sweet French Dressing: Mix ½ cup French Dressing and 2 tablespoons powdered sugar.   ABOUT ½ CUP DRESSING.

Tomato Dressing: Mix ½ cup French Dressing and ½ cup catsup.   ABOUT 1 CUP DRESSING.

CLASSIC FRENCH DRESSING

¼ cup vegetable or olive oil
 2 tablespoons tarragon or wine vinegar
½ teaspoon salt
 1 small clove garlic, crushed
   Generous dash of freshly ground pepper

For marinade, mix all ingredients. For dressing, toss salad greens (about 12 cups) with oil just until leaves glisten. Mix vinegar, salt, garlic and pepper; toss with salad mixture.   ABOUT ⅓ CUP DRESSING.

ITALIAN DRESSING

 1 cup vegetable oil
¼ cup lemon juice
¼ cup white vinegar
 1 teaspoon salt
 1 teaspoon sugar
½ teaspoon dry mustard
½ teaspoon onion salt
½ teaspoon paprika
½ teaspoon dried oregano leaves
⅛ teaspoon ground thyme leaves
 2 cloves garlic, crushed

Shake all ingredients in tightly covered jar; refrigerate at least 2 hours. Shake before serving. 1½ CUPS DRESSING.

SEASONED SALAD OIL

Shake 1 cup vegetable oil and 2 cloves garlic, cut into fourths, or 1 small onion, sliced, in tightly covered jar. Let stand at least 4 days.   1 CUP DRESSING.

GREEN GODDESS DRESSING

 1 cup mayonnaise or salad dressing
½ cup dairy sour cream
⅓ cup finely snipped parsley
 3 tablespoons finely snipped chives
 3 tablespoons anchovy paste or finely
    chopped anchovy fillets
 3 tablespoons tarragon or wine vinegar
 1 tablespoon lemon juice
¼ teaspoon salt
⅛ teaspoon freshly ground pepper

Mix all ingredients; refrigerate.   2 CUPS DRESSING.

COOKED SALAD DRESSING

¼ cup all-purpose flour
2 tablespoons sugar
1 teaspoon salt
1 teaspoon dry mustard
1½ cups milk
2 egg yolks, slightly beaten
⅓ cup vinegar
1 tablespoon margarine or butter

Mix flour, sugar, salt and mustard in 2-quart saucepan. Stir in milk gradually. Heat to boiling over medium heat, stirring constantly. Boil and stir 1 minute. Stir at least half of the hot mixture into egg yolks gradually. Blend into hot mixture in saucepan. Boil and stir 1 minute. Remove from heat; stir in vinegar and margarine. Cool slightly; refrigerate. ABOUT 2 CUPS DRESSING.

ZESTY LETTUCE DRESSINGS

Cut 1 medium head iceberg lettuce into 6 wedges. Place wedges cut sides down on salad plates. Make 3 or 4 vertical cuts almost to bottom of each wedge. Spoon one of the dressings (below) onto wedges. 6 SERVINGS.

Cheese-Olive Dressing: Mix 1 package (3 ounces) cream cheese, softened, and ¼ cup half-and-half; stir in ¼ cup chopped ripe or pimiento-stuffed olives.

Chili Dressing: Mix 1 carton (8 ounces) unflavored yogurt, 1 tablespoon chili sauce and 1 teaspoon onion salt.

Cucumber Dressing: Mix ¼ medium cucumber, chopped (about ½ cup), ¼ cup dairy sour cream, ¼ cup mayonnaise or salad dressing and ½ teaspoon salt.

Curry Dressing: Mix ½ cup Italian Dressing (page 157), ¼ teaspoon curry powder and dash of cayenne red pepper.

Dill Dressing: Mix ½ cup Classic French Dressing (page 157) and ½ teaspoon dried dill weed.

Red and White Dressing: Top wedges with ½ to ¾ cup Blue Cheese Dressing (right). Drizzle with Tomato Dressing (page 157).

Thousand Island Dressing: Top wedges with ½ to ¾ cup Thousand Island Dressing (right).

MAYONNAISE DRESSINGS

Cranberry Dressing (for fruit salads): Mix 1 cup mayonnaise or salad dressing, ¼ cup cranberry juice cocktail and ½ teaspoon poppy seed or celery seed. Cover and refrigerate at least 4 hours. ABOUT 1 CUP DRESSING.

Creamy Onion Dressing (for green, vegetable, meat or seafood salads): Mix 1 cup mayonnaise or salad dressing, ½ cup dairy sour cream and 2 green onions, finely chopped (about 2 tablespoons). Refrigerate at least 4 hours. 1¼ CUPS DRESSING.

Fruited Cream Dressing (for fruit salads): Mix ½ cup mayonnaise or salad dressing, 2 tablespoons orange juice, dash of salt and dash of paprika. Fold in ¼ cup chilled whipping cream, whipped. ¾ CUP DRESSING.

Parsley Cheese Dressing (for vegetable, meat or seafood salads): Mix 1 cup mayonnaise or salad dressing, ¼ cup pasteurized process sharp American cheese spread and 1 tablespoon snipped parsley. Cover and refrigerate at least 4 hours. ABOUT 1 CUP DRESSING.

Russian Dressing (for green or vegetable salads): Mix ½ cup mayonnaise or salad dressing, ¼ cup chili sauce, few drops onion juice and, if desired, 1 teaspoon lemon juice. ¾ CUP DRESSING.

Thousand Island Dressing (for green or vegetable salads): Mix ½ cup mayonnaise or salad dressing, 1 tablespoon chili sauce, 1 tablespoon chopped pimiento-stuffed olives, 1 teaspoon snipped chives, 1 hard-cooked egg, chopped, ¼ teaspoon paprika and salt and pepper to taste. Thin with whipping cream if desired. ¾ CUP DRESSING.

Tomato-Cucumber Dressing (for green, vegetable, meat or seafood salads): Mix 1 cup mayonnaise or salad dressing, ½ cup each drained diced tomato and cucumber, 1 teaspoon finely chopped onion and dash of salt. 1¾ CUPS DRESSING.

BLUE CHEESE DRESSING

¾ cup crumbled blue cheese
1 package (3 ounces) cream cheese, softened
½ cup mayonnaise or salad dressing
⅓ cup half-and-half

Reserve ⅓ cup blue cheese. Beat remaining blue cheese and cream cheese on low speed. Add mayonnaise and half-and-half; beat on medium speed until creamy. Stir in reserved blue cheese. Cover and refrigerate at least 3 hours. ABOUT 1⅔ CUPS DRESSING.

BUTTERMILK DRESSING

¾ cup mayonnaise or salad dressing
½ cup buttermilk
1 teaspoon dried parsley flakes
½ teaspoon instant minced onion
1 clove garlic, crushed
½ teaspoon salt
  Dash of ground pepper

Shake all ingredients in tightly covered jar; refrigerate at least 2 hours. Shake before serving. 1¼ CUPS DRESSING.

Mayonnaise-Buttermilk Dressing: Increase mayonnaise to 1 cup and decrease buttermilk to ¼ cup.

FLUFFY YOGURT DRESSING

Beat 1 carton (8 ounces) unflavored yogurt (1 cup) and 3 tablespoons raspberry or strawberry jam or orange marmalade with hand beater. Refrigerate any leftover dressing.   ABOUT 1 CUP DRESSING.

HONEY-PEANUT DRESSING

Mix ¼ cup honey, ¼ cup creamy peanut butter and 1 tablespoon lemon juice.   ½ CUP DRESSING.

1-2-3 FRUIT DRESSING

Mix 1 cup sugar, 1 egg, well beaten, and juice and grated peels of 1 lemon, 1 lime and 1 orange in saucepan. Heat to boiling over medium heat, stirring constantly. Boil and stir 1 minute; cool. Refrigerate any leftover dressing.   1½ CUPS DRESSING.

LIMEADE DRESSING

⅓ cup frozen limeade or lemonade
    concentrate (thawed)
⅓ cup honey
⅓ cup vegetable oil
1 teaspoon celery or poppy seed

Mix all ingredients with hand beater.   1 CUP DRESSING.

Grape-Cherry-Nut Salads (page 153) with Limeade Dressing

Broccoli with Cheese Sauce (page 169)

Quick Sweet-and-Sour Beets (page 168)

Okra Skillet (page 180)

Creole Lima Beans (page 167)

Polynesian Pea Pods (page 176)

Brandied Carrots (page 172)

Hot Relish Tray (page 174)

Corn Sesame Sauté (page 176)

Asparagus Dress-ups (page 164)

VEGETABLES

CANNED VEGETABLES

Drain vegetable liquid into saucepan. Heat to boiling; boil until liquid is reduced to half. Add vegetable; heat through.

Heat vegetables such as tomatoes or cream-style corn in saucepan. Sprinkle with salt and pepper.

Can Size	Number of Servings
8 ounces	2
16 ounces	3 or 4
29 ounces	5 to 7

FROZEN VEGETABLES

Prepare frozen vegetable as directed on package. Read carefully—directions vary from brand to brand.

NOTE: To use part of package, saw or cut frozen block of vegetable. Also consider frozen vegetables packaged in large-size bags; contents can be separated easily into exact amounts.

CEREAL TOPPING

Mix ½ cup crushed toasted oat cereal, corn puff cereal or whole wheat flake cereal, 1 tablespoon margarine or butter, melted, and ⅛ teaspoon salt. Sprinkle over hot cooked vegetables or creamed vegetables.   ½ CUP TOPPING.

Marjoram Cereal Topping: Mix in ⅛ teaspoon dried marjoram leaves.

Oregano Cereal Topping: Mix in ¼ teaspoon dried oregano leaves and ⅛ teaspoon dried basil leaves.

Sage Cereal Topping: Mix in ¼ teaspoon dried sage leaves and ⅛ teaspoon dry mustard.

DILL CROUTON TOPPING

½ cup croutons
1 tablespoon margarine or butter, melted
¼ teaspoon dried dill weed
⅛ teaspoon salt

Mix all ingredients. Sprinkle over hot cooked vegetables.   ½ CUP TOPPING.

CRUMB TOPPING

Mix ½ cup dry bread crumbs, 1 tablespoon margarine or butter, melted, and ⅛ teaspoon salt. Sprinkle over hot cooked vegetables or creamed vegetables.   ½ CUP TOPPING.

Nutmeg Crumb Topping: Mix in ⅛ teaspoon ground nutmeg.

BUTTER SAUCES FOR VEGETABLES

Drawn Butter: Heat margarine or butter over low heat until melted.

Browned Butter (Beurre Noisette): Heat margarine or butter over low heat until light brown.

Black Butter (Beurre Noir): Heat ⅓ cup margarine or butter over low heat until golden brown or microwave uncovered in 1-pint glass measuring cup about 3½ minutes. Stir in 1 tablespoon vinegar or lemon juice; heat until bubbly or microwave uncovered 15 seconds. Add dash each of salt and pepper. Serve immediately.

Maître d'Hôtel Butter: Blend 3 tablespoons margarine or butter, softened, 1 tablespoon lemon juice, 1 tablespoon snipped parsley, ½ teaspoon salt and ⅛ teaspoon pepper.

QUICK GLORIFIED BUTTERS

Heat ¼ cup margarine or butter over low heat until melted or microwave uncovered in 1-cup glass measuring cup until hot and bubbly, about 45 seconds. Mix with one of the following:

Almonds: 1 tablespoon chopped toasted almonds

Capers: 1 tablespoon finely chopped capers

Celery Seed: 1 teaspoon celery seed

Cheese: 2 tablespoons grated Parmesan cheese

Chive-Parsley: 1 tablespoon snipped chives, 1 tablespoon snipped parsley and ½ teaspoon salt

Curry: ¼ teaspoon curry powder

Garlic: ¼ teaspoon garlic powder

Horseradish: 1 tablespoon prepared horseradish

Lemon: 1 teaspoon grated lemon peel, 2 tablespoons lemon juice and, if desired, 1 tablespoon snipped chives

Poppy Seed: 1 teaspoon poppy seed, 2 tablespoons lemon juice and dash of cayenne red pepper

VEGETABLE COMBOS

Cook vegetables separately, then serve them mixed together. For added mealtime variety, try:

☐ Green cabbage and red cabbage

☐ Diced carrots in nest of French-style green beans

☐ Carrot slices and Brussels sprouts or lima beans

☐ Celery and carrots, mushrooms or Brussels sprouts

☐ Corn and green lima beans or green peas

☐ Green lima beans in acorn squash halves

☐ Green peas and acorn squash rings, carrots, cauliflower, mushrooms or onions

☐ Summer squash, tomatoes and onions

☐ Tomatoes and okra or zucchini

☐ Baked stuffed tomatoes and buttered green peas

NOTE: For herbs, spices, sauces and crumb or cereal toppings to complement each vegetable, see "Ways to Serve" under individual vegetable listings.

CREAMED VEGETABLES

Stir 2 cups cooked vegetable(s) into Thin White Sauce (below). 4 TO 6 SERVINGS.

THIN WHITE SAUCE

1 tablespoon margarine or butter
1 tablespoon flour
¼ teaspoon salt
⅛ teaspoon pepper
1 cup milk

Heat margarine in saucepan over low heat until melted. Blend in flour, salt and pepper. Cook over low heat, stirring constantly, until smooth and bubbly; remove from heat. Stir in milk. Heat to boiling, stirring constantly. Boil and stir 1 minute.

■ **To Microwave:** Microwave margarine uncovered in 1-pint glass measuring cup until melted, about 30 seconds. Stir in flour, salt and pepper with fork. Stir in milk. Microwave uncovered, stirring every minute, until thickened, 3 to 3½ minutes.

Au Gratin Vegetables: Add 1 teaspoon dry mustard to flour mixture and stir 1 cup shredded process American cheese into hot sauce. Cook, stirring constantly, until cheese is melted. Pour vegetable mixture into ungreased 1-quart casserole; sprinkle with ½ cup Cereal Topping or Crumb Topping (page 161). Cook uncovered in 325° oven until heated through, about 15 minutes.

Scalloped Vegetables: Pour vegetable mixture into ungreased 1-quart casserole; sprinkle with ½ cup Cereal Topping or Crumb Topping (page 161). Cook uncovered in 325° oven until heated through, about 15 minutes.

Vegetables in Cheese Sauce: Add 1 teaspoon dry mustard to flour mixture and stir 1 cup shredded process American cheese (about 4 ounces) into hot sauce. Cook, stirring constantly, until cheese is melted.

ARTICHOKES—JERUSALEM

Amount for 4 servings: 1½ pounds.

Season available: November through January.

When shopping: Look for firm, mold-free tubers.

Ways to serve: Buttered, with salt and pepper . . . Varied with lemon juice and snipped parsley . . . Creamed, French fried or baked.

TO PREPARE
Pare thinly. Leave whole, slice or dice.

TO COOK
Heat 1 inch salted water (½ teaspoon salt to 1 cup water) to boiling. Add artichokes. Cover and heat to boiling. Cook until crisp-tender, 15 to 35 minutes.

TO MICROWAVE
Cover and microwave Jerusalem artichokes (¼-inch slices) and ¼ cup water in 1½-quart glass casserole 3 minutes; stir. Cover and microwave until crisp-tender, 3 to 4 minutes longer. Let stand 1 minute; drain.

French (globe) artichokes, Jerusalem artichokes

ARTICHOKES—FRENCH (GLOBE)

Amount for 4 servings: 4 (1 per serving).

Season available: September to May.

When shopping: Look for plump, heavy globes, compact scales (leaves); brown spots, indicating frost, do not impair quality.

Slice 1 inch off top of artichoke; snip off leaf points.

TO COOK

Allow 1 artichoke for each serving. Remove any discolored leaves and the small leaves at base of artichoke; trim stem even with base of artichoke. Cutting straight across, slice 1 inch off top; discard top. Snip off points of the remaining leaves with scissors. Rinse artichoke under cold water.

To prevent leaves from spreading during cooking, tie string around artichoke and from top to bottom to hold leaves in place. Invert cleaned artichoke in bowl containing 1 tablespoon lemon juice for each quart water to prevent discoloration.

Artichokes should be cooked in large kettle. For 4 medium artichokes, heat 6 quarts water, ¼ cup vegetable oil, 2 tablespoons lemon juice, 1 clove garlic, cut into fourths, and 1 teaspoon salt to boiling. Add artichokes. Heat to boiling; reduce heat. Simmer uncovered, rotating occasionally, until leaves pull out easily and bottom is tender when pierced with a knife, 30 to 40 minutes. Remove artichokes carefully from water (use tongs or two large spoons); place upside down to drain.

To reach artichoke's "heart," slice off the fuzzy choke.

TO SERVE HOT

Remove string but do not remove choke. (Choke is the fuzzy growth covering artichoke heart.) Place artichoke upright on plate. Accompany with a small cup of Classic Hollandaise Sauce (page 164) or one of the Quick Glorified Butters (page 161).

TO SERVE COLD

Cool artichokes; cover and refrigerate at least 4 hours. Remove string. Cut out choke if desired. Open each artichoke like a flower to reach the interior. Pull out tender center cone of leaves; scrape off exposed choke with spoon. Replace cone of leaves if desired.

Place each artichoke in center of a luncheon plate or special artichoke plate. Accompany with a small cup of Classic Hollandaise Sauce (page 164) or one of the Quick Glorified Butters (page 161). If choke has been removed, the cavity can be filled with the sauce. (Or cut artichoke into halves and serve on the plate with the main course; provide a small plate for the leaves.)

TO EAT

Pluck leaves one at a time. Dip base of leaf into a sauce or lemon butter. Turn leaf meaty side down and draw between teeth, scraping off meaty portion. Discard leaf on plate.

When all outer leaves have been removed, a center cone of small light-colored leaves covering the fuzzy center choke will be exposed (unless, of course, the choke has been removed before serving).

Pull or cut off cone of leaves. Slice off fuzzy choke with knife and fork; discard. Cut the remaining "heart," the prize section, into bite-size pieces; dip into sauce.

ASPARAGUS

Amount for 4 servings: 1½ pounds.

Season available: February through June.

When shopping: Look for smooth, round, tender green spears with closed tips.

Ways to serve: Buttered, with salt and pepper . . . Varied with dash of lemon juice or mace or sprinkled with buttered crumbs . . . Topped with Thin White Sauce (page 162) . . . Seasoned with allspice, dill weed, marjoram or savory.

TO PREPARE

Break off tough ends as far down as stalks snap easily. Wash asparagus. Remove scales if sandy or tough. (If necessary, remove sand particles with a vegetable brush.) For spears, tie whole stalks in bundles with string or hold together with band of aluminum foil. Or cut stalks into 1-inch pieces.

TO COOK

Spears: Heat 1 inch salted water (½ teaspoon salt to 1 cup water) to boiling in deep narrow pan or coffeepot. Place asparagus upright in pan. Heat to boiling; cook uncovered 5 minutes. Cover and cook until stalk ends are crisp-tender, 7 to 10 minutes longer; drain.

Pieces: Cook lower stalk pieces uncovered in 1 inch boiling salted water (½ teaspoon salt to 1 cup water) 6 minutes. Add tips. Cover and cook until crisp-tender, 5 to 8 minutes longer; drain.

TO MICROWAVE

Cover and microwave asparagus (spears or pieces) and ¼ cup water in 2-quart glass casserole 4 minutes; turn asparagus over. Cover and microwave until crisp-tender, 4 to 6 minutes longer. Let stand 1 minute; drain.

ASPARAGUS DRESS-UPS

Cook 1 pound fresh asparagus, then:

□ Toss with 1 tablespoon margarine or butter and 1 tablespoon half-and-half. Sprinkle with ¼ teaspoon salt and ¼ teaspoon ground nutmeg.

□ Top with ¼ cup cashews and 2 tablespoons finely chopped onion that have been browned in 2 tablespoons margarine or butter.

□ Sprinkle with ¼ teaspoon seasoned salt, dash of pepper and, if desired, 1 tablespoon chopped pimiento. Serve hot or cold.

ASPARAGUS WITH WINE SAUCE

1½ pounds fresh asparagus*
¼ cup dry white wine**
 1 tablespoon instant minced onion
¾ cup mayonnaise or salad dressing
 1 tablespoon lemon juice
 2 hard-cooked eggs, chopped

Prepare and cook asparagus spears as directed at left.

Pour wine on onion in saucepan. Stir in mayonnaise and lemon juice; heat just to boiling. Stir in eggs gently. Serve hot over asparagus.   4 TO 6 SERVINGS.

*2 packages (10 ounces each) frozen asparagus spears, cooked and drained, or 2 cans (15 ounces each) asparagus spears, heated and drained, can be substituted for the fresh asparagus.

**2 tablespoons apple juice can be substituted for the wine; increase lemon juice to 2 tablespoons.

OVEN ASPARAGUS

Prepare 1 to 1¼ pounds fresh asparagus spears as directed at left except—do not tie stalks in bundles. Arrange asparagus in ungreased oblong baking dish, 12x7½x2 inches. Cover and cook in 400° oven until tender, 20 to 30 minutes. Serve with Classic Hollandaise Sauce (below).   4 SERVINGS.

CLASSIC HOLLANDAISE SAUCE

Stir 2 egg yolks, slightly beaten, and 3 tablespoons lemon juice vigorously in 1-quart saucepan with wooden spoon. Add ¼ cup margarine or butter. Heat over very low heat, stirring constantly, until margarine is melted. Add ¼ cup margarine or butter, stirring vigorously until margarine is melted and sauce thickens. (Be sure margarine melts slowly; this gives eggs time to cook and thicken sauce without curdling.) Serve hot or at room temperature.   ¾ CUP SAUCE.

NOTE: Leftover sauce can be covered and stored in refrigerator several days. Before serving, stir in 1 teaspoon hot water.

■ **To Microwave:** Microwave ½ cup margarine or butter uncovered in 1-pint glass measuring cup until melted, 45 to 60 seconds. Add lemon juice. Beat in egg yolks gradually with fork. Microwave uncovered, stirring every 15 seconds, until thickened, about 1 minute. (Do not overcook or sauce will curdle.) Let stand 4 minutes before serving.

Skillet Asparagus

BEANS—GREEN AND WAX

Amount for 4 servings: 1 pound.

Season available: All year (peak—summer).

When shopping: Look for bright color, crisp pods.

Ways to serve: Buttered, with salt and pepper . . . Tossed with bacon or ham drippings or crumbled crisply fried bacon . . . Seasoned with basil, dill, marjoram, nutmeg, savory or thyme . . . Sprinkled with buttered bread crumbs.

TO PREPARE
Wash beans and remove ends. Leave beans whole or cut French style into lengthwise strips or crosswise into 1-inch pieces.

TO COOK
Heat beans and 1 inch salted water (½ teaspoon salt to 1 cup water) to boiling.

Green beans: Cook uncovered 5 minutes. Cover and cook until tender, whole or cut 10 to 15 minutes, French style 5 to 10 minutes; drain.

Wax beans: Cover and cook until tender, whole or cut 15 to 20 minutes, French style 10 to 15 minutes; drain.

TO MICROWAVE
Cover and microwave beans (1-inch pieces) and ¼ cup water in 1½-quart glass casserole 6 minutes; stir. Cover and microwave until tender, 5 to 7 minutes longer. Let stand 1 minute; drain.

SKILLET ASPARAGUS

Prepare 2 pounds fresh asparagus spears as directed on page 164 except—cut each stalk diagonally into 1-inch pieces.

Heat ⅓ cup margarine or butter and ⅓ cup water to boiling in 12-inch skillet. Add asparagus, ½ teaspoon salt and ⅛ teaspoon pepper. Cover and cook over high heat until asparagus is crisp-tender, 5 to 8 minutes (do not overcook).   6 SERVINGS

With frozen asparagus: Use 2 packages (10 ounces each) frozen cut asparagus. Melt the margarine with the salt and pepper and omit the ⅓ cup water.

QUICK ASPARAGUS AU GRATIN

This quick cheese sauce with its crunchy topping adds a glamorous touch to beans, broccoli, Brussels sprouts, carrots, cauliflower, celery, mushrooms, peas or potatoes.

  1 **pound fresh asparagus***
  1 **can (11 ounces) condensed Cheddar
      cheese soup**
  ½ **teaspoon dry mustard**
  ½ **teaspoon Worcestershire sauce**
  ½ **cup Cereal Topping or Crumb Topping
      (page 161)**

Prepare and cook asparagus spears as directed on page 164.

Mix soup, mustard and Worcestershire sauce; stir gently into asparagus. Pour into ungreased 1-quart casserole. Sprinkle with Cereal Topping. Cook uncovered in 325° oven until hot, 15 to 20 minutes.   4 TO 6 SERVINGS.

*1 package (10 ounces) frozen asparagus spears, cooked and drained, can be substituted for the fresh asparagus.

ALMOND-CRUNCH WAX BEANS

  1 **pound fresh wax beans**
  ½ **cup water**
  2 **tablespoons margarine or butter**
  ¾ **teaspoon salt**
  3 **tablespoons toasted slivered almonds**

Prepare beans in 1-inch pieces as directed above. Cook and stir beans, water, margarine and salt in 12-inch skillet over medium heat until margarine is melted. Cover and cook until beans are tender, 20 to 25 minutes. Stir in almonds.   3 OR 4 SERVINGS.

With canned beans: Use 1 can (15½ ounces) cut wax beans, drained. Omit water; decrease salt to ¼ teaspoon and cook until beans are heated through.

With frozen beans: Use 1 package (9 ounces) frozen cut wax beans. Omit water; decrease salt to ¼ teaspoon and cook 12 to 15 minutes.

Bean-Mushroom Medley

BEAN-MUSHROOM MEDLEY

8 ounces fresh green beans, cut into 1-inch
   pieces (about 1½ cups)
2 fresh medium carrots, cut crosswise into
   halves, then into ⅜-inch strips
1 medium onion, cut into ¼-inch slices
8 ounces fresh mushrooms, cut into ¼-inch
   slices (about 3 cups)
¼ cup margarine or butter
1 teaspoon salt
½ teaspoon monosodium glutamate
¼ teaspoon garlic salt
⅛ teaspoon white pepper

Heat 1 inch water to boiling in 2-quart saucepan.
Add beans and carrots. Heat to boiling; reduce
heat. Cover and simmer, stirring occasionally, until
almost tender, about 12 minutes; drain.

Cook and stir onion and mushrooms in margarine
in 10-inch skillet over medium heat until almost
tender, about 5 minutes; reduce heat. Cover and
cook 3 minutes.

Stir in beans, carrots, salt, monosodium glutamate,
garlic salt and white pepper. Cover and cook over
medium heat 5 minutes.   5 OR 6 SERVINGS.

GREEN BEANS CAESAR

1½ pounds fresh green beans*
2 tablespoons vegetable oil
1 tablespoon vinegar
1 tablespoon instant minced onion
¼ teaspoon salt
1 clove garlic, crushed
⅛ teaspoon pepper
2 tablespoons dry bread crumbs
2 tablespoons grated Parmesan cheese
1 tablespoon margarine or butter,
   melted
Paprika

Prepare and cook beans, cut into 1-inch pieces, as
directed on page 165.

Toss beans, oil, vinegar, onion, salt, garlic and
pepper. Pour into ungreased 1-quart casserole.
Mix bread crumbs, cheese and margarine; sprinkle
over beans. Sprinkle with paprika. Cook uncovered
in 350° oven until heated through, 15 to 20
minutes.   4 TO 6 SERVINGS.

*2 packages (9 ounces each) frozen cut green beans,
cooked and drained, can be substituted for the fresh
green beans.

BEANS—GREEN LIMAS

Amount for 4 servings: 3 pounds (unshelled).

Season available: July through November.

When shopping: Look for broad, thick, shiny pods that are plump with large seeds.

Ways to serve: Seasoned with snipped parsley, savory or sage . . . In a cream or butter sauce.

TO PREPARE

Wash and shell lima beans just before cooking. To shell beans, remove thin outer edge of pod with sharp knife or scissors. Beans will slip out.

TO COOK

Heat 1 inch salted water (½ teaspoon salt to 1 cup water) to boiling. Add beans. Heat to boiling; cook uncovered 5 minutes. Cover and cook until tender, 15 to 20 minutes longer; drain.

TO MICROWAVE

Cover and microwave lima beans and ½ cup water in 1-quart glass casserole 6 minutes; stir. Cover and microwave 6 minutes longer; stir. Cover and microwave until tender, 4 to 6 minutes longer. Let stand 1 minute; drain.

SAUCY LIMA BEANS

3 pounds fresh lima beans*
½ cup mayonnaise or salad dressing
2 tablespoons milk
1 teaspoon prepared mustard

Prepare and cook beans as directed above. Heat mayonnaise, milk and mustard, stirring constantly; pour over hot beans. Sprinkle with paprika if desired. 4 SERVINGS.

*1 package (10 ounces) frozen baby lima beans, cooked and drained, can be substituted for the fresh lima beans.

PERKY LIMA BEANS

3 pounds fresh lima beans*
2 tablespoons margarine or butter, softened
1 teaspoon sugar
1 teaspoon dry mustard
1 teaspoon lemon juice
¼ teaspoon salt

Prepare and cook beans as directed above. Stir in remaining ingredients. 4 SERVINGS.

*1 can (15 ounces) lima beans, heated and drained, or 1 package (10 ounces) frozen baby lima beans, cooked and drained, can be substituted for the fresh lima beans.

HICKORY LIMAS

Prepare and cook 3 pounds fresh lima beans as directed at left.* Stir in ¼ cup pasteurized process cheese spread with hickory smoke flavor and 2 tablespoons milk. Heat, stirring constantly, until cheese spread is melted and smooth. 4 SERVINGS.

*1 can (15 ounces) lima beans, heated and drained, or 1 package (10 ounces) frozen baby lima beans, cooked and drained, can be substituted for the fresh beans.

Creamy Lima Beans: Substitute pasteurized process Neufchâtel cheese spread with olives and pimientos or pasteurized process cheese spread with blue cheese for cheese spread with hickory smoke flavor. Increase milk to 3 tablespoons.

CREOLE LIMA BEANS

1 can (8 ounces) stewed tomatoes
1 package (10 ounces) frozen lima beans
1 large stalk celery, chopped (about ¾ cup)
¾ teaspoon salt
⅛ teaspoon pepper

Heat tomatoes to boiling. Stir in remaining ingredients. Heat to boiling, separating beans with fork; reduce heat. Cover and simmer until beans are tender, about 5 minutes. 5 SERVINGS.

THREE-BEAN CASSEROLE

1 package (10 ounces) frozen lima beans
1 package (9 ounces) frozen cut green beans
1 package (9 ounces) frozen cut wax beans
2 tablespoons margarine or butter
2 tablespoons flour
¾ teaspoon salt
½ teaspoon monosodium glutamate
⅛ teaspoon pepper
1 cup milk
½ cup grated Parmesan or Romano cheese

Cook beans as directed on packages except—omit salt; drain. (If beans have the same cooking time, they can be cooked together.) Place in ungreased square baking dish, 8x8x2 inches.

Heat margarine in 2-quart saucepan over low heat until melted. Stir in flour, salt, monosodium glutamate and pepper. Cook, stirring constantly, until mixture is smooth and bubbly. Remove from heat; stir in milk. Heat to boiling, stirring constantly. Boil and stir 1 minute. Pour over beans. Sprinkle with cheese. Cook uncovered in 375° oven until bubbly and brown, about 20 minutes. 8 SERVINGS.

BEETS

Amount for 4 servings: 5 medium (about 1¼ pounds).

Season available: All year (peak—June and July).

When shopping: Look for firm, round, smooth beets of a deep red color; fresh tops.

Ways to serve: Buttered, with salt and pepper ... Seasoned with dill, caraway seed, bay leaf, cloves, basil, savory, mint or nutmeg ... Tossed with orange peel or lemon peel ... Pickled or glazed.

TO PREPARE

Cut off all but 2 inches of beet tops. Wash beets and leave whole, with root ends attached.

TO COOK

Heat 6 cups water, 1 tablespoon vinegar (to preserve color) and 1 teaspoon salt to boiling. Add beets. Cover and heat to boiling. Cook until tender, 35 to 45 minutes; drain. Run cold water over beets; slip off skins and remove root ends. Slice, dice or cut into shoestring pieces.

BEETS IN SOUR CREAM

　5　fresh medium beets (about 1¼ pounds)*
　2　tablespoons margarine or butter
　2　teaspoons flour
　2　tablespoons vinegar
　1　tablespoon sugar
　¼　teaspoon salt
　¼　teaspoon dried dill weed
　⅛　teaspoon pepper
　½　cup dairy sour cream
　3　tablespoons half-and-half

Prepare and cook beets as directed above; cut into shoestring pieces.

Heat margarine in 2-quart saucepan until melted. Blend in flour. Cook over low heat, stirring constantly, until mixture is smooth and bubbly. Remove from heat; stir in vinegar, sugar, salt, dill weed and pepper. Heat to boiling, stirring constantly. Boil and stir 1 minute. Stir in beets; heat through. Mix sour cream and half-and-half; heat through over low heat. Pour over hot beets. 4 SERVINGS.

*1 can (16 ounces) shoestring beets, drained, can be substituted for the fresh beets.

HARVARD BEETS

　5　fresh medium beets (about 1¼ pounds)
　1　tablespoon cornstarch
　1　tablespoon sugar
　¾　teaspoon salt
　　Dash of pepper
　⅔　cup water
　¼　cup vinegar

Prepare and cook beets as directed at left; cut into slices.

Mix cornstarch, sugar, salt and pepper in saucepan. Stir water and vinegar gradually into cornstarch mixture. Cook, stirring constantly, until mixture thickens and boils. Boil and stir 1 minute. Stir in beets; heat through. 4 SERVINGS.

With canned beets: Use 1 can (16 ounces) sliced beets, drained (reserve liquid). Add enough water to reserved liquid to measure ⅔ cup; substitute for the water.

Orange Beets: Substitute packed brown sugar for the sugar and ¾ cup orange juice for the water. Decrease vinegar to 1 tablespoon and add 1 teaspoon grated orange peel to the cornstarch mixture.

QUICK SWEET-AND-SOUR BEETS

Drain 1 jar (16 ounces) pickled beets, reserving syrup. Mix reserved syrup and 1 tablespoon cornstarch in 2-quart saucepan. Cook, stirring constantly, until mixture thickens and boils. Boil and stir 1 minute. Stir in beets and 1 can (11 ounces) mandarin orange segments, drained, or 1 can (8¼ ounces) pineapple chunks, drained; heat through. 4 SERVINGS.

QUICK BORSCH

　1　can (10½ ounces) condensed beef broth
　　　(about 1¼ cups)
　1　can (16 ounces) shoestring beets
　1　cup shredded cabbage
　2　tablespoons finely chopped onion
　1　teaspoon sugar
　1　teaspoon lemon juice
　　Dairy sour cream

Heat broth, beets (with liquid), cabbage, onion and sugar to boiling; reduce heat. Simmer uncovered 5 minutes. Stir in lemon juice; refrigerate until chilled. Top each serving with spoonful of sour cream. 3 OR 4 SERVINGS (ABOUT 1 CUP EACH).

BROCCOLI

Amount for 4 servings: 1½ pounds.

Season available: All year.

When shopping: Look for firm, compact dark green clusters. Avoid thick, tough stems.

Ways to serve: Buttered . . . Topped with Quick Glorified Butters (page 161), Classic Hollandaise Sauce (page 164) or grated cheese . . . Seasoned with nutmeg or oregano . . . Creamed.

TO PREPARE

Trim off large leaves; remove tough ends of lower stems. Wash broccoli. If stems are thicker than 1 inch, make lengthwise gashes in each stem.

TO COOK

Heat 1 inch salted water (½ teaspoon salt to 1 cup water) to boiling. Add broccoli. Cover and heat to boiling. Cook until stems are tender, 12 to 15 minutes; drain.

TO MICROWAVE

Cover and microwave broccoli (1-inch pieces or thin spears) and ¼ cup water in 3-quart glass casserole 5 minutes; stir. Cover and microwave until stems are tender, 4 to 6 minutes longer. Let stand 1 minute; drain.

ITALIAN BROCCOLI

Prepare and cook 1½ pounds fresh broccoli as directed above.*

Cook and stir broccoli in 3 tablespoons olive oil, margarine or butter until broccoli is delicate brown. Sprinkle with 2 tablespoons grated Parmesan cheese.   4 SERVINGS.

*1 package (10 ounces) frozen broccoli spears, cooked and drained, can be substituted for the fresh broccoli.

BROCCOLI ELEGANT

1½ pounds fresh broccoli*
 ½ can (11-ounce size) condensed
      Cheddar cheese soup (⅔ cup)
 3 tablespoons milk
 2 tablespoons sliced ripe olives

Prepare and cook broccoli as directed above.

Mix soup and milk in saucepan. Stir in broccoli and olives; heat through.   4 SERVINGS.

*1 package (10 ounces) frozen broccoli spears, cooked and drained, can be substituted for the fresh broccoli.

SAVORY BROCCOLI

Cook 1 package (10 ounces) frozen chopped broccoli as directed on package; drain. Stir in 1 tablespoon margarine or butter and ¾ teaspoon dried dill weed or ⅛ teaspoon ground allspice.   3 OR 4 SERVINGS.

BROCCOLI WITH CHEESE SAUCE

1½ pounds fresh broccoli*
 6 ounces process American cheese, sliced
 ⅓ cup milk
 ¼ teaspoon onion salt
 1 drop red pepper sauce (optional)

Prepare and cook broccoli as directed at left.

Heat remaining ingredients over medium heat, stirring frequently, until cheese is melted and mixture is smooth, 6 to 8 minutes. Pour cheese sauce over broccoli.   4 SERVINGS.

*1 package (10 ounces) frozen broccoli spears, cooked and drained, can be substituted for the fresh broccoli.

BROCCOLI WITH MUSTARD SAUCE

1½ pounds fresh broccoli*
 1 tablespoon margarine or butter
 1 tablespoon half-and-half
 ½ teaspoon dry mustard
 1 teaspoon sugar
 ⅛ teaspoon pepper

Prepare and cook broccoli as directed at left.

Stir in margarine. Mix remaining ingredients; pour over broccoli.   4 SERVINGS.

*1 package (10 ounces) frozen broccoli spears, cooked and drained, can be substituted for the fresh broccoli.

Make gashes in thick broccoli stems for even cooking.

BRUSSELS SPROUTS

Amount for 4 servings: 1½ pounds.

Season available: Fall and winter.

When shopping: Look for unblemished bright green sprouts; compact leaves.

Ways to serve: Buttered, with salt and pepper . . . Seasoned with garlic salt, basil, caraway seed, cumin, dill, marjoram, sage or savory . . . Creamed . . . With Cheese Sauce (page 173).

TO PREPARE

Remove any discolored leaves. Cut off stem ends; wash sprouts.

TO COOK

Heat 1 inch salted water (½ teaspoon salt to 1 cup water) to boiling. Add Brussels sprouts. Cover and heat to boiling. Cook until tender, 8 to 10 minutes; drain.

TO MICROWAVE

Cover and microwave Brussels sprouts and ¼ cup water in 1½-quart glass casserole 4 minutes; stir. Cover and microwave until tender, 3 to 4 minutes longer. Let stand 1 minute; drain.

BRUSSELS SPROUTS PARISIENNE

1½ **pounds fresh Brussels sprouts***
  2 **tablespoons margarine or butter**
  2 **tablespoons flour**
 ¼ **teaspoon salt**
 ⅛ **teaspoon ground nutmeg**
   Dash of pepper
  1 **can (13¾ ounces) chicken broth**
    (about 1¾ cups)
  2 **egg yolks, well beaten**
 ¼ **cup toasted slivered almonds**

Prepare and cook Brussels sprouts as directed above.

Heat margarine in 2-quart saucepan over low heat until melted. Blend in flour, salt, nutmeg and pepper. Cook over low heat, stirring constantly, until mixture is smooth and bubbly; remove from heat. Stir in broth. Heat to boiling, stirring constantly. Boil and stir 1 minute. Stir at least half of the hot mixture gradually into egg yolks; blend into hot mixture in saucepan. Boil and stir 1 minute longer. Stir in almonds and Brussels sprouts; heat through.
4 TO 6 SERVINGS.

*2 packages (10 ounces each) frozen Brussels sprouts, cooked and drained, can be substituted for the fresh Brussels sprouts.

CABBAGE—
GREEN, SAVOY AND RED

Amount for 4 servings: 1 medium head (about 1½ pounds).

Season available: All year.

When shopping: Look for firm, heavy heads of fresh, good color.

Ways to serve: Green or Savoy—Buttered, with salt and pepper . . . Seasoned with caraway or celery seed . . . Topped with Cheese Sauce (page 173) . . . Wedges, cooked in water with ham or corned beef . . . Shredded, creamed or scalloped; Red—Buttered, with salt and pepper . . . Shredded, seasoned with caraway or celery seed or crumbled crisply fried bacon.

TO PREPARE

Remove outside leaves; wash cabbage. Cut into wedges; remove core after cooking. Or shred cabbage and discard core.

TO COOK

Green or Savoy: Heat 1 inch (½ inch for shredded) salted water (½ teaspoon salt to 1 cup water) to boiling. Add cabbage. Cover and heat to boiling. Cook until crisp-tender, wedges 10 to 12 minutes, shredded about 5 minutes; drain.

Red: Heat 1 inch (½ inch for shredded) salted water (½ teaspoon salt to 1 cup water) and 2 tablespoons vinegar or lemon juice to boiling. Add cabbage. Cover and heat to boiling. Cook until crisp-tender, wedges about 20 minutes, shredded about 10 minutes; drain.

TO MICROWAVE

Cover and microwave cabbage (wedges or shredded) and 2 tablespoons water in 3-quart glass casserole 5 minutes; turn casserole one quarter turn (stir for shredded). Cover and microwave until crisp-tender, 4 to 6 minutes longer. Let stand 1 minute; drain.

ITALIAN CABBAGE WEDGES

Prepare and cook 1 large head green cabbage (about 2 pounds), cut into 6 wedges, as directed above.

Place cabbage wedges on serving plate. Place a 1-ounce slice mozzarella cheese on each cabbage wedge. Garnish each with strip of pimiento and sprinkle with dried oregano leaves if desired.
6 SERVINGS.

Chinese-style Vegetables

CHINESE-STYLE VEGETABLES

1 small head green cabbage (about 1 pound)
1 tablespoon shortening
2 medium stalks celery, cut into thin
    diagonal slices (about 1 cup)
1 medium green pepper, cut into thin
    diagonal slices (about 1 cup)
1 large onion, chopped (about ¾ cup)
1 teaspoon salt
⅛ teaspoon pepper

Prepare 3 cups finely shredded cabbage as directed on page 170.

Heat shortening in 10-inch skillet until melted. Stir in cabbage, celery, green pepper and onion. Cover and cook over medium heat, stirring several times, until vegetables are tender, about 5 minutes. Sprinkle with salt and pepper.   4 SERVINGS.

HEARTY VEGETABLE SOUP

2 cans (12 ounces each) vegetable juice
    cocktail
2 cups water
1 small head green cabbage (about 1 pound),
    finely chopped
1 medium onion, sliced
3 small or 2 medium carrots, sliced (about 1 cup)
1 medium stalk celery, chopped (about ½ cup)
2 tablespoons instant beef or chicken
    bouillon

Heat all ingredients to boiling; reduce heat. Cover and simmer 1 hour.   8 SERVINGS (ABOUT 1 CUP EACH).

NOTE: To chop cabbage in blender, see page 138.

SWEET-SOUR RED CABBAGE

1 medium head red cabbage (about
    1½ pounds)
4 slices bacon, diced
¼ cup packed brown sugar
2 tablespoons flour
½ cup water
¼ cup vinegar
1 teaspoon salt
⅛ teaspoon pepper
1 small onion, sliced

Prepare and cook 5 cups shredded cabbage as directed on page 170. (Be sure to add the 2 tablespoons vinegar or lemon juice to the salted water.)

Fry bacon until crisp; drain on paper towels. Drain fat from skillet, reserving 1 tablespoon. Stir brown sugar and flour into fat in skillet. Add water, vinegar, salt, pepper and onion. Cook, stirring frequently, until mixture thickens, about 5 minutes.

Stir bacon and sauce mixture into hot cabbage in saucepan; heat through. Garnish with additional crisply fried diced bacon if desired.   6 SERVINGS.

CABBAGE—
CHINESE OR CELERY

Amount for 4 servings: 1 medium head.

Season available: All year.

When shopping: Look for crisp, green heads, either firm or leafy.

Ways to serve: Buttered, with salt and pepper . . . Sprinkled with grated cheese or buttered bread crumbs . . . Topped with Classic Hollandaise Sauce (page 164) or Cheese Sauce (page 173).

TO PREPARE
Remove root ends. Wash cabbage; shred.

TO COOK
Heat ½ inch salted water (½ teaspoon salt to 1 cup water) to boiling. Add cabbage. Cover and heat to boiling. Cook until crisp-tender, 4 to 5 minutes; drain.

TO MICROWAVE
Cover and microwave cabbage and 2 tablespoons water in 2-quart glass casserole 2 minutes; stir. Cover and microwave until crisp-tender, 2 to 3 minutes longer. Let stand 1 minute; drain.

CARROTS

Amount for 4 servings: 1¼ pounds.

Season available: All year.

When shopping: Look for firm, nicely shaped carrots of good color.

Ways to serve: Buttered, with salt and pepper . . . Sprinkled with snipped parsley, mint, chives or cut green onion . . . Topped with Lemon Butter or Browned Butter (page 161) . . . Seasoned with basil, chervil, ginger, rosemary, savory or thyme . . . Creamed or mashed.

TO PREPARE

Scrape carrots and remove ends. Leave carrots whole, shred or cut lengthwise into ⅜-inch strips or crosswise into ¼-inch slices.

TO COOK

Heat 1 inch salted water (½ teaspoon salt to 1 cup water) to boiling. Add carrots. Cover and heat to boiling. Cook until tender, whole 25 minutes, shredded 5 minutes, lengthwise strips 18 to 20 minutes, crosswise slices 12 to 15 minutes; drain.

TO MICROWAVE

Cover and microwave carrots (¼-inch slices) in 1½-quart glass casserole 5 minutes; stir. Cover and microwave until tender, 5 to 7 minutes longer. Let stand 1 minute; drain.

CHIVE-BUTTERED CARROTS

1½ pounds fresh carrots*
¼ cup margarine or butter
¼ teaspoon seasoned salt
⅛ teaspoon pepper
1 tablespoon snipped chives

Prepare and cook whole carrots as directed above.

Heat margarine in 10-inch skillet until melted; add carrots. Sprinkle with seasoned salt, pepper and chives. Heat, turning occasionally to coat with margarine, until carrots are hot.   5 OR 6 SERVINGS.

With frozen carrots: Use 2 packages (10 ounces each) frozen carrots in butter sauce, cooked; sprinkle with seasoned salt, pepper and chives.

*2 cans (16 ounces each) whole carrots, drained, can be substituted for the fresh carrots.

BRANDIED CARROTS

1¼ pounds fresh carrots
¼ cup margarine or butter, melted
¼ cup brandy or pineapple juice
1 teaspoon sugar
1 teaspoon salt

Prepare carrots, cut into 2½x¼-inch strips, as directed at left.

Place carrots in ungreased square pan, 8x8x2 inches. Mix remaining ingredients; pour over carrots. Cover and cook in 375° oven until carrots are tender, about 40 minutes.   4 SERVINGS.

GLAZED CARROTS

1½ pounds fresh carrots
⅓ cup packed brown sugar
½ teaspoon salt
½ teaspoon grated orange peel
2 tablespoons margarine or butter

Prepare and cook carrots, cut into lengthwise strips, as directed at left.

Cook and stir brown sugar, salt and orange peel in margarine in 12-inch skillet until bubbly. Add carrots; cook over low heat, stirring occasionally, until carrots are glazed and heated through, about 5 minutes.   5 OR 6 SERVINGS.

CARROT-BACON SKILLET

1½ pounds fresh carrots
3 slices bacon
½ teaspoon salt
  Dash of pepper
¼ cup snipped parsley

Prepare and cook 4 cups shredded carrots as directed at left.

Fry bacon in 10-inch skillet until crisp; drain on paper towels. Drain fat from skillet, reserving 2 tablespoons. Stir carrots, salt and pepper into fat in skillet; heat through. Crumble bacon; sprinkle bacon and parsley over carrots.   5 OR 6 SERVINGS.

CAULIFLOWER

Amount for 4 servings: 1 medium head (about 2 pounds).

Season available: All year.

When shopping: Look for clean, nonspreading flower clusters (the white portion); green "jacket" leaves.

Ways to serve: Buttered, with salt and pepper . . . Topped with buttered crumbs, grated cheese or Cheese Sauce (below) . . . Seasoned with basil, curry powder, nutmeg, celery seed or poppy seed . . . Creamed . . . Raw, as a relish.

TO PREPARE

Remove outer leaves and stalk. Cut off any discoloration; wash cauliflower. Leave whole or separate into flowerets.

TO COOK

Heat 1 inch salted water (½ teaspoon salt to 1 cup water) to boiling. Add cauliflower. Cover and heat to boiling. Cook until tender, whole 20 to 25 minutes, flowerets 10 to 12 minutes; drain.

TO MICROWAVE

Cover and microwave cauliflower (whole or flowerets) and 2 tablespoons water in 2-quart glass casserole 6 minutes; turn casserole one quarter turn (stir flowerets). Cover and microwave until tender, 5 to 7 minutes longer. Let stand 1 minute; drain.

GLORIFIED CHEESE CAULIFLOWER

Prepare and cook 1 medium head cauliflower (about 2 pounds) as directed above for whole cauliflower. Pour Cheese Sauce (below) over hot cauliflower; sprinkle with paprika if desired.
4 SERVINGS.

CHEESE SAUCE

- 2 tablespoons margarine or butter
- 2 tablespoons flour
- 1 teaspoon dry mustard
- ¼ teaspoon salt
   Dash of pepper
- 1 cup milk
- 1 cup shredded process sharp American cheese (about 4 ounces)
- 5 drops red pepper sauce

Heat margarine over low heat until melted. Blend in flour, mustard, salt and pepper. Cook over low heat, stirring constantly, until mixture is smooth and bubbly; remove from heat. Stir in milk. Heat to boiling, stirring constantly. Boil and stir 1 minute. Stir in cheese and pepper sauce. Cook and stir over low heat until cheese is melted.

■ **To Microwave:** Microwave margarine uncovered in 1-pint glass measuring cup until melted, about 30 seconds. Stir in flour, mustard, salt and pepper with fork. Gradually stir in milk. Microwave uncovered 1 minute; stir. Microwave uncovered 1 minute longer; stir. Add cheese and pepper sauce. Microwave uncovered until thickened, 1 to 1½ minutes.

CREAMY CAULIFLOWER SOUP

- 1 medium head cauliflower (about 2 pounds)
- 2 cups water
- 1 large stalk celery, chopped (about ¾ cup)
- 1 medium onion, chopped (about ½ cup)
- 1 tablespoon lemon juice
- 2 tablespoons margarine or butter
- 2 tablespoons flour
- 2½ cups water
- 1 tablespoon instant chicken bouillon
- ¾ teaspoon salt
- ⅛ teaspoon pepper
   Dash of ground nutmeg
- ½ cup whipping cream

Prepare cauliflower as directed at left; separate into flowerets.

Heat 2 cups water to boiling in 3-quart saucepan. Add cauliflower, celery, onion and lemon juice. Cover and heat to boiling. Cook until tender, about 10 minutes; do not drain. Press cauliflower mixture through food mill. (Or place in blender container. Cover and blend until uniform consistency.)

Heat margarine in 3-quart saucepan over low heat until melted. Stir in flour. Cook, stirring constantly, until mixture is smooth and bubbly; remove from heat. Stir in 2½ cups water. Heat to boiling, stirring constantly. Boil and stir 1 minute. Stir in cauliflower mixture, instant bouillon, salt, pepper and nutmeg. Heat just to boiling. Stir in cream; heat but do not boil. Serve with grated cheese if desired.   8 SERVINGS.

Creamy Broccoli Soup: Substitute 1½ pounds broccoli, cut up, for the cauliflower; omit lemon juice.

Creamy Cabbage Soup: Substitute 1 medium head green cabbage (about 1½ pounds), shredded, for the cauliflower; decrease cooking time to 5 minutes.

CELERY

Types: Pascal (green), Golden (bleached).

Amount for 4 servings: 1 medium bunch.

Season available: All year.

When shopping: Look for crisp, unblemished stalks; fresh leaves.

Ways to serve: Buttered, with salt and pepper . . . Creamed or braised . . . Seasoned with mustard . . . Raw, as a relish.

TO PREPARE
Remove leaves and trim off root ends. Remove any coarse strings. Wash celery. Cut stalks into 1-inch pieces (about 4 cups).

TO COOK
Heat 1 inch salted water (½ teaspoon salt to 1 cup water) to boiling. Add celery pieces. Cover and heat to boiling. Cook until tender, 15 to 20 minutes; drain.

TO MICROWAVE
Cover and microwave celery and 2 tablespoons water in 1½-quart casserole 4 minutes; stir. Cover and microwave until tender, 3 to 5 minutes longer. Let stand 1 minute; drain.

GOLDEN CELERY

   1 medium bunch celery
   1 small onion, chopped (about ¼ cup)
   1 tablespoon margarine or butter
   1 tablespoon flour
   ¼ teaspoon salt
   ⅛ teaspoon pepper
   1 cup milk
   1 cup shredded process American cheese
       (about 4 ounces)
   1 teaspoon dry mustard
   1 jar (2 ounces) sliced pimiento, drained

Prepare and cook 4 cups celery pieces as directed above.

Cook and stir onion in margarine in 10-inch skillet until tender; remove from heat. Stir in flour, salt and pepper. Cook over low heat, stirring constantly, until mixture is bubbly; remove from heat. Stir in milk. Heat to boiling, stirring constantly. Boil and stir 1 minute.

Stir in cheese and mustard. Cook and stir over low heat until cheese is melted. Stir in celery and pimiento; heat through.   4 SERVINGS.

HOT RELISH TRAY

   1 can (16 ounces) whole carrots
   2 medium stalks celery, cut into ¼-inch
       diagonal slices (about 1 cup)
   ½ cup sweet pickle sticks or watermelon
       pickles
   ½ teaspoon salt

Mix carrots (with liquid) and remaining ingredients in saucepan; heat through.   4 SERVINGS.

CRUNCHY CELERY SKILLET

   10 medium stalks celery, cut into ¼-inch
       diagonal slices (about 5 cups)
    1 can (8 ounces) water chestnuts, drained
       and sliced
    1 tablespoon instant chicken bouillon
    ½ teaspoon salt
    ½ teaspoon celery salt
    1 teaspoon vegetable oil
    1 jar (2 ounces) sliced pimiento, drained

Cook and stir celery, water chestnuts, instant bouillon, salt and celery salt in oil over medium heat, turning vegetables constantly with pancake turner, until celery is crisp-tender, about 10 minutes. Stir in pimiento; heat through.   5 SERVINGS.

CELERY ROOT (CELERIAC)

Amount for 4 servings: 1½ pounds.

Season available: October through April.

When shopping: Look for firm, clean roots.

Ways to serve: Buttered . . . Marinated in French dressing, as a salad (Grape-Celery Salads, page 317) . . . Raw, as a relish.

TO PREPARE
Cut off leaves and root fibers. Scrub; do not pare.

TO COOK
Heat enough salted water to cover celery root (½ teaspoon salt to 1 cup water) to boiling. Add celery root. Heat to boiling. Cook until tender, 40 to 60 minutes; drain. Pare and slice.

TO MICROWAVE
Cover and microwave celery root (½-inch pieces) and ¼ cup water in 1½-quart glass casserole 4 minutes; stir. Cover and microwave until crisp-tender, 4 to 6 minutes longer. Let stand 1 minute; drain.

Glorified Cheese Cauliflower (page 173) and Crunchy Celery Skillet (page 174)

Chinese pea pods, mushrooms

CHINESE PEA PODS

Amount for 4 servings: 1 pound.

Season available: All year.

When shopping: Look for flat, crisp, bright pods.

Ways to serve: Buttered . . . With water chestnuts, almonds or mushrooms.

TO PREPARE
Wash pods; remove tips and strings.

TO COOK
Heat 1 inch salted water (½ teaspoon salt to 1 cup water) to boiling. Add pea pods. Heat to boiling. Cook uncovered, stirring occasionally, until crisp-tender, 2 to 3 minutes; drain.

TO MICROWAVE
Cover and microwave pea pods and ¼ cup water in 2-quart glass casserole 3 minutes; stir. Cover and microwave until crisp-tender, 2 to 4 minutes longer. Let stand 1 minute; drain.

POLYNESIAN PEA PODS

8 ounces fresh Chinese pea pods*
1 can (8¼ ounces) pineapple chunks, drained
2 tablespoons margarine or butter
¼ teaspoon salt

Prepare and cook pea pods as directed above. Cook and stir pineapple in margarine in 1-quart saucepan until hot. Add pea pods and salt; toss and heat.   4 SERVINGS.

*1 package (7 ounces) frozen Chinese pea pods, cooked and drained, can be substituted for the fresh pea pods.

CORN

Amount for 4 servings: 4 to 8 ears.

Season available: May through December.

When shopping: Look for bright green husks, fresh-looking silk, plump but not too large kernels.

Ways to serve: On the cob—with butter, salt and pepper . . . Seasoned with basil, cayenne red pepper, celery seed, chili powder or rosemary.

TO PREPARE
Refrigerate unhusked corn until ready to use. Corn is best when eaten as soon after picking as possible. Husk ears and remove silk just before cooking.

TO COOK
Place corn in enough *unsalted* cold water to cover (salt toughens corn). Add 1 tablespoon sugar and 1 tablespoon lemon juice to each gallon of water. Heat to boiling; boil uncovered 2 minutes. Remove from heat; let stand 10 minutes before serving.

TO MICROWAVE
Wrap corn in waxed paper; twist ends. Microwave until tender, 7 to 9 minutes. Let stand 1 minute.

CORN SESAME SAUTE

3 ears fresh corn
3 tablespoons margarine or butter
1 clove garlic, crushed
2 tablespoons sesame seed
2 tablespoons chopped green pepper
½ teaspoon salt
¼ teaspoon dried basil leaves
⅛ teaspoon pepper

Prepare corn as directed above. Cut enough kernels from corn to measure 1½ cups.

Cook and stir corn and remaining ingredients over medium heat until margarine is melted; reduce heat. Cover and cook until tender, about 15 minutes.   4 SERVINGS.

With canned corn: Use 1 can (12 ounces) whole kernel corn with peppers, drained. Decrease margarine to 1 tablespoon and omit green pepper. Cook and stir all ingredients except corn over medium heat until sesame seed is toasted. Stir in corn; heat through.

With frozen corn: Use 1 package (10 ounces) frozen whole kernel corn. Cook, stirring occasionally, until corn is tender, about 7 minutes.

SUMMER SUCCOTASH

4 ears fresh corn
3 pounds fresh lima beans (about 2 cups shelled)
⅓ cup cut-up lean salt pork or bacon
1 small onion, chopped (about ¼ cup)
½ cup half-and-half
¼ teaspoon salt
⅛ teaspoon pepper

Prepare corn as directed on page 176. Cut enough kernels from corn to measure 2 cups. Mix beans, pork and onion in 3-quart saucepan; add enough water to cover. Heat to boiling; reduce heat. Cover and simmer until beans are tender, 20 to 25 minutes. Stir in corn. Heat to boiling; reduce heat. Cover and simmer until corn is tender, about 5 minutes; drain. Stir in half-and-half, salt and pepper. Heat, stirring occasionally, until hot.
6 SERVINGS.

CHILI CORN

Prepare and cook 3 ears fresh corn* as directed on page 176. Cut enough kernels from corn to measure 1½ cups. Stir in 1 tablespoon margarine or butter, ¼ teaspoon chili powder and ¼ cup sliced ripe olives.   3 OR 4 SERVINGS.

*1 package (10 ounces) frozen whole kernel corn, cooked and drained, can be substituted for the fresh corn.

TOMATOED CORN

4 ears fresh corn*
¼ cup margarine or butter
1 small onion, chopped (about ¼ cup)
½ small green pepper, chopped
2 teaspoons sugar
½ teaspoon salt
¼ teaspoon ground cumin
1 large tomato, cut up

Prepare corn as directed on page 176. Cut enough kernels from corn to measure 2 cups.

Cook and stir all ingredients except tomato over medium heat until margarine is melted. Cover and cook over low heat 10 minutes. Stir in tomato. Cover and cook 5 minutes longer.   4 SERVINGS.

With canned corn: Decrease margarine to 3 tablespoons; stir in 1 can (16 ounces) whole kernel corn, drained, with the tomato.

*1 package (10 ounces) frozen whole kernel corn can be substituted for the fresh corn.

SCALLOPED CORN

4 ears fresh corn*
1 small onion, chopped (about ¼ cup)
½ small green pepper, chopped
2 tablespoons margarine or butter
2 tablespoons flour
1 teaspoon salt
½ teaspoon paprika
¼ teaspoon dry mustard
   Dash of pepper
¾ cup milk
1 egg, slightly beaten
⅓ cup cracker crumbs
1 tablespoon margarine or butter, melted

Prepare and cook corn as directed on page 176. Cut enough kernels from corn to measure 2 cups.

Cook and stir onion and green pepper in 2 tablespoons margarine until onion is tender; remove from heat. Stir in flour, salt, paprika, mustard and pepper. Cook over low heat, stirring constantly, until mixture is bubbly; remove from heat. Stir in milk gradually. Heat to boiling, stirring constantly. Boil and stir 1 minute. Stir in corn and egg. Pour into ungreased 1-quart casserole.

Mix crumbs and 1 tablespoon melted margarine; sprinkle over corn. Cook uncovered in 350° oven until bubbly, 30 to 35 minutes.   4 SERVINGS.

*1 package (10 ounces) frozen whole kernel corn, cooked and drained, or 1 can (16 ounces) whole kernel corn, drained, can be substituted for the fresh corn.

Cheese Scalloped Corn: Fold ½ cup shredded natural Cheddar cheese into the sauce mixture.

CORN OYSTERS

1 cup bacon fat
1 cup vegetable oil
1 cup all-purpose flour
1 teaspoon baking powder
1 teaspoon salt
2 eggs, slightly beaten
1 can (16 ounces) whole kernel corn, drained
   (reserve ¼ cup liquid)

Heat fat and oil in 10-inch skillet to 375°. Mix flour, baking powder, salt, eggs and reserved corn liquid. Stir in corn. Drop by rounded tablespoonfuls into hot fat. Fry until golden brown, 4 to 5 minutes; drain on paper towels.   2 DOZEN CORN OYSTERS.

Nutmeg Corn Oysters: Stir in 1 teaspoon ground nutmeg with the flour.

EGGPLANT

Amount for 4 servings: 1 medium (about 1½ pounds).

Season available: All year (peak—July, August, September).

When shopping: Look for smooth, firm eggplants of an even dark purple.

Ways to serve: Buttered, with salt and pepper . . . Sprinkled with grated Parmesan cheese, snipped chives or parsley . . . Seasoned with allspice, chili powder, curry powder, garlic, oregano or rosemary . . . Panfried, French fried, stuffed or scalloped.

TO PREPARE

Just before cooking, wash eggplant and, if desired, pare. Cut eggplant into ½-inch cubes, strips or ¼-inch slices.

TO COOK

To Boil: Heat small amount salted water (½ teaspoon salt to 1 cup water) to boiling. Add eggplant. Cover and heat to boiling. Cook until tender, 5 to 8 minutes; drain.

To Fry: Cook and stir eggplant in margarine, butter or bacon fat until tender, 5 to 10 minutes.

TO MICROWAVE

Cover and microwave eggplant (¼-inch slices) in 2-quart glass casserole until tender, 5 to 7 minutes. Let stand 1 minute.

RATATOUILLE

1 medium eggplant (about 1½ pounds)
2 small zucchini (about ½ pound)
1 medium green pepper, chopped (about 1 cup)
1 medium onion, finely chopped (about ½ cup)
4 medium tomatoes, each cut into fourths
¼ cup vegetable oil
1 clove garlic, crushed
2 teaspoons salt
¼ teaspoon pepper

Prepare 5 cups cubed eggplant as directed above. Prepare 2 cups sliced zucchini as directed on page 188.

Cook and stir all ingredients until heated through. Cover and cook over medium heat, stirring occasionally, until vegetables are crisp-tender, about 10 minutes.　6 TO 8 SERVINGS.

PECAN EGGPLANT

¼ cup margarine or butter
1 medium eggplant (about 1½ pounds), cut into ½-inch slices
1 cup half-and-half
¾ teaspoon salt
½ teaspoon paprika
⅛ teaspoon pepper
½ cup chopped pecans

Heat margarine in 10-inch skillet over low heat until melted. Add eggplant. Cook, turning once, until golden brown. Place in ungreased oblong baking dish, 13½x9x2 inches. Pour half-and-half over eggplant. Sprinkle with remaining ingredients. Cook uncovered in 300° oven until half-and-half is absorbed, about 1 hour.
4 SERVINGS.

MUSHROOM-STUFFED EGGPLANT

1 medium eggplant (about 1½ pounds)
1 jar (4½ ounces) sliced mushrooms, drained
¼ cup all-purpose flour
¼ cup margarine or butter
2 tablespoons finely chopped green pepper
2 tablespoons finely chopped onion
1 clove garlic, crushed
1 teaspoon salt
⅛ teaspoon pepper
¼ cup half-and-half
1 jar (2 ounces) chopped pimiento, drained
1 tablespoon grated Parmesan cheese or 2 tablespoons buttered bread crumbs

Wash eggplant; cut a large lengthwise slice from eggplant. Remove and cube enough eggplant from shell to measure 3 cups.

Mix eggplant, mushrooms, flour, margarine, green pepper, onion, garlic, salt and pepper in 10-inch skillet. Cook and stir over medium heat until mixture is browned. Remove from heat; stir in half-and-half and pimiento. Fill eggplant shell with mixture; sprinkle with cheese. Cook uncovered in 350° oven until eggplant is tender, 40 to 45 minutes.　4 TO 6 SERVINGS.

GREENS

Types: Mild-flavored—Beet Tops, Chicory (outer leaves), Collards, Escarole, Lettuce (outer leaves), Spinach; Strong-flavored—Kale, Mustard Greens, Swiss Chard, Turnip Greens.

Amount for 4 servings: 2 pounds.

Season available: All year.

When shopping: Look for tender, young, unblemished leaves of bright green color.

Ways to serve: Seasoned with dill, marjoram, mint, nutmeg, rosemary or onion . . . With lemon juice or vinegar, bacon, horseradish, chili sauce or grated cheese . . . Raw, in salads.

TO PREPARE

Remove root ends and imperfect leaves. Wash several times in water, lifting out each time; drain.

TO COOK

Cover and cook with just the water that clings to leaves until tender, spinach 3 to 10 minutes, beet tops 5 to 15 minutes, chicory, escarole and lettuce 15 to 20 minutes, collards 10 to 15 minutes, Swiss chard and mustard greens 15 to 20 minutes, turnip greens and kale 15 to 25 minutes; drain.

TO MICROWAVE

Place greens (beet tops, chicory, escarole, lettuce or spinach) with just the water that clings to the leaves in 3-quart glass casserole. Cover and microwave 6 minutes; stir. Cover and microwave 6 minutes longer; stir. Cover and microwave until tender, 3 to 6 minutes longer. Let stand 1 minute; drain.

SPINACH GOURMET

1 pound fresh spinach or Swiss chard
1 can (4 ounces) button mushrooms, drained
1 teaspoon instant minced onion
1 small clove garlic, crushed
½ teaspoon salt
   Dash of pepper
⅓ cup dairy sour cream
1 tablespoon half-and-half or milk

Prepare and cook spinach as directed above; chop and drain completely. Mix spinach, mushrooms, onion, garlic, salt and pepper in saucepan. Blend sour cream and half-and-half; pour over spinach mixture. Heat just to boiling.   4 SERVINGS.

With frozen spinach: Use 1 package (10 ounces) frozen chopped spinach, cooked and drained, and add 2 tablespoons margarine or butter.

SPINACH WITH BACON

1 slice bacon, cut up
1 small onion, thinly sliced
1 pound spinach
¼ teaspoon salt
   Dash of pepper

Cook and stir bacon and onion in 10-inch skillet until bacon is crisp. Add about half of the spinach, the salt and pepper. Cover and cook over medium heat 2 minutes. Add remaining spinach. Cover and cook, stirring occasionally, until spinach is tender, 3 to 10 minutes.   3 OR 4 SERVINGS.

SWISS CHARD BAKE

2 pounds fresh Swiss chard or spinach
1 can (8 ounces) water chestnuts, drained and
   thinly sliced
1 can (10¾ ounces) condensed cream of
   celery soup

Prepare and cook Swiss chard or spinach as directed at left; chop and drain completely.

Place Swiss chard in ungreased baking dish, 10x6x1½ inches. Arrange water chestnuts on Swiss chard; spread soup over top. Cook uncovered in 350° oven until hot, 25 to 30 minutes.   6 SERVINGS.

LEEKS

Amount for 4 servings: 2 pounds.

Season available: All year (peak—October through May).

When shopping: Look for bright green tops and white bulbs.

Ways to serve: Sprinkled with grated Parmesan cheese . . . Seasoned with basil, ginger, rosemary or thyme . . . Raw, in salads.

TO PREPARE

Remove green tops to within 2 inches of white part; peel outside layer of bulbs. Wash leeks.

TO COOK

Heat 1 inch salted water (½ teaspoon salt to 1 cup water) to boiling. Add leeks. Cover and heat to boiling. Cook until tender, 12 to 15 minutes; drain.

TO MICROWAVE

Cover and microwave leeks and ¼ cup water in 3-quart glass casserole 3 minutes; turn leeks over. Cover and microwave until tender, 3 to 4 minutes longer. Let stand 1 minute; drain.

MUSHROOMS

Amount for 4 servings: 1 pound.

Season available: All year.

When shopping: Look for creamy white to light brown caps, closed around the stems; if slightly open, gills should be light pink or tan.

Ways to serve: Sautéed, as a hot vegetable or meat accompaniment . . . Seasoned with marjoram, oregano, rosemary, savory or tarragon . . . Creamed, scalloped or combined with other hot cooked vegetables—peas, green beans, lima beans . . . Stuffed.

TO PREPARE
Wash mushrooms and trim off stem ends. Do not peel. Slice parallel to stem if desired.

TO COOK
Heat ¼ cup margarine or butter in 10-inch skillet until bubbly. Cook mushrooms over medium heat, stirring occasionally, until tender, 6 to 8 minutes.

TO MICROWAVE
Cover and microwave mushrooms (¼-inch slices) in 2-quart glass casserole until tender, 4 to 5 minutes. Let stand 1 minute; drain. Stir in 3 tablespoons margarine or butter.

ORIENTAL MUSHROOMS

 1 pound fresh mushrooms*
 1 small onion, chopped (about
    ¼ cup)
¼ cup margarine or butter
 2 teaspoons flour
½ cup water
 1 beef bouillon cube or 1 teaspoon
    instant beef bouillon
 1 tablespoon soy sauce
    Toasted slivered almonds

Prepare mushrooms as directed above, slicing parallel to stems.

Cook and stir onion in margarine in 12-inch skillet until tender. Stir in mushrooms. Sprinkle flour over mixture; stir until mushrooms are coated. Add water, bouillon cube and soy sauce, stirring until bouillon cube is dissolved. Cook over medium heat about 3 minutes. Sprinkle with slivered almonds.   4 TO 6 SERVINGS.

*2 jars (4½ ounces each) sliced mushrooms, drained, can be substituted for the fresh mushrooms.

OKRA

Amount for 4 servings: 1 pound.

Season available: June through November.

When shopping: Look for tender, unblemished, bright green pods, less than 4 inches long.

Ways to serve: Varied with dash of vinegar or lemon juice . . . In soups and casseroles . . . Combined with tomatoes.

TO PREPARE
Wash okra; remove ends and cut into ½-inch slices.

TO COOK
Heat 1 inch salted water (½ teaspoon salt to 1 cup water) to boiling. Add okra. Cover and heat to boiling. Cook until tender, about 10 minutes; drain.

TO MICROWAVE
Cover and microwave okra and ¼ cup water in 1½-quart glass casserole 3 minutes; stir. Cover and microwave until tender, 2 to 3 minutes longer. Let stand 1 minute; drain.

ONION-FRIED OKRA

 1 pound fresh okra
½ cup white cornmeal
½ teaspoon onion salt
⅛ teaspoon pepper
½ cup vegetable oil

Prepare okra as directed above. Mix cornmeal, onion salt and pepper. Toss okra and cornmeal mixture until okra is completely coated. Cook and stir okra in vegetable oil until brown.   4 SERVINGS.

OKRA SKILLET

¾ pound fresh okra
 2 to 3 ears fresh corn
¼ cup finely cut-up lean salt pork (about
    ¼ pound)
 1 medium onion, chopped (about ½ cup)
 4 medium tomatoes, each cut into eighths
    Dash of pepper

Prepare 2 cups sliced okra as directed above. Prepare corn as directed on page 176. Cut enough kernels from corn to measure 1 cup. Cook and stir pork and onion in 10-inch skillet until pork is golden; stir in okra. Cook over medium-high heat, stirring constantly, 3 minutes. Stir in tomatoes and corn. Cover and simmer until corn is tender, 10 to 15 minutes. Stir in pepper.   4 SERVINGS.

ONIONS

Types: Dry, small white (for whole-cooked); yellow or red (domestic, for seasoning); Spanish, Bermuda, Italian (sweet, for raw or French-fried slices).

Amount for 4 servings: 1½ pounds.

Season available: All year.

When shopping: Look for firm, well-shaped onions with unblemished, papery skins.

Ways to serve: Buttered, with salt and pepper . . . Seasoned with basil, ginger, oregano or thyme . . . Creamed, scalloped, au gratin, fried, baked, stuffed, or sliced and French fried.

TO PREPARE
Peel onions under running cold water (to prevent eyes from watering).

TO COOK
To Boil: Heat several inches salted water (½ teaspoon salt to 1 cup water) to boiling. Add onions. Cover and heat to boiling. Cook until tender, small 15 to 20 minutes, large 30 to 35 minutes; drain.

To Bake: Place large onions in ungreased baking dish. Pour water into dish to ¼-inch depth. Cover; cook in 350° oven until tender, 40 to 50 minutes.

TO MICROWAVE
Cover and microwave whole small onions of similar size and ¼ cup water in 2-quart glass casserole 3 minutes; stir. Cover and microwave until tender, 3 to 5 minutes longer. Let stand 1 minute; drain.

FRENCH-FRIED ONION RINGS

  3 **large Spanish or Bermuda onions**
      Vegetable oil
 ½ **cup milk**
  1 **egg**
 ¾ **cup all-purpose flour***
 ½ **teaspoon salt**

Prepare onions as directed above; cut into ¼-inch slices and separate into rings. Heat oil (1 inch) in 3-quart saucepan to 375°. Beat remaining ingredients with hand beater until smooth. Dip each ring into batter, letting excess drip into bowl.

Fry a few onion rings at a time in hot oil, turning once, until golden brown, about 2 minutes; drain.   4 SERVINGS.

*If using self-rising flour, omit salt.

NOTE: To keep fried onion rings warm, place in 300° oven until ready to serve.

CLOVED ONIONS

1½ pounds small white onions*
 3 tablespoons margarine or butter
 ⅛ teaspoon ground cloves
 ⅓ cup packed brown sugar

Prepare and boil onions as directed on page 181.

Heat margarine and cloves over medium heat, stirring occasionally, until margarine is melted. Add onions; stir gently until coated.

Sprinkle brown sugar over onions. Cook, turning frequently, until golden and glazed, about 5 minutes.   4 SERVINGS.

*1 can (16 ounces) whole onions, drained, can be substituted for the fresh onions.

BROILED ONIONS AND POTATOES

Shape aluminum foil into a broiler pan, 11x7x1½ inches. Place 1 can (16 ounces) whole onions, drained, and 1 can (16 ounces) whole potatoes, drained, in foil pan; dot with 1 or 2 tablespoons margarine or butter, softened.

Set oven control to broil and/or 550°. Place pan on rack in broiler pan. Broil 3 inches from heat 4 minutes. Turn potatoes and onions; sprinkle with seasoned salt and paprika. Broil until heated through, about 3 minutes longer.   4 SERVINGS.

DELUXE CREAMED ONIONS

1½ to 2 pounds small white onions*
 2 tablespoons margarine or butter
 2 tablespoons flour
 ½ teaspoon salt
 ⅛ teaspoon pepper
1½ cups half-and-half
1½ cups shredded carrots

Prepare and boil onions as directed on page 181.

Heat margarine over low heat until melted. Blend in flour, salt and pepper. Cook over low heat, stirring constantly, until mixture is smooth and bubbly; remove from heat. Stir in half-and-half. Heat to boiling, stirring constantly. Boil and stir 1 minute. Stir in carrots and cook 5 minutes longer. Pour sauce over hot onions.   4 TO 6 SERVINGS.

*2 cans (16 ounces each) whole onions, heated and drained, can be substituted for the fresh onions.

Green onion, leeks

ONIONS—GREEN

Amount for 4 servings: 2 bunches.

Season available: All year (peak—May through August).

When shopping: Look for crisp green tops; 2 to 3 inches of white root.

Ways to serve: Buttered, with salt and pepper . . . Sprinkled with grated Parmesan cheese . . . Raw, as a relish or in salads.

TO PREPARE

Wash onions; remove any loose layers of skin. Leave about 3 inches of green tops.

TO COOK

Heat 1 inch salted water (½ teaspoon salt to 1 cup water) to boiling. Add green onions. Cover and heat to boiling. Cook just until tender, 8 to 10 minutes; drain.

TO MICROWAVE

Cover and microwave green onions and 2 tablespoons water in 1½-quart glass casserole just until tender, 1 to 2 minutes. Let stand 1 minute; drain.

MICROWAVE RECIPE TESTING

All microwave recipes in this book were tested using 100% settings—High, Full, Normal or Number 10. For best results, use one of these settings. When tested, foods normally stored at room temperature or in the refrigerator were prepared at those same temperatures.

PARSNIPS

Amount for 4 servings: 1½ pounds (about 6).

Season available: All year.

When shopping: Look for firm, nicely shaped, unblemished parsnips that are not too wide.

Ways to serve: Buttered, with salt and pepper . . . Sprinkled with parsley . . . Baked or mashed.

TO PREPARE

Scrape or pare. Leave whole or cut into halves, fourths, slices or ¼-inch lengthwise strips.

TO COOK

Heat 1 inch salted water (½ teaspoon salt to 1 cup water) to boiling. Add parsnips. Cover and heat to boiling. Cook until tender, about 30 minutes; drain.

TO MICROWAVE

Cover and microwave parsnips (¼-inch slices) and ¼ cup water in 1½-quart glass casserole 4 minutes; stir. Cover and microwave until tender, 4 to 6 minutes longer. Let stand 1 minute; drain.

PARSNIP CAKES

1¼ pounds fresh parsnips (about
    5 medium)
2 tablespoons flour
½ teaspoon salt
    Dash of pepper
2 tablespoons margarine or butter,
    softened
1 tablespoon chopped onion
1 egg, beaten
    Dried bread crumbs or cracker
    crumbs
¼ cup shortening

Prepare and cook whole parsnips as directed above; mash parsnips.

Mix parsnips, flour, salt, pepper, margarine, onion and egg. Shape parsnip mixture into 8 patties; coat with bread crumbs. Heat shortening in 10-inch skillet over low heat. Add parsnip patties. Cook over medium heat, turning once, until golden brown, about 5 minutes. 4 SERVINGS.

PEAS—GREEN

Amount for 4 servings: 3 pounds.

Season available: September to June (peak—April and May).

When shopping: Look for bright green pods, well filled and tender.

Ways to serve: Buttered, with salt and pepper . . . Seasoned with allspice, basil, chervil, marjoram, mint, rosemary, savory, thyme or tarragon . . . Creamed or topped with Lemon Butter or Maître d'Hôtel Butter (page 161) . . . Combined with other vegetables such as carrots, onions or mushrooms.

TO PREPARE

Wash and shell peas just before cooking.

TO COOK

Heat 1 inch salted water (½ teaspoon salt to 1 cup water) to boiling. Add peas. Heat to boiling; cook uncovered 5 minutes. Cover and cook until tender, 3 to 7 minutes longer. If desired, add ½ teaspoon sugar and a few pea pods or lettuce leaf to boiling water for added flavor; drain.

TO MICROWAVE

Cover and microwave peas and ¼ cup water in 1½-quart glass casserole 5 minutes; stir. Cover and microwave until tender, 5 to 6 minutes longer. Let stand 1 minute; drain.

CURRIED PEAS

3 pounds fresh green peas*
2 tablespoons chopped onion
2 tablespoons margarine or butter
2 tablespoons flour
½ teaspoon curry powder
¼ teaspoon salt
1½ cups milk

Prepare and cook peas as directed above.

Cook and stir onion in margarine until tender; remove from heat. Stir in flour, curry powder and salt. Cook over low heat, stirring constantly, until mixture is bubbly; remove from heat. Stir in milk. Heat to boiling, stirring constantly. Boil and stir 1 minute. Gently stir in peas and heat through.
4 SERVINGS.

*1 package (10 ounces) frozen green peas, cooked and drained, or 1 can (17 ounces) green peas, drained, can be substituted for the fresh peas.

PEPPERS—GREEN BELL

Amount for 4 servings: 4 green peppers.

Season available: April through December.

When shopping: Look for well-shaped, shiny, medium to dark green peppers with firm sides.

Ways to serve: Stuffed and baked . . . Fried or cooked in seasoned sauce.

TO PREPARE
Wash peppers; remove stems, seeds and membranes. Leave whole to stuff and bake; cut into thin slices or rings to fry.

TO COOK
To Bake: Parboil peppers until crisp-tender, 3 to 5 minutes; stuff and bake.

To Fry: Fry pepper slices or rings in small amount of margarine or butter until crisp-tender and light brown, 3 to 5 minutes.

SPANISH PEPPERS

3 medium green peppers
2 medium stalks celery, cut into ¼-inch
    diagonal slices (about 1 cup)
1 small onion, finely chopped (about
    ¼ cup)
2 tablespoons vegetable oil
½ teaspoon dried basil leaves
1 teaspoon salt
    Dash of pepper
1 can (15 ounces) tomato sauce
    Garlic Croutons (below)

Prepare green peppers, cut into ½-inch strips, as directed above.

Cook and stir green peppers, celery and onion in oil over medium heat until onion is tender. Stir in basil, salt, pepper and tomato sauce. Cover and cook over medium heat until green peppers are tender, about 10 minutes. Sprinkle with Garlic Croutons.   4 TO 6 SERVINGS.

GARLIC CROUTONS
Heat 2 tablespoons margarine or butter until melted; stir in ¼ teaspoon garlic powder. Add 1 cup toasted bread cubes; toss.

POTATOES—SMALL NEW

Amount for 4 servings: 1½ pounds (10 to 12).

Season available: Spring and summer.

When shopping: Look for nicely shaped, smooth, firm potatoes with unblemished skins, free from discoloration.

Ways to serve: Buttered, with salt and pepper . . . Seasoned with snipped parsley, chives or green onion, paprika or lemon juice . . . Creamed and often combined with peas.

TO PREPARE
Wash potatoes lightly and leave whole. If desired, pare narrow strip around centers.

TO COOK
Heat 1 inch salted water (1 teaspoon salt to 1 cup water) to boiling. Add potatoes. Cover and heat to boiling. Cook until tender, 20 to 25 minutes; drain.

TO MICROWAVE
Prick potatoes of similar size with fork to allow steam to escape. Arrange potatoes about 1 inch apart in circle on paper towel in microwave. Microwave until tender, 10 to 12 minutes. Let stand 1 minute.

LEMON-CHIVE POTATOES

1½ pounds new potatoes (10 to 12 small)
 2 tablespoons margarine or butter
 ½ teaspoon grated lemon peel
 1 tablespoon lemon juice
 2 teaspoons snipped chives
 ½ teaspoon salt
 ⅛ teaspoon pepper
   Dash of ground nutmeg

Prepare and cook new potatoes as directed above; keep warm. Heat remaining ingredients just to boiling. Turn hot potatoes into serving dish; pour lemon butter over potatoes.   4 SERVINGS.

ABOUT POTATOES
New potatoes should be used within a few days but baking potatoes (with thick, netted skin and shallow eyes) will keep in a cool, dry place several months. Potatoes furnish carbohydrates (for energy), vitamin B (helps body use protein) and vitamin C. A medium baked potato has 90 calories. Cook and eat potatoes in their skins for added flavor.

POTATOES—WHITE

Amount for 4 servings: 1½ pounds (about 4 medium).

Season available: All year.

When shopping: Look for well-shaped, smooth, firm potatoes with unblemished skins, free from discoloration.

Ways to serve: Buttered, with salt and pepper . . . Seasoned with bay leaf, caraway seed, dill, mint, poppy seed or sage . . . Baked, creamed, fried, scalloped or mashed.

TO PREPARE

For Boiling: Wash potatoes. Leave skins on whenever possible or pare thinly and remove eyes. Leave whole or cut into large pieces.

For Baking: Scrub potatoes and, if desired, rub with shortening for softer skins. Prick with fork to allow steam to escape.

TO COOK

To Boil: Heat 1 inch salted water (½ teaspoon salt to 1 cup water) to boiling. Add potatoes. Cover and heat to boiling. Cook until tender, whole 30 to 35 minutes, pieces 20 to 25 minutes; drain.

To Bake: Cook in 375° oven 1 to 1¼ hours, in 350° oven 1¼ to 1½ hours, in 325° oven about 1½ hours.

TO MICROWAVE

Prick potatoes of similar size with fork to allow steam to escape. Arrange potatoes about 1 inch apart in circle on paper towel in microwave. Microwave until tender, 11 to 13 minutes. Let stand 1 minute.

MASHED POTATOES

  2 **pounds potatoes (about 6 medium)**
 ⅓ **to ½ cup milk**
 ¼ **cup margarine or butter, softened**
 ½ **teaspoon salt**
   Dash of pepper

Prepare and boil pared potatoes as directed above. Shake pan gently over low heat to dry potatoes.

Mash potatoes until no lumps remain. Beat in milk in small amounts. (Amount of milk needed to make potatoes smooth and fluffy depends on kind of potatoes.) Add margarine, salt and pepper; beat vigorously until potatoes are light and fluffy. Dot with margarine or sprinkle with paprika, snipped parsley, watercress or chives if desired.   4 TO 6 SERVINGS.

Duchess Potatoes: Beat 2 eggs; add to Mashed Potatoes and beat until blended. Drop mixture by spoonfuls in mounds onto ungreased cookie sheet, or form rosettes or pipe border around meat or fish, using decorators' tube with tip. Brush mounds, rosettes or border with melted margarine or butter; Cook uncovered in 425° oven until potatoes are light brown, about 15 minutes.   9 OR 10 MOUNDS OR ROSETTES.

Riced Mashed Potatoes: Put potatoes through ricer instead of mashing. Add milk, margarine, salt and pepper; beat until fluffy.

CREAMY SCALLOPED POTATOES

  2 **pounds potatoes (about 6 medium)**
  3 **tablespoons margarine or butter**
  3 **tablespoons flour**
  1 **teaspoon salt**
 ¼ **teaspoon pepper**
 2½ **cups milk**
  1 **small onion, finely chopped (about**
     ¼ cup)
  1 **tablespoon margarine or butter**

Prepare potatoes as directed at left for boiling; cut into enough thin slices to measure about 4 cups.

Heat 3 tablespoons margarine in saucepan over low heat until melted. Blend in flour, salt and pepper. Cook over low heat, stirring constantly, until mixture is smooth and bubbly; remove from heat. Stir in milk. Heat to boiling, stirring constantly. Boil and stir 1 minute.

Arrange potatoes in greased 2-quart casserole in 3 layers, topping each of the first two layers with ½ of the onion and ⅓ of the white sauce. Top with remaining potatoes and sauce. Dot with 1 tablespoon margarine. Cover and cook in 325° oven 40 minutes or in 350° oven 30 minutes. Uncover and cook until potatoes are tender, 60 to 70 minutes longer. Let stand 5 to 10 minutes before serving. 6 SERVINGS.

Scalloped Potatoes for Three: Use 1 pound potatoes, 2 tablespoons margarine, 2 tablespoons flour, ½ teaspoon salt, ⅛ teaspoon pepper, 1½ cups milk, 2 tablespoons onion and 1 teaspoon margarine. Prepare as directed except—layer half of the potatoes, all of the onion and half of the sauce in greased 1-quart casserole. Top with remaining potatoes and sauce. Dot with margarine. Cover and cook in 350° oven 30 minutes; uncover and cook 35 minutes. Do not let stand before serving.

AU GRATIN POTATOES

2 pounds potatoes (about 6 medium)
1 medium onion, chopped (about
    ½ cup)
¼ cup margarine or butter
1 tablespoon flour
1 teaspoon salt
¼ teaspoon pepper
2 cups milk
2 cups shredded natural sharp
    Cheddar cheese (about 8 ounces)
¼ cup fine dry bread crumbs
    Paprika

Prepare potatoes as directed on page 185 for boiling; cut into enough thin slices to measure about 4 cups.

Cook and stir onion in margarine in 2-quart saucepan until onion is tender. Stir in flour, salt and pepper. Cook over low heat, stirring constantly, until mixture is bubbly; remove from heat. Stir in milk and 1½ cups of the cheese. Heat to boiling, stirring constantly. Boil and stir 1 minute. Place potatoes in ungreased 1½-quart casserole. Pour cheese sauce on potatoes. Cook uncovered in 325° oven 1 hour 20 minutes or in 375° oven 1 hour.

Mix remaining cheese and the bread crumbs; sprinkle over potatoes. Sprinkle with paprika. Cook uncovered until top is brown and bubbly, 15 to 20 minutes longer.   6 SERVINGS.

BUFFET POTATOES

2 pounds potatoes (about 6 medium)
    Pepper
1 teaspoon salt
3 tablespoons snipped parsley
1 small onion, chopped (about ¼ cup)
¾ cup shredded sharp process cheese
    (about 3 ounces)
3 tablespoons margarine or butter
¾ cup half-and-half

Prepare potatoes as directed on page 185 for boiling; cut into lengthwise strips, ¼ to ⅜ inch wide.

Arrange potatoes in greased 2-quart casserole in 3 layers, topping each layer with dash of pepper and ⅓ each of the salt, parsley, onion and cheese. Dot with margarine and pour half-and-half over potatoes. Cover and cook in 325° oven 1 hour 10 minutes or in 350° oven 1 hour. Uncover and cook until potatoes are tender, about 30 minutes longer.
6 TO 8 SERVINGS.

TWICE-BAKED POTATOES

Prepare and bake 4 large baking potatoes as directed on page 185.

Increase oven temperature to 400°. Cut thin lengthwise slice from each potato; scoop out inside, leaving a thin shell. Mash potatoes until no lumps remain. Beat in ⅓ to ½ cup milk in small amounts. (Amount of milk needed to make potatoes smooth and fluffy depends on kind of potatoes.) Add ¼ cup margarine or butter, softened, ½ teaspoon salt and dash of pepper; beat vigorously until potatoes are light and fluffy.

Fill shells with potatoes. Sprinkle with shredded cheese if desired. Cook uncovered until filling is golden, about 20 minutes.   4 SERVINGS.

Pepper or Pimiento Potatoes: Stir ½ small green pepper, finely chopped (about ¼ cup), or ¼ cup drained chopped pimiento into mashed potato mixture.

BAKED POTATOES WITH TOPPERS

Prepare and bake 4 to 6 large baking potatoes as directed on page 185. To serve, cut crisscross gashes in tops; squeeze gently until some potato pops up through opening. Top with 1 cup dairy sour cream mixed with one of the following: ¼ cup grated Parmesan cheese; 1 teaspoon curry powder and ½ teaspoon salt; or 2 tablespoons snipped chives and 1 teaspoon salt.   4 TO 6 SERVINGS.

SKILLET CREAMED POTATOES

2 pounds potatoes (about 6 medium)*
2 cups dairy sour cream
1 small onion, finely chopped (about
    ¼ cup)
2 tablespoons finely chopped
    pimiento-stuffed olives
1 teaspoon salt
½ teaspoon pepper

Prepare and boil potatoes as directed on page 185; cut into ½-inch cubes. Mix remaining ingredients in 10-inch skillet. Add potatoes; heat over medium heat, stirring frequently, until sour cream bubbles and potatoes are heated through. Garnish with paprika, snipped parsley and sliced pimiento-stuffed olives if desired.   6 SERVINGS.

*2 cans (16 ounces each) whole potatoes can be substituted for the fresh potatoes.

POTATO PANCAKES

Serve with applesauce or as a tasty side dish with steak, a roast, ham slice or your favorite barbecued meat.

- 2 pounds potatoes (about 6 medium)
- 1 egg
- ⅓ cup finely chopped onion
- 3 tablespoons flour
- 1 teaspoon salt
- ¼ cup margarine or butter

Prepare potatoes as directed on page 185 for boiling; shred enough to measure 4 cups. Drain completely.

Beat egg in small mixer bowl until thick and lemon colored. Mix in potatoes, onion, flour and salt. Heat margarine in 12-inch skillet over low heat until melted. Shape potato mixture into 8 patties; place in skillet. Cook over medium heat, turning once, until golden brown, about 5 minutes.   8 SERVINGS.

HASHED BROWNS

- 1½ pounds potatoes (about 4 medium)
- 2 tablespoons finely chopped onion
- ½ teaspoon salt
- ⅛ teaspoon pepper
- 2 tablespoons margarine or butter
- 2 tablespoons vegetable oil or bacon fat

Prepare and boil potatoes as directed on page 185; cool slightly. Shred enough to measure 4 cups.

Toss potatoes, onion, salt and pepper. Heat margarine and oil in 10-inch skillet. Pack potato mixture firmly in skillet, leaving a ½-inch space around edge. Cook over low heat until bottom crust is brown, 10 to 15 minutes. Cut potato mixture into fourths; turn. Add 1 tablespoon vegetable oil if necessary. Cook until brown, 12 to 15 minutes longer.   4 TO 6 SERVINGS.

NOTE: Potato mixture can be kept in one piece if desired. To turn, invert onto plate and slide back into skillet.

FRENCH-FRIED POTATOES

Prepare 1½ pounds potatoes (about 4 medium) as directed on page 185 for boiling; cut into lengthwise strips, ¼ to ⅜ inch wide.

Fill deep-fat fryer or deep saucepan ½ full with vegetable oil or shortening; heat to 375°. Fill basket ¼ full with potatoes. Slowly lower into hot oil. (If oil bubbles excessively, raise and lower basket several times.) Use long-handled fork to keep potatoes separated. Fry until potatoes are golden, 5 to 7 minutes. Drain; repeat. Sprinkle with salt.
4 SERVINGS.

RAW FRIES

The secrets are a heavy skillet, steady heat and the patience not to turn the potatoes until they're brown.

- 2 pounds potatoes (about 6 medium)
- 2 tablespoons shortening or vegetable oil
- 1 large onion, thinly sliced (optional)
- 1½ teaspoons salt
  Pepper
- 2 tablespoons margarine or butter

Prepare potatoes as directed on page 185 for boiling; cut into enough thin slices to measure about 4 cups.

Heat shortening in 10-inch skillet until melted. Layer ⅓ each of the potato and onion slices in skillet; sprinkle with ½ teaspoon salt and dash of pepper. Repeat 2 times. Dot top layer with margarine. Cover and cook over medium heat 20 minutes. Uncover and cook, turning once, until potatoes are brown.   4 TO 6 SERVINGS.

Raw Fries

Summer and winter squashes

SQUASH—SUMMER

Types: White—Cymling, Pattypan and Scalloped; Yellow—Straightneck and Crookneck; Light green—Chayote; Dark green—Zucchini.

Amount for 4 servings: 2 pounds.

Season available: All year (peak—summer).

When shopping: Look for firm, well-shaped squash with shiny, smooth skins. Should seem heavy for size.

Ways to serve: Buttered, with salt and pepper . . . Seasoned with basil, marjoram, oregano or rosemary . . . Sprinkled with grated Parmesan or shredded mozzarella cheese . . . Baked, mashed or fried . . . Topped with Cheese Butter or Chive-Parsley Butter (page 161).

TO PREPARE
Wash squash; remove stem and blossom ends but do not pare. Cut into ½-inch slices or cubes.

TO COOK
Heat 1 inch salted water (½ teaspoon salt to 1 cup water) to boiling. Add squash. Cover and heat to boiling. Cook until tender, slices 12 to 15 minutes, cubes 7 to 8 minutes; drain.

TO MICROWAVE
Cover and microwave squash (½-inch slices) and ¼ cup water in 2-quart glass casserole 4 minutes; stir. Cover and microwave until tender, 3 to 5 minutes longer (pattypan 5 to 7 minutes). Let stand 1 minute; drain.

BROILED ZUCCHINI
Prepare 2 pounds zucchini (about 8 small) as directed at left except—cut each zucchini lengthwise into halves. Brush each cut side with margarine or butter, melted; sprinkle with salt and pepper. Set oven control to broil and/or 550°. Broil 5 to 6 inches from heat until zucchini is tender, 10 to 12 minutes.   4 SERVINGS.

ZUCCHINI-PEPPER SKILLET
1 pound zucchini (about 4 small)
1 onion, thinly sliced
1 small green pepper, chopped
2 tablespoons vegetable oil
1 clove garlic, crushed
1 teaspoon salt
⅛ teaspoon pepper
2 tomatoes, cut into wedges

Prepare zucchini as directed at left except—cut into ¼-inch slices. Cook and stir zucchini, onion, green pepper, oil, garlic, salt and pepper in 10-inch skillet until heated through. Cover and cook over medium heat, stirring occasionally, until vegetables are crisp-tender, about 5 minutes.

Add tomatoes. Cover and cook over low heat just until tomatoes are heated through, about 3 minutes. Sprinkle with snipped parsley and grated Parmesan cheese if desired.   4 SERVINGS.

Yellow Squash Skillet: Substitute 1 pound yellow summer squash (about 2 medium) for the zucchini and 1 teaspoon ground ginger for the garlic; omit pepper.

HARVEST ZUCCHINI
1¼ pounds zucchini (about 5 small)
⅓ cup finely chopped onion
¼ cup margarine or butter
½ cup dairy sour cream
2 tablespoons milk
2 teaspoons paprika
2 teaspoons poppy seed
1 teaspoon salt
1 teaspoon monosodium glutamate

Prepare 4 cups sliced zucchini as directed at left. Cook and stir zucchini and onion in margarine in 10-inch skillet until margarine is melted. Cover and cook, stirring occasionally, until zucchini is tender. Mix remaining ingredients; stir gently into zucchini and heat through.   4 SERVINGS.

CONTINENTAL ZUCCHINI

1 pound zucchini (about 4 small)
1 can (12 ounces) whole kernel corn, drained
1 jar (2 ounces) chopped pimiento, drained
2 medium cloves garlic, crushed
2 tablespoons vegetable oil
1 teaspoon salt
¼ teaspoon pepper
½ cup shredded mozzarella cheese (about
   2 ounces)

Prepare 3 cups cubed zucchini as directed on page 188. Mix zucchini, corn, pimiento, garlic, oil, salt and pepper in skillet. Cover and cook over medium heat, stirring occasionally, until zucchini is crisp-tender, about 10 minutes. Stir in cheese; heat through.   4 TO 6 SERVINGS.

SQUASH—WINTER

Types: Large—Banana, Buttercup, Hubbard; Medium—Acorn (Table Queen or Des Moines), Butternut.

Amount for 4 servings: 3 pounds

Season available: October through February.

When shopping: Look for good yellow-orange color; hard, tough rinds; squash that is heavy.

Ways to serve: Buttered, with salt and pepper . . . Removed from rind and mashed with cream, nutmeg, brown sugar, crumbled crisply fried bacon, candied ginger, grated orange peel or orange juice.

TO PREPARE

Large: Cut squash into serving pieces; remove seeds and fibers. For boiling, pare squash if desired; cut into slices or cubes.

Medium: Cut each squash lengthwise into halves; remove seeds and fibers.

TO COOK

To Bake: Place squash in ungreased baking dish, 13½x9x2 inches. Sprinkle cut sides with salt and pepper; dot with margarine or butter. Pour water into dish to ¼-inch depth. Cover and cook until tender, in 400° oven 30 to 40 minutes, in 350° oven about 40 minutes or in 325° oven about 45 minutes.

To Boil (for large squash): Heat 1 inch salted water (½ teaspoon salt to 1 cup water) to boiling. Add squash. Cover and heat to boiling. Cook until tender, 15 to 20 minutes; drain.

TO MICROWAVE

Acorn Squash: Prick whole squash of similar size. Arrange at least 1 inch apart diagonally in microwave. Microwave 6 minutes; turn squash over. Microwave until tender, 7 to 9 minutes longer; cool slightly. Cut into halves; remove seeds.

Hubbard Squash: Prepare as directed above except— decrease second microwave time to 6 to 8 minutes.

MAPLE BAKED ACORN SQUASH

Cut 2 acorn squash (1 to 1½ pounds each) into halves; remove seeds and fibers. Place squash cut sides up in ungreased baking pan. Spoon 1 tablespoon maple-flavored or maple syrup and 1 tablespoon cream into each half. Cook uncovered in 350° oven until tender, about 1 hour.   4 SERVINGS.

SQUASH AND APPLE BAKE

2 pounds butternut or buttercup squash
½ cup packed brown sugar
¼ cup margarine or butter, melted
1 tablespoon flour
1 teaspoon salt
½ teaspoon ground mace
2 baking apples, cored and cut into ½-inch
   slices

Cut each squash into halves; remove seeds and fibers. Pare squash. Cut into ½-inch slices.

Mix brown sugar, margarine, flour, salt and mace. Arrange squash in ungreased oblong baking dish, 12x7½x2 inches; top with apple slices. Sprinkle sugar mixture over top. Cover and cook in 350° oven until squash is tender, 50 to 60 minutes. 6 SERVINGS.

GOURMET GOLDEN SQUASH

3 pounds Hubbard squash*
1 cup dairy sour cream
2 tablespoons margarine or butter
1 medium onion, finely chopped
1 teaspoon salt
¼ teaspoon pepper

Prepare and boil cubed squash as directed at left.

Mash squash; stir in remaining ingredients. Turn mixture into ungreased 1-quart casserole. Cook uncovered in 400° oven until hot, 20 to 30 minutes.   6 SERVINGS.

*2 packages (12 ounces each) frozen cooked squash, thawed, can be substituted for the fresh squash.

SWEET POTATOES— JERSEY SWEETS, YAMS

Amount for 4 servings: 2 pounds (about 6 medium).

Season available: All year.

When shopping: Look for smooth, even-colored skins; potatoes that are firm and nicely shaped.

Ways to serve: Buttered, with salt and pepper . . . Mashed or candied . . . In soufflés.

TO PREPARE
Wash sweet potatoes but do not pare.

TO COOK
Heat enough salted water to cover potatoes (½ teaspoon salt to 1 cup water) to boiling. Add potatoes. Cover and heat to boiling. Cook until tender, 30 to 35 minutes; drain. Slip off skins. Leave potatoes whole, slice or mash.

TO MICROWAVE
Prick 4 medium sweet potatoes of similar size (about 1½ pounds) to allow steam to escape. Arrange sweet potatoes about 1 inch apart in circle on paper towel in microwave. Microwave until tender, 8 to 9 minutes. Let stand 1 minute.

SWEET POTATO CHIPS

Cut 4 pared medium sweet potatoes or yams (about 1 pound) into ¹⁄₁₆-inch slices. Soak in 2 quarts iced water 1 hour. Drain and pat dry. Heat vegetable oil or shortening (2 to 3 inches) in deep-fat fryer or heavy saucepan to 360°. Fry potato slices until light brown around edges, 1 to 2 minutes; drain on paper towels. Sprinkle with salt. Keep warm in oven. 2 TO 4 SERVINGS.

STORING VEGETABLES

Most vegetables (except root vegetables) should be refrigerated to help preserve freshness and nutrients. Store cleaned vegetables in crisper or plastic bags. Artichokes (globe) should not be stored more than a few days. Green peas or limas in the pod should be stored without shelling. Use within 2 days. Carrots without tops stay fresh longer than those with tops. Sweet potatoes, winter squash, eggplant, rutabagas and onions should be stored at about 60°—not in the refrigerator.

SWEET POTATO MALLOW

1 pound sweet potatoes or yams (about 3 medium)*
½ cup dairy sour cream
1 egg yolk
½ teaspoon salt
¼ teaspoon ground mace
¾ cup miniature marshmallows

Prepare and cook sweet potatoes as directed at left.

Beat sweet potatoes, sour cream, egg yolk, salt and mace in small mixer bowl on medium speed until smooth. Pour into buttered 1-quart casserole; top with marshmallows. Cook uncovered in 350° oven until marshmallows are puffed and golden brown, about 30 minutes. 4 SERVINGS.

*1 can (17 ounces) vacuum-packed sweet potatoes can be substituted for the fresh sweet potatoes.

CANDIED SWEET POTATOES

2 pounds sweet potatoes or yams (about 6 medium)*
½ cup packed brown sugar
3 tablespoons margarine or butter
3 tablespoons water
½ teaspoon salt

Prepare and cook sweet potatoes as directed at left; cut crosswise into ½-inch slices.

Mix brown sugar, margarine, water and salt in 8-inch skillet. Cook over medium heat, stirring constantly, until smooth and bubbly. Add sweet potato slices; stir gently until glazed and heated through. 4 TO 6 SERVINGS.

*1 can (17 ounces) vacuum-packed sweet potatoes, cut into ½-inch slices, can be substituted for the fresh sweet potatoes.

Orange Sweet Potatoes: Substitute 3 tablespoons orange juice for the water and mix in 1 tablespoon grated orange peel.

Pineapple Sweet Potatoes: Omit water and mix in 1 can (8¼ ounces) crushed pineapple (with syrup).

Spicy Sweet Potatoes: Stir ½ teaspoon ground cinnamon or ¼ teaspoon ground allspice, cloves, mace or nutmeg into sugar mixture in skillet.

TOMATOES

Amount for 4 servings: 2 pounds (about 6 medium).

Season available: Summer and fall.

When shopping: Look for nicely ripened, well-shaped tomatoes; fully ripe tomatoes should be slightly soft, have a rich red color.

Ways to serve: Buttered, with salt and pepper . . . Seasoned with allspice, basil, bay leaf, chives, fennel, marjoram, oregano, sage or tarragon . . . Fried, broiled, baked or stewed.

TO PREPARE

Wash tomatoes; cut into fourths or ¾-inch slices. Peel tomatoes before cutting if desired. To remove skin easily, dip tomato into boiling water 30 seconds, then into cold water. Or scrape surface of tomato with blade of knife to loosen; peel.

TO COOK

Cover and cook tomatoes *without water* over low heat, stirring occasionally, until tender, 8 to 10 minutes.

TO MICROWAVE

Cover and microwave tomatoes (8 wedges or ½-inch slices) in 2-quart glass casserole 4 minutes for wedges, 3 minutes for slices. Stir and break up wedges with fork or turn casserole one quarter turn for slices. Cover and microwave until tender, wedges 3 to 4 minutes, slices 2 to 3 minutes. Let stand 1 minute.

STEWED TOMATOES

3 ripe large tomatoes (about 1½ pounds)*
⅓ cup finely chopped onion
2 tablespoons chopped green pepper
1 tablespoon sugar
½ teaspoon salt
⅛ teaspoon pepper
1 cup soft bread cubes

Remove stem end from each tomato; peel tomatoes and cut into small pieces.

Mix tomatoes, onion, green pepper, sugar, salt and pepper. Cover and heat to boiling; reduce heat. Simmer until onion and green pepper are tender, 8 to 10 minutes. Stir in bread cubes.   4 OR 5 SERVINGS.

*1 can (16 ounces) peeled tomatoes can be substituted for the fresh tomatoes.

EASY PANFRIED TOMATOES

4 firm ripe or green medium tomatoes
    (about 1½ pounds)
½ cup all-purpose flour*
1 teaspoon salt
¼ teaspoon pepper
⅓ cup margarine or butter

Prepare tomato slices as directed at left.

Mix flour, salt and pepper. Dip tomato slices into flour mixture. Heat margarine in 10-inch skillet until melted. Add tomato slices; cook, turning once, until golden brown.   3 OR 4 SERVINGS.

*If using self-rising flour, omit salt.

BAKED STUFFED TOMATOES

6 medium tomatoes (about 2 pounds)
½ small green pepper, finely chopped
    (about ¼ cup)
¼ cup grated Parmesan cheese
⅓ cup croutons
1 teaspoon salt

Remove stem ends from tomatoes; cut thin slice from bottom of each tomato to prevent tipping. Remove pulp from each tomato, leaving a ½-inch wall; chop enough pulp to measure ⅓ cup.

Mix tomato pulp, green pepper, cheese, croutons and salt. Fill tomatoes with tomato-cheese mixture. Place filled tomatoes in ungreased oblong baking dish, 12x7½x2 inches. Cook uncovered in 350° oven until tomatoes are heated through, about 20 minutes. Garnish with parsley sprigs or crumbled crisply fried bacon if desired.   6 SERVINGS.

Baked Stuffed Tomatoes

TURNIPS, RUTABAGAS (YELLOW TURNIPS) AND KOHLRABI

Amount for 4 servings: Turnips—2 pounds (about 6 medium); Rutabagas—1 large or 2 medium; Kohlrabi—4 to 6 medium.

Season available: Turnips—all year; Rutabagas—fall through early spring; Kohlrabi—summer and fall.

When shopping: Look for turnips that are smooth, round and firm, with fresh tops; look for rutabagas that are heavy, well shaped (round or elongated) and smooth; look for kohlrabi that are young and small (not over 3 inches in diameter).

Ways to serve: Seasoned with dill, poppy seed, thyme . . . Mashed and, if desired, seasoned with cream and nutmeg . . . Varied with snipped onion or chives and dash of Worcestershire sauce . . . Raw, as a relish.

TO PREPARE

Turnips: If necessary, cut off tops. Wash turnips and pare thinly; leave whole or cut into cubes.

Rutabagas: Wash rutabagas and pare thinly. Cut into ½-inch cubes or 2-inch pieces.

Kohlrabi: Trim off root ends and vinelike stems. Wash and pare. Cube or cut into ¼-inch slices.

TO COOK

Heat 1 inch salted water (½ teaspoon salt to 1 cup water) to boiling. Add turnips, rutabagas or kohlrabi. Cover and heat to boiling; cook until tender—turnips: whole 25 to 30 minutes, cubes 15 to 20 minutes; rutabagas: cubes 20 to 25 minutes, pieces 30 to 40 minutes; kohlrabi: 25 minutes. Drain.

TO MICROWAVE

Turnips: Cover and microwave turnips (½-inch pieces) and ¼ cup water in 3-quart glass casserole 5 minutes; stir. Cover and microwave 5 minutes longer; stir. Cover and microwave until tender, 2 to 4 minutes longer. Let stand 1 minute; drain.

Rutabagas: Cover and microwave rutabagas (½-inch cubes) and ¼ cup water in 3-quart glass casserole 6 minutes; stir. Cover and microwave 6 minutes longer; stir. Cover and microwave until tender, 5 to 6 minutes longer. Let stand 1 minute; drain.

Kohlrabi: Cover and microwave kohlrabi (¼-inch slices) and ¼ cup water in 1½-quart glass casserole 3 minutes; stir. Cover and microwave until tender, 3 to 5 minutes longer. Let stand 1 minute; drain.

RUTABAGA-POTATO WHIP

1 pound potatoes (about 3 medium)
1 large rutabaga (about 2 pounds)
1 teaspoon sugar
3 tablespoons margarine or butter
1 teaspoon salt
⅛ teaspoon pepper

Prepare and cook cut-up potatoes as directed on page 185. Prepare and cook cubed rutabaga as directed at left except—add 1 teaspoon sugar to water.

Mash potatoes and rutabaga together until no lumps remain. Beat in margarine, salt and pepper until mixture is smooth and fluffy. (Beat in enough hot milk to make mixture smooth and fluffy if necessary.)   6 SERVINGS.

MUSTARD KOHLRABI

4 to 6 medium kohlrabi
2 tablespoons margarine or butter
1 tablespoon prepared mustard
½ teaspoon salt

Prepare and cook sliced kohlrabi as directed at left.

Heat margarine in 8-inch skillet until melted. Stir in mustard and salt. Add kohlrabi and toss. Cook, turning slices, until golden brown.   4 SERVINGS.

Pictured opposite: Blueberry Muffins (page 199), Fruited Wreath (page 217), Crescent Rolls (page 212) and Sourdough Bread (211)

BREADS, PASTA AND RICE

QUICK BREADS

BAKING POWDER BISCUITS

For tender, flaky biscuits, cut in the shortening with two knives, a fork or a pastry blender. Knead the dough gently, but do knead it—this improves the texture of the biscuits.

⅓ cup shortening
1¾ cups all-purpose flour*
2½ teaspoons baking powder
¾ teaspoon salt
¾ cup milk

Heat oven to 450°. Cut shortening into flour, baking powder and salt with pastry blender until mixture resembles fine crumbs. Stir in just enough milk so dough leaves side of bowl and rounds up into a ball. (Too much milk makes dough sticky, not enough makes biscuits dry.)

Turn dough onto lightly floured surface. Knead lightly 10 times. Roll ½ inch thick. Cut with floured 2-inch biscuit cutter. Place on ungreased cookie sheet about 1 inch apart for crusty sides, touching for soft sides. Bake until golden brown, 10 to 12 minutes. Immediately remove from cookie sheet. ABOUT 1 DOZEN BISCUITS.

*If using self-rising flour, omit baking powder and salt.

Buttermilk Biscuits: Decrease baking powder to 2 teaspoons and add ¼ teaspoon baking soda to the flour mixture. Substitute buttermilk for the milk. (If buttermilk is thick, it may be necessary to add slightly more than ¾ cup.)

Cheese Biscuits: Stir in ½ cup shredded sharp cheese.

Chive-Yogurt Biscuits: Substitute 1 cup unflavored yogurt for the milk; stir in 1 tablespoon plus 1 teaspoon snipped chives with the yogurt.

Cornmeal Biscuits: Substitute ½ cup cornmeal for ½ cup of the flour. Sprinkle cookie sheet with cornmeal; place biscuits on cookie sheet and sprinkle with additional cornmeal.

Drop Biscuits: Increase milk to 1 cup. Drop dough by spoonfuls onto greased cookie sheet. (If desired, first drop dough into sesame seed; coat all sides.)

Herb Biscuits: Add 1¼ teaspoons caraway seed, ½ teaspoon crumbled leaf sage and ¼ teaspoon dry mustard to the dry ingredients.

Rye Biscuits: Substitute ¾ cup rye flour for ¾ cup of the all-purpose flour.

Sour Cream-Chive Biscuits: Substitute 1 cup dairy sour cream for the milk; stir in 1 tablespoon plus 1 teaspoon snipped chives with the sour cream.

Stir-n-Roll Biscuits: Substitute vegetable oil for the shortening; stir in all at once with the milk. Roll dough between sheets of waxed paper on dampened surface.

Wheat Germ Biscuits: Add ¼ cup wheat germ to the dry ingredients.

Whole Wheat Biscuits: Substitute whole wheat flour for the all-purpose flour.

MICROWAVE REHEAT DIRECTIONS

	Room Temperature	Frozen
BAKING POWDER BISCUITS		
1 biscuit	10–15 seconds	20–25 seconds
2 biscuits	20–30 seconds	35–40 seconds
3 biscuits	30–35 seconds	55–60 seconds

BISCUIT STICKS

Heat oven to 450°. Heat ⅓ cup margarine or butter in square pan, 9x9x2 inches, in oven until melted; remove from oven.

Prepare Baking Powder Biscuits dough (left). Turn dough onto lightly floured surface. Knead lightly 10 times. Roll into 8-inch square. Cut dough into halves; cut each half into eight 1-inch strips. Dip strips into margarine, coating all sides. Arrange strips in 2 rows in pan. Bake until golden brown, about 15 minutes.   16 STICKS.

Baking Powder Biscuits

1. Cut in shortening until mixture resembles fine crumbs.

2. Round up dough; knead lightly 10 times.

3. Cut with floured cutter; keep rounds close together.

4. For crusty sides, bake biscuits 1 to 2 inches apart.

BUTTONS AND BOWKNOTS

⅓ cup shortening
1¾ cups all-purpose flour*
2 tablespoons sugar
2½ teaspoons baking powder
1 teaspoon ground nutmeg
¾ teaspoon salt
⅛ teaspoon ground cinnamon
1 egg
½ cup milk
¼ cup margarine or butter, melted
About ½ cup sugar

Heat oven to 400°. Cut shortening into flour, 2 tablespoons sugar, the baking powder, nutmeg, salt and cinnamon until mixture resembles fine crumbs. Stir in egg and just enough milk so dough leaves side of bowl. Turn dough onto lightly floured surface. Knead lightly 10 times. Roll ½ inch thick. Cut with floured doughnut cutter.

Hold opposite ends of each ring and twist to form a figure "8." Place Bowknots and Buttons (holes) on ungreased cookie sheet. Bake until golden brown, 8 to 10 minutes. Dip into margarine, then into about ½ cup sugar.   ABOUT 10 BUNS.

*If using self-rising flour, omit baking powder and salt.

DUMPLINGS

Dumplings are cooked on top of bubbling stews—10 minutes uncovered for lightness and 10 minutes covered to cook them through.

3 tablespoons shortening
1½ cups all-purpose flour*
2 teaspoons baking powder
¾ teaspoon salt
¾ cup milk

Cut shortening into flour, baking powder and salt until mixture resembles fine crumbs. Stir in milk. Drop dough by spoonfuls onto hot meat or vegetables in boiling stew (do not drop directly into liquid). Cook uncovered 10 minutes. Cover and cook about 10 minutes longer.   8 TO 10 DUMPLINGS.

*If using self-rising flour, omit baking powder and salt.

Cheese Dumplings: Add ¼ cup shredded sharp cheese (about 1 ounce) to the dry ingredients.

Herb Dumplings: Add ½ teaspoon herbs (such as dried sage leaves, celery seed or dried thyme leaves) to the dry ingredients.

Parsley Dumplings: Add 3 tablespoons snipped parsley or chives to the dry ingredients.

FLUFFY FRENCH TOAST

½ cup all-purpose flour*
1 tablespoon plus 1½ teaspoons sugar
¼ teaspoon salt
2 cups milk
6 eggs
18 slices French bread, each 1 inch thick
1 tablespoon margarine or butter

Beat flour, sugar, salt, milk and eggs with hand beater until smooth. Soak bread in egg mixture until saturated.

Heat margarine in skillet until melted. Cook bread until golden brown, about 12 minutes on each side.   18 SLICES.

*If using self-rising flour, omit salt.

NOTE: To make a honey spread for French toast, pancakes and waffles, beat ¼ cup margarine or butter and ¼ cup honey with fork in bowl. Sprinkle with a little nutmeg.

OVEN FRENCH TOAST

3 eggs
¾ cup milk
1 tablespoon sugar
¼ teaspoon salt
8 slices white bread

Heat oven to 500°. Butter cookie sheet generously. Beat eggs, milk, sugar and salt with fork. Heat cookie sheet in oven 1 minute; remove from oven. Dip bread into egg mixture; arrange on hot cookie sheet. Drizzle any remaining egg mixture over bread. Bake until bottoms are golden brown, 5 to 8 minutes. Turn bread; bake until golden brown, 2 to 4 minutes longer.   8 SLICES.

Do-ahead Tip: After dipping, arrange bread in ungreased oblong baking dish, 13½x9x2 inches, overlapping edges slightly. Drizzle any remaining egg mixture over bread. Cover and refrigerate no longer than 24 hours. Bake on cookie sheet or cook in skillet as directed, using pancake turner to prevent tearing saturated bread.

Skillet French Toast: Heat 1 tablespoon margarine or butter in skillet over medium heat until melted. Dip bread into egg mixture; cook until golden brown, about 4 minutes on each side.

CRISP WAFFLES

2 eggs
1¾ cups milk
½ cup margarine or butter, melted, or
    vegetable oil
2 cups all-purpose flour*
4 teaspoons baking powder
1 tablespoon sugar
½ teaspoon salt

Heat waffle iron. Beat eggs with hand beater until fluffy; beat in remaining ingredients just until smooth. Pour batter from cup or pitcher onto center of hot waffle iron. Bake until steaming stops, about 5 minutes. Remove waffle carefully.
THREE 10-INCH WAFFLES.

*If using self-rising flour, omit baking powder and salt.

Do-ahead Tip: After baking, cool waffles and wrap individually in aluminum foil; freeze. To heat, unwrap and bake on ungreased cookie sheet in 400° oven until hot, 8 to 10 minutes.

Blueberry Waffles: Sprinkle 2 to 4 tablespoons fresh or frozen blueberries (thawed and well drained) over batter immediately after pouring it onto the iron.

Bran Waffles: Sprinkle 2 tablespoons whole bran cereal or bran flakes over batter immediately after pouring it onto the iron.

Cheese and Bacon Waffles: Stir in 1 cup shredded sharp cheese (about 4 ounces). Arrange 4 short slices bacon, crisply fried, on batter immediately after pouring it onto the iron.

Cornmeal Waffles: Substitute 1½ cups cornmeal for 1½ cups of the flour.

Granola Waffles: Sprinkle 2 tablespoons granola over batter immediately after pouring it onto the iron.

Ham Waffles: Stir in 1 package (3 ounces) sliced smoked ham, cut up.

Nut Waffles: Sprinkle 2 to 4 tablespoons coarsely chopped nuts over batter immediately after pouring it onto the iron.

Orange Waffles: Substitute orange juice for the milk and beat in 2 to 3 tablespoons grated peel.

Puffy Waffles: Decrease milk to 1½ cups.

Whole Wheat Waffles: Substitute whole wheat flour for the all-purpose flour and packed brown sugar for the granulated sugar. If desired, sprinkle 2 tablespoons wheat germ or sesame seed over batter immediately after pouring it onto the iron.

PANCAKES

1 egg
1 cup all-purpose flour*
¾ cup milk
2 tablespoons shortening, melted, or
  vegetable oil
1 tablespoon sugar
3 teaspoons baking powder
½ teaspoon salt

Beat egg with hand beater until fluffy; beat in remaining ingredients just until smooth. For thinner pancakes, stir in additional ¼ cup milk. Grease heated griddle if necessary. (To test griddle, sprinkle with few drops water. If bubbles skitter around, heat is just right.)

Pour about 3 tablespoons batter from tip of large spoon or from pitcher onto hot griddle. Cook pancakes until puffed and dry around edges. Turn and cook other sides until golden brown. (To keep pancakes hot, stack on hot plate with paper towels in between.) ABOUT NINE 4-INCH PANCAKES.

*If using self-rising flour, omit baking powder and salt.

Applesauce Pancakes: Decrease milk to ½ cup. Beat in ½ cup applesauce and ¼ teaspoon ground cinnamon. ABOUT 11 PANCAKES.

Banana Pancakes: Beat in 1 medium banana, cut into ¼-inch pieces (about ½ cup), and ¼ teaspoon ground nutmeg. ABOUT 11 PANCAKES.

Blueberry Pancakes: Stir in ½ cup fresh or frozen blueberries (thawed and well drained).

Buckwheat Pancakes: Substitute ½ cup buckwheat flour and ½ cup whole wheat flour for the all-purpose flour. Use 1 cup milk. If desired, sprinkle 1 teaspoon whole bran or wheat germ over each pancake before turning. ABOUT 10 PANCAKES.

Buttermilk Pancakes: Substitute 1 cup buttermilk for the milk. Decrease baking powder to 1 teaspoon and beat in ½ teaspoon baking soda. ABOUT 10 PANCAKES.

Cheese Pancakes: Omit sugar. Stir in 1 cup shredded Swiss or American cheese (about 4 ounces). ABOUT 11 PANCAKES.

Cornmeal Pancakes: Substitute ½ cup cornmeal for ½ cup of the flour. Substitute dark molasses for the sugar if desired. ABOUT 11 PANCAKES.

Ham Pancakes: Omit sugar. Stir in ⅓ to ½ cup ground or cut-up fully cooked ham.

Nut Pancakes: Stir in ¼ to ½ cup broken or chopped nuts.

Oatmeal Pancakes: Substitute ½ cup quick-cooking oats and ½ cup whole wheat flour for the all-purpose flour. Substitute honey for the sugar if desired.

Orange-Coconut Pancakes: Beat in 2 tablespoons frozen orange juice concentrate (thawed) and ½ cup flaked coconut.

Peach Pancakes: Beat in ¼ teaspoon ground cinnamon. Stir in 1 medium peach, peeled and cut up (about ⅔ cup).

Rye Pancakes: Substitute ½ cup rye flour for ½ cup of the all-purpose flour. Use 1 cup milk. Beat in 1 tablespoon grated orange peel. Stir in ½ cup raisins if desired. ABOUT 11 PANCAKES.

Whole Wheat Pancakes: Substitute whole wheat flour for the all-purpose flour and packed brown sugar for the granulated sugar. If desired, sprinkle sesame seed generously over pancakes before turning.

Yogurt Pancakes: Substitute 1¼ cups unflavored yogurt for the milk. Decrease baking powder to 2 teaspoons and beat in ¼ teaspoon baking soda. ABOUT 12 PANCAKES.

MICROWAVE REHEAT DIRECTIONS

	Room Temperature	Frozen
PANCAKES		
1 pancake	20–30 seconds	35–45 seconds
2 pancakes	35–45 seconds	1–1½ minutes
4 pancakes	1–1½ minutes	1½–2 minutes

Whole Wheat Pancakes

Lift with wide spatula to keep shape.

Do not prick when lifting from oil.

Cake Doughnuts

CAKE DOUGHNUTS

Vegetable oil
3⅓ **cups all-purpose flour***
 1 **cup sugar**
 3 **teaspoons baking powder**
½ **teaspoon salt**
½ **teaspoon ground cinnamon**
¼ **teaspoon ground nutmeg**
 2 **tablespoons shortening**
 2 **eggs**
¾ **cup milk**

Heat oil (2 to 3 inches) in deep-fat fryer or heavy kettle to 375°. Beat 1½ cups of the flour and the remaining ingredients in large mixer bowl on low speed, scraping bowl constantly, 30 seconds. Beat on medium speed, scraping bowl occasionally, 2 minutes. Stir in remaining flour. Turn dough onto well-floured cloth-covered board; roll around lightly to coat with flour. Roll gently ⅜ inch thick.

Cut with floured doughnut cutter. Slide doughnuts into hot oil with wide spatula. Turn doughnuts as they rise to surface. Fry until golden brown, 1 to 1½ minutes on each side. Remove from oil; do not prick doughnuts. Drain on paper towels. Serve plain, sugared or frosted.   2 DOZEN DOUGHNUTS.

*If using self-rising flour, omit baking powder and salt.

Buttermilk Doughnuts: Decrease baking powder to 2 teaspoons and beat in 1 teaspoon baking soda. Substitute buttermilk for the milk. Do not use self-rising flour.

NOTE: To dress up Cake Doughnuts, shake one at a time in a bag with powdered sugar. Roll warm Raised Doughnuts (page 217) in granulated sugar. To glaze, mix 1 cup powdered sugar and ⅓ cup boiling water; dip warm doughnuts into warm glaze. Sprinkle with chopped nuts if desired.

MUFFINS

1 egg
¾ cup milk
½ cup vegetable oil
2 cups all-purpose* or whole wheat flour
⅓ cup sugar
3 teaspoons baking powder
1 teaspoon salt

Heat oven to 400°. Grease bottoms only of about 12 medium muffin cups, 2½x1¼ inches. Beat egg; stir in milk and oil. Stir in remaining ingredients all at once just until flour is moistened (batter will be lumpy). Fill muffin cups about ¾ full. Bake until golden brown, about 20 minutes. Immediately remove from pan. ABOUT 1 DOZEN MUFFINS.

*If using self-rising flour, omit baking powder and salt.

Apple-Nut Muffins: Stir in 1 medium apple, pared and chopped, with the milk and ½ teaspoon ground cinnamon with the flour. Substitute packed brown sugar for the granulated sugar. Sprinkle tops with mixture of ¼ cup brown sugar, ¼ cup chopped nuts and ½ teaspoon cinnamon before baking.

Banana Muffins: Decrease milk to ⅓ cup; stir in 1 cup mashed bananas (2 to 3 medium) with the milk. Substitute packed brown sugar for the sugar.

Blueberry Muffins: Stir in 1 cup fresh or ¾ cup frozen blueberries (thawed and well drained) with the milk.

Buttermilk Muffins: Substitute buttermilk for the milk. Decrease baking powder to 2 teaspoons and stir in ½ teaspoon baking soda with the flour.

Cranberry-Orange Muffins: Stir in 1 cup cranberry halves and 1 tablespoon grated orange peel with the milk. Sprinkle tops with sugar before baking.

Date-Nut Muffins: Stir in ½ cup cut-up pitted dates and ⅓ cup chopped nuts with the milk.

French Puffs: Immediately roll hot muffins in about ½ cup margarine or butter, melted, then in mixture of ½ cup sugar and 1 teaspoon ground cinnamon.

Granola Muffins: Decrease milk to ½ cup, flour to 1 cup and sugar to 3 tablespoons. Stir in 2 cups granola with the flour. Do not reheat in microwave.

Honey Muffins: Substitute honey for the sugar; stir in honey and 2 tablespoons grated orange peel with the milk. Spoon 1 teaspoon orange marmalade onto batter in each cup before baking.

Molasses-Bran Muffins: Pour the milk on 1½ cups whole bran cereal; let stand 1 minute. Stir in with the oil. Decrease flour to 1¼ cups and substitute molasses for the sugar.

Oatmeal-Raisin Muffins: Stir in 1 cup raisins with the milk. Decrease flour to 1 cup; stir in 1 cup quick-cooking oats, ½ teaspoon ground nutmeg and ¼ teaspoon ground cinnamon with the flour.

Prune-Apricot Muffins: Stir in ½ cup cut-up dried prunes and ½ cup cut-up dried apricots with the milk.

Pumpkin Muffins: Do not use whole wheat flour. Stir in ½ cup pumpkin and ½ cup raisins with the milk and 2 teaspoons pumpkin pie spice with the flour. Sprinkle tops with sugar before baking if desired.

Rye Muffins: Substitute rye flour for the all-purpose flour; stir in 1 tablespoon caraway seed with the flour.

Surprise Muffins: Fill muffin cups about half full. Spoon 1 teaspoon strawberry jam onto batter in each cup; top with enough batter to fill cups about ¾ full.

MICROWAVE REHEAT DIRECTIONS

MUFFINS	Room Temperature	Frozen
1 muffin	10–15 seconds	20–25 seconds
2 muffins	20–30 seconds	35–40 seconds
4 muffins	30–35 seconds	55–60 seconds

POPOVERS

2 eggs
1 cup all-purpose flour*
1 cup milk
½ teaspoon salt

Heat oven to 450°. Generously grease six 6-ounce custard cups or 8 medium muffin cups, 2½x1¼ inches. Beat eggs slightly; beat in flour, milk and salt just until smooth (do not overbeat).

Fill custard cups about ½ full, muffin cups about ¾ full. Bake 20 minutes. Decrease oven temperature to 350°; bake custard cups 20 minutes longer, muffin cups 15 minutes longer. Immediately remove from cups; serve hot. 6 OR 8 POPOVERS.

*Do not use self-rising flour in this recipe.

Yorkshire Pudding: The traditional English accompaniment for roast beef is simply popover batter baked in the meat drippings. Directions for preparing it with the meat are on page 10.

SOUR CREAM COFFEE CAKE

1½ cups sugar
¾ cup margarine or butter, softened
3 eggs
1½ teaspoons vanilla
3 cups all-purpose* or whole wheat flour
1½ teaspoons baking powder
1½ teaspoons baking soda
¾ teaspoon salt
1½ cups dairy sour cream
    Filling (below)
    Light Brown Glaze (below)

Heat oven to 350°. Grease tube pan, 10x4 inches, 12-cup bundt cake pan or 2 loaf pans, 9x5x3 inches. Beat sugar, margarine, eggs and vanilla in large mixer bowl on medium speed, scraping bowl occasionally, 2 minutes. Beat in flour, baking powder, baking soda and salt alternately with sour cream on low speed. Prepare Filling.

For tube or bundt cake, spread ⅓ of the batter (about 2 cups) in pan and sprinkle with ⅓ of the Filling (about 6 tablespoons); repeat 2 times. For loaves, spread ¼ of the batter (about 1½ cups) in each pan and sprinkle each with ¼ of the Filling (about 5 tablespoons); repeat.

Bake until wooden pick inserted near center comes out clean, about 1 hour. Cool slightly; remove from pan(s). Cool 10 minutes; drizzle with Light Brown Glaze.   14 TO 16 SERVINGS.

*If using self-rising flour, omit baking powder, baking soda and salt.

FILLING

Mix ½ cup packed brown sugar, ½ cup finely chopped nuts and 1½ teaspoons ground cinnamon.

LIGHT BROWN GLAZE

¼ cup margarine or butter
2 cups powdered sugar
1 teaspoon vanilla
1 to 2 tablespoons milk

Heat margarine in 1½-quart saucepan over medium heat until delicate brown. Stir in powdered sugar and vanilla. Stir in milk, 1 tablespoon at a time, until glaze is smooth and of desired consistency.

Molasses-Sour Cream Coffee Cake: Substitute ½ cup light molasses for ½ cup of the sugar. Increase baking soda to 2 teaspoons and decrease sour cream to 1⅓ cups. Bake 55 to 60 minutes. (If using self-rising flour, omit baking powder and salt and decrease baking soda to 1 teaspoon.)

DANISH PUFF

A flaky pastry crust with a custardlike top.

½ cup margarine or butter, softened
1 cup all-purpose flour*
2 tablespoons water
½ cup margarine or butter
1 cup water
1 teaspoon almond extract
1 cup all-purpose flour*
3 eggs
    Powdered Sugar Glaze (below)
    Chopped nuts

Heat oven to 350°. Cut ½ cup margarine into 1 cup flour until particles are size of small peas. Sprinkle 2 tablespoons water over flour mixture; mix. Gather pastry into a ball; divide into halves. Pat each half into rectangle, 12x3 inches, on ungreased cookie sheet. Rectangles should be about 3 inches apart.

Heat ½ cup margarine and 1 cup water to rolling boil; remove from heat. Quickly stir in almond extract and 1 cup flour. Stir vigorously over low heat until mixture forms a ball, about 1 minute; remove from heat. Add eggs; beat until smooth and glossy. Spread half of the topping over each rectangle. Bake until topping is crisp and brown, about 1 hour; cool. (Topping will shrink and fall, forming the custardy top.) Spread with Powdered Sugar Glaze; sprinkle with nuts.   2 COFFEE CAKES (5 OR 6 SERVINGS EACH).

*Self-rising flour can be used in this recipe.

POWDERED SUGAR GLAZE

Mix 1½ cups powdered sugar, 2 tablespoons margarine, softened, and 1½ teaspoons vanilla. Stir in 1 to 2 tablespoons warm water, 1 teaspoon at a time, until glaze is of desired consistency.

Individual Danish Puffs: Pat pastry by rounded teaspoonfuls into 3-inch circles. Spread a rounded tablespoonful topping over each circle, extending it just beyond edge of circle. Bake 30 minutes. 2 DOZEN PUFFS.

MICROWAVE REHEAT DIRECTIONS

	Room Temperature	Frozen
SOUR CREAM COFFEE CAKE (without glaze)		
1 slice	15–20 seconds	25–30 seconds
2 slices	25–30 seconds	50–60 seconds
4 slices	45–50 seconds	1¼ minutes

STREUSEL COFFEE CAKE

    Streusel (below)
    2 cups all-purpose flour*
    1 cup sugar
    3 teaspoons baking powder
    1 teaspoon salt
    ⅓ cup margarine or butter,
        softened
    1 cup milk
    1 egg

Heat oven to 350°. Prepare Streusel. Beat remaining ingredients in large mixer bowl on low speed 30 seconds. Beat on medium speed, scraping bowl occasionally, 2 minutes. Spread half of the batter in greased oblong pan, 13x9x2 inches, or square pan, 9x9x2 inches; sprinkle with half of the Streusel. Top with remaining batter; sprinkle with remaining Streusel. Bake until wooden pick inserted in center comes out clean, 35 to 40 minutes.   9 TO 12 SERVINGS.

*If using self-rising flour, omit baking powder and salt.

STREUSEL
    ½ cup chopped nuts
    ⅓ cup packed brown sugar
    ¼ cup all-purpose flour
    ½ teaspoon ground cinnamon
    3 tablespoons firm margarine or
        butter

Mix all ingredients until crumbly.

Blueberry Coffee Cake: Omit Streusel. Spread half of the batter in pan; sprinkle with 1 cup fresh or frozen blueberries (thawed and well drained). Top with remaining batter; sprinkle with 1 cup fresh or frozen blueberries (thawed and well drained). Bake oblong about 35 minutes, square about 45 minutes. Drizzle warm coffee cake with mixture of 1 cup powdered sugar, 1 teaspoon grated lemon peel and 1 to 2 tablespoons lemon juice.

Orange Coffee Cake: Substitute ½ cup orange juice for ½ cup of the milk. Beat in 2 to 3 tablespoons grated orange peel.

Peanut Butter and Jelly Coffee Cake: Substitute crunchy peanut butter for the margarine. After sprinkling with remaining Streusel, drop ¼ cup grape jelly by teaspoonfuls onto top. Bake oblong about 30 minutes, square about 45 minutes.

Pineapple Coffee Cake: After sprinkling with remaining Streusel, spread 1 can (8¼ ounces) crushed pineapple, well drained, over top. Bake oblong about 45 minutes, square about 1 hour.

Raisin-Spice Coffee Cake: Beat in 1 teaspoon ground cinnamon, ¼ teaspoon ground nutmeg and ¼ teaspoon ground allspice. Stir ½ cup raisins into the batter.

Whole Wheat Coffee Cake: Substitute 1 cup whole wheat flour for 1 cup of the all-purpose flour in batter. Substitute whole wheat flour for the all-purpose flour in Streusel. Bake about 45 minutes.

MICROWAVE REHEAT DIRECTIONS

	Room Temperature	Frozen
STREUSEL COFFEE CAKE		
1 piece	10 seconds	*
2 pieces	15 seconds	*
3 pieces	25 seconds	*

*Not recommended; topping or frosting will overheat.

UPSIDE-DOWN COFFEE CAKE

    Streusel (left)
    ¼ cup margarine or butter
    ½ cup packed brown sugar
    2 medium apples, thinly sliced
    Streusel Coffee Cake batter (left)

Heat oven to 350°. Prepare Streusel. Heat margarine in square pan, 9x9x2 inches, in oven until melted; sprinkle with brown sugar. Arrange apples in pan.

Prepare Streusel Coffee Cake batter; spread over apples. Sprinkle with Streusel. Bake until wooden pick inserted in center comes out clean, about 50 minutes. Immediately invert pan on heatproof serving plate. Let pan remain a minute so butterscotch can drizzle over coffee cake.   9 SERVINGS.

ADDED NUTRIENTS IN FLOUR

When you're shopping, look for that very important word "enriched" on packages of flour, cake mixes and baking mixes. Enriched white flour contains about seven times as much thiamin as unenriched white flour. We need thiamin in our diet to help change food into energy. In addition, enriched white flour has nearly five times as much riboflavin (needed for healthy skin and for changing food into energy) and more than three times as much iron (needed to help build red cells) as unenriched white flour.

STEAMED BROWN BREAD

2 cups buttermilk
1 cup all-purpose* or rye flour
1 cup cornmeal
1 cup whole wheat flour
1 cup raisins (optional)
¾ cup molasses
2 teaspoons baking soda
1 teaspoon salt

Grease 4 cans, 4¼x3 inches (16-ounce vegetable cans), or a 7-inch tube mold. Beat all ingredients in large mixer bowl on low speed, scraping bowl constantly, 30 seconds. Beat on medium speed, scraping bowl constantly, 30 seconds longer. Fill cans about ⅔ full. Cover tightly with aluminum foil.

Place cans on rack in Dutch oven or steamer; pour boiling water around cans to level of rack. Cover Dutch oven. Keep water boiling over low heat until wooden pick inserted in center of bread comes out clean, about 3 hours. (Add boiling water during steaming if necessary.) Immediately unmold bread.   4 LOAVES.

*If using self-rising flour, decrease baking soda to 1 teaspoon and omit salt.

Baked Brown Bread: Heat oven to 325°. Pour batter into greased 2-quart casserole. Bake about 1 hour.

IMPROVISING A STEAMER

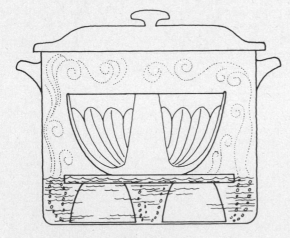

If you don't have a regular steamer pan, you can improvise one quite easily using a Dutch oven or large saucepan with a tight-fitting cover. Place a wire rack in pan about 1 to 2 inches from the bottom. If rack is not adjustable, simply balance it on custard cups as shown.

PUMPKIN BREAD

⅔ cup shortening
2⅔ cups sugar
4 eggs
1 can (16 ounces) pumpkin
⅔ cup water
3⅓ cups all-purpose flour*
2 teaspoons baking soda
1½ teaspoons salt
½ teaspoon baking powder
1 teaspoon ground cinnamon
1 teaspoon ground cloves
⅔ cup coarsely chopped nuts
⅔ cup raisins

Heat oven to 350°. Grease bottoms only of 2 loaf pans, 9x5x3 inches, or 3 loaf pans, 8½x4½x2½ inches. Mix shortening and sugar in large bowl. Add eggs, pumpkin and water. Blend in flour, baking soda, salt, baking powder, cinnamon and cloves. Stir in nuts and raisins. Pour into pans. Bake until wooden pick inserted in center comes out clean, about 1 hour 10 minutes; cool slightly. Loosen sides of loaves from pans; remove from pans. Cool completely before slicing. To store, wrap and refrigerate no longer than 10 days.

*If using self-rising flour, omit baking soda, salt and baking powder.

Zucchini Bread: Substitute 3 cups shredded zucchini (about 2 medium) for the pumpkin. Blend in 2 teaspoons vanilla with the cloves. Decrease baking time to 60 to 70 minutes.

MICROWAVE REHEAT DIRECTIONS

	Room Temperature	Frozen
PUMPKIN BREAD		
1 slice	15–20 seconds	15–20 seconds
2 slices	20–25 seconds	30–35 seconds
4 slices	45–50 seconds	45–55 seconds

NUT BREAD BUTTERS

Almond Butter: Mix ½ cup margarine or butter, softened, 1 tablespoon finely chopped almonds and ½ teaspoon almond extract.

Date Butter: Mix ½ cup margarine or butter, softened, and ¼ cup finely cut-up dates.

Orange Butter: Mix ½ cup margarine or butter, softened, 1 tablespoon orange juice and 1 teaspoon grated orange peel.

NUT BREAD

2½ cups all-purpose flour*
½ cup granulated sugar
½ cup packed brown sugar
3½ teaspoons baking powder
1 teaspoon salt
3 tablespoons vegetable oil
1¼ cups milk
1 egg
1 tablespoon plus 1 teaspoon grated
     orange peel
1 cup chopped nuts

Heat oven to 350°. Grease bottom only of loaf pan, 9x5x3 inches, or 2 loaf pans, 8½x4½x2½ inches. Mix all ingredients; beat 30 seconds. Pour into pan(s). Bake until wooden pick inserted in center comes out clean, 9-inch loaf 55 to 65 minutes, 8-inch loaves 55 to 60 minutes; cool slightly. Loosen sides of loaf from pan; remove from pan. Cool completely before slicing. To store, wrap and refrigerate no longer than 1 week.

*If using self-rising flour, omit baking powder and salt.

Apricot Nut Bread: Mix in 1 cup finely cut-up dried apricots.

Banana Nut Bread: Decrease milk to ⅓ cup and omit orange peel. Mix in 1¼ cups mashed bananas (2 to 3 medium). Bake 9-inch loaf 65 to 70 minutes.

Cherry Nut Bread: Omit orange peel and use almonds. Mix in ½ teaspoon almond extract. Stir in 1 jar (10 ounces) maraschino cherries, chopped and drained on paper towels. Bake 9-inch loaf 65 to 70 minutes.

Cranberry-Cheese Nut Bread: Decrease nuts to ½ cup. Stir in 1½ cups shredded Cheddar cheese (about 6 ounces) and 1 cup cranberries, cut into halves. Bake 9-inch loaf 65 to 70 minutes.

Date Nut Bread: Omit milk. Mix 1½ cups boiling water and 1½ cups cut-up dates; cool. Stir into the batter.

Whole Wheat Raisin Bread: Substitute 2¾ cups whole wheat flour for the all-purpose flour and honey for the brown sugar. Mix in 1 cup raisins.

Apricot Nut Bread

CORN BREAD

1½ cups cornmeal
 ½ cup all-purpose flour*
 2 teaspoons baking powder
 1 teaspoon sugar
 1 teaspoon salt
 ½ teaspoon baking soda
 ¼ cup shortening or bacon fat
1½ cups buttermilk
 2 eggs

Heat oven to 450°. Mix all ingredients; beat vigorously 30 seconds. Pour into greased round layer pan, 9x1½ inches, or square pan, 8x8x2 inches. Bake until golden brown, 25 to 30 minutes. Serve warm.   9 TO 12 SERVINGS.

*If using self-rising flour, decrease baking powder to 1 teaspoon and omit salt.

Bacon Corn Bread: Decrease salt to ¾ teaspoon and use bacon fat. Stir in 4 slices bacon, crisply fried and crumbled (about ⅓ cup).

Chili Corn Bread: Stir in 1 can (4 ounces) chopped green chilies, drained on paper towels, and ½ teaspoon chili powder.

Corn Muffins: Fill 14 greased medium muffin cups, 2½x1¼ inches, about ⅞ full. Bake about 20 minutes.

Corn Sticks: Fill 18 greased corn stick pans about ⅞ full. Bake 12 to 15 minutes.

Double Corn Bread: Stir in 1 can (7 or 8 ounces) whole kernel corn, well drained. Pour batter into greased square pan, 9x9x2 inches. Bake about 25 minutes.

Onion-Cheese Corn Bread: Stir in ½ cup shredded process sharp American cheese (about 2 ounces) and 3 medium green onions, chopped (about ¼ cup).

Skillet Corn Bread: Pour batter into greased 10-inch ovenproof skillet. Bake about 20 minutes.

Corn Bread as a base for asparagus and cheese sauce, with Canadian-style bacon and a melon salad

FLUFFY SPOON BREAD

A soufflé-type spoon bread; it's spooned onto plate and eaten with a fork.

1½ cups boiling water
 1 cup cornmeal
 1 tablespoon margarine or butter, softened
 3 eggs, separated
 1 cup buttermilk
 1 teaspoon salt
 1 teaspoon sugar
 1 teaspoon baking powder
 ¼ teaspoon baking soda
    Margarine or butter

Heat oven to 375°. Stir boiling water into cornmeal; continue stirring until mixture is lukewarm. Blend in 1 tablespoon margarine and the egg yolks. Stir in buttermilk, salt, sugar, baking powder and baking soda. Beat egg whites just until soft peaks form; fold into batter. Pour into greased 2-quart casserole. Bake until knife inserted near center comes out clean, 45 to 50 minutes. Serve with margarine.

MICROWAVE REHEAT DIRECTIONS

	Room Temperature	Frozen
CORN BREAD		
1 piece	15 seconds	40–45 seconds
2 pieces	20–25 seconds	1¼–1½ minutes
4 pieces	55–60 seconds	2–2¼ minutes

CORNMEAL MUSH

¾ cup cornmeal
¾ cup cold water
2½ cups boiling water
¾ teaspoon salt
2 tablespoons margarine or butter
Flour
Maple-flavored Syrup (below)

Mix cornmeal and cold water in saucepan. Stir in boiling water and salt. Cook, stirring constantly, until mixture thickens and boils; reduce heat. Cover and simmer 10 minutes. Spread in greased loaf pan, 9x5x3 or 8½x4½x2½ inches. Cover and refrigerate until firm, at least 12 hours but no longer than 2 weeks.

Invert pan to unmold; cut loaf into ½-inch slices. Heat margarine in 10-inch skillet until melted. Coat slices with flour; cook in margarine over low heat until brown on both sides. Serve hot with Maple-flavored Syrup.   4 SERVINGS.

MAPLE-FLAVORED SYRUP

1 cup light corn syrup
1 tablespoon margarine or butter
¼ teaspoon maple flavoring
⅛ teaspoon vanilla

Heat corn syrup and margarine over low heat, stirring occasionally, until margarine is melted. Stir in maple flavoring and vanilla.

GNOCCHI

Serve Gnocchi as a first course or a side dish.

2½ cups milk
1 cup white cornmeal
1 tablespoon margarine or butter
2 eggs, well beaten
¼ teaspoon salt
2 tablespoons margarine or butter
¼ to ½ cup grated Parmesan cheese
Tomato sauce (optional)

Heat milk to scalding in 2-quart saucepan; reduce heat. Sprinkle cornmeal slowly into hot milk, stirring constantly. Cook, stirring constantly, until thick, about 5 minutes (spoon will stand upright in the mixture); remove from heat. Mix in 1 tablespoon margarine, the eggs and salt; beat until smooth. Spread in greased square pan, 8x8x2 inches; cool. Refrigerate until firm, 2 to 3 hours.

Heat oven to 425°. Cut cornmeal mixture into sixteen 1½-inch circles. Place 4 circles in each ungreased individual casserole. (If individual casseroles are not available, place circles in baking pan or ovenproof skillet.) Dot with 2 tablespoons margarine and sprinkle with cheese. Bake until hot, 10 to 12 minutes.

Set oven control to broil and/or 550°. Broil gnocchi with tops 2 to 3 inches from heat until golden brown, about 2 minutes. Serve with tomato sauce.   4 SERVINGS.

1. The cornmeal mixture for Gnocchi is very stiff.

2. Golden-brown Gnocchi prepared in a baking pan.

HUSH PUPPIES

   Vegetable oil
2¼ cups yellow cornmeal
 1 teaspoon salt
 2 tablespoons finely chopped onion
 ¾ teaspoon baking soda
1½ cups buttermilk

Heat oil (1 inch) to 375°. Mix cornmeal, salt, onion and baking soda. Stir in buttermilk. Drop by spoonfuls into hot oil. Fry until brown, about 2 minutes.   ABOUT 2 DOZEN HUSH PUPPIES.

TORTILLAS

1½ cups cold water
 1 cup all-purpose flour*
 ½ cup cornmeal
 ¼ teaspoon salt
 1 egg

Heat 8-inch skillet over medium-low heat just until hot. Grease skillet if necessary. (To test skillet, sprinkle with few drops water. If bubbles skitter around, heat is just right.)

Beat all ingredients with hand beater until smooth. Pour scant ¼ cup of the batter into skillet; immediately rotate skillet until batter forms very thin tortilla about 6 inches in diameter. Cook tortilla until dry around edge, about 2 minutes. Turn and cook other side until golden, about 2 minutes longer.   ABOUT 1 DOZEN TORTILLAS.

*Do not use self-rising flour in this recipe.

NOTE: To store, stack tortillas, placing waxed paper between each. Wrap and freeze no longer than 3 months. When ready to use, separate tortillas and thaw covered at room temperature about 30 minutes.

ABOUT TORTILLAS
Tortillas (Mexican pancakes) are served most simply like hot biscuits, for each person to butter, roll up and eat. If you dip a tortilla in sauce, sprinkle it with cheese, roll it and top it with more sauce, cheese and chopped onion, then bake it, you have an Enchilada (page 31). A tortilla wrapped around mashed refried beans or chili-flavored ground meat, topped with chopped onion and cheese, baked, then served on shredded lettuce with a hot sauce is a Burrito (page 33).

FRITTERS AND DEEP-FRIED FOODS

FRITTER BATTER
 1 cup all-purpose flour*
 1 teaspoon baking powder
 1 teaspoon salt**
 2 eggs
 ½ cup milk
 1 teaspoon vegetable oil

THIN BATTER
 1 cup all-purpose flour*
 1 teaspoon baking powder
 ½ teaspoon salt**
 1 egg
 1 cup milk
 ¼ cup vegetable oil

Prepare food to be fried (see suggested foods below). Thaw frozen foods completely before frying. Dry food completely before dipping into batter. Use Fritter Batter with chopped or shredded foods; use Thin Batter when you want to retain shape of food.

Heat vegetable oil (2 to 3 inches) in deep-fat fryer or kettle to 375°. Beat batter ingredients in bowl with hand beater until smooth.

To prepare fritters: Stir about 1 cup suggested food into Fritter Batter; drop by level tablespoonfuls into hot oil and fry until completely cooked, about 5 minutes. Drain.

Suggested foods for fritters: Chopped cooked shrimp or ham, cubed luncheon meat; corn; chopped apple or banana, pineapple cubes.

To deep-fry foods: Coat suggested food with flour. Dip food into Thin Batter with tongs or fork, allowing excess batter to drip into bowl; fry in hot oil until golden brown. Drain.

Suggested foods for deep-frying: Whole shrimp, scallops, oysters, fish fillets, chicken pieces (partially cooked), cutlets; eggplant slices, cauliflowerets, onion rings, zucchini slices; pineapple slices, bananas (cut into fourths), apple slices, apricot halves.

*If using self-rising flour, omit baking powder and salt.
**If adding salted foods to the batter, omit salt.

YEAST BREADS

ABOUT BREAD BAKING

INGREDIENTS

Flour: All-purpose flour contains gluten, the bread builder. Gluten traps the gas formed by the yeast and gives elasticity to the dough. Recipes seldom give exact amounts of the second addition of flour because temperature and humidity affect the dough's softness. (On a humid day, more flour is needed.) You'll learn to adjust by "feel."

Yeast: Yeast is a live plant that gives off a gas that makes dough rise. It comes two ways: active dry or compressed cake. (One packet of dry equals one ⅗-ounce cake.) Our recipes use active dry and follow the traditional method of first dissolving the yeast in warm water. The dissolving liquid should be 105 to 115°, since yeast is very sensitive. Too much heat will kill it; cold will stunt its growth.

Liquids: Water and milk are most commonly used. Water gives bread an especially crisp crust; milk, a velvety texture and added nutrients.

Sweeteners: Sugar, honey and molasses "feed" yeast, enhance flavor, help brown the crust.

Salt: Salt controls growth of the yeast.

Fats: These contribute tenderness and flavor.

HANDLING THE DOUGH

Kneaded Dough: The bread is brought to life by the centuries-old rhythm of push-and-pull, fold-and-press known as kneading. The dough is worked until springy, blistered with tiny bubbles under the surface and satin-smooth on top.

Batter Dough: Because less flour is used and the dough is stickier, these breads are beaten with a mixer with the first addition of flour instead of being kneaded. They are generally not shaped and when baked have a more open-grained texture.

Roll Dough: Dough for rolls should be softer than for kneaded breads. Add the second amount of flour slowly. Add just enough so that the dough can be handled without sticking. After kneading, the dough is shaped. If it is too elastic and springs back, let it rest 10 minutes, then shape. To cut, use a very sharp knife or kitchen scissors.

Refrigerating Dough: If you want to make your dough now and bake later, the refrigerator can hold dough made with water (except for plain bread dough) as long as 5 days. However, if milk and at least ¼ cup sugar are used, the limit is 3 days. To prepare dough, grease the top well, cover with moisture-proof wrap and then a damp cloth. Keep the cloth damp. When you're ready to bake, shape the dough and let it rise until double, 1½ to 2 hours.

Interruptions while Baking: If you're called away while beating or kneading dough, just pick up where you left off. Dough will wait as long as 15 minutes. If you can't shape dough after it has doubled, just punch it down to get out the air, cover and let rise again. The next rising will take less time.

PANS

Use loaf pans of the size specified in the recipe. The pans should have anodized aluminum or darkened metal exteriors to help absorb heat and give loaves a good brown crust. (A nonstick coating on the inside will not change the baking characteristics of the pan.) A shiny metal pan can be darkened by heating it about 5 hours in a 350° oven.

BAKING

Stagger loaf pans on a lower shelf of the oven so that they do not touch either the sides of the oven or each other. The top of each pan should be level with, or slightly above, the middle of the oven. If baking round loaves on a cookie sheet, place the sheet on the center rack of the oven.

To test a loaf for doneness, tap the crust. It will have a hollow sound when done.

To cool bread, remove loaves from pans immediately and place on wire racks away from draft. If you like a soft crust, brush the loaf with shortening and cover with a towel for a few minutes.

STORING

Store breads in airtight containers; breads are best if not stored in the refrigerator.

FREEZING

Bake breads before freezing; breads baked after freezing will be smaller and tougher. Overwrap the bread you buy if it is to stay in the freezer for more than 1 week. Cool baked loaves completely, then slice (this saves thawing time later). Rolls and coffee cake slices can be individually wrapped for quick thawing. Seal all breads tightly in moistureproof wrap or bags. Freeze up to 9 months.

To thaw, let bread stand wrapped at room temperature about 3 hours or toast frozen slices in toaster. Or make lunch box sandwiches with frozen bread. Thaw and heat breads in 350° oven.

TIPS FOR YEAST BREADS

1. Water used to dissolve granular yeast should be 105 to 115°. Use a thermometer or test a drop on inside of wrist (water should feel very warm but not hot).

2. After the first addition of flour, beat ingredients with electric mixer or wooden spoon. Batter breads require especially vigorous beating.

3. To knead, fold dough toward you, then push away with heels of hands in rocking motion. Rotate a quarter turn; repeat until dough is smooth and blistered.

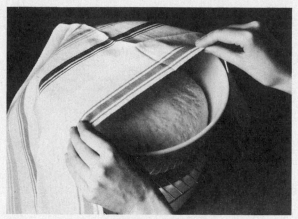

4. To let dough rise, cover and keep in a warm, draft-free place. If necessary, place bowl of dough on a wire rack over a bowl of warm water.

5. Dough should rise until double. Test by pressing fingertips ½ inch into dough; indentation will remain if dough has doubled.

6. To punch down dough, plunge fist into center of dough. Fold over and form into a ball. This releases large air bubbles to produce a finer texture.

WHITE BREAD

- 2 packages active dry yeast
- ¾ cup warm water (105 to 115°)
- 2 cups lukewarm milk (scalded then cooled)
- 3 tablespoons sugar
- 3 tablespoons shortening
- 1 tablespoon salt
- 7 to 8 cups all-purpose flour*
  Margarine or butter, softened

Dissolve yeast in warm water in large bowl. Stir in milk, sugar, shortening, salt and 4 cups of the flour. Beat until smooth. Mix in enough remaining flour to make dough easy to handle.

Turn dough onto lightly floured surface; knead until smooth and elastic, about 10 minutes. Place in greased bowl; turn greased side up. Cover; let rise in warm place until double, about 1 hour. (Dough is ready if indentation remains when touched.)

Punch down dough; divide into halves. Roll each half into rectangle, 18x9 inches. Fold 9-inch sides crosswise into thirds, overlapping ends. Roll up tightly, beginning at narrow end. Pinch edge of dough into roll to seal well; press in ends of roll. Press each end with side of hand to seal; fold ends under.

Place loaves seam sides down in 2 greased loaf pans, 9x5x3 or 8½x4½x2½ inches. Brush lightly with margarine. Let rise until double, about 1 hour.

Heat oven to 425°. Place loaves on low rack so that tops of pans are in center of oven. Pans should not touch each other or sides of oven. Bake until loaves are deep golden brown and sound hollow when tapped, 25 to 30 minutes. Immediately remove from pans. Brush tops of loaves with margarine; cool on wire racks.   2 LOAVES.

*If using self-rising flour, omit salt.

Cinnamon-Raisin Bread: Mix in 1½ cups raisins with the second addition of flour. Mix ¼ cup sugar and 2 teaspoons ground cinnamon. After rolling dough into rectangles, sprinkle each with 1 tablespoon water and half of the sugar mixture.

Cornmeal Bread: Substitute 1 cup cornmeal for 1 cup of the second addition of flour. Sprinkle greased pans with cornmeal and sprinkle tops of loaves with cornmeal before baking.

Cracked Wheat Bread: Substitute packed brown sugar for the granulated sugar. Substitute 2⅔ cups cracked wheat for 2⅔ cups of the second addition of flour. If desired, mix in ½ cup wheat germ with the second addition of flour.

Egg Bread: Decrease milk to 1¾ cups; stir in 2 eggs.

Herb Bread: Stir in 2 teaspoons caraway seed, ½ teaspoon dried sage leaves and ½ teaspoon ground nutmeg with the first addition of flour.

Oatmeal Bread: Substitute packed brown sugar for the granulated sugar. Substitute 1 cup quick-cooking oats for 1 cup of the second addition of flour. Sprinkle greased pans with oats and sprinkle tops of loaves with oats before baking.

Raisin Bread: Mix in 1½ cups raisins.

Rye Bread: Substitute ¼ cup dark molasses for the sugar. Stir in 2 tablespoons caraway seed with the first addition of flour. Substitute 3 to 4 cups rye flour for the second addition of all-purpose flour. Do not roll into rectangles. Shape each half of dough into round loaf, tucking in at bottom to resemble giant mushroom cap. Pinch to seal. Bake on greased cookie sheet.

Whole Wheat Bread: Substitute ¼ cup honey for the sugar and whole wheat flour for the all-purpose flour.

1. Roll up dough tightly to prevent large air holes in bread.

2. Pinch length of roll to seal. Press ends to seal; fold under loaf.

3. Bake loaves with tops of pans in the center of the oven.

Rye Bread (page 209), Cheese Casserole Bread and Onion-Dill Casserole Bread

CASSEROLE BREAD

1 package active dry yeast
½ cup warm water (105 to 115°)
½ cup lukewarm milk (scalded then cooled)
⅔ cup margarine or butter, softened
2 eggs
1 teaspoon salt
3 cups all-purpose flour*
   Margarine or butter, softened

Dissolve yeast in warm water in large mixer bowl. Add milk, ⅔ cup margarine, the eggs, salt and 1 cup of the flour. Beat on low speed, scraping bowl constantly, 30 seconds. Beat on medium speed, scraping bowl occasionally, 2 minutes. Stir in remaining flour until smooth. Scrape batter from side of bowl. Cover; let rise in warm place until double, about 30 minutes. (Batter is ready if indentation remains when touched with floured finger.)

Stir down batter by beating about 25 strokes. Spread evenly in greased 2-quart casserole. Cover; let rise until double, about 40 minutes.

Heat oven to 375°. Place loaf on low rack so that top of casserole is in center of oven. Casserole should not touch sides of oven. Bake until loaf is brown and sounds hollow when tapped, 40 to 45 minutes. Immediately remove from casserole. Brush top of loaf with margarine; cool on wire rack. To serve, cut into wedges with serrated knife.

*If using self-rising flour, omit salt.

Cheese Casserole Bread: Stir in 1 cup shredded Cheddar or Swiss cheese (about 4 ounces) and ½ teaspoon pepper with the second addition of flour.

Onion-Dill Casserole Bread: Stir in 1 small onion, finely chopped (about ¼ cup), and 1 tablespoon dried dill weed with the second addition of flour. Brush top of loaf with margarine and sprinkle with sesame seed or poppy seed before baking.

Taco Casserole Bread: Substitute ½ cup cornmeal for ½ cup of the second addition of flour. Stir in 1 cup shredded hot pepper cheese (about 4 ounces) and 2 to 4 tablespoons chopped green chilies, drained on paper towels, with the second addition of flour. Brush top of loaf with margarine and sprinkle with cornmeal before baking.

Whole Wheat Casserole Bread: Substitute 1½ cups whole wheat flour for 1½ cups of the second addition of all-purpose flour.

MICROWAVE REHEAT DIRECTIONS

	Room Temperature	Frozen
CASSEROLE BREAD		
1 slice	10-15 seconds	30-35 seconds
2 slices	15-20 seconds	35-40 seconds
4 slices	25-30 seconds	1¼ minutes

SOURDOUGH BREAD

Your homemade sourdough will be crispy, tangy and delicious, but a home oven cannot duplicate the special San Francisco bakery loaf.

1 cup Sourdough Starter (below)
2½ cups all-purpose flour*
2 cups warm water (105 to 115°)
3¾ to 4¼ cups all-purpose flour*
3 tablespoons sugar
1 teaspoon salt
¼ teaspoon baking soda
3 tablespoons vegetable oil
  Cold water

Mix 1 cup Sourdough Starter, 2½ cups flour and 2 cups warm water in 3-quart glass bowl with wooden spoon until smooth. Cover; let stand in warm, draft-free place 8 hours.

Add 3¾ cups of the flour, the sugar, salt, baking soda and oil to mixture in bowl; stir with wooden spoon until smooth and flour is completely absorbed. (Dough should be just firm enough to gather into a ball. If necessary, add remaining ½ cup flour gradually, stirring until all flour is absorbed.)

Turn dough onto heavily floured surface, knead until smooth and elastic, about 10 minutes. Place in greased bowl; turn greased side up. Cover; let rise in warm place until double, about 1½ hours. (Dough is ready if indentation remains when touched.)

Punch down dough; divide into halves. Shape each half into a round, slightly flat loaf. Do not tear dough by pulling. Place loaves in opposite corners of greased cookie sheet. Make three ¼-inch-deep slashes in each loaf. Let rise until double, about 45 minutes.

Heat oven to 375°. Brush loaves with cold water. Place cookie sheet in center of oven. Cookie sheet should not touch sides of oven. Bake, brushing occasionally with water, until loaves sound hollow when tapped, about 50 minutes. Remove from cookie sheet; cool on wire racks.   2 LOAVES.

SOURDOUGH STARTER

1 teaspoon active dry yeast
¼ cup warm water (105 to 115°)
¾ cup milk
1 cup all-purpose flour*

Dissolve yeast in warm water in 3-quart glass bowl. Stir in milk. Stir in flour gradually. Beat until smooth. Cover with towel or cheesecloth; let stand in warm, draft-free place until starter begins to ferment, about 24 hours (bubbles will appear on surface of starter). If starter has not begun fermentation after 24 hours, discard and begin again. If fermentation has begun, stir well; cover tightly with plastic wrap and return to warm, draft-free place. Let stand until foamy, 2 to 3 days.

When starter has become foamy, stir well; pour into 1-quart crock or glass jar with tightly fitting cover. Store in refrigerator. Starter is ready to use when a clear liquid has risen to top. Stir before using. Use 1 cup starter in recipe; reserve remaining starter. Add ¾ cup milk and ¾ cup flour to reserved starter. Store covered at room temperature until bubbles appear, about 12 hours; refrigerate.

Use starter regularly, every week to 10 days. If the volume of the breads you bake begins to decrease, dissolve 1 teaspoon active dry yeast in ¼ cup warm water. Stir in ½ cup milk, ¾ cup flour and the remaining starter.

*Do not use self-rising flour in this recipe.

NOTE: Start bread at night to bake in the morning—or vice versa. Before adding the milk and flour to remaining starter, bake your bread and judge the volume.

NATURAL GRAINS AND FLOURS

Rediscovering these natural flours of yesterday is one of today's delights:

Whole wheat (or *graham*) is made from the entire wheat berry after it has been thoroughly cleaned, while *cracked wheat* is cleaned wheat cracked or cut into angular fragments. Milled from rye grain, *rye* is usually mixed with wheat for bread baking. *Buckwheat* is made from the triangular seeds of the buckwheat plant. Known by its "speckles," it is a robust favorite for pancakes. Ground from whole raw soybeans, *soy flour* is slightly sweet-tasting. *Cornmeal* (ground corn) and *rolled oats* (oat groats pressed between rollers) give crunchy sweetness to breads. The germinating portion of the wheat kernel, *wheat germ*, adds texture and some protein.

Some of these flours and grains do not have enough gluten and are combined with all-purpose flour.

REFRIGERATOR ROLL DOUGH

   1 package active dry yeast
1½ cups warm water (105 to 115°)
   1 cup unseasoned lukewarm mashed
       potatoes
⅔ cup sugar
⅔ cup shortening
   2 eggs
1½ teaspoons salt
   6 to 7 cups all-purpose flour*

Dissolve yeast in warm water in large bowl. Stir in potatoes, sugar, shortening, eggs, salt and 3 cups of the flour. Beat until smooth. Mix in enough remaining flour to make dough easy to handle. Turn dough onto lightly floured surface; knead until smooth and elastic, about 5 minutes. Place in greased bowl; turn greased side up. Cover bowl tightly; refrigerate at least 8 hours but no longer than 5 days.

Punch down dough; divide into 4 equal parts. Use ¼ of the dough for any Dinner Roll recipe (below) unless otherwise noted.

*If using self-rising flour, omit salt.

Bran Refrigerator Roll Dough: Increase water to 2 cups; pour ½ cup over ¾ cup whole bran cereal. Let stand 1 minute; stir in with remaining water.

Whole Wheat Refrigerator Roll Dough: Substitute 3 to 4 cups whole wheat flour for the second addition of all-purpose flour.

DINNER ROLLS

Brown-and-Serve Rolls: Shape Refrigerator Roll Dough (above) as directed in any roll recipe below. Let rise 1 hour. Heat oven to 275°. Bake 20 minutes (do not allow to brown). Remove from pans; cool to room temperature. Wrap in aluminum foil. Store in refrigerator no longer than 8 days or freeze no longer than 2 months. At serving time, heat oven to 400°. Bake until brown, 8 to 12 minutes.

Casseroles: Shape ¼ of Refrigerator Roll Dough (above) into 1-inch balls. Place in lightly greased round layer pan, 9x1½ inches. Brush with margarine or butter, softened. Let rise 1 hour. Heat oven to 400°. Bake until golden brown, about 15 minutes.   3 DOZEN ROLLS.

Cloverleaf Rolls: Shape ¼ of Refrigerator Roll Dough (above) into 1-inch balls. Place 3 balls in each greased medium muffin cup, 2½x1¼ inches. Brush with margarine or butter, softened. Let rise 1 hour. Heat oven to 400°. Bake until golden brown, 15 to 20 minutes.   1 DOZEN ROLLS.

Crescent Rolls: Roll ¼ of Refrigerator Roll Dough (left) into 12-inch circle on floured surface. Spread with margarine, softened. Cut into 16 wedges. Roll up tightly, beginning at rounded edges, stretching dough as it is rolled. Place rolls with points underneath on greased cookie sheet; curve slightly. Brush with margarine, softened. Let rise 1 hour. Heat oven to 400°. Bake 15 minutes.   16 ROLLS.

Fan Tans: Roll ¼ of Refrigerator Roll Dough (left) into rectangle, 13x9 inches, on well-floured surface. Spread with 2 to 3 tablespoons margarine or butter, softened. Cut lengthwise into 6 strips, each about 1½ inches wide. Stack strips evenly; cut into 12 pieces, each about 1 inch wide. Place cut sides down in greased medium muffin cups, 2½x1¼ inches. Brush with margarine or butter, softened. Let rise 1 hour. Heat oven to 400°. Bake until golden brown, 15 to 20 minutes.   1 DOZEN ROLLS.

Four-Leaf Clovers: Shape ¼ of Refrigerator Roll Dough (left) into 2-inch balls. Place each ball in greased medium muffin cup, 2½x1¼ inches. With scissors, snip each ball completely into halves, then into quarters. Brush with margarine or butter, softened. Let rise 1 hour. Heat oven to 400°. Bake until golden brown, 15 to 20 minutes.   8 TO 10 ROLLS.

Pan Biscuits: Use half of Refrigerator Roll Dough (left). Roll dough into rectangle, 13x9 inches, on well-floured surface. Place in greased oblong pan, 13x9x2 inches. Cut dough into rectangles, each about 3x2½ inches. Brush with margarine or butter, softened. Let rise 1 hour. Heat oven to 400°. Bake 25 minutes.   15 ROLLS.

Parker House Rolls: Roll ¼ of Refrigerator Roll Dough (left) into rectangle, 12x9 inches, on well-floured surface. Cut into 3-inch circles with floured cutter. Brush with margarine or butter, softened. Make crease across each circle; fold so top half slightly overlaps bottom half. Press edges together. Place close together in greased square pan, 9x9x2 inches. Brush with margarine or butter, softened. Let rise 1 hour. Heat oven to 400°. Bake until golden brown, 15 to 20 minutes.   1 DOZEN ROLLS.

MICROWAVE REHEAT DIRECTIONS

	Room Temperature	Frozen
DINNER ROLLS		
1 roll	10–15 seconds	20–25 seconds
2 rolls	15–20 seconds	25–30 seconds
4 rolls	25–30 seconds	35–40 seconds

NOTE: Breads should be reheated uncovered on absorbent paper (paper towels, napkins).

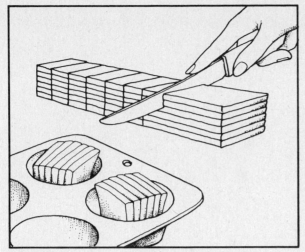

Fan Tans

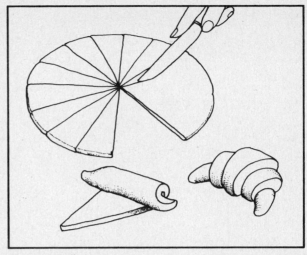

Crescent Rolls

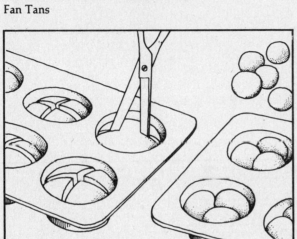

Four-Leaf Clovers and Cloverleaf Rolls

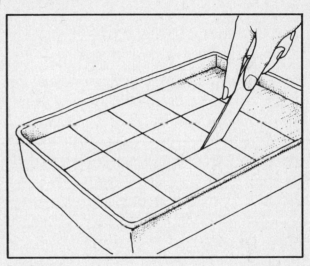

Pan Biscuits

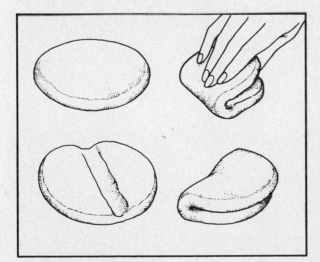

Parker House Rolls

Casseroles

Orange Rolls (page 215), Raised Doughnuts (page 217), Cinnamon Rolls (page 215) and Cheese-filled Rolls (page 215)

SWEET ROLL DOUGH

1 package active dry yeast
½ cup warm water (105 to 115°)
½ cup lukewarm milk (scalded then cooled)
⅓ cup sugar
⅓ cup shortening, or margarine or butter, softened
1 teaspoon salt
1 egg
3½ to 4 cups all-purpose flour*

Dissolve yeast in warm water in large bowl. Stir in milk, sugar, shortening, salt, egg and 2 cups of the flour. Beat until smooth. Mix in enough remaining flour to make dough easy to handle.

Turn dough onto lightly floured surface; knead until smooth and elastic, about 5 minutes. Place in greased bowl; turn greased side up. Cover; let rise in warm place until double, about 1½ hours. (Dough is ready if an indentation remains when touched.)

Punch down dough. Shape, let rise and bake as directed.

*If using self-rising flour, omit salt.

Do-ahead Tip: After kneading, dough can be covered and refrigerated in greased bowl no longer than 4 days.

CHEESE-FILLED ROLLS

1 package (8 ounces) cream cheese, softened
¼ cup sugar
3 tablespoons flour
1 egg yolk
½ teaspoon grated lemon peel
1 tablespoon lemon juice
½ Sweet Roll Dough (above)
½ cup jam
¼ cup chopped nuts

Beat cream cheese and sugar until light and fluffy. Stir in flour, egg yolk, lemon peel and lemon juice.

Roll dough into 15-inch square on lightly floured surface. Cut into twenty-five 3-inch squares. Place on greased cookie sheets. Spoon about 1 tablespoon cream cheese mixture onto center of each square. Bring 2 diagonally opposite corners to center of each square, overlapping slightly; pinch. Let rise until double, about 40 minutes.

Heat oven to 375°. Bake until golden brown, 12 to 15 minutes. Heat jam until melted; brush lightly over hot rolls and sprinkle with chopped nuts.
25 ROLLS.

ORANGE ROLLS

3 tablespoons margarine or butter, softened
1 tablespoon grated orange peel
2 tablespoons orange juice
1½ cups powdered sugar
½ Sweet Roll Dough (left)

Beat margarine, orange peel, orange juice and powdered sugar until smooth and creamy. Roll dough into rectangle, 12x7 inches, on lightly floured surface; spread with half of the orange mixture. Roll up tightly, beginning at 12-inch side. Pinch edge of dough into roll to seal well. Stretch roll to make even. Cut into twelve 1-inch slices. Place slightly apart in greased round layer pan, 8x1½ inches. Let rise until double, about 40 minutes.

Heat oven to 375°. Bake until golden brown, 20 to 25 minutes. Frost with remaining orange mixture while warm.   1 DOZEN ROLLS.

CINNAMON ROLLS

½ Sweet Roll Dough (left)
2 tablespoons margarine or butter, softened
¼ cup sugar
2 teaspoons ground cinnamon
Glaze (page 219)

Roll dough into rectangle, 15x9 inches, on lightly floured surface; spread with margarine. Mix sugar and cinnamon; sprinkle over rectangle. Roll up tightly, beginning at 15-inch side. Pinch edge of dough into roll to seal well. Stretch roll to make even. Cut into nine 1½-inch slices. Place slightly apart in greased square pan, 9x9x2 inches, or in greased medium muffin cups, 2½x1¼ inches. Let rise until double, about 40 minutes.

Heat oven to 375°. Bake until golden brown, 25 to 30 minutes. Spread rolls with Glaze while warm.
9 ROLLS.

Butterscotch-Pecan Rolls: Before rolling dough into rectangle, heat ¼ cup margarine or butter until melted; stir in ½ cup packed brown sugar, 2 tablespoons corn syrup and ½ cup pecan halves. Spread in pan. Roll dough, slice, let rise and bake as directed. Immediately invert pan on heatproof serving plate. Let pan remain a minute so butterscotch can drizzle over rolls.

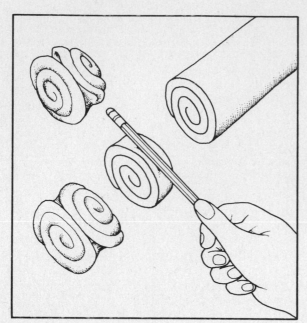

For butterfly "wings," press pencil almost through dough in center of each slice.

BUTTERFLY ROLLS

½ Sweet Roll Dough (page 215)
  Margarine or butter, softened
½ cup sugar
1 teaspoon ground cinnamon
⅓ cup all-purpose flour
2 tablespoons sugar
2 tablespoons firm margarine or butter
1½ teaspoons ground cinnamon
  Glaze (page 219)

Roll dough into rectangle, 18x9 inches, on lightly floured surface; spread with margarine. Mix ½ cup sugar and 1 teaspoon cinnamon; sprinkle over rectangle. Roll up tightly, beginning at 18-inch side. Pinch edge of dough into roll to seal well. Stretch roll to make even. Cut into eighteen 1-inch slices. Place pencil in center of each slice parallel to cut sides; press almost through dough. Place on greased cookie sheet.

Mix flour, 2 tablespoons sugar, 2 tablespoons margarine and 1½ teaspoons cinnamon until crumbly; sprinkle over rolls. Let rise until double, about 40 minutes.

Heat oven to 375°. Bake until golden brown, about 12 minutes. Drizzle rolls with Glaze while warm. 1½ DOZEN ROLLS.

HONEY HORNS

  Topping (below)
  Sweet Roll Dough (page 215)
¼ cup margarine or butter, softened
½ cup sugar
2 teaspoons ground cinnamon

Prepare Topping; cool slightly. Divide dough into 3 equal parts. Roll each part into 10-inch circle on lightly floured surface. Spread about 1 tablespoon margarine and 2 tablespoons Topping over each circle. Mix sugar and cinnamon; sprinkle each circle with about 3 tablespoons of mixture. Cut each circle into 12 wedges. Roll up tightly, beginning at rounded sides. Place rolls with points underneath in spoke fashion in 3 greased round layer pans, 8 or 9x1½ inches; curve slightly. Let rise in warm place until double, about 45 minutes.

Heat oven to 400°. Bake 10 minutes; spread with remaining Topping. Bake until golden brown, about 10 minutes longer. Immediately remove from pans. 3 DOZEN ROLLS.

TOPPING

⅓ cup sugar
¼ cup finely chopped nuts
¼ cup honey
3 tablespoons margarine or butter
⅛ teaspoon ground cinnamon

Heat all ingredients to boiling, stirring frequently.

HOT CROSS BUNS

½ Refrigerator Roll Dough (page 212)
¾ cup raisins
⅓ cup chopped citron
¼ teaspoon ground nutmeg
1 egg white, slightly beaten
  Quick Frosting (below)

Turn dough onto well-floured surface. Squeeze raisins, citron and nutmeg into dough. Cut dough into 24 equal pieces. Shape each piece into a ball; place about 2 inches apart on greased cookie sheet. Snip a cross on top of each ball with scissors. Cover; let rise until double, about 1 hour.

Heat oven to 375°. Brush tops of buns with egg white. Bake until golden brown, about 20 minutes. When cool, frost crosses on tops of buns with Quick Frosting. 2 DOZEN BUNS.

QUICK FROSTING

Mix ¾ cup powdered sugar, 2 teaspoons water or milk and ¼ teaspoon vanilla until frosting is smooth and of spreading consistency.

BALLOON BUNS

- ½ Refrigerator Roll Dough (page 212)
- 1 cup sugar
- 1 tablespoon ground cinnamon
- 18 large marshmallows
- ½ cup margarine or butter, melted

Roll dough ⅛ inch thick on well-floured surface. Cut into eighteen 3½-inch circles with floured cutter. Mix sugar and cinnamon. Dip each marshmallow into margarine, then into sugar-cinnamon mixture. Wrap each dough circle around marshmallow, pinching together tightly at bottom. Dip roll into margarine, then into sugar-cinnamon mixture. Place in greased medium muffin cups, 2½x1¼ inches. Let rise until double, about 1 hour.

Heat oven to 375°. Bake until golden brown, 20 to 25 minutes.   1½ DOZEN ROLLS.

RAISED DOUGHNUTS

Roll ½ Refrigerator Roll Dough (page 212) ⅜ inch thick on well-floured surface. Cut with floured doughnut cutter. Cover; let rise on floured surface until double, about 1 hour.

Heat vegetable oil (2 to 3 inches) in deep-fat fryer or heavy saucepan to 375°. Slide doughnuts into hot oil with wide spatula. Turn doughnuts as they rise to surface. Fry until golden brown, 1 to 1½ minutes on each side. Remove from oil; do not prick doughnuts. Drain on paper towels. Dip doughnuts in Vanilla Glaze (below) or roll in sugar while warm.   ABOUT 20 DOUGHNUTS.

VANILLA GLAZE

Mix 1¾ cups powdered sugar, ¼ cup water or milk and ¼ teaspoon vanilla until glaze is smooth and of desired consistency.

Raised Bismarcks: Roll dough ¼ inch thick and cut with 2½-inch cutter. Let rise until double, about 1 hour. Fry until golden brown, about 1½ minutes on each side.

When cool, cut a 1-inch slit in side of each Bismarck through to center. Insert about 1 teaspoon jelly through slit to center, using a baster or spoon. Close slit; dip Bismarcks in Vanilla Glaze or sugar. ABOUT 2 DOZEN BISMARCKS.

FRUITED WREATHS

- 2 packages active dry yeast
- ½ cup warm water (105 to 115°)
- 1¼ cups buttermilk
- 2 eggs
- 5½ cups all-purpose flour*
- ½ cup margarine or butter, softened
- ½ cup sugar
- 2 teaspoons baking powder
- 2 teaspoons salt
- ½ cup chopped pecans
- 1 tablespoon grated lemon peel
- 1 cup chopped mixed candied fruit

Dissolve yeast in warm water in large mixer bowl. Add buttermilk, eggs, 2½ cups of the flour, the margarine, sugar, baking powder and salt. Beat on low speed, scraping bowl constantly, 30 seconds. Beat on medium speed, scraping bowl occasionally, 2 minutes. Stir in remaining flour, the pecans, lemon peel and candied fruit (dough should remain soft and slightly sticky).

Turn dough onto floured surface; knead 5 minutes. Divide dough into halves. Roll each half into rectangle, 18x3 inches. Cut into 3 strips, each 18x1 inch; braid loosely. Twirl braid into wreath shape on greased cookie sheet; pinch ends to seal. Let rise in warm place until double, about 1 hour.

Heat oven to 375°. Bake until golden brown, 20 to 30 minutes. Brush with butter or margarine if desired.   2 COFFEE CAKES.

*If using self-rising flour, omit baking powder and salt.

LATTICE COFFEE CAKES

- Sweet Roll Dough (page 215)
- 2 tablespoons margarine or butter, softened
- ½ cup sugar
- 2 teaspoons ground cinnamon

Divide dough into halves. Roll each half into 8-inch square on lightly floured surface. Cut each square into eight 1-inch strips. Place 4 strips in each of 2 greased square pans, 8x8x2 inches; weave in 4 cross strips to make lattice.

Spread with margarine. Mix sugar and cinnamon; sprinkle half of the mixture over each coffee cake. Let rise until double, about 40 minutes. Bake until golden brown, 25 to 30 minutes.   2 COFFEE CAKES (9 SERVINGS EACH).

HUNGARIAN COFFEE CAKE

Sweet Roll Dough (page 215)
½ cup margarine or butter, melted
¾ cup sugar
1 teaspoon ground cinnamon
½ cup finely chopped nuts

Shape dough into 1½-inch balls. Dip into margarine, then into mixture of sugar, cinnamon and nuts. Place a single layer of balls in well-greased 10-inch tube pan so they just touch. (If pan has removable bottom, line with aluminum foil.) Top with another layer of balls. Let rise until double, about 40 minutes.

Heat oven to 375°. Bake until golden brown, 35 to 40 minutes. (If coffee cake browns too quickly, cover loosely with aluminum foil.) Loosen from pan. Immediately invert pan on serving plate. Let pan remain a minute so butter-sugar mixture can drizzle over coffee cake. To serve, break coffee cake apart with 2 forks.   1 COFFEE CAKE.

BUTTER DRESS-UPS

Would you like to make your dinner rolls or sweet breads extra special? Dress them up with butter curls or butter balls. It's so easy!

To make butter curls, let butter curler stand in hot water for at least 10 minutes. Pull curler firmly across surface of ¼-pound bar of firm butter. (Butter should not be too cold or curls will break.) Drop curls into iced water; cover and refrigerate. Dip curler into hot water before making each curl.

To make butter balls, scald a pair of wooden butter paddles in boiling water for 30 seconds; chill in iced water. Cut ¼-pound bar of firm butter into 1-inch squares. Cut each square into halves; stand one half upright on paddle. Smack butter between paddles. Holding bottom paddle steady, rotate top paddle quickly to form a ball. If butter clings to paddles, dip them into hot water, then into iced water. Drop each finished ball into iced water and refrigerate.

GRANOLA ORANGE COFFEE CAKE

Streusel (below)
1 package active dry yeast
¾ cup warm water (105 to 115°)
3 tablespoons sugar
1 teaspoon salt
1 egg
¼ cup shortening
Grated peel of 1 orange
2 cups all-purpose flour*
½ cup granola, crushed
Orange Glaze (below)

Prepare Streusel. Dissolve yeast in warm water in large mixer bowl. Add sugar, salt, egg, shortening, orange peel and 1¼ cups of the flour. Beat on medium speed, scraping bowl frequently, 2 minutes. Stir in remaining flour and the granola.

Drop half of the batter by tablespoonfuls into greased square pan, 8x8x2 inches, spreading to edges of pan; sprinkle with half of the Streusel. Drop remaining batter by tablespoonfuls into pan; sprinkle with remaining Streusel. Press Streusel into batter with back of spoon. Cover; let rise in warm place until double, 40 to 50 minutes.

Heat oven to 375°. Bake until golden brown, 30 to 35 minutes. Loosen sides of coffee cake from pan; remove from pan. Cool on wire rack. Drizzle with Orange Glaze while warm.   9 SERVINGS.

*If using self-rising flour, omit salt.

STREUSEL
¼ cup all-purpose flour
¼ cup packed brown sugar
1 teaspoon ground cinnamon
¼ cup firm margarine or butter
½ cup granola, crushed

Mix flour, brown sugar, cinnamon and margarine until crumbly. Mix in granola.

ORANGE GLAZE
Mix ½ cup powdered sugar and 1 tablespoon plus 1 teaspoon orange juice.

SWEDISH TEA RING

Roll ½ Sweet Roll Dough (page 215) into rectangle, 15x9 inches, on lightly floured surface. Spread with one of the fillings (below and right). Roll up tightly, beginning at 15-inch side. Pinch edge of dough into roll to seal well. Stretch roll to make even. With sealed edge down, shape into ring on lightly greased cookie sheet. Pinch ends together. With scissors, make cuts ⅔ of the way through ring at 1-inch intervals. Turn each section on its side. Let rise until double, about 40 minutes.

Heat oven to 375°. Bake until golden brown, 25 to 30 minutes. (If tea ring browns too quickly, cover loosely with aluminum foil.) Spread ring with Glaze (right) and, if desired, decorate with nuts or cherries while warm.   1 COFFEE CAKE.

APRICOT-CHERRY FILLING

Mix ½ cup finely cut-up dried apricots and ½ cup finely chopped maraschino cherries, drained on paper towels.

CINNAMON-RAISIN FILLING

    2 tablespoons margarine or butter, softened
 ½ cup packed brown sugar
    2 teaspoons ground cinnamon
 ½ cup raisins

Spread margarine over rectangle; sprinkle with brown sugar, cinnamon and raisins.

DATE FILLING

 1 cup cut-up dates
 ¼ cup sugar
 ⅓ cup water
 ⅓ cup coarsely chopped nuts

Cook dates, sugar and water over medium heat, stirring constantly, until thickened. Stir in nuts; cool.

GLAZE

Mix 1 cup powdered sugar, 1 tablespoon milk and ½ teaspoon vanilla until glaze is smooth and of desired consistency.

Cut into ring at intervals.

Turn sections on sides.

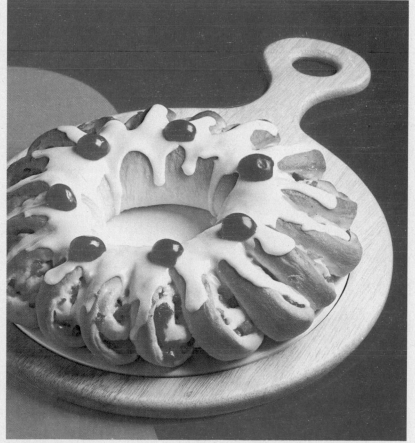

Swedish Tea Ring

Clockwise from bowl with Noodles Romanoff (page 222): orzo, little shells, cavatelli, farfallette, ziti, rigatoni, spaghettini, lasagne. Center, left to right: manicotti, mostaccioli (penne), egg noodles.

PASTA

TO COOK MACARONI, SPAGHETTI AND NOODLES

Traditional Method: Add 1 tablespoon salt to 3 quarts rapidly boiling water in deep kettle. Add 7 or 8 ounces macaroni, spaghetti or noodles to water gradually so that water continues to boil. (If spaghetti strands are left whole, place one end in water; as they soften, gradually coil them into kettle until submerged.)

Boil uncovered, stirring occasionally, just until tender* (7 to 10 minutes or as directed on package). Test by cutting several strands with fork against side of kettle. Drain quickly in colander or sieve. If macaroni product is to be used in a salad, rinse in cold water.   4 TO 6 SERVINGS.

Easy Method: Drop 7 or 8 ounces macaroni, spaghetti or noodles into 6 cups rapidly boiling salted water (4 teaspoons salt). Heat to rapid boiling. Cook, stirring constantly, 3 minutes.* Cover tightly. Remove from heat and let stand 10 minutes. Drain. If macaroni product is to be used in a salad, rinse in cold water.   4 TO 6 SERVINGS.

*For thicker macaroni products, such as lasagne, kluski noodles, etc., follow manufacturer's directions.

NOTE: Toss cooked and drained macaroni, spaghetti or noodles with 3 tablespoons margarine or butter; this will keep pieces separated.

SPAGHETTI WITH TOMATO SAUCE

    1 clove garlic, cut into halves
    2 tablespoons olive oil
    2 cans (16 ounces each) whole tomatoes
    1 medium onion, chopped (about ½ cup)
    1 tablespoon margarine or butter
    1 teaspoon salt
    ½ teaspoon sugar
    ½ teaspoon dried basil leaves
    ¼ teaspoon dried rosemary leaves (optional)
       Dash of pepper
    16 ounces uncooked spaghetti
       Grated Parmesan or Romano cheese

Cook and stir garlic in oil in 3-quart saucepan over low heat until garlic is brown; discard garlic. Stir in tomatoes (with liquid), onion, margarine, salt, sugar, basil, rosemary and pepper; break up tomatoes with fork. Heat to boiling; reduce heat. Simmer uncovered, stirring frequently, until sauce thickens, 40 to 50 minutes. (If a smoother sauce is desired, place in blender container; cover and blend on low speed 15 seconds.)

Cook spaghetti as directed at left. Serve sauce over hot spaghetti; sprinkle with cheese.   6 SERVINGS.

Spaghetti with Broccoli-Tomato Sauce: Cook 1 package (10 ounces) frozen broccoli spears as directed on package; drain. Arrange broccoli on hot spaghetti; top with sauce.

Spaghetti with Garden Sauce: Stir in 1 small carrot, finely chopped, and 1 medium stalk celery, finely chopped, with the tomatoes.

SPAGHETTI WITH MUSHROOMS

    7 ounces uncooked spaghetti
    5 ounces mushrooms, sliced (about 2 cups)
    2 tablespoons margarine or butter
    2 tablespoons flour
    2 tablespoons lemon juice
    ½ teaspoon salt
    ¼ teaspoon pepper
    2 cups milk
    3 tablespoons snipped parsley

Cook spaghetti as directed at left. Cook and stir mushrooms in margarine in 3-quart saucepan over medium heat until tender. Stir in flour, lemon juice, salt and pepper. Cook over low heat, stirring constantly, until mixture is smooth and bubbly; remove from heat.

Gradually stir in milk. Heat to boiling, stirring constantly. Boil and stir 1 minute. Stir in hot spaghetti and parsley. Cover and let stand 10 minutes.   4 TO 6 SERVINGS.

PASTA YIELDS

Kind of Pasta	Cooked	
	Cups	Servings
Macaroni		
6 or 7 ounces or 2 cups uncooked	4	4 to 6
Spaghetti		
7 or 8 ounces	4	4 to 6
Egg Noodles		
8 ounces or 4 to 5 cups uncooked	4 to 5	4 to 6

CHEESE SPAGHETTI TOSS

16 ounces uncooked thin spaghetti
½ pound bacon, cut into ½-inch squares
½ cup dry white wine or dry vermouth
3 eggs, well beaten
1 cup grated Romano or Parmesan cheese
   Pepper

Cook spaghetti as directed on page 221; drain but do not rinse. Return to pan. Fry bacon over medium heat until almost crisp; drain on paper towels. Stir wine into hot bacon fat. Heat to boiling. Boil and stir 3 minutes. Stir wine mixture and bacon into spaghetti. Add eggs and ½ cup of the cheese; toss over low heat until egg adheres to spaghetti and appears cooked. Serve with remaining cheese and the pepper.   4 SERVINGS.

TOMATOED MACARONI

1 can (16 ounces) whole tomatoes
2 tablespoons margarine or butter
1 teaspoon salt
¼ teaspoon dried oregano leaves
7 ounces uncooked elbow macaroni
   (about 2 cups)
   Grated Parmesan or Romano cheese

Heat tomatoes (with liquid), margarine, 1 teaspoon salt and the oregano to boiling; reduce heat. Simmer uncovered, stirring occasionally, 10 to 12 minutes.

Cook macaroni as directed on page 221. Arrange in serving dish; pour sauce on hot macaroni and sprinkle with cheese. Garnish with parsley sprigs if desired.   6 SERVINGS.

NOODLES ROMANOFF

8 ounces uncooked wide egg noodles
2 cups dairy sour cream
¼ cup grated Parmesan cheese
1 tablespoon snipped chives
1 teaspoon salt
⅛ teaspoon pepper
1 large clove garlic, crushed
2 tablespoons margarine or butter
¼ cup grated Parmesan cheese

Cook noodles as directed on page 221. Mix sour cream, ¼ cup cheese, the chives, salt, pepper and garlic. Stir margarine into hot noodles; stir in sour cream mixture. Arrange on warm platter; sprinkle with ¼ cup cheese.   6 TO 8 SERVINGS.

EGG NOODLE RING

Heat oven to 375°. Cook 8 ounces wide egg noodles as directed on page 221. Stir in 2 to 3 tablespoons margarine or butter. Press noodles in buttered 1½-quart ring mold. Place ring mold in pan of hot water (1 inch deep). Bake 20 minutes. Invert warm serving plate on mold; turn over. Remove ring mold. 5 OR 6 SERVINGS.

NOODLES ALFREDO

8 ounces uncooked wide egg noodles
½ cup margarine or butter
½ cup half-and-half
1 cup grated Parmesan cheese
1 tablespoon dried parsley flakes
¼ teaspoon salt
   Dash of pepper

Cook noodles as directed on page 221. Heat margarine and half-and-half in 1-quart saucepan over low heat until margarine is melted. Stir in remaining ingredients; keep warm over low heat. Pour sauce over hot noodles, stirring gently until noodles are well coated.   5 OR 6 SERVINGS.

TANGY NOODLES

Cook 5 ounces noodles as directed on page 221. Toss hot noodles with ¼ cup Italian salad dressing.   4 TO 6 SERVINGS.

STIR-INS FOR NOODLES

Cook 8 ounces noodles as directed on page 221, then stir in one of the following:

Almonds: ¼ cup slivered almonds browned in 2 tablespoons margarine or butter.

Browned Buttered Crumbs: ½ cup dry bread crumbs browned in 2 tablespoons margarine or butter.

Herbs: ½ teaspoon *each* thyme leaves, basil leaves, snipped parsley and snipped chives stirred into 2 tablespoons margarine or butter, melted.

Onion and Green Pepper: ¼ cup chopped green pepper and 2 tablespoons chopped onion cooked and stirred in 2 tablespoons margarine or butter until onion is tender.

Parmesan: 2 tablespoons margarine or butter, then ¼ cup grated Parmesan cheese.

Poppy Seed: 2 teaspoons poppy seed and 1 tablespoon margarine or butter.

1. Make a well in center of flour. Add egg yolks, egg and salt; mix well. Mix in water, 1 tablespoon at a time.

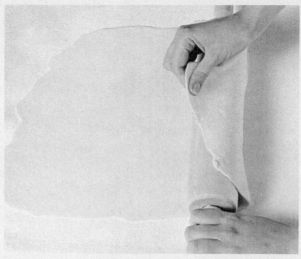

2. Roll thin rectangle of dough around rolling pin; remove pin. Or fold loosely into thirds and cut.

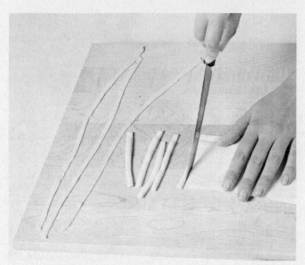

3. Use a sharp knife to cut dough into strips. Cut a few at a time, then shake out and place on towel.

4. Cook noodles until tender. Drain quickly but thoroughly in colander or sieve.

EGG NOODLES

2 cups all-purpose* or whole wheat flour
3 egg yolks
1 egg
2 teaspoons salt
¼ to ½ cup water

Make a well in center of flour. Add egg yolks, egg and salt; mix thoroughly. Mix in water, 1 tablespoon at a time, until dough is stiff but easy to roll.

Divide dough into 4 equal parts. Roll dough, one part at a time, into paper-thin rectangle on well-floured cloth-covered board (keep remaining dough covered). Loosely fold rectangle lengthwise into thirds; cut crosswise into ⅛-inch strips for narrow noodles, ¼-inch strips for wide noodles. Shake out strips and place on towel until stiff and dry, about 2 hours.

Break dry strips into smaller pieces. Cook in 3 quarts boiling salted water (1 tablespoon salt) until tender, 12 to 15 minutes; drain. (To cook half of the noodles, use 2 quarts water and 2 teaspoons salt.) ABOUT 6 CUPS NOODLES.

*If using self-rising flour, omit salt.

Do-ahead Tip: After drying, noodles can be covered and stored no longer than 1 month.

RICE

KINDS OF RICE

Don't buy just one kind of rice—enjoy them all! Choose the rice to fit your purpose:

Regular Rice: The hull and the bran have been removed by polishing. Short grain rice is less expensive than long grain; it is used for casseroles, puddings and creamy desserts. Long grain rice is a better all-purpose rice and cooks fluffier, flakier and drier; it is used for curries, Chinese dishes and as a side dish. One cup uncooked yields about 3 cups cooked.

Parboiled (Converted) Rice: This type contains the vitamins found in the husk of brown rice, but is polished like white rice. It can be substituted for regular rice, but the cooking time is longer. One cup uncooked yields about 3½ cups cooked.

Precooked (Instant) Rice: Commercially cooked, rinsed and dried. It is good as part of a main dish—and quick to fix at any time. One cup uncooked yields about 2 cups cooked.

Brown Rice: A vitamin-rich whole grain, with only the outer hull removed. It has a nutty flavor and is used as a side dish. Store in refrigerator. One cup uncooked yields about 4 cups cooked.

Wild Rice: Long grained and dark greenish-brown in color. (And not really rice, but the seed of an aquatic grass.) Expensive, it is often sold combined with brown rice. Four ounces uncooked yields about 3 cups cooked.

RICE TIPS

To Reheat Cooked Rice: Heat cooked rice in top of double boiler over hot water until rice is hot and fluffy, about 10 minutes. Or place rice in heavy pan with tightly fitted cover. Sprinkle water over rice, using about 2 tablespoons water to 1 cup rice. Cover; heat over low heat until hot and fluffy, 5 to 8 minutes.

To Refrigerate Cooked Rice: Place rice in bowl and cover tightly or wrap completely to prevent drying out. Keeps 4 to 5 days.

To Freeze Cooked Rice: Store rice in covered freezer container or wrap well. Keeps up to 6 months.

COOK-INS FOR RICE

A simple way to change the flavor and color of a plain rice is to vary the cooking liquid. Try any one of the following substitutions:

☐ Chicken or beef broth or bouillon for the water

☐ Chicken consommé diluted as directed on can for the water

☐ Apple juice for half of the water

☐ Orange juice for half of the water

☐ Pineapple juice for half of the water

☐ Tomato juice for half of the water

STIR-INS FOR RICE

For color, flavor or just for a change.

Prepare 3 cups hot cooked rice (page 225); stir in one of the following:

Almond: ½ cup slivered almonds browned in 2 tablespoons margarine or butter.

Bacon: 4 slices bacon, diced, crisply fried and drained.

Browned Butter: ¼ cup margarine or butter heated until light brown.

Carrot: ½ cup shredded carrot and 2 tablespoons margarine or butter, melted.

Lemon: 2 teaspoons lemon juice and 2 tablespoons margarine or butter, melted.

Marmalade: ¼ cup marmalade and 2 tablespoons margarine or butter, melted.

Mushroom: 1 can (3 or 4 ounces) sliced mushrooms or mushroom stems and pieces, drained, heated in 2 tablespoons margarine or butter.

Olive: ½ cup chopped ripe or pimiento-stuffed olives or 10 pitted ripe or pimiento-stuffed olives, sliced.

Onion: 2 tablespoons finely chopped onion cooked in 2 tablespoons margarine or butter until tender.

Parsley: 2 tablespoons snipped parsley.

AT-A-GLANCE RICE YIELDS

Yield	Rice	Water	Salt
For about 1 cup cooked rice:			
Regular white rice	⅓ cup	⅔ cup	¼ teaspoon
Parboiled rice	¼ cup	⅔ cup	¼ teaspoon
Precooked (instant) rice	½ cup	½ cup	¼ teaspoon
For about 1½ cups cooked rice:			
Regular white rice	½ cup	1 cup	½ teaspoon
Parboiled rice	⅓ cup	1 cup	¼ teaspoon
Precooked (instant) rice	¾ cup	¾ cup	¼ teaspoon
For about 2 cups cooked rice:			
Regular white rice	⅔ cup	1⅓ cups	½ teaspoon
Parboiled rice	½ cup	1¼ cups	½ teaspoon
Precooked (instant) rice	1 cup	1 cup	½ teaspoon
For about 3 cups cooked rice:			
Regular white rice	1 cup	2 cups	1 teaspoon
Parboiled rice	¾ cup	2 cups	1 teaspoon
Precooked (instant) rice	1½ cups	1½ cups	1 teaspoon
Wild rice	1 cup	2½ cups	1 teaspoon
For about 4 cups cooked rice:			
Regular white rice	1⅓ cups	2⅔ cups	1 teaspoon
Parboiled rice	1 cup	2½ cups	1 teaspoon
Precooked (instant) rice	2 cups	2 cups	1 teaspoon
Brown rice	1 cup	2½ cups	1 teaspoon

TO COOK RICE

Refer to the chart above for the right amount of rice.

Regular Rice: Heat rice, water and salt to boiling, stirring once or twice; reduce heat. Cover and simmer 14 minutes. (Do not lift cover or stir.) Remove from heat. Fluff rice lightly with fork; cover and let steam 5 to 10 minutes.

Parboiled (Converted) and Precooked (Instant) Rice: Follow package directions.

Brown Rice: Follow directions for Regular Rice (above) except — increase cooking time to 30 to 40 minutes.

Wild Rice: Wash wild rice by placing in wire strainer; run cold water through it, lifting rice with fingers to clean thoroughly. Heat rice, water and salt to boiling, stirring once or twice; reduce heat. Cover and simmer until tender, 40 to 50 minutes. After cooking rice 30 minutes, check to see that rice is not sticking to pan. Add ¼ cup water if necessary.

OVEN-STEAMED RICE

Heat oven to 350°. Mix 2 cups boiling water, 1 cup uncooked regular rice and 1 teaspoon salt in ungreased 1-quart casserole or oblong baking dish, 12x7½x2 inches. Cover and bake until liquid is absorbed, 25 to 30 minutes.   4 TO 6 SERVINGS.

NOTE: For large quantities, double or triple all ingredients and bake in 3-quart casserole.

Flavored Oven-steamed Rice: Substitute chicken or beef bouillon for the water and add seasonings such as dried chervil leaves, curry powder, dried dill weed, onion, orange peel, parsley or saffron.

RICE RING

Prepare 4 cups rice (left). Press lightly in wellgreased 4-cup ring mold. Keep hot until serving time. Invert warm serving plate on mold; turn over. Remove ring mold.   8 SERVINGS.

Herbed Rice Puffs

RICE MEDLEY

    1 can (17 ounces) peas and tiny onions,
       drained (reserve liquid)
1½ cups uncooked instant rice
    1 teaspoon margarine or butter
    ½ teaspoon salt
    1 small carrot, shredded
       (about 3 tablespoons)

Add enough water to reserved vegetable liquid to measure 1½ cups; pour into 2-quart saucepan. Heat to boiling. Stir in peas, rice, margarine, salt and carrot. Heat to boiling; remove from heat. Cover and let stand until liquid is absorbed and rice is tender, about 10 minutes.   4 TO 6 SERVINGS.

TOMATOED RICE
WITH ARTICHOKES

    1 can (14 ounces) artichoke hearts
    1 can (16 ounces) stewed tomatoes
1½ cups uncooked instant rice
    1 tablespoon dried shredded green onion
       or 3 fresh green onions, chopped
    ¼ teaspoon salt

Mix artichoke hearts (with liquid), tomatoes, rice, onion and salt in 10-inch skillet. Heat to boiling, stirring frequently; reduce heat. Cover and simmer until rice is tender, about 10 minutes.   4 OR 5 SERVINGS.

HERBED RICE PUFFS

    1 egg
    1 cup cooked brown or white rice (page 225)
    ⅛ teaspoon poultry seasoning
    ⅛ teaspoon salt
    ½ cup grated Parmesan cheese
    ⅓ cup dry bread crumbs
       Vegetable oil

Beat egg; stir in rice, poultry seasoning, salt and cheese. Refrigerate at least 1 hour. Shape by rounded teaspoonfuls into fifteen 1-inch balls. Roll in bread crumbs.

Heat oil (2 to 3 inches) in 2-quart saucepan to 375°. Fry rice balls until golden brown; drain.   15 RICE PUFFS.

Do-ahead Tip: After frying, puffs can be covered and refrigerated no longer than 12 hours. To heat, bake on ungreased cookie sheet in 350° oven until hot, 10 to 12 minutes.

HOPPIN' JOHN

    ½ pound dried black-eyed peas (about
       1 cup)
3½ cups water
    ¼ pound slab bacon, lean salt pork or
       smoked pork
    1 onion, sliced
    ¼ to ½ teaspoon very finely chopped fresh
       hot pepper or ⅛ to ¼ teaspoon crushed
       dried hot pepper
    ½ cup uncooked long grain rice
    1 teaspoon salt
       Pepper

Heat peas and water to boiling in 2-quart saucepan. Boil 2 minutes; remove from heat. Cover and let stand 1 hour.

Cut bacon into 8 pieces. Stir bacon, onion and hot pepper into peas. Heat to boiling; reduce heat. Cover and simmer until peas are tender, 1 to 1½ hours.

Stir in rice, salt and pepper. Cover and simmer, stirring occasionally, until rice is tender, about 25 minutes. Stir in additional water, if necessary, to cook rice.   6 TO 8 SERVINGS.

RISOTTO MILANESE

1 small onion, finely chopped (about ¼ cup)
1 tablespoon chopped beef marrow
   (optional)
2 tablespoons margarine or butter
1 can (10½ ounces) condensed beef broth
   (about 1¼ cups)
1 soup can water
1 cup uncooked parboiled (converted) rice
⅓ cup dry white wine
   Dash of ground saffron
1 to 2 tablespoons margarine or butter
½ cup grated Parmesan cheese

Cook and stir onion and beef marrow in 2 table-spoons margarine in 10-inch skillet over medium heat until onion is tender, about 2 minutes. Heat broth and water just to boiling; remove from heat.

Stir rice into onion-marrow mixture; cook and stir 1 minute. Stir in wine; cook until wine is almost absorbed, about 1 minute. Stir in 1¼ cups of the broth; stir saffron into remaining broth.

Cook rice mixture uncovered until broth is almost absorbed, about 10 minutes. Stir in remaining broth. Cook until broth is absorbed and rice is tender, about 15 minutes; remove from heat. Stir in 1 to 2 tablespoons margarine and the cheese.
4 TO 6 SERVINGS.

Shrimp Risotto: Substitute 1 can (10¾ ounces) condensed chicken broth for the beef broth and ground thyme for the saffron. Stir in 1 can (4½ ounces) tiny shrimp, rinsed and drained, and 1 tablespoon snipped parsley.   3 SERVINGS.

FRIED RICE

1 small onion, chopped (about ¼ cup)
2 tablespoons chopped green pepper
2 tablespoons vegetable oil
2 cups cooked rice (page 225)
1 can (8½ ounces) water chestnuts, drained
   and thinly sliced
1 can (4 ounces) mushroom stems and pieces,
   drained
2 tablespoons soy sauce
3 eggs, beaten

Cook and stir onion and green pepper in oil in 10-inch skillet until onion is tender, about 3 minutes. Stir in rice, water chestnuts, mushrooms and soy sauce. Cook over low heat, stirring frequently, 5 to 7 minutes. Stir in eggs; cook and stir until eggs are done, 4 to 5 minutes longer.   4 OR 5 SERVINGS.

FIESTA RICE

1 medium onion, finely chopped
½ small green pepper, chopped
3 tablespoons margarine or butter
1 can (16 ounces) stewed tomatoes
1 teaspoon salt
⅛ teaspoon pepper
3 cups cooked rice (page 225)

Cook and stir onion and green pepper in margarine in 10-inch skillet until onion is tender. Stir in tomatoes, salt, pepper and rice. Simmer uncovered over low heat until hot, about 15 minutes.
6 SERVINGS.

CURRIED RICE

1 tablespoon finely chopped onion
2 tablespoons margarine or butter
½ to 1 teaspoon curry powder
¼ teaspoon salt
¼ teaspoon pepper
3 cups hot cooked white or brown rice
   (page 225)
¼ cup toasted slivered almonds
¼ cup chopped pimiento-stuffed olives or
   pitted ripe olives

Cook and stir onion in margarine until onion is tender. Stir in curry powder, salt and pepper. Stir into hot rice. Sprinkle with almonds and olives.
4 SERVINGS.

INDIAN PILAF

¾ cup uncooked regular rice
1 small onion, chopped (about ¼ cup)
2 tablespoons margarine or butter
¼ teaspoon salt
¼ teaspoon ground allspice
¼ teaspoon ground turmeric
⅛ teaspoon curry powder
   Dash of pepper
3½ cups chicken broth
¼ cup slivered blanched almonds

Heat oven to 350°. Cook and stir rice and onion in margarine until rice is yellow and onion is tender. Stir in salt, allspice, turmeric, curry powder and pepper; pour into ungreased 1-quart casserole.

Heat broth to boiling; stir into rice mixture. Cover and bake until liquid is absorbed, about 35 minutes. Stir in almonds.   4 TO 6 SERVINGS.

Brown Rice Indian Pilaf: Substitute brown rice for the regular rice. Bake about 1 hour 5 minutes.

BULGUR PILAF

2 tablespoons finely chopped onion
2 tablespoons chopped green pepper
2 tablespoons margarine or butter
2 cups chicken broth
1 cup uncooked bulgur wheat
1 can (3 ounces) sliced mushrooms, drained
½ teaspoon salt
  Dash of pepper

Cook and stir onion and green pepper in margarine in 10-inch skillet until onion is tender. Stir in remaining ingredients. Cover; heat to boiling. Reduce heat; simmer 15 minutes.   4 SERVINGS.

NOTE: Bulgur wheat, sometimes called parboiled wheat, is whole wheat that has been cooked, dried, partly debranned and cracked into coarse, angular fragments. It resembles whole wheat in nutritive properties and is used as an alternate for rice in many recipes. This ancient food originated in the Near East.

WILD RICE WITH MUSHROOMS AND ALMONDS

1 cup uncooked wild rice
½ cup slivered almonds
2 tablespoons snipped chives or chopped
    green onion
1 can (8 ounces) mushroom stems and
    pieces, drained
¼ cup margarine or butter
3 cups chicken broth

Cook and stir wild rice, almonds, chives and mushrooms in margarine until almonds are golden brown, about 20 minutes.

Heat oven to 325°. Pour wild rice mixture into ungreased 1½-quart casserole. Heat broth to boiling; stir into wild rice mixture. Cover and bake until all liquid is absorbed and wild rice is tender and fluffy, about 1½ hours.   6 TO 8 SERVINGS.

SAVORY RICE BLEND

For economy, combine wild rice with regular rice.

¼ cup uncooked wild rice
1 medium stalk celery, chopped
    (about ½ cup)
1 small onion, chopped (about ¼ cup)
3 tablespoons margarine or butter
2½ cups chicken broth
1 tablespoon dried parsley flakes
½ teaspoon salt
½ teaspoon bottled brown bouquet sauce
¼ teaspoon ground sage
¼ teaspoon dried basil leaves
1 can (4 ounces) mushroom stems and
    pieces, drained
¾ cup uncooked regular rice
1 cup dairy sour cream (optional)

Heat oven to 350°. Cook and stir wild rice, celery and onion in margarine until onion is tender. Pour into ungreased 1½-quart casserole. Heat broth to boiling; pour over wild rice mixture. Stir in parsley, salt, bouquet sauce, sage, basil and mushrooms. Cover and bake 45 minutes.

Stir in regular rice. Cover and bake until all liquid is absorbed and rice is tender, 40 to 45 minutes longer. Stir in sour cream.   7 SERVINGS.

BARLEY PILAF FOR TWO

1 tablespoon margarine or butter
⅓ cup uncooked barley
1 tablespoon instant minced onion
1 teaspoon instant chicken bouillon
¼ teaspoon celery salt
⅛ teaspoon pepper
1 cup boiling water
1 tablespoon snipped parsley

Heat oven to 325°. Mix all ingredients except parsley in ungreased 2½-cup casserole. Cover and bake until barley is done, about 1 hour. Stir in parsley.   2 SERVINGS.

Pictured opposite: Spicy Prune Ring Cake (page 237), Farm-style Oatmeal Cookies (page 274) and Summer Jewel Tarts (page 304)

DESSERTS

CAKES

ABOUT CAKE BAKING

NO GUESSWORK, PLEASE!

Begin at the beginning. Read through the recipe carefully; assemble *all* utensils and ingredients; heat the oven; prepare the pans. Be sure all ingredients are at room temperature. (Please forgive us if we insist: Don't make changes in the recipes!)

Like any art, cake baking is exacting. Because you are working with a delicately balanced formula, the ingredients must be measured exactly (with no substitutions), the directions followed carefully and the correct pans used. Stick to these few rules and you can be sure of success.

POINTERS ON PANS

□ For good size, shape and texture, always use pans of the size called for. A cake baked in too large a pan will be pale, flat and shrunken; baked in too small or too shallow a pan, it will bulge over and lose its shape. Layer pans should be at least 1½ inches deep; square or oblong, 2 inches deep; pound or loaf, more than 2 inches deep.

□ Shiny metal pans are preferred for cake baking because they reflect heat away from the cake and produce a light brown, tender crust. Do *not* use darkened metal or enamel pans.

□ Never fill cake pans more than half full. If you are using an odd-shaped pan (lamb, bell, star, heart, Christmas tree), measure the capacity by filling with water, then measure the water and use half that amount of batter. (Use the rest for cupcakes.)

PREPARING THE PANS

□ For layer, square and oblong cakes and two-egg chiffon cakes, grease bottoms and sides of pans generously with shortening. (Do not use margarine, butter or oil.) Dust each greased pan with flour, shaking pan until bottom and sides are well coated. Shake out excess flour. When using pans with a nonstick coating, follow the manufacturer's directions.

□ For classic angel food and chiffon cakes, do not grease and flour the pans. The batter must cling to the side and tube to rise properly.

□ For fruitcakes, line pans with aluminum foil, then grease. Leave short "ears" so you can lift the cake out easily. If you intend to store the fruitcake, extend the foil well over the sides of the pan. When the cake has cooled, bring foil up and over the top and seal.

□ Jelly roll pans should first be lined with waxed paper or aluminum foil, then greased.

CUTTING CAKES

□ Use a sharp, thin knife to cut shortening-type cakes, a long serrated knife for angels and chiffons. If the frosting sticks, dip the knife in hot water and wipe with a damp paper towel after cutting each slice.

STORING CAKES

□ Cool unfrosted cakes thoroughly before storing. If covered warm, they become sticky.

□ Keep cake with a creamy-type frosting under a cake safe (or large inverted bowl) or cover loosely with aluminum foil, plastic wrap or waxed paper.

□ Serve cake with a fluffy-type frosting the day it's made. If you must store the cake overnight, use a cake safe or inverted bowl, but slip a knife under the edge so the container is not airtight.

□ Cakes with whipped cream toppings or cream fillings should be kept in the refrigerator.

FREEZING AND THAWING CAKES

□ Unfrosted cakes and cupcakes freeze better than frosted cakes. Allow the cakes to cool thoroughly. Place in rigid containers to prevent crushing, then cover with aluminum foil or plastic wrap. It's smart to package cake in family portions or single pieces that thaw out quickly and are nice for the lunch box. Properly packaged, unfrosted cakes can be kept frozen 4 to 6 months.

□ Of the frosted cakes, those with creamy-type frostings freeze best. Fluffy-type and whipped cream frostings freeze well but tend to stick to the covering. To reduce stickiness, freeze the cake before wrapping. Or insert wooden picks around the top and side of the cake to hold the wrapping away from the frosting. Frozen frosted cakes keep for 2 to 3 months.

□ Do not freeze cakes with custard or fruit fillings. They tend to become soggy while thawing.

□ Do not freeze cake batter.

□ To thaw, let the wrapped frozen cake stand at room temperature as follows: 2 hours for frosted cakes, 1 hour for unfrosted layers, 30 minutes for cupcakes. (Do not thaw in oven.) Cakes with whipped cream toppings or fillings should be thawed in the refrigerator for 3 to 4 hours. If you do not need the whole cake, cut individual pieces; they will thaw in about 5 minutes.

TIPS FOR CAKE BAKING

1. Use shiny metal pans. If using a heatproof glass pan, reduce oven temperature by 25°.

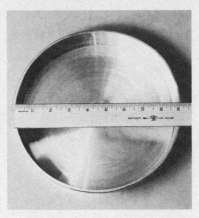

2. Be sure pan is correct size. To check size, measure across top of pan from inside edge to inside edge.

3. To determine batter amount for odd-shaped pan, fill with water; measure. Use half as much batter.

4. Grease bottoms and sides of pans generously with shortening. (Do not use margarine, butter or oil.)

5. To flour pans, tap and shake to cover completely. Invert pan and shake out excess flour.

6. Pans should be placed in middle of oven and at least 1 inch from edge. Do not let pans touch.

7. To store cake with creamy-type frosting, loosely cover with foil or plastic wrap, or use a cake safe.

8. To store cake with fluffy-type frosting, slip knife under cake safe so it will *not* be airtight.

9. Store cake with whipped cream frosting in the refrigerator. Cover with inverted bowl if desired.

TIPS FOR LAYER CAKES

1. Cool layers in pans on wire racks about 5 minutes. Cover another rack with a towel; place towel side down on top of layer and invert as a unit. Remove pan.

2. Place original rack on bottom of layer; turn over both racks so layer is right side up. Repeat with other layer(s). Allow layers to cool completely on racks.

BEST CHOCOLATE CAKE

1 cup all-purpose* or cake flour
1 cup sugar
½ teaspoon baking soda
½ teaspoon salt
¼ teaspoon baking powder
¼ cup plus 2 tablespoons water
¼ cup plus 2 tablespoons buttermilk
¼ cup shortening
1 egg
½ teaspoon vanilla
2 ounces melted unsweetened chocolate (cool)

Heat oven to 350°. Grease and flour square pan, 8x8x2 or 9x9x2 inches. Beat all ingredients in large mixer bowl on low speed, scraping bowl constantly, 30 seconds. Beat on high speed, scraping bowl occasionally, 3 minutes. Pour into pan.

Bake until wooden pick inserted in center comes out clean, 30 to 35 minutes; cool. Frost with ½ recipe Chocolate-Nut Butter Frosting (page 251).

*If using self-rising flour, omit baking soda, salt and baking powder.

Brownie-Nut Cake: Add ½ cup chopped nuts before beating. Bake 35 to 40 minutes. Frost with Glossy Chocolate Frosting (page 251) if desired.

New Orleans Spice Cake: Omit vanilla and add ½ teaspoon ground cloves before beating. Frost with Cocoa Butter Frosting (page 251) if desired.

Whole Wheat Chocolate Cake: Substitute ½ cup whole wheat flour for ½ cup of the all-purpose flour and use ½ cup plus 2 tablespoons all-purpose flour. Frost with ½ recipe Peanut Butter Frosting (page 251) if desired.

CHOCOLATE LOAF CAKE

1½ cups all-purpose flour*
1 cup sugar
¾ cup milk
¼ cup margarine or butter, softened
¼ cup shortening
4 egg yolks
2 teaspoons baking powder
1 teaspoon almond extract or vanilla
½ teaspoon salt
2 ounces melted unsweetened chocolate (cool)

Heat oven to 350°. Grease and flour loaf pan, 9x5x3 inches. Beat all ingredients in large mixer bowl on low speed, scraping bowl constantly, 30 seconds. Beat on medium speed, scraping bowl occasionally, 3 minutes. Pour into pan.

Bake until wooden pick inserted in center comes out clean, 65 to 70 minutes. Cool 10 minutes; remove from pan. Cool completely. Frost with Vanilla Butter Frosting (page 251) if desired.

*If using self-rising flour, omit baking powder and salt. Bake 60 to 65 minutes.

BEATING BY HAND

Our one-bowl method was developed with the electric mixer in mind but you can also mix by hand. Stir the ingredients to moisten and blend them; then beat 150 strokes for *every* minute of beating time (3 minutes equals 450 strokes). You'll need practice before this seems easy; while you're practicing, cake volume may suffer.

GERMAN CHOCOLATE CAKE

This is the grass-roots recipe that swept the country to become a classic.

- ½ cup boiling water
- 1 bar (4 ounces) sweet cooking chocolate
- 2 cups sugar
- 1 cup margarine or butter, softened
- 4 egg yolks
- 1 teaspoon vanilla
- 2½ cups cake flour
- 1 teaspoon baking soda
- 1 teaspoon salt
- 1 cup buttermilk
- 4 egg whites, stiffly beaten
  Coconut-Pecan Frosting (below)

Heat oven to 350°. Grease 2 square pans, 8x8x2 or 9x9x2 inches, or 3 round layer pans, 8 or 9x1½ inches. Line bottoms of pans with waxed paper. Pour boiling water on chocolate in small bowl, stirring until chocolate is melted; cool.

Mix sugar and margarine in large mixer bowl until light and fluffy. Beat in egg yolks 1 at a time. Beat in chocolate and vanilla on low speed. Mix in flour, baking soda and salt alternately with buttermilk, beating after each addition until batter is smooth. Fold in egg whites. Divide batter among pans.

Bake until wooden pick inserted in center comes out clean, 8-inch square layers 45 to 50 minutes, 9-inch square layers 40 to 45 minutes, 8-inch round layers 35 to 40 minutes, 9-inch round layers 30 to 35 minutes; cool. Fill layers and frost top of cake with Coconut-Pecan Frosting.

COCONUT-PECAN FROSTING

- 1 cup sugar
- 1 cup evaporated milk
- ½ cup margarine or butter
- 3 egg yolks
- 1 teaspoon vanilla
- 1⅓ cups flaked coconut
- 1 cup chopped pecans

Mix sugar, milk, margarine, egg yolks and vanilla in 1-quart saucepan. Cook over medium heat, stirring occasionally, until thick, about 12 minutes. Stir in coconut and pecans. Beat until frosting is of spreading consistency.

CHOCOLATE-CHERRY CAKE

- 1⅔ cups all-purpose flour*
- 1 cup packed brown sugar
- ¼ cup cocoa
- 1 teaspoon baking soda
- ½ teaspoon salt
- ⅓ cup chopped unblanched almonds
- 1 jar (4 ounces) maraschino cherries, drained and chopped (reserve syrup)
- ⅓ cup vegetable oil
- 1 teaspoon vinegar
- ½ teaspoon vanilla

Heat oven to 350°. Mix flour, brown sugar, cocoa, baking soda, salt and almonds with fork. Add enough water to reserved cherry syrup to measure 1 cup. Stir syrup-water mixture and the remaining ingredients into flour mixture. Pour into ungreased square pan, 8x8x2 inches.

Bake until wooden pick inserted in center comes out clean, 35 to 40 minutes. Sprinkle with powdered sugar if desired.

*Do not use self-rising flour in this recipe.

NOTE: Cake can be mixed in pan if desired.

Chocolate Chip Cake: Omit cocoa, cherries and vanilla. Substitute chopped walnuts for the almonds and 1 cup water for the syrup-water mixture. Sprinkle ⅓ cup miniature chocolate chips over batter in pan.

Chocolate-Mint Cake: Omit almonds and cherries. Substitute 1 cup water for the syrup-water mixture. Stir in ½ teaspoon peppermint extract with the remaining ingredients.

Maple-Nut Cake: Omit cocoa, cherries and vanilla. Substitute ½ cup chopped pecans for the almonds and 1 cup water for the syrup-water mixture. Stir in ½ teaspoon maple flavoring with the remaining ingredients.

Oatmeal-Molasses Cake: Omit cocoa, almonds, cherries and vanilla. Stir ¾ cup quick-cooking oats and 1 teaspoon ground allspice into the flour mixture. Substitute 1 cup water for the syrup-water mixture. Stir in 2 tablespoons dark molasses with the remaining ingredients.

Pumpkin Cake: Omit cocoa, almonds, cherries and vanilla. Stir 1 teaspoon ground allspice into the flour mixture. Substitute ½ cup water for the syrup water mixture. Stir in ½ cup canned pumpkin pie mix with the remaining ingredients.

COCOA FUDGE CAKE

1⅔ cups all-purpose flour* or 2 cups
    cake flour
1½ cups sugar
 ⅔ cup cocoa
1½ teaspoons baking soda
 1 teaspoon salt
1½ cups buttermilk
 ½ cup shortening
 2 eggs
 1 teaspoon vanilla

Heat oven to 350°. Grease and flour oblong pan, 13x9x2 inches, 2 round layer pans, 8 or 9x1½ inches, or 12-cup bundt cake pan. Beat all ingredients in large mixer bowl on low speed, scraping bowl constantly, 30 seconds. Beat on high speed, scraping bowl occasionally, 3 minutes. Pour into pan(s).

Bake until wooden pick inserted in center comes out clean, oblong 35 to 40 minutes, layers 30 to 35 minutes, bundt cake 40 to 45 minutes; cool. Frost with White Mountain Frosting (page 253) or Mocha Butter Frosting (page 251) if desired.

*If using self-rising flour, decrease baking soda to ¾ teaspoon and omit salt.

Chocolate-Almond Cake: Substitute almond extract for the vanilla and add ½ cup chopped roasted almonds before mixing.

Cocoa Fudge Cupcakes: Pour batter into paper-lined muffin cups, 2½x1¼ inches, filling each half full. Bake 20 minutes.   2½ DOZEN CUPCAKES.

Red Devils Food Cake: Substitute ½ cup packed brown sugar for ½ cup of the granulated sugar and 2 ounces melted unsweetened chocolate (cool) for the cocoa. Frost with Cherry-Nut Frosting (page 253) if desired.

Small Cocoa Fudge Cake: Cut all ingredients in half except—if using all-purpose flour, use 1 cup. Pour batter into greased and floured square pan, 8x8x2 inches. Bake about 30 minutes. Frost with ½ recipe Broiled Butterscotch Frosting (page 254).

SHORTENINGS

When a recipe calls for margarine, softened, use only stick-type (not whipped) margarine.

When a recipe calls for shortening or margarine or butter, do not substitute oil, even when the shortening, margarine or butter is melted.

BANANA-NUT CAKE

For best flavor, be sure the bananas you use for cakes, cookies and quick breads are fully ripened.

2⅓ cups all-purpose flour*
1⅔ cups sugar
1¼ cups mashed bananas (about 3 medium)
 ⅔ cup shortening
 ⅔ cup buttermilk
 3 eggs
1¼ teaspoons baking powder
1¼ teaspoons baking soda
 1 teaspoon salt
 ⅔ cup finely chopped nuts

Heat oven to 350°. Grease and flour oblong pan, 13x9x2 inches, or two 9-inch or three 8-inch round layer pans. Beat all ingredients in large mixer bowl on low speed, scraping bowl constantly, 30 seconds. Beat on high speed, scraping bowl occasionally, 3 minutes. Pour into pan(s).

Bake until wooden pick inserted in center comes out clean, oblong 45 to 50 minutes, layers 35 to 40 minutes; cool. Frost with Vanilla Butter Frosting (page 251) if desired.

*If using self-rising flour, omit baking powder, baking soda and salt.

DATE CAKE

1⅔ cups all-purpose flour*
 1 cup sugar
 1 teaspoon baking soda
 ½ teaspoon salt
 1 cup water
 ¼ cup shortening
 1 egg
 1 teaspoon vanilla
 1 cup cut-up dates
 ½ cup finely chopped nuts

Heat oven to 350°. Grease and flour square pan, 9x9x2 inches. Beat all ingredients in large mixer bowl on low speed, scraping bowl constantly, 30 seconds. Beat on high speed, scraping bowl occasionally, 3 minutes. Pour into pan.

Bake until wooden pick inserted in center comes out clean, 45 to 50 minutes; cool. Frost with ½ recipe Lemon Butter Frosting (page 251) if desired.

*If using self-rising flour, decrease baking soda to ¼ teaspoon, omit salt and use 2 eggs.

Whole Wheat Date Cake: Substitute ⅔ cup whole wheat flour for ⅔ cup of the all-purpose flour.

Applesauce Cake

APPLESAUCE CAKE

2½ cups all-purpose* or cake flour
 2 cups sugar
1½ teaspoons baking soda
1½ teaspoons salt
 ¼ teaspoon baking powder
 ¾ teaspoon ground cinnamon
 ½ teaspoon ground cloves
 ½ teaspoon ground allspice
1½ cups applesauce
 ½ cup water
 ½ cup shortening
 2 eggs
 1 cup raisins
 ½ cup chopped walnuts

Heat oven to 350°. Grease and flour oblong pan, 13x9x2 inches, or 2 round layer pans, 8 or 9x1½ inches. Beat all ingredients in large mixer bowl on low speed, scraping bowl constantly, 30 seconds. Beat on high speed, scraping bowl occasionally, 3 minutes. Pour into pan(s).

Bake until wooden pick inserted in center comes out clean, oblong 60 to 65 minutes, layers 50 to 55 minutes; cool. Frost with Butterscotch Meringue (page 254) if desired.

*Do not use self-rising flour in this recipe.

Small Applesauce Cake: Cut all ingredients in half. Pour batter into greased and floured square pan, 9x9x2 inches. Bake 50 to 55 minutes.

Whole Wheat Applesauce Cake: Substitute 1¼ cups whole wheat flour for 1¼ cups of the all-purpose flour and decrease sugar to 1⅔ cups. Do not use cake flour.

PINEAPPLE UPSIDE-DOWN CAKE

When you use canned fruits in upside-down cakes, be thrifty—save the leftover syrup for gelatin desserts, fruit drinks or party punches.

 ¼ cup margarine or butter
 ½ cup packed brown sugar
 1 can (8¼ ounces) sliced pineapple, drained
 7 maraschino cherries
 6 pecan halves
   Dinette Cake batter (page 248)

Heat oven to 350°. Heat margarine in round layer pan, 9x1½ inches, in oven until melted. Sprinkle brown sugar over margarine. Place 1 pineapple slice in center of pan. Cut remaining slices into halves; arrange halves cut sides out around pineapple in center of pan. Place cherries in center or curves of pineapple slices; arrange pecans around center slice. Prepare Dinette Cake batter; pour over fruit in pan.

Bake until wooden pick inserted in center comes out clean, about 45 minutes. Invert onto heatproof plate. Let pan remain a few minutes. Serve warm and, if desired, with whipped cream.   9 SERVINGS.

Williamsburg Orange Cake

WILLIAMSBURG ORANGE CAKE

2½ cups all-purpose flour* or 2¾ cups
    cake flour
1½ cups sugar
1½ teaspoons baking soda
¾ teaspoon salt
1½ cups buttermilk
½ cup margarine or butter, softened
¼ cup shortening
3 eggs
1½ teaspoons vanilla
1 cup golden raisins, cut up
½ cup finely chopped nuts
1 tablespoon grated orange peel
    Williamsburg Butter Frosting (below)

Heat oven to 350°. Grease and flour oblong pan, 13x9x2 inches, or two 9-inch or three 8-inch round layer pans. Beat all ingredients except frosting in large mixer bowl on low speed, scraping bowl constantly, 30 seconds. Beat on high speed, scraping bowl occasionally, 3 minutes. Pour into pan(s).

Bake until wooden pick inserted in center comes out clean, oblong 45 to 50 minutes, layers 30 to 35 minutes; cool. Frost with Williamsburg Butter Frosting.

*Do not use self-rising flour in this recipe.

WILLIAMSBURG BUTTER FROSTING

½ cup margarine or butter, softened
4½ cups powdered sugar
4 to 5 tablespoons orange-flavored liqueur
    or orange juice
1 tablespoon grated orange peel

Mix margarine and powdered sugar. Beat in liqueur and orange peel.

ORANGE RING CAKE

Heat oven to 350°. Grease and flour tube pan, 10x4 inches, or 12-cup bundt cake pan. Prepare Williamsburg Orange Cake (above), using all-purpose flour. Pour into pan.

Bake until wooden pick inserted in center comes out clean, 55 to 60 minutes. Cool 20 minutes; remove from pan. Cool completely. Spread Orange Buttermilk Glaze (page 254) over top of cake if desired.

Whole Wheat Orange Ring Cake: Substitute 1¼ cups whole wheat flour for 1¼ cups of the all-purpose flour. Spread Light Brown Glaze (page 268) over top of cake if desired.

SPICY PRUNE CAKE

1 cup boiling water
1 cup cut-up pitted uncooked prunes
2 cups all-purpose flour*
1½ cups sugar
1¼ teaspoons baking soda
1 teaspoon salt
1 teaspoon ground cinnamon
1 teaspoon ground nutmeg
1 teaspoon ground cloves
½ cup vegetable oil
3 eggs
1 teaspoon vanilla
1 cup chopped nuts
    Lemon Swirl Frosting (page 251)

Pour boiling water on prunes in large mixer bowl; let stand 1 hour.

Heat oven to 350°. Grease and flour oblong pan, 13x9x2 inches. Beat prunes and remaining ingredients except frosting on low speed, scraping bowl constantly, 1 minute. Beat on medium speed, scraping bowl occasionally, 2 minutes. Pour into pan.

Bake until wooden pick inserted in center comes out clean, 45 to 50 minutes; cool. Frost with Lemon Swirl Frosting.

*If using self-rising flour, decrease baking soda to ½ teaspoon and omit salt.

Spicy Apple Cake: Decrease boiling water to ⅓ cup and substitute 2 cups finely chopped pared apples (about 2 medium) for the prunes. Do not let apples stand. Decrease sugar to 1¼ cups.

Spicy Carrot Cake: Decrease boiling water to ⅓ cup and substitute 2 cups finely shredded carrots (about 4 medium) for the prunes. Do not let carrots stand. Decrease sugar to 1¼ cups.

Spicy Prune Ring Cake: Pour batter into greased and floured 9- or 12-cup bundt cake pan or tube pan, 10x4 inches. Bake 50 to 55 minutes. Cool 10 minutes; remove from pan. Cool completely. Frost with Orange Glaze (page 254).

Spicy Rhubarb Cake: Decrease boiling water to ⅓ cup and substitute 2 cups frozen rhubarb, rinsed, drained and chopped, for the prunes. Do not let rhubarb stand. Decrease sugar to 1¼ cups.

Spicy Zucchini Cake: Decrease boiling water to ⅓ cup and substitute 2 cups finely chopped zucchini (about 3 medium) for the prunes. Do not let zucchini stand. Decrease sugar to 1¼ cups.

YELLOW FRUITCAKE

Make fruitcakes 3 to 4 weeks in advance and let them mellow in their wraps. For a richer flavor, pour wine or brandy over the cake before wrapping or wrap in wine-dampened cloths. Overwrap and store in refrigerator.

    3 cups all-purpose flour*
 1½ cups sugar
 1½ teaspoons baking powder
   ¾ teaspoon salt
   ¾ cup shortening
   ¾ cup margarine or butter, softened
   ⅔ cup orange juice
    9 eggs
  16 ounces candied cherries, cut into halves
       (about 2½ cups)
  15 ounces golden raisins (about 3 cups)
  12 ounces candied pineapple, cut up (about
       2 cups)
    4 ounces candied citron, cut up (about
       ⅔ cup)
    4 ounces candied orange peel, cut up
       (about ⅔ cup)
   ¾ cup flaked coconut
    8 ounces blanched whole almonds (about
       1½ cups)
    8 ounces pecan halves (about 2 cups)

Heat oven to 275°. Line 2 loaf pans, 9x5x3 inches,** with aluminum foil; grease. Beat all ingredients except fruits and nuts in large mixer bowl on low speed, scraping bowl constantly, 30 seconds. Beat on high speed, scraping bowl occasionally, 3 minutes. Mix batter into fruits and nuts in large bowl. Spread in pans.

Bake until wooden pick inserted in center comes out clean, 2½ to 3 hours. If necessary, cover with aluminum foil during last hour of baking to prevent excessive browning. Remove from pans; cool. Wrap in plastic wrap or aluminum foil and store in refrigerator 3 to 4 weeks or freeze.   2 FRUITCAKES.

*Do not use self-rising flour in this recipe.
**Do not use 8½x4½x2½-inch loaf pans.

Whole Wheat Fruitcake: Substitute 1½ cups whole wheat flour for 1½ cups of the all-purpose flour. Decrease sugar to 1¼ cups.

JEWELED FRUITCAKE

Always serve fruitcake thinly sliced; cut with a non-serrated or electric knife.

    8 ounces dried apricots (about 2 cups)
    8 ounces pitted dates (about 1½ cups)
    1 cup red and green maraschino cherries
    9 ounces Brazil nuts (about 1½ cups)
    5 ounces red and green candied pineapple,
       cut up (about 1 cup)
   ¾ cup all-purpose flour*
   ¾ cup sugar
   ½ teaspoon baking powder
   ½ teaspoon salt
    3 eggs
 1½ teaspoons vanilla

Heat oven to 300°. Line loaf pan, 9x5x3 or 8½x4½x2½ inches, with aluminum foil; grease. Mix all ingredients. Spread in pan.

Bake until wooden pick inserted in center comes out clean, about 1¾ hours. If necessary, cover with aluminum foil during last 30 minutes of baking to prevent excessive browning. Remove from pan; cool. Wrap in plastic wrap; store in refrigerator.

*If using self-rising flour, omit baking powder and salt.

GLAZES FOR FRUITCAKES

Pour a thin glaze over your favorite fruitcake after storing. Each of the following is enough for one fruitcake. To decorate, dip undersides of cut candied fruit in additional glaze and press on top of cake.

Jelly Glaze: Heat ¼ cup apple or currant jelly over low heat, stirring occasionally, until smooth.

Sweet Glaze: Heat 2 tablespoons light corn syrup and 1 tablespoon water just to boiling. Cool to lukewarm.

BAKING CHART FOR FRUITCAKES

Pan Size	Temperature	Baking Time
16-ounce vegetable can	275°	2 to 2½ hours
Miniature loaf pans, 4½x2¾x1¼ inches	275°	1 to 1½ hours
Muffin cups	275°	40 to 50 minutes

NOTE: Cans must be from heat-processed foods. Fill well-greased cans, pans and muffin cups almost full.

Jeweled Fruitcake

Christmas Snow Cake

Cat Cake

Musical Birthday Cake

SILVER WHITE CAKE

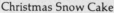

    2 cups all-purpose flour* or 2¼ cups
        cake flour
1½ cups sugar
3½ teaspoons baking powder
    1 teaspoon salt
    ½ cup shortening
    1 cup milk
    1 teaspoon vanilla
    4 egg whites

Heat oven to 350°. Grease and flour oblong pan, 13x9x2 inches, or 2 round layer pans, 9x1½ inches. Beat flour, sugar, baking powder, salt, shortening, milk and vanilla in large mixer bowl on low speed, scraping bowl constantly, 30 seconds. Beat on high speed, scraping bowl occasionally, 2 minutes. Add egg whites; beat on high speed, scraping bowl occasionally, 2 minutes. Pour into pan(s).

Bake until wooden pick inserted in center comes out clean, oblong 35 to 40 minutes, layers 30 to 35 minutes; cool. Frost with Pink Mountain Frosting (page 253) if desired.

*Do not use self-rising flour in this recipe.

Lady Baltimore Cake: Bake Silver White Cake in layer pans. Prepare White Mountain Frosting (page 253). For filling, remove 1 cup frosting; stir in ½ cup chopped walnuts, ⅓ cup cut-up raisins and ⅓ cup figs, cut into strips. Fill layers with half of the filling; spread remaining filling over top of cake. Frost side and top of cake with remaining frosting.

Lemon-filled Silver White Cake: Spread oblong cake or fill layers with Clear Lemon Filling (page 245) and frost with White Mountain Frosting (page 253). Sprinkle frosted cake with about 1 cup flaked or shredded coconut if desired.

Silver White Cupcakes: Pour batter into paper-lined medium muffin cups, 2½x1¼ inches, filling each about half full. Bake 20 minutes.   ABOUT 2 DOZEN CUPCAKES.

Small Silver White Cake: Cut all ingredients in half and bake in greased and floured square pan, 8x8x2 or 9x9x2 inches. Frost with Quick Fudge Frosting (page 253) if desired.

Special Filbert Cake: Add 1 cup ground filberts or hazelnuts with the dry ingredients.

CHRISTMAS SNOW CAKE

Grease and flour 2 round layer pans, 8 or 9x1½ inches. Prepare Silver White Cake (left) or your favorite cake; pour into pans. Bake as directed. Remove from pans; cool.

Fill and frost with White Mountain Frosting (page 253); sprinkle with flaked coconut.

Place piece of plain paper on back of cake pan and cut out circle the size of cake. Draw Christmas tree in center of paper; cut out tree. Place circle with tree pattern on cake. Sprinkle Tinted Coconut (below) in pattern, carefully following outline. Fill base of tree with shaved chocolate. Remove circle.

Roll red gumdrops on granulated sugar until flat. Cut star in each gumdrop with small star cutter. Insert small red candles in gumdrop stars and place on branches of tree. Decorate tree with silver dragées if desired.

TINTED COCONUT

Place ½ cup coconut in jar or plastic bag. Mix 1 or 2 drops green food color and ½ teaspoon water. Add to coconut. Screw on lid or fold over top of bag and shake until coconut is uniformly colored.

MUSICAL BIRTHDAY CAKE

Grease and flour oblong pan, 13x9x2 inches. Prepare Silver White Cake (page 240) or your favorite cake; pour into pan. Bake as directed. Remove from pan; cool. Place cake upside down on large tray or plate.

Prepare Vanilla Butter Frosting (page 251); tint if desired. Frost sides and top of cake.

Prepare Chocolate Decorators' Frosting (page 253). With frosting in decorators' tube or envelope cone (page 252), make a treble clef and staff (5 horizontal lines with 4 spaces between) on cake. Write "Happy Birthday to You" below staff. Press small gumdrops into oval shapes and place on lines to resemble notes of song. Place birthday candles to right of gumdrop notes. Additional candles can be placed around edges of cake if desired.

CAT CAKE

Heat oven to 350°. Grease and flour 2 round layer pans, 8x1½ inches. Prepare Silver White Cake (page 240), Cocoa Fudge Cake (page 234) or Starlight Cake (page 247); pour into pans. Bake as directed. Remove from pans; cool.

Use 1 layer for body. Cut other layer as shown in diagram. Arrange layer and pieces on large tray or cardboard covered with aluminum foil as shown in diagram. Join all parts and frost sides and top of cake with Chocolate Butter Frosting (page 251).

Sprinkle with toasted coconut if desired. Use gumdrops for eyes and nose and black shoestring licorice for whiskers, lines on eyes and paws.

HEART CAKE

Heat oven to 350°. Grease and flour square pan, 8x8x2 inches, and round layer pan, 8x1½ inches. Prepare Silver White Cake (page 240). Divide batter evenly between pans. Bake until wooden pick inserted in center comes out clean, 25 to 30 minutes. Remove from pans; cool.

Place square layer on large tray or plate. Cut round layer into halves. Place cut edge of each half against adjacent sides of square layer to form heart. Frost with Pink Mountain Frosting (page 253). Garnish with chopped nuts, toasted or untoasted slivered almonds or coconut if desired.

CHRISTMAS TREE CAKE

Heat oven to 350°. Grease and flour oblong pan, 13x9x2 inches. Prepare Silver White Cake (page 240); pour into pan. Sprinkle batter with 2 tablespoons green sugar and 2 tablespoons multicolored nonpareils. Cut through batter with spatula to swirl. Bake as directed. Remove from pan; cool.

Cover large tray or piece of cardboard with aluminum foil or foil wrapping paper. Cut cake as shown in diagram.

Prepare White Mountain Frosting (page 253). Tint frosting green with 1 or 2 drops green food color. Arrange cake pieces A and B on tray to make tree shape (see diagram); frost. Place piece C on top; frost sides and top, making strokes through frosting to resemble tree branches.

Sprinkle cake with green sugar. Insert 3 candy canes in end of cake to make trunk. Decorate trunk with chocolate-coated candies if desired.

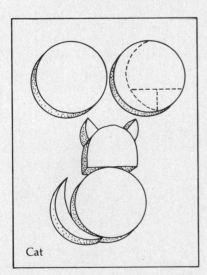

Cat

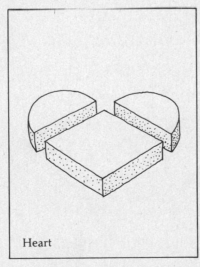

Heart

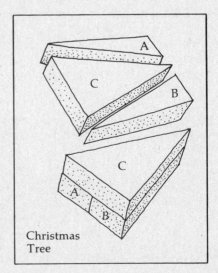

Christmas Tree

ABOUT ANGEL, SPONGE AND CHIFFON CAKES

Angel cakes are made without leavening, shortening or egg yolks. *Sponge cakes* use both the whites and yolks of eggs. Sometimes leavening is called for, but shortening is never used. *Chiffon cakes* depend on meringue for lightness; they also use egg yolks, leavening and shortening. For best results, follow the success tips (right).

☐ Bake cakes in tube pans on bottom rack in oven.

☐ Don't peek until minimum baking time is up.

☐ Foam-type cakes baked in oblong, layer or jelly roll pans are done when a wooden pick inserted in center comes out clean.

☐ To remove cooled cake from tube pan, loosen by moving spatula or table knife up and down against side of pan. Next, turn pan over and hit one side against counter. The cake will slip out.

TIPS FOR ANGEL FOOD AND CHIFFON CAKES

1. Egg whites must be beaten until stiff peaks form. Be sure egg whites are at room temperature.

2. To fold, cut down through center of beaten egg whites, along bottom and up side; rotate ¼ turn. Repeat.

3. Use spatula to break down large air pockets and to seal batter against side of pan and tube.

4. To test angel cake for doneness, touch cracks. They should feel dry; no imprint should remain.

5. Cool cake upside down in pan. Support tube on funnel or bottle so cake does not touch counter.

6. Invert cooled cake on waxed paper. Brush loose crumbs from top and side before frosting.

7. To split cake, measure even widths and mark with picks; cut across cake, sawing lightly.

8. Coat side with thin layer of frosting to seal in crumbs; swirl more up side, forming a slight ridge.

9. Pour or spoon small amount of glaze on top of cake; spread, allowing some to drizzle down side.

ANGEL FOOD CAKE DELUXE

1 cup cake flour
1½ cups powdered sugar
1½ cups egg whites (about 12)
1½ teaspoons cream of tartar
1 cup granulated sugar
¼ teaspoon salt
1½ teaspoons vanilla
½ teaspoon almond extract

Heat oven to 375°. Mix flour and powdered sugar. Beat egg whites and cream of tartar in large mixer bowl on medium speed until foamy. Beat in granulated sugar on high speed, 2 tablespoons at a time; continue beating until stiff and glossy. Add salt, vanilla and almond extract with the last addition of sugar. Do not underbeat.

Sprinkle flour-sugar mixture, ¼ cup at a time, over meringue, folding in just until flour-sugar mixture disappears. Push batter into ungreased tube pan, 10x4 inches. Cut gently through batter with metal spatula.

Bake until cracks feel dry and top springs back when touched lightly, 30 to 35 minutes. Invert pan on funnel; let hang until cake is cold. Remove from pan. Spread top of cake with Butter-Rum Glaze (page 254) if desired.

Brown Sugar Angel Food Cake: Substitute 1¼ cups packed brown sugar for the powdered sugar and ¾ cup packed brown sugar for the granulated sugar. Beat flour and 1¼ cups brown sugar with hand beater until no longer lumpy (break up any remaining lumps with fingers). Serve with Toffee Topping (below) if desired.

Toffee Topping: Chill 6 bars (¾ ounce each) chocolate-covered toffee candy; crush bars. Beat 2 cups chilled whipping cream and ½ cup powdered sugar in chilled bowl until stiff. Fold in crushed candy. Refrigerate at least 1 hour before serving; refrigerate any leftover topping.

Coconut Angel Food Cake: Fold in 1 cup shredded coconut, ½ cup at a time, after folding in flour-sugar mixture. Bake 35 to 45 minutes. Serve with Almond Fluff (below) if desired.

Almond Fluff: Beat 2 cups chilled whipping cream in chilled bowl until stiff. Fold in ½ cup white crème de cacao. Refrigerate at least 1 hour before serving. Garnish each serving with ½ teaspoon toasted diced almonds. Refrigerate any leftover fluff.

DAFFODIL CAKE

Heat oven to 375°. Prepare Angel Food Cake Deluxe (left) as directed except—after preparing meringue, beat 4 egg yolks until very thick and lemon colored, about 5 minutes; reserve. Finish preparing batter. Pour ⅓ of the batter into another bowl; fold in egg yolks. Spoon yellow and white batters alternately into pan. Cut through batters gently to swirl. Bake as directed.

SUNSHINE CAKE

1 cup egg whites (about 8)
½ teaspoon cream of tartar
½ teaspoon salt
1½ cups sugar
5 egg yolks
1 cup all-purpose flour*
2 tablespoons water
½ teaspoon almond extract
½ teaspoon lemon extract
½ teaspoon vanilla

Heat oven to 325°. Beat egg whites, cream of tartar and salt in large mixer bowl on medium speed until foamy. Beat in 1 cup of the sugar on high speed, 1 tablespoon at a time; continue beating until stiff and glossy. Do not underbeat. Reserve meringue.

Beat egg yolks in small mixer bowl until very thick and lemon colored, about 5 minutes. Beat in remaining ½ cup sugar gradually. Beat in flour alternately with water and flavorings on low speed. Fold egg yolk mixture into reserved meringue. Spread in ungreased tube pan, 10x4 inches. Cut gently through batter with metal spatula.

Bake until top springs back when touched lightly, 60 to 65 minutes. Invert pan on funnel; let hang until cake is cold. Remove. Top with fruit and Sweetened Whipped Cream (page 244) if desired.

*If using self-rising flour, omit salt.

EGG SIZES

Eggs are available most often in these sizes: extra-large (27 to 29 ounces per dozen), large (24 to 26 ounces per dozen) and medium (21 to 23 ounces per dozen). Our recipes are tested with large eggs. Two eggs equal ⅓ to ½ cup; 3 eggs, ½ to ⅔ cup; 4 eggs, ⅔ to 1 cup. Egg whites equal about 2 tablespoons each; yolks, 1½ tablespoons. Let whites come to room temperature before beating.

HOT WATER SPONGE CAKE

3 eggs
¾ cup sugar
⅓ cup hot water or hot milk
1 teaspoon vanilla
½ teaspoon lemon extract
1¼ cups cake flour
1½ teaspoons baking powder
½ teaspoon salt
Sweetened Whipped Cream (below)

Heat oven to 350°. Grease and flour square pan, 8x8x2 or 9x9x2 inches. Beat eggs in small mixer bowl on high speed 5 minutes; pour into large mixer bowl. Beat in sugar gradually. Beat in water, vanilla and lemon extract on low speed. Beat in flour, baking powder and salt on low speed; beat just until batter is smooth. Pour into pan.

Bake until top springs back when touched lightly in center, 25 to 30 minutes; cool. Serve with Sweetened Whipped Cream and, if desired, whole or sliced strawberries.

SWEETENED WHIPPED CREAM

For 1 cup whipped cream: Beat ½ cup chilled whipping cream and 1 tablespoon granulated or powdered sugar in chilled bowl until stiff.

For 1½ cups whipped cream: Use ¾ cup chilled whipping cream and 2 tablespoons sugar.

For 2⅓ cups whipped cream: Use 1 cup chilled whipping cream and 3 tablespoons sugar.

Flavored Whipped Cream: Beat one of the following into 1 cup whipping cream and sugar:

☐ ½ teaspoon almond extract
☐ ½ teaspoon ground cinnamon
☐ ½ teaspoon ground ginger
☐ 1 teaspoon grated lemon or orange peel
☐ ¼ teaspoon maple flavoring
☐ ½ teaspoon ground nutmeg
☐ ½ teaspoon peppermint extract
☐ ½ teaspoon rum flavoring
☐ 1 teaspoon vanilla

YARDSTICK FOR YIELDS

Size and kind	Servings
8- or 9-inch layer cake	10 to 16
8- or 9-inch square cake	9
13x9x2-inch oblong cake	12 to 15
10x4-inch tube cake	12 to 16

JELLY ROLL

3 eggs
1 cup granulated sugar
⅓ cup water
1 teaspoon vanilla
¾ cup all-purpose flour* or 1 cup cake flour
1 teaspoon baking powder
¼ teaspoon salt
About ⅔ cup jelly or jam
Powdered sugar

Heat oven to 375°. Line jelly roll pan, 15½x10½x1 inch, with aluminum foil or waxed paper; grease generously. Beat eggs in small mixer bowl on high speed until very thick and lemon colored, about 5 minutes. Pour eggs into large mixer bowl. Beat in granulated sugar gradually. Beat in water and vanilla on low speed. Add flour, baking powder and salt gradually, beating just until batter is smooth. Pour into pan.

Bake until wooden pick inserted in center comes out clean, 12 to 15 minutes. Immediately loosen cake from edges of pan; invert on towel sprinkled generously with powdered sugar. Carefully remove foil. Trim off stiff edges if necessary.

While hot, carefully roll cake and towel from narrow end. Cool on wire rack at least 30 minutes. Unroll cake; remove towel. Beat jelly slightly with fork to soften; spread over cake. Roll up; sprinkle with powdered sugar.   10 SERVINGS.

*If using self-rising flour, omit baking powder and salt.

Do-ahead Tip: Before sprinkling with powdered sugar or spreading with a glaze, jelly rolls can be wrapped and refrigerated no longer than 48 hours or frozen no longer than 1 month (place in box to prevent crushing). Let stand at room temperature 15 to 30 minutes before serving.

Rainbow Sherbet Roll: Omit jelly. After unrolling cake, spread raspberry sherbet on ⅓ of cake, orange sherbet on next ⅓ and lime sherbet on remaining cake. Roll up but do not sprinkle with powdered sugar. Place seam side down on piece of aluminum foil, 18x12 inches. Wrap securely in foil; freeze. Remove from freezer 15 minutes before serving.   12 SERVINGS.

Strawberry Roll: Omit jelly. About 1 hour before serving, beat ½ cup chilled whipping cream and 2 tablespoons powdered sugar until stiff. Spread on unrolled cake. Arrange 2 cups sliced fresh strawberries on whipped cream. Roll up; sprinkle with powdered sugar and refrigerate. Serve with Sweetened Whipped Cream (left).   8 TO 10 SERVINGS.

Roll hot cake on sugared towel.

Spread cooled cake with jelly; reroll.

Tart Lemon Cake Roll

TART LEMON CAKE ROLL

Prepare Jelly Roll (page 244) as directed except—substitute Clear Lemon Filling (below) for the jelly. Refrigerate cake roll at least 1 hour. Serve with Sweetened Whipped Cream (page 244) if desired.

CLEAR LEMON FILLING
¾ cup sugar
3 tablespoons cornstarch
¼ teaspoon salt
¾ cup water
1 teaspoon grated lemon peel
1 tablespoon margarine or butter
⅓ cup lemon juice
4 drops yellow food color (optional)

Mix sugar, cornstarch and salt in saucepan. Stir in water gradually. Cook, stirring constantly, until mixture thickens and boils. Boil and stir 5 minutes. Remove from heat; add lemon peel and margarine. Stir in lemon juice and food color; cool. If filling is too soft, refrigerate until set.

CHOCOLATE ROLL

Heat oven to 375°. Prepare Jelly Roll (page 244) as directed except—beat in ¼ cup cocoa with the flour. Substitute Cinnamon Whipped Cream (below) for the jelly and spread roll with Chocolate Glaze (page 254) instead of sprinkling with powdered sugar.

CINNAMON WHIPPED CREAM
Beat 1 cup chilled whipping cream, 3 tablespoons granulated or powdered sugar and ½ teaspoon ground cinnamon in chilled bowl until stiff.

Cherry-Almond Roll: Omit cinnamon in Cinnamon Whipped Cream. Fold ¼ cup chopped maraschino cherries and ¼ cup diced roasted almonds into the whipped cream.

Chocolate-Mint Roll: Omit Cinnamon Whipped Cream. Spread 1 pint vanilla ice cream, softened, on cake; sprinkle with ¼ cup crushed peppermint candy. Roll up; wrap in plastic wrap. Freeze until firm, about 6 hours. Sprinkle with powdered sugar. Garnish with mint leaves if desired.

Maple-Pecan Chiffon Cake

CHIFFON CAKE

  2 cups all-purpose flour* or 2¼ cups
      cake flour
1½ cups sugar
  3 teaspoons baking powder
  1 teaspoon salt
  ½ cup vegetable oil
  7 egg yolks (with all-purpose flour) or
      5 egg yolks (with cake flour)
  ¾ cup cold water
  2 tablespoons grated orange peel
  1 cup egg whites (about 8)
  ½ teaspoon cream of tartar
      Orange or Lemon Butter Frosting (right)

Heat oven to 325°. Mix flour, sugar, baking powder and salt. Beat in oil, egg yolks, water and orange peel with spoon until smooth. Beat egg whites and cream of tartar in large mixer bowl until stiff peaks form. Pour egg yolk mixture gradually over beaten egg whites, folding with rubber spatula just until blended. Pour into ungreased tube pan, 10x4 inches.

Bake until top springs back when touched lightly, about 1¼ hours. Invert pan on funnel; let hang until cake is cold. Remove from pan. Frost with Orange or Lemon Butter Frosting.

*If using self-rising flour, omit baking powder and salt.

ORANGE OR LEMON BUTTER FROSTING
Mix 3 cups powdered sugar, ⅓ cup margarine or butter, softened, 1 tablespoon plus 1½ teaspoons grated orange peel or lemon peel and about 3 tablespoons orange juice or lemon juice.

Chocolate Chip Chiffon Cake: Increase sugar to 1¾ cups. Omit orange peel and beat in 2 teaspoons vanilla. Just before pouring into pan, fold in 3 squares (1 ounce each) sweet, semisweet or unsweetened chocolate, shaved. Frost with Satiny Beige Frosting (page 253) if desired.

Lemon Chiffon Cake: Omit peel; beat in 2 teaspoons grated lemon peel and 2 teaspoons vanilla.

Maple-Pecan Chiffon Cake: Substitute ¾ cup packed brown sugar for ¾ cup of the granulated sugar and beat in 2 teaspoons maple flavoring. Just before pouring into pan, fold in 1 cup very finely chopped pecans. Frost with Maple-Nut Butter Frosting or French Silk Frosting (page 251) if desired.

Spice Chiffon Cake: Add 1 teaspoon ground cinnamon, ½ teaspoon ground nutmeg, ½ teaspoon ground allspice and ½ teaspoon ground cloves to the dry ingredients. Omit orange peel.

ORANGE CHIFFON LAYER CAKE

  2 eggs, separated
1½ cups sugar
2¼ cups cake flour
  3 teaspoons baking powder
  1 teaspoon salt
  ⅓ cup vegetable oil
      Grated peel of 1 orange
      Juice of 1 orange plus enough milk to
        measure 1 cup liquid

Heat oven to 350°. Grease and flour 2 round layer pans, 8 or 9x1½ inches. Beat egg whites on medium speed until foamy. Beat in ½ cup of the sugar on high speed, 1 tablespoon at a time; continue beating until very stiff and glossy. Do not underbeat.

Mix remaining sugar, the flour, baking powder and salt in large mixer bowl. Add oil and half of the liquid. Beat on low speed until moistened. Beat on high speed, scraping bowl constantly, 1 minute. Add remaining liquid, the peel and egg yolks. Beat on high speed, scraping occasionally, 1 minute. Fold in meringue. Pour into pans.

Bake until wooden pick inserted in center comes out clean, 25 to 30 minutes; cool. Frost with Pineapple Butter Frosting (page 251) if desired.

BONNIE BUTTER CAKE

1¾ cups sugar
⅔ cup margarine or butter, softened
2 eggs
1½ teaspoons vanilla
2¾ cups all-purpose flour* or 3 cups
    cake flour
2½ teaspoons baking powder
1 teaspoon salt
1¼ cups milk

Heat oven to 350°. Grease and flour oblong pan, 13x9x2 inches, or two 9-inch or three 8-inch round layer pans. Mix sugar, margarine, eggs and vanilla until fluffy. Beat on high speed, scraping bowl occasionally, 5 minutes. Beat in flour, baking powder and salt alternately with milk on low speed. Pour into pan(s).

Bake until wooden pick inserted in center comes out clean, oblong 45 to 50 minutes, layers 30 to 35 minutes; cool. Frost with Broiled Cereal Frosting (page 254) if desired.

*If using self-rising flour, omit baking powder and salt.

Whole Wheat Bonnie Butter Cake: Decrease sugar to 1½ cups. Substitute 1¼ cups whole wheat flour for 1¼ cups of the all-purpose flour. Do not use cake flour.

POUND CAKE

2¾ cups sugar
1¼ cups margarine or butter, softened
5 eggs
1 teaspoon vanilla
3 cups all-purpose flour*
1 teaspoon baking powder
¼ teaspoon salt
1 cup evaporated milk

Heat oven to 350°. Grease and flour tube pan, 10x4 inches, or 12-cup bundt cake pan. Beat sugar, margarine, eggs and vanilla in large mixer bowl on low speed, scraping bowl constantly, 30 seconds. Beat on high speed, scraping bowl occasionally, 5 minutes. Beat in flour, baking powder and salt alternately with milk on low speed. Pour into pan.

Bake until wooden pick inserted in center comes out clean, 70 to 80 minutes. Cool 20 minutes; remove from pan.

*Do not use self-rising flour in this recipe.

Mace Pound Cake: Beat in ½ teaspoon ground mace with the flour.

STARLIGHT CAKE

2 cups all-purpose flour*
1½ cups sugar
3½ teaspoons baking powder
1 teaspoon salt
½ cup shortening (half margarine or
    butter, softened, if desired)
1 cup milk
1 teaspoon vanilla
3 eggs

Heat oven to 350°. Grease and flour oblong pan, 13x9x2 inches, or 2 round layer pans, 8 or 9x1½ inches. Beat all ingredients in large mixer bowl on low speed, scraping bowl constantly, 30 seconds. Beat on high speed, scraping bowl frequently, 3 minutes. Pour into pan(s).

Bake until wooden pick inserted in center comes out clean, oblong 40 to 45 minutes, layers 30 to 35 minutes; cool. Frost with French Silk Frosting (page 251) if desired.

*If using self-rising flour, omit baking powder and salt.

Eggnog Cake: Substitute rum flavoring for the vanilla. Beat in 1 teaspoon ground nutmeg and ¼ teaspoon ground ginger. Frost with Cherry Butter Frosting (page 251) if desired.

Golden Starlight Cake: Substitute 2¼ cups cake flour for the all-purpose flour. Decrease baking powder to 3 teaspoons and increase vanilla to 1½ teaspoons. Decrease eggs to 2. Frost with Easy Penuche Frosting (page 253) if desired.

Orange Starlight Cake: Substitute 1 tablespoon grated orange peel for the vanilla. Frost with Browned Butter Frosting (page 251) if desired.

Starlight Cupcakes: Pour batter into paper-lined medium muffin cups, 2½x1¼ inches, filling each about half full. Bake 20 minutes. Frost with Mocha Butter Frosting (page 251) if desired.   3 DOZEN CUPCAKES.

Whole Wheat Starlight Cake: Substitute 1 cup whole wheat flour for 1 cup of the all-purpose flour and 1 cup packed brown sugar and ¼ cup granulated sugar for the 1½ cups granulated sugar. Frost with Broiled Peanut Butter Frosting (page 254) if desired.

FROSTING AN OBLONG CAKE

To frost sides as well as top, remove cake from pan and place *right side up* on tray. Frost when cool.

FROSTING CUPCAKES

Twirl top of each cupcake *very lightly* in a fluffy frosting—try White Mountain Frosting (page 253).

CHOCOLATE CHIP CAKE

    2 cups all-purpose flour*
    1 cup packed brown sugar
    ½ cup granulated sugar
    3 teaspoons baking powder
    1 teaspoon salt
    ½ teaspoon baking soda
    ½ cup shortening
    1¼ cups milk
    3 eggs
    ½ cup semisweet chocolate chips, finely
        chopped, or ½ cup miniature
        semisweet chocolate chips
    1½ teaspoons vanilla

Heat oven to 350°. Grease and flour oblong pan, 13x9x2 inches, or 2 round layer pans, 8 or 9x1½ inches. Beat all ingredients in large mixer bowl on low speed, scraping bowl constantly, 30 seconds. Beat on high speed, scraping bowl occasionally, 3 minutes. Pour into pan(s).

Bake until wooden pick inserted in center comes out clean, 40 to 45 minutes; cool. Frost with Chocolate Butter Frosting (page 251) if desired.

*If using self-rising flour, omit baking powder, salt and baking soda.

FROSTING A TWO-LAYER CAKE

Place layer upside down on plate. Using a flexible spatula, spread about ½ cup frosting to within ¼ inch of edge; top with second layer, right side up. Coat side with a thin layer of frosting; swirl more up side, forming a ¼-inch ridge. Frost top.

DINETTE CAKE

    1¼ cups all-purpose flour* or 1½ cups
        cake flour
    1 cup sugar
    1½ teaspoons baking powder
    ½ teaspoon salt
    ¾ cup milk
    ⅓ cup shortening
    1 egg
    1 teaspoon vanilla

Heat oven to 350°. Grease and flour square pan, 8x8x2 or 9x9x2 inches, or round layer pan, 9x1½ inches. Beat all ingredients in large mixer bowl on low speed, scraping bowl constantly, 30 seconds. Beat on high speed, scraping bowl occasionally, 3 minutes. Pour into pan.

Bake until wooden pick inserted in center comes out clean, square 35 to 40 minutes, round 35 minutes; cool. Frost with ½ recipe Broiled Coconut Frosting or Chocolate Chip Glaze (page 254) if desired.

*If using self-rising flour, omit baking powder and salt.

Spicy Raisin Cake: Use all-purpose flour and square pan, 8x8x2 or 9x9x2 inches. Omit vanilla and add 1 teaspoon ground cinnamon, ½ teaspoon ground nutmeg and ¼ teaspoon ground cloves. Stir in 1 cup raisins before pouring into pan.

Spicy Raisin Cupcakes: Pour Spicy Raisin Cake batter (above) into paper-lined medium muffin cups, 2½x1¼ inches, filling each about half full. 15 OR 16 CUPCAKES.

BOSTON CREAM PIE

Heat oven to 350°. Grease and flour round layer pan, 9x1½ inches. Prepare Dinette Cake (page 248). Bake as directed. Remove from pan; cool.

Split cake to make 2 thin layers. Fill layers with Cream Filling (below). Spread top with Chocolate Glaze (page 254). Refrigerate any leftover cake.

CREAM FILLING

⅓ cup sugar
2 tablespoons cornstarch
⅛ teaspoon salt
1½ cups milk
2 egg yolks, slightly beaten
2 teaspoons vanilla

Mix sugar, cornstarch and salt in 2-quart saucepan. Stir in milk gradually. Cook over medium heat, stirring constantly, until mixture thickens and boils. Boil and stir 1 minute. Stir at least half of the hot mixture gradually into egg yolks. Blend into hot mixture in saucepan. Boil and stir 1 minute. Remove from heat; stir in vanilla. Cool to room temperature.

Martha Washington's Pie: Substitute 1 cup jelly for the Cream Filling. Omit Chocolate Glaze; sprinkle top with powdered sugar.

LORD BALTIMORE CAKE

Heat oven to 350°. Bake Starlight Cake (page 247) in layer pans; cool. Prepare Lord Baltimore Frosting (below). Stir ½ cup toasted flaked coconut, ¼ cup each toasted chopped pecans, toasted chopped blanched almonds and chopped maraschino cherries into 1 cup of the frosting. Fill layers with half of the coconut mixture; spread remainder over top. Frost side and top of cake with remaining frosting.

LORD BALTIMORE FROSTING

½ cup sugar
¼ cup light corn syrup
2 tablespoons maraschino cherry syrup
2 egg whites
1 teaspoon vanilla

Mix sugar, corn syrup and cherry syrup in saucepan. Cover and heat to rolling boil over medium heat. Uncover and boil rapidly until candy thermometer registers 242° or until small amount of mixture dropped into very cold water forms a firm ball. Beat egg whites until stiff peaks form. Pour hot syrup very slowly into egg whites, beating constantly on medium speed. Beat on high speed until stiff peaks form. Beat in vanilla.

BURNT SUGAR CAKE

1½ cups sugar
½ cup boiling water
2 eggs, separated
½ cup margarine or butter, softened
1 teaspoon vanilla
2¼ cups all-purpose flour*
3 teaspoons baking powder
1 teaspoon salt
1 cup milk
Caramel Frosting (below)

Heat ½ cup of the sugar in heavy 8-inch skillet, stirring constantly, until sugar is melted and golden brown. Remove from heat; stir in boiling water slowly. Cook over low heat, stirring constantly, until sugar lumps are dissolved. Add enough water to syrup, if necessary, to measure ½ cup; cool.

Heat oven to 375°. Grease and flour two 9-inch or three 8-inch round layer pans. Beat egg whites in small mixer bowl on medium speed until foamy. Beat in ½ cup of the sugar on high speed, 1 tablespoon at a time; continue beating until very stiff and glossy. Do not underbeat.

Beat margarine, remaining ½ cup sugar, the egg yolks and vanilla in large mixer bowl on low speed, scraping bowl constantly, 30 seconds. Beat on high speed, scraping bowl occasionally, 5 minutes. Beat in syrup. Beat in flour, baking powder and salt alternately with milk. Fold in meringue. Pour into pans.

Bake until wooden pick inserted in center comes out clean, 20 to 25 minutes. Cool 10 minutes; remove from pans. Cool completely. Fill layers and frost cake with Caramel Frosting. Arrange pecan or walnut halves around top edge of cake if desired.

*If using self-rising flour, omit baking powder and salt.

CARAMEL FROSTING

2 tablespoons margarine or butter
⅔ cup packed dark brown sugar
⅛ teaspoon salt
⅓ cup whipping cream or evaporated milk
2⅓ to 2½ cups powdered sugar
½ teaspoon vanilla

Heat margarine in 2-quart saucepan until melted. Stir in brown sugar, salt and whipping cream. Heat to boiling, stirring constantly. Remove from heat; cool to lukewarm. Stir in enough powdered sugar gradually until of spreading consistency. Stir in vanilla.

CREATIVE CAKES—DESIGNED WITH FLAIR

Cookie Cutter Cake: Frost cake with white frosting. Dip a cookie cutter into liquid food color; press into frosting, making an imprint on top of cake. Repeat around top of cake, dipping cutter into food color each time.

Balloon Cake: Frost cake with a white frosting or one that has been delicately tinted with food color. On top of cake, arrange pastel mint-wafer "balloons." Use shoestring licorice for the balloon strings.

Abstract Cupcakes: Frost cupcakes with white frosting. Divide more frosting into several parts; tint each part a different color. Fill a decorators' tube with frosting; make bright designs on top of cupcakes.

Carnival Cake: Frost cake with fluffy-type white frosting. Mark top into 8 wedges. Form foil into a V-shape the same size as each wedge. Place on cake; sprinkle confetti candy within foil over every other wedge.

Spiral Cake: Frost a two-layer cake with a creamy-type frosting. Hold a flexible spatula at the center of the top of the cake; draw the spatula very slowly toward you, rotating cake plate as you do so.

Allegretti Cake: Frost cake with a fluffy-type white frosting. Melt 1 ounce unsweetened chocolate and ¼ teaspoon shortening. Using teaspoon, drizzle melted chocolate around top edge; let it run down side unevenly.

VANILLA BUTTER FROSTING

    3 cups powdered sugar
    ⅓ cup margarine or butter, softened
    1½ teaspoons vanilla
        About 2 tablespoons milk

Mix powdered sugar and margarine. Stir in vanilla and milk; beat until frosting is smooth and of spreading consistency.   FILLS AND FROSTS TWO 8- OR 9-INCH LAYERS OR FROSTS A 13x9-INCH CAKE.

NOTE: To fill and frost three 8-inch layers, use 4½ cups powdered sugar, ½ cup margarine or butter, softened, 2 teaspoons vanilla and about 3 tablespoons milk.

Browned Butter Frosting: Heat margarine over medium heat until delicate brown.

Cherry Butter Frosting: Stir in 2 tablespoons drained chopped maraschino cherries and 2 drops red food color.

Lemon Butter Frosting: Omit vanilla and substitute lemon juice for the milk. Stir in ½ teaspoon grated lemon peel.

Maple-Nut Butter Frosting: Substitute ½ cup maple-flavored syrup for the vanilla and milk. Stir in ¼ cup finely chopped nuts.

Orange Butter Frosting: Omit vanilla and substitute orange juice for the milk. Stir in 2 teaspoons grated orange peel.

Peanut Butter Frosting: Substitute peanut butter for the margarine and increase milk to ¼ to ⅓ cup.

Pineapple Butter Frosting: Omit vanilla and milk. Stir in ⅓ cup well-drained crushed pineapple.

GLOSSY CHOCOLATE FROSTING

    3 tablespoons shortening
    3 squares (1 ounce each) unsweetened
        chocolate
    2 cups powdered sugar
    ¼ teaspoon salt
    ⅓ cup milk
    1 teaspoon vanilla

Heat shortening and chocolate in saucepan over low heat until melted. Stir in remaining ingredients; beat until smooth. Place pan of frosting in bowl of ice and water; continue beating until frosting is smooth and of spreading consistency. Stir in ½ cup finely chopped nuts if desired.
FILLS AND FROSTS TWO 8- OR 9-INCH LAYERS OR FROSTS A 13x9-INCH CAKE.

CHOCOLATE BUTTER FROSTING

    ⅓ cup margarine or butter, softened
    2 ounces unsweetened melted chocolate
        (cool)
    2 cups powdered sugar
    1½ teaspoons vanilla
        About 2 tablespoons milk

Mix margarine and chocolate. Stir in powdered sugar. Beat in vanilla and milk until frosting is of spreading consistency.   FILLS AND FROSTS TWO 8- OR 9-INCH LAYERS OR FROSTS A 13x9-INCH CAKE.

NOTE: To frost three 8-inch layers, use ½ cup margarine or butter, softened, 3 ounces melted unsweetened chocolate (cool), 3 cups powdered sugar, 2 teaspoons vanilla and about 3 tablespoons milk.

Chocolate-Nut Butter Frosting: Stir in ¼ cup chopped nuts.

Cocoa Butter Frosting: Substitute ⅓ cup cocoa for the chocolate.

Mocha Butter Frosting: Stir in 1½ teaspoons instant powdered coffee with the sugar.

FRENCH SILK FROSTING

    2⅔ cups powdered sugar
    ⅔ cup margarine or butter, softened
    2 ounces melted unsweetened chocolate
        (cool)*
    ¾ teaspoon vanilla
    2 tablespoons milk

Beat powdered sugar, margarine, chocolate and vanilla in small mixer bowl on low speed. Add milk gradually; beat until smooth and fluffy.   FROSTS TWO 9-INCH LAYERS OR THREE 8-INCH LAYERS.

*1 bar (4 ounces) sweet cooking chocolate, melted and cooled, can be substituted for the unsweetened.

LEMON SWIRL FROSTING

    1 package (3 ounces) cream cheese, softened
    ½ cup margarine or butter, softened
    4 cups powdered sugar
    1 teaspoon vanilla
    2 to 3 teaspoons grated lemon peel
        About 3 tablespoons lemon juice

Beat all ingredients until frosting is fluffy and of spreading consistency. If necessary, stir in additional lemon juice, 1 teaspoon at a time.
FILLS AND FROSTS TWO 8- OR 9-INCH LAYERS OR FROSTS A 13x9-INCH CAKE.

USING A DECORATORS' TUBE AND FROSTING

Writing Tip: Use to make numbers, letters, borders, lattice work and delicate outlines.

Petal Tip: Use to make petals for roses and other flowers; also for borders and ribbons.

Star Tip: Use to pipe small borders around cake, also to make simple flowers, rosettes and fancy letters.

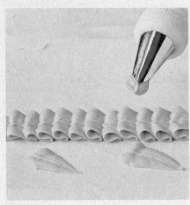

Leaf Tip: Use to make leaves and long, delicate petals; also for elaborate borders and designs.

Experiment with a variety of tips in a single design or pattern to create the desired effect.

Envelope Cone: Place about ⅓ cup frosting in envelope; fold sides. Snip off corner to make tip.

TO MAKE ROSES

Attach waxed paper to flower nail with frosting. With narrow end of petal tip up and turning nail slowly, press out frosting to form center.

To form first petal, make standing half-circle to one side of center. Add 2 more petals, forming triangle. Add more petals, overlapping.

Remove waxed paper with rose from nail; place on countertop until set. Carefully lift rose from paper with spatula and place on cake.

DECORATORS' FROSTING

Mix 2 cups powdered sugar and 2 to 3 tablespoons water—just enough to make a frosting that can be used easily in a decorators' tube or envelope cone (page 252) and yet hold its shape.

CHOCOLATE DECORATORS' FROSTING

Heat 1 square (1 ounce) unsweetened chocolate and 1 teaspoon margarine or butter until melted; remove from heat. Blend in 1 cup powdered sugar and 1 tablespoon hot water. Beat until smooth. If necessary, stir in hot water, 1 teaspoon at a time, until frosting is of desired consistency.

QUICK FUDGE FROSTING

½ cup granulated sugar
2 tablespoons cocoa
2 tablespoons margarine or butter
¼ cup milk
1 tablespoon light corn syrup
 Dash of salt
½ to ¾ cup powdered sugar
½ teaspoon vanilla

Mix granulated sugar and cocoa in saucepan. Stir in margarine, milk, corn syrup and salt; heat to boiling, stirring frequently. Boil vigorously, stirring occasionally, 3 minutes; cool. Beat in powdered sugar and vanilla.   FROSTS ONE 8- OR 9-INCH LAYER.

EASY PENUCHE FROSTING

½ cup margarine or butter
1 cup packed brown sugar
¼ cup milk
2 cups powdered sugar

Heat margarine in saucepan until melted. Stir in brown sugar. Heat to boiling, stirring constantly. Boil and stir over low heat 2 minutes. Stir in milk; heat to boiling. Remove from heat and cool to lukewarm. Stir in powdered sugar gradually. Place pan of frosting in bowl of ice and water; beat until frosting is smooth and of spreading consistency. If frosting becomes too stiff, heat slightly, stirring constantly.   FILLS AND FROSTS TWO 8- OR 9-INCH LAYERS OR FROSTS A 13x9-INCH CAKE.

WHITE MOUNTAIN FROSTING

½ cup sugar
¼ cup light corn syrup
2 tablespoons water
2 egg whites
1 teaspoon vanilla

Mix sugar, corn syrup and water in saucepan. Cover; heat to rolling boil over medium heat. Uncover; boil rapidly until candy thermometer registers 242° or until small amount of mixture dropped into very cold water forms a firm ball that holds its shape until pressed.

As mixture boils, beat egg whites until stiff peaks form. Pour hot syrup very slowly in thin stream into egg whites, beating constantly on medium speed. Add vanilla; beat on high speed until stiff peaks form.   FILLS AND FROSTS TWO 8- OR 9-INCH LAYERS OR FROSTS A 13x9-INCH CAKE.

Cherry-Nut Frosting: Stir in ¼ cup cut-up candied cherries and ¼ cup chopped nuts.

Chocolate Revel Frosting: Stir in ½ cup semisweet chocolate chips or 1 square (1 ounce) unsweetened chocolate, coarsely grated.

Cocoa Frosting: Sift ¼ cup cocoa over frosting and fold in until blended.

Coffee Frosting: Beat 1 teaspoon powdered instant coffee into Satiny Beige Frosting (below).

Lemon Frosting: Substitute 1 tablespoon lemon juice for the vanilla; beat in ¼ teaspoon grated lemon peel and 10 drops yellow food color with the lemon juice.

Maple-Pecan Frosting: Stir ¼ teaspoon maple flavoring and ½ cup chopped pecans into Satiny Beige Frosting (below).

Peppermint Frosting: Stir in ⅓ cup coarsely crushed peppermint candy (1 stick) or ½ teaspoon peppermint extract.

Pineapple Frosting: Substitute 1 teaspoon grated lemon peel for the vanilla and stir in 1 can (8¼ ounces) crushed pineapple, drained.

Pink Mountain Frosting: Beat in 8 drops red food color with the vanilla.

Raisin-Nut Frosting: Stir in ¼ cup snipped raisins and ¼ cup finely chopped nuts.

Satiny Beige Frosting: Substitute packed brown sugar for the granulated sugar and decrease vanilla to ½ teaspoon.

Tutti-Frutti Frosting: Fold in chopped nuts, cut-up dates, cut-up raisins and cut-up candied cherries.

CREAMY GLAZE

⅓ cup margarine or butter
2 cups powdered sugar
1½ teaspoons vanilla
2 to 4 tablespoons hot water

Heat margarine in saucepan until melted. Stir in powdered sugar and vanilla. Stir in water, 1 tablespoon at a time, until glaze is of desired consistency. GLAZES A 10-INCH CHIFFON OR ANGEL FOOD CAKE OR 12-CUP BUNDT CAKE.

Butter-Rum Glaze: Substitute 2 tablespoons light rum or 1½ teaspoons rum flavoring for the vanilla; stir in hot water, 1 teaspoon at a time, until glaze is of desired consistency.

Orange or Lemon Glaze: Add ½ teaspoon grated orange or lemon peel to melted margarine and substitute orange or lemon juice for the vanilla and water.

CHOCOLATE GLAZE

2 squares (1 ounce each) unsweetened chocolate
3 tablespoons margarine or butter
1 cup powdered sugar
¾ teaspoon vanilla
About 2 tablespoons hot water

Heat chocolate and margarine over low heat until melted. Remove from heat; stir in powdered sugar and vanilla. Stir in water, 1 teaspoon at a time, until glaze is of desired consistency. GLAZES ONE 8- OR 9-INCH LAYER.

ORANGE BUTTERMILK GLAZE

Mix 1½ cups powdered sugar, 2 tablespoons margarine or butter, softened, 1 tablespoon grated orange peel and 1 to 2 tablespoons buttermilk until glaze is of desired consistency. GLAZES A 10-INCH CHIFFON OR ANGEL FOOD CAKE OR 12-CUP BUNDT CAKE.

CHOCOLATE CHIP GLAZE

Heat ½ cup semisweet chocolate chips, 2 tablespoons margarine or butter and 1 tablespoon light corn syrup in 1-quart saucepan over low heat, stirring constantly, until chocolate is melted. Cool slightly. GLAZES ONE 8- OR 9-INCH LAYER.

BROILED BUTTERSCOTCH FROSTING

⅔ cup packed brown sugar
¼ cup margarine or butter, softened
1 cup chopped nuts
2 tablespoons milk

Mix brown sugar, margarine and nuts; stir in milk. Spread frosting over warm 13x9-inch cake. Set oven control to broil and/or 550°. Broil cake about 5 inches from heat until frosting bubbles and browns slightly, about 3 minutes. (Watch carefully—frosting burns easily.) FROSTS A 13x9-INCH CAKE.

Broiled Cereal Frosting: Substitute ½ cup whole wheat flake cereal for ½ cup of the nuts and increase milk to 3 tablespoons.

Broiled Coconut Frosting: Decrease nuts to ½ cup; add 1 cup flaked coconut and increase milk to 3 tablespoons.

BROILED PEANUT BUTTER FROSTING

⅔ cup packed brown sugar
¼ cup margarine or butter, softened
¼ cup peanut butter
3 tablespoons milk
1 cup finely chopped peanuts

Mix brown sugar, margarine, peanut butter and milk; stir in peanuts. Spread frosting over warm 13x9-inch cake. Set oven control to broil and/or 550°. Broil cake about 5 inches from heat until frosting bubbles and browns slightly, about 3 minutes. (Watch carefully—frosting burns easily.) FROSTS A 13x9-INCH CAKE.

BUTTERSCOTCH MERINGUE

2 egg whites
1 cup packed brown sugar
1 tablespoon lemon juice
½ cup finely chopped nuts

Just before cake is removed from oven, beat egg whites until foamy. Beat sugar and lemon juice gradually into egg whites until stiff. Carefully spread over *hot* 13x9-inch cake. Sprinkle with nuts. Bake in 400° oven until brown, 8 to 10 minutes. FROSTS A 13x9-INCH CAKE.

CAKE GARNISHES—PROFESSIONAL BUT EASY

Gumdrop Roses: For each rose, roll 4 large gumdrops on well-sugared board into ⅛-inch ovals. Sprinkle with sugar. Cut ovals into halves. Roll one half-oval tightly to form center of rose. Place more half-ovals around center, overlapping slightly; press together at base. Trim base. Cut leaves from rolled-out green gumdrops.

Brazil Nut Flowers: Place about 10 shelled Brazil nuts in 1 cup boiling water. Remove pan from heat and let stand about 5 minutes. Remove one nut at a time and quickly slice lengthwise (with vegetable parer), cutting off paper-thin curls. Arrange 6 or 7 Brazil nut curls around halved candied cherries.

Chocolate Curls: With a vegetable parer or thin, sharp knife, slice across block of sweet milk chocolate with long, thin strokes. Large-size milk chocolate candy bars can also be used. Lift curls with wooden picks.

Cherry Flowers: Snip well-drained red maraschino cherries into 6 sections, cutting about ¾ of the way through. Spread sections apart gently to resemble petals. Cut leaves from green maraschino cherries.

Citrus Decorations: Cut thin slices from an orange or a lemon. Using a small sharp knife or miniature cutter, cut a design of your choice around peel.

Frosted Grapes: Dip small clusters of green grapes into water, then dip into granulated or colored sugar. Dry clusters on wire racks before adding to cake.

Strawberry Shortcake

CAKE DESSERTS AND PUDDINGS

STRAWBERRY SHORTCAKES

1 quart strawberries, sliced
1 cup sugar
⅓ cup shortening
2 cups all-purpose flour*
2 tablespoons sugar
3 teaspoons baking powder
1 teaspoon salt
¾ cup milk
   Margarine or butter, softened
   Sweetened Whipped Cream (page 244)

Mix strawberries with 1 cup sugar; let stand 1 hour.

Heat oven to 450°. Cut shortening into flour, 2 tablespoons sugar, the baking powder and salt until mixture resembles fine crumbs. Stir in milk just until blended. Gently smooth dough into a ball on lightly floured cloth-covered board. Knead 20 to 25 times. Roll to ½-inch thickness; cut with floured 3-inch cutter. Place about 1 inch apart on ungreased cookie sheet.

Bake until golden brown, 10 to 12 minutes. Split crosswise while hot. Spread with margarine; fill and top with cream and strawberries.   6 SERVINGS.

*If using self-rising flour, omit baking powder and salt.

PEACH-CUSTARD KUCHEN

1 cup all-purpose flour*
2 tablespoons sugar
¼ teaspoon salt
⅛ teaspoon baking powder
¼ cup margarine or butter, softened
1½ cups sliced peaches (about 2 medium)
¼ cup plus 2 tablespoons sugar
1 teaspoon ground cinnamon
2 egg yolks
1 cup whipping cream

Heat oven to 400°. Mix flour, 2 tablespoons sugar, the salt and baking powder. Cut in margarine until mixture is crumbly. Pat mixture firmly in bottom and halfway up sides of ungreased square pan, 8x8x2 inches. Arrange peaches in pan. Mix ¼ cup plus 2 tablespoons sugar and the cinnamon; sprinkle over peaches. Bake 15 minutes.

Mix egg yolks and whipping cream; pour over peaches. Bake until custard is set and edges are light brown, 25 to 30 minutes. Serve warm. 9 SERVINGS.

*If using self-rising flour, omit salt and baking powder.

GINGERBREAD

2⅓ cups all-purpose flour*
⅓ cup sugar
1 cup molasses
¾ cup hot water
½ cup shortening
1 egg
1 teaspoon baking soda
1 teaspoon ground ginger
1 teaspoon ground cinnamon
¾ teaspoon salt

Heat oven to 325°. Grease and flour square pan, 9x9x2 inches. Beat all ingredients in large mixer bowl on low speed, scraping bowl constantly, 30 seconds. Beat on medium speed, scraping bowl occasionally, 3 minutes. Pour into pan.

Bake until wooden pick inserted in center comes out clean, about 50 minutes. Serve with Apricot-Cream Topping or Honey-Ginger Fluff (below) if desired.   9 SERVINGS.

*Do not use self-rising flour in this recipe.

APRICOT-CREAM TOPPING

Mix 1 cup apricot preserves or jelly, 1 tablespoon grated lemon peel and 2 tablespoons lemon juice. Cut warm gingerbread into squares; top with vanilla ice cream and sauce.

HONEY-GINGER FLUFF

Beat 2 cups chilled whipping cream, ¼ cup honey and ½ teaspoon ground ginger in chilled bowl until stiff. Refrigerate at least 1 hour before serving.

Whole Wheat Gingerbread: Substitute 1 cup whole wheat flour for 1 cup of the all-purpose flour. Decrease sugar to ¼ cup.

MICROWAVE REHEAT DIRECTIONS

	Room Temperature	Frozen
GINGERBREAD		
1 piece	15–20 seconds	30–35 seconds
2 pieces	25–30 seconds	50–55 seconds
4 pieces	80–85 seconds	90–95 seconds

HOT FUDGE SUNDAE CAKE

    1 cup all-purpose flour*
    ¾ cup granulated sugar
    2 tablespoons cocoa
    2 teaspoons baking powder
    ¼ teaspoon salt
    ½ cup milk
    2 tablespoons vegetable oil
    1 teaspoon vanilla
    1 cup chopped nuts (optional)
    1 cup packed brown sugar
    ¼ cup cocoa
    1¾ cups hottest tap water
      Ice cream

Heat oven to 350°. Mix flour, granulated sugar, 2 tablespoons cocoa, the baking powder and salt in ungreased square pan, 9x9x2 inches. Mix in milk, oil and vanilla with fork until smooth. Stir in nuts. Spread in pan. Sprinkle with brown sugar and ¼ cup cocoa. Pour hot water over batter.

Bake 40 minutes. While warm, spoon into dessert dishes and top with ice cream. Spoon sauce from pan onto each serving.   9 SERVINGS.

*If using self-rising flour, omit baking powder and salt.

Butterscotch Sundae Cake: Substitute 1 package (6 ounces) butterscotch chips (1 cup) for the nuts. Decrease brown sugar to ½ cup and the ¼ cup cocoa to 2 tablespoons.

Mallow Sundae Cake: Substitute 1 cup miniature marshmallows for the nuts.

Peanutty Sundae Cake: Substitute ½ cup peanut butter and ½ cup chopped peanuts for the nuts.

Raisin Sundae Cake: Substitute 1 cup raisins for the nuts.

ABOUT NUTS

Nuts are good vegetable sources of protein—so good that ½ cup of almonds, cashews or walnuts or ⅓ cup of peanuts can be used occasionally as a meat substitute. Look for shelled nuts that are plump and fairly uniform in color and size, not dark or shriveled. For attractive snacks, choose whole or half nuts. Broken pieces (less expensive), slivered and sliced nuts save time. Or chop nuts and freeze them in premeasured packets to save time later. Shelled nuts will keep fresh for several months if stored tightly covered in the refrigerator. Freezing or refrigerating unopened cans of nuts will keep them fresh for a longer time.

PLANTATION CAKE

    ⅔ cup shortening
    ½ cup packed brown sugar
    2 cups all-purpose flour*
    ¼ teaspoon salt
    ⅔ cup water
    ⅔ cup light molasses
    ¾ teaspoon baking soda
      Lemon Sauce (below)
      Cream Cheese Topping (below)

Heat oven to 350°. Beat shortening and brown sugar in small mixer bowl on high speed, scraping bowl occasionally, 5 minutes. Mix in flour and salt. Press half of the sugar mixture in greased square pan, 8x8x2 inches.

Mix water, molasses and baking soda; pour half over sugar mixture in pan. Sprinkle with half of the remaining sugar mixture. Pour remaining molasses mixture over top; sprinkle with remaining sugar mixture.

Bake 40 minutes. Serve warm with Lemon Sauce and Cream Cheese Topping.   9 SERVINGS.

*Do not use self-rising flour in this recipe.

LEMON SAUCE

    ½ cup sugar
    2 tablespoons cornstarch
    1 cup water
    2 tablespoons margarine or butter
    1 tablespoon grated lemon peel
    1 tablespoon lemon juice

Mix sugar and cornstarch in saucepan. Stir in water gradually. Cook over medium heat, stirring constantly, until mixture thickens and boils. Boil and stir 1 minute. Remove from heat; stir in remaining ingredients. Serve warm or cool.

■ **To Microwave:** Mix sugar and cornstarch in 1-quart glass measuring cup. Stir in remaining ingredients. Microwave uncovered, stirring every minute, 3½ minutes.

CREAM CHEESE TOPPING

Beat 2 packages (3 ounces each) cream cheese, softened, and 2 to 3 tablespoons milk until smooth and creamy.

Whole Wheat Plantation Cake: Substitute 1 cup whole wheat flour for 1 cup of the all-purpose flour.

LEMON PUDDING CAKE

2 eggs, separated
1 teaspoon grated lemon peel
¼ cup lemon juice
⅔ cup milk
1 cup sugar
¼ cup all-purpose flour*
¼ teaspoon salt

Heat oven to 350°. Beat egg whites until stiff peaks form. Beat egg yolks slightly. Beat in lemon peel, lemon juice and milk. Beat in remaining ingredients until smooth. Fold into beaten egg whites. Pour into ungreased 1-quart casserole. Place casserole in square pan, 9x9x2 inches, on oven rack; pour very hot water (1 inch deep) into pan.

Bake until golden brown, 45 to 50 minutes. Remove casserole from water. Serve warm or cool and, if desired, with whipped cream.   6 SERVINGS.

*If using self-rising flour, omit salt.

Lime Pudding Cake: Substitute 1½ teaspoons grated lime peel and ¼ cup lime juice for the lemon peel and lemon juice.

Saucy Pudding Cake: Increase milk to 1 cup.

CRANBERRY CAKE WITH GOLDEN SAUCE

2 cups all-purpose flour*
1¼ cups sugar
1 cup milk
2 tablespoons shortening
2 teaspoons baking powder
1 teaspoon vanilla
½ teaspoon salt
1 egg
2 cups cranberries
Golden Sauce (below)

Heat oven to 350°. Mix flour, sugar, milk, shortening, baking powder, vanilla, salt and egg; beat 30 seconds. Stir in cranberries. Pour into greased and floured square pan, 9x9x2 inches.

Bake until wooden pick inserted in center comes out clean, 40 to 45 minutes. Serve warm with Golden Sauce.   9 SERVINGS.

*If using self-rising flour, omit baking powder and salt.

GOLDEN SAUCE
Heat ½ cup sugar, ½ cup half-and-half, ½ cup margarine or butter and ½ teaspoon vanilla in 1-quart saucepan, stirring constantly, until margarine is melted.

DATE GEMS

1 cup all-purpose* or whole wheat flour
½ cup sugar
⅓ cup buttermilk
¼ cup shortening
1 egg
1 tablespoon grated orange peel
½ teaspoon baking soda
½ teaspoon baking powder
½ teaspoon salt
1 cup cut-up dates
¼ cup sugar
2 teaspoons cornstarch
¾ cup orange juice

Heat oven to 350°. Grease bottoms only of 10 medium muffin cups, 2½x1¼ inches. Beat flour, ½ cup sugar, the buttermilk, shortening, egg, orange peel, baking soda, baking powder, salt and dates in large mixer bowl on low speed, scraping bowl constantly, 30 seconds. Beat on high speed, scraping bowl occasionally, 2 minutes. Pour into muffin cups, filling each about ⅔ full. Bake until wooden pick inserted in center comes out clean, 25 to 30 minutes.

Mix ¼ cup sugar and the cornstarch in 1-quart saucepan. Stir in orange juice gradually. Cook over medium heat, stirring constantly, until mixture thickens and boils. Boil and stir 1 minute. Spoon sauce onto warm cupcakes.   10 CUPCAKES.

*If using self-rising flour, decrease baking soda to ¼ teaspoon and omit baking powder and salt.

MICROWAVE REHEAT DIRECTIONS

	Room Temperature	Frozen
PLANTATION CAKE		
1 square	15–20 seconds	35–40 seconds
2 squares	25–30 seconds	60–65 seconds
4 squares	50–55 seconds	85–90 seconds
CRANBERRY CAKE		
1 square	20–25 seconds	*
2 squares	30–35 seconds	*
4 squares	50–55 seconds	*
DATE GEMS		
1 cupcake	15–20 seconds	*
2 cupcakes	25–30 seconds	*
4 cupcakes	45–50 seconds	*

*Not recommended.

APPLE CRISP

4 cups sliced tart apples (about 4 medium)
⅔ to ¾ cup packed brown sugar
½ cup all-purpose flour*
½ cup oats
¾ teaspoon ground cinnamon
¾ teaspoon ground nutmeg
⅓ cup margarine or butter, softened

Heat oven to 375°. Arrange apples in greased square pan, 8x8x2 inches. Mix remaining ingredients; sprinkle over apples.

Bake until topping is golden brown and apples are tender, about 30 minutes. Serve warm and, if desired, with cream or ice cream.   6 SERVINGS.

*Self-rising flour can be used in this recipe.

■ **To Microwave:** Use ungreased 2-quart glass casserole or square glass baking dish, 8x8x2 inches. Microwave uncovered until apples are tender, about 12 minutes.

Apricot Crisp: Substitute 2 cans (16 ounces each) apricot halves, drained, for the apples and use the lesser amount of brown sugar.

Cherry Crisp: Substitute 1 can (21 ounces) cherry pie filling for the apples and use the lesser amount of brown sugar.

Peach Crisp: Substitute 1 can (29 ounces) sliced peaches, drained, for the apples and use the lesser amount of brown sugar.

Pineapple Crisp: Substitute 2 cans (13¼ ounces each) pineapple chunks, drained, or 2 cans (20 ounces each) crushed pineapple, drained, for the apples and use the lesser amount of brown sugar.

SELECTING APPLES

Choose apples that have a good color and feel firm. Store apples in the refrigerator to protect their crispness and tangy flavor. To keep pared apples from discoloring, sprinkle them with lemon juice or put them in water mixed with a little lemon juice.

There are many different apple varieties; each has its own distinctive texture, flavor and color. Good cooking apples include the Rome Beauty, Rhode Island Greening, Starr and Jersey Red varieties. Apples good for both eating and cooking include the Newtown Pippin, Golden Delicious, Cortland, Winesap and Northern Spy. Most of these varieties are widely available.

BLUEBERRY CRISP

3 cups blueberries or 1 package (16 ounces)
    frozen unsweetened blueberries
2 tablespoons lemon juice
⅔ cup packed brown sugar
½ cup all-purpose flour*
½ cup quick-cooking oats
⅓ cup margarine or butter, softened
¾ teaspoon ground cinnamon
¼ teaspoon salt
    Cream or ice cream

Heat oven to 375°. Arrange blueberries in ungreased square baking dish, 8x8x2 inches. Sprinkle with lemon juice. Mix brown sugar, flour, oats, margarine, cinnamon and salt; sprinkle on top.

Bake until topping is light brown and blueberries are hot, about 30 minutes. Serve warm with cream.   4 TO 6 SERVINGS.

*If using self-rising flour, omit salt.

■ **To Microwave:** Microwave uncovered in ungreased square glass baking dish, 8x8x2 inches, until blueberries are hot, 12 to 14 minutes.

RHUBARB CRISP

1½ pounds cut-up rhubarb (about 4 cups)
½ teaspoon salt
1⅓ to 2 cups sugar (depending on tartness of
    rhubarb)
¾ cup all-purpose flour*
1 teaspoon ground cinnamon
⅓ cup margarine or butter
    Sweetened Whipped Cream (page 244)

Heat oven to 350°. Arrange rhubarb in ungreased square baking dish, 8x8x2 inches; sprinkle with salt. Mix sugar, flour and cinnamon. Mix in margarine until mixture is crumbly; sprinkle over rhubarb.

Bake until topping is golden brown and rhubarb is tender, 40 to 50 minutes. Serve warm with Sweetened Whipped Cream.   6 SERVINGS.

*If using self-rising flour, omit salt.

■ **To Microwave:** Sprinkle crumb mixture over rhubarb in ungreased square glass baking dish, 8x8x2 inches. Sprinkle with ground cinnamon if desired. Microwave uncovered until rhubarb is tender, 12 to 14 minutes.

Granola Rhubarb Crisp: Mix in 1 cup granola with the sugar.

PEACH COBBLER

Two healthful basics—fruit and bread—are provided in each serving of this dessert.

½ cup sugar
1 tablespoon cornstarch
¼ teaspoon ground cinnamon
4 cups sliced peaches (about 6 medium)
1 teaspoon lemon juice
3 tablespoons shortening
1 cup all-purpose flour*
1 tablespoon sugar
1½ teaspoons baking powder
½ teaspoon salt
½ cup milk

Heat oven to 400°. Mix ½ cup sugar, the cornstarch and cinnamon in 2-quart saucepan. Stir in peaches and lemon juice. Cook, stirring constantly, until mixture thickens and boils. Boil and stir 1 minute. Pour into ungreased 2-quart casserole; keep peach mixture hot in oven.

Cut shortening into flour, 1 tablespoon sugar, the baking powder and salt until mixture resembles fine crumbs. Stir in milk. Drop dough by 6 spoonfuls onto hot peach mixture.

Bake until topping is golden brown, 25 to 30 minutes. Serve warm and, if desired, with Cinnamon Whipped Cream (page 245).   6 SERVINGS.

*If using self-rising flour, omit baking powder and salt.

Blueberry Cobbler: Omit cinnamon. Substitute 4 cups blueberries for the peaches.

Cherry Cobbler: Substitute 4 cups pitted red tart cherries for the peaches; increase sugar in cherry mixture to 1¼ cups, cornstarch to 3 tablespoons and substitute ¼ teaspoon almond extract for the lemon juice.

Plum Cobbler: Substitute 4 cups sliced plums (about 14 large) for the peaches; increase sugar in plum mixture to ¾ cup, cornstarch to 3 tablespoons and cinnamon to ½ teaspoon.

DATE PUDDING

    3 eggs
    1 cup sugar
    ¼ cup all-purpose flour*
    1 teaspoon baking powder
    ¼ teaspoon salt
    2½ cups cut-up dates
    1 cup chopped nuts
      Sweetened Whipped Cream (page 244)

Heat oven to 350°. Beat eggs until light and fluffy. Beat in sugar until mixture is thick. Stir in flour, baking powder and salt. Mix into egg-sugar mixture. Stir in dates and nuts. Spread in greased square pan, 9x9x2 inches. Bake 30 minutes. Cut into squares. Serve warm with Sweetened Whipped Cream.   9 TO 12 SERVINGS.

*If using self-rising flour, decrease baking powder to ½ teaspoon.

OZARK PUDDING

    ¾ cup sugar
    ⅓ cup all-purpose* or whole wheat flour
    1½ teaspoons baking powder
    ⅛ teaspoon salt
    1 egg
    1 teaspoon vanilla
    1 medium apple, finely chopped
    ½ cup chopped nuts

Heat oven to 350°. Beat sugar, flour, baking powder, salt, egg and vanilla in small mixer bowl on medium speed until smooth, about 1 minute. Stir in apple and nuts. Pour into greased 9-inch pie plate. Bake until golden brown, about 30 minutes. Cut into wedges. Serve warm.   6 SERVINGS.

*If using self-rising flour, decrease baking powder to 1 teaspoon and omit salt.

MICROWAVE REHEAT DIRECTIONS

	Room Temperature	Frozen
DATE PUDDING		
1 square	15–20 seconds	30–35 seconds
2 squares	25–30 seconds	50–55 seconds
4 squares	45–50 seconds	75–80 seconds
OZARK PUDDING		
1 wedge	15–20 seconds	30–35 seconds
2 wedges	25–30 seconds	50–55 seconds
4 wedges	45–50 seconds	75–80 seconds

BREAD PUDDING

    4 slices bread
    2 tablespoons margarine or butter,
      softened
    ⅓ cup packed brown sugar
    ½ teaspoon ground cinnamon
    ⅓ cup raisins
    3 eggs, slightly beaten
    ⅓ cup granulated sugar
    1 teaspoon vanilla
      Dash of salt
    2½ cups milk, scalded

Heat oven to 350°. Toast bread slices lightly. Spread slices with margarine; sprinkle with brown sugar and cinnamon. Cut each slice into 4 pieces. Arrange pieces sugared sides up in buttered 1½-quart casserole; sprinkle with raisins. Mix eggs, granulated sugar, vanilla and salt; slowly stir in milk. Pour over bread.

Place casserole in square pan, 9x9x2 inches, on oven rack; pour very hot water (1 inch deep) into pan. Bake until knife inserted halfway between center and edge comes out clean, 65 to 70 minutes. Remove casserole from hot water. Serve warm or cool.   6 TO 8 SERVINGS.

PINEAPPLE BREAD PUDDING

    ½ cup margarine or butter, softened
    1 cup sugar
    ½ teaspoon ground cinnamon
    4 eggs
    1 can (13¼ ounces) crushed pineapple,
      well drained
    2 cups ½-inch bread cubes (about 3 slices)
    ¼ cup chopped pecans

Heat oven to 325°. Beat margarine, sugar and cinnamon in large mixer bowl on medium speed, scraping bowl constantly, 1 minute. Add eggs; beat on high speed, scraping bowl occasionally, until mixture is light and fluffy, about 2 minutes. Fold in pineapple, bread cubes and pecans. Pour into buttered 1½-quart casserole.

Bake until knife inserted in center comes out clean, 40 to 45 minutes. Serve with Caramel Fluff (below) if desired.   4 TO 6 SERVINGS.

CARAMEL FLUFF

Beat 2 cups chilled whipping cream, ¾ cup packed brown sugar and 1 teaspoon vanilla in chilled bowl until stiff. Refrigerate at least 1 hour before serving; refrigerate any leftover fluff.

YAM PUDDING

3½ cups grated uncooked yams or sweet
    potatoes (about 2 pounds)
1¼ cups milk
½ cup light corn syrup
3 eggs, beaten
2 tablespoons margarine or butter, softened
½ cup packed brown sugar
1 teaspoon ground cinnamon
½ teaspoon salt
½ teaspoon ground nutmeg
   Cream or ice cream

Heat oven to 325°. Grease square baking dish, 8x8x2 inches. Mix all ingredients except cream; pour into dish. Bake until knife inserted halfway between center and edge comes out clean, about 1 hour. Serve with cream.　6 TO 8 SERVINGS.

STEAMED FIG PUDDING

1 cup boiling water
1 cup snipped dried figs
2 tablespoons shortening
1½ cups all-purpose flour*
1 cup sugar
1 teaspoon baking soda
1 teaspoon salt
1 cup chopped nuts
1 egg
   Creamy Sauce (below)

Pour boiling water on figs; stir in shortening. Mix flour, sugar, baking soda, salt and nuts in 2-quart bowl. Stir in fig mixture and egg. Pour into well-greased 6-cup mold. Cover tightly with aluminum foil. Place mold on rack in Dutch oven or steamer; pour boiling water into Dutch oven halfway up mold. Cover Dutch oven. Keep water boiling over low heat 2 hours.

Remove mold from Dutch oven and let stand 5 minutes; unmold. Serve warm with Creamy Sauce. 8 SERVINGS.

*Do not use self-rising flour in this recipe.

CREAMY SAUCE
Beat ¾ cup powdered sugar and ¾ cup margarine or butter, softened, in 1-quart saucepan until smooth and creamy. Stir in ¾ cup whipping cream. Heat to boiling, stirring occasionally.

Whole Wheat Steamed Fig Pudding: Substitute ¾ cup whole wheat flour for ¾ cup of the all-purpose flour.

MOLASSES DUFF

1 egg
2 tablespoons shortening
½ cup boiling water
½ cup molasses
2 tablespoons sugar
1⅓ cups all-purpose flour*
1 teaspoon baking soda
¼ teaspoon salt
   Hard Sauce (below) or Lemon Sauce
   (page 258)

Beat egg in small mixer bowl on high speed until very thick and lemon colored, about 5 minutes. Heat shortening in boiling water until melted. Beat shortening mixture, molasses, sugar, flour, baking soda and salt into egg on low speed. Pour into well-greased 4-cup mold. Cover tightly with aluminum foil.

Place mold on rack in Dutch oven or steamer; pour boiling water into Dutch oven halfway up mold. Cover Dutch oven. Keep water boiling over low heat until wooden pick inserted in center of pudding comes out clean, about 1½ hours.

Remove mold from Dutch oven and let stand 5 minutes; unmold. Serve warm with Hard Sauce. 6 SERVINGS.

*Do not use self-rising flour in this recipe.

HARD SAUCE
Beat ½ cup margarine or butter, softened, in small mixer bowl on high speed until very creamy, fluffy and light in color, about 5 minutes. Beat in 1 cup powdered sugar gradually. Stir in 2 teaspoons vanilla or 1 tablespoon brandy or sherry or 1 teaspoon grated orange peel and 1 tablespoon orange juice. Refrigerate about 1 hour.

Whole Wheat Molasses Duff: Substitute ¾ cup whole wheat flour for ¾ cup of the all-purpose flour.

FLAMING A STEAMED PUDDING
For a dramatic dinner finale, dim the lights and flame the steamed pudding. Heat ¼ cup brandy in a tiny long-handled pan; ignite with a long fireplace match and pour over the warm unmolded pudding. The alcohol burns off—but the flavor remains. Or soak sugar cubes—enough to surround the unmolded pudding—in lemon extract. The cubes needn't touch; light just one.

BAKED CUSTARD

Choose desserts that furnish important nutrients as well as good flavor. Custard, with milk and eggs, is a rich protein source.

　3　eggs, slightly beaten
　⅓　cup sugar
　　　Dash of salt
　1　teaspoon vanilla
　2½　cups milk, scalded
　　　Ground nutmeg

Heat oven to 350°. Mix eggs, sugar, salt and vanilla. Stir in milk gradually. Pour into six 6-ounce custard cups; sprinkle with nutmeg. Place cups in oblong pan, 13x9x2 inches, on oven rack. Pour very hot water into pan to within ½ inch of tops of cups.

Bake until knife inserted halfway between center and edge comes out clean, about 45 minutes. Remove cups from water. Serve warm or chilled.　6 SERVINGS.

Caramel Custard: Before preparing custard, heat ½ cup sugar in heavy 1-quart saucepan over low heat, stirring constantly, until sugar is melted and golden brown. Divide syrup among custard cups; tilt cups to coat bottoms. Allow syrup to harden in cups about 10 minutes. Pour custard mixture over syrup; bake. Unmold and serve warm or, if desired, refrigerate and unmold at serving time. Caramel syrup will run down sides of custard, forming a sauce.

Marshmallow Custard: Before preparing custard, place ¼ cup miniature marshmallows in each cup.

Place pan with filled custard cups on oven rack, then add very hot water to within ½ inch of tops of cups.

WHIPPED CREAM KNOW-HOW

Whipped cream is an important ingredient in many of our recipes—and, as a topping, dresses up just about any dessert. For success, remember these pointers: The cream you use should have at least 35% butterfat content. It should be thoroughly chilled, along with the bowl and beaters. Don't overbeat, or the whipped cream will separate. And remember that whipping causes cream to double in volume. For do-ahead instant toppings: Freeze whipped cream in small mounds, then package. Plop an individual mound on each dessert serving.

CREAMY VANILLA PUDDING

　⅓　cup sugar
　2　tablespoons cornstarch
　⅛　teaspoon salt
　2　cups milk
　2　egg yolks, slightly beaten
　2　tablespoons margarine or butter, softened
　2　teaspoons vanilla

Mix sugar, cornstarch and salt in 2-quart saucepan. Stir in milk gradually. Cook over medium heat, stirring constantly, until mixture thickens and boils. Boil and stir 1 minute. Stir at least half of the hot mixture gradually into egg yolks. Blend into hot mixture in saucepan. Boil and stir 1 minute. Remove from heat; stir in margarine and vanilla. Pour into dessert dishes. Cool slightly; refrigerate.　4 SERVINGS.

Butterscotch Pudding: Substitute ⅔ cup packed brown sugar for the granulated sugar and decrease vanilla to 1 teaspoon.

Chocolate Pudding: Increase sugar to ½ cup and stir ⅓ cup cocoa into sugar mixture. Omit margarine.

CHOCOLATE CREME

　1　bar (4 ounces) sweet cooking chocolate
　⅔　cup half-and-half
　2　tablespoons sugar
　2　egg yolks, slightly beaten
　½　teaspoon vanilla

Heat chocolate, half-and-half and sugar over medium heat, stirring constantly, until chocolate is melted and mixture simmers. Beat into egg yolks gradually. Stir in vanilla. Pour into demitasse cups or other small dessert dishes; refrigerate. Garnish with whipped cream if desired.　4 SERVINGS.

AMBROSIA TAPIOCA

½ cup sugar
¼ cup quick-cooking tapioca
Dash of salt
2½ cups orange juice
1 cup orange sections
¼ cup cut-up dates
¼ cup flaked coconut

Mix sugar, tapioca, salt and orange juice in 2-quart saucepan. Let stand 5 minutes. Heat to boiling over medium heat, stirring constantly.

Cool slightly. Stir in orange sections and dates. Refrigerate at least 1 hour. Spoon tapioca into dessert dishes; sprinkle with coconut.   6 SERVINGS.

BROWN RICE PUDDING

½ cup uncooked regular or quick-cooking
    brown rice
3 tablespoons honey
3 tablespoons margarine or butter
¼ teaspoon ground cinnamon
¾ cup milk
¼ cup raisins (optional)
    Cream
    Honey or brown sugar

Cook rice as directed on page 225. Stir in 3 tablespoons honey, the margarine, cinnamon, milk and raisins. Heat to boiling; reduce heat. Cook over low heat, stirring occasionally, until of desired consistency, 10 to 15 minutes. Serve warm with cream and honey.   3 OR 4 SERVINGS.

GLORIFIED RICE

1 cup cold cooked white or brown rice
    (page 225)
⅓ cup sugar
1 can (13¼ ounces) crushed pineapple,
    drained
½ teaspoon vanilla
⅓ cup miniature marshmallows
2 tablespoons drained chopped maraschino
    cherries
1 cup chilled whipping cream

Mix rice, sugar, pineapple and vanilla. Add marshmallows and cherries. Beat whipping cream in chilled bowl until stiff; fold into rice mixture. 6 TO 8 SERVINGS.

BAKED RICE PUDDING

½ cup uncooked regular rice
1 cup water
½ cup sugar
1 tablespoon cornstarch
    Dash of salt
2 eggs, separated
2½ cups milk
1 tablespoon lemon juice
½ cup raisins
¼ cup sugar

Mix rice and water in saucepan. Heat to boiling, stirring once or twice. Reduce heat; cover and simmer 14 minutes without removing cover. All water should be absorbed.

Heat oven to 350°. Mix ½ cup sugar, the cornstarch and salt. Beat egg yolks slightly. Beat egg yolks and milk into sugar mixture with hand beater. Stir in rice, lemon juice and raisins. Pour into ungreased 1½-quart casserole. Place casserole in square pan, 9x9x2 inches, on oven rack; pour very hot water (1 inch deep) into pan.

Bake, stirring occasionally, until pudding is creamy and most liquid is absorbed, about 1½ hours. Remove casserole from oven but not from pan of hot water.

Increase oven temperature to 400°. Beat egg whites on medium speed until foamy. Beat in ¼ cup sugar on high speed, 1 tablespoon at a time; continue beating until stiff and glossy. Do not underbeat. Spread over pudding. Bake until meringue is golden brown, 8 to 10 minutes. Serve warm.   6 TO 8 SERVINGS.

NOTE: Omit meringue if desired. Just before serving, sprinkle pudding with cinnamon or nutmeg.

TYPES OF RICE

Be sure the type of rice you use is the type specified in the recipe. Cooking times and the characteristics of the finished dish will vary. Short grain regular rice, often less expensive, is ideal for use in casseroles, puddings and creamy desserts. Long grain regular rice is most often used as a side dish, as is parboiled (converted) rice, which takes longer to cook. Instant (precooked) rice is quick cooking but does not retain as separate a grain. Brown rice has a nutty flavor and, except for its instant form, requires the most time to cook. For complete cooking directions for all rice types, see page 225.

COOKIES

ABOUT COOKIE MAKING

Cookies are classified by the way they're formed—drop, bar, molded, refrigerated, rolled, pressed. Many can be made with a direct substitution of whole wheat flour (noted in recipes). Drop cookies made with stone-ground whole wheat flour may spread more and have a coarser texture than cookies made with all-purpose flour.

Follow the recipe: Read through the recipe. Then heat the oven. Assemble and measure the ingredients (putting them all on a tray provides a built-in double check). Collect the utensils.

Use a good cookie sheet: For evenly browned cookies, choose shiny, bright cookie sheets at least 2 inches narrower and shorter than the oven. (Do not grease unless called for in the recipe.) Always place dough on a cool cookie sheet; dough spreads on a hot one. It saves time to work with 3 or 4 cookie sheets—you can fill and bake at the same time.

The "test" cookie: Bake one cookie. If it spreads more than desired, add 1 to 2 tablespoons of flour to the dough. If it's too dry, add 1 to 2 tablespoons of cream or milk. Liquid proportions are affected by egg size and dryness of flour. Flour stored in humid conditions will absorb less liquid.

Rolling and shaping: When rolling dough, use a pastry cloth and a stockinet-covered rolling pin. These will make the rolling easier and help prevent the dough from sticking. When shaping dough for molded, drop or refrigerator cookies, make each the same size and thickness to assure uniform baking.

Baking: For delicate brown cookies, place one cookie sheet at a time on the center oven rack. Check at the end of the minimum time—a minute can make a difference. Don't overbake. Unless otherwise directed, immediately remove cookies with wide spatula from sheet onto wire racks.

Storing: Store crisp, thin cookies in a container with a loose-fitting cover. If they soften, recrisp by placing in a 300° oven for 3 to 5 minutes. Store soft cookies in a tightly covered container. If changed frequently, a piece of bread or apple placed in the container helps keep the cookies soft.

Freezing baked cookies: Both frosted and unfrosted cookies can be frozen and stored from 2 to 12 months. Arrange baked cookies in a sturdy box lined with plastic wrap or aluminum foil; separate layers with wrap. Seal wrap. Close box, label and freeze. Thaw cookies by allowing them to stand uncovered on serving plate for about 20 minutes.

Freezing cookie dough: Package dough for drop cookies in an airtight container or wrap. Thaw until just soft enough to spoon onto sheet. Shape dough for refrigerator cookies in rolls; wrap and freeze. Thaw rolls just enough to slice easily.

CHOCOLATE CHIP COOKIES

½ cup granulated sugar
½ cup packed brown sugar
⅓ cup margarine or butter, softened
⅓ cup shortening
1 egg
1 teaspoon vanilla
1½ cups all-purpose* or whole wheat flour
½ teaspoon baking soda
½ teaspoon salt
½ cup chopped nuts
1 package (6 ounces) semisweet
    chocolate chips

Heat oven to 375°. Mix sugars, margarine, shortening, egg and vanilla. Stir in remaining ingredients.

Drop dough by rounded teaspoonfuls about 2 inches apart onto ungreased cookie sheet. Bake until light brown, 8 to 10 minutes. Cool slightly before removing from cookie sheet.   ABOUT 3½ DOZEN COOKIES.

*If using self-rising flour, omit baking soda and salt.

Peppermint Chocolate Chip Cookies: Stir in ⅓ cup crushed peppermint candy with the remaining ingredients.

Be sure to drop dough by rounded teaspoonfuls.

Pumpkin Cookies and Carrot-Coconut Cookies

PUMPKIN COOKIES

1 cup sugar
1 cup canned pumpkin
½ cup shortening
1 tablespoon grated orange peel
2 cups all-purpose* or whole wheat flour
1 teaspoon baking powder
1 teaspoon baking soda
1 teaspoon ground cinnamon
¼ teaspoon salt
½ cup raisins
½ cup chopped nuts
   Light Brown Glaze (page 268)

Heat oven to 375°. Mix sugar, pumpkin, shortening and orange peel. Stir in flour, baking powder, baking soda, cinnamon and salt. Stir in raisins and nuts.

Drop dough by teaspoonfuls onto ungreased cookie sheet. Bake until light brown, 8 to 10 minutes. Immediately remove from cookie sheet; cool. Spread with Light Brown Glaze.   ABOUT 4 DOZEN COOKIES.

*If using self-rising flour, omit baking powder, baking soda and salt.

Chocolate Chip-Pumpkin Cookies: Substitute ½ cup semisweet chocolate chips for the raisins.

CARROT-COCONUT COOKIES

The next time you make carrots for dinner, cook some extra for use in these cookies.

1 cup mashed cooked carrots (about
   4 medium)
¾ cup sugar
1 cup shortening (part margarine or butter,
   softened)
2 eggs
2 cups all-purpose* or whole wheat flour
2 teaspoons baking powder
½ teaspoon salt
¾ cup shredded or flaked coconut
½ recipe Orange Butter Frosting
   (page 251)

Heat oven to 400°. Mix carrots, sugar, shortening and eggs. Stir in flour, baking powder and salt. Stir in coconut.

Drop dough by teaspoonfuls about 2 inches apart onto ungreased cookie sheet. Bake until almost no indentation remains when touched, about 8 minutes.

Immediately remove from cookie sheet; cool. Frost with Orange Butter Frosting.   ABOUT 5 DOZEN COOKIES.

*If using self-rising flour, omit baking powder and salt.

CHOCOLATE DROP COOKIES

1 cup sugar
½ cup margarine or butter, softened
1 egg
2 ounces melted unsweetened chocolate
    (cool)
⅓ cup buttermilk or water
1 teaspoon vanilla
1¾ cups all-purpose* or whole wheat flour
½ teaspoon baking soda
½ teaspoon salt
1 cup chopped nuts (optional)
    Chocolate Frosting (below)

Heat oven to 400°. Mix sugar, margarine, egg, chocolate, buttermilk and vanilla. Stir in flour, baking soda, salt and nuts.

Drop dough by rounded teaspoonfuls about 2 inches apart onto ungreased cookie sheet. Bake until almost no indentation remains when touched, 8 to 10 minutes. Immediately remove from cookie sheet; cool. Frost with Chocolate Frosting.   ABOUT 4½ DOZEN COOKIES.

*If using self-rising flour, omit baking soda and salt.

CHOCOLATE FROSTING

2 squares (1 ounce each) unsweetened
    chocolate
2 tablespoons margarine or butter
3 tablespoons water
    About 2 cups powdered sugar

Heat chocolate and margarine over low heat until melted. Remove from heat; stir in water and powdered sugar.

Chocolate-Cherry Drop Cookies: Omit nuts. Stir in 2 cups cut-up candied or maraschino cherries. Use Chocolate Frosting.

Cocoa Drop Cookies: Increase margarine to ⅔ cup; omit chocolate and stir in ½ cup cocoa.

Double Chocolate Drops: Stir in 1 package (6 ounces) semisweet chocolate chips.

DROP COOKIES

If the cookie edges are dark and crusty, the cookies were overbaked or the sheet was too large for the oven. Overbaking results in a dry, hard cookie; underbaking, a doughy cookie. When excessive spreading occurs, either the dough was too warm or the cookie sheet was too hot.

BROWN SUGAR DROPS

1 cup packed brown sugar
½ cup shortening
¼ cup buttermilk or water
1 egg
1¾ cups all-purpose flour*
½ teaspoon baking soda
½ teaspoon salt
    Light Brown Glaze (below)

Mix brown sugar, shortening, buttermilk and egg. Stir in flour, baking soda and salt. Cover and refrigerate at least 1 hour.

Heat oven to 400°. Drop dough by rounded teaspoonfuls about 2 inches apart onto ungreased cookie sheet. Bake until almost no indentation remains when touched, 8 to 10 minutes. Immediately remove from cookie sheet; cool. Spread with Light Brown Glaze.   ABOUT 3 DOZEN COOKIES.

LIGHT BROWN GLAZE

¼ cup margarine or butter
2 cups powdered sugar
1 teaspoon vanilla
1 to 2 tablespoons milk

Heat margarine in 1½-quart saucepan over medium heat until delicate brown. Stir in powdered sugar and vanilla. Stir in milk until smooth.

*If using self-rising flour, omit baking soda and salt.

Applesauce Drops: Substitute ½ cup applesauce for the buttermilk. Stir in 1 cup raisins, 1 teaspoon ground cinnamon and ¼ teaspoon ground cloves with the flour.   ABOUT 4 DOZEN COOKIES.

Coconut Drops: Stir in ½ cup shredded coconut and ½ cup chopped nuts.

Chocolate Chip-Cherry Drops: Stir in ½ cup semisweet chocolate chips and ½ cup cut-up maraschino cherries.   ABOUT 4 DOZEN COOKIES.

Holiday Fruit Drops: Stir 1 cup candied cherries, cut into halves, 1 cup cut-up dates and ¾ cup broken pecans into dough. Place pecan half on each cookie. Omit glaze.   ABOUT 4 DOZEN COOKIES.

Jeweled Drops: Stir in 1½ to 2 cups cut-up gumdrops. Omit glaze.

Wheat Cereal Drops: Decrease flour to 1 cup. Stir in 1 cup oats, ½ cup whole wheat flake cereal and ½ cup coarsely chopped salted peanuts with the flour. Bake 12 to 14 minutes.

Whole Wheat Drops: Substitute whole wheat flour for the all-purpose flour. Do not refrigerate dough.

EASY FILLED COOKIES

Prepare Date-Nut Filling (below). Prepare double recipe of Brown Sugar Drops (page 268) except—stir in 1 teaspoon vanilla and ⅛ teaspoon ground cinnamon with the salt. Do not refrigerate dough.

Heat oven to 400°. Drop dough by teaspoonfuls about 2 inches apart onto ungreased cookie sheet. Place ½ teaspoon filling on each teaspoonful of dough and cover with ½ teaspoon dough. Bake until almost no indentation remains when touched, 10 to 12 minutes. Immediately remove from cookie sheet.   ABOUT 5½ DOZEN COOKIES.

DATE-NUT FILLING
  2 cups snipped dates
 ¾ cup sugar
 ¾ cup water
 ½ cup chopped nuts

Heat dates, sugar and water, stirring constantly, until mixture thickens. Stir in nuts; cool.

HERMITS
  1 cup packed brown sugar
 ¼ cup shortening
 ¼ cup margarine or butter, softened
 ¼ cup cold coffee
  1 egg
 ½ teaspoon baking soda
 ½ teaspoon salt
 ½ teaspoon ground cinnamon
 ½ teaspoon ground nutmeg
 1¾ cups all-purpose flour*
 1¼ cups raisins
 ¾ cup chopped nuts

Heat oven to 375°. Mix brown sugar, shortening, margarine, coffee, egg, baking soda, salt, cinnamon and nutmeg. Stir in remaining ingredients.

Drop dough by rounded teaspoonfuls about 2 inches apart onto ungreased cookie sheet. Bake until almost no indentation remains when touched, 8 to 10 minutes. Immediately remove from cookie sheet.   ABOUT 4 DOZEN COOKIES.

*If using self-rising flour, omit baking soda and salt.

Bran Hermits: Omit nuts. Stir in 1¼ cups whole bran cereal with the remaining ingredients.

Mincemeat Hermits: Stir in 1 cup mincemeat.

VERSATILE COOKIE MIX
  4 cups all-purpose* or whole wheat flour
 1¼ cups granulated sugar
 1¼ cups packed brown sugar
  3 teaspoons baking powder
 1½ teaspoons salt
 1½ cups shortening

Mix flour, sugars, baking powder and salt. Cut in shortening until mixture resembles fine crumbs.

Place desired amounts of mix in containers. Seal tightly, label and refrigerate no longer than 10 weeks.   9 TO 10 CUPS COOKIE MIX.

*If using self-rising flour, omit baking powder and salt.

BANANA COOKIES
 2½ cups cookie mix
 ½ cup mashed banana (about 1 small)
  1 teaspoon vanilla
  1 egg
 ½ cup chopped nuts

Heat oven to 375°. Mix all ingredients. Drop dough by rounded teaspoonfuls about 2 inches apart onto ungreased cookie sheet. Bake until light brown, 12 to 15 minutes. Immediately remove from cookie sheet.   ABOUT 3 DOZEN COOKIES.

PEANUT BUTTER COOKIES
  2 cups cookie mix
 ½ cup crunchy peanut butter
  1 egg
  1 teaspoon vanilla

Heat oven to 375°. Mix all ingredients. Shape dough by teaspoonfuls into balls. Place about 2 inches apart on ungreased cookie sheet; flatten in crisscross pattern with fork dipped in flour. Bake until light brown, 10 to 12 minutes. Immediately remove from cookie sheet; cool.   ABOUT 2 DOZEN COOKIES.

SPICE COOKIES
 2½ cups cookie mix
  1 egg
 ½ teaspoon ground cinnamon
 ½ teaspoon lemon extract
 ½ cup raisins
 ½ cup chopped nuts

Heat oven to 375°. Mix all ingredients. Drop dough by rounded teaspoonfuls about 2 inches apart onto ungreased cookie sheet. Bake until light brown, 12 to 15 minutes. Immediately remove from cookie sheet.   ABOUT 2½ DOZEN COOKIES.

GINGER CREAMS

½ cup sugar
½ cup water
½ cup molasses
⅓ cup shortening
1 egg
2 cups all-purpose* or whole wheat flour
1 teaspoon ground ginger
½ teaspoon salt
½ teaspoon baking soda
½ teaspoon ground nutmeg
½ teaspoon ground cloves
½ teaspoon ground cinnamon

Mix sugar, water, molasses, shortening and egg. Stir in remaining ingredients. Cover; refrigerate 1 hour.

Heat oven to 400°. Drop dough by teaspoonfuls 2 inches apart onto ungreased cookie sheet. Bake until almost no indentation remains when touched, about 8 minutes. Immediately remove from cookie sheet; cool.   ABOUT 4 DOZEN COOKIES.

*If using self-rising flour, omit salt and baking soda.

OATMEAL-WHEAT COOKIES

½ cup granulated sugar
½ cup packed brown sugar
½ cup shortening
1 egg
½ teaspoon vanilla
1 cup all-purpose flour*
½ teaspoon baking soda
¼ teaspoon baking powder
¼ teaspoon salt
1 cup quick-cooking oats
1 cup whole wheat flake cereal
½ cup shredded coconut

Heat oven to 375°. Mix sugars, shortening, egg and vanilla. Stir in remaining ingredients (dough will be stiff). Drop dough by rounded teaspoonfuls 2 inches apart onto ungreased cookie sheet. Bake until set but not hard, 9 to 11 minutes. Cool about 3 minutes before removing from cookie sheet.
ABOUT 3 DOZEN COOKIES.

*If using self-rising flour, omit baking soda, baking powder and salt.

Cereal Cookies: Omit oats and increase whole wheat flake cereal to 2 cups.

Whole Wheat-Oatmeal Cookies: Mix in 2 tablespoons milk with the vanilla and substitute whole wheat flour for the all-purpose flour.

COCONUT MERINGUE BARS

2 cups all-purpose flour*
½ cup granulated sugar
½ cup packed brown sugar
¾ cup margarine or butter, softened
1 teaspoon baking powder
3 eggs, separated
1 teaspoon vanilla
¼ teaspoon baking soda
¼ teaspoon salt
1 package (6 ounces) semisweet chocolate chips
1 cup flaked coconut
¾ cup coarsely chopped nuts
1 cup packed brown sugar

Heat oven to 350°. Beat flour, granulated sugar, ½ cup brown sugar, the margarine, baking powder, egg yolks, vanilla, baking soda and salt on medium speed, scraping bowl occasionally, 2 minutes. Press in greased oblong pan, 13x9x2 inches; sprinkle with chocolate chips, coconut and nuts.

Beat egg whites until foamy. Beat in 1 cup brown sugar, 1 tablespoon at a time; continue beating until stiff and glossy. Spread over mixture in pan. Bake 35 to 40 minutes. Cool; cut into bars, about 3x1 inch.   32 COOKIES.

*If using self-rising flour, omit baking powder, baking soda and salt.

Chocolate Meringue Bars: Increase chocolate chips to 2 packages and omit coconut.

LEMON SQUARES

1 cup all-purpose flour*
½ cup margarine or butter, softened
¼ cup powdered sugar
2 eggs
1 cup granulated sugar
½ teaspoon baking powder
¼ teaspoon salt
2 teaspoons grated lemon peel (optional)
2 tablespoons lemon juice

Heat oven to 350°. Mix flour, margarine and powdered sugar. Press in ungreased square pan, 8x8x2 or 9x9x2 inches, building up ½-inch edges. Bake 20 minutes. Beat remaining ingredients until light and fluffy, about 3 minutes. Pour over hot crust. Bake until no indentation remains when touched lightly in center, about 25 minutes. Cool; cut into about 1½-inch squares.   25 COOKIES.

*If using self-rising flour, omit baking powder and salt.

MIXED NUT SQUARES

  2 cups all-purpose* or whole wheat flour
  1 cup packed brown sugar
  1 cup margarine or butter, softened
  1 teaspoon vanilla
  ¼ teaspoon salt
  1 egg yolk
  1 package (6 ounces) butterscotch chips
  ½ cup light corn syrup
  2 tablespoons margarine or butter
  1 tablespoon water
  1 can (13 ounces) salted mixed nuts

Heat oven to 350°. Mix flour, brown sugar, 1 cup margarine, the vanilla, salt and egg yolk. Press in ungreased oblong pan, 13x9x2 inches. Bake until light brown, about 25 minutes; cool.

Mix butterscotch chips, corn syrup, 2 tablespoons margarine and the water in saucepan. Cook over medium heat, stirring occasionally, until butterscotch chips are melted; cool. Spread over cooled base in pan. Sprinkle nuts on top; press gently into topping. Refrigerate until topping is firm, about 1 hour. Cut into about 1½-inch squares.   4 DOZEN COOKIES.

*Do not use self-rising flour in this recipe.

BUTTERSCOTCH BROWNIES

  ¼ cup shortening
  1 cup packed brown sugar
  1 egg
  1 teaspoon vanilla
  ¾ cup all-purpose* or whole wheat flour
  1 teaspoon baking powder
  ½ teaspoon salt
  ½ cup chopped nuts

Heat oven to 350°. Heat shortening over low heat until melted; remove from heat. Mix in brown sugar, egg and vanilla. Stir in remaining ingredients. Spread in greased square pan, 8x8x2 inches. Bake 25 minutes. Cut into about 2-inch squares while warm.   16 COOKIES.

*If using self-rising flour, omit baking powder and salt.

Brazil Nut Bars: Substitute ¾ cup ground Brazil nuts for the nuts.

Butterscotch-Date Brownies: Decrease vanilla to ½ teaspoon; stir in ½ cup snipped dates with the remaining ingredients.

Coconut-Butterscotch Brownies: Decrease vanilla to ½ teaspoon. Substitute cookie coconut for nuts.

BROWNIES

  2 squares (1 ounce each) unsweetened
      chocolate
  ⅓ cup shortening
  1 cup sugar
  2 eggs
  ½ teaspoon vanilla
  ¾ cup all-purpose* or whole wheat flour
  ½ teaspoon baking powder
  ½ teaspoon salt
  ½ cup chopped nuts

Heat oven to 350°. Heat chocolate and shortening in 2-quart saucepan over low heat, stirring constantly, until melted; remove from heat. Mix in sugar, eggs and vanilla. Stir in remaining ingredients. Spread in greased pan, 8x8x2 inches.

Bake until brownies begin to pull away from sides of pan, 30 to 35 minutes. Cool slightly. Frost with ½ recipe Glossy Chocolate Frosting (page 251) if desired. Cut into about 2-inch squares.
16 COOKIES.

*If using self-rising flour, omit baking powder and salt.

Fudgy Brownies: Substitute ½ cup margarine or butter for the shortening. Increase vanilla to 1 teaspoon. Decrease flour to ½ cup and salt to ¼ teaspoon. Omit baking powder. Spread in greased square pan, 9x9x2 inches, or oblong baking dish, 12x7½x2 inches. Bake 20 to 25 minutes.

Peanut Butter Brownies: Decrease the shortening to 2 tablespoons and omit the nuts. Stir in 2 tablespoons peanut butter and ¼ cup chopped peanuts with the flour.

Brownies

Coconut Chews

COCONUT CHEWS

- ¾ cup powdered sugar
- ¾ cup shortening (half margarine or butter, softened)
- 1½ cups all-purpose* or whole wheat flour
- 2 eggs
- 1 cup packed brown sugar
- 2 tablespoons flour
- ½ teaspoon baking powder
- ½ teaspoon salt
- ½ teaspoon vanilla
- ½ cup chopped walnuts
- ½ cup flaked coconut

Heat oven to 350°. Mix powdered sugar and shortening. Stir in 1½ cups flour. Press in ungreased oblong pan, 13x9x2 inches. Bake until golden brown, 12 to 15 minutes.

Mix remaining ingredients. Spread over baked layer. Bake 20 minutes; cool. Frost with Orange-Lemon Frosting (below) if desired. Cut into bars, about 3x1 inch.   32 COOKIES.

*Self-rising flour can be used in this recipe.

ORANGE-LEMON FROSTING
Mix 1½ cups powdered sugar, 2 tablespoons margarine or butter, melted, 3 tablespoons orange juice and 1 teaspoon lemon juice.

Pecan Chews: Substitute 1 cup chopped pecans for the walnuts and coconut.

DATE BARS

- Date Filling (below)
- 1 cup packed brown sugar
- ½ cup margarine or butter, softened
- ¼ cup shortening
- 1¾ cups all-purpose* or whole wheat flour
- 1 teaspoon salt
- ½ teaspoon baking soda
- 1½ cups quick-cooking oats

Prepare Date Filling. Heat oven to 400°. Mix brown sugar, margarine and shortening. Mix in remaining ingredients. Press half of the mixture in greased oblong pan, 13x9x2 inches; spread with filling. Top with remaining crumbly mixture, pressing lightly.

Bake until light brown, 25 to 30 minutes. Cut into bars, about 2x1½ inches, while warm.   3 DOZEN COOKIES.

*If using self-rising flour, omit salt and baking soda.

DATE FILLING
Heat 1 pound dates, cut up (about 3 cups), 1½ cups water and ¼ cup sugar over low heat, stirring constantly, until thickened, about 10 minutes; cool.

Jam Bars: Substitute 1 cup jam for the Date Filling.

TOFFEE BARS

- 1 cup packed brown sugar
- 1 cup margarine or butter, softened
- 1 egg yolk
- 1 teaspoon vanilla
- 2 cups all-purpose* or whole wheat flour
- ¼ teaspoon salt
- 1 bar (4 ounces) milk chocolate candy
- ½ cup chopped nuts

Heat oven to 350°. Mix brown sugar, margarine, egg yolk and vanilla. Stir in flour and salt. Press in greased oblong pan, 13x9x2 inches.

Bake until very light brown, 25 to 30 minutes (crust will be soft). Remove from oven; immediately place separated pieces of chocolate candy on crust. Let stand until soft; spread evenly. Sprinkle with nuts. Cut into bars, about 2x1½ inches, while warm. 32 COOKIES.

*If using self-rising flour, omit salt.

Spicy Bars: Stir in 1 teaspoon ground ginger with the salt. Omit chocolate and substitute ¼ cup chopped salted nuts and ¼ cup flaked coconut for the nuts.

THUMBPRINT COOKIES

¼ cup packed brown sugar
¼ cup shortening
¼ cup margarine or butter, softened
1 egg, separated
½ teaspoon vanilla
1 cup all-purpose* or whole wheat flour
¼ teaspoon salt
¾ cup finely chopped nuts
  Jelly

Heat oven to 350°. Mix brown sugar, shortening, margarine, egg yolk and vanilla. Mix in flour and salt until dough holds together. Shape dough into 1-inch balls.

Beat egg white slightly. Dip each ball into egg white; roll in nuts. Place about 1 inch apart on ungreased cookie sheet; press thumb deeply in center of each. Bake until light brown, 8 to 9 minutes.

Immediately remove from cookie sheet; cool. Fill thumbprints with jelly.   ABOUT 3 DOZEN COOKIES.

*If using self-rising flour, omit salt.

RUSSIAN TEACAKES

1 cup margarine or butter, softened
½ cup powdered sugar
1 teaspoon vanilla
2¼ cups all-purpose* or whole wheat
    flour
¼ teaspoon salt
¾ cup finely chopped nuts
  Powdered sugar

Heat oven to 400°. Mix margarine, ½ cup powdered sugar and the vanilla. Mix in flour, salt and nuts until dough holds together.

Shape dough into 1-inch balls. Place about 1 inch apart on ungreased cookie sheet. Bake until set but not brown, 10 to 12 minutes.

Roll in powdered sugar while warm; cool. Roll in powdered sugar again.   ABOUT 4 DOZEN COOKIES.

*Do not use self-rising flour in this recipe.

Ambrosia Balls: Omit nuts. Mix in 1 cup flaked coconut and 1 tablespoon grated orange peel.

Surprise Candy Teacakes: Decrease nuts to ½ cup. Cut 12 vanilla caramels into 4 pieces each or cut 1 bar (4 ounces) sweet cooking chocolate into ½-inch squares. Mold portions of dough around pieces of caramels or chocolate to form 1-inch balls.

PEANUT BUTTER COOKIES

½ cup granulated sugar
½ cup packed brown sugar
½ cup shortening
½ cup peanut butter
1 egg
1¼ cups all-purpose* or whole wheat flour
¾ teaspoon baking soda
½ teaspoon baking powder
¼ teaspoon salt
  Jelly or jam

Mix sugars, shortening, peanut butter and egg. Stir in flour, baking soda, baking powder and salt. Cover and refrigerate at least 3 hours.

Heat oven to 375°. Shape dough into ¾-inch balls. Place 2 inches apart on ungreased cookie sheet. Bake until set but not hard, about 10 minutes.

Cool slightly before removing from cookie sheet; cool completely. Put cookies together in pairs with jelly.   ABOUT 4½ DOZEN SANDWICH COOKIES.

*If using self-rising flour, omit baking soda, baking powder and salt.

Crisscross Peanut Butter Cookies: Shape dough into 1¼ inch balls. Place about 3 inches apart on ungreased cookie sheet. Flatten in crisscross pattern with fork dipped in flour. Bake 10 to 12 minutes.   ABOUT 3 DOZEN COOKIES.

Peanut Butter Thumbprints: Shape dough into 1-inch balls. Roll balls in ½ cup finely chopped peanuts. Place about 3 inches apart on ungreased cookie sheet; press thumb deeply in center of each. Bake 10 to 12 minutes. Fill thumbprints with jelly.   ABOUT 3½ DOZEN COOKIES.

Peanut Butter Cookies

VANILLA CRISPIES

1 cup sugar
1 cup margarine or butter, softened
1 egg
2 teaspoons vanilla
2 cups all-purpose* or whole wheat flour
½ teaspoon baking soda
½ teaspoon cream of tartar

Mix sugar, margarine, egg and vanilla. Stir in remaining ingredients. Cover and refrigerate at least 1 hour.

Heat oven to 375°. Shape dough into 1-inch balls. Place about 2 inches apart on ungreased cookie sheet. Flatten with bottom of glass dipped in sugar. Bake until light brown, 8 to 10 minutes. Immediately remove from cookie sheet. ABOUT 6 DOZEN COOKIES.

*If using self-rising flour, omit baking soda and cream of tartar.

Brown Sugar Crispies: Substitute ½ cup packed brown sugar for ½ cup of the granulated sugar.

MOLASSES CRINKLES

1 cup packed brown sugar
¾ cup shortening
¼ cup molasses
1 egg
2¼ cups all-purpose flour*
2 teaspoons baking soda
1 teaspoon ground cinnamon
1 teaspoon ground ginger
½ teaspoon ground cloves
¼ teaspoon salt
Granulated sugar

Mix brown sugar, shortening, molasses and egg. Mix in flour, baking soda, cinnamon, ginger, cloves and salt. Cover and refrigerate at least 1 hour.

Heat oven to 375°. Shape dough by rounded teaspoonfuls into balls. Dip tops in granulated sugar. Place balls sugared sides up about 3 inches apart on lightly greased cookie sheet. Bake just until set, 10 to 12 minutes. Immediately remove from cookie sheet. ABOUT 4 DOZEN COOKIES.

*If using self-rising flour, decrease baking soda to 1 teaspoon and omit salt.

Whole Wheat Molasses Crinkles: Mix in 2 tablespoons milk with the egg and substitute whole wheat flour for the all-purpose flour.

FARM-STYLE OATMEAL COOKIES

2 cups packed brown sugar
1 cup lard or shortening
½ cup buttermilk
1 teaspoon vanilla
4 cups quick-cooking oats
1¾ cups all-purpose* or whole wheat flour
1 teaspoon baking soda
¾ teaspoon salt

Heat oven to 375°. Mix brown sugar, lard, buttermilk and vanilla. Stir in remaining ingredients.

Shape dough into 1-inch balls. Place about 3 inches apart on ungreased cookie sheet. Flatten cookies with bottom of glass dipped in water. Bake until golden brown, 8 to 10 minutes. Immediately remove from cookie sheet. ABOUT 7 DOZEN COOKIES.

*If using self-rising flour, omit baking soda and salt.

VANILLA REFRIGERATOR COOKIES

1 cup sugar
1 cup margarine or butter, softened
1½ teaspoons vanilla
2 eggs
3 cups all-purpose* or whole wheat flour
1 teaspoon salt
½ teaspoon baking soda

Mix sugar, margarine, vanilla and eggs. Mix in remaining ingredients. Divide dough into 3 equal parts. Shape each part into roll 1½ inches in diameter and about 7 inches long. Wrap; refrigerate at least 4 hours but no longer than 6 weeks.

Heat oven to 400°. Cut rolls into ⅛-inch slices. Place about 1 inch apart on ungreased cookie sheet. Bake until set, 8 to 10 minutes. Immediately remove from cookie sheet. ABOUT 7 DOZEN COOKIES.

*If using self-rising flour, omit salt.

Cookie Tarts: Spoon 1 teaspoon jelly or preserves onto half of the slices; top with remaining slices. Seal edges. Cut slits in tops so filling shows. ABOUT 3½ DOZEN SANDWICH COOKIES.

Crunchy Peanut Cookies: Substitute ½ cup crunchy peanut butter for ½ cup of the margarine and packed brown sugar for the granulated sugar.

Nut Cookies: Mix in ½ cup chopped blanched almonds or black walnuts with the flour.

Orange-Almond Cookies: Mix in 1 tablespoon grated orange peel with the margarine and ½ cup chopped blanched almonds with the flour.

Cut chilled dough for Pinwheels into ⅛-inch slices.

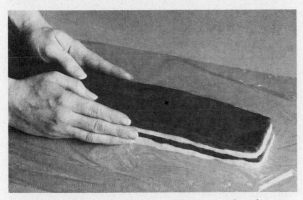

For Ribbon Bar Cookies, press and even up dough strips.

CHOCOLATE REFRIGERATOR COOKIES

1½ cups powdered sugar
1¼ cups margarine or butter, softened
 1 egg
 3 cups all-purpose* or cake flour
½ cup cocoa
¼ teaspoon salt
1½ cups finely chopped pecans
    Fudge Frosting (right)

Mix powdered sugar, margarine and egg. Mix in flour, cocoa and salt. Cover and refrigerate at least 1 hour but no longer than 6 weeks.

Divide dough into halves; shape each half into roll 1½ inches in diameter. Roll in pecans. Wrap and refrigerate at least 8 hours.

Heat oven to 400°. Cut rolls into ⅛-inch slices. (If dough crumbles while cutting, let warm slightly.) Place about 1 inch apart on ungreased cookie sheet. Bake until set, about 8 minutes.

Immediately remove from cookie sheet; cool. Frost with Fudge Frosting.   ABOUT 8 DOZEN COOKIES.

*Do not use self-rising flour in this recipe.

FUDGE FROSTING

 1 cup sugar
⅓ cup milk
¼ cup shortening
 2 squares (1 ounce each) unsweetened
    chocolate
¼ teaspoon salt
 1 teaspoon vanilla

Heat sugar, milk, shortening, chocolate and salt to rolling boil, stirring occasionally. Boil, without stirring, 1 minute. Place saucepan in bowl of ice and water; beat until frosting is thick. Stir in vanilla.

Pinwheels: Omit ½ cup cocoa and the pecans. After dough is mixed, divide into halves. Stir ¼ cup cocoa into one half. Refrigerate at least 1 hour. Roll plain dough into rectangle, 16x9 inches, on lightly floured board. Roll chocolate dough same size; place on plain dough. Roll doughs ³⁄₁₆ inch thick. Roll up tightly, beginning at wide side. Wrap, refrigerate, slice and bake as directed. Do not frost.

Ribbon Bar Cookies: Omit ½ cup cocoa. After dough is mixed, divide into halves. Stir ¼ cup cocoa into one half. Refrigerate at least 1 hour. Shape each half into 2 strips, each 2½ inches wide and 16 inches long, on very lightly floured board. Layer strips, alternating colors. Press together. Wrap, refrigerate, slice and bake as directed. Do not frost.
ABOUT 5½ DOZEN COOKIES.

CANDIED FRUIT COOKIES

 1 cup powdered sugar
 1 cup margarine or butter, softened
 1 egg
2¼ cups all-purpose flour*
¼ teaspoon cream of tartar
½ cup chopped pecans
½ cup chopped mixed candied fruit
 1 cup candied whole cherries

Mix powdered sugar, margarine and egg. Mix in remaining ingredients. Divide dough into halves; shape each half into roll 1½ inches in diameter. Wrap and refrigerate at least 4 hours.

Heat oven to 375°. Cut rolls into ⅛-inch slices. Place about 1 inch apart on ungreased cookie sheet. Bake until set, about 8 minutes. Immediately remove from cookie sheet.   6 DOZEN COOKIES.

*Self-rising flour can be used in this recipe.

Do-ahead Tip: After shaping into rolls, dough can be refrigerated or frozen no longer than 6 weeks. Unwrap and thaw frozen dough before slicing.

SUGAR COOKIES

1½ cups powdered sugar
 1 cup margarine or butter, softened
 1 egg
 1 teaspoon vanilla
 ½ teaspoon almond extract
2½ cups all-purpose* or whole wheat flour
 1 teaspoon baking soda
 1 teaspoon cream of tartar
   Granulated sugar

Mix powdered sugar, margarine, egg, vanilla and almond extract. Mix in flour, baking soda and cream of tartar. Cover and refrigerate at least 2 hours. Heat oven to 375°. Divide dough into halves. Roll each half ³⁄₁₆ inch thick on lightly floured cloth-covered board. Cut into shapes.

Sprinkle with granulated sugar; place on lightly greased sheet. Bake until edges are light brown, 7 to 8 minutes.   ABOUT 5 DOZEN 2-INCH COOKIES.

*If using self-rising flour, omit baking soda and cream of tartar.

JUMBO MOLASSES COOKIES

 1 cup sugar
 ½ cup shortening
 1 cup dark molasses
 ½ cup water
 4 cups all-purpose* or whole wheat flour
1½ teaspoons salt
 1 teaspoon baking soda
1½ teaspoons ground ginger
 ½ teaspoon ground cloves
 ½ teaspoon ground nutmeg
 ¼ teaspoon ground allspice
   Sugar

Mix 1 cup sugar and the shortening. Mix in remaining ingredients except sugar. Cover and refrigerate at least 2 hours. (It is not necessary to refrigerate whole wheat dough.)

Heat oven to 375°. Roll dough ¼ inch thick on well-floured cloth-covered board; cut into 3-inch circles. Sprinkle with sugar; place about 1½ inches apart on ungreased sheet. Bake until almost no indentation remains when touched, 10 to 12 minutes. Cool 2 minutes before removing from sheet; cool on wire rack.   ABOUT 3 DOZEN COOKIES.

*If using self-rising flour, omit salt and baking soda.

Ice-cream Sandwiches: Cut round bulk ice cream into slices; place each slice between 2 cookies. Freeze at least 1 hour.

CRISP GINGER COOKIES

 ⅓ cup molasses
 ¼ cup shortening
 2 tablespoons packed brown sugar
1¼ cups all-purpose* or whole wheat flour
 ½ teaspoon salt
 ¼ teaspoon baking soda
 ¼ teaspoon baking powder
 ¼ teaspoon ground cinnamon
 ¼ teaspoon ground ginger
 ¼ teaspoon ground cloves
   Dash of ground nutmeg
   Dash of ground allspice
   Easy Creamy Frosting (below)

Mix molasses, shortening and brown sugar. Mix in remaining ingredients except frosting. Cover and refrigerate at least 4 hours.

Heat oven to 375°. Roll dough ⅛ inch thick or paper thin on floured cloth-covered board. Cut with floured 3-inch cutter. Place about ½ inch apart on ungreased cookie sheet. Bake until light brown, ⅛-inch-thick cookies about 8 minutes, paper-thin cookies about 5 minutes.

Immediately remove from cookie sheet; cool. Frost with Easy Creamy Frosting.   ABOUT 1½ DOZEN ⅛-INCH-THICK COOKIES, ABOUT 3 DOZEN PAPER-THIN COOKIES.

*If using self-rising flour, omit salt, baking soda and baking powder.

EASY CREAMY FROSTING

 1 cup powdered sugar
 ½ teaspoon vanilla
 ¼ teaspoon salt
 1 to 2 tablespoons half-and-half

Mix powdered sugar, vanilla and salt. Stir in half-and-half until frosting is smooth and of spreading consistency.

ROLLED COOKIES

Here are a few helpful tips: To prevent dough from sticking, rub flour into stockinet on rolling pin and lightly into pastry cloth. If you're handling chilled dough, roll only part of it at a time; keep the remainder chilled. Roll lightly and evenly to ensure that cookies bake evenly. (The thinner you roll, the crisper the cookies.) Dip cookie cutter into flour. Shake off excess, then cut dough. (Cut cookies close together.) To maintain shapes, lift cookies to cookie sheet with a spatula.

Gingerbread People

GINGERBREAD PEOPLE

1½ cups dark molasses
  1 cup packed brown sugar
  ⅔ cup cold water
  ⅓ cup shortening
  7 cups all-purpose flour*
  2 teaspoons baking soda
  1 teaspoon salt
  1 teaspoon ground allspice
  2 teaspoons ground ginger
  1 teaspoon ground cloves
  1 teaspoon ground cinnamon
    Decorators' Frosting (page 253)

Mix molasses, brown sugar, water and shortening. Mix in remaining ingredients except frosting. Cover and refrigerate at least 2 hours.

Heat oven to 350°. Roll dough ¼ inch thick on floured board. Cut with floured gingerbread cutter or other favorite shaped cutter. Place about 2 inches apart on lightly greased cookie sheet. Bake until no indentation remains when touched, 10 to 12 minutes; cool. Decorate with Decorators' Frosting. ABOUT 2½ DOZEN 2½-INCH COOKIES.

*If using self-rising flour, omit baking soda and salt.

Gingerbread Cookies: Decrease flour to 6 cups. Roll dough ½ inch thick and cut with floured 2½-inch round cutter. Place about 1½ inches apart on lightly greased cookie sheet. Bake about 15 minutes.

SCOTCH SHORTBREAD

Heat oven to 350°. Mix ¾ cup margarine or butter, softened, and ¼ cup sugar. Mix in 2 cups all-purpose flour.* (If dough is crumbly, mix in 1 to 2 tablespoons margarine or butter, softened.)

Roll dough about ½ inch thick on lightly floured cloth-covered board. Cut into small shapes (leaves, ovals, squares, triangles, etc.). Place about ½ inch apart on ungreased cookie sheet. Bake until set, about 20 minutes. Immediately remove from cookie sheet.   ABOUT 2 DOZEN 1½x1-INCH COOKIES.

*Do not use self-rising flour in this recipe.

SPRITZ

1 cup margarine or butter, softened
½ cup sugar
2¼ cups all-purpose flour*
½ teaspoon salt
1 egg
1 teaspoon almond extract or vanilla

Heat oven to 400°. Mix margarine and sugar. Mix in remaining ingredients.

Place dough in cookie press; form desired shapes on ungreased cookie sheet. Bake until set but not brown, 6 to 9 minutes. Immediately remove from cookie sheet.   ABOUT 5 DOZEN COOKIES.

*Do not use self-rising flour in this recipe.

Bow Tie Cookies: Stir 2 ounces melted unsweetened chocolate (cool) into margarine mixture. Place dough in cookie press with star plate; form 2½-inch bow ties on ungreased cookie sheet. Place cinnamon candy in center. Bake 9 to 10 minutes. ABOUT 3 DOZEN COOKIES.

Chocolate Spritz: Stir 2 ounces melted unsweetened chocolate (cool) into margarine mixture.

Christmas Decorated Spritz: Before baking, top cookies with currants, raisins, candies, nuts, slices of candied fruits or candied fruit peels arranged in attractive patterns. Or after baking, decorate with colored sugars, nonpareils, red cinnamon candies and finely chopped nuts. Use drop of corn syrup to hold decorations on baked cookies.

ORANGE CRISPS

½ cup granulated sugar
½ cup packed brown sugar
½ cup shortening
½ cup margarine or butter, softened
2 teaspoons grated orange peel
1 tablespoon orange juice
1 egg
2½ cups all-purpose flour*
¼ teaspoon baking soda
¼ teaspoon salt

Heat oven to 375°. Mix sugars, shortening and margarine. Mix in remaining ingredients.

Place dough in cookie press; form desired shapes on ungreased cookie sheet. (If dough is too stiff, mix in 1 egg yolk. If dough is not stiff enough, mix in small amount of flour.) Bake until edges are light brown, 8 to 10 minutes.   ABOUT 6 DOZEN COOKIES.

*If using self-rising flour, omit baking soda and salt.

Lemon Crisps: Substitute lemon juice and lemon peel for the orange juice and orange peel.

PRESSED COOKIES

Follow the directions that come with your cookie press but keep these tips in mind:

□ Use shortening, margarine or butter at room temperature. Cream the shortening-sugar mixture until light and fluffy.

□ Test the dough for consistency before adding all the flour. To do this, put a small amount in the cookie press and squeeze out. The dough should be soft and pliable but not crumbly.

□ If dough is too stiff, add 1 egg yolk. If dough is too soft, add 1 to 2 tablespoons flour.

□ Chill dough only when specified in the recipe; otherwise, use at room temperature.

□ Be sure your cookie sheet is cool. Hold press so that it rests on sheet, unless using star or bar plate.

□ Do not raise press from the cookie sheet before enough dough has been turned out to form the cookie *on* the sheet. For some cookies, it may be necessary to wait a moment to allow the dough to adhere to the sheet before lifting press.

□ Do not force the press down heavily on the sheet. If the dough is of the right consistency, it won't be necessary to force either press or handle.

Dip the hot rosette iron into batter until ⅔ covered.

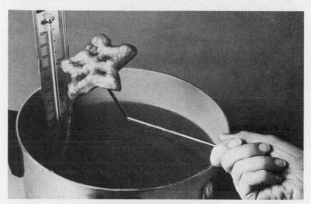

After removing rosette from fat, invert iron to drain.

ROSETTES

  Vegetable oil
1 egg
1 tablespoon sugar
½ teaspoon salt
1 tablespoon vegetable oil
½ cup water or milk
½ cup all-purpose flour*

Heat oil (2 to 3 inches) in small deep saucepan to 400°. Beat egg, sugar and salt in small deep bowl. Beat in 1 tablespoon oil, the water and flour until smooth. Heat rosette iron by placing in hot oil 1 minute. Tap excess oil from iron on paper towels; dip hot iron into batter just to top edge (don't go over top). Fry until golden brown, about 30 seconds. Immediately remove rosette; invert on paper towel to cool. (If rosette is not crisp, stir in small amount of water or milk.)

Heat iron in hot oil and tap on paper towels before making each rosette. (If iron is not hot enough, batter will not stick.) Just before serving, sprinkle with powdered sugar if desired.   18 ROSETTES.

*If using self-rising flour, omit salt.

FRUIT DESSERTS

FRESH FRUIT PLATE

Choose a variety of well-chilled fresh fruit (whole strawberries with stems, orange slices, grapefruit sections, blueberries, dark sweet cherries, clusters of grapes, melon balls, cubes or slices, apple wedges,* banana slices*). Arrange fruit on tray, assorted plates or lazy Susan. Serve with Pineapple Tower and two or three of the sauces (below) for dipping.

*Dip into lemon or pineapple juice to prevent discoloration.

PINEAPPLE TOWER

Cut cone-shaped wedge around "eye" or groups of 2 "eyes," spacing cuts evenly around entire pineapple. Cut off any core from each wedge. Insert plastic or wooden pick in rind side of each wedge; replace in pineapple. To eat, guests pull out wedges and dip into powdered sugar.

CINNAMON SOUR CREAM SAUCE

Mix 1 cup dairy sour cream, 2 tablespoons sugar, ½ teaspoon ground cinnamon and ⅛ teaspoon ground nutmeg.

SOUR CREAM SAUCE

Mix 1 cup dairy sour cream and 2 tablespoons packed dark brown sugar.

VELVET FRUIT SAUCE

Mix 1 package (8 ounces) cream cheese, softened, and ¾ cup dairy sour cream. Beat in small mixer bowl on high speed until light and smooth.

COOKED DRIED FRUIT

Prepare fruits such as apples, apricots, figs, peaches, pears or prunes as directed on package. Or soak in cold water until plump; simmer in same water in tightly covered saucepan until tender, 30 to 45 minutes. Sweeten to taste.

■ **To Microwave:** Place fruits in ungreased 1½-quart glass casserole; add enough cold water just to cover. Soak 30 minutes. Cover and microwave until tender, 11 to 12 minutes.

BAKED FRESH FRUIT COMPOTE

1 jar (10 ounces) currant jelly
½ cup water
4 plums, cut into halves
2 pears, cut into halves
2 peaches, cut into halves

Heat jelly and water over low heat, stirring occasionally, until smooth. Arrange fruits cut sides down in ungreased oblong baking dish, 12x7½x2 inches, or 1½-quart casserole. Pour hot syrup over fruits. Cover and bake in 350° oven until fruits are tender when pierced with fork, 25 to 30 minutes.   4 TO 6 SERVINGS.

Fresh Fruit Compote: Mix all ingredients in saucepan. Cover and heat to boiling; reduce heat. Simmer until fruits are tender, about 10 minutes.

RUM POT

Allow at least 4 weeks before serving the fruit from your rum pot so that you can keep supplementing it with fruits and sugar.

1 can (16 ounces) sliced peaches, drained
1 can (13¼ ounces) pineapple chunks,
    drained
2 cups sugar
1 cup rum
1 can (about 16 ounces) sliced pears, drained
1 can (about 17 ounces) apricot halves,
    drained
2 cups sugar
1 package (10 ounces) frozen raspberries,
    thawed

Place peaches and pineapple in 2- to 3-quart sterilized glass or glazed pottery container. Add 2 cups sugar and the rum. (Fruit should be completely covered with rum; add more rum if necessary.) Cover container loosely. Let stand at room temperature, stirring several times to dissolve sugar, 2 weeks. (Stir carefully to avoid breaking up fruit.)

After 2 weeks, add pears, apricots and 2 cups sugar. (Fruit should always be completely covered; add rum if necessary.) Let stand at room temperature, stirring several times to dissolve sugar, 2 weeks longer.

After 2 weeks, stir in raspberries. Use as topping for ice cream, cake or pudding. The Rum Pot will keep several weeks if stored in refrigerator. Serve at room temperature for best flavor.   15 TO 20 SERVINGS.

FRUIT AND CHEESE TRAY

Arrange a variety of fresh fruit and cheese on tray. Serve with dessert plates and small knives. Select fruit in season: apples, bananas, cherries, grapes, oranges, pears, pineapple, raspberries, strawberries, tangerines. Fill in spaces on tray with dates, figs, prunes and nuts.

As a guide, choose at least one soft, one semisoft and one firm-to-hard cheese, some mild and some sharp. Cheese should be served at room temperature. Try one of the following combinations:

Gourmandise (soft; cherry brandy flavored); Port du Salut (semisoft; mild to robust); and Swiss (firm to hard; mild, nutty, sweet) or Fontina (firm to hard; mellow, scattered "eyes")

Liederkranz (soft; edible crust, pungent); Bel Paese (semisoft; mild); and Cheddar (firm to hard; mild to very sharp) or Gruyère (firm to hard; nutty, sharper than Swiss)

Camembert (soft; edible crust, pungent) or Brie (soft; edible crust, pungent); Blue (firm to hard; tangy, sharp); and Edam or Gouda (firm to hard; inedible casing, mild)

If desired, serve cheese with assortment of crackers and a dessert wine such as cream (sweet) sherry, port, Marsala, Madeira or Tokay. Serve wine at room temperature or chilled.

FRESH FRUIT MEDLEY

1 cup seedless green grapes
1 cup cantaloupe balls or pineapple cubes
1 cup strawberries
1 can (6 ounces) frozen fruit juice concentrate
    (pineapple, orange, lemonade or
      cranberry juice cocktail), partially thawed

Divide fruit among 6 dessert dishes. Just before serving, spoon 1 to 2 tablespoons fruit concentrate onto each serving.   6 SERVINGS.

RAW APPLESAUCE

3 medium eating apples, cut up
¼ cup light corn syrup
2 tablespoons lemon juice
2 teaspoons sugar
   Dash of salt

Place half of the apples and the remaining ingredients in blender container. Cover and blend on high speed until smooth, 1 to 2 minutes. Add remaining apples; repeat.   ABOUT 2 CUPS.

APPLESAUCE

4 medium cooking apples, each cut
   into fourths
½ cup water
½ cup packed brown sugar or ⅓ to
   ½ cup granulated sugar
¼ teaspoon ground cinnamon
⅛ teaspoon ground nutmeg

Heat apples and water to boiling over medium heat; reduce heat. Simmer uncovered, stirring occasionally to break up apples, until tender, 5 to 10 minutes. Stir in remaining ingredients. Heat to boiling; boil and stir 1 minute.   ABOUT 3 CUPS.

BAKED CINNAMON APPLES

Core baking apples (Rome Beauty, Golden Delicious, Greening) and pare 1-inch strip of skin from around middle of each apple or pare upper half of each to prevent splitting. Place apples upright in ungreased baking dish. Place 1 to 2 tablespoons granulated or packed brown sugar, 1 teaspoon margarine or butter and ⅛ teaspoon ground cinnamon in center of each apple. Pour water (¼ inch deep) into baking dish.

Bake uncovered in 375° oven until tender when pierced with fork, 30 to 40 minutes. (Time will vary with size and variety of apple.) Spoon syrup in dish over apples several times during baking if desired.

■ **To Microwave:** Prepare 1, 2 or 4 apples as directed except—do not pour water into dish. Microwave uncovered until tender when pierced with fork, 1 apple 2 to 4 minutes, 2 apples 3 to 5 minutes and 4 apples 6 to 8 minutes.

Baked Granola Apples: Omit cinnamon. Place 1 tablespoon granola, slightly crushed, 2 teaspoons packed brown sugar and 1 teaspoon margarine or butter in center of each apple.

Baked Grenadine Apples: Substitute grenadine syrup for the sugar. Spoon syrup in dish over apples several times during baking.

Baked Honey Apples: Substitute honey for the sugar.

FRUIT IN SOUR CREAM

    2 cups seedless green grapes or 2 cans
        (8 ounces each) seedless grapes, drained
    1 can (13¼ ounces) pineapple chunks,
        drained
    3 tablespoons packed brown sugar
    ⅓ cup dairy sour cream
    1 tablespoon packed brown sugar

Mix grapes and pineapple. Mix 3 tablespoons brown sugar and the sour cream. Toss with grapes and pineapple; refrigerate. Just before serving, sprinkle with 1 tablespoon brown sugar. 4 SERVINGS.

Peaches in Sour Cream: Substitute 3 peaches, sliced, for the grapes and pineapple. Spoon sour cream mixture onto each serving; sprinkle with brown sugar. Serve immediately.

Strawberries in Sour Cream: Substitute 3 cups strawberry halves for the grapes and pineapple.

Strawberries to Dip: Divide 1 pint unhulled chilled strawberries among dessert dishes. Serve with sour cream and brown sugar. Guests spoon some of each onto dessert plates and dip strawberries into sour cream, then into brown sugar.

BROILED GRAPEFRUIT

Cut 2 grapefruit into halves; remove seeds. Cut around edges and sections to loosen; remove centers. Sprinkle each half with 1 tablespoon packed brown sugar.

Set oven control to broil and/or 550°. Broil grapefruit 4 to 6 inches from heat until juice bubbles and edges of peels turn light brown, 5 to 10 minutes. Serve hot.   4 SERVINGS.

■ **To Microwave:** Microwave grapefruit halves in glass serving dishes or cereal bowls until hot, 2 to 3 minutes.

SPARKLING MELON COMPOTE

    2 packages (12 ounces each) frozen melon
        balls, partially thawed and drained
    1 pint lime sherbet
    1 cup sparkling catawba grape juice or
        ginger ale, chilled

Divide melon balls among 4 dessert dishes. Top each with 1 scoop sherbet; pour about ¼ cup grape juice over sherbet.   4 SERVINGS.

MELON WITH SHERBET BALLS

    Raspberry-Currant Sauce (below)
    3 small cantaloupes
    ½ pint lemon sherbet
    ½ pint lime sherbet
    ½ pint orange sherbet

Prepare Raspberry-Currant Sauce. Cut cantaloupes into halves; remove seeds and fibers. Make small balls of sherbet with scoop or spoon; divide among cantaloupe halves. Serve with Raspberry-Currant Sauce or sprinkle 1 teaspoon orange-flavored liqueur over each serving.   6 SERVINGS.

RASPBERRY-CURRANT SAUCE

    1 package (10 ounces) frozen raspberries,
        thawed, or 1 cup fresh raspberries
    ½ cup currant jelly
    1 tablespoon water
    1½ teaspoons cornstarch

Heat raspberries (with syrup) and jelly to boiling. Mix water and cornstarch; stir into raspberries. Heat to boiling, stirring constantly. Boil and stir 1 minute. Cool; press through sieve to remove seeds.

GLAZED ORANGES

    6 large seedless oranges
    1 cup sugar
    ½ cup water
    ¼ cup light corn syrup
    1 to 3 drops each red and yellow food color
    1 tablespoon orange-flavored liqueur or
        1 teaspoon orange extract
    2 tablespoons toasted slivered almonds
        (optional)

With vegetable parer or sharp knife, cut slivers of peel from one of the oranges, being careful not to cut into white membrane; reserve peel. Pare all of the oranges, cutting only deep enough to remove *all* of the white membrane.

Mix sugar, water and corn syrup in saucepan. Cook until candy thermometer registers 230 to 234° or until syrup spins a 2-inch thread when dropped from a spoon. Stir in food color, reserved slivered peel and the liqueur. Place oranges in syrup; turn to coat all sides. Remove oranges to shallow dish or pan. Spoon syrup onto oranges until well glazed. Refrigerate, spooning syrup onto oranges occasionally.

To serve, place each orange in dessert dish. Pour syrup over each serving and sprinkle with almonds.   6 SERVINGS.

Rum Pot (page 280), Glazed Oranges (page 282) and Crimson Pears (page 285)

Flaming Peaches

FLAMING PEACHES

½ cup water
¼ cup apricot jam
3 tablespoons sugar
4 large fresh peaches, sliced, or 1 can
    (28 ounces) sliced peaches, drained
1 teaspoon lemon juice
¼ cup brandy
1 quart vanilla ice cream

Simmer water, jam and sugar over low heat until syrupy, about 5 minutes. Stir in peaches; cook over low heat until almost tender, about 3 minutes. (If using canned peaches, cook only long enough to heat through.) Stir in lemon juice.

Heat brandy in saucepan until warm; ignite and pour over peaches. Stir well before serving. Spoon peaches and syrup onto each serving of ice cream. Garnish with whipped cream and toasted slivered almonds if desired.   4 TO 6 SERVINGS.

NOTE: To prepare at table, assemble all ingredients and utensils on large serving tray. Simmer water, jam and sugar in chafing dish over direct heat until syrupy, 5 to 10 minutes. Add peaches; cook until tender, 3 to 5 minutes. Continue as directed.

CHERRIES JUBILEE

To make sure the ice cream is hard when the hot cherry sauce is added, spoon serving-size portions onto cookie sheet and freeze several hours before serving.

¼ cup rum
2 cups pitted dark sweet cherries*
¾ cup currant jelly
1 teaspoon grated orange peel
¼ cup brandy
    Vanilla ice cream

Pour rum over cherries; refrigerate 4 hours.

Just before serving, heat jelly in chafing dish or saucepan over low heat until melted. Stir in cherry mixture and orange peel. Cook, stirring constantly, until mixture simmers. Heat brandy in saucepan until warm; ignite and pour over cherries. Serve hot over ice cream.   8 TO 10 SERVINGS.

*1 can (16 ounces) pitted dark sweet cherries can be substituted for the fresh cherries. Drain cherries, reserving ¼ cup syrup. Mix reserved cherry syrup and the rum; pour over cherries.

GRANOLA PEACHES

 1 can (29 ounces) peach halves, drained
 2 tablespoons packed brown sugar
 ⅔ cup granola
 ¼ cup packed brown sugar
 3 tablespoons margarine or butter, melted
 2 tablespoons broken pecans
   Vanilla ice cream

Set oven control to broil and/or 550°. Place peach halves cut sides up in ungreased square pan, 8x8x2 inches; sprinkle with 2 tablespoons brown sugar. Broil about 5 inches from heat until light brown, 2 to 3 minutes.

Mix granola, ¼ cup brown sugar, the margarine and pecans; spoon onto peaches. Broil until mixture is bubbly and brown, about 1 minute longer. Serve with ice cream.   5 OR 6 SERVINGS.

HONEY-SAUTERNE PEACHES

Mix ¼ cup honey and ¼ cup sauterne or other sweet white wine. Slice 4 peaches; divide among 4 dessert dishes. Spoon 2 tablespoons honey mixture onto each serving.   4 SERVINGS.

Honey-Sauterne Pears: Substitute pears for the peaches.

Honey-Sauterne Pineapple: Substitute ½ cup pineapple chunks for the peaches.

Honey-Sauterne Strawberries: Substitute ½ cup strawberries for the peaches.

PEACHES RIVIERA

Place 2 peach halves* in each of 4 dessert dishes. Heat ⅓ cup raspberry jelly until melted; pour over peaches. Refrigerate several hours. Top each serving with scoop of vanilla or pistachio ice cream. 4 SERVINGS.

*Dip fresh peach halves into lemon juice to prevent discoloration.

Brandied Peaches Riviera: Use bottled brandied peaches and stir 1 tablespoon brandy syrup into melted raspberry jelly. (Any remaining brandied peach syrup can be served over ice cream or fruit.) Or mix canned peach halves (with syrup) and ⅓ cup brandy; refrigerate at least 24 hours.

CRIMSON PEARS

 ¼ cup sugar
 ¼ cup water
 2 tablespoons lemon juice
 6 large pears
 1 package (10 ounces) frozen raspberries,
   thawed

Heat oven to 350°. Mix sugar, water and lemon juice in ungreased 2-quart casserole until sugar is dissolved. Pare pears (do not core or remove stems). Arrange pears in casserole, turning to coat with sugar mixture. Cover and bake until pears are tender when pierced with fork, 45 to 60 minutes.

Carefully remove pears; drain sugar mixture from casserole. Return pears to casserole. Sieve raspberries over pears; turn pears to coat with raspberry syrup. Cool 30 minutes. Refrigerate, turning pears occasionally to coat evenly with raspberry syrup, about 12 hours. To serve, place pears upright in dessert dishes or serving dish. Pour raspberry syrup over each pear.   6 SERVINGS.

APRICOT-GLAZED PEARS

Mix ⅓ cup orange juice and ⅓ cup apricot jam in ungreased square baking dish, 8x8x2 or 9x9x2 inches, or 2-quart casserole. Place 4 pears, cut into halves, cut sides down in sauce. Cover and bake in 350° oven until pears are tender when pierced with fork, 25 to 30 minutes. Serve warm or chilled. Garnish with dollops of whipped cream and dash of ground nutmeg if desired.   4 SERVINGS.

Apricot-glazed Peaches: Substitute 4 peaches, cut into halves, for the pears.

PEARS POACHED IN RED WINE

 6 small pears, cut into halves
   Juice of 1 lemon
 2 cups dry red wine
1⅓ cups sugar
 1 two-inch stick cinnamon

Dip pears into lemon juice. Heat remaining ingredients in 10-inch skillet, stirring constantly, until sugar is dissolved and mixture boils; reduce heat and add pears. Simmer uncovered until pears are soft but not mushy when pierced with sharp knife, about 15 minutes. Cool pears in syrup until lukewarm; discard cinnamon. Remove pears to dessert dishes with slotted spoon. Spoon syrup onto pears. Serve warm or chilled.   6 SERVINGS.

MINTED PINEAPPLE SPEARS

Cut thick slice from top and bottom of 1 pineapple. Remove rind by cutting down pineapple in long wide strokes; remove eyes. Cut pineapple lengthwise into spears; discard core. Place 2 or 3 spears on each plate. Sprinkle each serving with 1 teaspoon crème de menthe; refrigerate.   4 to 6 servings.

MANDARIN PLUMS

    2 cans (16 ounces each) purple plums,
        drained (reserve syrup)
    1 can (11 ounces) mandarin orange
        segments, drained
    ¼ cup sugar
    ½ teaspoon ground cinnamon
    ¼ teaspoon ground ginger

Mix plums and orange segments in ungreased 1½-quart casserole. Mix reserved plum syrup and the remaining ingredients; pour over fruits. Cover and bake in 350° oven until hot, about 30 minutes. Serve warm.   4 to 6 servings.

COOKED PLUMS

    2 cups water
    ¾ to 1 cup sugar
    2 tablespoons lemon juice
    ⅛ teaspoon salt
        Dash of ground allspice
    2 sticks cinnamon
    2 pounds plums (Santa Rosa, Greengage,
        Damson, Italian prune)

Heat water, sugar, lemon juice, salt, allspice and cinnamon to boiling in 3-quart saucepan. Add plums. Cook uncovered over medium heat just until plums are tender, about 15 minutes. Cool; refrigerate. Serve as breakfast fruit, dessert or meat accompaniment.   8 servings.

PRUNES IN PORT

Heat 1 pound prunes, 2 cups port or other sweet red wine and ½ cup water to boiling in 2-quart saucepan; reduce heat. Cover and simmer until tender, 10 to 15 minutes. Cool; refrigerate. Serve as relish or dessert.

NOTE: If pitted prunes are used, decrease prunes to 12 ounces. Simmer 5 minutes.

Prunes in Claret: Substitute 2 cups claret or other dry red wine for the port; stir ⅓ cup sugar into prune mixture after simmering.

BAKED PRUNE WHIP

    1 cup cut-up cooked prunes
    3 egg whites
    ⅓ cup sugar
    ¼ teaspoon salt
    1 tablespoon lemon juice
    ¼ cup chopped pecans
        Sweetened Whipped Cream (page 244) or
            Soft Custard (page 349)

Beat prunes, egg whites, sugar and salt until stiff. Fold in lemon juice and pecans. Pour into ungreased 1½-quart casserole. Place casserole in pan on oven rack. Pour very hot water (1 inch deep) into pan. Bake uncovered in 350° oven until puffed and thin film has formed on top, 30 to 35 minutes. Serve warm with Sweetened Whipped Cream.   4 to 6 servings.

COOKED RHUBARB

Cut enough rhubarb into 1-inch pieces to measure 4 cups. Heat ¾ to 1 cup sugar and ½ cup water to boiling, stirring occasionally; reduce heat. Add rhubarb. Simmer uncovered until rhubarb is tender and slightly transparent, about 10 minutes. Stir in few drops red food color if desired.   5 servings.

STRAWBERRIES ROMANOFF

    1 quart strawberries
    ½ cup powdered sugar
    1 cup chilled whipping cream
    ¼ cup orange-flavored liqueur or orange
        juice

Sprinkle strawberries with powdered sugar; stir gently. Cover and refrigerate 2 hours.

Just before serving, beat whipping cream in chilled bowl until stiff. Stir in liqueur gradually. Fold in strawberries.   6 servings.

RHUBARB FACTS

Rhubarb is a vegetable, but we cook, eat and enjoy it as a fruit. Look for fresh, firm, crisp and tender stalks. Color? Usually pink or cherry red, although some good-quality stems will be predominantly light green. Rhubarb wilts rapidly at room temperature so you should always refrigerate it. From a nutrition standpoint, rhubarb contributes to the daily ration of vitamins A and C.

WATERMELON SUPREME

1 large oblong watermelon
1 cantaloupe
1 honeydew melon
1 pineapple
2 peaches or nectarines
2 cups blueberries
    Honey-Lime Sauce or Aloha Sauce (right)

Cut top third lengthwise from watermelon; cover and refrigerate to use as desired. Scoop balls from larger section of watermelon. Remove seeds; cover balls and refrigerate. Scoop remaining pulp from watermelon with large spoon to form shell. (For decorative edge on shell, cut a saw-toothed or scalloped design.) Drain shell. Cut thin slice from bottom of shell to keep it from tipping; refrigerate.

Scoop melon balls from cantaloupe and honeydew melon (about 3 cups each). Remove rind and core from pineapple. Cut fruit into bite-size pieces. Mix with cantaloupe and honeydew melon balls; cover and refrigerate.

Just before serving, slice peaches. Drain melon balls and pineapple pieces. Mix all fruit in large bowl. Drizzle with Honey-Lime Sauce. Pour fruit into watermelon shell. Garnish with mint leaves, if desired, and serve immediately.   20 SERVINGS.

HONEY-LIME SAUCE
Mix ½ cup white wine or ginger ale, 3 tablespoons honey and 2 tablespoons lime juice.

ALOHA SAUCE
⅔ cup sugar
⅓ cup water
2 tablespoons strained orange juice
2 tablespoons strained lemon juice
2 tablespoons strained lime juice

Mix all the ingredients until sugar is dissolved.

Banana Cream Pie (page 302) and Fresh Rhubarb Pie (page 297)

PIES AND PASTRY

STANDARD PASTRY

8- OR 9-INCH ONE-CRUST PIE
⅓ cup plus 1 tablespoon shortening or
⅓ cup lard
1 cup all-purpose flour*
½ teaspoon salt
2 to 3 tablespoons cold water

8- OR 9-INCH TWO-CRUST PIE
⅔ cup plus 2 tablespoons shortening or
⅔ cup lard
2 cups all-purpose flour*
1 teaspoon salt
4 to 5 tablespoons cold water

Cut shortening into flour and salt until particles are size of small peas. Sprinkle in water, 1 tablespoon at a time, tossing with fork until all flour is moistened and pastry almost cleans side of bowl (1 to 2 teaspoons water can be added if necessary).

Gather pastry into a ball; shape into flattened round on lightly floured cloth covered board. (For Two-Crust Pie, divide pastry into halves and shape into 2 rounds.) Roll pastry 2 inches larger than inverted pie plate with floured stockinet-covered rolling pin. Fold pastry into quarters; unfold and ease into plate, pressing firmly against bottom and side.

For One-Crust Pie: Trim overhanging edge of pastry 1 inch from rim of plate. Fold and roll pastry under, even with plate; flute (see page 291). Fill and bake as directed in recipe.

For Baked Pie Shell: Prick bottom and side thoroughly with fork. Bake at 475° until light brown, 8 to 10 minutes; cool.

For Two-Crust Pie: Turn desired filling into pastry-lined pie plate. Trim overhanging edge of pastry ½ inch from rim of plate. Roll other round of pastry. Fold into quarters; cut slits so steam can escape. Place over filling and unfold. Trim overhanging edge of pastry 1 inch from rim of plate. Fold and roll top edge under lower edge, pressing on rim to seal; flute (see page 291). Cover edge with 2- to 3-inch strip of aluminum foil to prevent excessive browning; remove foil during last 15 minutes of baking. Bake as directed in recipe.

*If using self-rising flour, omit salt. Pie crusts made with self-rising or whole wheat flour differ in flavor and texture from those made with all-purpose flour.

NOTE: If possible, hook fluted edge over edge of pie plate to prevent shrinking and help pastry retain its shape.

Whole Wheat Pastry: Prepare filling before preparing pastry. Substitute whole wheat flour for the all-purpose flour or substitute stone-ground whole wheat flour for half of the all-purpose flour. Fold rolled pastry in half instead of into quarters.

OIL PASTRY

8- OR 9-INCH ONE-CRUST PIE
1 cup plus 2 tablespoons all-purpose flour*
⅓ cup vegetable oil
½ teaspoon salt
2 to 3 tablespoons cold water

8- OR 9-INCH TWO-CRUST PIE
1¾ cups all-purpose flour*
½ cup vegetable oil
1 teaspoon salt
3 to 4 tablespoons cold water

Mix flour, oil and salt until particles are size of small peas. Sprinkle in water, 1 tablespoon at a time, mixing until all flour is moistened and pastry almost cleans side of bowl. (If pastry seems dry, 1 to 2 tablespoons oil can be added. Do not add water.) Gather pastry into a ball.

For One-Crust Pie: Shape pastry into flattened round. (For Two-Crust Pie, divide pastry into halves; place 1 half cut side down and flatten into round.) Place flattened round between two 15-inch lengths of waxed paper (for 9-inch pie, tape 2 pieces together to make wider strips).

Wipe table with damp cloth to prevent paper from slipping. Roll pastry 2 inches larger than inverted pie plate. Peel off top paper. Place pastry paper side up in plate. Peel off paper. Ease pastry loosely into plate.

Trim and complete as directed for Standard Pastry (left) except—increase baking time for Baked Pie Shell to 12 to 15 minutes.

For Two-Crust Pie: Roll top crust in same way as bottom crust. Cut slits after peeling off top paper. Place pastry paper side up on filling; peel off paper. Trim and complete as directed (left).

*Do not use quick-mixing or whole wheat flour in this recipe. If using self-rising flour, omit salt. Pie crusts made with self-rising flour differ in flavor and texture from those made with all-purpose flour.

TIPS FOR PASTRY MAKERS

1. Sprinkle in water, 1 tablespoon at a time; toss with fork after each addition until flour is moistened. Mix lightly until pastry clings together.

2. After pastry is thoroughly mixed, press firmly together into a ball with hands. Handle pastry just as you would a snowball.

3. When rolling out pastry, keep circular by occasionally pushing edge in gently with cupped hands. Lift occasionally to prevent sticking.

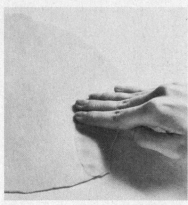

4. If patching is necessary, cut piece of pastry to fit irregular edge or tear. Moisten edge of area to be patched and press piece firmly into place.

5. For best results, select heat-resistant glass plates for pie baking. Darkened pans and dull-finished aluminum pans are also good.

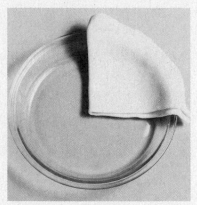

6. Fold rolled-out pastry into quarters and carefully place in pie plate with point in center; unfold and trim as directed on page 291.

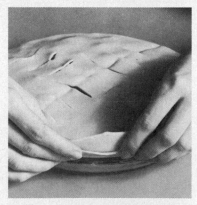

7. For two-crust pie, leave 1-inch rim of top pastry beyond edge of plate. Fold and roll rim under edge of bottom pastry, pressing to seal.

8. While pinching the top and bottom edges together, form a stand-up rim on edge of plate to seal pastry and to make fluting easier.

9. Crimp a 2- to 3-inch strip of foil over fluted edge to prevent over-browning. Remove foil 15 minutes before end of baking time.

FLUTED AND DECORATED PASTRY EDGES

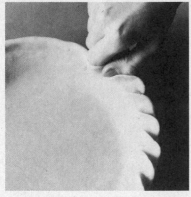

Rope: Place thumb on pastry rim at an angle. Pinch pastry by pressing knuckle down into pastry toward thumb.

Ruffle: Place thumb and index finger about 1 inch apart on pastry rim. With other index finger, pull pastry toward outside.

Pinch: Place index finger on inside of pastry rim, thumb and index finger on outside. Pinch pastry into V-shape; pinch again to sharpen.

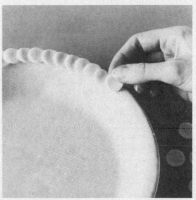

Fork: Flatten pastry evenly on rim of pie plate. Press firmly around edge with tines of fork. (Dip into flour occasionally to prevent sticking.)

Spoon Scallop: Trim pastry over hang so it is ¼ inch from rim of pie plate. Cut edge with tip of inverted teaspoon. If desired, mark with fork.

Cutouts: Trim pastry overhang even with plate. Moisten pastry cutouts and place on moistened rim, overlapping slightly. Press into place.

FROZEN PASTRY CIRCLES

Prepare Standard Pastry for two 8- or 9-inch Two-Crust Pies (page 289). Divide pastry into 4 equal parts. Roll each part 2 inches larger than inverted 8- or 9-inch pie plate.

Stack circles, placing waxed paper between each, on ungreased cookie sheet. Freeze uncovered 1 hour. Wrap stack; label and return to freezer. To prevent breaking, store on flat surface.

For Baked Pie Shell or One-Crust Baked Pie: Remove 1 Frozen Pastry Circle from freezer; place on pie plate. Thaw uncovered at room temperature until soft, about 20 minutes. Heat oven to 475°. Gently ease pastry into plate. Trim overhanging edge of pastry 1 inch from rim of plate. Fold and roll pastry under, even with plate; flute. (For One-Crust Baked Pie, continue as directed in recipe.) For Baked Pie Shell, prick bottom and side thoroughly with fork. Bake until light brown, 8 to 10 minutes.

For Two-Crust Pie: Remove 2 Frozen Pastry Circles from freezer; place one on pie plate and one on flat surface. Thaw uncovered at room temperature until soft, about 20 minutes. Heat oven to temperature designated in recipe. Gently ease pastry into plate. Trim overhanging edge of pastry ½ inch from rim of plate. Pour filling into pastry-lined pie plate. Fold other circle into quarters; cut slits so steam can escape. Place over filling and unfold. Trim overhanging edge of pastry 1 inch from rim of plate. Fold and roll top edge under lower edge, pressing on rim to seal securely; flute. Bake as directed.

ABOUT FROZEN PIES

☐ To prevent soggy crust, bake pies before freezing.

☐ Freeze pies first, then wrap and store. Use heavy-weight plastic wrap (seal with freezer tape), heavy-duty aluminum foil (seal with a double fold), plastic bags or other airtight containers. Label and date. Frozen pies will keep 4 to 6 months.

☐ Freeze pie shells unbaked or baked. Frozen baked shells will keep 4 months; unbaked 2 months.

☐ Do *not* freeze custard, cream or meringue-topped pies. Custard and cream fillings separate; meringues toughen and shrink.

☐ Do *not* thaw unbaked shells—pop right in the oven.

☐ To thaw baked pie shells, unwrap and let stand at room temperature. Or heat in 350° oven about 6 minutes.

☐ Bake pies in aluminum foil pie pans if desired. Since these pans are shiny and reflect heat, place on cookie sheet so bottom crust will brown evenly.

☐ To heat baked pies, unwrap and let stand 30 minutes; heat in 350° oven just until warm. Place foil pans on cookie sheet.

FLAVORED PASTRY

Stir one of the following into flour for Pastry for 8- or 9-inch One-Crust Pie (page 289). Double the amount for 8- or 9-inch Two-Crust Pie (page 289).

☐ 1 teaspoon celery seed

☐ ½ cup shredded Cheddar cheese

☐ 1 teaspoon ground cinnamon

☐ 1½ teaspoons shredded lemon or orange peel

☐ 2 tablespoons finely chopped nuts

☐ 1 tablespoon toasted sesame seed

☐ 2 tablespoons wheat germ

PASTRY SCRAPS

Heat oven to 475°. Gather leftover rolled pastry into a ball; shape into flattened round. Roll ⅛ inch thick. Cut into small desired shapes. Prick and sprinkle with sesame, celery or poppy seed; seasoned, onion or garlic salt; finely chopped nuts; wheat germ; cinnamon-sugar; or grated Parmesan cheese and paprika. Place on ungreased cookie sheet; bake 8 to 10 minutes. Use as an appetizer, "crackerlike" salad accompaniment, dessert or anytime snack.

CRUNCHY PIE CRUSTS

Name	Crumbs	Sugar	Margarine or Butter	Baking Temperature and Time
Graham Cracker				
8-inch	1¼ cups (about 16 squares)	2 tablespoons	¼ cup, melted	350° 10 minutes
9-inch	1½ cups (about 20 squares)	3 tablespoons	⅓ cup, melted	350° 10 minutes
Cookie*				
9-inch	1½ cups		¼ cup, melted	350° 10 minutes
Granola				
9-inch	2 cups crushed granola	2 tablespoons	¼ cup, melted	350° 6-8 minutes
Nut				
9-inch	1½ cups ground nuts	3 tablespoons	2 tablespoons, softened	400° 6-8 minutes

*Vanilla or chocolate wafers or gingersnaps

Heat oven. Mix crumbs, sugar and margarine. Reserve 3 tablespoons mixture for topping if desired. Press remaining mixture firmly against bottom and side of pie plate. Bake as directed; cool.

1. **Lattice Top:** Place 5 to 7 strips on filling; fold back alternate strips as each cross-strip is added.

2. **Diamond Top:** Weave or lay second half of pastry strips diagonally across first strips on filling.

3. **Twister Top:** Twist strips as they are placed on filling. Fold trimmed edge of lower crust over strips and flute.

4. **Spiral Top:** Place twisted strip in spiral on filling, then place a strip around edge, pressing to seal.

LATTICE TOP

Prepare pastry as directed for Two-Crust Pie (page 289) except—leave 1-inch overhang on lower crust. After rolling circle for top crust, cut circle into strips about ½ inch wide. Pastry wheel can be used for more decorative strips.

Place 5 to 7 strips (depending on size of pie) across filling in pie plate. Weave a cross-strip through center by first folding back every other strip going the other way. Continue weaving until lattice is complete, folding back alternate strips each time cross-strip is added. (To save time, do not weave strips. Simply lay second half of strips across first strips.) Trim ends of strips.

Fold trimmed edge of lower crust over ends of strips, building up a high edge. (A juicy fruit pie is more likely to bubble over when topped by lattice than when juices are held in by a top crust. Be sure to build up high pastry edge.) Seal and flute.

Diamond Top: Weave or lay second half of the strips diagonally across first strips.

Twister Top: Twist strips as pictured above.

Spiral Top: Beginning with 1 strip and from center of pie, twist strip and place in spiral on pie, adding strips by moistening ends and pinching. Moisten trimmed edge of lower crust; place tightly twisted pastry strip around edge, pressing to seal.

Fresh Apple Pie

FRESH APPLE PIE

8-INCH

Pastry for 8-inch Two-Crust Pie (page 289)
½ cup sugar
3 tablespoons flour*
¼ teaspoon ground nutmeg
¼ teaspoon ground cinnamon
Dash of salt
5 cups thinly sliced pared tart apples
   (about 5 medium)
1 tablespoon margarine or butter

9-INCH

Pastry for 9-inch Two-Crust Pie (page 289)
¾ cup sugar
¼ cup all-purpose flour*
½ teaspoon ground nutmeg
½ teaspoon ground cinnamon
Dash of salt
6 cups thinly sliced pared tart apples (about
   6 medium)
2 tablespoons margarine or butter

Heat oven to 425°. Prepare pastry. Mix sugar, flour, nutmeg, cinnamon and salt. Stir in apples. Turn into pastry-lined pie plate; dot with margarine. Cover with top crust that has slits cut in it; seal and flute. Cover edge with 3-inch strip of aluminum foil; remove foil during last 15 minutes of baking. Bake until crust is brown and juice begins to bubble through slits in crust, 40 to 50 minutes.

*If using self-rising flour, omit salt.

Apple-Cheese Pie: Prepare 9-inch pie as directed except—pour half of the apple mixture into pastry-lined pie plate; cover with 5 slices process American cheese and top with remaining apples.

Canned Apple Pie: Prepare 9-inch pie as directed except—substitute 2 cans (20 ounces each) pie-sliced apples, drained, for the fresh apples.

Dutch Apple Pie: Prepare 9-inch pie as directed except—make extra large slits in top crust; 5 minutes before end of baking, pour ½ cup whipping cream through slits in top crust. Best served warm.

French Apple Pie: Prepare pastry for 9-inch One-Crust Pie (page 289); omit margarine and top apple filling with Crumb Topping: Mix 1 cup all-purpose flour, ½ cup firm margarine or butter and ½ cup packed brown sugar until crumbly. Bake 50 minutes. Cover topping with aluminum foil during last 10 minutes of baking. Best served warm.

Green Apple Pie: Prepare pie as directed except—increase sugar ½ cup and use green apples.

FRESH BLUEBERRY PIE

8-INCH

Pastry for 8-inch Two-Crust Pie (page 289)
⅓ cup sugar
¼ cup all-purpose flour
½ teaspoon ground cinnamon (optional)
3 cups fresh blueberries
1 teaspoon lemon juice
1 tablespoon margarine or butter

9-INCH

Pastry for 9-inch Two-Crust Pie (page 289)
½ cup sugar
⅓ cup all-purpose flour
½ teaspoon ground cinnamon (optional)
4 cups fresh blueberries
1 tablespoon lemon juice
2 tablespoons margarine or butter

Heat oven to 425°. Prepare pastry. Mix sugar, flour and cinnamon. Stir in blueberries. Turn into pastry-lined pie plate; sprinkle with lemon juice and dot with margarine. Cover with top crust that has slits cut in it; seal and flute.

Cover edge with 2- to 3-inch strip of aluminum foil to prevent excessive browning; remove foil during last 15 minutes of baking.

Bake until crust is brown and juice begins to bubble through slits in crust, 35 to 45 minutes.

Canned Blueberry Pie: Substitute drained canned blueberries for the fresh blueberries.

Frozen Blueberry Pie: Substitute unsweetened frozen blueberries, partially thawed, for the fresh blueberries. (One 12-ounce package frozen blueberries yields 2½ cups.)

Plum Pie: Substitute 4 cups purple plum slices for the blueberries and add the cinnamon.

Strawberry Pie: Substitute 4 cups sliced strawberries for the blueberries and omit the cinnamon.

KNOW YOUR APPLES

A good apple pie starts with good apples—tart, firm, juicy apples. Those rated excellent for pies are Cortland, Rhode Island Greening, McIntosh and Yellow Transparent. Those rated very good are Golden Delicious, Jersey Red, Jonathan, Lodi, Rome Beauty and Starr. Note: One pound equals 3 medium apples or 3 cups sliced apples.

FRESH PEACH PIE

8-INCH

Pastry for 8-inch Two-Crust Pie
(page 289)
4 cups sliced fresh peaches
(about 7 medium)
1 teaspoon lemon juice
⅔ cup sugar
3 tablespoons flour
¼ teaspoon ground cinnamon
1 tablespoon margarine or butter

9-INCH

Pastry for 9-inch Two-Crust Pie
(page 289)
5 cups sliced fresh peaches
(about 9 medium)
1 teaspoon lemon juice
1 cup sugar
¼ cup all-purpose flour
¼ teaspoon ground cinnamon
2 tablespoons margarine or butter

Heat oven to 425°. Prepare pastry. Mix peaches and lemon juice. Mix sugar, flour and cinnamon; stir into peaches. Turn into pastry-lined pie plate; dot with margarine. Cover with top crust that has slits cut in it; seal and flute. Cover edge with 2- to 3-inch strip of aluminum foil to prevent excessive browning; remove foil during last 15 minutes of baking.

Bake until crust is brown and juice begins to bubble through slits in crust, 35 to 45 minutes. Serve with ice cream and Raspberry-Currant Sauce (page 282) if desired.

Apricot Pie: Prepare 9-inch pie as directed except—substitute 5 cups apricot halves for the peaches.

Brown Sugar Peach Pie: Prepare 9-inch pie as directed except—substitute ¾ cup packed brown sugar for the granulated sugar.

Canned Peach Pie: Prepare 9-inch pie as directed except—substitute 2 cans (29 ounces each) sliced peaches, drained, for the fresh peaches and decrease sugar to ½ cup.

Frozen Peach Pie: Prepare 9-inch pie as directed except—substitute 3 packages (12 ounces each) frozen sliced peaches, partially thawed and drained, for the fresh; decrease sugar to ½ cup.

Peach-Apricot Pie: Substitute ¼ cup apricot jam or preserves and ¾ cup packed brown sugar for the granulated sugar; stir jam into peaches and lemon juice before mixing in flour and cinnamon.

Peach-Green Apple Pie: Prepare 9-inch pie as directed except—substitute 2 cups sliced fresh peaches (about 3 medium) and 2 cups thinly sliced pared green apples (about 2 medium) for the 5 cups sliced peaches. Omit lemon juice. Sprinkle fruit mixture with ¼ cup sliced almonds and dot with 1 tablespoon margarine or butter.

CHERRY PIE

8-INCH

Pastry for 8-inch Two-Crust Pie
(page 289)
1⅓ cups sugar
⅓ cup all-purpose flour
2 cans (16 ounces each) pitted red tart
cherries, drained
¼ teaspoon almond extract
2 tablespoons margarine or butter

9-INCH

Pastry for 9-inch Two-Crust Pie
(page 289)
1⅓ cups sugar
⅓ cup all-purpose flour
2 cans (16 ounces each) pitted red tart
cherries, drained
¼ teaspoon almond extract
2 tablespoons margarine or butter

Heat oven to 425°. Prepare pastry. Mix sugar and flour. Stir in cherries. Turn into pastry-lined pie plate; sprinkle with almond extract and dot with margarine. Cover with top crust that has slits cut in it; seal and flute. Cover edge with 2- to 3-inch strip of aluminum foil to prevent excessive browning; remove foil during last 15 minutes of baking.

Bake until crust is brown and juice begins to bubble through slits in crust, 35 to 45 minutes.

Fresh Cherry Pie: Prepare 9-inch pie as directed except—substitute 4 cups fresh red tart cherries, pitted, for the canned cherries.

Frozen Cherry Pie: Prepare 9-inch pie as directed except—substitute 2 cans (20 ounces each) frozen pitted red tart cherries, thawed and drained, for the canned cherries and decrease sugar to ½ cup.

FRESH RHUBARB PIE
8-INCH
Pastry for 8-inch Two-Crust Pie
(page 289)
1 to 1¼ cups sugar
¼ cup all-purpose flour
¼ teaspoon grated orange peel (optional)
3 cups cut-up rhubarb (½-inch pieces)
1 tablespoon margarine or butter

9-INCH
Pastry for 9-inch Two-Crust Pie
(page 289)
1⅓ to 1⅔ cups sugar
⅓ cup all-purpose flour
½ teaspoon grated orange peel (optional)
4 cups cut-up rhubarb (½-inch pieces)
2 tablespoons margarine or butter

Heat oven to 425°. Prepare pastry. Mix sugar, flour and orange peel. Turn half of the rhubarb into pastry-lined pie plate; sprinkle with half of the sugar mixture. Repeat with remaining rhubarb and sugar mixture; dot with margarine. Cover with top crust that has slits cut in it; seal and flute. Sprinkle with sugar if desired. Cover edge with 2- to 3-inch strip of aluminum foil to prevent excessive browning; remove foil during last 15 minutes of baking.

Bake until crust is brown and juice begins to bubble through slits in crust, 40 to 50 minutes.

Frozen Rhubarb Pie: Prepare 9-inch pie as directed except—decrease sugar to ⅔ cup and substitute 8 cups frozen rhubarb (32 ounces), partially thawed, for the fresh rhubarb.

Rhubarb-Blueberry Pie: Substitute fresh or frozen blueberries (thawed) for half of the rhubarb and use the lesser amount of sugar.

Rhubarb-Strawberry Pie: Substitute sliced strawberries for half of the rhubarb and use the lesser amount of sugar.

TOP CRUST PLUS
It's easy to give top crusts a blue-ribbon look. Take your choice—shiny, sugary or glazed. For a shiny top, brush the crust lightly with milk before baking. For a sugary crust, use your fingers or a pastry brush to moisten crust lightly with water, then sprinkle on a little sugar. To glaze a crust, brush lightly with beaten egg (or egg yolk mixed with a little water) before baking.

STRAWBERRY GLACE PIE
9-inch Baked Pie Shell (page 289)
6 cups strawberries (about 1½ quarts)
1 cup sugar
3 tablespoons cornstarch
½ cup water
1 package (3 ounces) cream cheese, softened

Bake pie shell. Mash enough strawberries to measure 1 cup. Mix sugar and cornstarch in 2-quart saucepan. Stir in water and strawberries gradually. Cook over medium heat, stirring constantly, until mixture thickens and boils. Boil and stir 1 minute; cool.

Beat cream cheese until smooth; spread on bottom of pie shell. Fill shell with remaining strawberries; pour cooked strawberry mixture over top. Refrigerate until set, at least 3 hours.

Peach Glacé Pie: Substitute 5 cups sliced peaches (7 medium) for the strawberries. To prevent discoloration, use an ascorbic acid mixture as directed on package.

Raspberry Glacé Pie: Substitute raspberries for the strawberries.

CREAMY CHEESECAKE PIE
Graham Cracker Crust (page 292)
2 packages (8 ounces each) cream cheese, softened
2 eggs
¾ cup sugar
2 teaspoons vanilla
½ teaspoon grated lemon peel
Cheesecake Topping (below)

Heat oven to 350°. Prepare crust but do not bake. Beat cream cheese slightly. Add eggs, sugar, vanilla and lemon peel; beat until light and fluffy. Pour into crust. Bake until firm, about 25 minutes. Spread Cheesecake Topping carefully over pie; cool. Refrigerate at least 8 hours. Serve with sweetened strawberries if desired.   8 SERVINGS.

CHEESECAKE TOPPING
Mix 1 cup dairy sour cream, 2 tablespoons sugar and 2 teaspoons vanilla.

PECAN PIE

Pastry for 9-inch One-Crust Pie
  (page 289)
3 eggs
⅔ cup sugar
½ teaspoon salt
⅓ cup margarine or butter, melted
1 cup corn syrup
1 cup pecan halves or broken pecans

Heat oven to 375°. Prepare pastry. Beat eggs, sugar, salt, margarine and syrup with hand beater. Stir in pecans. Pour into pastry-lined pie plate.

Bake until set, 40 to 50 minutes. Cool slightly. Serve warm or refrigerate.

Do-ahead Tip: After baking, cool pie 2 hours. Freeze uncovered at least 3 hours. Wrap and return to freezer. Store no longer than 1 month. Unwrap pie and thaw in refrigerator 20 minutes.

Brandy Pecan Pie: Decrease corn syrup to ¾ cup and beat in ¼ cup brandy.

Chocolate Pecan Pie: Melt 2 squares (1 ounce each) unsweetened chocolate with the margarine.

Honey Pecan Pie: Substitute ½ cup honey for ½ cup of the corn syrup.

Peanut Pie: Substitute 1 cup salted peanuts for the pecans.

Sunflower Nut Pie: Substitute 1 cup toasted sunflower nuts for the pecans.

SOUTHERN PEANUT BUTTER PIE

Pastry for 9-inch One-Crust Pie
  (page 289)
⅔ cup sugar
½ teaspoon salt
1 cup dark corn syrup
⅓ cup creamy peanut butter
3 eggs
1 cup salted peanuts

Heat oven to 375°. Prepare pastry. Beat sugar, salt, corn syrup, peanut butter and eggs; stir in peanuts. Pour into pastry-lined pie plate.

Bake until crust is golden brown, 40 to 50 minutes. (Center of filling may be slightly soft but will become firm as pie cools.) Cool slightly; refrigerate. Serve with Sweetened Whipped Cream (page 244) or ice cream if desired.

SPICY WALNUT-RAISIN PIE

Pastry for 8-inch One-Crust Pie
  (page 289)
2 eggs
½ cup sugar
¼ teaspoon salt
¼ teaspoon ground cinnamon
¼ teaspoon ground nutmeg
¼ teaspoon ground cloves
¾ cup corn syrup
¼ cup margarine or butter, melted
⅓ cup coarsely chopped walnuts
⅓ cup raisins

Heat oven to 375°. Prepare pastry. Beat eggs, sugar, salt, cinnamon, nutmeg, cloves, corn syrup and margarine with hand beater. Stir in walnuts and raisins. Pour into pastry-lined pie plate.

Bake until filling is set, 40 to 50 minutes. Serve warm or refrigerate.

CUSTARD PIE

Refrigerate cream and custard pie fillings; they should never be allowed to stand at room temperature.

8-INCH

Pastry for 8-inch One-Crust Pie
  (page 289)
3 eggs
⅓ cup sugar
¼ teaspoon salt
¼ teaspoon ground nutmeg
1¾ cups milk
1 teaspoon vanilla

9-INCH

Pastry for 9-inch One-Crust Pie
  (page 289)
4 eggs
⅔ cup sugar
½ teaspoon salt
¼ teaspoon ground nutmeg
2⅔ cups milk
1 teaspoon vanilla

Heat oven to 450°. Prepare pastry. Beat eggs slightly with hand beater; beat in remaining ingredients. Pour into pastry-lined pie plate. Bake 20 minutes.

Reduce oven temperature to 350°. Bake until knife inserted halfway between center and edge comes out clean, 8-inch pie 10 minutes longer, 9-inch pie 15 to 20 minutes longer.

SOUR CREAM-RAISIN PIE

 9-inch Baked Pie Shell (page 289)
1 tablespoon plus 1½ teaspoons cornstarch
1 cup plus 2 tablespoons sugar
¼ teaspoon salt
¾ teaspoon ground nutmeg
1½ cups dairy sour cream
3 egg yolks
1½ cups raisins
1 tablespoon lemon juice
 Brown Sugar Meringue (page 300)

Bake pie shell. Heat oven to 400°. Mix cornstarch, sugar, salt and nutmeg in 2-quart saucepan. Stir in sour cream. Stir in egg yolks, raisins and lemon juice. Cook over medium heat, stirring constantly, until mixture thickens and boils. Boil and stir 1 minute. Pour into pie shell.

Spoon meringue onto hot pie filling; spread over filling, sealing meringue to edge of crust to prevent shrinking or weeping. Bake until delicate brown, about 10 minutes. Cool away from draft.

PUMPKIN PIE

8-INCH

 Pastry for 8-inch One-Crust Pie
  (page 289)
1 egg
1¼ cups canned pumpkin or Cooked
  Pumpkin (right)
⅔ cup sugar
¼ teaspoon salt
¾ teaspoon ground cinnamon
¼ teaspoon ground ginger
⅛ teaspoon ground cloves
1¼ cups evaporated milk

9-INCH

 Pastry for 9-inch One-Crust Pie
  (page 289)
2 eggs
1 can (16 ounces) pumpkin or 2 cups
  Cooked Pumpkin (right)
¾ cup sugar
½ teaspoon salt
1 teaspoon ground cinnamon
½ teaspoon ground ginger
¼ teaspoon ground cloves
1⅔ cups evaporated milk

Heat oven to 425°. Prepare pastry. Beat egg(s) slightly with hand beater; beat in remaining ingredients. Place pastry-lined pie plate on oven rack; pour in filling. Bake 15 minutes.

Reduce oven temperature to 350°. Bake until knife inserted in center comes out clean, 8-inch pie 35 minutes longer, 9-inch pie 45 minutes longer; cool. Serve with Sweetened Whipped Cream (page 244) if desired.

COOKED PUMPKIN

To Boil: Heat 1 inch salted water (½ teaspoon salt to 1 cup water) to boiling. Cut 1¼ pounds pumpkin into 1-inch pieces (about 1½ cups pared) for 8-inch pie or cut 2 pounds pumpkin into 1-inch pieces (about 2½ cups pared) for 9-inch pie. Add to boiling water. Cover and heat to boiling. Cook until tender, about 30 minutes; drain. Mash pumpkin until no lumps remain. 1¼ OR 2 CUPS MASHED COOKED PUMPKIN.

To Bake: Heat oven to 400°. Cut 1 small pumpkin (about 4 pounds) into halves; remove seeds and fiber. Place pumpkin cut sides up in oblong baking dish; pour water (¼ inch deep) into dish.

Cover and bake until tender, about 1 hour. Scoop pumpkin from shells; mash until no lumps remain. ABOUT 4 CUPS MASHED COOKED PUMPKIN.

NOTE: 1 pound pared pumpkin yields about 1 cup mashed cooked pumpkin.

Sweet Potato Pie: Substitute mashed cooked sweet potatoes (page 190) for the pumpkin.

Sweet Potato Pie

ABOUT MERINGUE PIES

There's no mystery to making a perfect meringue pie. With a little care and these clues, the delicate topping will be light as air, high and golden brown every time.

☐ Separate eggs carefully. (It's easier to do when they're cold.) Even a speck of yolk can hold down the peaks.

☐ Wait until the egg whites come to room temperature before beating. They'll be higher and lighter.

☐ Beat in the sugar *gradually*—and continue beating until it's completely dissolved.

☐ Spread the meringue over a *hot* filling, right to the crust all the way around.

☐ Watch baking time.

☐ Avoid drafts; a chill may make meringue shrink.

Beat egg whites and cream of tartar until foamy.

MERINGUE FOR PIE

8-INCH PIE
  2 egg whites
  ¼ teaspoon cream of tartar
  ¼ cup sugar
  ¼ teaspoon vanilla

9-INCH PIE
  3 egg whites
  ¼ teaspoon cream of tartar
  6 tablespoons sugar
  ½ teaspoon vanilla

Beat egg whites and cream of tartar until foamy. Beat in sugar, 1 tablespoon at a time; continue beating until stiff and glossy. Do not underbeat. Beat in vanilla.

Brown Sugar Meringue: Substitute packed brown sugar for the granulated sugar.

Continue beating until mixture stands in stiff peaks.

MERINGUE PIE SHELL

Heat oven to 275°. Generously butter 9-inch pie plate. Beat 2 egg whites and ¼ teaspoon cream of tartar in small mixer bowl until foamy. Beat in ½ cup sugar, 1 tablespoon at a time; continue beating until stiff and glossy. Do not underbeat. Spoon into pie plate, pressing meringue against bottom and side.

Bake 45 minutes. Turn off oven; leave meringue in oven with door closed 45 minutes. Remove from oven; finish cooling away from draft.

Spread meringue over filling; seal to edge of crust.

LEMON MERINGUE PIE

8-INCH

    8-inch Baked Pie Shell (page 289)
1   cup sugar
¼   cup cornstarch
1   cup water
2   egg yolks, slightly beaten
2   tablespoons margarine or butter
1   teaspoon grated lemon peel
⅓   cup lemon juice
2   drops yellow food color (optional)
    Meringue for 8-inch Pie (page 300)

9-INCH

    9-inch Baked Pie Shell (page 289)
1½ cups sugar
⅓   cup plus 1 tablespoon cornstarch
1½ cups water
3   egg yolks, slightly beaten
3   tablespoons margarine or butter
2   teaspoons grated lemon peel
½   cup lemon juice
2   drops yellow food color (optional)
    Meringue for 9-inch Pie (page 300)

Bake pie shell. Heat oven to 400°. Mix sugar and cornstarch in 1½-quart saucepan. Stir in water gradually. Cook over medium heat, stirring constantly, until mixture thickens and boils. Boil and stir 1 minute. Stir at least half of the hot mixture gradually into egg yolks. Blend into hot mixture in saucepan. Boil and stir 1 minute. Remove from heat; stir in margarine, lemon peel, lemon juice and food color. Pour into pie shell.

Spoon meringue onto hot pie filling; spread over filling, carefully sealing meringue to edge of crust to prevent shrinking or weeping.

Bake until delicate brown, about 10 minutes. Cool away from draft.

Lime Meringue Pie: Prepare 9-inch pie as directed except—decrease cornstarch to ⅓ cup and omit margarine. Substitute lime peel for the lemon peel, ¼ cup lime juice for the lemon juice and green food color for the yellow food color.

DIVINE LIME PIE

    Meringue Pie Shell (page 300)
4   egg yolks
½   cup sugar
¼   teaspoon salt
⅓   cup fresh lime juice (2 to 3 limes)
2   or 3 drops green food color
1   cup chilled whipping cream
1   tablespoon grated lime peel

Bake pie shell. Beat egg yolks in small mixer bowl until light and lemon colored. Mix sugar, salt, lime juice and egg yolks in saucepan. Cook over medium heat, stirring constantly, until mixture thickens, about 5 minutes. Cool; stir in food color.

Beat whipping cream in chilled bowl until stiff. Fold in lime mixture and grated lime peel. Spoon into meringue shell; refrigerate at least 4 hours. Garnish with Sweetened Whipped Cream (page 244) and grated lime peel or lime twist if desired.

CHOCOLATE ANGEL PIE

    Meringue Pie Shell (page 300)
1   bar (4 ounces) sweet cooking chocolate
3   tablespoons hot water
1   teaspoon vanilla
1   cup chilled whipping cream

Bake pie shell. Heat chocolate in hot water in saucepan over low heat, stirring constantly, until melted. Cool to room temperature. Stir in vanilla.

Beat whipping cream in chilled bowl until stiff. Fold in chocolate mixture. Spoon into pie shell; refrigerate at least 12 hours. Garnish with whipped cream, chopped nuts or grated chocolate if desired.

CHOCOLATE TIPS

Here are two simple but successful ways to melt chocolate squares or chips. You can melt them in a heavy saucepan over low heat—just make sure the pan is heavy and the heat is low. The other way is a little more trouble but there's no danger of scorching: Melt chocolate in a small heatproof bowl or in the top of a double boiler over hot—not boiling—water.

Chocolate equivalent quantities: 1 package (6 ounces) semisweet chocolate chips equals 1 cup; 1 square (1 ounce) unsweetened chocolate equals 1 envelope (1 ounce) premelted chocolate; 1 package (8 ounces) unsweetened chocolate equals 8 squares (1 ounce each).

VANILLA CREAM PIE

8-INCH

8-inch Baked Pie Shell (page 289)
½ cup sugar
3 tablespoons cornstarch
¼ teaspoon salt
2 cups milk
3 egg yolks, slightly beaten
1 tablespoon margarine or butter, softened
1 tablespoon vanilla
Sweetened Whipped Cream (page 244)

9-INCH

9-inch Baked Pie Shell (page 289)
⅔ cup sugar
¼ cup cornstarch
½ teaspoon salt
3 cups milk
4 egg yolks, slightly beaten
2 tablespoons margarine or butter, softened
1 tablespoon plus 1 teaspoon vanilla
Sweetened Whipped Cream (page 244)

Bake pie shell. Mix sugar, cornstarch and salt in 1½-quart saucepan. Stir in milk gradually. Cook over medium heat, stirring constantly, until mixture thickens and boils. Boil and stir 1 minute. Stir at least half of the hot mixture gradually into egg yolks. Blend into hot mixture in saucepan. Boil and stir 1 minute. Remove from heat; stir in margarine and vanilla. Pour into pie shell; press plastic wrap onto filling. Refrigerate at least 2 hours but no longer than 48 hours. Remove plastic wrap; top pie with whipped cream.

Banana Cream Pie: Prepare 9-inch pie as directed except—press plastic wrap onto filling in saucepan; cool to room temperature. Slice 2 large bananas into pie shell; pour filling over bananas. Refrigerate until serving time; top pie with whipped cream and garnish with banana slices.

Butterscotch Cream Pie: Prepare 9-inch pie as directed except—substitute 1 cup packed brown sugar for the sugar; decrease vanilla to 1 teaspoon.

Chocolate Cream Pie: Prepare 9-inch pie as directed except—increase sugar to 1½ cups and cornstarch to ⅓ cup. Stir in 2 squares (1 ounce each) unsweetened chocolate, cut up, after stirring in milk or stir in 2 envelopes (1 ounce each) premelted chocolate with the vanilla. Omit margarine.

Coconut Cream Pie: Prepare 9-inch pie as directed except—decrease vanilla to 2 teaspoons and stir ¾ cup flaked coconut into pudding. Sprinkle whipped cream with ¼ cup flaked coconut.

CHOCOLATE-ALMOND PIE

Almond Crunch Crust (below)
1½ cups miniature marshmallows or
     16 large marshmallows
½ cup milk
1 bar (8 ounces) milk chocolate
1 cup chilled whipping cream

Bake pie crust. Heat marshmallows, milk and chocolate in saucepan over low heat, stirring constantly, just until chocolate and marshmallows are melted and mixture is smooth. Refrigerate, stirring occasionally, until mixture mounds slightly when dropped from a spoon.

Beat whipping cream in chilled bowl until stiff. Fold chocolate mixture into whipped cream. Pour into pie crust. Refrigerate until set, about 8 hours.

ALMOND CRUNCH CRUST

Heat oven to 400°. Mix 1½ cups ground blanched almonds, 3 tablespoons sugar and 2 tablespoons margarine or butter, softened. Press mixture firmly against bottom and side of ungreased 9-inch pie plate. Bake until light brown, 6 to 8 minutes; cool.

GRASSHOPPER PIE

Chocolate Cookie Crust or Graham
     Cracker Crust (page 292)
32 large marshmallows or 3 cups
     miniature marshmallows
½ cup milk
¼ cup crème de menthe
3 tablespoons white crème de cacao
1½ cups chilled whipping cream
     Few drops green food color
     (optional)

Bake pie crust. Heat marshmallows and milk over medium heat, stirring constantly, just until marshmallows are melted. Refrigerate until thickened; stir in liqueurs.

Beat whipping cream in chilled bowl until stiff. Fold marshmallow mixture into whipped cream; fold in food color. Pour into crust. Sprinkle with grated semisweet chocolate if desired. Refrigerate until set, at least 3 hours.

Alexander Pie: Substitute dark crème de cacao for the crème de menthe and brandy for the white crème de cacao.

Cherry Cordial Pie: Substitute ½ cup cherry liqueur for the crème de menthe and white crème de cacao and red food color for the green food color.

PINK PEPPERMINT PIE

Graham Cracker Crust or Chocolate
Cookie Crust (page 292)
24 large marshmallows
½ cup milk
1 teaspoon vanilla
⅛ teaspoon salt
6 drops peppermint extract
6 drops red food color
1 cup chilled whipping cream
2 tablespoons crushed peppermint candy

Bake pie crust. Heat marshmallows and milk in saucepan over low heat, stirring constantly, just until marshmallows are melted. Remove from heat; stir in vanilla, salt, peppermint extract and food color. Refrigerate, stirring occasionally, until mixture mounds slightly when dropped from a spoon.

Beat whipping cream in chilled bowl until stiff. Stir marshmallow mixture until blended; fold into whipping cream. Pour into crust. Refrigerate at least 12 hours. Just before serving, sprinkle with crushed candy.

FROSTY PUMPKIN PIE

9-inch Baked Pie Shell (page 289) or
Graham Cracker Crust (page 292)
1 pint vanilla ice cream
2 to 3 tablespoons chopped crystallized
ginger
1 cup canned or Cooked Pumpkin (page 299)
1 cup sugar
1 teaspoon pumpkin pie spice
½ teaspoon ground ginger
½ teaspoon salt
½ cup chopped walnuts
1 cup chilled whipping cream

Bake pie shell. Soften ice cream slightly; quickly fold in crystallized ginger. Spread in pie shell. Freeze until ice cream is solid.

Mix pumpkin, sugar, pumpkin pie spice, ground ginger, salt and walnuts. Beat whipping cream in chilled bowl until stiff; fold into pumpkin mixture. Pour over ice cream in pie shell. Freeze several hours. Remove from freezer 10 to 15 minutes before serving.

Pink Peppermint Pie

BAKED TART SHELLS

Prepare pastry as directed for 8- or 9-inch One-Crust Pie (page 289) except—roll into 13-inch circle about ⅛ inch thick.

Cut circle into 4½-inch rounds; fit rounds over backs of muffin cups or small custard cups, making pleats so pastry will fit closely. (If using individual pie pans or tart pans, cut pastry rounds 1 inch larger than inverted pans; fit into pans.) Prick thoroughly with fork to prevent puffing.

Heat oven to 475°. Place on ungreased cookie sheet. Bake until light brown, 8 to 10 minutes. Cool before removing from pans. Fill each tart with ⅓ to ½ cup of favorite filling.   6 TART SHELLS.

SWEDISH ALMOND TARTS

    Foil Tart Shells (below)
 2 egg whites
 ¼ cup sugar
 ½ cup ground blanched almonds
 6 tablespoons raspberry jam

Heat oven to 375°. Prepare tart shells; reserve pastry scraps.

Beat egg whites until foamy. Add sugar gradually; beat until stiff peaks form. Fold in almonds. Spread 1 tablespoon jam over bottom of each tart shell; spoon in ⅓ cup almond filling and spread evenly.

Roll pastry scraps; cut into ¼-inch strips. Crisscross 2 strips on each filled tart. Place on ungreased cookie sheet. Bake until filling is delicate golden brown, 20 to 25 minutes. Cool; remove foil. 6 TARTS.

FOIL TART SHELLS

Prepare pastry as directed for 9-inch One-Crust Pie (page 289) except—divide into 6 equal parts. Place each part on 5-inch square of heavy-duty aluminum foil; roll each into circle about 5 inches in diameter. Trim edges of foil and pastry to make neat circle. Shape foil and pastry together into tart by turning up 1½-inch edge; flute.

JIFFY TARTS

Prepare Baked Tart Shells (above), then fill with a scoop of ice cream topped with your favorite dessert sauce (garnish with chopped nuts or coconut) or fresh fruit (berries and peaches are especially good). Or fill shells with sweetened fresh or well-drained canned fruit; dot with jelly.

SUMMER JEWEL TARTS

    Baked Tart Shells (left)
 ½ cup seedless green grapes
 1 medium peach, sliced (about ¾ cup)
 ½ cup raspberries or sliced strawberries
 1 small banana, sliced (about ¾ cup)
    Orange Glacé (below)
 ½ cup blueberries

Bake tart shells. Toss grapes, peach slices, raspberries and banana slices with Orange Glacé. Fill tart shells with fruit mixture. Top with blueberries; refrigerate.   6 TARTS.

ORANGE GLACE

Mix ¼ cup sugar, 1 tablespoon cornstarch and dash of salt in saucepan. Stir in ⅓ cup orange juice and 3 tablespoons water. Cook over medium heat, stirring constantly, until mixture thickens and boils. Boil and stir 1 minute; cool.

APPLE SQUARES WITH CARDAMOM SAUCE

    Pastry for 8- or 9-inch Two-Crust Pie
      (page 289)
 2 or 3 medium apples, each cut into
      16 slices
 8 teaspoons sugar
 8 teaspoons margarine or butter
    Cardamom Sauce (below)

Heat oven to 425°. Prepare pastry as directed except—roll each round into rectangle, 16x8 inches. Cut each rectangle crosswise into 4 strips, 8x4 inches. Place 6 apple slices on half of each strip; sprinkle with 1 teaspoon sugar and dot with 1 teaspoon margarine. Moisten edges of strips with water; fold pastry over apple slices and press edges together with floured fork to seal. Cut slits or apple shapes in tops of pastry squares. Place on ungreased cookie sheet. Bake until light brown, 15 to 20 minutes. Serve warm with Cardamom Sauce. 8 SQUARES.

CARDAMOM SAUCE

 ⅔ cup packed brown sugar
 1 tablespoon cornstarch
 ⅔ cup water
 1 tablespoon lemon juice
 2 teaspoons margarine or butter
 ¼ teaspoon ground cardamom or
      cinnamon

Mix brown sugar and cornstarch in saucepan; stir in remaining ingredients. Heat to boiling, stirring constantly. Boil and stir 1 minute. Serve warm.

Join pastry corners on top.

Pinch pastry edges to seal.

Apple Dumplings—made with Whole Wheat Pastry

DATE TURNOVERS

  1 package (8 ounces) dates, cut up
½ cup chopped apple (about ½ medium
      apple)
¼ cup chopped walnuts
⅛ teaspoon salt
  1 teaspoon grated orange peel
⅓ cup orange juice
    Pastry for 9-inch Two-Crust Pie
      (page 289)
    Orange Glaze (below)

Heat oven to 450°. Mix dates, apple, walnuts, salt, orange peel and orange juice. Prepare pastry as directed except—after rolling, cut each round into eight 4½-inch rounds. Place about 1 tablespoon date mixture on half of each round; fold over pastry and press edges with fork to seal. Prick tops; place on ungreased cookie sheet.

Bake until light brown, 15 to 20 minutes. Cool slightly; spread Orange Glaze over tops. Serve warm or cool.   16 TURNOVERS.

ORANGE GLAZE
Mix 1 cup powdered sugar, 1 tablespoon margarine or butter, softened, and 1 tablespoon orange juice until smooth.

APPLE DUMPLINGS

    Pastry for 8- or 9-inch Two-Crust Pie
      (page 289)
  6 baking apples (each about 3 inches in
      diameter), cored
  3 tablespoons raisins
  3 tablespoons chopped nuts
  2 cups packed brown sugar
  1 cup water

Heat oven to 425°. Prepare pastry as directed except—roll ⅔ into 14-inch square; cut into 4 squares. Roll remaining pastry into rectangle, 14x7 inches; cut into 2 squares. Place apple on each square.

Mix raisins and nuts; fill each apple. Moisten corners of pastry squares; bring 2 opposite corners up over apple and pinch. Repeat with remaining corners; pinch edges of pastry to seal. Place dumplings in ungreased oblong baking dish, 12x7½x2 inches, or square pan, 9x9x2 inches.

Heat brown sugar and water to boiling; carefully pour around dumplings. Bake, spooning syrup over dumplings 2 or 3 times, until crust is golden and apples are tender, about 40 minutes. Serve warm or cool with cream or Sweetened Whipped Cream (page 244) if desired.   6 DUMPLINGS.

CREAM PUFFS

½ cup water
¼ cup margarine or butter
½ cup all-purpose flour*
2 eggs
    Cream Filling (below) or Sweetened
        Whipped Cream (page 244)
    Powdered sugar

Heat oven to 400°. Heat water and margarine to rolling boil in saucepan. Stir in flour. Stir vigorously over low heat until mixture forms a ball, about 1 minute; remove from heat. Beat in eggs, all at once; continue beating until smooth. Drop dough by scant ¼ cupfuls about 3 inches apart onto ungreased cookie sheet.

Bake until puffed and golden, 35 to 40 minutes. Cool away from draft. Cut off tops; pull out any filaments of soft dough. Fill puffs with Cream Filling. Replace tops; dust with powdered sugar. Refrigerate until serving time.   6 CREAM PUFFS.

*Self-rising flour can be used in this recipe.

CREAM FILLING

⅓ cup sugar
2 tablespoons cornstarch
⅛ teaspoon salt
2 cups milk
2 egg yolks, slightly beaten
2 tablespoons margarine or butter, softened
2 teaspoons vanilla

Mix sugar, cornstarch and salt in 2-quart saucepan. Stir in milk gradually. Cook over medium heat, stirring constantly, until mixture thickens and boils. Boil and stir 1 minute. Stir at least half of the hot mixture gradually into egg yolks. Blend into hot mixture. Boil and stir 1 minute. Remove from heat; stir in margarine and vanilla; cool.

Chocolate Eclairs: Drop dough by scant ¼ cupfuls onto ungreased cookie sheet. Shape each into finger 4½ inches long and 1½ inches wide with spatula. Bake; cool. Fill puffs with Cream Filling (above). Frost with Chocolate Frosting (below). Refrigerate until serving time.   6 ECLAIRS.

Quick Cream Puffs: Omit Cream Filling. Fill puffs with ice cream or fruit pie filling. Frost with Chocolate Frosting (below) or dust with powdered sugar.

Chocolate Frosting: Heat ½ square (½ ounce) unsweetened chocolate and ½ teaspoon margarine or butter over low heat until melted. Remove from heat; stir in ½ cup powdered sugar and about 1 tablespoon hot water. Beat until smooth.

SPECIAL DESSERTS

CREPES

1½ cups all-purpose flour*
1 tablespoon sugar
½ teaspoon baking powder
½ teaspoon salt
2 cups milk
2 eggs
2 tablespoons margarine or butter, melted
½ teaspoon vanilla

Mix flour, sugar, baking powder and salt. Stir in remaining ingredients. Beat with hand beater until smooth. Lightly butter 6- to 8-inch skillet; heat over medium heat until bubbly. Pour scant ¼ cup of the batter into skillet; *immediately* rotate skillet until thin film covers bottom.

Cook until light brown. Run wide spatula around edge to loosen; turn and cook other side until light brown. Stack crepes, placing waxed paper between each. Keep covered.

If desired, thinly spread applesauce, sweetened strawberries, currant jelly, or raspberry jam on warm crepes; roll up. (Be sure to fill crepes so the more attractive side is on the outside.) Sprinkle with powdered sugar.   12 CREPES.

*If using self-rising flour, omit baking powder and salt.

CREPES SUZETTE

Crepes (above)
⅔ cup margarine or butter
¾ teaspoon grated orange peel
⅔ cup orange juice
¼ cup sugar
⅓ cup brandy
⅓ cup orange-flavored liqueur

Prepare Crepes. Heat margarine, orange peel, orange juice and sugar to boiling in 10-inch skillet, stirring occasionally. Boil and stir 1 minute. Reduce heat and simmer. Heat brandy and liqueur in saucepan but do not boil.

Fold crepes into fourths; place in hot orange sauce and turn once. Arrange crepes around edge of skillet. Pour warm brandy mixture into center of skillet and ignite. Spoon flaming sauce over crepes. Place 2 crepes on each dessert plate; spoon warm sauce onto crepes.   6 SERVINGS.

CREPES CHANTILLY

Crepes (left)
¾ cup chilled whipping cream
¼ cup powdered sugar
¾ cup sliced fresh strawberries
Powdered sugar

Prepare Crepes. Beat whipping cream and ¼ cup powdered sugar in chilled bowl until stiff. Fold in strawberries. Spoon about 2 tablespoons of the strawberry mixture onto each crepe; roll up. Place 2 crepes seam sides down on each dessert plate; sprinkle with powdered sugar.   6 SERVINGS.

CHERRY BLINTZES

6 Crepes (left)
½ cup dry cottage cheese
¼ cup dairy sour cream
1 tablespoon sugar
½ teaspoon vanilla
¼ teaspoon grated lemon peel
2 tablespoons margarine or butter
½ cup dairy sour cream
½ can (21-ounce size) cherry pie filling

Prepare Crepes except—brown only one side. Cool, keeping crepes covered to prevent them from drying out.

Mix cottage cheese, ¼ cup sour cream, the sugar, vanilla and lemon peel. Spoon about 1½ tablespoons of the cheese mixture onto browned side of each crepe. Fold sides of crepe up over filling, overlapping edges; roll up.

Heat margarine in skillet over medium heat until bubbly. Place blintzes seam sides down in skillet. Cook, turning once, until golden brown. Top each with rounded tablespoon of sour cream and about 3 tablespoons pie filling.   3 SERVINGS.

DO-AHEAD CREPES

Crepes on call, whenever you want them! Serve these elegant little pancakes even on a busy day. The secret? Make crepes ahead, then refrigerate or freeze them. Stack 6 to 8 together, with a layer of waxed paper between each. Wrap and refrigerate for several days. For long-term storage, wrap, label and freeze. When ready to use, thaw (wrapped) at room temperature about 3 hours. Crepes freeze well, but should not be stored in the freezer for more than 3 months.

POTS DE CREME AU CHOCOLAT

⅔ cup semisweet chocolate chips
1 cup half-and-half
2 eggs
3 tablespoons sugar
　Dash of salt
2 tablespoons rum (optional)

Heat oven to 350°. Heat chocolate chips and half-and-half, stirring constantly, until chocolate is melted and mixture is smooth. Cool slightly. Beat remaining ingredients; gradually stir into chocolate mixture. Pour into 4 ungreased 6-ounce custard cups or 4 or 5 ovenproof pot de crème cups.

Place cups in baking pan on oven rack. Pour boiling water into pan to within ½ inch of tops of cups. Bake 20 minutes. Cool slightly. Cover and refrigerate at least 4 hours but no longer than 24 hours.　4 OR 5 SERVINGS.

CHOCOLATE FONDUE

12 ounces milk chocolate, semisweet
　　chocolate chips or sweet cooking
　　chocolate
½ cup half-and-half
2 to 3 tablespoons orange-flavored liqueur,
　　kirsch, brandy or white crème de
　　menthe or 2 teaspoons instant coffee or
　　¼ teaspoon ground cinnamon
　Dippers (fruit,* cake cubes, miniature
　　doughnuts, pretzels, cookies)

Heat chocolate and half-and-half in heavy saucepan over low heat, stirring constantly, until chocolate is melted and mixture is smooth. Remove from heat; stir in liqueur. Pour into fondue pot or chafing dish to keep warm.

Guests select Dippers and place on dessert plates; then, with fondue forks or bamboo skewers, they dip each into chocolate mixture. If mixture becomes too thick, stir in small amount of half-and-half. If desired, Dippers can be rolled in granola, chopped peanuts, chopped salted cashews or cookie coconut after coating with chocolate mixture.　6 TO 8 SERVINGS.

*Strawberries, banana slices, pineapple chunks, mandarin orange segments, orange sections, apple wedges, grapes, maraschino cherries and melon balls. Dip the bananas and apples into lemon or pineapple juice to prevent discoloration.

CHOCOLATE SOUFFLE

⅓ cup sugar
⅓ cup cocoa
¼ cup all-purpose flour
1 cup milk
3 egg yolks
2 tablespoons margarine or butter, softened
1 teaspoon vanilla
4 egg whites
¼ teaspoon cream of tartar
⅛ teaspoon salt
3 tablespoons sugar
　Best Sauce or Amber Sauce (below)

Mix ⅓ cup sugar, the cocoa and flour in saucepan. Stir in milk gradually. Heat to boiling, stirring constantly. Remove from heat. Beat egg yolks with fork. Beat in about ⅓ of the cocoa mixture. Stir in remaining cocoa mixture gradually. Stir in margarine and vanilla. Cool slightly.

Place oven rack in lowest position. Heat oven to 350°. Butter and sugar 6-cup soufflé dish. Make 4-inch band of triple thickness aluminum foil 2 inches longer than circumference of dish. Butter and sugar one side of band. Extend dish by securing band buttered side in around outside edge.

Beat egg whites, cream of tartar and salt in large mixer bowl until foamy. Beat in 3 tablespoons sugar, 1 tablespoon at a time; continue beating until stiff and glossy. Do not underbeat. Stir about ¼ of the egg whites into chocolate mixture. Fold in remaining egg whites. Carefully pour into dish. Place dish in square pan, 9x9x2 inches, on oven rack; pour very hot water (1 inch deep) into pan. Bake 1¼ hours. Serve immediately with Best Sauce.　6 SERVINGS.

BEST SAUCE

Beat ½ cup powdered sugar and ½ cup margarine or butter, softened, in saucepan until creamy. Beat ½ cup chilled whipping cream in chilled bowl until stiff. Fold whipped cream into sugar mixture. Heat to boiling, stirring occasionally.

AMBER SAUCE

1 cup packed brown sugar or granulated
　　sugar
½ cup light corn syrup
½ cup half-and-half
¼ cup margarine or butter

Mix all ingredients in 1-quart saucepan. Cook over low heat, stirring occasionally, 5 minutes.

Do-ahead Tip: Before baking, soufflé can be covered and refrigerated no longer than 6 hours.

COMPANY CHEESECAKE

1¼ cups graham cracker crumbs (about
      15 squares) or 1¼ cups finely crushed
      whole wheat flake cereal
2 tablespoons sugar
3 tablespoons margarine or butter, melted
2 packages (8 ounces each) plus 1 package
      (3 ounces) cream cheese, softened
1 cup sugar
2 teaspoons grated lemon peel
¼ teaspoon vanilla
3 eggs
1 cup dairy sour cream or Cherry,
      Strawberry or Blueberry Glaze (below)

Heat oven to 350°. Mix cracker crumbs, 2 table-spoons sugar and the margarine. Press in bottom of 9-inch springform pan. Bake 10 minutes; cool.

Heat oven to 300°. Beat cream cheese in large mixer bowl. Add 1 cup sugar gradually, beating until fluffy. Add lemon peel and vanilla. Beat in 1 egg at a time. Pour over crumb mixture.

Bake until center is firm, about 1 hour. Cool to room temperature. Refrigerate at least 3 hours but no longer than 10 days. Loosen edge of cheesecake with knife before removing side of pan. Top with sour cream or glaze.   12 SERVINGS.

CHERRY GLAZE

1 can (16 ounces) pitted red tart cherries,
      drained (reserve syrup)
½ cup sugar
2 tablespoons cornstarch
4 drops red food color

Add enough water to reserved cherry syrup to measure 1 cup. Mix sugar and cornstarch in saucepan. Stir in syrup mixture. Cook, stirring constantly, until mixture thickens and boils. Boil and stir 1 minute. Remove from heat; stir in cherries and food color. Cool completely.

STRAWBERRY GLAZE

Arrange 1 cup sliced strawberries on cheesecake. Heat ⅔ cup strawberry jelly and 1 teaspoon lemon juice, stirring constantly, until jelly is melted and smooth. Remove from heat; let stand 5 minutes. Pour over strawberries just before serving.

BLUEBERRY GLAZE

Drain 1 can (16 ounces) blueberries, reserving liquid. Add enough water to liquid to measure 1 cup. Mix ½ cup sugar and 2 tablespoons cornstarch in saucepan. Stir in the 1 cup liquid. Cook, stirring constantly, until mixture thickens and boils. Boil and stir 1 minute. Stir in blueberries; cool.

NUT-CRACKER SWEET TORTE

6 eggs, separated
½ cup sugar
2 tablespoons vegetable oil
1 tablespoon rum flavoring
½ cup sugar
¼ cup all-purpose flour*
1¼ teaspoons baking powder
1 teaspoon ground cinnamon
½ teaspoon ground cloves
1 cup fine graham cracker crumbs (about
      12 squares)
1 square (1 ounce) unsweetened chocolate,
      grated
1 cup finely chopped nuts
      Rum-flavored Whipped Cream (below)

Heat oven to 350°. Line bottoms of 2 round layer pans, 8 or 9x1½ inches, with aluminum foil. Beat egg whites in large mixer bowl until foamy. Beat in ½ cup sugar, 1 tablespoon at a time; continue beating until stiff and glossy.

Beat egg yolks, oil and rum flavoring in small mixer bowl on low speed until blended. Add ½ cup sugar, the flour, baking powder, cinnamon and cloves; beat on medium speed 1 minute. Fold egg yolk mixture into egg whites. Fold in cracker crumbs, chocolate and nuts. Pour into pans.

Bake until top springs back when touched lightly, 30 to 35 minutes. Immediately invert pans, resting rims on edges of 2 inverted pans. Cool completely.

Loosen edges of layers with knife; invert pan and hit sharply on table. Remove foil. Split cake to make 4 layers.

Fill layers and frost top of torte with Rum-flavored Whipped Cream. Garnish with chocolate curls if desired. Refrigerate at least 7 hours. (Torte mellows and becomes moist.)   12 SERVINGS.

*If using self-rising flour, decrease baking powder to 1 teaspoon.

RUM-FLAVORED WHIPPED CREAM

Beat 2 cups chilled whipping cream, ½ cup powdered sugar and 2 teaspoons rum flavoring in chilled bowl until stiff.

Company Cheesecake (page 309), Grenadine Ice-cream Mold (page 312) and Orange-Cinnamon Meringue (page 311)

MERINGUE SHELL

Heat oven to 275°. Cover cookie sheet with heavy brown paper. Beat 3 egg whites and ¼ teaspoon cream of tartar in small mixer bowl until foamy. Beat in ¾ cup sugar, 1 tablespoon at a time; continue beating until stiff and glossy. Do not underbeat. Shape meringue on brown paper into 9-inch circle with back of spoon, building up side.

Bake 1½ hours. Turn off oven; leave meringue in oven with door closed 1 hour. Finish cooling meringue at room temperature. If desired, fill meringue with ice cream and top with fresh berries, cut-up fruit or Fudge Sauce or Butterscotch-Rum Sauce (page 314). 8 TO 10 SERVINGS.

Cinnamon-Peach Meringue: Mix ½ teaspoon ground cinnamon with the sugar before beating into egg whites. Fill baked meringue with vanilla ice cream and top with sliced peaches.

Coffee-Peach Meringue: Mix 1 teaspoon powdered instant coffee with sugar. Beat ½ cup chilled whipping cream, 1 tablespoon sugar and ¼ teaspoon ground ginger in chilled bowl until stiff. Fill meringue with whipped cream and sliced peaches.

Crème de Menthe Meringue: Fold 1 square (1 ounce) unsweetened chocolate, coarsely grated, into meringue after beating. Fill baked meringue with French vanilla ice cream and top with green crème de menthe.

Heart Meringue: Fold several drops red food color into meringue. Shape into heart shape, building up side. Fill baked meringue with strawberry ice cream and top with sliced strawberries.

Individual Heart Meringues: Fold several drops red food color into meringue after beating. Drop meringue by ⅓ to ½ cupfuls onto brown paper. Shape into heart shapes, building up sides. Bake 55 minutes. Turn off oven; leave meringues in oven with door closed until meringues are cool. Fill baked meringues with strawberry or vanilla ice cream and top with strawberries. 8 SHELLS.

Individual Meringues: Drop meringue by ⅓ cupfuls onto brown paper. Shape into circles, building up sides. Bake 1 hour. Turn off oven; leave meringues in oven with door closed 1½ hours. Finish cooling at room temperature. 8 TO 10 SHELLS.

Orange-Cinnamon Meringue: Mix ½ teaspoon ground cinnamon with the sugar before beating into egg whites. Fill baked meringue with orange sherbet and sprinkle with chopped nuts.

CHERRY-BERRIES ON A CLOUD

    6 egg whites
    ½ teaspoon cream of tartar
    ¼ teaspoon salt
    1¾ cups sugar
    2 packages (3 ounces each) cream cheese, softened
    1 cup sugar
    1 teaspoon vanilla
    2 cups chilled whipping cream
    2 cups miniature marshmallows
       Cherry-Berry Topping (below)

Heat oven to 275°. Grease oblong pan, 13x9x2 inches. Beat egg whites, cream of tartar and salt until foamy. Beat in 1¾ cups sugar, 1 tablespoon at a time; beat until stiff and glossy. Do not underbeat. Spread in pan. Bake 1 hour. Turn off oven; leave in oven with door closed at least 12 hours.

Mix cream cheese, 1 cup sugar and the vanilla. Beat whipping cream in chilled bowl until stiff. Fold whipped cream and marshmallows into cream cheese mixture. Spread over meringue; refrigerate at least 12 hours. Cut into serving pieces and top with Cherry-Berry Topping. 10 TO 12 SERVINGS.

CHERRY-BERRY TOPPING

Mix 1 can (21 ounces) cherry pie filling, 2 cups sliced strawberries or 1 package (16 ounces) frozen strawberries (thawed) and 1 teaspoon lemon juice.

COFFEE MALLOW

    32 large marshmallows or 3 cups miniature marshmallows
    ⅔ cup water
    2 tablespoons instant coffee
    1 cup chilled whipping cream
       Sweetened Whipped Cream (page 244)
       Roasted diced almonds

Mix marshmallows, water and coffee in saucepan. Cook over medium heat, stirring occasionally, until marshmallows are melted. Refrigerate until mixture mounds slightly when dropped from a spoon.

Beat whipping cream in chilled bowl until stiff. Fold marshmallow mixture into whipped cream. Pour into square pan, 8x8x2 inches. Freeze until firm, about 4 hours. Top with Sweetened Whipped Cream and almonds. 9 SERVINGS.

Orange Mallow: Substitute 1 teaspoon grated orange peel and ⅔ cup orange juice for the water and coffee. Omit Sweetened Whipped Cream and almonds.

PINEAPPLE REFRIGERATOR DESSERT

1¼ cups graham cracker crumbs (about
  15 squares) or 1½ cups granola,
  crushed
¼ cup margarine or butter, melted
2 tablespoons granulated sugar
1 cup powdered sugar
½ cup margarine or butter, softened
1 egg
1 cup chilled whipping cream
1 can (20 ounces) crushed pineapple, well
  drained
  Sweetened Whipped Cream (page 244)
  Maraschino cherries

Mix cracker crumbs, ¼ cup margarine and the granulated sugar. Press half of the crumb mixture firmly in ungreased square pan, 8x8x2 inches. Beat powdered sugar, ½ cup margarine and the egg in small mixer bowl until light and fluffy. Spread carefully over crumb mixture.

Beat whipping cream in chilled bowl until stiff; fold in pineapple. Spread over sugar mixture. Sprinkle remaining crumb mixture over top. Cover and refrigerate at least 12 hours. Cut into squares; top each with Sweetened Whipped Cream and maraschino cherry. 9 SERVINGS.

Banana Refrigerator Dessert: Substitute a mixture of ½ cup chopped nuts, 1 banana, mashed, and ¼ cup maraschino cherries, cut into fourths and drained, for the pineapple.

GRENADINE ICE-CREAM MOLD

1 pint vanilla ice cream, slightly softened
¼ cup orange-flavored liqueur
¾ cup flaked coconut
2 tablespoons diced roasted almonds
2 teaspoons powdered sugar
½ cup chilled whipping cream
¼ cup grenadine syrup
1 tablespoon orange-flavored liqueur

Mix ice cream, ¼ cup liqueur, the coconut, almonds and powdered sugar. Beat whipping cream in chilled bowl until stiff. Fold whipped cream into ice-cream mixture; pour into 4-cup mold. Cover and freeze until ice-cream mixture is firm, at least 8 hours.

Mix syrup and 1 tablespoon liqueur. Unmold dessert on plate with rim and spoon sauce over dessert. 6 TO 8 SERVINGS.

FRUITY SOFT ICE CREAM

This frozen dessert thickens in the blender container and is ready to spoon out in less than a minute.

1 cup chilled whipping cream
¾ cup nonfat dry milk
¼ cup sugar
1 package (16 ounces) frozen unsweetened
  raspberries, strawberries or boysenberries

Place whipping cream, dry milk and sugar in blender container. Cover and blend on high speed 10 seconds. Add about ½ cup of the raspberries. Cover and blend on high speed 10 seconds; stir. Repeat with remaining raspberries, about ½ cup at a time. Serve immediately or, for firmer consistency, freeze 1 hour. 6 SERVINGS.

Spiced Apple Soft Ice Cream: Substitute 1 package (16 ounces) frozen unsweetened apple slices for the raspberries. Add 1 teaspoon pumpkin pie spice.

Yogurt Fruit Shakes: Substitute 1 cup unflavored yogurt for the whipping cream and, if desired, 2 packages (10 ounces each) frozen quick-thaw peaches for the strawberries.

SHERBET POLKA-DOT DESSERT

2 pints lime sherbet
2 pints raspberry sherbet
2 pints orange sherbet
2 quarts chocolate chip ice cream
1½ cups chilled whipping cream
½ teaspoon almond extract

Working quickly, make balls of sherbet with small ice-cream scoop (#40) or teaspoon; place in chilled jelly roll pan. Freeze until balls are firm, about 4 hours.

Slightly soften ice cream; beat until fluffy. Layer sherbet balls in chilled tube pan, 10x4 inches, alternating colors and filling in spaces between balls in each layer with ice cream. Freeze until firm, at least 12 hours. (Dessert can be covered and frozen several days.)

Beat whipping cream and almond extract in chilled bowl until stiff. Unmold dessert and frost with whipped cream. 20 SERVINGS.

Ice-cream Polka-dot Dessert: Substitute 1 quart chocolate ice cream, 1 quart pistachio or mint ice cream and 1 quart strawberry ice cream for the 3 sherbets. Substitute 2 quarts vanilla ice cream for the chocolate chip ice cream.

FRENCH VANILLA ICE CREAM

1 cup milk
½ cup sugar
¼ teaspoon salt
3 egg yolks, beaten
1 tablespoon vanilla
2 cups chilled whipping cream

For crank-type freezer: Mix milk, sugar, salt and egg yolks in saucepan. Cook over medium heat, stirring constantly, just until bubbles appear around edge. Cool to room temperature. Stir in vanilla and whipping cream.

Pour into freezer can; put dasher in place. Cover and adjust crank. Place can in freezer tub. Fill freezer tub ⅓ full of ice; add remaining ice alternately with layers of rock salt (6 parts ice to 1 part rock salt). Turn crank until it turns with difficulty. Drain water from freezer tub. Remove lid; take out dasher. Pack mixture down; replace lid. Repack in ice and rock salt. Let stand to ripen several hours.
1 QUART ICE CREAM.

For refrigerator: Mix milk, sugar, salt and egg yolks in saucepan. Cook over medium heat, stirring constantly, just until bubbles appear around edge. Cool to room temperature. Stir in vanilla.

Pour into ice cube tray. Freeze until mixture is mushy and partially frozen, 30 to 60 minutes. Beat whipping cream in chilled bowl until soft peaks form. Spoon partially frozen mixture into another chilled bowl; beat until smooth. Fold in whipped cream. Pour into 2 ice cube trays; cover to prevent crystals from forming. Freeze, stirring frequently during first hours, until firm, 3 to 4 hours.
1 QUART ICE CREAM.

Chocolate Ice Cream: Increase sugar to 1 cup and decrease vanilla to 1 teaspoon. Stir 2 squares (1 ounce each) unsweetened chocolate, melted,* into hot milk mixture in saucepan.

Frozen Custard Ice Cream: Decrease salt to ⅛ teaspoon and cream to 1 cup.

Frozen Strawberry Ice Cream: Decrease vanilla to 1 teaspoon. Stir in 1 package (16 ounces) frozen strawberry halves (thawed) after adding cream. Stir in few drops red food color if desired.

Nut Brittle Ice Cream: Stir in 1 cup crushed almond, pecan or peanut brittle after adding cream.

Peach Ice Cream: Decrease vanilla to 1 teaspoon. Mash 4 or 5 peaches to yield 2 cups. Stir ½ cup sugar into peaches. Stir in peaches after adding cream.

Pistachio Ice Cream: Stir in ½ cup chopped pistachio nuts or almonds, ½ teaspoon almond extract and few drops green food color after adding cream.

Strawberry Ice Cream: Decrease vanilla to 1 teaspoon. Mash 1 pint strawberries with ½ cup sugar; stir into milk mixture after adding cream. Stir in few drops red food color if desired.

Vanilla Bean Ice Cream: Omit vanilla. Add one 3-inch piece of vanilla bean to milk mixture before cooking. Before cooling, remove bean and split lengthwise into halves. Scrape the seeds into cooked mixture with tip of small knife; discard bean.

Wintergreen or Peppermint Ice Cream: Decrease vanilla to 1 teaspoon. Stir in ½ cup crushed wintergreen or peppermint candy sticks after adding cream. Stir in few drops green or red food color.

*Do not use premelted chocolate.

With crank freezer, scrape ice cream from dasher; pack ice cream down and replace lid.

Refrigerator ice cream must be partly frozen until mushy, then beaten until smooth.

PHILADELPHIA ICE-CREAM SUNDAES

1 quart whipping cream
¾ cup sugar
2 tablespoons vanilla
⅛ teaspoon salt
    Fudge Sauce or Butterscotch-Rum
        Sauce (below)

Mix whipping cream, sugar, vanilla and salt. Pour into freezer; put dasher in. Cover can and adjust crank. Place can in tub. Fill tub ⅓ full of ice; add remaining ice alternately with rock salt (6 parts ice to 1 part rock salt). Turn crank until it turns with difficulty. Drain water from tub. Remove lid; take out dasher. Pack mixture down; replace lid. Repack in ice and salt. Let stand several hours. Serve with Fudge Sauce.   1½ QUARTS ICE CREAM.

FUDGE SAUCE

1 can (13 ounces) evaporated milk
2 cups sugar
4 squares (1 ounce each) unsweetened
    chocolate
¼ cup margarine or butter
1 teaspoon vanilla
½ teaspoon salt

Heat milk and sugar to rolling boil, stirring constantly. Boil and stir 1 minute. Add chocolate; stir until melted. Beat over heat until smooth. Remove from heat; stir in margarine, vanilla and salt.

BUTTERSCOTCH-RUM SAUCE

⅔ cup sugar
⅓ cup margarine or butter
⅓ cup buttermilk
2 teaspoons light corn syrup
¼ teaspoon baking soda
1 tablespoon rum or 1 teaspoon rum
    flavoring

Heat sugar, margarine, buttermilk, corn syrup and baking soda to boiling over medium heat, stirring constantly. Boil, stirring frequently, 5 minutes. Remove from heat; stir in rum. Cool completely.

BISCUIT TORTONI

⅔ cup vanilla wafer or macaroon cookie
    crumbs (about 12 cookies)
¼ cup cut-up red candied cherries
½ cup chopped salted almonds
1 quart vanilla ice cream, slightly softened
    Red and green candied cherries

Mix cookie crumbs, cut-up cherries and almonds. Fold into ice cream. Divide ice-cream mixture among 8 paper-lined medium muffin cups, 2½x1¼ inches. Arrange red cherry half and slices of green cherry on each to resemble flower. Freeze until firm, about 4 hours.   8 SERVINGS.

CRANBERRY ICE

1 pound cranberries
2 cups water
2 cups sugar
¼ cup lemon juice
1 teaspoon grated orange peel
2 cups cold water

Cook cranberries in 2 cups water until skins are broken, about 10 minutes. Rub cranberries through sieve to make smooth pulp. Stir in sugar, lemon juice and orange peel. Stir in 2 cups cold water. Pour into square baking dish, 8x8x2 inches. Freeze, stirring several times to keep mixture smooth, until firm. Let stand at room temperature about 10 minutes before serving.   8 SERVINGS.

WATERMELON ICE

Remove seeds from 8 cups 1-inch pieces watermelon (about ½ medium watermelon). Place half of the watermelon pieces, 1 cup sugar and ¼ cup lemon juice in blender container. Cover and blend on high speed until mixture is smooth and sugar is dissolved; repeat with remaining watermelon. Pour into 2 ice cube trays. Freeze until firm around edges, about 2 hours.   ABOUT 1 QUART DESSERT.

Pictured opposite: Sangría Punch (page 346), Peanut Brittle (page 339), Chilled Avocado Soup (page 318) and Polynesian Shrimp Dip (page 323)

APPETIZERS,
SNACKS AND BEVERAGES

APPETIZERS AND SNACKS

First Course Favorites

Give your meal a happy head start with any one of these special openers. Many are perfect for the formality of a first course at the table, curtain-raisers for the good meal to come. Or sometimes you may prefer to serve in the living room, to get the good talk started. Whether you choose an elegant traditional appetizer or offer soup in small mugs, these recipes will wake up appetites—and say "welcome" at the same time.

GRAPEFRUIT CUP

2 grapefruit
1 pint strawberries
¼ cup sugar
1 teaspoon aromatic bitters

Cut grapefruit into halves. Cut around edges and membranes to remove grapefruit sections. Place sections in bowl. Remove membranes from grapefruit shells and reserve shells.

Cut strawberries into halves and place in bowl with grapefruit sections. Sprinkle sugar and bitters over fruit; toss. Cover and refrigerate. Just before serving, fill grapefruit shells with fruit mixture. Garnish with mint leaves if desired.   4 SERVINGS.

SPARKLING FRUIT COMPOTE

3 medium peaches
2 cups sliced strawberries
2 cups blueberries
2 cups melon balls
3 medium bananas
1 bottle (25.6 ounces) pink sparkling
   catawba grape juice, chilled

Slice peaches into bowl. Top peach slices with strawberries, blueberries and melon balls. Cover and refrigerate.

Just before serving, slice bananas into fruit mixture. Pour grape juice on fruit.   8 TO 10 SERVINGS.

PAPAYAS WITH LIME WEDGES

Cut 2 large papayas lengthwise into halves; remove seeds. Cut each half lengthwise into slices. Arrange slices on 4 lettuce-lined salad plates. Serve with lime wedges.   4 SERVINGS.

COCONUT FRUIT CUPS

3 small coconuts
1 medium pineapple
¼ cup orange-flavored liqueur or orange
   juice
Whole strawberries

Break coconuts crosswise into halves. (You'll need a hammer for this job.) Remove coconut meat; reserve shells. Cover and refrigerate half of the coconut meat for future use. Cut remaining coconut meat into bite-size pieces.

Remove rind from pineapple and cut fruit into bite-size pieces as directed on page 156. Mix coconut meat and pineapple; add liqueur and toss. Cover and refrigerate.

Just before serving, fill coconut shells with fruit mixture. Top with whole strawberries and, if desired, garnish with a mint sprig.   6 SERVINGS.

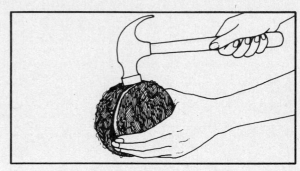

Tap around middle of coconut with a hammer. When you reach starting point give an extra tap (or use saw).

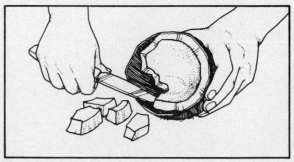

Pry out coconut meat with a sturdy knife.

FRUIT SOUP

    3 tablespoons sugar
    3 tablespoons cornstarch
    ⅛ teaspoon salt
    1¼ cups medium red or rosé wine
    1 cup water
    1½ cups cranberry juice
    3 to 3½ cups assorted fresh fruit

Mix sugar, cornstarch and salt in 3-quart saucepan; stir in wine and water. Heat to boiling, stirring constantly. Boil and stir 1 minute. Remove from heat; stir in cranberry juice. Cover loosely and refrigerate until chilled.

Stir in fruit. Serve with sour cream or whipped cream if desired.   6 SERVINGS.

MELON AND PROSCIUTTO

Cut 1 cantaloupe, casaba, honeydew or Spanish melon (about 3 pounds) into halves; scoop out seeds and fibers. Cut each half lengthwise into 6 wedges; remove rind. Cut crosswise slits 1½ inches apart in each melon wedge.

Cut ¼ pound thinly sliced prosciutto (Italian ham) into 1-inch strips. Place several slices of ham over each wedge; push ham into slits.   12 SERVINGS.

Melon and Prosciutto Bites: Cut melon into bite-size pieces. Wrap each piece in strips of prosciutto; secure with wooden picks.   12 SERVINGS.

ASPARAGUS WITH CURRIED MAYONNAISE

    ½ cup mayonnaise or salad dressing
    ¼ teaspoon curry powder
    1 package (10 ounces) frozen asparagus
        spears
      Pimiento strips

Mix mayonnaise and curry powder. Cover and refrigerate at least 4 hours. Cook asparagus as directed on package; drain and refrigerate.

Place ¼ of asparagus on each plate. Top with curried mayonnaise; crisscross pimiento strips on mayonnaise.   4 SERVINGS.

Asparagus with Crab-Curry Mayonnaise: Increase mayonnaise to ¾ cup. Mix 2 teaspoons dry white wine (optional) and 1 can (7½ ounces) crabmeat, drained and cartilage removed, into mayonnaise with the curry powder.   6 SERVINGS.

CELERY VICTOR

    1 bunch celery
    1 can (10½ ounces) condensed beef broth
        (about 1¼ cups)
      Italian salad dressing
      Pimiento strips

Trim root end from celery bunch but do not separate stalks. Remove coarse outer stalks and leaves, reserving leaves for garnish. Cut celery bunch crosswise once so bottom section is 5 inches long. (Refrigerate top section for future use.) Cut bottom section into fourths; tie each with string.

Pour broth into skillet; add celery bundles. Cover; heat to boiling. Boil 15 minutes. Drain celery; place in shallow dish. Pour salad dressing over celery. Refrigerate, turning bundles once or twice, 3 hours.

To serve, place 1 bundle cut side down on each plate; remove string. Top with pimiento strips and garnish with reserved celery leaves.   4 SERVINGS.

GRAPE-CELERY SALADS

    ½ cup water
    2 teaspoons lemon juice
    ½ teaspoon celery salt
      Dash of pepper
    1 large stalk celery, cut into ½-inch pieces
        (about ½ cup), or 1 small celery root, cut
        into ½-inch cubes (about 1 cup)
    ¼ cup clear French salad dressing
    1 can (8¼ ounces) pineapple chunks, chilled
        and drained
    1 cup halved Tokay grapes or seedless green
        grapes, chilled
    ¼ cup toasted slivered almonds
    ¼ cup mayonnaise or salad dressing
    4 or 5 lettuce cups

Heat water, lemon juice, celery salt and pepper to boiling in 1-quart saucepan. Add celery; simmer uncovered 5 minutes. Drain; turn into shallow glass dish. Pour French salad dressing over celery. Refrigerate, stirring occasionally, at least 2 hours.

Just before serving, drain celery. Stir in pineapple, grapes and almonds. Add mayonnaise; toss. Spoon into lettuce cups. Garnish with small clusters of grapes if desired.   4 OR 5 SERVINGS.

NOTE: Celery root (or celeriac) has an edible knob that can be peeled, cut up, braised and marinated to add crispness and a delicate flavor to salads. Choose small roots; they are more tender.

VICHYSSOISE

1 medium onion, sliced
2 teaspoons margarine or butter
2 medium potatoes, thinly sliced
1 small stalk celery, chopped (about ¼ cup)
1 can (10¾ ounces) chicken broth (about
    1¼ cups)
¼ teaspoon salt
1 cup half-and-half
¼ teaspoon salt
⅛ teaspoon pepper
½ to ⅔ cup half-and-half
    Snipped chives

Cook and stir onion and margarine in 3-quart saucepan over medium heat until onion is tender; reduce heat. Stir in potatoes, celery, broth and ¼ teaspoon salt. Cover and simmer until potatoes are soft, 30 to 40 minutes.

Press potato mixture through sieve. Return potato mixture to saucepan. Stir in 1 cup half-and-half, ¼ teaspoon salt and the pepper. Heat over medium heat, stirring constantly, until hot and bubbly. (At this point, soup can be served hot if desired.) Cover and refrigerate soup at least 4 hours.

Just before serving, stir ½ to ⅔ cup half-and-half into soup. Sprinkle with chives and, if desired, paprika.   6 SERVINGS (ABOUT ½ CUP EACH) COLD, 3 SERVINGS (ABOUT 1 CUP EACH) HOT.

CHILLED AVOCADO SOUP

 2 medium avocados
1½ cups water
 1 cup milk
 2 tablespoons lemon juice
2½ teaspoons seasoned salt
    Dash of red pepper sauce
 1 medium tomato, chopped

Cut avocados lengthwise into fourths. Press avocados through sieve. Beat in water, milk and lemon juice gradually until smooth. Mix in seasoned salt and pepper sauce; stir in tomato. Refrigerate until chilled. Garnish each serving with lemon slices if desired.   8 SERVINGS (ABOUT ½ CUP EACH).

Blender Avocado Soup: Place avocados, water and milk in blender container. Cover and blend on high speed until smooth. Mix in lemon juice, seasoned salt and pepper sauce. Stir in tomato; refrigerate.

GAZPACHO

1½ cups tomato juice
 1 beef bouillon cube
 1 tomato, chopped
 ¼ cup chopped cucumber
 2 tablespoons chopped green pepper
 2 tablespoons chopped onion
 2 tablespoons wine vinegar
 1 tablespoon vegetable oil
 ½ teaspoon salt
 ½ teaspoon Worcestershire sauce
 3 drops red pepper sauce
    Accompaniments (herbed croutons and
        about ⅓ cup each chopped cucumber,
        tomato, green pepper and onion)

Heat tomato juice to boiling. Add bouillon cube; stir until dissolved. Stir in remaining ingredients except Accompaniments. Refrigerate several hours. Serve with Accompaniments.   5 SERVINGS (ABOUT ½ CUP EACH).

FRENCH ONION SOUP

3 medium onions, sliced
2 tablespoons margarine or butter
4 cups Beef Consommé (below)
1 teaspoon Worcestershire sauce
2 thin slices French bread, toasted
    Grated Parmesan cheese

Cover and cook onions in margarine in 3-quart saucepan over low heat, stirring occasionally, 30 minutes. Add consommé and Worcestershire sauce; heat to boiling. Reduce heat; cover and simmer 30 minutes.

Place ½ slice toasted bread in each of 4 soup bowls; pour hot soup over toast and sprinkle toast with cheese.   4 SERVINGS (ABOUT 1 CUP EACH).

BEEF CONSOMME

2 cans (10½ ounces each) condensed beef
    broth (about 2½ cups)
1 soup can water
1 small onion, sliced (about ¼ cup)
1 small carrot, sliced (about ¼ cup)
1 small stalk celery, sliced (about ¼ cup)
2 sprigs parsley
1 small bay leaf
⅛ teaspoon dried thyme leaves

Heat all ingredients to boiling; reduce heat. Cover and simmer 30 minutes; strain.

Gazpacho

HOT SHERRIED MADRILENE

Heat 1 can (13 ounces) clear madrilene and 1 can (13 ounces) red madrilene to boiling. Remove from heat; stir in ¼ cup sherry and serve immediately.   5 SERVINGS (ABOUT ⅔ CUP EACH).

Hot Lemon Madrilene: Increase clear madrilene to 2 cans and omit red madrilene. Substitute 2 teaspoons lemon juice for the sherry. Garnish with thin lemon slices if desired.

JELLIED TOMATO MADRILENE

Serve this hot-weather soup in a small bowl placed in a larger bowl filled with crushed ice.

    2 envelopes unflavored gelatin
        (2 tablespoons)
  2¼ cups tomato juice
    3 chicken bouillon cubes
    2 cups boiling water
    ½ teaspoon grated onion
    ⅛ teaspoon salt
      Dash of pepper

Sprinkle gelatin on tomato juice to soften. Dissolve bouillon cubes in water; stir into gelatin mixture until gelatin is dissolved. Stir in onion, salt and pepper. Cool; refrigerate until set.

To serve, break up jellied madrilene with fork; garnish with lemon wedges if desired.   8 SERVINGS (ABOUT ½ CUP EACH).

Jellied Tomato Madrilene

CAVIAR CLASSIC

Mound crushed ice in large glass bowl; place dish of chilled black or red caviar in center of ice. (Or leave caviar in original container.) If desired, sprinkle caviar with sieved hard-cooked eggs, finely chopped onion or snipped chives. Serve with lemon wedges and crisp toast triangles or black bread. Allow 1 tablespoon caviar per serving.

SHRIMP COCKTAIL

    1 bottle (12 ounces) chili sauce
    1 to 2 tablespoons prepared horseradish
    1 tablespoon lemon juice
    ½ teaspoon Worcestershire sauce
    ¼ teaspoon salt
      Dash of pepper
  36 cooked medium shrimp, chilled

Mix chili sauce, horseradish, lemon juice, Worcestershire sauce, salt and pepper; refrigerate until chilled. To serve as individual appetizers, mix shrimp with sauce. For a party snack, fill large bowl with crushed ice and place a dish of sauce in center; arrange shrimp on ice. Serve with wooden picks for dipping shrimp into sauce.   6 SERVINGS.

CLAMS ON THE HALF SHELL

Wash 36 shell clams (littlenecks or cherrystones), discarding any broken-shell or open (dead) clams. Hold clam in palm of hand with shell's hinge against palm. Insert slender, strong, sharp knife between halves of the shell and cut around clam, twisting knife slightly to pry open shell. Cut both muscles from shell. Remove only half of the shell.

Place a bed of crushed ice in each of 6 shallow bowls or plates. Arrange 6 half-shell clams on ice around small container of cocktail sauce. Garnish with lemon wedges if desired.   6 SERVINGS.

OYSTERS ON THE HALF SHELL

For each serving, scrub 5 or 6 medium oysters in shells under running cold water. Break off thin end of shell with hammer. Force a table knife or shucking knife between shell at broken end; pull apart. Cut oyster at muscle to separate from shell. Remove any bits of shell. Place oyster on deep half of shell; discard other half. Arrange shells on crushed ice. Garnish with parsley and lemon wedges. Serve with rye bread and cocktail sauce.

Force a table knife (or shucking knife) between oyster shell at broken end; pull halves of shell apart.

To eat this French delicacy, grasp snail shell firmly with holder; remove meat with the long-handled fork.

OYSTERS ROCKEFELLER

      Rock salt
12 medium oysters in shells
 2 tablespoons finely chopped onion
 2 tablespoons snipped parsley
 2 tablespoons finely chopped celery
¼ cup margarine or butter
½ cup chopped fresh or frozen spinach
      (partially thawed and drained)
⅓ cup dry bread crumbs
¼ teaspoon salt
 7 drops red pepper sauce
      Dash of ground anise

Fill three 9-inch pie plates ½ inch deep with rock salt; sprinkle with water. Scrub and prepare oysters as directed for Oysters on the Half Shell (page 320). Arrange filled shells on rock salt base.

Heat oven to 450°. Cook and stir onion, parsley and celery in margarine until onion is tender. Mix in remaining ingredients. Spoon about 1 tablespoon spinach mixture onto oyster in each shell. Bake 10 minutes.   2 SERVINGS.

Oysters Parmesan: Omit spinach mixture. Spoon 1 teaspoon dairy sour cream onto oyster in each shell. Mix ½ cup grated Parmesan cheese, ¼ cup cracker crumbs, ¼ cup margarine or butter, melted, and ½ teaspoon dry mustard. Spoon about 2 teaspoons cheese mixture onto each oyster.

ESCARGOTS (SNAILS)

⅔ cup margarine or butter, softened
 2 cloves garlic, crushed
 1 teaspoon dried parsley flakes
 1 teaspoon finely chopped green onion
½ teaspoon salt
⅛ teaspoon pepper
 1 package (2 dozen) snail shells
 1 can (4½ ounces) natural snails, drained
      and rinsed
 2 tablespoons dry white wine or apple
      juice

Heat oven to 400°. Mix margarine, garlic, parsley, onion, salt and pepper. Spoon small amount of margarine mixture into each snail shell; insert snail and top each with remaining margarine mixture.

Pour wine into baking dish, 8x8x2 inches, or into each section of snail plates; arrange filled shells open ends up in dish or plates. Bake until margarine mixture is bubbly, about 10 minutes.   4 TO 6 SERVINGS.

NOTE: Canned snails and packages of snail shells are available in specialty food stores, as are snail holders, long slender forks and specially grooved plates designed to prevent the shells from rattling and tipping as they're baked and served. If you don't have snail plates and forks, you can serve snails on salad plates with small cocktail forks.

Dips and Spreads

What do you dip in a dip? Something crisp! Raw asparagus, sliced mushrooms, thin strips of turnip or zucchini, carrot and celery sticks, cauliflowerets, radishes. And something crunchy: not just chips—but pretzels, snacks and cracker "scoops."

GUACAMOLE

  2 avocados, cut up
  1 medium onion, finely chopped (about ½ cup)
  1 or 2 green chili peppers, finely chopped
  1 tablespoon lemon juice
  1 teaspoon salt
  ½ teaspoon coarsely ground pepper
  ½ teaspoon ascorbic acid mixture
  1 medium tomato, finely chopped (about ¾ cup)

Beat avocados, onion, peppers, lemon juice, salt, pepper and ascorbic acid mixture until creamy. Stir in tomato. Cover and refrigerate at least 1 hour. Serve with corn chips.   ABOUT 2 CUPS DIP.

Bacon Guacamole: Stir in 2 slices bacon, crisply fried and crumbled.

Creamy Guacamole: Stir in ¼ cup mayonnaise or salad dressing and ½ teaspoon garlic salt.

COTTAGE CHEESE-CHIVE DIP

  1 cup creamed cottage cheese
  1 tablespoon lemon juice
  1 tablespoon milk
  ¼ teaspoon garlic salt
  1 tablespoon snipped chives

Place cottage cheese, lemon juice, milk and garlic salt in blender container. Cover and blend on high speed, stopping blender occasionally to scrape sides, until smooth, about 2 minutes. Pour into small bowl; stir in chives. Refrigerate at least 1 hour.   ABOUT 1 CUP DIP.

Cheese-Chive Dip: Add 3 tablespoons shredded American or grated Parmesan or Romano cheese with the cottage cheese.

Chutney-Chive Dip: Add ½ teaspoon curry powder with the cottage cheese. Stir in 3 tablespoons chutney and ¼ cup chopped salted cashews or peanuts.

Vegetable-Chive Dip: Stir in ½ to 1 cup shredded carrots, sliced radishes, chopped celery or green pepper and ½ to 1 teaspoon lemon juice.

CHEESE SPREAD DIP

  1 jar (8 ounces) pasteurized process cheese spread
  2 tablespoons dry white wine
  2 teaspoons prepared mustard
  ½ teaspoon Worcestershire sauce
    Dash of cayenne red pepper

Mix all ingredients. Cover and refrigerate at least 1 hour.   ABOUT 1 CUP DIP.

Clam Dip: Stir in 1 can (8 ounces) minced clams, drained.

Garden Dip: Stir in 1 cup fresh or frozen (thawed) green peas.

FRUIT STACK DIPPERS

 30 seedless green grapes (about ½ cup)
 30 pineapple chunks, each about ¾ inch wide (¼ pineapple), or 1 can (8¼ ounces) sliced pineapple, drained and each slice cut into eighths
 26 mandarin orange segments or 1 can (11 ounces) mandarin orange segments, drained
 15 strawberries, cut into halves (about 1 cup)
 24 cheese cubes, each about ¾ inch thick (about 8 ounces caraway, colby, Cheddar, Monterey Jack or cream cheese)
    Lime-Yogurt Dip (below)

Alternate 3 pieces of any combination of fruit and cheese on plastic or wooden picks. Serve with Lime-Yogurt Dip.   ABOUT 40 APPETIZERS.

LIME-YOGURT DIP

Mix ½ cup unflavored yogurt, 1 tablespoon honey and grated peel of 1 medium lime.

Fruit Stack Dippers

CHEESE-SOUR CREAM DIP

¾ cup shredded sharp Cheddar or process
   American cheese
¾ cup dairy sour cream
½ teaspoon Worcestershire sauce
¼ teaspoon salt (optional)
¼ teaspoon dry mustard

Mix all ingredients. Cover and refrigerate at least 1 hour. (For a thinner dip, stir in 1 to 2 teaspoons milk.) Garnish with snipped parsley if desired. ABOUT 1 CUP DIP.

Blue Cheese-Sour Cream Dip: Substitute ¼ cup crumbled blue cheese for the Cheddar cheese.

Dried Beef-Sour Cream Dip: Omit cheese and salt. Mix in 1 package (2½ ounces) dried beef, snipped.

Liverwurst-Sour Cream Dip: Omit cheese. Mash ¼ cup liverwurst with fork. Mix in liverwurst and 2 tablespoons pickle relish.

Olive-Sour Cream Dip: Omit cheese. Mix in ⅓ cup sliced pitted ripe or pimiento-stuffed olives.

Onion-Sour Cream Dip: Omit cheese, salt and mustard. Mix in 2 tablespoons onion soup mix.

Red Bean-Sour Cream Dip: Omit cheese. Mix in 1 can (8 ounces) kidney beans, drained, 4 slices bacon, crisply fried and crumbled, and 2 tablespoons chopped green pepper.

POLYNESIAN SHRIMP DIP

Cut 1-inch slice from top of pineapple, leaving green leaves on top. Cut out and remove fruit from pineapple, leaving ½-inch shell. Remove core from fruit and cut remaining pineapple into bite-size pieces.

Place pitted ripe olive in curve of each cleaned cooked shrimp; secure with wooden pick. (You will need about 1 cup shrimp.*) Place pineapple pieces on picks. Attach rows of shrimp and pineapple in spiral design to shell of pineapple.

Place custard cup of Curry Dip (below) in pineapple; cover with pineapple top if desired. Serve immediately or cover completely with plastic wrap and refrigerate. 6 SERVINGS.

*From ¾ pound fresh or frozen raw shrimp (in shells), 1 package (7 ounces) frozen peeled shrimp or 1 can (4½ or 5 ounces) shrimp.

CURRY DIP
Mix 1 cup dairy sour cream, ¾ teaspoon curry powder and ¼ teaspoon salt.

SANTA FE BEAN DIP

1 can (11 ounces) condensed black bean soup
1 can (8 ounces) tomato sauce
½ cup shredded Cheddar cheese (about
   2 ounces)
1 to 1½ teaspoons chili powder
2 tablespoons shredded Cheddar cheese

Heat soup, tomato sauce, ½ cup cheese and the chili powder just to boiling over medium heat, stirring frequently. Sprinkle with 2 tablespoons cheese. ABOUT 2 CUPS DIP.

Bean-with-Bacon Dip: Substitute 1 can (11½ ounces) condensed bean with bacon soup for the black bean soup. Before heating, place soup, tomato sauce, ½ cup cheese and the chili powder in blender container. Cover and blend on high speed until smooth, about 10 seconds.

CHEESE FONDUE DIP

2 tablespoons margarine or butter
2 cups shredded sharp process American
   cheese (about 8 ounces)
3 to 5 drops red pepper sauce
⅓ cup dry white wine
   Dippers (green pepper, zucchini and
   celery sticks, cherry tomato halves,
   rye bread cubes)

Heat margarine in 1-quart saucepan over low heat until melted. Stir in cheese gradually until melted. Add pepper sauce; stir in wine slowly. Heat, stirring constantly, until hot. Pour into ceramic fondue pot or chafing dish; keep warm over low heat. Use long-handled forks to spear Dippers, then dip and swirl in fondue with stirring motion to keep fondue from sticking. ABOUT 1½ CUPS DIP.

■ **To Microwave:** Microwave margarine uncovered in 1½-quart glass bowl 30 seconds. Stir in cheese. Microwave 30 seconds; stir. Microwave 30 seconds longer. Add pepper sauce; stir in wine slowly. Microwave until hot, 30 seconds.

Chili Fondue Dip: Stir in 1 can (4 ounces) whole green chilies, drained and chopped, after stirring in the wine.

Lobster Fondue Dip: Stir in 1 can (5 ounces) lobster, drained and broken into small pieces, after stirring in the wine.

Pepperoni Fondue Dip: Stir in ¾ cup finely snipped pepperoni or salami and 1 small clove garlic, finely chopped, after stirring in the wine.

CREAM CHEESE-TUNA DIP

¼ cup milk
1 package (8 ounces) cream cheese, softened
½ cup mayonnaise or salad dressing
¼ cup chopped green onions (with tops)
2 teaspoons prepared horseradish
⅛ teaspoon red pepper sauce
   Dash of Worcestershire sauce
1 can (6½ ounces) tuna, drained
   Paprika

Stir milk, 1 tablespoon at a time, into cream cheese. Mix in mayonnaise, onions, horseradish, pepper sauce and Worcestershire sauce. Stir in tuna; sprinkle with paprika. Cover and refrigerate at least 1 hour. ABOUT 2½ CUPS DIP.

Cream Cheese-Crab Dip: Substitute 1 can (7 ounces) crabmeat, drained and cartilage removed, for the tuna.

Cream Cheese-Deviled Ham Dip: Mix in 1 tablespoon prepared mustard with the mayonnaise. Substitute 1 can (4½ ounces) deviled ham for the tuna.

Cream Cheese-Shrimp Dip: Substitute 1 can (4½ ounces) tiny shrimp, drained, for the tuna.

SALMON PARTY SPREAD

1 package (8 ounces) cream cheese, softened
1 can (16 ounces) salmon, drained and
   flaked
1 tablespoon lemon juice
1 tablespoon grated onion
¼ teaspoon liquid smoke
¼ teaspoon salt

Mix all ingredients. Pack in 3 individual soufflé dishes or 1-cup containers. Cover and refrigerate at least 8 hours but no longer than 4 days. Sprinkle with snipped parsley if desired. 3 CUPS SPREAD.

Salmon Party Ball: Shape salmon mixture into a ball. After refrigerating, roll ball in mixture of ½ cup chopped nuts and 3 tablespoons snipped parsley.

PARTY CHEESE BALL

2 packages (8 ounces each) cream cheese
¾ cup crumbled blue cheese (about
   4 ounces)
1 cup shredded sharp Cheddar cheese
   (about 4 ounces)
1 small onion, finely chopped (about
   ¼ cup)
1 tablespoon Worcestershire sauce
   Finely snipped parsley

Place cheeses in small mixer bowl; let stand at room temperature until softened. Beat in onion and Worcestershire sauce on low speed. Beat on medium speed, scraping bowl frequently, until fluffy. Cover and refrigerate at least 8 hours.

Shape mixture into 1 large ball or into thirty to thirty-six 1-inch balls. Roll in parsley; place on serving plate. Cover and refrigerate until firm, about 2 hours. To serve small balls, insert wooden pick in each. ABOUT 12 SERVINGS.

INDIVIDUAL APPETIZER PATES

1 package (8 ounces) frozen chicken livers,
   thawed
½ cup water
1 chicken bouillon cube or 1 teaspoon
   instant chicken bouillon
1 small onion, chopped (about ¼ cup)
¼ teaspoon dried thyme leaves
3 slices bacon, crisply fried and
   crumbled
¼ cup margarine or butter, softened
¼ teaspoon dry mustard
⅛ teaspoon garlic salt
   Dash of pepper

Mix chicken livers, water, bouillon cube, onion and thyme in 1-quart saucepan. Heat to boiling; reduce heat. Simmer uncovered until livers are done, about 15 minutes. Cool mixture; drain and reserve ¼ cup broth.

Mix chicken livers, reserved broth and the remaining ingredients in small mixer bowl or blender container. Beat on low speed of mixer and then on high speed until creamy, or beat in blender until smooth, about 30 seconds. Divide mixture among eight 1½-inch paper nut cups. Cover and refrigerate at least 3 hours.

At serving time, remove paper cups and invert molded pâté on individual plates. Garnish with parsley if desired. 8 SERVINGS.

Pick-up Nibbles

Party guests will welcome an array of bite-size, fingertip tidbits. Put your friends at ease with these crowd-pleasers.

SAUSAGE SMORGASBORD

    Salami Wedges (below)
    Cream Cheese Balls (below)
    Sausage Frills (below)
8 ounces natural Cheddar cheese
8 ounces Swiss cheese
8 ounces caraway cheese
¾ pound hard summer sausage, sliced

Prepare Salami Wedges, Cream Cheese Balls and Sausage Frills; cover and refrigerate.

Cut cheeses into ½-inch cubes. Arrange wedges, balls, frills, cheese cubes and sausage in attractive pattern on large serving platter. Cover and refrigerate until serving time. Serve with assorted breads if desired.   8 TO 10 SERVINGS.

SALAMI WEDGES

Spread 1 package (3 ounces) cream cheese, softened, over 9 slices salami (each 4½ inches); stack and top with a plain slice salami. Cover and refrigerate. Just before serving, cut into 12 wedges.

CREAM CHEESE BALLS

1 package (8 ounces) cream cheese, softened
1 teaspoon prepared horseradish
    Chopped radishes
½ teaspoon curry powder
    Chopped pitted ripe olives
½ teaspoon celery seed
    Chopped sweet pickles

Cut cream cheese into 3 equal parts. Stir horseradish into 1 part; shape into 1-inch balls and roll in chopped radishes. Stir curry powder into second part; shape into 1-inch balls and roll in chopped olives. Stir celery seed into remaining part; shape into 1-inch balls and roll in chopped pickles.

SAUSAGE FRILLS

Spread your favorite cheese spread in a strip across center of each of 6 slices large bologna. Fold bologna lengthwise down center of cheese. Keeping rounded edges of folded bologna together, "pleat" into thirds. Secure each fan at pointed end with wooden pick.

STUFFED CELERY STICKS

7 medium stalks celery
½ cup shredded Swiss cheese (about 2 ounces)
½ cup finely chopped fully cooked ham
⅓ cup mayonnaise or salad dressing
½ teaspoon prepared mustard

Cut celery into 3-inch pieces (make sure celery is completely dry). Mix remaining ingredients; spread about 1 tablespoon in each piece of celery. Cover and refrigerate 1 hour.   ABOUT 14 APPETIZERS.

CHERRY TOMATO BLOSSOMS

1 pint medium to large cherry tomatoes (about 24)
2 ounces cheese (caraway, colby, Cheddar, Monterey Jack or cream cheese), cut into ½-inch cubes (about 24)
    Parsley sprigs

Place tomatoes stem sides down; cut each almost through to bottom into fourths (larger tomatoes can be cut into sixths). Place cheese cube in center of each tomato. Top with small parsley sprigs.
ABOUT 24 APPETIZERS.

GARLIC OLIVES

1 can (7¾ ounces) ripe olives, drained
1 jar (7 ounces) green olives, drained
½ cup vinegar
½ cup olive oil
½ cup vegetable oil
1 small onion, sliced
1 clove garlic, sliced

Split olives slightly; place in jar with remaining ingredients. Cover tightly and shake. Refrigerate at least 2 hours.   3 CUPS OLIVES.

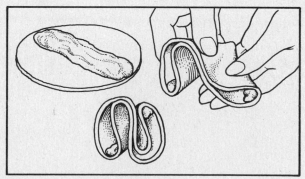

To form Sausage Frill (left), "pleat" into an S-shape.

PARTY FINGER FOODS

Stuffed Mushrooms (page 329)

Sesame Seed Squares (page 328)

Olive-Cheese Balls (page 328)

Deviled Eggs (page 327)

Shrimp-Bacon Bites (page 330)

Pickled Eggs (page 327)

Cherry Tomato Blossoms (page 325)

Bambinos (page 328)

Little Pecan Sandwiches (page 327)

PICKLED BEETS

2 cans (16 ounces each) sliced beets
1½ cups sugar
¾ cup vinegar
2 three-inch sticks cinnamon

Drain beets, reserving liquid in saucepan. Add sugar, vinegar and cinnamon sticks to reserved liquid. Heat to boiling, stirring constantly. Pour over beets; cool. Cover and refrigerate at least 8 hours.   ABOUT 3 CUPS BEETS.

PICKLED GREEN BEANS

1 can (16 ounces) cut green beans, drained
½ small onion, sliced and separated into
    rings
¼ cup vinegar
3 tablespoons dry white wine
1 teaspoon salt
¼ teaspoon dried dill weed

Place beans in 1-quart jar. Heat remaining ingredients to boiling; pour into jar. Cover and refrigerate, shaking several times, at least 24 hours. Drain before serving.   4 TO 6 SERVINGS.

Pickled Artichokes: Substitute 1 can (14 ounces) artichoke hearts, drained and cut into halves, for the beans. Omit dill weed.

Pickled Mushrooms: Substitute 36 small mushroom caps or 16 large mushrooms, cut into halves, for the green beans. Omit dill weed. Heat 2 tablespoons soy sauce with the remaining ingredients.

PICKLED EGGS

6 hard-cooked eggs
1 cup cider vinegar
1 cup beet liquid
⅓ cup granulated sugar or packed brown
    sugar
½ teaspoon salt
1 small onion, chopped (about ¼ cup)
4 whole cloves
    Shredded greens

Place peeled eggs in bowl or jar. Mix vinegar, beet liquid, sugar, salt, onion and cloves; pour over eggs. Cover and refrigerate at least 2 days. Slice eggs; serve on greens.   6 SERVINGS.

Spiced Pickled Eggs: Substitute 2 cups white vinegar for the cider vinegar and beet liquid.

DEVILED EGGS

6 hard-cooked eggs
½ teaspoon salt
½ teaspoon dry mustard
¼ teaspoon pepper
3 tablespoons mayonnaise, salad dressing,
    vinegar or half-and-half

Cut peeled eggs lengthwise into halves. Slip out yolks; mash with fork. Mix in salt, mustard, pepper and mayonnaise. Fill whites with egg yolk mixture, heaping it lightly. Arrange eggs on large serving plate. Cover and refrigerate no longer than 24 hours.   6 SERVINGS.

Catsup Deviled Eggs: Decrease salt to ¼ teaspoon and substitute ¼ cup plus 1 tablespoon catsup for the mayonnaise.

Deviled Eggs with Olives: Decrease salt to ¼ teaspoon, omit mustard and mix ¼ cup finely chopped ripe olives and ⅛ teaspoon curry powder into the egg yolk mixture.

Party Deviled Eggs: Garnish each deviled egg half with cooked shrimp, rolled anchovy fillet or sliced pimiento-stuffed olive.

Zesty Deviled Eggs: Decrease salt to ¼ teaspoon and mix ½ cup finely shredded process American cheese (about 2 ounces), 2 tablespoons snipped parsley or 1 teaspoon prepared horseradish into the egg yolk mixture.

LITTLE PECAN SANDWICHES

Spread ¼ teaspoon anchovy paste, bacon-flavored cheese spread or cream cheese, softened, on 1 large pecan half; top with another pecan half to make a tiny "sandwich."

SAVORY ALMONDS

1 cup blanched almonds
2 tablespoons margarine or butter
1 teaspoon salt
½ teaspoon ground ginger

Heat oven to 350°. Place almonds and margarine in shallow pan. Bake, stirring occasionally, until golden brown, about 20 minutes. Drain on paper towels. Sprinkle salt and ginger over almonds; toss. Serve warm.   1 CUP SNACK.

Garlic Almonds: Omit salt and substitute garlic salt for the ginger.

BAMBINOS

4 dozen Melba or cracker rounds
¾ cup catsup
  About 2 ounces thinly sliced pepperoni
1 cup shredded mozzarella cheese (about
    4 ounces)
  Dried oregano leaves

Heat oven to 400°. Spread rounds with catsup; top with pepperoni slices. Sprinkle cheese and oregano over pepperoni. Bake on ungreased cookie sheet until cheese is melted, 3 to 5 minutes.   4 DOZEN CANAPES.

SESAME SEED SQUARES

Heat oven to 350°. Bake 2 tablespoons sesame seed on ungreased cookie sheet until golden, about 10 minutes; cool. Cut 1 package (3 ounces) cream cheese into 9 squares. Roll each cheese square in sesame seed. Dip into soy sauce; refrigerate. At serving time, dip cheese squares into soy sauce and garnish each with parsley sprig if desired.
9 CHEESE SQUARES.

Dried Beef Squares: Omit sesame seed and soy sauce. Dip cheese squares into 2 tablespoons finely snipped dried beef.

POPCORN

Pour ½ cup popcorn and ¼ cup vegetable oil into Dutch oven; tilt pan to distribute popcorn. Cover and cook over medium-high heat until 1 kernel pops. Remove from heat; let stand 1 minute. Return to heat; cook, shaking pan occasionally, until popcorn stops popping.   ABOUT 12 CUPS POPCORN.

PARMESAN-CURRY POPCORN

½ cup margarine or butter, melted
⅓ cup grated Parmesan cheese
½ teaspoon salt
¼ teaspoon curry powder
12 cups Popcorn (above)

Mix margarine, cheese, salt and curry powder. Pour over Popcorn; toss.   12 CUPS POPCORN.

TOASTED CEREAL SNACK

4 cups toasted oat cereal
2 cups pretzel sticks
1 cup Spanish peanuts
¼ cup margarine or butter
1 tablespoon Worcestershire sauce
1 teaspoon paprika
1 teaspoon garlic salt

Heat oven to 275°. Mix cereal, pretzel sticks and peanuts in ungreased oblong pan, 13x9x2 inches. Heat margarine in 1-quart saucepan until melted; remove from heat. Stir in Worcestershire sauce, paprika and garlic salt. Pour over cereal mixture, tossing until thoroughly coated. Bake, stirring occasionally, 30 minutes.

Snack can be stored in airtight container about 1 week or frozen in airtight container about 2 weeks. If frozen, thaw at room temperature or heat in 275° oven about 5 minutes.   ABOUT 7½ CUPS SNACK.

NOTE: This recipe can be doubled. Mix cereal, pretzel sticks and peanuts in 2 ungreased oblong pans, 13x9x2 inches. Stagger pans in oven. Continue as directed.

■ **To Microwave:** Mix cereal, pretzel sticks and peanuts in 4-quart glass bowl. Microwave margarine uncovered in 1-cup glass measuring cup until melted, about 30 seconds. Stir in Worcestershire sauce, paprika and garlic salt. Pour over cereal mixture, tossing until thoroughly coated. Microwave uncovered, stirring every 2 minutes, until hot and crispy, 5 to 6 minutes.

OLIVE-CHEESE BALLS

2 cups shredded sharp natural Cheddar
    cheese (about 8 ounces)
1¼ cups all-purpose flour*
½ cup margarine or butter, melted
  About 36 small pimiento-stuffed olives,
    drained

Mix cheese and flour; mix in margarine. (Work dough with hands if it seems dry.) Mold 1 teaspoon dough around each olive; shape into a ball. Place 2 inches apart on ungreased cookie sheet. Cover and refrigerate at least 1 hour.

Heat oven to 400°. Bake until set, 15 to 20 minutes.   3 TO 4 DOZEN APPETIZERS.

*Do not use self-rising flour in this recipe.

BISCUIT PARTY SNACKS

⅓ cup shortening
1¾ cups all-purpose flour*
2½ teaspoons baking powder
¾ teaspoon salt
½ cup shredded sharp cheese (about 2 ounces)
¾ cup milk
1 can (4½ ounces) deviled ham
½ teaspoon prepared horseradish

Heat oven to 450°. Cut shortening into flour, baking powder and salt with pastry blender until mixture resembles fine crumbs. Stir in cheese and just enough milk so dough leaves side of bowl and rounds up into a ball. (Too much milk makes dough sticky; not enough milk makes biscuits dry.)

Turn dough onto lightly floured cloth-covered board. Knead lightly 10 times. Divide into halves; roll each half into 8-inch square. Place 1 square on ungreased cookie sheet. Mix deviled ham and horseradish; spread over dough on cookie sheet. Top with other half. Cut into 1-inch squares. Bake until golden brown, 10 to 12 minutes. Immediately remove from cookie sheet. 64 APPETIZERS.

*If using self-rising flour, omit baking powder and salt.

STUFFED MUSHROOMS

1 pound medium mushrooms
1 small onion, chopped (about ¼ cup)
½ small green pepper, chopped (about ¼ cup)
3 tablespoons margarine or butter
1½ cups soft bread crumbs
½ teaspoon salt
½ teaspoon dried thyme leaves
¼ teaspoon ground turmeric
¼ teaspoon pepper
1 tablespoon margarine or butter

Heat oven to 350°. Cut stems from mushrooms; finely chop enough stems to measure ⅓ cup.

Cook and stir chopped mushroom stems, onion and green pepper in 3 tablespoons margarine until tender, about 5 minutes; remove from heat. Stir in bread crumbs, salt, thyme, turmeric and pepper.

Heat 1 tablespoon margarine in shallow baking dish until melted. Fill mushroom caps with stuffing mixture; place mushrooms filled sides up in baking dish. Bake 15 minutes. Set oven control to broil and/or 550°. Broil 3 to 4 inches from heat 2 minutes. Serve hot. ABOUT 3 DOZEN APPETIZERS.

LITTLE WIENER KABOBS

30 cocktail wieners
4 dill pickles, cut into ¾-inch pieces (about ¾ cup)
1 can (4 ounces) button mushrooms, drained
1 pint small cherry tomatoes (about 40)
15 large pimiento-stuffed olives
1 medium green pepper, cut into ¾-inch squares (about 24)
Lemon Butter (below)

Heat oven to 450°. Alternate 2 wieners and the vegetables on each skewer; place on rack in broiler pan. Brush with Lemon Butter. Bake until hot, 4 to 6 minutes. 15 KABOBS.

LEMON BUTTER
Heat 2 tablespoons margarine or butter, 1 teaspoon lemon juice and dash of red pepper sauce until margarine is melted.

RUMAKI

6 chicken livers
4 water chestnuts
Teriyaki Sauce (below)
6 slices bacon
Brown sugar

Cut chicken livers into halves; cut each water chestnut into 3 pieces. Pour Teriyaki Sauce on livers and water chestnuts in bowl. Refrigerate at least 4 hours; drain.

Cut bacon slices into halves. Wrap a piece of liver and a piece of water chestnut in each bacon piece. Secure with wooden pick; roll in brown sugar.

Set oven control to broil and/or 550°. Broil 3 to 4 inches from heat, turning occasionally, until bacon is crisp, about 10 minutes. 12 APPETIZERS.

TERIYAKI SAUCE
¼ cup vegetable oil
¼ cup soy sauce
2 tablespoons catsup
1 tablespoon vinegar
¼ teaspoon pepper
2 cloves garlic, crushed

Mix all ingredients.

NOTE: To cook on a hibachi, place over hot coals; cook, turning frequently, 15 to 20 minutes.

SHRIMP-BACON BITES

1 cup cleaned cooked shrimp*
½ clove garlic, slivered
½ cup chili sauce
8 to 10 slices bacon

Mix shrimp and garlic; pour chili sauce on mixture. Cover and refrigerate, stirring occasionally, several hours.

Cut bacon slices into halves. Fry bacon until partially cooked; drain. Wrap each shrimp in bacon piece; secure with wooden pick.

Set oven control to broil and/or 550°. Broil 2 to 3 inches from heat until bacon is crisp. 16 TO 20 APPETIZERS.

*From ¾ pound fresh or frozen raw shrimp (in shells), 1 package (7 ounces) frozen peeled shrimp or 1 can (4½ or 5 ounces) shrimp.

COCKTAIL MEATBALLS

1 pound hamburger
½ cup dry bread crumbs
⅓ cup finely chopped onion
¼ cup milk
1 egg
1 tablespoon snipped parsley
1 teaspoon salt
½ teaspoon Worcestershire sauce
⅛ teaspoon pepper
¼ cup shortening
1 bottle (12 ounces) chili sauce
1 jar (10 ounces) grape jelly

Mix hamburger, bread crumbs, onion, milk, egg, parsley, salt, Worcestershire sauce and pepper; gently shape into 1-inch balls.

Cook meatballs in shortening in 12-inch skillet until brown. Remove meatballs from skillet; drain fat. Heat chili sauce and jelly in skillet, stirring constantly, until jelly is melted. Add meatballs and stir until coated. Simmer uncovered 30 minutes. Serve hot in chafing dish. 5 DOZEN MEATBALLS.

Cocktail Sausages: Substitute 4 cans (4 ounces each) Vienna sausages, cut crosswise into halves, for the meatballs. Decrease simmering time to 20 minutes.

Cocktail Wieners: Substitute 4 jars (4 ounces each) cocktail wieners for the meatballs. Decrease simmering time to 20 minutes.

BROILED HAM ON PICKS

Trim fat from 1 fully cooked center-cut smoked ham slice, ¾ inch thick (about 1½ pounds). Cut ham into 1-inch pieces. Secure on wooden picks and arrange in shallow pan. Prepare Zesty Bar-B-Q Sauce (below).

Set oven control to broil and/or 550°. Broil ham pieces 2 to 3 inches from heat until hot, 2 to 3 minutes. Serve with Zesty Bar-B-Q Sauce. ABOUT 40 APPETIZERS.

ZESTY BAR-B-Q SAUCE

½ cup catsup
¼ cup vinegar
2 tablespoons chopped onion
1 tablespoon Worcestershire sauce
2 teaspoons packed brown sugar
¼ teaspoon dry mustard
1 clove garlic, crushed

Heat all ingredients to boiling over medium heat, stirring constantly; reduce heat. Simmer uncovered, stirring occasionally, 15 minutes.

GLAZED CHICKEN WINGS

3 pounds chicken wings (17 or 18)
⅓ cup soy sauce
2 tablespoons vegetable oil
2 tablespoons chili sauce
¼ cup honey
1 teaspoon salt
½ teaspoon ground ginger
¼ teaspoon garlic powder
¼ teaspoon cayenne red pepper (optional)

For easier handling as a finger food, separate chicken wings at joints. Mix remaining ingredients; pour on chicken. Cover and refrigerate, turning chicken occasionally, at least 1 hour.

Heat oven to 375°. Drain chicken, reserving marinade. Place chicken on rack in foil-lined broiler pan. Bake 30 minutes. Brush chicken with reserved marinade. Turn chicken and bake, brushing occasionally with marinade, until tender, about 30 minutes. 17 OR 18 APPETIZERS.

Do-ahead Tip: After baking, chicken can be covered and refrigerated no longer than 24 hours. To heat, bake uncovered in 375° oven until hot, about 7 minutes.

DEVILED PUFFS

1 cup water
½ cup margarine or butter
1 cup all-purpose flour*
4 eggs
3 cans (4½ ounces each) deviled ham
1 tablespoon prepared horseradish
¾ teaspoon pepper
¾ teaspoon onion salt
⅓ cup dairy sour cream

Heat oven to 400°. Heat water and margarine to rolling boil in 3-quart saucepan. Stir in flour. Stir vigorously over low heat until mixture forms a ball, about 1 minute; remove from heat. Beat in eggs, all at once, until smooth and glossy.

Drop dough by slightly rounded teaspoonfuls onto ungreased cookie sheet. Bake until puffed, golden brown and dry, about 25 minutes. Cool on wire racks away from draft.

Blend deviled ham, horseradish, pepper, onion salt and sour cream; refrigerate. Just before serving, cut off tops of puffs with sharp knife; remove any filaments of soft dough. Fill each puff with slightly rounded teaspoonful of ham mixture.   ABOUT 6 DOZEN APPETIZERS.

*Self-rising flour can be used in this recipe.

TINY COCKTAIL BUNS

½ Refrigerator Roll Dough (page 212)
1 egg yolk
1 tablespoon water
   Poppy or sesame seed

Shape dough into 1-inch balls; place on greased cookie sheet. Beat egg yolk and water; brush tops of balls with egg mixture. Sprinkle with poppy seed. Let rise until double, about 1 hour. Heat oven to 400°. Bake until golden brown, about 15 minutes.   ABOUT 4 DOZEN BUNS.

Tiny Cocktail Rolls: Roll dough into rectangle, 13x10 inches, on well-floured surface. Place on greased cookie sheet. Cut into 1-inch squares with knife dipped in flour. Brush with egg mixture and sprinkle with poppy seed. Continue as directed. ABOUT 11 DOZEN ROLLS.

Fold in the folded edges to meet in the center.

Fold rectangle as if closing a book, then flatten; repeat.

PARMESAN FANS

1 cup margarine or butter
1½ cups all-purpose flour*
½ cup dairy sour cream
¾ cup grated Parmesan cheese

Cut margarine into flour until mixture resembles fine crumbs. Blend in sour cream. Divide pastry into 4 equal parts; wrap each part and refrigerate at least 8 hours.

Heat oven to 350°. Roll each part pastry into rectangle, 12x6 inches, on well-floured cloth-covered board. Sprinkle with 2 tablespoons of the cheese. Fold ends to meet in center, forming a square. Sprinkle with 1 tablespoon of the cheese. Fold in folded edges to meet in center. Fold lengthwise in half (as if you were closing a book). Flatten lightly; fold lengthwise again. Cut ³⁄₁₆-inch slices on folded edge; place on ungreased cookie sheet. Bring ends together to form a fan shape. Bake until light brown, 20 to 25 minutes.   ABOUT 4 DOZEN APPETIZERS.

*If using self-rising flour, decrease baking time slightly.

Party Sandwiches

Be your own caterer! These sandwiches look so pretty and professional that everyone will think you had them specially made. Vary your canapé bases and be sure to add the garnishes for identification and color.

CANAPE TOAST BASES

Remove crusts from slices of sandwich bread. Cut each slice into 4 squares or cut with round, star or other shaped cutter. Heat small amount of margarine or butter in skillet until melted; toast bread cutouts in skillet over low heat until brown on one side. Just before serving, spread untoasted side with desired spread.

Broiled Canapé Toast Bases: Set oven control to broil and/or 550°. Lightly brush one side with margarine or butter, melted, after cutting bread into shapes. Broil 3 to 4 inches from heat until golden brown on buttered side, 3 to 4 minutes.

SMOKED TURKEY CANAPES

1 package (3 ounces) smoked sliced turkey, finely chopped
1 small stalk celery, finely chopped (about ¼ cup)
1 tablespoon finely chopped onion
⅓ cup mayonnaise or salad dressing
⅛ teaspoon liquid smoke
Canapé Toast Bases (above) or crackers

Mix turkey, celery, onion, mayonnaise and liquid smoke. Cover and refrigerate at least 3 hours. Serve on Canapé Toast Bases.   ABOUT 16 CANAPES.

SMOKED SALMON CANAPES

2 packages (3 ounces each) cream cheese, softened
2 teaspoons prepared mustard
25 Canapé Toast Bases (above)
1 can (3⅔ ounces) smoked salmon, drained
Parsley sprigs

Blend cream cheese and mustard; spread part of mixture thinly on Canapé Toast Bases. Place piece of salmon on each toast base; top with dot of remaining cream cheese mixture. Or pipe all the cream cheese mixture around base. Top each canapé with parsley sprig.   25 CANAPES.

CAVIAR CANAPES

Divide 2 jars (2 ounces each) red caviar among 20 Canapé Toast Bases (left); spread evenly. If desired, cut a lemon into ⅛-inch slices; make very tiny lemon wedges by cutting along membrane lines and place 2 wedges on each canapé.   20 CANAPES.

CRABMEAT SPREAD

1 can (7½ ounces) crabmeat, drained and cartilage removed
⅓ cup mayonnaise or salad dressing
1 tablespoon capers
Snipped parsley

Mix crabmeat, mayonnaise and capers. Sprinkle canapés with parsley and, if desired, garnish with additional capers.   ABOUT 1 CUP SPREAD (ENOUGH FOR 4 DOZEN 1-INCH CANAPES).

CLAM-CREAM CHEESE SPREAD

1 package (8 ounces) cream cheese, softened
1 can (8 ounces) minced clams, rinsed and drained
½ teaspoon seasoned salt
¼ teaspoon Worcestershire sauce
¼ teaspoon onion juice
Ripe olive slices

Mix cream cheese and clams. Stir in seasoned salt, Worcestershire sauce and onion juice. Top canapés with olive slices.   ABOUT 1¼ CUPS SPREAD (ENOUGH FOR 5 DOZEN 1-INCH CANAPES).

CHICKEN-HAM-CHEESE SPREAD

1 can (5 ounces) boned chicken, rinsed and finely chopped
½ cup finely chopped fully cooked ham
½ cup shredded sharp Cheddar cheese (about 2 ounces)
1 teaspoon salt
Dash of pepper
Snipped parsley

Mix chicken, ham, cheese, salt and pepper. Sprinkle canapés with parsley.   ABOUT 1¼ CUPS SPREAD (ENOUGH FOR 5 DOZEN 1-INCH CANAPES).

CHILI-HAM SPREAD

1 can (4½ ounces) deviled ham
1 tablespoon mayonnaise or salad dressing
¼ teaspoon onion juice
1 teaspoon finely chopped chili peppers
    Green olive slices

Mix deviled ham, mayonnaise, onion juice and chili peppers. Top canapés with olive slices. ABOUT ½ CUP SPREAD (ENOUGH FOR 2 DOZEN 1-INCH CANAPES).

LIVERWURST-MUSHROOM SPREAD

¼ pound liverwurst
1 can (4 ounces) mushroom stems and
    pieces, drained and finely chopped
1 teaspoon chili sauce
    Chopped hard-cooked egg yolk

Mash liverwurst with fork until smooth. Stir in mushrooms and chili sauce. Sprinkle canapés with egg yolk. ABOUT 1 CUP SPREAD (ENOUGH FOR 4 DOZEN 1-INCH CANAPES).

KIPPERED HERRING SPREAD

1 can (3¼ ounces) kippered herring, drained
¼ teaspoon vinegar
¼ teaspoon red pepper sauce
    Chopped hard-cooked egg yolk

Mix herring, vinegar and pepper sauce. Sprinkle canapés with egg yolk. ABOUT ¼ CUP SPREAD (ENOUGH FOR 1 DOZEN 1-INCH CANAPES).

FREEZER CANAPE TRAY

Trim crust from day-old unsliced loaf white, whole wheat or rye sandwich bread. Cut loaf horizontally into ½-inch slices. Spread margarine or butter, softened, on each slice; cut into desired shapes. Spread 1 level teaspoonful of one of the canapé spreads (above and page 332) to the edge of each canapé. Use two or more of the canapé spreads for a tasty and attractive tray.

Place desired number of canapés on cardboard tray; cover with plastic wrap. Wrap with aluminum foil and freeze.

Forty-five minutes before serving, remove from freezer and remove aluminum foil. Let stand at room temperature covered with plastic wrap.

PARTY SANDWICH LOAF

Trim crust from 1 loaf unsliced sandwich bread. Cut loaf horizontally into 4 slices. Spread 3 slices with margarine or butter, softened.

Place 1 buttered slice on tray or platter. Spread evenly with Shrimp Salad Spread (below). Top with second slice and spread evenly with Olive-Nut Spread (below). Top with third slice and spread evenly with Deviled Ham Spread (below). Top with unbuttered bread slice.

Mix 2 packages (8 ounces each) cream cheese, softened, and ½ cup half-and-half. (A few drops food color can be added to tint mixture a delicate color.) Frost top and sides of loaf with cream cheese mixture. Refrigerate until frosting is set, about 30 minutes. Wrap loaf in a damp cloth and refrigerate at least 2½ hours. Just before serving, top loaf with thinly sliced carrots, green onions or radishes, parsley sprigs or celery leaves. 12 TO 14 SLICES.

SHRIMP SALAD SPREAD

1 can (4½ ounces) shrimp, rinsed and
    drained
1 hard-cooked egg, finely chopped
2 tablespoons finely chopped celery
1 tablespoon lemon juice
⅛ teaspoon salt
    Dash of pepper
3 tablespoons mayonnaise or salad dressing

Mix all ingredients.

OLIVE-NUT SPREAD

1 package (3 ounces) cream cheese, softened
½ cup finely chopped walnuts
¼ cup chopped pimiento-stuffed olives
2 tablespoons milk

Mix all ingredients.

DEVILED HAM SPREAD

1 can (4½ ounces) deviled ham
¼ cup dairy sour cream
2 tablespoons sweet pickle relish, drained
1 tablespoon grated onion
    Dash of red pepper sauce

Mix all ingredients.

PARTY SANDWICH PREPARATION TIPS

1. Trim sandwich loaf, removing all traces of crust.

2. For a cutting guide, mark loaf with wooden picks.

PARTY SANDWICH LOAF

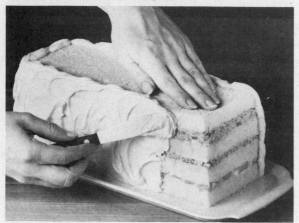

Cover loaf with a thin layer of frosting, then swirl on more. Just before serving, add garnish.

OPEN-FACE SANDWICHES

Garnishes add color and sparkle; key them to the shapes of the Open-face Sandwiches.

PINWHEEL SANDWICHES

Pinwheel and Ribbon Sandwiches can be made ahead, frozen, defrosted 1 to 2 hours, then cut.

RIBBON SANDWICHES

If you cut the Ribbon Sandwiches into halves, you will get 10 dozen sandwiches from 2 bread loaves.

OPEN-FACE SANDWICHES

Trim crusts from slices of bread. The easiest shape to work with is a square sandwich loaf. Cut bread into desired shapes and spread with any of the spreads suggested on pages 332–33.

Top sandwiches with sliced pimiento-stuffed olives or pitted ripe olives, mushroom slices, anchovies, parsley, pimiento, radish slices, sweet pickle slices, shredded cheese or egg slices.

PINWHEEL SANDWICHES

Trim crust from 1 loaf unsliced sandwich bread. Cut loaf horizontally into ¼-inch slices. Spread each slice with 2 tablespoons margarine or butter, softened, and ½ cup of one of the spreads suggested on pages 332–33.

Cut each slice crosswise into halves. Roll up tightly, beginning at narrow end. Secure with wooden picks. Cut each roll into slices about ½ inch thick.   6 SANDWICHES PER ROLL.

RIBBON SANDWICHES

Trim crusts from 1 loaf white and 1 loaf whole wheat unsliced sandwich bread. Cut each loaf horizontally into 6 slices.

For each ribbon loaf, spread each of 2 slices white and 1 slice whole wheat bread with ½ cup of one of the spreads suggested on pages 332–33. Assemble loaf, alternating white and whole wheat slices; top with unspread whole wheat slice. Cut loaves into slices about ½ inch thick; cut each slice crosswise into halves.   3 LOAVES (ABOUT 10 DOZEN SANDWICHES).

CHECKERBOARD SANDWICHES

Cut ribbon loaf (above) into ½-inch slices. Spread margarine or butter, softened, on 1 slice; top with a second slice, placing the dark strip on top of the light. Press together gently but firmly. Spread margarine or butter, softened, on second slice; top with a third slice with the light strip on top of the dark. Press together gently but firmly. Cut into 4 slices; cut each slice into 2 sandwiches.   ABOUT 5½ DOZEN SANDWICHES.

CHECKERBOARD SANDWICHES

Slice ribbon loaf ½ inch thick.

Stack slices, alternating light and dark.

Slice again; cut slices into halves if desired.

Apricot Balls, Caramel Corn (page 340); Spiced Nuts, Candied Orange Peel (page 339); Chocolate Fudge (page 338)

Candy and Sweet Snacks

To brighten up a kitchen, there's nothing like an old-fashioned candy-making session. And isn't there someone you know who'd treasure a sweet gift?

ABOUT CANDY MAKING

☐ Use the recommended size cooking pan. A pan larger or smaller than the kind specified can affect the cooking time and quality of the candy.

☐ Never double a recipe. If a larger amount of candy is desired, make another batch or two.

☐ Use a good, dependable candy thermometer; it is an inexpensive but wise investment. Be sure that it stands upright in the cooking mixture. The bulb should not rest on the bottom of the pan. Read the thermometer at eye level and watch the temperature closely—once it reaches 200°, it soars quickly.

☐ Test candy carefully. If you do not have a thermometer, use the cold water test. Remove candy from heat and drop a small amount of the mixture from a clean spoon into a cupful of very cold water (see chart below).

☐ Both humidity and altitude affect candy. If it is rainy, cook candy to a degree or so higher than the recipe indicates. Consult an altitude table to determine the boiling point in your area. You may want to test the temperature of boiling water before you make candy. If the water boils at 210° instead of the norm of 212°, for example, subtract 2 degrees from the temperature specified in the recipe.

HOW TO TEST CANDY

Stage	Cold Water Test	Temperature
Soft Ball	Can be picked up but flattens	234° to 240°
Firm Ball	Holds its shape until pressed	242° to 248°
Hard Ball	Holds its shape but is pliable	250° to 268°
Soft Crack	Separates into hard but not brittle threads	270° to 290°
Hard Crack	Separates into hard and brittle threads	300° to 310°

CREAMY CARAMELS

½ cup finely chopped nuts
2 cups sugar
¾ cup light corn syrup
½ cup margarine or butter
2 cups half-and-half

Butter square pan, 8x8x2 inches. Spread nuts in pan. Heat sugar, corn syrup, margarine and 1 cup of the half-and-half to boiling in 3-quart saucepan over medium heat, stirring constantly. Stir in remaining half-and-half. Cook over medium heat, stirring frequently, to 245° on candy thermometer or until small amount of mixture dropped into very cold water forms a firm ball. Immediately spread over nuts in pan. Cool; cut into about 1-inch squares.   3 DOZEN CANDIES.

Chocolate Caramels: Heat 2 squares (1 ounce each) unsweetened chocolate with the sugar.

TOFFEE

1 cup chopped pecans
¾ cup packed brown sugar
½ cup margarine or butter
½ cup semisweet chocolate chips

Butter square pan, 9x9x2 inches. Spread pecans in pan. Heat sugar and margarine to boiling in 1-quart saucepan, stirring constantly. Boil over medium heat, stirring constantly, 7 minutes. Immediately spread mixture over pecans in pan.

Sprinkle chocolate chips over hot mixture; place cookie sheet over pan until chocolate chips are melted. Spread melted chocolate over candy. Cut into about 1½-inch squares while hot. Refrigerate until firm.   3 DOZEN CANDIES.

Toffee

Divinity

CHOCOLATE FUDGE

2 cups sugar
⅔ cup milk
2 ounces unsweetened chocolate or
    ⅓ cup cocoa
2 tablespoons corn syrup
¼ teaspoon salt
2 tablespoons margarine or butter
1 teaspoon vanilla
½ cup coarsely chopped nuts

Butter loaf pan, 9x5x3 inches. Heat sugar, milk, chocolate, corn syrup and salt in 3-quart saucepan over medium heat, stirring constantly, until chocolate is melted and sugar is dissolved. Cook, stirring occasionally, to 234° on candy thermometer or until small amount of mixture dropped into very cold water forms a soft ball that flattens when removed from water. Remove from heat; add margarine.

Cool, without stirring, to 120° (bottom of pan will be lukewarm). Add vanilla; beat continuously with wooden spoon until candy is thick and no longer glossy, 5 to 10 minutes (mixture will hold its shape when dropped from spoon). Quickly stir in nuts. Spread in pan. Cool until firm. Cut into about 1-inch squares.   32 CANDIES.

Pecan Roll: Substitute 1 cup packed brown sugar for 1 cup of the sugar and omit chocolate. Shape candy into 12-inch roll and roll in ½ cup finely chopped pecans. Wrap and refrigerate until firm. Cut into ¼-inch slices.   ABOUT 4 DOZEN CANDIES.

Penuche: Substitute 1 cup packed brown sugar for 1 cup of the sugar and omit chocolate.

DIVINITY

2⅔ cups sugar
⅔ cup light corn syrup
½ cup water*
2 egg whites
1 teaspoon vanilla
⅔ cup broken nuts

Heat sugar, corn syrup and water in 2-quart saucepan over low heat, stirring constantly, until sugar is dissolved. Cook, without stirring, to 260° on candy thermometer or until small amount of mixture dropped into very cold water forms a hard ball. Remove from heat.

Beat egg whites until stiff peaks form; continue beating while pouring hot syrup in a thin stream into egg whites. Add vanilla; beat until mixture holds its shape and becomes slightly dull (mixture may become too stiff for mixer). Fold in nuts. Drop mixture from tip of buttered spoon onto waxed paper.   ABOUT 4 DOZEN CANDIES.

*Use 1 tablespoon less water on humid days.

TING-A-LINGS

Heat 1 package (12 ounces) semisweet chocolate chips or 12 ounces milk chocolate until melted. Stir gradually into 4 cups whole wheat flake cereal until flakes are well coated. Drop mixture by tablespoonfuls onto waxed paper-lined cookie sheets. Refrigerate until firm, about 2 hours.   ABOUT 3½ DOZEN CANDIES.

THREE-MINUTE FUDGE

⅔ cup evaporated milk
1⅔ cups sugar
½ teaspoon salt
2 cups miniature marshmallows, or
    16 large marshmallows, cut into fourths
1½ packages (6 ounces each) semisweet
    chocolate chips (about 1½ cups)
1 teaspoon vanilla
½ cup chopped nuts

Mix milk, sugar and salt in 2-quart saucepan. Heat to boiling over low heat. Boil and stir 3 minutes or until candy thermometer registers 225°. Remove from heat; add marshmallows, chocolate chips, vanilla and nuts, stirring until marshmallows and chocolate are melted. Pour into buttered square pan, 9x9x2 inches. Refrigerate until firm. Cut into about 1½-inch squares.   3 DOZEN CANDIES.

OATMEAL-CHOCOLATE CLUSTERS

1 package (6 ounces) semisweet chocolate
    chips
⅓ cup margarine or butter
16 large marshmallows
½ teaspoon vanilla
2 cups oats
1 cup flaked coconut

Heat chocolate chips, margarine and marshmallows in 3-quart saucepan over low heat, stirring constantly, until smooth; remove from heat. Mix in vanilla, oats and coconut. Drop mixture by teaspoonfuls onto waxed paper and shape into clusters with hands. Refrigerate until firm, about 30 minutes.   ABOUT 3½ DOZEN CANDIES.

Bran-Chocolate Clusters: Substitute ½ cup whole bran cereal for ½ cup of the oats.

CANDIED ORANGE PEEL

Cut peel of each of 3 oranges into 4 sections with sharp knife. Remove peel carefully with fingers. Scrape white membrane from peel with spoon (back of peel will appear porous when membrane is removed). Cut peel lengthwise into strips ¼ inch wide. Heat peel and 8 cups water to boiling in 3-quart saucepan; reduce heat. Simmer uncovered 30 minutes; drain. Repeat simmering process.

Heat 2 cups sugar and 1 cup water to boiling in 2-quart saucepan, stirring constantly, until sugar is dissolved. Add peel. Simmer uncovered, stirring occasionally, 45 minutes. Drain in strainer. Roll peel in 1½ cups sugar; spread on waxed paper to dry.   ABOUT 9 OUNCES CANDY.

Candied Grapefruit Peel: Substitute 2 large grapefruit for the oranges. Repeat simmering process 3 times.

SPICED NUTS

1 tablespoon egg white
2 cups pecans or walnuts
¼ cup sugar
1 tablespoon ground cinnamon

Heat oven to 300°. Mix egg white and pecans until pecans are coated and sticky.

Mix sugar and cinnamon; sprinkle over pecans, stirring until sugar mixture completely coats pecans. Spread on ungreased cookie sheet. Bake 20 minutes.   ABOUT 2 CUPS SNACK.

TAFFY

1 cup sugar
¾ cup light corn syrup
⅔ cup water
1 tablespoon cornstarch
2 tablespoons margarine or butter
1 teaspoon salt
2 teaspoons vanilla

Butter square pan, 8x8x2 inches. Mix sugar, corn syrup, water, cornstarch, margarine and salt in 2-quart saucepan. Heat to boiling over medium heat, stirring constantly. Cook, without stirring, to 256° on candy thermometer or until small amount dropped into very cold water forms a hard ball. Remove from heat; stir in vanilla. Pour into pan.

When just cool enough to handle, pull taffy until satiny, light in color and stiff. If taffy becomes sticky, butter hands lightly. Pull into long strips ½ inch wide. Cut strips into pieces with scissors. Wrap pieces individually in plastic wrap or waxed paper (candy must be wrapped to hold its shape).   ABOUT 1 POUND CANDY.

PEANUT BRITTLE

The key to "brittleness" is thinness. Warming the cookie sheet helps in spreading the candy in a thin layer.

1½ teaspoons baking soda
1 teaspoon water
1 teaspoon vanilla
1½ cups sugar
1 cup water
1 cup light corn syrup
3 tablespoons margarine or butter
1 pound shelled unroasted peanuts

Butter 2 cookie sheets, 15½x12 inches; keep warm. Mix baking soda, 1 teaspoon water and the vanilla; reserve. Mix sugar, 1 cup water and the corn syrup in 3-quart saucepan. Cook over medium heat, stirring occasionally, to 240° on candy thermometer or until small amount of syrup dropped into very cold water forms a soft ball that flattens when removed from water.

Stir in margarine and peanuts. Cook, stirring constantly, to 300° or until small amount of mixture dropped into very cold water separates into threads that are hard and brittle (watch carefully so mixture does not burn). Immediately remove from heat; stir in baking soda mixture.

Pour half of the candy mixture onto each cookie sheet and quickly spread about ¼ inch thick. Cool; break into pieces.   ABOUT 2 POUNDS CANDY.

APRICOT BALLS

1 package (8 ounces) dried apricots,
    ground or finely cut up
2½ cups flaked coconut
¾ cup sweetened condensed milk
⅔ cup finely chopped nuts

Mix apricots, coconut and milk. Shape mixture into 1-inch balls; roll each in nuts. Let stand until firm, about 2 hours.   ABOUT 4 DOZEN CANDIES.

Apricot-Nut Balls: Mix the nuts into fruit mixture and roll balls in powdered sugar.

Tangy Apricot Balls: Mix 2 tablespoons lemon juice into fruit mixture.

FONDANT-STUFFED DATES

4½ cups powdered sugar
⅔ cup sweetened condensed milk
1 teaspoon vanilla
1 teaspoon almond extract
4 dozen pitted dates
   Granulated or powdered sugar

Blend powdered sugar, milk, vanilla and almond extract. Knead fondant until smooth and creamy. Wrap in aluminum foil or plastic wrap and refrigerate 24 hours.

Fill each date with fondant; roll in granulated sugar.   ABOUT 4 DOZEN CANDIES.

CARAMEL APPLES

Remove stems and blossom ends of 4 or 5 apples (make sure apples are completely dry).

Heat 1 package (14 ounces) caramel candies, ½ teaspoon salt and 2 tablespoons water in top of double boiler over hot water, stirring frequently, until caramels are melted and mixture is smooth. Remove from heat.

Keeping sauce over hot water, place each apple in hot caramel sauce, spooning sauce over apple until it is completely coated. Insert wooden skewer in stem end; remove from sauce and place on waxed paper. Refrigerate until caramel coating is firm.
4 OR 5 CARAMEL APPLES.

Chocolate-Caramel Apples: Heat ¼ cup semisweet chocolate chips with the caramel candies.

CARAMEL POPCORN BALLS

½ cup packed brown sugar
½ cup dark corn syrup
¼ cup margarine or butter
½ teaspoon salt
8 cups Popcorn (page 328)

Heat brown sugar, corn syrup, margarine and salt to simmering in 4-quart Dutch oven over medium-high heat, stirring constantly. Add Popcorn. Cook, stirring constantly, until Popcorn is well coated, about 2 minutes. Cool slightly.

Dip hands in cold water; shape mixture into 2-inch balls. Place on waxed paper; cool completely. Wrap individually in plastic wrap or place in plastic bags and tie.   ABOUT 6 POPCORN BALLS.

Caramel Corn: Heat oven to 300°. Butter cookie sheet. Mix 1 cup pecan halves and ½ cup blanched almonds with Popcorn. Immediately after cooking, spread mixture on cookie sheet. Bake 15 minutes. Cool 10 minutes; loosen mixture from cookie sheet with spatula. Let stand at room temperature 1 hour to harden. Store uncovered.

GRANOLA

1 cup quick-cooking oats
½ cup whole bran cereal
½ cup whole wheat flour
½ cup flaked coconut
¼ cup coarsely chopped slivered almonds or
    salted peanuts
½ cup vegetable oil, margarine or butter
½ cup honey
1 teaspoon vanilla or almond extract
¼ cup raisins

Heat oven to 300°. Mix oats, cereal, flour, coconut and almonds in ungreased oblong pan, 13x9x2 inches. Heat oil and honey in 1-quart saucepan over medium heat until hot and bubbly; stir in vanilla. Pour honey mixture over oat mixture; stir. Bake until light brown, 30 to 35 minutes. (Granola will darken while cooling.) Stir in raisins; cool 15 minutes.

Loosen granola from pan with spatula; cool to room temperature. Break granola into pieces. Cover and store no longer than 1 week.   ABOUT 5 CUPS SNACK.

BEVERAGES

ABOUT COFFEE

☐ Start with a thoroughly clean coffee maker. Wash after each use with hot, soapy water and rinse well with hot water; never scour with an abrasive pad. When cleaning an automatic coffee maker, follow the manufacturer's directions.

☐ Always use fresh coffee and freshly drawn cold water. Never use hot water, especially in automatic coffee makers; it changes percolating time.

☐ Serve steaming-hot coffee as soon as possible after brewing. If coffee must stand any length of time, remove grounds and hold coffee at serving temperature over very low heat.

☐ Keep ground coffee tightly covered.

PREPARATION METHODS

Automatic: Follow manufacturer's directions for selecting grind of coffee (special ones are available), measuring and brewing the coffee and holding the coffee at serving temperature.

Drip: Measure cold water into kettle and heat to boiling. Meanwhile, preheat coffeepot by rinsing with very hot water. Measure drip-grind coffee into filter paper in cone or into filter section of coffeepot, depending on the type of drip pot used. Pour measured fresh boiling water into upper container; cover. When dripping is completed, remove upper container and filter section and serve coffee.

Vacuum: Measure fresh cold water into lower bowl and heat to boiling. Place filter in upper bowl; add fine or drip-grind coffee. Remove boiling water from heat; reduce heat. Insert upper bowl with a slight twist. Return to heat. Let water rise into upper bowl; stir. Remove from heat. Coffee should return to lower bowl within 2 minutes. Remove upper bowl and serve coffee.

COFFEE CHART

Strength of Brew	For each serving* Ground Coffee	Water
Weak	1 level tablespoon	¾ cup
Medium	2 level tablespoons	¾ cup
Strong	3 level tablespoons	¾ cup

*Best general recommendation.

INSTANT COFFEE

In the cup: Place 1 to 2 teaspoons instant coffee in each cup. Fill with boiling water; stir.

In the pot: Place 2 to 4 tablespoons instant coffee in heatproof container. Stir in part of 4 cups cold water; add remaining water. Heat *just* to boiling but do not boil. (Or heat water to boiling; remove from heat and stir in coffee. Cover and let stand 3 minutes.)   6 SERVINGS (ABOUT ⅔ CUP EACH).

■ **To Microwave:** For each serving, mix ¾ to 1 cup water and 1 teaspoon instant coffee in glass cup. Microwave uncovered until hot, 2 to 2½ minutes.

DEMITASSE

Prepare coffee as directed at left, using ¼ cup ground coffee for each ¾ cup water. Demitasse is served in small cups, often with a twist of lemon peel. Sugar may be offered; cream usually is not.

INSTANT DEMITASSE

Place ½ cup instant coffee in heatproof container. Stir in 1 quart boiling water. Cover and let stand 5 minutes.   12 SERVINGS (ABOUT ⅓ CUP EACH).

NOTE: For smaller amounts, use 2 teaspoons instant coffee and ⅓ cup boiling water for each serving.

CALIFORNIA COFFEE

For each serving, pour 2 tablespoons brandy into mug. Fill ⅔ full with hot strong coffee (left). Top with 1 scoop (about ¼ cup) chocolate ice cream.

California Coffee

Spiced Coffee

SPICED COFFEE

2 cups water
1 tablespoon packed brown sugar
2 three-inch sticks cinnamon
   Peel of 1 orange
¼ teaspoon whole allspice
1 tablespoon instant coffee

Heat water, brown sugar, cinnamon, orange peel and allspice to boiling. Strain; pour liquid over coffee in heatproof container and stir until coffee is dissolved.   6 SERVINGS (ABOUT ⅓ CUP EACH).

Café Brûlot: Double recipe and serve in heatproof bowl. Stir in 2 tablespoons brandy. Garnish with 3 small clove-studded oranges.

ICED COFFEE

Prepare strong coffee (page 341). Fill tall glass with crushed ice. Pour hot coffee over ice. Serve with sugar and cream or whipped cream if desired.

Or prepare medium coffee (page 341); cool. Pour into ice cube trays; freeze. Pour freshly brewed medium coffee over coffee cubes in tall glass.

CAFE AU LAIT

Prepare coffee as directed on page 341, using ¾ cup ground coffee and 3 cups water. Heat 3 cups milk. Pour equal amounts of hot coffee and hot milk *simultaneously* from separate pots into each cup. 8 SERVINGS (ABOUT ¾ CUP EACH).

Capuccino-style Café au Lait: Stir 1 teaspoon ground cinnamon into ground coffee.

IRISH COFFEE

1 cup chilled whipping cream
¼ cup powdered sugar
1 teaspoon vanilla
¾ cup ground coffee
3 cups water
½ cup Irish whiskey or brandy
4 to 8 teaspoons granulated sugar

Beat whipping cream, powdered sugar and vanilla in chilled small mixer bowl until stiff; refrigerate.

Prepare coffee as directed on page 341, using ¾ cup coffee and 3 cups water.

Heat 4 mugs or Irish coffee glasses by rinsing with boiling water; drain. Place 2 tablespoons whiskey and 1 to 2 teaspoons granulated sugar in each mug; stir. Pour hot coffee into each mug. Top with whipped cream; serve immediately.   4 SERVINGS (ABOUT ¾ CUP EACH).

EGG COFFEE FOR A CROWD

5 quarts water
1½ cups regular-grind coffee
1 egg
¾ cup water

Heat 5 quarts water to boiling. Mix coffee, egg and ¾ cup water; pour into boiling water. Heat to rolling boil (coffee mixture will sink to bottom). Remove from heat; add ½ cup cold water to settle grounds.   30 SERVINGS (ABOUT ⅔ CUP EACH).

COFFEE ITALIAN STYLE

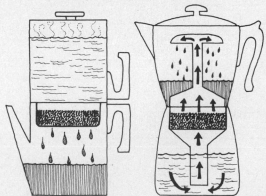

The first must for good Italian coffee is dark Italian-roast coffee beans. In the Neapolitan drip pot (left), hot water drips down through the basket of fine coffee grains. In the espresso machine (right), pressure forces steam and boiling water up through the grains.

DESSERT COFFEE MIX

Place ¼ cup freeze-dried coffee, ½ cup sugar and ½ cup cocoa in blender container. Cover and blend on high speed 15 seconds; stir. Cover and blend on high speed 15 seconds longer. Store in tightly covered container.

For each serving, place 2 teaspoons mix in cup. Fill with boiling water. For 6 servings (about ⅔ cup each), place ¼ cup mix in heatproof container; add 4 cups boiling water.   ABOUT 1 CUP MIX.

Café au Lait Coffee Mix: Substitute nonfat dry milk for the cocoa.   ABOUT ⅔ CUP MIX.

Cardamom Coffee Mix: Omit cocoa. Add ½ teaspoon ground cardamom and ¼ teaspoon ground mace to ingredients in blender container.   ABOUT ½ CUP MIX.

Lemon Coffee Mix: Omit cocoa. Increase coffee to ½ cup. Add 1 package (3 ounces) lemon-flavored gelatin to ingredients in blender container. ABOUT ½ CUP MIX.

Spice Coffee Mix: Omit cocoa. Add ¼ teaspoon ground cinnamon, ¼ teaspoon ground nutmeg and ¼ teaspoon ground allspice to ingredients in blender container.   ABOUT ½ CUP MIX.

LARGE-QUANTITY COFFEE

Measure regular-grind coffee into a clean cloth sack; fill only half full to allow for expansion of coffee and free circulation of water. (Soak and rinse sack thoroughly before using.) Tie sack, allowing sufficient length of cord for fastening to handle.

Heat measured amount of cold water to full rolling boil; reduce heat. Tie sack to handle; submerge in water. Keep kettle over low heat. Brew, pushing sack up and down frequently for proper extraction, 6 to 8 minutes. When coffee is done, remove sack, permitting all extract to drain into kettle.

COFFEE-MAKING CHART

People	Servings (⅔ cup each)	Ground Coffee	Water
12	23	2 cups	4 quarts
25	46	4 cups	8 quarts

Note: For 25 people, based on half the people using cream and sugar, you will need 1½ cups cream (1 tablespoon per cup) and ½ cup or 25 cubes sugar (1 teaspoon per cup).

ABOUT TEA

The tea you buy is a delicate blend of some 20 to 30 varieties. Quality varies according to the soil, climate and altitude in which it is grown and the age and size of the leaves when they are picked.

Broadly classified, there are three types: black, oolong and green.

Black tea derives its color from a special processing treatment in which the leaves are allowed to oxidize. This turns the leaves black and produces a rich brew.

Oolong tea is semioxidized. Its leaves are brown and green. It brews light in color.

Green tea is not oxidized, thus the leaves remain green. The brew is pale green in color.

PREPARATION METHOD

Whether you use loose tea or tea bags, the preparation method is the same:

☐ Start with a spotlessly clean teapot made of glass, china or earthenware. Add rapidly boiling water; allow to stand a few minutes then pour out.

☐ Heat cold water to a full rolling boil.

☐ Add tea or bags to the warm pot, allowing 1 teaspoon of loose tea or 1 tea bag for each cup of tea desired. Pour boiling water over the tea (¾ cup for each cup of tea); let stand 3 to 5 minutes to bring out the full flavor. Stir the tea once to ensure uniform strength.

☐ Do not judge the strength of tea by its color; you must taste it.

☐ Strain the tea or remove tea bags. Serve with sugar and milk or lemon if desired.

Instant tea, a concentrate, should be prepared according to the directions on the jar.

SPICED ORANGE TEA

4 cups boiling water
4 teaspoons loose tea
6 whole cloves, broken into pieces
½ teaspoon dried orange peel
⅛ teaspoon ground cinnamon

Pour boiling water over tea, cloves, orange peel and cinnamon in heatproof container. Cover and let stand until desired strength, 3 to 5 minutes. Stir and strain.   6 SERVINGS (ABOUT ⅔ CUP EACH).

ICED TEA

Prepare tea as directed on page 343 except—double the amount of tea. Strain tea over ice in pitcher or into ice-filled glasses.

NOTE: Tea that has been steeped too long or refrigerated will become cloudy. Pour a small amount of boiling water into tea to make clear again.

DO-AHEAD ICED TEA

Use 2 teaspoons loose tea or 2 tea bags for each cup of cold water. Place tea in glass container; add water. Cover and refrigerate at least 24 hours. Serve over crushed ice.

LEMON ICED TEA

- 4 cups boiling water
- 8 tea bags or 2 tablespoons plus
  - 2 teaspoons loose tea
- 2 medium lemons
- ½ to ¾ cup sugar
- 1 tray ice cubes (about 14)

Pour boiling water on tea bags; let stand until desired strength, 3 to 5 minutes. Cool to room temperature.

Cut peel of each lemon in continuous motion to form a spiral. Squeeze juice from lemons. Mix lemon peel, lemon juice, sugar and ice cubes in 2-quart pitcher; stir in tea. Serve immediately in ice-filled glasses.   8 SERVINGS (ABOUT 1 CUP EACH).

LEMONADE

Mix 3 cups water, 1 cup lemon juice (about 4 lemons) and ½ cup sugar. Serve over ice.
5 SERVINGS (ABOUT ¾ CUP EACH).

Limeade: Substitute lime juice (about 10 limes) for the lemons and increase sugar to ¾ cup.

Minted Lemonade: Bruise mint leaves in glasses before pouring Lemonade. Garnish with mint.

Pink Lemonade: Add 2 tablespoons grenadine syrup (optional) and 2 or 3 drops red food color.

FROZEN DAIQUIRI COCKTAILS

Mix 2 cups light rum, 2 cans (6 ounces each) frozen lemonade concentrate and 2¼ cups water; pour into ice cube tray. Freeze until slushy. Serve with short straws.   8 SERVINGS (ABOUT ¾ CUP EACH).

BUBBLY APPLE DRINK

Mix 1 bottle (7 ounces) lemon-lime carbonated beverage, chilled (about 1 cup), and ½ cup apple juice, chilled. Serve immediately in stemmed glasses and, if desired, garnish with thin lemon slices.   3 SERVINGS (ABOUT ½ CUP EACH).

CORAL COOLER

- 2¼ cups unsweetened pineapple juice
- 1 bottle (10 ounces) grapefruit carbonated beverage
- ¼ cup maraschino cherry juice
- 4 maraschino cherries

Mix pineapple juice, carbonated beverage and cherry juice; pour into ice-filled glasses. Top each with maraschino cherry.   4 SERVINGS (ABOUT ¾ CUP EACH).

CRANBERRY FROST

For each serving, place 1 scoop lemon, lime or orange sherbet or vanilla ice cream in tall glass. Fill with cranberry juice cocktail, chilled.

ORANGE-CHAMPAGNE SWIZZLE

Mix 2 cups champagne or ginger ale, chilled, and 1 can (6 ounces) frozen orange juice concentrate, thawed. Serve immediately.   4 SERVINGS (ABOUT ¾ CUP EACH).

GRAPE JUICE CRUSH

- 1 bottle (24 ounces) grape juice, chilled
- 1 cup orange juice, chilled
- ¼ cup lemon juice, chilled
- ½ cup sugar
- 1 quart ginger ale, chilled

Mix juices and sugar, stirring until sugar is dissolved. Just before serving, stir in ginger ale. Serve over ice.   8 SERVINGS (ABOUT 1 CUP EACH).

FOAMY REFRESHER

Place 2 teaspoons instant tea in large pitcher. Add 1 bottle (10 ounces) grapefruit carbonated beverage; stir. Pour into ice-filled glasses.   2 SERVINGS (ABOUT ¾ CUP EACH).

CARROT-PINEAPPLE COOLER

For each serving, place 1 medium carrot, sliced (about ½ cup), ¾ cup pineapple juice, 1 teaspoon honey (optional) and 3 or 4 ice cubes in blender container. Cover and blend on high speed 30 seconds.   ABOUT 1¼ CUPS BEVERAGE.

RED-EYE COCKTAILS

Mix 1½ cups tomato juice, chilled, and 2 cans (12 ounces each) beer, chilled. Pour into chilled glasses. Serve immediately with red pepper sauce, salt, pepper and green onions for stirrers.   6 SERVINGS (ABOUT ¾ CUP EACH).

SPARKLING RED ROUSER

This recipe can be tripled and served in a small punch bowl over Vegetable Ice Ring (right).

Just before serving, mix 2 bottles (7 ounces each) lemon-lime carbonated beverage (about 2 cups) and 1 can (8 ounces) tomato sauce. Serve over ice.   4 SERVINGS (ABOUT ½ CUP EACH).

TOMATO BOUILLON

    4 cups tomato juice
    3 cans (10½ ounces each) condensed beef
        broth (about 3¾ cups)
    1 tablespoon lemon juice
    ½ teaspoon Worcestershire sauce
    ½ teaspoon prepared horseradish
    ½ cup dry sherry (optional)

Heat tomato juice, broth, lemon juice, Worcestershire sauce and horseradish over low heat, stirring occasionally, 30 minutes. Just before serving, stir in sherry.   15 SERVINGS (ABOUT ½ CUP EACH).

POW!

    2 cans (10½ ounces each) condensed beef
        broth (about 2½ cups)
    1 cup tomato juice (optional)
    1 cup water
    1½ teaspoons prepared horseradish
    ½ teaspoon dried dill weed

Heat all ingredients to simmering. Serve hot or cold.   6 SERVINGS (ABOUT ¾ CUP EACH).

■ **To Microwave:** Microwave all ingredients uncovered 4 minutes.

COOL CUCUMBER COCKTAIL

    2 medium cucumbers
    1½ cups buttermilk
    1 teaspoon instant minced onion
    1 teaspoon lemon juice or Worcestershire
        sauce
    1 teaspoon salt
    ⅛ teaspoon pepper

Cut 4 to 6 thin slices from 1 cucumber and reserve for garnish. Pare remaining cucumbers; cut cucumbers into ¾-inch slices.

Pour ¼ cup of the buttermilk into blender container; add half of the cucumber slices. Cover and blend until smooth. Add remaining slices, the onion, lemon juice, salt and pepper. Cover and blend until smooth, about 1 minute. Stir in remaining buttermilk. Cover and refrigerate until chilled but no longer than 48 hours. Serve in cups and garnish each with reserved cucumber slice.   4 TO 6 SERVINGS (ABOUT ½ CUP EACH).

VEGETABLE COCKTAIL

    2 cans (46 ounces each) vegetable juice
        cocktail
    ½ cup margarine or butter, softened
    1 tablespoon Worcestershire sauce
    1 teaspoon salt
    1 teaspoon celery salt
    ½ teaspoon dried oregano leaves
    5 drops red pepper sauce

Mix all ingredients in Dutch oven. Cover; heat to boiling. Reduce heat; simmer uncovered, stirring occasionally, 10 minutes.   15 SERVINGS (ABOUT ¾ CUP EACH).

NOTE: A 15-cup automatic percolator (with basket removed) can be used. Pour ingredients into percolator and let perk 1 cycle.

VEGETABLE ICE RING

Arrange slices of cucumbers and radishes, carrot curls and sprigs of parsley in bottom of ring mold that will fit into punch bowl. Add small amount of water (about ½ inch); freeze.

When frozen, add additional vegetables and water to fill mold ¾ full; freeze. At serving time, unmold and float curved side up in punch bowl.

Vegetable Ice Cubes: Prepare as directed except—arrange vegetables in each square of ice cube tray.

SANGRIA PUNCH

⅔ cup lemon juice
⅓ cup orange juice
¼ cup sugar
1 bottle (⅘ quart) dry red wine

Strain juices; add sugar, stirring until dissolved. Just before serving, mix juice mixture and wine in pitcher. Add ice; serve in punch cups. Decorate cups with twists of lemon peel if desired.   6 TO 8 SERVINGS (ABOUT ½ CUP EACH).

APPLE-ORANGE PUNCH

1 can (6 ounces) frozen orange juice
    concentrate, thawed
1 can (6 ounces) frozen lemonade
    concentrate, thawed
1 quart apple juice, chilled
2 quarts ginger ale, chilled
1 pint lemon or orange sherbet

Mix concentrates and apple juice in large punch bowl. Just before serving, stir in ginger ale. Spoon sherbet into bowl.   28 SERVINGS (ABOUT ½ CUP EACH).

SPARKLING CRANBERRY PUNCH

2 quarts cranberry juice cocktail, chilled
1 can (6 ounces) frozen pink lemonade
    concentrate, thawed
1 quart sparkling water, chilled

Mix cranberry juice cocktail and lemonade concentrate in large punch bowl. Just before serving, stir in sparkling water.   25 SERVINGS (ABOUT ½ CUP EACH).

Cran-Ale Punch: Substitute 2 cans (12 ounces each) beer, chilled, for the sparkling water. 14 SERVINGS (ABOUT ½ CUP EACH).

RASPBERRY SHRUB

Cook 4 packages (10 ounces each) frozen raspberries, thawed, 10 minutes. Rub through strainer with wooden spoon; cool. Add 1 can (6 ounces) frozen lemonade concentrate, thawed. Just before serving, stir in 2 quarts ginger ale, chilled.   24 SERVINGS (ABOUT ½ CUP EACH).

LUAU WATERMELON PUNCH

1 large watermelon (about 15 inches long
    and 7 inches wide)
1 can (6 ounces) frozen lemonade
    concentrate, partially thawed
1⅓ cups chilled orange-flavored liqueur
    Mint sprigs

Cut top third lengthwise from watermelon. Scoop melon balls from top piece (about 2½ cups); reserve. Scoop remaining pulp from top with large spoon; remove seeds. Discard shell.

Cut thin slice from underside of bottom piece of watermelon to keep it from tipping. Scoop pulp from bottom piece with large spoon, leaving ½ inch pulp on shell. Cut pulp (including pulp from top shell) into smaller pieces (about 18 cups); remove seeds.

Place lemonade concentrate and about 3 cups pulp pieces in blender container. Cover and blend on high speed until uniform consistency, about 5 seconds. Repeat with remaining pulp pieces (1 cup pulp mixture should remain in blender container each time for easy blending). Cover and refrigerate shell and pulp mixture.

Just before serving, stir liqueur into pulp mixture; pour into shell. Secure melon balls and mint sprigs on wooden picks and insert around edge of shell.   32 SERVINGS (ABOUT ½ CUP EACH).

Luau Watermelon Coolers: Use ½ small watermelon (about 6 cups pulp pieces). Decrease lemonade concentrate to ¼ cup and liqueur to ½ cup. Blend as directed above. Refrigerate until cold. Serve in chilled glasses.   4 SERVINGS (ABOUT 1¼ CUPS EACH).

WASSAIL

1 gallon apple cider
2 teaspoons whole cloves
2 teaspoons whole allspice
2 three-inch sticks cinnamon
⅔ cup sugar
2 oranges, studded with cloves

Heat cider, cloves, allspice, cinnamon and sugar to boiling; reduce heat. Cover and simmer 20 minutes. Strain punch and pour into punch bowl. Float oranges in bowl.   32 SERVINGS (ABOUT ½ CUP EACH).

CRANBERRY-APPLE PUNCH

3 quarts water
2 cups sugar
2 cups strong tea
2 cans (6 ounces each) frozen lemonade
    concentrate, thawed
2 quarts cranberry juice cocktail
1 quart apple juice
2 cups orange juice

Heat water and sugar to boiling, stirring constantly, until sugar is dissolved; cool.

Prepare tea as directed on page 343, using 1 tablespoon loose tea or 3 tea bags and 2 cups boiling water; cool. Refrigerate all ingredients. Just before serving, mix in large punch bowl.   60 SERVINGS (ABOUT ½ CUP EACH).

PINK PUNCH

Chill 1 bottle (25.6 ounces) pink sparkling catawba grape juice. Cut 1 package (10 ounces) frozen raspberries into fourths. Place raspberries and 1 cup grape juice in blender container. Cover and blend on high speed 15 seconds; strain. Pour remaining grape juice into small punch bowl or pitcher. Stir in raspberry mixture. Serve immediately.   8 SERVINGS (ABOUT ½ CUP EACH).

PINEAPPLE-CITRUS PUNCH

3 cups pineapple juice, chilled
3 cups orange-grapefruit juice, chilled
1 quart lemon-lime carbonated beverage,
    chilled
1 cup lime or lemon sherbet

Mix juices and carbonated beverage in large punch bowl. Spoon scoops of sherbet into bowl. Serve immediately.   19 SERVINGS (ABOUT ½ CUP EACH).

ICE RING FOR PUNCH BOWL

Arrange thin citrus slices and maraschino cherries or strawberries in an attractive design in 6- to 6½-cup ring mold. Pour water into mold to partially cover fruit; freeze.

When frozen, add water to fill mold ¾ full; freeze. At serving time, unmold and float fruit side up in punch bowl.

If you prefer, freeze ring without decoration. Or instead of freezing water, freeze part of a nonsparkling punch recipe itself; this will keep punch cold without diluting it.

NOTE: Packages of frozen melon balls, mixed fruit, raspberries or strawberries can be floated in fruit punches instead of an ice ring. As the fruit thaws, it becomes a garnish for the punch.

Cranberry-Apple Punch

Pineapple-Citrus Punch

Clockwise from top: Iced Tea (page 344), Raspberry Shrub (page 346), Orange-Champagne Swizzle (page 344), Lemonade (page 344), Sparkling Cranberry Punch (page 346), Ice-cream Soda (page 349) and Limeade (page 344)

BRANDY CREAM

Place 1 pint vanilla ice cream in small mixer bowl; cut ice cream into fourths. Let stand until slightly softened, about 10 minutes. Add 2 to 4 tablespoons brandy; beat on low speed 30 seconds. Cover and freeze until thick, 3 to 5 hours.

Just before serving, stir gently and pour into chilled glasses. Sprinkle with shaved chocolate if desired.   4 SERVINGS (ABOUT ½ CUP EACH).

Fruit Brandy Cream: Substitute apricot-, peach- or cherry-flavored brandy for the brandy.

SOUTHERN CUSTARD EGGNOG

   Soft Custard (below)
1 cup chilled whipping cream
2 tablespoons powdered sugar
½ teaspoon vanilla
½ cup rum
1 or 2 drops yellow food color (optional)
   Ground nutmeg

Prepare Soft Custard. Just before serving, beat whipping cream, powdered sugar and vanilla in chilled small mixer bowl until stiff. Stir rum and food color into chilled custard. Stir 1 cup of the whipped cream gently into custard.

Pour eggnog into small punch bowl. Drop remaining whipped cream in 4 or 5 mounds onto eggnog. Sprinkle nutmeg on whipped cream mounds. Serve immediately.   10 SERVINGS (ABOUT ½ CUP EACH).

SOFT CUSTARD

3 eggs, slightly beaten
⅓ cup sugar
   Dash of salt
2½ cups milk
1 teaspoon vanilla

Mix eggs, sugar and salt in heavy 2-quart saucepan. Stir in milk gradually. Cook over low heat, stirring constantly, until mixture just coats a metal spoon, 15 to 20 minutes.

Remove custard from heat; stir in vanilla. Place saucepan in cold water until custard is cool. (If custard curdles, beat vigorously with hand beater until smooth.) Cover and refrigerate at least 2 hours but no longer than 24 hours.

BUTTERMILK ORANGE SHAKES

1 cup buttermilk
1 scoop vanilla ice cream (about ½ cup)
½ cup orange juice
2 tablespoons packed brown sugar

Place all ingredients in blender container. Cover and blend on high speed until smooth. (Or beat all ingredients with hand beater.)   2 SERVINGS (ABOUT ¾ CUP EACH)..

YOGURT BANANA SIPS

1 cup unflavored yogurt
1 medium banana, sliced (about 1 cup)
¼ cup packed brown sugar
¼ teaspoon vanilla
   Dash of ground nutmeg (optional)
2 ice cubes

Place all ingredients in blender container. Cover and blend on high speed until smooth, about 30 seconds.   2 SERVINGS (ABOUT ¾ CUP EACH).

Yogurt Strawberry Sips: Substitute 1 cup strawberries, sliced, for the banana. Omit nutmeg and ice cubes.

ICE-CREAM SODAS

For each serving, place 2 to 3 tablespoons syrup or ice-cream topping (any flavor) or ¼ cup crushed fruit and 1 teaspoon sugar in tall glass. Fill half full with chilled sparkling water. Add 1 scoop ice cream; stir. Fill glass with sparkling water.

CHOCOLATE MILK SHAKES

Place ¾ cup milk and ¼ cup chocolate-flavored syrup in blender container. Cover and blend on high speed 2 seconds. Add 3 scoops vanilla ice cream. Cover and blend on low speed until smooth, about 5 seconds longer.   2 SERVINGS (ABOUT 1 CUP EACH).

Cherry Milk Shakes: Substitute cherry ice-cream topping for the chocolate-flavored syrup.

Chocolate Malts: Add 1 tablespoon instant malted milk with the syrup.

Pineapple Milk Shakes: Substitute pineapple ice-cream topping for the chocolate-flavored syrup.

HOT COCOA

⅓ cup sugar
⅓ cup cocoa
¼ teaspoon salt
1½ cups water
4½ cups milk
¼ teaspoon vanilla (optional)

Mix sugar, cocoa and salt in 2-quart saucepan. Add water. Heat to boiling, stirring constantly. Boil and stir 2 minutes. Stir in milk; heat through but do not boil. Stir in vanilla.

Just before serving, beat with hand beater until foamy or stir until smooth.   9 SERVINGS (ABOUT ⅔ CUP EACH).

FRENCH CHOCOLATE

¼ cup semisweet chocolate chips
2 tablespoons light corn syrup
2 tablespoons water
¼ teaspoon vanilla
½ cup chilled whipping cream
2 cups milk

Heat chocolate chips, corn syrup and water over low heat, stirring constantly, until chocolate is melted and mixture is smooth. Stir in vanilla; refrigerate.

Beat whipping cream in chilled small mixer bowl until stiff, adding chilled chocolate gradually. Continue beating until mixture mounds when dropped from a spoon; refrigerate.

Just before serving, heat milk through but do not boil. Fill cups half full with whipped cream mixture. Fill cups with milk; stir.   4 SERVINGS (ABOUT ¾ CUP EACH).

MEXICAN CHOCOLATE

1½ ounces unsweetened chocolate
¼ cup sugar
1 tablespoon plus 2 teaspoons instant coffee
½ teaspoon ground cinnamon
¼ teaspoon ground nutmeg
  Dash of salt
¾ cup water
2 cups milk
  Whipped cream

Heat chocolate, sugar, coffee, cinnamon, nutmeg, salt and water in 1½-quart saucepan over low heat, stirring constantly, until chocolate is melted and mixture is smooth. Heat to boiling; reduce heat. Simmer uncovered, stirring constantly, 4 minutes.

Stir in milk; heat through. Just before serving, beat with hand beater until foamy. Top with whipped cream.   5 SERVINGS (ABOUT ⅔ CUP EACH).

HOT CHOCOLATE

2 ounces unsweetened chocolate
1 cup water
¼ cup sugar
  Dash of salt
3 cups milk

Heat chocolate and water in 1½-quart saucepan, stirring constantly, until chocolate is melted and mixture is smooth. Stir in sugar and salt. Heat to boiling; reduce heat. Simmer uncovered, stirring constantly, 4 minutes.

Stir in milk; cover and heat through but do not boil. Just before serving, beat with hand beater until foamy.   6 SERVINGS (ABOUT ⅔ CUP EACH).

SPECIAL HELPS

MEAL PLANNING

MEATS

What do meats do for you? Build and repair body tissues; regulate body; help convert food to energy.

How much meat do you need each day? Not as much as you might think: Adults need 2 or more servings daily (pregnant and nursing women, 3 or more).

What is an average adult serving? Two to 3 ounces cooked lean meat, not counting bone or fat.

SAMPLE SERVING

Choose 2 or more each day:

1. 1 small chicken leg or thigh or ½ small chicken breast; 2 slices (4x2x¼ inch) beef, veal, lamb, pork, ham, liver or other organ meats, chicken, turkey, duck, game hen

2. 2 frankfurters

3. 4 fish sticks

4. 1 hamburger patty, 3x½ inch

5. ⅓ cup canned tuna or salmon

6. 2 eggs

As occasional substitutes: 1 cup cooked dried beans or lentils, ⅓ cup peanuts, 4 tablespoons imitation bacon, 4 tablespoons peanut butter.

The servings listed above may seem small but they are nutritionally adequate. Some people will eat more than two servings a day.

BREADS AND CEREALS

What do breads and cereals do for you? Provide energy; help regulate vital body processes; help convert food into energy.

How much do you need? Adults: 4 servings daily of enriched, restored, fortified or whole grain products.

SAMPLE SERVING

These must be enriched, restored or fortified, or made with enriched whole grain flour.

1. ½ to ¾ cup cooked rice or pasta

2. 1 roll, biscuit or muffin or 1 slice whole wheat or enriched bread

3. 1 pancake or waffle

4. 1 cup ready-to-eat cereal or ½ to ¾ cup cooked cereal, cornmeal or grits

5. 1 tablespoon wheat germ

Sample servings of meats

Sample servings of breads and cereals

Sample servings of fruits and vegetables

FRUITS AND VEGETABLES

What do fruits and vegetables do for you? Help maintain healthy gums and body tissues, normal night vision and healthy skin.

How much do you need each day? Adults need 4 or more servings: a source of vitamin C every day and a source of vitamin A every other day. Fruits and vegetables not listed here also contribute valuable nutrients.

Good sources of vitamin C: cantaloupes, grapefruit, grapefruit juice, lemons, lemon juice, oranges, orange juice, papayas, strawberries, broccoli, Brussels sprouts, green peppers.

Good sources of vitamin A: cantaloupes, mangoes, carrots, collard greens, kale, mustard greens, pumpkin, spinach, sweet potatoes, turnip greens, winter squash.

SAMPLE SERVING
Choose 4 or more each day:
1. ½ cup cooked vegetables
2. ¼ medium cantaloupe
3. ½ banana or 1 medium fruit or 12 grapes or cherries or 1 cup berries or ½ cup fruit juice
4. 1 cup raw leafy vegetable

MILK

What do foods in the milk group do for you? Help build and maintain healthy bones and teeth; help build and repair body tissues; help convert food into energy.

Types of milk: Whole milk (3% or more butterfat, fortified with vitamin D); 2% milk (2% butterfat —look for 2% milk fortified with vitamins D and A); fortified skim milk (virtually fat free); fortified nonfat dry milk; buttermilk; evaporated milk.

Cheese, yogurt and other milk products can be substituted for part of these daily requirements. See equivalents (left): 1 cup buttermilk, 1 cup yogurt, 1½ cups cottage cheese, 2 one-inch cubes Cheddar cheese or 1 one-ounce slice Swiss cheese equals 1 cup milk in calcium.

How much do you need each day? Children under 9 need 2 to 3 cups; children 9 to 12, 3 or more cups; teen-agers, 4 or more cups; adults, 2 or more cups (pregnant and nursing women, 4 or more cups).

NOTE: For variety and additional food energy, you can include butter, margarine, oil, sauces, sweets and extra servings of foods from the 4 groups.

Foods containing calcium equivalent to 1 cup milk

SAMPLE DAILY MENU PLAN

Breakfast	Lunch	Dinner
Citrus Fruit or Juice	Meat, Fish, Poultry or Cheese*	Meat, Fish, Poultry or Cheese
Cereal with Milk	Vegetable and/or Salad	Green or Yellow Vegetable and
Egg or Meat	Breads, Noodles or Rice	Salad (or two vegetables)
Toast, Quick Bread or Grits	Fruit Milk	Breads, Noodles or Rice
Tea, Coffee or Milk		Fruit or Dessert (optional)
		Milk

*Legumes (dried peas or beans) or peanut butter can be substituted.

Note: Don't underestimate the importance of breakfast. After going without food all night, the body's energy needs a pickup. Whatever is nutritious and tastes good will do the job.

NUTRIENTS IN FOODS

Proteins: It is wise to combine complete proteins from meats, eggs and cheese with incomplete proteins from breads, cereals, dried beans and peas.

Carbohydrates: Starches (pasta and bread) and sugars (fruits and sweets) supply carbohydrates.

Fats: Fatty meats, most cheeses and nuts are some important sources of fats.

Vitamins: Citrus fruits are an important source of vitamin C; liver, deep yellow and dark green vegetables, whole and enriched grains, milk and eggs are excellent sources of other vitamins.

Minerals: Important sources are seafood, milk and milk products, whole and enriched grains and eggs.

Water: Fruits, vegetables and milk are important sources.

FIBER CONTENT IN FOODS

Impressive evidence has recently been revealed that indicates food fiber may play a more important and beneficial role in the diet than formerly believed. In our diets, fiber is derived mainly from whole grain cereals and breads, fruits and vegetables and nuts. For example, bran cereals, whole wheat breads and other foods made from whole wheat grains, such as whole ground cornmeal, whole rolled oats and brown rice, retain the outer coat of the cereal grain, which contains the most fiber. Fruits and vegetables contain fiber, although in variable amounts, as do roasted nuts, sesame seed, sunflower seeds and nuts, and coconut.

NONMEAT PROTEIN FOODS

With food prices soaring and nutrition high on the concerned cook's list, it is timely to learn the protein value of nonmeat foods:

	Amount	Protein Grams
Milk (all kinds)	1 cup	9
Cottage cheese	¼ cup	8
Cheese		
Cheddar	1 ounce	7
Swiss	1 ounce	8
Egg	1	6
Yogurt	½ cup	4
Peanut butter	2 tablespoons	8
Imitation bacon	2 tablespoons	8
Soybeans	½ cup cooked	8
Lentils	½ cup cooked	8
Peas, dried	½ cup cooked	8
Flour	½ cup	7
Oatmeal	1 cup cooked	5
Cornmeal	1 cup cooked	3
Bread		
brown	1 slice	3
white	1 slice	2
Noodles	½ cup cooked	3
Rice	½ cup cooked	2

For comparison, there are 17 grams protein in a 3-ounce cooked hamburger, 18 grams protein in a 3-ounce chicken drumstick, 25 grams protein in 1 thick (3.5 ounces) pork chop, 5 grams protein in 1 breaded fish stick and 16 grams protein in 2 ounces canned tuna. Daily meals and snacks should provide an adult about 65 grams of protein.

CALORIES DO COUNT

When you are counting calories, choose very lean, well-trimmed meats, poultry and fish without skin, broiled or baked—not fried or deep fried; all vegetables (eat less often corn, kidney and lima beans, peas, potatoes and winter squash); fresh and/or unsweetened canned fruits or juices; fruits rich in vitamin C (oranges, grapefruit, strawberries, cantaloupes); whole grain, enriched, restored or fortified cereals and breads; fortified skim, buttermilk, nonfat dry milk; dry or 2% creamed cottage cheese, farmer or pot cheese, Neufchâtel and other low-calorie cheeses.

MEAT
Bacon (2 slices) 100
Baked ham (3 ounces) 245
Beef (3 ounces)
    hamburger, broiled 245
    T-bone steak, broiled 400
Frankfurters (2) 310
Lamb chop (3 ounces), broiled 300
Pork chop (3 ounces), broiled 320
Spareribs (6 medium) 245

FISH AND SEAFOOD
Fish sticks (4) 160
Salmon, canned (3 ounces) 120
Shrimp, canned (3 ounces) 100
Tuna, water packed (3 ounces) 110

POULTRY
Chicken breast (3 ounces), broiled 100
Chicken drumstick (3 ounces meat), broiled 110
Turkey (3 ounces) 160

CHEESE AND EGGS
American cheese (1 slice) 105
Cottage cheese (¼ cup) 60
Egg (1 large) 80
Fried or scrambled egg 110
Omelet (2 eggs) 215

VEGETABLES
Asparagus (½ cup) 20
Beets (½ cup), Carrots (½ cup) 30
Broccoli (½ cup), Cabbage (½ cup) 20
Cauliflower (½ cup) 10
Celery (1 stalk) 5
Corn (5-inch ear) 70
Green beans (½ cup) 20
Lettuce, iceberg (¼ head) 15
Peas (½ cup) 60
Potatoes
    baked (medium) 90
    French-fried (10 pieces) 155
    mashed, with milk and butter (½ cup) 95
Spinach (½ cup) 20
Tomato (1 small) 30

FRUITS
Apple (2½-inch), Orange (3-inch) 70
Banana (6x1½ inches) 85
Grapefruit (half, 4¼-inch) 60
Peach (2-inch) 35
Pear (3x2½ inches) 100

BREADS
Biscuit (1 medium) 140
Graham cracker (1 medium) 30
Pancake (4-inch) 60
Saltine (1 square) 20
Sweet roll 135
Waffle (5½x4½ inches) 210
White, whole wheat, raisin, rye (1 slice) 60

CEREALS
Oatmeal, cooked (½ cup) 65
Toasted oat cereal (1 cup) 98
Whole wheat flake cereal (1 cup) 101

DESSERTS
Brownie (2-inch square) 145
Cake (2-inch piece)
    angel food, unfrosted 110
    chocolate, with chocolate frosting 445
Cookie (3-inch) 120
Gelatin, flavored (½ cup) 70
Ice cream (½ cup), Ice milk (½ cup) 140
Pie (⅐ of 9-inch)
    apple 345
    lemon meringue 305
    pecan (⅑ of 9-inch) 490
Sherbet (½ cup) 130

BEVERAGES
Chocolate malted milk 500
Cola-type (8 ounces) 95
Lemonade (1 cup) 110
Milk (1 cup)
    skim 90
    2% 140
    whole 160
Orange juice (½ cup) 55
Tomato juice (½ cup) 20

Note: These caloric values are averages not specifically calculated for the recipes in this book.

KITCHEN HELPS

KEEPING FOOD SAFE

KEEP FOOD HOT OR COLD

The most perishable foods are those containing eggs, milk (creamed foods, cream pies), seafood (seafood salads), meat and poultry. When you shop, pick up your meat and poultry selections last. Take them straight home and refrigerate them.

Don't allow hot or cold foods to remain at room temperature for more than 2 hours; bacteria thrive in lukewarm food. These germs seldom change the taste, odor or appearance of food. A standard rule, recommended by the U.S. Department of Agriculture, is that hot foods should be kept hot (above 140°) and cold foods cold (below 40°).

Once food has been cooked, keep it hot until serving time or refrigerate as soon as possible. If it will not raise the refrigerator temperature above 45°, hot food can be placed immediately in the refrigerator. If you must refrigerate large quantities of hot food, first quickly reduce the temperature: Fill the sink or a large bowl with cold water and ice and place the container in it. Refrigerate leftovers from meals immediately.

KEEP FOOD CLEAN

Germs are a natural part of the environment; you will have to keep washing them off things, especially your hands. If you keep germs off meat, poultry and dairy products, you will avoid problems. Keep utensils, platters, hands and countertops soap-and-hot-water clean. Don't handle food if you have infected cuts or sores on your hands.

Be careful not to transfer germs from raw meat to cooked meat. Do not, for example, carry raw hamburgers to the grill on a platter then later serve the cooked meat on the same (unwashed) platter.

Another hazard to food is a wooden chopping board used for raw meat or poultry as well as other foods. For meats, a hard plastic cutting board is less porous and safer to use. Wash cutting boards with a mixture of 2 teaspoons chlorine bleach and 1 teaspoon vinegar to a gallon of water.

Use disposable paper towels when working with or cleaning up after raw foods.

Keep pets out of the kitchen. Teach children to wash their hands after playing with pets.

FOOD SAFETY TIPS

Ground Meat: Cook thoroughly—it's handled often in preparation and germs can get mixed into it. Don't eat raw ground meat—it's not safe!

Ham: Know what kind of ham you're buying; some are fully cooked but others need cooking. Check the label. If you have any doubts, cook it.

Luncheon Meat, Frankfurters: Refrigerate; use within a week. Use a fork or tongs when you handle the meat.

Poultry: Cook all poultry products as long as directions require. Refrigerate cooked poultry, stuffing and giblets as soon as possible in separate containers; use within a few days or freeze.

Canned Foods: Do not buy or use food from leaking, bulging or dented cans or jars with cracks or loose or bulging lids. If you are in doubt about a can of food, don't taste it! Return it to your grocer and report it to your local health authority.

Milk: Since fresh milk products are highly perishable, refrigerate them as soon after purchase as possible. (The longer the exposure to light and heat, the greater the nutritional loss.) Store in covered containers and use within 5 days. Unopened evaporated milk and nonfat dry milk may be stored in a cool area for several months. Unopened dry *whole* milk, which contains fat, should be refrigerated; use within a few weeks.

NOTE: For *Food Safety in the Family* (free), write to the Animal and Plant Health Inspection Service, USDA, Washington, D.C. 20250.

PACK SAFE LUNCHES

☐ Scrub fruits and vegetables well before packing.

☐ Use fully cooked foods (bologna, frankfurters, canned meats and poultry). They keep well.

☐ Wash vacuum bottles and rinse with boiling water after each use. Be sure soups, stews or chili are boiling hot when poured into vacuum bottles.

☐ Lunch boxes insulate better than lunch bags.

KEEP FOOD SAFE AT BUFFETS

Serve food in small dishes, refilling frequently from stove or refrigerator. Or keep foods hot in electric frypans or chafing dishes or on hot trays. Do not depend on warming units that use small candles.

Refrigerate desserts made with eggs, milk or cream; potato salads; and salads made with seafood, poultry or meat. Ideally, chill both food and dish before serving. Serve cold foods over crushed ice.

COMMON FOOD EQUIVALENTS

	Amount	Approximate Measure
Cheese, American or Cheddar	4 ounces	1 cup shredded
Cheese, cottage	1 pound	2 cups
Cheese, cream	3-ounce package	6 tablespoons
	8-ounce package	1 cup (16 tablespoons)
Chocolate, unsweetened	8-ounce package	8 squares (1 ounce each)
Chocolate chips	6-ounce package	1 cup
Coconut, shredded or flaked	4-ounce can	about 1⅓ cups
Coffee, ground	1 pound	80 tablespoons
Cream, dairy sour	8 ounces	1 cup
Cream, whipping	½ pint	1 cup (2 cups whipped)
Flour, all-purpose	1 pound	about 3½ cups
Flour, cake	1 pound	about 4 cups
Lemon juice	1 medium lemon	2 to 3 tablespoons
Lemon peel, lightly grated	1 medium lemon	1½ to 3 teaspoons
Margarine or other shortening	1 pound	2 cups
Marshmallows	1 large	10 miniature
	about 11 large or 110 miniature	1 cup
Nuts		
almonds	1 pound	1 to 1¾ cups nutmeats
	1 pound shelled	3½ cups
peanuts	1 pound	2¼ cups nutmeats
	1 pound shelled	3 cups
pecans	1 pound	2¼ cups nutmeats
	1 pound shelled	4 cups
walnuts	1 pound	1⅔ cups nutmeats
	1 pound shelled	4 cups
Onion	1 medium	½ cup chopped
Orange juice	1 medium orange	⅓ to ½ cup
Orange peel, lightly grated	1 medium orange	1 to 2 tablespoons
Pasta (see page 221)		
Rice (see page 225)		
Sugar, brown	1 pound	2¼ cups (firmly packed)
Sugar, granulated	1 pound	2 cups
Sugar, powdered	1 pound	about 4 cups

EQUIVALENT MEASURES

3 teaspoons	=	1 tablespoon (15 mL)
16 tablespoons	=	1 cup (about 250 mL)
2 cups	=	1 pint (about 500 mL)
4 cups (2 pints)	=	1 quart (about 1 L)
4 quarts (liquid)	=	1 gallon (about 4 L)
4 tablespoons	=	¼ cup (about 50 mL)
5⅓ tablespoons	=	⅓ cup (about 80 mL)

EMERGENCY SUBSTITUTIONS

An emergency is the only excuse for using a substitute ingredient—recipe results will vary. Following are some stand-ins for staples.

For	Use
1½ teaspoons cornstarch	1 tablespoon flour
1 whole egg	2 egg yolks plus 1 tablespoon water (in cookies) or 2 egg yolks (in custards and similar mixtures)
1 cup fresh whole milk	½ cup evaporated milk plus ½ cup water or 1 cup reconstituted nonfat dry milk plus 2 teaspoons margarine or butter
1 ounce unsweetened chocolate	3 tablespoons cocoa plus 1 tablespoon fat
1 cup honey	1¼ cups sugar plus ¼ cup liquid

FOOD PREPARATION TIPS

Peeling Tomatoes: Place in boiling water 1 minute; plunge into cold water. Slip off skin with knife point.

Deveining Shrimp: Make a shallow cut lengthwise down back; remove sand vein with point of knife.

Cutting on the diagonal: Use a very sharp knife; keep angle of the blade almost parallel to cutting surface.

Bread Crumbs: For soft crumbs, pull bread into pieces. For dry crumbs, dry bread in low oven; crush.

Croutons: Trim bread and cut into cubes; toast in 300° oven. Add cubes to melted margarine and toss.

Coating Chicken: Place seasonings, crumbs or flour in plastic or paper bag. Shake a few pieces at a time.

Adding Food Color: Add liquid color drop by drop. Add paste color (from specialty stores) sparingly.

Tinting Coconut: Add a few drops of liquid food color to coconut in a jar; shake until evenly tinted.

Melting Chocolate: Place in small heatproof bowl or in top of double boiler over hot (not boiling) water.

TERMS YOU NEED TO KNOW

FOR PREPARING INGREDIENTS

Crush: Press to extract juice with garlic press, mallet or side of knife (garlic).

Snip: Cut into very small pieces with scissors (parsley, chives).

Chop: Cut into pieces with a knife or other sharp tool (hold end of knife tip on the board with one hand; move the blade up and down with the other).

Cut up: Cut into pieces with scissors (dried fruits, marshmallows).

Dice: Cut into small cubes (less than ½ inch).

Cube: Cut into cubes ½ inch or larger.

Sliver: Cut into long thin pieces (almonds).

Julienne: Cut into matchlike sticks (cooked meat, cheese).

Grate: Cut into tiny particles, using small holes of grater (lemon peel).

Shred: Cut into thin pieces, using large holes of grater or shredder (cheese).

Pare: Cut off outer covering with a knife or other sharp tool (potatoes, apples).

Peel: Strip off outer covering (oranges).

FOR COMBINING INGREDIENTS

Arranged from the gentlest action to the most vigorous.

Toss: Tumble ingredients lightly with a lifting motion (salads).

Fold: Combine ingredients lightly by a combination of two motions: one cuts vertically through mixture; the other slides the spatula across the bottom of the bowl and up the side, turning over (chiffon cakes, soufflés).

Cut in: Distribute solid fat in dry ingredients by chopping with knives or pastry blender (pastry, biscuits).

Stir: Combine ingredients with a figure "8" or circular motion until of uniform consistency.

Mix: Combine in any way that distributes all ingredients evenly.

Blend: Thoroughly combine all ingredients until very smooth and uniform.

Beat: Make mixture smooth by a vigorous over-and-over motion with a spoon, whip or beater.

Whip: Beat rapidly to incorporate air.

FOR COOKING

Cook and stir: Cook in small amount of shortening, stirring occasionally, until tender (onion). We use this term rather than sauté.

Brown: Cook until food changes color, usually in small amount of fat over moderate heat (meat).

Scald: Heat milk to just below the boiling point. Tiny bubbles form at edge.

Simmer: Cook in liquid just below the boiling point. Bubbles form slowly and collapse *below* the surface.

Boil: Heat until bubbles rise continuously and break on the surface of liquid (*rolling boil:* bubbles form rapidly).

OTHER TERMS

Cool: Allow to come to room temperature.

Refrigerate: Place in refrigerator to chill or to store.

Marinate: Let food stand in liquid that will add flavor or tenderize.

Baste: Spoon a flavoring ingredient over food during cooking period.

Toast: Brown in oven or toaster (bread, nuts).

HOW TO CHOOSE A RECIPE

There's more to reading a recipe than just giving it a quick once-over. Actually, you have to think of it in terms of

- □ servings
- □ type of cooking involved
- □ equipment needed
- □ timing

Check the servings in the recipe and consider the number you are planning for. If the recipe is larger, will leftovers keep in the refrigerator for the next day's meal? Will the food reheat well?

Check the ingredients. Are they in season? Expensive or a bargain? Fit the recipe to your budget and to the occasion.

Be sure you have on hand all the utensils and equipment you'll need. (See Choosing Cooking Equipment, page 365.)

Check the timetable of your recipe. Match your recipe to the free time you have. If you are combining two recipes, such as a meat roast with baked vegetables, be sure that the baking temperatures of both are compatible.

INGREDIENTS— HINTS TO HELP YOU

Ascorbic Acid: The vitamin C ingredient used to preserve the color of fruits and vegetables (usually sold with canning supplies.)

Baking Powder: All our testing has been done with double-acting baking powder. Do not use single-acting baking powder.

Cheese: Many of our recipes call for natural or process cheese; be sure to use the type specified. They vary in fat and moisture content as well as in texture and flavor.

Chocolate: Our recipes call for unsweetened, semisweet and sweet cooking chocolate; be sure to use the type specified.

When "melted unsweetened chocolate (cool)" is called for, you can either melt and cool the unsweetened squares or use the envelopes of pre-melted chocolate. (We do not recommend the use of premelted chocolate when the ingredient listing specifies squares.)

Cocoa: When our recipes call for cocoa, we mean the unsweetened product; do not use instant cocoa mix.

Cream: Whipping (30 to 35% butterfat), coffee (about 20% butterfat), half-and-half (10 to 12% butterfat), dairy sour (20% butterfat). Do not substitute one for another. Our recipes do not call for cream that has been soured.

Eggs: The eggs used in our bakings are medium to large Grade A eggs. (When the exact size is essential to the success of a recipe, as in the case of cakes, we have also given a cup measurement.) If you use larger or smaller eggs, measure them—1 medium-to-large egg equals about ¼ cup.

Flour: When our recipes call for all-purpose flour, either the regular or quick-mixing type can be used unless the recipe includes another recommendation.

Regular or stone-ground flour can be used when recipes call for whole wheat flour. Occasionally there is an adjustment for stone-ground or other whole wheat flours; this is noted in the recipes.

Specific directions for the use of self-rising flour are included in each recipe using more than ¼ cup. With lesser amounts, you can substitute self-rising flour without other recipe adjustments. Cake flour should be used when it is called for in recipes. (See Measuring Ingredients, page 361; we do not recommend sifting flour.)

Gelatin: Unflavored gelatin is packaged in envelopes, each containing about 1 tablespoon. (We usually call for the entire package.) Flavored gelatin contains sugar, color and flavoring.

Herbs: Ground herbs should be used in the recipes unless another form is specified. If you substitute fresh herbs, increase the amount.

Milk: Our testing has been done with fresh whole milk. When buttermilk is called for, use commercial-cultured buttermilk. (Do not substitute soured milk for buttermilk.) To substitute evaporated milk for fresh milk, mix with an equal amount of water.

Shortening: When a recipe calls for shortening, we refer to the type sold in 1- or 3-pound cans. In baked goods, such as cakes, you can substitute margarine or butter for up to half the amount.

If a recipe calls for "margarine or butter, softened," use only stick-type (not whipped) margarine.

Vegetable oil is any oil of vegetable origin. Use oil only when called for; do not use as a substitute for other shortenings, even when they are melted.

Sugar: When sugar is listed in a recipe, use granulated (cane or beet) sugar. Brown sugar and powdered sugar are always specified in recipes. When more than one type of sugar is used in any recipe, all types are designated. (Do not sift any sugar unless it is necessary to remove lumps.)

FOOD ADDITIVES

An additive is just what the word says—it is anything that is put into food that adds to such qualities as flavor, freshness, texture, color, keepability, ease of preparation or nutritive value. Some additives are natural, some are manufactured. All are chemicals—but don't let that word frighten you. Our bodies are made up of chemicals, and every nutrient we consume—whether protein, carbohydrate, fat or whatever—is really a chemical.

The addition of vitamin D to milk prevents bone-crippling rickets in babies. Iodine in salt has done much to reduce goiter in this country. Additives such as cinnamon or synthetic flavorings make food taste better. An additive such as baking powder makes layer cakes rise.

Other additives keep bread from molding, pudding from separating, shortening from spoiling. As necessary, they help food travel, thicken, gel, spread or brown—all with the assurance that the government rules and standards that help guard food safety are being met.

MEASURING INGREDIENTS — THE RIGHT WAY

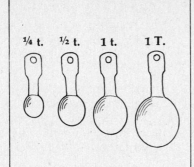

Graduated Spoons: To measure thin liquids, pour into the appropriate spoon until full.

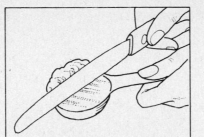

For dry ingredients and thick liquids: Pour or scoop into appropriate spoon until full, then level. If your set of spoons does not have a ⅛-teaspoon measure, use the ¼ teaspoon; fill, then remove half. Note: A dash is less than ⅛ teaspoon.

Glass Measuring Cup: For measuring liquids. Read the measurement at eye level.

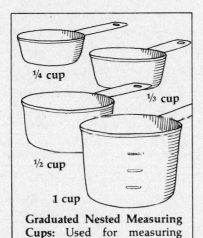

Graduated Nested Measuring Cups: Used for measuring nonliquids.

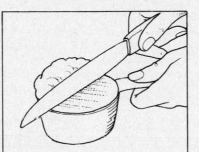

For all-purpose flour, quick-mixing flour and granulated sugar: Dip cup into ingredient to fill, then level with straight-edged spatula or knife. (Do not sift flour to measure or combine with other ingredients.)

For cake flour, powdered sugar and biscuit baking mix: Lightly spoon into cup, then level. (Sift powdered sugar only if lumpy.)

For cereals and dry bread crumbs: Pour into cup, then level. (This method can also be used for measuring powdered sugar and quick-mixing flour.)

For nuts, coconut, shredded cheese, cut-up or small fruit and soft bread crumbs: Spoon into cup and pack down lightly.

For brown sugar, fats and shortening: Spoon into cup and pack down firmly. (When a recipe calls for melted shortening, it can be measured before or after melting.)

METRICS IN THE KITCHEN

The metric system is arriving gradually, but don't panic—you have plenty of time to master it. Total United States conversion may take a decade. And learning the system is easy: All metric measurements are divisible by 10.

In the kitchen, you needn't worry about conversion tables. Keep your present cup, tablespoon and teaspoon measures for conventional cookbooks. Then, when metric recipes are available, spend a minimal amount for a set of metric measures—and convert with ease. Instead of converting a recipe from one system to another, you'll be matching metric measures with metric recipes. Test kitchens will have had to convert and retest recipes, so the work will have been done for you. All you need are the metric measures and a sense of adventure.

The following metric recipe is an example of what you'll be seeing. If you have metric measures, try it.

CHOCOLATE CHIP COOKIES

250 mL granulated sugar
250 mL packed brown sugar
150 mL shortening
150 mL margarine or butter, softened
2 eggs
10 mL vanilla
750 mL all-purpose flour
5 mL baking soda
5 mL salt
250 mL chopped nuts
2 packages (170 g each) semisweet
   chocolate chips

Heat oven to 190°C. Mix sugars, shortening, margarine, eggs and vanilla thoroughly. Stir in remaining ingredients.

Drop dough by rounded teaspoonfuls about 5 cm apart onto ungreased cookie sheet. Bake until light brown, 8 to 10 minutes. Cool slightly before removing from cookie sheet.   ABOUT 100 COOKIES.

METRIC TEMPERATURES

Degrees Celsius (°C) is the metric unit of measure for temperature. Water boils at 100°C (212°F) and freezes at 0°C (32°F) at sea level. Other everyday examples of degrees Celsius are: −40°F and −40°C are the same; a very cold day, −20°C; room temperature, 20°C; body temperature, 37°C. Cooking temperatures: rare beef, 60°C; medium beef, 70°C; well-done beef, 80°C. A very slow oven, 120°C; slow oven, 142°C; moderate oven, 180°C; hot oven, 210°C; very hot oven, 230°C.

THE BASIC UNITS

The liter (volume), gram (weight) and meter (length, width, depth) are the basic units of metric measure. All increase or decrease in units of 10.

METRIC VOLUME (Dry and Liquid Ingredients)

The liter (L) is the basic unit for measuring dry and liquid ingredients. It is a little larger than a quart. Recipes will usually use the milliliter (mL), which is .001 liter.

Metric Quantity	Equivalent
1 mL*	slightly less than ¼ teaspoon
2 mL*	slightly less than ½ teaspoon
5 mL*	1 teaspoon
15 mL*	1 tablespoon
25 mL*	1 tablespoon plus 2 teaspoons
50 mL*	¼ cup minus 2 teaspoons
125 mL*	½ cup plus 1½ teaspoons
250 mL*	1 cup plus 1 tablespoon
500 mL	1 pint plus 2 tablespoons
1 L (1000 mL)	1 quart plus ¼ cup

*These are the measures expected to be available.

NOTE: We are not adopting the European method of weighing ingredients for recipes.

METRIC WEIGHT

The gram (g) is the basic unit for measuring solids by weight. Over 500, the term for weight changes to *kilogram* (kg) and the decimal system is used. Meat, butter, cheese and packaged goods are sold by gram and kilogram.

Metric Quantity	Equivalent
30 g	1 ounce plus a large pinch
125 g	¼ pound plus about ¼ ounce
250 g	½ pound plus less than an ounce
500 g	1 pound plus 1⅔ ounces
0.750 kg	1½ pounds plus about 2½ ounces
1 kg (1000 g)	2 pounds plus about 3½ ounces

METRIC DIMENSIONS (Length, Width, Depth)

The meter (m) is the basic unit for measuring length, width and depth. However, the centimeter (cm), .01 meter, is used most often. In addition, the millimeter (mm), .001 meter, will be used.

Metric Measure	Equivalent
6.0 mm	about ¼ inch
2.5 cm	slightly less than 1 inch
15.0 cm	6 inches
30.0 cm	slightly less than 1 foot
1.0 m	slightly longer than 1 yard

HIGH-ALTITUDE COOKING

People who live in a high-altitude area face some unique cooking problems. Certain foods and methods of preparation are affected by the pressure of high altitudes and recipes must be adjusted.

If you're new to a high-altitude area, call the Home Service Department of the local utility company or the State Extension Office for recipe booklets and help in solving specific problems. Recipes for high-altitude cooking are also available from Colorado State University, Fort Collins, Colorado 80521.

Here are a few guidelines to help you:

Vegetables: Because the boiling point of water is lower at high altitudes, vegetables (fresh or frozen) take longer to become tender and cooking time must be increased.

Eggs: Again, because water boils at a lower temperature, the cooking time for eggs in the shell must be increased. Keep a record for the future.

Meats: Meats cooked in boiling liquid or steam take longer to cook than at sea level, sometimes quite a bit longer. Meats cooked in the oven also take longer to cook than at sea level. Use a meat thermometer and record the time needed as a guide for future use.

Deep-fried Foods: To prevent food from becoming too dark before it is cooked through, the temperature of the fat should be lower than at sea level. Fry several pieces at a lower temperature, then check doneness in the middle.

Candy and Cooked Frostings: The mixture should be cooked to a lower temperature. If you use a thermometer, first check the boiling temperature of water in your area, then subtract this temperature from 212°F. Subtract the same number of degrees from the temperature cited in the recipe. (Or use the cold water test for candy.)

Yeast Breads: At high altitudes, if room temperature is very warm, overrising can occur. Allow dough to rise *just* until doubled.

Mixes: Many mixes that require adjustment for high altitudes have specific directions right on the package. Be sure to look for them.

Cakes: Use recipes especially developed for high altitudes. Your best source is the Home Service Department of your local utility company. At the right, however, are two basic recipes for your files.

APPLESAUCE CAKE

For altitudes of 3,500 to 6,500 feet.

2⅔ cups all-purpose flour*
 2 cups sugar
 1 teaspoon baking soda
1½ teaspoons salt
 ¼ teaspoon baking powder
 ¾ teaspoon ground cinnamon
 ½ teaspoon ground cloves
 ½ teaspoon ground allspice
1½ cups applesauce
 ½ cup water
 ½ cup shortening
 2 eggs
 1 cup raisins
 ½ cup chopped walnuts

Heat oven to 375°. Grease and flour oblong pan, 13x9x2 inches, or two 9-inch or three 8-inch round layer pans. Beat all ingredients in large mixer bowl on low speed, scraping bowl constantly, 30 seconds. Beat on high speed, scraping bowl occasionally, 3 minutes. Pour into pan(s).

Bake until wooden pick inserted in center comes out clean, oblong 60 to 65 minutes, 9-inch layers 50 to 55 minutes, 8-inch layers 40 to 50 minutes; cool.

*Do not use self-rising flour in this recipe.

BONNIE BUTTER CAKE

For altitudes of 3,500 to 6,500 feet.

1¼ cups plus 2 tablespoons sugar
 ⅔ cup margarine or butter, softened
 2 eggs
1½ teaspoons vanilla
 3 cups all-purpose flour*
2¼ teaspoons baking powder
 1 teaspoon salt
1⅓ cups milk

Heat oven to 375°. Grease and flour two 9-inch or three 8-inch round layer pans. Mix sugar, margarine, eggs and vanilla until fluffy. Beat on high speed, scraping bowl occasionally, 5 minutes. Beat in flour, baking powder and salt alternately with milk on low speed. Pour into pans.

Bake until wooden pick inserted in center comes out clean, 30 to 35 minutes; cool.

*If using self-rising flour, omit baking powder and salt.

HELPFUL EQUIPMENT EXTRAS

Mallet: Use to crush (candy, ice) or to pound thin (meat, poultry).

Garlic Press: Use to crush whole garlic cloves or to extract juice.

Wire Strainer: Use to drain foods. Use a colander for large amounts.

Kitchen Shears: Use to snip (parsley, chives) or to cut (dates).

French Knives: Use two to chop finely; hold tips down, moving handles.

Apple Corer: Use to core (apples, pears). Some corers also slice.

Pastry Brush: Use to grease (pans, cookie sheets) or to brush on glazes.

Wire Whip or Whisk: Use to blend (sauces, gravies) or to whip (cream).

Vegetable Parer: Use to pare (fruits, too) or to make chocolate curls.

Scoops: Use to serve or shape foods (meatballs, cookies).

Decorators' Tube: Use for decorating tasks or to stuff (celery, eggs).

Grinders: Use for many foods. Some have a choice of blades.

CHOOSING COOKING EQUIPMENT

We have used standard equipment in the preparation of all the recipes in this book. (Standard sizes are usually marked on the back of a pan; if not, measure from inside rim to inside rim.) Where applicable, choices of pans have been given. Other substitutions affect baking temperature and time and are not recommended.

Some of the equipment called for throughout the book is described below. Equipment related to specific bakings (breads, pies, cakes, cookies) is described in the pertinent chapters.

FOR COOKING AND BAKING

Baking Dish: Heat-resistant dish with low sides. (For information about microwave utensils, see page 367.)

Baking Pan: The standard metal pans in the size specified. We have given choices wherever possible; it is best not to make substitutions. If glass is used, it may be necessary to reduce the oven temperature 25°.

Bundt Cake Pan: Pan with a tube in the middle and scalloped sides (the capacity should be correct; measure by cups).

Casserole: Heat-resistant dish with deep sides.

Double Boiler: Because of advances in the heat control of ranges, we have eliminated the use of the double boiler in many recipes. It is, however, essential in a few.

Dutch Oven: Deep cooking utensil with tight-fitting cover.

FOR PREPARATION

Measuring Cups and Spoons: See page 361.

Rotary Beater: Standard electric mixer, hand electric mixer or hand (nonelectric) beater. In some cases, only one type of beater is suitable, and it is so specified in the recipe.

Mixer Bowl: The sturdy bowl that is sold with standard electric mixers. When our recipes call for a bowl, use any container in which you can combine the necessary ingredients.

THE WELL-STOCKED KITCHEN

A well-stocked kitchen means more than food. It's neither crammed with gadgets nor Mother Hubbard bare. When it comes to utensils, rely on day-to-day, do-almost-everything basics:

For measuring: Nested dry measuring cups; liquid measuring cups; measuring spoons; flexible metal spatula (for leveling off ingredients)

For preparation: Mixing bowls; wooden spoons; metal spoons; slotted spoon; rubber scraper; cutting board; chef's knife; serrated knife; paring knives; utility knife (long, narrow-handled); can opener; bottle and jar opener; long-handled fork; spatulas; tongs; kitchen scissors; vegetable parer; vegetable brush; pastry brush; skewers; grater/shredder; pepper mill; strainer; colander; electric mixer; hand beater; toaster; rolling pin and cover; pastry cloth; pastry blender; kitchen timer

For top-of-the-range cooking: Covered skillets (8-inch and either a 10- or 12-inch); covered saucepans (1- and 2-quart and either a 3- or 4-quart); Dutch oven

For baking: Covered casseroles (1-, 2- and 3-quart); baking dishes (2- and 3-quart); custard cups; baking pans (8-inch square, 9-inch square and 13x9x2 inches); cookie sheets; biscuit and cookie cutters; round layer pans (9x1½ inches); loaf pan (9x5x3 inches); tube pan (10x4 inches); jelly roll pan (15½x10½x1 inch); roasting pan (with rack); muffin pan; pie plates; wire cooling racks; pot holders; meat thermometer

Special utensils: Griddle; electric blender; electric skillet; food chopper or grinder; gelatin molds; soufflé dish; ladle; wire whip; baster; ice-cream scoop; garlic press; melon-ball cutter; thermometers (candy and/or deep fat); pressure cooker; springform pan (9x3 inches)

OVEN CARE

Oven thermostats can go on the blink, so it's a good idea to check the temperature from time to time. Place a portable oven thermometer on a centered rack, set the oven temperature, wait 10 or 15 minutes and check the thermometer. If the temperatures don't match, adjust the setting accordingly and maintain the adjustment until the necessary repairs have been made.

Sprinkle salt on any oven spill as soon as possible. Chances are you'll be able to lift it out easily after the oven cools.

Keep your oven clean by wiping the walls while they are still warm with a cloth wrung out in a mild solution of water and vinegar or baking soda. When using a commercial oven cleaner, follow the directions exactly.

MICROWAVE COOKING

This cool, convenient new way of cooking simplifies life. It saves time. It doesn't heat the kitchen. It means fewer dishes to wash. It virtually eliminates the chore of oven scouring. It prevents waste because generally you are cooking only what you will eat. It consumes less energy—from 25 to 75% of the energy required for conventional cooking—because only the food (not the oven cavity or the utensils) is heated.

There are differences. Meats cooked less than 10 minutes usually do not brown nor do crisp crusts form on breads or other baked goods. In those instances, complementary cooking is the answer. For example: Use the microwave first for speed in cooking the apples in a pie, then brown the crust in a conventional oven. (Toppings, sauces and cereal crumbs add eye appeal to foods that do not brown.)

HOW DO MICROWAVES WORK?

There's nothing magical about microwaves. They are simply electromagnetic waves of energy, very similar to radio and television waves. The magnetron tube converts regular electricity into microwaves. These microwaves, which are deflected by metal, bounce off the walls, floor and ceiling of the cavity in an irregular pattern. When they encounter any matter containing moisture (specifically food), they are absorbed into it. A stirrer fan further deflects the microwaves so that they penetrate the food from all sides. The microwaves agitate and vibrate the moisture molecules at such a rate that friction is created; the friction, in turn, creates heat and the heat cooks the food.

In conventional cooking methods, heat is applied to the food; with microwave cooking, heat is generated within the food. Unlike a conventional oven, the microwave never heats up. Because microwaves permeate the food only about 1 inch, the additional heating occurs by conduction and/or convection. This same conduction heats the dishes that hold the food—so do remember to use hot pads.

MICROWAVE COOKING PRINCIPLES

As the volume of food increases, so must the cooking time. . . . The colder the starting temperature of the food, the longer it takes to cook. . . . Microwaves move readily throughout porous food, but merely agitate the outside of dense food; the inside cooks as heat is transferred to the center. . . . The higher the sugar or fat content, the faster the food cooks. (The sugary frosting on sweet rolls heats more quickly than the bread. A slice of fatty meat cooks faster than a lean portion.)

ARE MICROWAVES SAFE?

Cautious scientists agree that microwaves are as safe as other household cooking appliances. Actually, no other appliance has so much safety built into it. The FDA offers these tips:

☐ When you unpack the microwave, examine it for evidence of shipping damage.

☐ Follow manufacturer's instruction manual for use and care of the microwave.

☐ Clean door, seals and inside of microwave with water and mild detergent. Grease around door seal can cause excess radiation emission. Do not clean with scouring pads or other abrasives.

☐ Never insert objects through door grill or around door seal. Never allow even a paper towel to stick out of the door.

☐ Never tamper with or deactivate safety interlocks.

☐ Never operate an empty microwave.

☐ Have the microwave checked regularly by a microwave technician for wear, damage, tampering and radiation emission.

ARRANGING FOODS

Food is usually arranged in a ring shape. The energy then can penetrate the food from all sides and cook it more evenly. When some foods are cooked in square baking dishes, the corners tend to overcook. Use round dishes for most baked foods. It may be necessary to place a glass in the center of the dish to ensure even cooking.

TO COVER OR NOT TO COVER?

Coverings are often used to keep moisture in and to prevent liquid food from spattering. "Cover" in a microwave recipe means that no steam or moisture should escape. Use a fitted lid or cover the container with plastic wrap, sealing well. "Cover loosely" means that a certain amount of moisture and steam should be permitted to escape from the food. Put the lid on slightly ajar or cover with waxed paper or a paper towel. Or use plastic wrap and turn the corners back.

PREPARING MICROWAVE MEALS

Microwave meals generally are prepared in a sequence different from conventionally cooked meals. Because foods are microwaved one at a time, start with the one that is least likely to be served hot, retains heat longer or reheats well. This sequence is a guide: desserts; large cuts of meat; potatoes and smaller cuts of meat; vegetables and fish; foods to be reheated, including breads.

Stop! These utensils are not suitable for microwaving.

Go ahead with these for microwave heating and cooking.

MICROWAVE UTENSILS

Utensils appropriate for use in the microwave allow the microwaves to pass through easily into the food. There are many specially developed microwave-suitable products on the market, but chances are that you already have plenty of excellent utensils in your kitchen. For microwaving, use these:

Glassware: Suitable for both heating and cooking. For cooking, it's best to use oven-tempered glass. Keep in mind that cooked food becomes very hot and that heat is transferred to the utensil; thus, the material must be strong enough to withstand high temperatures.

Paper: Good for brief heating of many types of foods—muffins, rolls, sandwiches. For cooking, use the more durable paper products or containers designed for microwaving.

Dishwasher-safe plastic containers: Suitable for quick reheatings only. Don't cook in them; the hot food can distort and melt the plastic. More durable plastic utensils have been developed for microwaving.

Ceramic plates and casseroles: Suitable for use only if they contain no metals.

China: Good only if it contains no metal decorations or trims.

Avoid the following utensils for microwave heating and cooking:

Metal pans: Microwaves cannot penetrate metal; rather, they are deflected by it. Consult your microwave manual for guidelines about metal.

Ceramic plates and casseroles containing metals: Unsuitable for use.

To test a container for metal content, put 1 cup of water in a glass measuring cup and place it on or near the container in question. Microwave 1 minute on the 100% setting. If the container becomes warm, don't use it.

China with even a tiny fleck of gold trim: This trim can cause "arcing" and do more damage than a larger all-metal utensil.

MICROWAVE TESTING FOR THIS BOOK

All the microwave recipes in this book were developed and tested in countertop microwaves with wattage outputs of 600 to 700 watts. A variety of brands and models were used and, although they had different features and power levels, all recipes were tested using 100% settings—High, Full, Normal or Number 10. For best results, use one of these settings.

If your microwave has a wattage output rating of less than 600 watts, some increase in the suggested cooking time may be necessary. For testing, foods normally stored at room temperature were used at that temperature, while foods normally refrigerated were prepared at that temperature.

CANNING AND FREEZING

SELECTING PRODUCE

The Agricultural Marketing Service of the U.S. Department of Agriculture has established grade standards for most fresh fruits and vegetables. The grades are based on the product's color, size, shape, maturity and number of defects. The most commonly used grades are U.S. Fancy, U.S. No. 1 and U.S. No. 2. If the package bears the official USDA grade shield or the statement "Packed under Continuous Inspection of the U.S. Department of Agriculture" or "USDA Inspected," the shopper can buy with greater confidence.

When selecting fruits and vegetables for canning and freezing, it is not necessary to purchase the highest grade. It is more important to look for produce that appears fresh; avoid any that is wilted or has spots of decay. For successful canning or freezing, use produce at the peak of quality (never overripe) and gather or purchase only as much as you can handle within 2 or 3 hours.

FOR CANNING SUCCESS

□ To avoid spoilage, select only sound, unbruised foods at the peak of ripeness (do not can overripe fruits, especially tomatoes). Process immediately.

□ Thoroughly wash or peel any fruits or vegetables that have been sprayed with insecticides.

□ Make small batches and never double a recipe.

□ Use only standard jars and lids intended for home preserving and follow the manufacturer's instructions for sealing the jars.

□ Do *not* reuse sealing lids or cracked, chipped jars, or jars not designed for canning.

□ Jars used for jam and jelly preserving must be sterilized; jars used in boiling water processing do not need sterilization.

□ Use open-kettle (hot-pack) canning only for jellies and jams. Use the boiling water method only for fruits and tomatoes and for pickles preserved in vinegar. Use a pressure canner for other vegetables and for meats, poultry and fish.

□ Have the seal and pressure gauge on the pressure canner checked regularly for accuracy.

□ Do not overpack jars; allow adequate headspace (see individual recipes).

AT-A-GLANCE FRUIT AND VEGETABLE YIELDS

Produce	Amount (1 bushel) Pounds	Canned Yield Quarts	Frozen Yield Quarts
Apples	48	16 to 20	16 to 20
applesauce	48	15 to 18	15 to 18
Apricots	22 (1 lug)	7 to 11	12 to 14
Cherries	56	22 to 23*	18 to 22
	22 (1 lug)	9 to 11*	8 to 10
Peaches	48	18 to 24	16 to 24
	22 (1 lug)	8 to 12	8 to 10
Pears	50	20 to 25	18 to 24
	35 (1 box)	14 to 17	12 to 16
Plums	56	24 to 30	22 to 28
	24 (1 lug)	12	10 to 12
Beans, green or wax	30	12 to 22	15 to 22
Beets, without tops	52	14 to 24	17 to 22
Carrots, without tops	50	17 to 20	16 to 20
Corn, in husks	35	6 to 10	7 to 9
Peas, green, in pods	30	5 to 10	6 to 8
Squash, summer	40	10 to 20	16 to 20
Squash, winter	11	**	4
Tomatoes	53	14 to 22	**

*Unpitted **Not recommended

HOW TO CAN PEACHES

1. After washing and draining peaches, fill canner half full with water; put canner on to heat. Prepare Medium Syrup (page 371).

2. After dipping peaches into boiling water 30 to 60 seconds and then into cold water, drain and slip off skins. Cut into halves; remove pits.

3. Drop pitted, peeled peach halves into mixture of 1 gallon water and 2 tablespoons each salt and vinegar; rinse peaches before packing.

4. With layers overlapping, pack peaches cavity sides down in hot jars placed on board or cloth. Leave ½-inch headspace in jars.

5. Cover peaches with boiling syrup, leaving ½-inch headspace in each jar. Each pint takes ½ to ¾ cup syrup, each quart 1 to 1½ cups syrup.

6. Run rubber spatula or table knife gently between peaches and jar to release air bubbles. Add more hot syrup if necessary.

7. Wipe rims and screw threads of jars with clean, damp cloth. Put lids on; screw bands tightly and evenly to hold rubber sealing rings in place.

8. Stand filled jars on rack in hot water in canner. Add hot (not boiling) water to cover jars by 1 to 2 inches; heat to steady, gentle boil.

9. Process pints 24 minutes, quarts 30 minutes. Remove jars; cool 12 hours. Test for seal; remove bands and store in cool, dry place.

NOTE: See page 371 for preparation of jars and boiling water processing.

HOW TO CAN TOMATOES

1. Wash and drain enough fresh, firm, red-ripe tomatoes* for one canner load. Place in wire basket.

2. After dipping into boiling water 30 seconds to loosen skins, dip into cold water; drain. Slip off skins.

3. Cut out cores and trim any green spots. Pack small tomatoes whole, large ones in halves or wedges.

4. Pack tomatoes in hot jars, pressing tomatoes to fill spaces with juice to ½ inch of tops of jars.

5. Add ½ teaspoon salt per pint. Run rubber spatula between tomatoes and jar to release air bubbles.

6. After wiping rims and threads of jars with damp cloth, add lids, rubber sides down; screw bands tightly.

7. Stand filled jars on rack in hot water in canner. Add hot water to cover jars by 1 to 2 inches.

8. Put cover on canner. Heat water to steady, gentle boil. Process pints 40 minutes, quarts 50 minutes.

9. After removing jars and cooling 12 hours, test each seal (page 371). Remove bands; store in cool place.

NOTE: See page 371 for preparation of jars and boiling water processing.

*In recent years, there has been a varying acidity level in tomatoes. Use only regular size ripe tomatoes; avoid yellow and small tomatoes. The Extension Service of the USDA recommends any of the following additions: citric acid (available in drugstores) at a ratio of ¼ teaspoon per pint or ½ teaspoon per quart; or bottled or frozen lemon juice at a ratio of 1 teaspoon per pint, 2 teaspoons per quart; or 5% vinegar, same ratio as for lemon juice. Any of these additions will alter the taste only slightly. Commercially prepared tablets containing salt and citric acid are available and can be added to jars before processing.

BOILING WATER PROCESSING FOR FRUITS AND TOMATOES

This process is also called water-bath processing. You will need a large kettle with a cover and a rack. The kettle should be deep enough that the jars will be covered by 1 to 2 inches of water. In addition, you will need a ladle with a lip, a jar lifter and two large measuring cups—one for dry ingredients and one for liquids. Work quickly; prepare no more food than you can process at one time.

To prepare jars and boiling water bath: Examine tops and edges of standard jars to see that there are no nicks, cracks or sharp edges on sealing surfaces. Wash jars in hot, soapy water. Rinse; cover with hot water. Let jars remain in hot water until ready to use. Prepare lids as directed by manufacturer. About 10 minutes before ready to use, fill kettle half full with hot water; heat. (The water should be hot but not boiling when jars are placed in kettle.) Remove jars; invert jars on folded towel to drain.

To raw pack: Put cold raw fruits in jars and cover with boiling hot syrup, juice or water. For tomatoes, press down in the containers so they are covered with their own juice; add no liquid.

To hot pack: Heat fruits in syrup or water, or steam or juice them before packing. Juicy fruits and tomatoes can be preheated without added liquid and packed in the juice that cooks out.

To fill jars: Pack each hot jar to within ¼ inch of top. Wipe top and screw threads of jar with damp cloth. Place hot metal lid on jar with sealing compound next to glass; screw metal band down firmly. As each jar is sealed, place on rack in kettle, allowing enough space for water to circulate.

To process: When jars are in kettle, add hot (not boiling) water to cover them by 1 to 2 inches. Cover kettle. Heat water to boiling; reduce heat to steady but gentle boil. Start counting processing time; process as directed for each product. Remove jars. If center of lid is down and will not move, jar is sealed. Or tap center of lid with a spoon: a clear ringing sound means a good seal.

To cool jars: Place jars upright, not touching, on rack or folded cloth; keep out of drafts, but do not cover. Test for seal after 12 hours (caps or lids will be depressed in centers and will not move when pressed; lids with wire clamps and rubber seals will not leak when inverted). If seal is incomplete, empty jar; repack and reprocess food as if fresh, or refrigerate for immediate use. Remove screw bands from sealed jars. Label jars with product name and date. Store in a cool, dry place. Use within one year.

SUGAR SYRUPS

These are used for canning and freezing fruits.

For fruits to be canned, light corn syrup or mild-flavored honey can be substituted for as much as half of the sugar. For fruits to be frozen, corn syrup can replace up to one fourth of the sugar.

Syrup	Yield
Light	
2 cups sugar, 4 cups water	5 cups
Medium	
3 cups sugar, 4 cups water	5½ cups
Heavy	
4¾ cups sugar, 4 cups water	6½ cups

Cook sugar and water until sugar is dissolved. For canning, keep syrup hot until needed but do not boil down. For freezing, refrigerate until ice cold. The usual proportion of sugar to fruit for canned fruits is ½ to ¾ cup sugar for each quart of fruit. Types of syrup for various fruits are shown below:

Fruit	Syrup
Apples	Light
Grapes, rhubarb	Light or medium
Apricots, cherries, grapefruit, pears, prunes	Medium
Berries, figs, peaches, plums	Medium or heavy

To help maintain quality of canned fruits, ¼ teaspoon ascorbic acid, dissolved in ¼ cup cold water, can be added for each quart of fruit.

TIMETABLE FOR BOILING WATER BATH

High-Acid Produce	Minutes	
	Pints	Quarts
Apples	15	20
Applesauce	25	25
Apricots	25	30
Cherries	20	25
Peaches	25	30
Pears	25	30
Plums	20	25
Tomato Juice	35	35
Tomatoes	40	45

FOOD SAFETY GUIDE

Keep hot foods hot, cold foods cold! The following indicates food temperature zones for control of bacteria.

°F

240 Canning temperatures for low-acid vegetables, meat and poultry in steam-pressure canner.

212 Canning temperatures for fruits, tomatoes and pickles in water-bath canner. Boiling point of water.

165 Cooking temperatures destroy most bacteria. Time required to kill bacteria decreases as temperature is increased.

140 Warming temperatures prevent growth but allow survival of some bacteria.

125 Some bacterial growth may occur. Many bacteria survive.

DANGER ZONE

60 Foods held more than 2 hours in this zone are subject to rapid growth of bacteria and production of toxins by some bacteria.

40 Some growth of food poisoning bacteria may occur.

32 Cold temperatures permit slow growth of some bacteria that cause spoilage.

0 Freezing temperatures stop growth of bacteria, but may allow bacteria to survive. (Do not store food above 10° for more than a few weeks.)

INFORMATION SOURCES

For canning information and recipes, write for: *Home Canning of Fruits and Vegetables*, USDA Bulletin G8 (20 cents) or *How to Make Jellies, Jams and Preserves*, USDA Bulletin G56 (40 cents). For freezing information, write for: *Home Freezing of Fruits and Vegetables*, USDA Bulletin G10 (55 cents). Send check or money order to the Superintendent of Documents, U.S. Government Printing Office, Washington, D.C. 20402.

TIMETABLE FOR PRESSURE CANNING

Low-Acid Produce	Minutes at 10 Pounds Pressure	
	Pints	Quarts
Beans, green	20	25
Beets	30	35
Carrots	25	30
Corn, whole kernel	55	*
Peas	40	40
Pumpkin or winter squash	55	90
Squash, summer	25	30

*Corn should be canned in pints because the longer processing time for quarts causes the corn to darken.

CANNING FOODS SAFELY

	Safe Method
Acid Foods: Fruits, tomatoes, pickles	Boiling water bath (212°) or pressure canner at 5 pounds pressure
Low-Acid Foods: Meats, poultry, fish, vegetables (except tomatoes)	Pressure canner *only* at 10 pounds pressure (240°)

A higher acidity level in foods such as fruits and tomatoes helps stop the growth of dangerous bacteria. These foods are safe if processed in a boiling water bath (212°) or at 5 pounds pressure in a pressure canner. Failure to do this may allow growth of yeasts, molds or bacteria that can cause spoilage.

Foods in the low-acid group above *must* be processed at a heat of 240°, which can be reached only with steam under 10 pounds pressure in a pressure canner. This high temperature will destroy dangerous heat-resistant, botulism-producing bacteria.

Processing times for foods vary because the rate of heat transfer is not the same in all vegetables and fruits. Recommended processing times are based on the length of time needed to reach the proper temperature in the slowest heating part of the container.

PRESSURE CANNER PROCESSING

Prepare jars as directed on page 371. Follow the manufacturer's instructions for opening and closing the canner. Follow Timetable on page 372.

Have 2 to 3 inches of hot water in pressure canner. Stand the jars on a rack so they are not touching each other or sides of canner. Fasten lid to canner.

Turn heat on until steam flows from vent in a steady stream (10 minutes or more after steam first appears). At first a mixture of steam and air will be released as a white vapor or cloud. When air is all driven out, the steam from the vent will become nearly invisible. It is then time to put on or close the petcock or pressure regulator. All air must be exhausted from canner to make certain the internal temperature of pressure canner reaches 240°.

Raise pressure rapidly to 2 pounds less than required; reduce heat and bring up the last 2 pounds slowly to avoid overpressure. Fluctuating pressure is one cause of liquid loss from jars, so hold the pressure steady.

When processing time is up, remove the canner from heat and allow the pressure to return to zero. Do *not* attempt to cool the pressure canner with cold water.

When the pressure registers zero, wait 1 to 2 minutes, then slowly remove or open the petcock or pressure regulator. Unfasten the cover and tilt the far side up so that any steam escapes away from you. Remove each jar with tongs or lift out in wire basket. Place the jars upright on a dry, nonmetallic surface. Towels, boards or newspapers can be used. Space the jars for free air circulation.

HOW TO CAN GREEN BEANS

1. Wash fresh, tender, crisp beans in several changes of water; drain, trim ends and cut into 1-inch pieces.

2. Boil beans 5 minutes before packing or pack raw into hot jars. Add ½ teaspoon salt per pint of beans.

3. Add boiling water to within 1 inch of jar tops. Wipe tops, add lids, seal sides down; screw on bands.

4. Place jars in pressure canner in 2 to 3 inches hot water. Process according to manufacturer's directions.

5. Remove from heat; let pressure fall to zero. Wait 2 minutes; slowly open vent, open canner, remove jars.

6. Do not tighten bands; let jars stand 12 hours. Press center of lid; if down and stays down, jar is sealed.

NOTE: See page 371 for preparation of jars and above for pressure canner processing.

Pickles—Fresh-pack Dill, Watermelon Rind, Chunk (page 377); Peach Jam (page 375) and Plum Jelly (page 376)

JAMS, JELLIES AND PICKLES

ABOUT JAMS AND JELLIES

Containers: For jams and jellies firm enough to be sealed with paraffin, use glasses or straight-sided containers. For soft jams and preserves, use canning jars with lids that can be sealed tightly. In warm, humid climates, use canning jars with tight seals for all jams, conserves and marmalades.

To prepare jelly jars or glasses:
1. Examine tops and edges of standard jars; discard any with chips or cracks (which prevent an air-tight seal).
2. Wash in hot, soapy water; rinse well.
3. Place in pan with rack or folded cloth on bottom.
4. Cover with hot (not boiling) water; heat to boiling.
5. After boiling gently 15 minutes, cover and let stand in hot water in pan.
6. About 5 minutes before filling, remove from hot water; invert on folded towel to drain away from draft. Prepare lids as directed by manufacturer.

To seal with lids: Use only standard home canning jars and lids. Fill one hot sterilized jar at a time, leaving the amount of headspace specified in recipe. Wipe tops and screw threads of jars with damp cloth. Place hot metal lid on jar with sealing compound next to glass. Screw band tightly; stand jar upright to cool. Work quickly when packing and sealing. Shake jars of jam occasionally as they cool to keep fruit from floating to top.

To seal with paraffin: Ladle fruit mixture into hot sterilized glasses, leaving the amount of headspace specified in recipe. Hold ladle close to tops to prevent air bubbles from forming in jelly or jam. Use only enough paraffin to make a 1/8-inch layer; it must touch side of glass and be even for a good seal. Prick any air bubbles—they prevent a proper seal. Check seal when paraffin has hardened.

Before storing: Let jellied fruit products stand at least 8 hours to avoid breaking the gel. Cover with metal or paper lids. Store in a cool, dry place. The shorter the storage time, the better the eating.

EQUIPMENT FOR JELLY MAKING

You will need a large kettle with a broad, flat bottom. This will allow the sugar and juice mixture to boil quickly and evenly. You will also need a long-handled spoon for skimming the jelly, a pair of tongs for removing the glasses from the hot water and a can and a small pan for heating the paraffin.

STRAWBERRY JAM

Mix 8 cups strawberries (about 4 pints), crushed, 5 cups sugar and 2 tablespoons lemon juice in Dutch oven. Heat to boiling over high heat, stirring frequently. Boil, stirring frequently, until translucent and jam is thick, about 25 minutes. Quickly skim off foam. Immediately pour jam into hot sterilized jars, leaving 1/4-inch headspace. Wipe rims of jars. Seal as directed (left).   ABOUT 5 HALF-PINTS JAM.

Cherry Jam: Substitute 8 cups cut-up cherries (about 4 pounds) for the strawberries. Boil 30 minutes.

Peach Jam: Substitute 8 cups cut-up peeled peaches (about 12 medium) for the strawberries.

Raspberry Jam: Substitute 8 cups raspberries (about 4 pints), crushed, for the strawberries.

PINEAPPLE-RHUBARB JAM

1 pineapple
1 orange
1 lemon
7 cups cut-up rhubarb
7 cups sugar

Remove top from pineapple. Cut pineapple into wedges and remove core. Cut rind and eyes from wedges. Cut unpeeled orange and lemon into quarters; discard seeds. Grind pineapple, orange and lemon in food chopper, using medium blade. Mix with rhubarb and sugar. Cover and refrigerate at least 5 hours.

Heat fruit mixture to boiling in Dutch oven. Boil gently over medium heat, stirring frequently, until jam thickens, about 25 minutes. Quickly skim off foam. Immediately pour jam into hot sterilized jars, leaving 1/4-inch headspace. Wipe rims of jars. Seal as directed (left).   ABOUT 3 HALF-PINTS JAM.

CHOOSING A PINEAPPLE

Pineapples are available year-round, but peak in April and May. Choose a mature, fragrant pineapple. The color of most mature pineapples (depending on the variety) will be orange-yellow, golden yellow or reddish brown, but some pineapples are green when fully ripened and are so labeled. Look for a firm pineapple that feels heavy for its size, and has plump, glossy eyes or pips. Bruised or discolored fruits are susceptible to decay.

APPLE JELLY

Heat 4 pounds apples (about 18), cut into fourths, and 5 cups water to boiling; reduce heat. Cover and simmer until apples are ·soft, about 20 minutes. Strain but do not press pulp through strainer. Strain juice through 2 thicknesses of cheesecloth.

Mix 3 cups apple juice and 3 cups sugar in Dutch oven. Heat to boiling, stirring constantly; reduce heat. Cook until candy or jelly thermometer registers 220°; remove from heat. Quickly skim off foam. Immediately pour jelly into hot sterilized jars, leaving ½-inch headspace. Wipe rims of jars. Seal as directed (page 375).   ABOUT 4 HALF-PINTS JELLY.

HERB JELLY

    2 tablespoons herbs (dried marjoram leaves
        for orange juice, whole cloves for
        tangerine juice, dried tarragon leaves
        for grape juice)
    2 cups water
    1 can (6 ounces) frozen orange, tangerine
        or grape juice concentrate, thawed
    1 package (1¾ ounces) powdered fruit
        pectin
    3¾ cups sugar

Tie herbs in cheesecloth bag. Heat water to boiling; remove from heat. Drop cheesecloth bag into water. Cover and let stand 10 minutes. Squeeze cheesecloth bag into water.

Mix herb water, juice concentrate and pectin in saucepan until pectin is dissolved. Heat over high heat, stirring constantly, to rolling boil, about 2 minutes. Add sugar. Heat to rolling boil, stirring constantly; remove from heat. Quickly skim off foam. Immediately pour jelly into hot sterilized jars, leaving ½-inch headspace. Wipe rims. Seal as directed (page 375).   ABOUT 4 HALF-PINTS JELLY.

Fruit Jelly: Omit herbs.

PORT WINE JELLY

Heat 3 cups sugar and 2 cups port wine in top of double boiler over rapidly boiling water, stirring constantly, until sugar is dissolved, about 3 minutes. Remove from heat. Quickly stir in ½ bottle (6-ounce size) liquid pectin. Immediately pour jelly into hot sterilized jars, leaving ½-inch headspace. Wipe rims of jars. Seal as directed (page 375).
4 OR 5 HALF-PINTS JELLY.

PLUM JELLY

    5 pounds plums, crushed (about
        4½ quarts)
    1 cup water
    6 cups sugar
    ½ bottle (6-ounce size) liquid pectin

Heat plums and water to boiling in Dutch oven; reduce heat. Cover and simmer 10 minutes. Strain but do not press pulp through strainer. Strain juice through 2 thicknesses of cheesecloth.

Mix 3 cups plum juice and the sugar. Heat, stirring constantly, to full rolling boil that cannot be stirred down. Add pectin. Heat to full rolling boil. Boil 1 minute; remove from heat. Quickly skim off foam. Immediately pour jelly into hot sterilized jars, leaving ½-inch headspace. Wipe rims. Seal as directed (page 375).   ABOUT 6 HALF-PINTS JELLY.

APPLE BUTTER

    4 quarts sweet apple cider
    3 quarts pared and quartered cooking
        apples (about 4 pounds)
    2 cups sugar
    1 teaspoon ground cinnamon
    1 teaspoon ground ginger
    ½ teaspoon ground cloves

Heat cider to boiling in 5-quart Dutch oven. Boil uncovered until cider measures 2 quarts, about 1¼ hours. Add apples. Heat to boiling; reduce heat. Simmer uncovered, stirring frequently, until apples are soft and can be broken apart with spoon, about 1 hour. (Apples can be pressed through sieve or food mill at this point for smooth apple butter.)

Stir in remaining ingredients. Heat to boiling; reduce heat. Simmer uncovered, stirring frequently, until no liquid separates from pulp, about 2 hours. Heat to boiling. Pour into hot sterilized jars, leaving ¼-inch headspace. Wipe rims of jars. Seal and process in boiling water bath 10 minutes (page 371).   ABOUT 3½ PINTS APPLE BUTTER.

NOTE: Good apples for cooking are Beacon, Cortland, Jonathan, McIntosh, Rhode Island Greening, Rome Beauty and York Imperial.

FRESH-PACK DILL PICKLES

36 to 40 pickling cucumbers (3 to 3½ inches)
7½ cups water
5 cups vinegar (5 to 6% acidity)
½ cup plus 2 tablespoons pickling or
    noniodized salt
6 heads dill
6 slices onion, ½ inch thick

Wash and scrub cucumbers carefully. Cut ¼-inch slice from blossom end of each cucumber. Mix water, vinegar and salt in Dutch oven; heat to boiling. Place dill head and onion slice in each of 6 hot quart jars. Pack cucumbers in jars, leaving ½-inch headspace. Cover with boiling brine, leaving ½-inch headspace. Wipe rims of jars. Seal and process in boiling water bath 10 minutes (page 371). ABOUT 6 QUARTS PICKLES.

Garlic-Dill Pickles: Add 2 cloves garlic to each jar with the dill and onion.

CHUNK PICKLES

24 pickling cucumbers (about 3 inches long)
½ cup pickling or noniodized salt
8 cups water
2½ cups sugar
2 cups vinegar (5 to 6% acidity)
¼ cup mustard seed
1 tablespoon celery seed
1 teaspoon curry powder

Wash and scrub cucumbers carefully; cut into 1-inch chunks. Dissolve salt in water; pour over cucumbers. Cover and let stand 5 hours.

Drain cucumbers; rinse thoroughly and place in Dutch oven. Heat remaining ingredients to boiling, stirring constantly, until sugar is dissolved. Pour over cucumbers; heat to boiling. Pack cucumbers in hot jars, leaving ½-inch headspace. Cover with boiling brine, leaving ½-inch headspace. Wipe rims of jars. Seal and process in boiling water bath 10 minutes (page 371). 5 OR 6 HALF-PINTS PICKLES.

DILL PICKLE SUCCESS TIPS

Choose a pickling variety of cucumbers. Pickle within 24 hours of harvesting or immediately after buying. Use special canning salt or noniodized salt to prevent cloudiness and soft water to prevent discoloration. Use standard canning jars, jar lifters and tongs for handling the hot lids and bands. Place the hot jars on folded newspapers.

WATERMELON RIND PICKLES

¼ cup pickling or noniodized salt
8 cups cold water
4 quarts 1-inch cubes pared watermelon
    rind
1 piece gingerroot
3 sticks cinnamon, broken
2 tablespoons whole cloves
8 cups cider vinegar (5 to 6% acidity)
9 cups sugar

Dissolve salt in cold water; pour over watermelon rind in Dutch oven. Add more water, if necessary, to cover rind. Let stand in cool place 8 hours.

Drain rind; cover with cold water. Heat to boiling. Boil just until tender, 10 to 15 minutes; drain. Tie spices in cheesecloth bag. Heat cheesecloth bag, vinegar and sugar to boiling; boil 5 minutes. Reduce heat; add rind. Simmer uncovered 1 hour. Remove cheesecloth bag. Immediately pack mixture in hot jars, leaving ¼-inch headspace. Wipe rims of jars. Seal and process in boiling water bath 10 minutes (page 371). 7 OR 8 PINTS PICKLES.

CORN RELISH

9 ears corn, husked
1½ cups sugar
3 tablespoons flour
2 tablespoons pickling or noniodized salt
2 teaspoons dry mustard
1 teaspoon ground turmeric
3 cups white vinegar (5 to 6% acidity)
3 medium onions, chopped
2 red sweet peppers, chopped
1 green pepper, chopped
1 small head green cabbage, chopped

Place corn in Dutch oven; add enough cold water to cover. Heat to boiling; boil 3 minutes. Cool; cut enough kernels from corn to measure 5 cups.

Mix sugar, flour, salt, mustard and turmeric in Dutch oven; stir in vinegar. Heat to boiling. Add vegetables; simmer uncovered 25 minutes. Immediately pack mixture in hot jars, leaving ¼-inch headspace. Wipe rims of jars. Seal and process in boiling water bath 15 minutes (page 371). 5 OR 6 PINTS RELISH.

NOTE: Onions, peppers and cabbage can be ground in food grinder, using coarse blade, or chopped in blender, following manufacturer's directions.

FREEZING

FREEZING FRUIT

Assemble all the equipment you will need. Make and refrigerate the syrup (page 371); if using an ascorbic acid mixture, do not add it to the syrup until just before using. Choose fully ripened (never overripe) fruits and keep them as cold as possible until you put them in the freezer.

Wash a small quantity of fruit at a time to prevent bruising. Lift fruit out of the water and drain thoroughly. Work quickly.

Fruit for freezing is usually prepared much as fruit for serving. Large pieces freeze better if cut into smaller pieces or crushed.

Peel, pit and slice fruit as desired. It is best to prepare enough fruit for only a few containers at one time, especially those fruits that darken rapidly. Two or three quarts is a good amount to freeze at one time.

PACKING THE FRUIT

Most fruits have better texture and flavor if packed in sugar or syrup. Some can be packed without sweetening. See chart below for recommended type of syrup and amount of sugar. Use Medium Syrup (page 371) for most fruits. For some mild-flavored fruits, lighter syrups can be used. For each pint of fruit, ½ to ⅔ cup syrup will be needed.

Fruits packed in syrup are usually best for desserts; those packed in sugar or unsweetened are best for most cooking purposes (pies, fillings, jams).

Using one of the methods described below, pack fruit in containers. (For information about container, see page 380.) Place a small piece of crumbled parchment paper or freezer wrap on top and press fruit down into syrup. Leave ½-inch headspace; seal. Freeze at once.

Syrup Pack: Pack fruit in containers; add syrup. Be sure syrup covers fruit so that top pieces will not change in color or flavor. Seal and freeze.

Sugar Pack: Sprinkle cut fruit with sugar; mix gently with a large spoon until juice is drawn out and sugar is dissolved. Pack fruit and juice in containers. Seal and freeze.

Unsweetened Pack: Pack prepared fruit in containers without juice or sugar. Or pack crushed or sliced fruit in its own juice without sweetening. Seal and freeze.

ASCORBIC ACID

Most fruits will darken during freezing. Ascorbic acid (vitamin C) can be used to help preserve flavor as well as color, adding nutritive value at the same time. Buy ascorbic acid compounds intended for use in home food preservation (available at your grocer's) and follow the manufacturer's directions.

For syrup pack, the ascorbic acid mixture is dissolved in a small amount of cold water or in the syrup. For sugar pack, it is dissolved in water then sprinkled over the fruit just before adding the sugar. For the unsweetened pack, the dissolved mixture is sprinkled over the fruit and mixed well just before packing.

SWEETENING FRUITS FOR FREEZING

Fruit	Syrup Pack: Type of Syrup*	Sugar Pack: Sugar for Each Pint	Unsweetened	Ascorbic Acid
Apples	Medium	¼ cup	omit sugar	yes
Apricots	Medium	¼ cup	**	yes
Berries	Medium/Heavy	⅓ cup	omit sugar	no
Cherries, sweet	Medium	⅓ cup	**	yes
Cranberries	Medium/Heavy	**	omit sugar	no
Peaches	Medium	⅓ cup	cover with cold water	yes
Pineapple	Light	**	omit sugar	no
Plums	Medium	**	omit sugar	yes
Raspberries	Medium	⅓ cup	omit sugar	no
Rhubarb	Medium	**	omit sugar	no
Strawberries	Heavy	⅓ cup	omit sugar	no

*See page 371 for Sugar Syrups. **Other methods preferred.

BLANCHING VEGETABLES

All vegetables must be blanched before freezing to preserve nutritional value, fresh color and flavor. Blanching is quick, partial cooking that stops the enzyme action that causes ripening and maturing in vegetables. It also stabilizes the vitamin content.

For home freezing, the best way to heat almost all vegetables is in boiling water. Use a blancher with a basket and cover. Or fit a wire basket into a large kettle.

For each pound of prepared vegetables, use at least 1 gallon of boiling water in the blancher or kettle. Blanch only 1 pound at a time. Put vegetables in blanching basket and lower into the boiling water. Cover and start counting time immediately. Keep over high heat for the time given in directions for vegetable you are freezing.

Immediately plunge vegetables into a large quantity of cold water (60° or below). Change water frequently or use running cold water or iced water. It will take about twice as long to cool the food as it does to heat it. Remove from water, drain and cool at room temperature. If desired, freeze on cookie sheet to keep vegetables from sticking together.

Pack the cold or frozen vegetables in bags or other containers. Leave ½-inch headspace and seal by twisting and folding back top of bag. Freeze at once. The packaging keeps the food moist and preserves food value, flavor, color and texture.

TIMETABLE FOR BLANCHING VEGETABLES

Asparagus, medium stalks	3 minutes
Beans, green or wax	3 minutes
Beans, lima, medium	3 minutes
Beets, medium	45 to 50 minutes
Broccoli, 1½-inch flowerets	3 minutes
Brussels sprouts, medium heads	4 minutes
Carrots, whole, small	5 minutes
diced, sliced, strips	2 minutes
Cauliflower, 1-inch pieces	3 minutes
Corn, sweet, on the cob, medium	9 minutes
whole kernel or cream style	4 minutes
Peas, green	1½ minutes
Peppers, halves	3 minutes
slices	2 minutes
Pumpkin	until soft
Squash, summer, ½-inch slices	3 minutes
Squash, winter, ½-inch slices	until soft
Sweet potatoes	until tender

BLANCHING VEGETABLES

You'll need either (1) a blancher with a basket or (2) a large aluminum or enamelware kettle and a colander. For the cold plunge, use a large bowl or the kitchen sink.

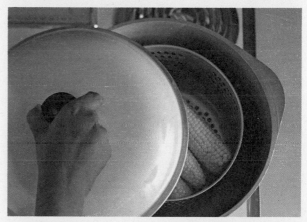

Lower no more than 1 pound of vegetables into boiling water. Keep the heat high, cover and start counting as the vegetables touch the water (see Timetable, left).

When blanching time is over, immediately plunge the vegetables into very cold or iced water. Leave about twice as long as you did in boiling water.

COOLING FOODS FOR FREEZING

The less time that food spends at temperatures between 45 and 140°, the better. If you allow foods to remain at these temperatures for more than 3 to 4 hours, they may not be safe to eat, so speed the cooling process.

Hot foods can be placed right in the refrigerator provided they don't raise the refrigerator temperature above 45°.

A large quantity of hot food should be cooled in a big bowl (or a sink) filled with cold water and ice that almost reaches the top of the food container. Replace ice as it melts; freeze the food as soon as it is cool.

WRAPPING FOODS FOR FREEZING

To maintain the high quality of food in the freezer, it is necessary to use good packaging and wrapping materials. Select them on the basis of convenience of use, space occupied in the freezer and cost. Freezer wraps and containers should be airtight, moistureproof and vaporproof. The best materials for freezing are heavy-duty aluminum foil, heavyweight plastic wrap and freezer bags or containers.

When you wrap, press out the air and wrap tightly. Fragile foods are an exception—they may need to be protected with a box. You can place the freezer-wrapped food in the box or overwrap the box. To freeze food in a container, see page 379.

EASY FREEZING TRICKS

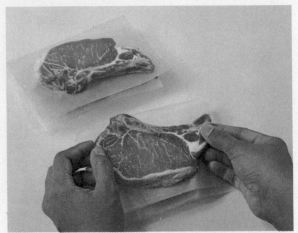

A double layer of waxed paper or freezer wrap between hamburger, chops or steaks makes separating easy.

Or freeze on cookie sheets, then transfer to freezer bags. Foods won't stick together; take out just what you want.

To free a baking pan for other uses, line with heavy aluminum foil; fill with food (Lasagne, page 54, is shown). Cook the food, wrap, cool quickly. Freeze until set.

Remove frozen block from pan; label, date and return to freezer. To use, remove foil, place in original baking dish and reheat. (For Lasagne, see Do-ahead Tip, page 54).

WISE BUYING FOR YOUR FREEZER

Take advantage of your supermarket's "specials" and of the foods that cost less because they are in season. This way you can enjoy the best foods at the lowest prices all the time.

Make sure the food you buy is in top condition. You may want to package it in smaller portions for freezing or prepare a freezer recipe. Whatever you do, get the food into the freezer as fast as you can.

LABELING FOODS FOR FREEZING

Label your packages before you put them in the freezer. Don't rely on your memory—especially if you make good use of your freezer and keep it well stocked. For labeling you will need labels, a grease pencil or a felt-tipped pen (to avoid moisture smudges) and freezer tape. Keep these handy with your packaging materials so you won't be tempted to smuggle an unlabeled package into the freezer. Include this information:

Name of Recipe: If you have more than one package from the same recipe, note that on the label.

Last-Stage Ingredients: Write down and keep your own instructions for reheating or additional ingredients that are needed before serving.

Number of Servings: Write down the number of servings your package contains; when you freeze meat, note its weight.

Storage Time: Figure out when your package should be used and put that "use before" date on your label. (If you leave your package in the freezer beyond the recommended storage time, your food won't spoil—but it may begin to lose some of its moisture, flavor or texture.)

FAST FREEZING

Thawing then refreezing is not recommended, so use meal-size containers and, at any one time, freeze only as much food as you can place against a freezing surface. The faster your food freezes, the better it retains flavor and texture. For fast freezing, food packages should be in direct contact with a freezing surface, at least 1 inch apart so the air can circulate.

Arrange large frozen packages on bottom of freezer and crushable ones on top. (Once the food is frozen solid, you can stack packages.)

FREEZING LARGE QUANTITIES

When you want to freeze food in large quantities, guard against a rise of temperature in your freezer. Reduce your freezer temperature to -10° or lower about 24 hours before you put a large amount of unfrozen food into your freezer. This way, your food will be frozen solid in 10 to 12 hours.

DO-AHEAD MAIN DISHES

If you freeze dishes made from your own favorite recipes, these suggestions may be helpful:

☐ Slightly undercook meats, pasta and vegetables before freezing to prevent overcooking when reheating. When you prepare a double batch—one to eat and one to freeze—set the freezer batch aside a few minutes before it is fully cooked.

☐ Season lightly and add more seasonings just before serving. Pepper and some other spices become strong and bitter when frozen.

☐ Add crumb and cheese toppings to frozen foods just before reheating.

☐ While thawing, sauces and gravies may appear curdled but you can stir them smooth.

Good do-ahead main dishes are cooked chicken and turkey casseroles . . . almost any kind of cooked meat stew or goulash . . . most vegetables used in stew or goulash—peas, carrots, celery, onions . . . meat loaves (baked) . . . cooked dried beans (cook until barely tender before freezing).

DO-AHEAD SANDWICHES

Freeze 1 to 3 weeks' supply of sandwiches. Spread bread slices to the edges with margarine or butter. Sliced meat, poultry, cheese, cheese spread, peanut butter, salmon and tuna freeze well. Moisten with applesauce, fruit juice or dairy sour cream, not mayonnaise, salad dressing or jelly. Don't use fresh vegetables or cooked egg whites. Freezer-wrap sandwiches individually. Place sandwich in lunchbox unthawed—it will defrost in about 3 hours.

DON'T FREEZE THESE

Some foods are not recommended for freezing. Cooked egg whites become tough. Salad greens become soggy; raw tomatoes, limp and watery. Raw apples and grapes become soft and mushy. And fried foods may taste warmed over when reheated.

ABOUT YOUR FREEZER

BUYING A FREEZER

When buying a freezer, you have a choice of three basic types: the refrigerator with a freezer unit; the upright freezer with shelves from top to bottom; and the freezer chest with baskets and dividers.

If you have limited floor space or don't need a great deal of freezer space, the refrigerator-freezer may be your best bet. In a refrigerator-freezer, the storage capacity of your freezer will be between 2 and 10 cubic feet. A model with a freezer unit that is completely insulated from the refrigerator is desirable because such freezers can maintain a constant temperature of 0°. If your freezing compartment does not remain at 0°, the food you store should be used within a week or two.

You may need the freezer space provided by an upright freezer or a freezer chest. You may not be certain, however, about which size freezer you should buy. In addition to questions of floor space and price, let yourself be guided by the size of your family—allow 5 cubic feet per person—and the amount of preplanning you want to do.

FREEZER TEMPERATURE

The temperature for freezing and storing food is 0° or lower. At a low temperature (0°), foods freeze faster with less breakdown in their cellular structure; they are more likely to retain true flavor and firm texture.

Chest and upright freezers (and the fully insulated refrigerator-freezers) are designed to stay at a constant 0° temperature. It is important that you know exactly what temperature is maintained in your freezer. We strongly recommend that you buy a freezer thermometer. Check the thermometer often, and make sure that your freezer actually maintains a temperature of 0° or lower.

DEFROSTING AND CLEANING

Above all, read the manufacturer's instructions.

Unless you have a self-defrosting freezer, defrost it as soon as you see thick frost. Transfer the frozen foods to the refrigerator. If necessary, pile frozen foods into a laundry basket and cover with newspapers or a blanket. To speed defrosting, have an electric fan blow into the freezer, or place pans of warm water in the freezer. Wash with a solution of 3 tablespoons baking soda to 1 quart water, or with a mild detergent solution. Dry thoroughly before resetting temperature control.

EMERGENCIES

In case of power failure or mechanical defect, keep the freezer closed. In a full freezer that is kept at 0°, little or no thawing will take place within the first 12 to 20 hours.

If it appears that your freezer will be out of commission for more than a day and it is full of food, you will want to take action. You can remove the contents of your freezer to a frozen food locker. Or you can buy dry ice. Wear heavy gloves when you handle dry ice. Lay cardboard over the packages in your freezer and place the dry ice on the cardboard; do not place it directly on the packages. A 50-pound block of dry ice will prevent foods from thawing for 2 to 3 days.

INDEX

A

Acorn squash, 189
  maple baked, 189
Additives, 360
Alexander pie, 302
Almond(s). *See also* Nut(s).
  chocolate-, pie, 302
  -crunch wax beans, 165
  fluff, 243
  garlic, 327
  orange-, cookies, 274
  savory, 327
  tarts, Swedish, 304
Ambrosia balls, 273
Ambrosia salads, 152
Ambrosia tapioca, 265
Angel food cakes, 243
  about, 242
Antipasto platter, vegetable, 142
Appetizer(s), 316–35. *See also* Beverages; Canapé(s); Dip(s); Snacks; Spread(s).
  beverages, 345
  caviar classic, 320
  clams on the half shell, 320
  coconut fruit cups, 316
  escargots, 321
  first course, 316–21
  fruit
    compote, sparkling, 316
    soup, 317
  grapefruit cup, 316
  melon and prosciutto, 317
  oysters
    on the half shell, 320
    Parmesan, 321
    Rockefeller, 321
  papayas with lime wedges, 316
  pâtés, individual, 324
  salad(s)
    asparagus with crab-curry mayonnaise, 317
    asparagus with curried mayonnaise, 317
    celery Victor, 317
    grape-celery, 317
    tangy shrimp, 132
  sandwiches, party, 332–35
  shrimp cocktail, 320

Appetizer(s) *(cont.)*
  soup(s). *See also* Soup(s).
    avocado, 318
    beef consommé, 318
    fruit, 317
    gazpacho, 318
    madrilene, 320
    onion, French, 318
    vichyssoise, 318
Apple(s). *See also* Applesauce; Green apple.
  about, 260, 295
  baked, 281
  butter, 376
  cake, spicy, 237
  caramel, 340
  -cheese coleslaw, 138
  chocolate-caramel, 340
  crisp, 260
  drink, bubbly, 344
  dumplings, 305
  jelly, 376
  -nut muffins, 199
  -orange-grape salad, 152
  -orange punch, 346
  pies, 295
  -raisin stuffing, 85
  salad, double, 152
  squares with cardamom sauce, 304
  squash and, bake, 189
  Waldorf salad(s), 152
    molded, 147
Applesauce, 281
  cakes, 235
    high altitude, 363
  drops, 268
  meat loaf, 26
  pancakes, 197
Apricot
  balls, 340
  -cinnamon mold, 147
  crisp, 260
  glaze, 58
  -glazed peaches, 285
  -glazed pears, 285
  -nut balls, 340
  nut bread, 203
  pie, 296
  prune-, muffins, 199
Artichoke(s), French (globe), 163. *See also* Jerusalem artichokes.
  chicken-, salads, 82
  chicken-, skillet, 93
  crabmeat-, salads, 82
  pickled, 327
  shrimp-, salads, 82
  tomatoed rice with, 226

Ascorbic acid, 360, 378
Asparagus, 164
  au gratin, quick, 165
  chicken-, bake, 96
  dress-ups, 164
  oven, 164
  skillet, 165
  with crab-curry mayonnaise, 317
  with curried mayonnaise, 317
  with wine sauce, 164
Aspic, tangy tomato, 145
Avocado(s)
  -apple salad, tossed, 135
  California salad, 152
  cheeseburgers, 30
  -citrus salad, 152
  crab-, salads, 80
  -grapefruit salad, tossed, 135
  guacamole, 322
  Mexican salad, 144
  preparing, 144
  -radish salad, tossed, 135
  salad, tossed, 135
  soups, 318

B

Bacon. *See also* Canadian-style bacon.
  about, 94
  -and-egg bean salads, 137
  -cauliflower toss, 135
  cheese and, waffles, 196
  club sandwich(es), 91
    cheese, 119
  cooking, 56
  corn bread, 204
  curls, 56
  guacamole, 322
  omelet, 107
  rumaki, 329
  shrimp-, bites, 330
  Spanish rice, 56
  -turkey club salad, 56
  -wrapped hamburgers, 30
Baking powder, 360
Baking powder biscuits, 194
Bambinos, 328
Banana
  cream pie, 302
  muffins, 199
  nut bread, 203
  -nut cake, 234
  pancakes, 197
  -pineapple salad, 152
  refrigerator dessert, 312
  sips, yogurt, 349

Banana squash, 189
Barbecue sauce, 19
  zesty, 16
Barley
  beef-, vegetable soup, 24
  pilaf for two, 228
Batter
  fritter, 206
  thin, 206
Batter breads. *See* Casserole bread(s).
Bean(s). *See also names of beans.*
  and egg salad, 126
  baked, 121
    Boston, 121
    soy, 121
  bonanza, 137
  burritos, meaty, 33
  cheesy, quick, 121
  chili, 31
  dip, Santa Fe, 323
  dried, 121–26
  green. *See* Green bean(s).
  -mushroom medley, 166
  red, -sour cream dip, 323
  refried, 33
  salads, 126, 137
  skillet, 122
  soups, 125–26
  tomatoed, 122
  wax. *See* Wax bean(s).
  -with-bacon dip, 323
Bean sprout, spinach-, salad, 132
Béarnaise sauce, 10
Beef, 8–40
  and mushroom salads, 20
  -bean combo, 35
  beer stew, 52
  brisket barbecue, 13
  -bulgur salad, 16
  buying, 14
  California stir-fry, 14
  carving, 9
  consommé, 318
  corned. *See* Corned beef.
  cuts, 11
  dried. *See* Dried beef.
  fondue, 21
  ground. *See* Hamburger; Hamburgers.
  hash, 14
  kabobs, 20
    wine-marinated, 29
  leftovers, 14–16
  meat loaf. *See* Meat loaf(-ves).
  meatballs. *See* Meatball(s).
  microwaving, 38

*Whole wheat flour is used in many recipes throughout the book; check the ingredient lists.

Use caution. Start with a small amount, especially if you're using dried herbs. If the taste is too delicate, you can always add more.

HERBS AND SPICES

 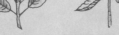 

	ALLSPICE	BASIL	CHILI POWDER	CINNAMON	CLOVES	DILL SEED AND WEED
MEATS AND MAIN DISHES	Pot Roasts Meat Loaf Meatballs Ham	Beef Pork Lamb Pizza Spaghetti	Meat Loaf Hamburgers Cheese Fondue Welsh Rabbit	Ham Pork Chops Sauerbraten	Corned Beef Ham Tongue Baked Beans	Beef Steaks Lamb Chops Lamb Steaks Rice Dishes

SEAFOOD, POULTRY AND EGGS	Poached Fish
	  Fillets
	Chicken Fricassee
	Egg Dishes
		Fish Fillets
		Tuna
		Shellfish
		Fried Chicken
		Creamed Eggs
		Omelets
		Soufflés
			Shrimp
			Barbecued
			  Chicken
			Fried Chicken
			Scrambled Eggs
				Sweet-and-Sour
				  Shrimp
				Stewed Chicken
					Baked Fish
					  Fillets
					Roast Chicken
					Chicken a la King
						Seafood Cocktails
						Salmon
						Shellfish
						Chicken
						Deviled Eggs

SOUPS, STEWS AND SAUCES	Potato Soup Oyster Stew Barbecue Sauce Tomato Sauces Cranberry Sauce	Manhattan Clam Chowder Tomato Soup Vegetable Soup Beef Stew Spaghetti Sauce	Pea Soup Beef Stew Chili Cheese Sauces Gravy	Fruit Soup Beef Stew	Bean Soup Onion Soup Pea Soup Tomato Sauces	Borsch Split Pea Soup Lamb Stew Drawn Butter Gravy

SALADS AND SALAD DRESSINGS	Cottage Cheese
	Cabbage
	Fruit
		Seafood
		Cucumber
		Tomato
		Tomato Aspic
		French Dressing
		Russian Dressing
			Cottage Cheese
			Potato
			French Dressing
			Guacamole
				Fruit	Spiced Fruit
					Fruit Salad
					  Dressings
						Seafood
						Cottage Cheese
						Potato
						French Dressing
						Sour Cream
						  Dressings

VEGETABLES	Eggplant Parsnips Spinach Squash Turnips	Asparagus Green Beans Squash Tomatoes Wax Beans	Cauliflower Corn Lima Beans Onions Peas	Carrots Onions Spinach Squash Sweet Potatoes	Beets Carrots Onions Squash Sweet Potatoes	Cabbage Carrots Cauliflower Peas Potatoes Sauerkraut
BREADS AND BEVERAGES	Coffee Cakes Sweet Rolls		Biscuits French Bread	Biscuits Nut Bread Sweet Rolls Tea Coffee Hot Chocolate	Coffee Cakes Nut Bread Sweet Rolls Fruit Punch	Onion Rolls
DESSERTS	Fruitcake Steamed Pudding Tapioca Pudding Mince Pie Pumpkin Pie	Fruit Compotes		Chocolate Pudding Rice Pudding Apple Desserts Fruit Compotes	Chocolate Cake Gingerbread Applesauce Pears Chocolate Sauce	Green Apple Pie